The

A SHAAR PRESS PUBLICATION

Betrayal

a novel by
M. Kenan

Translated by Libby Lazewnik

© Copyright 2010 by Shaar Press

First edition – Four impressions / May 2010 — December 2020
Fifth impression / May 2022

ALL RIGHTS RESERVED
No part of this book may be reproduced IN ANY FORM, scan, photocopy, electronic media, for use with digital retrieval systems, as an audio or video recording, or otherwise – EVEN FOR PERSONAL, STUDY GROUP, OR CLASSROOM USE – without WRITTEN permission from the copyright holder, except by a reviewer who wishes to quote brief passages in connection with a review written for inclusion in magazines or newspapers..

THE RIGHTS OF THE COPYRIGHT HOLDER WILL BE STRICTLY ENFORCED.

This is a work of fiction. Names, characters, places, and incidents are either the product of the author's imagination or are used fictitiously. Any resemblance to actual persons, living or dead, or locales is entirely coincidental.

Published by **SHAAR PRESS**
Distributed by MESORAH PUBLICATIONS, LTD.
313 Regina Avenue / Rahway, N.J. 07065 / (718) 921-9000

Distributed in Israel by SIFRIATI / A. GITLER
POB 2351 / Bnei Brak 51122

Distributed in Europe by LEHMANNS
Unit E, Viking Business Park, Rolling Mill Road / Jarrow, Tyne and Wear, NE32 3DP/ England

Distributed in Australia and New Zealand by GOLDS WORLD OF JUDAICA
3-13 William Street / Balaclava, Melbourne 3183 / Victoria Australia

Distributed in South Africa by KOLLEL BOOKSHOP
Ivy Common / 105 William Road / Norwood 2192, Johannesburg, South Africa

ITEM CODE: BETRH
ISBN 10: 1-4226-0985-5
ISBN 13: 978-1-4226-0985-9

Printed in the United States of America
Custom bound by Sefercraft, Inc. / 313 Regina Avenue / Rahway, N.J. 07065

AUTHOR'S NOTE

Historians differ as to whether there was ever a powerful Jewish kingdom known as Khazar.

Rav Chasdai's letters to the king of Khazar (recorded in the *Sefer Kuzari* by Rabbi Yehudah HaLevi) lend credence to the opinion that it did exist. However, solid historical evidence of their lifestyle, reigning family, and customs has not survived the passage of time.

The kingdom of Khazar presented to you on these pages is not based on historical fact, and any resemblance between it and the Khazar kingdom on the Krim Peninsula during the years in question is intended to be symbolic.

Prominent Characters

(listed in order of appearance)

ROYAL FAMILY

Reuel II — king (*khagan*) of Khazar
Brachia — late king of Khazar, Reuel's father
Yosef I — Reuel's ancestor, convert to Judaism
Basya — deceased wife of Reuel, mother of Istrak and Tur
Istrak — Reuel's firstborn and heir; son of Basya
Sarah — present queen
Michoel — 12-year-old son of Reuel and Sarah
Tur — 14-year-old daughter of Reuel and Basya
Lissia — 3-year-old daughter of Reuel and Sarah
Binyamin — 6-year-old son of Reuel and Sarah
Unmar — 8-year-old daughter of Reuel and Sarah
Yekavel — 9-year-old son of Reuel and Sarah
Rena — missing sister of Reuel, presumed deceased

NOBLEMEN AND THEIR FAMILIES

Lord Elranan Shefer — Reuel's brother-in-law (brother of the late queen, Basya) and study partner; governor of the central region
Pinras — Istrak's cousin and mentor; 26-year-old son of Khazar's prime minister (*bek*), Lord Eshal Bluadian
Meshuel Min-Hagai — the father of Tur's *chasan*
Ruben Min-Hagai — Tur's *chasan*
Lord Eshal Bluadian — prime minister (*bek*) of Khazar; Reuel's brother-in-law (husband of Reuel's sister)
Lord Elnatan — minister of education
Lord Bastian Makan — minister of war; commander of the Khazar army; Reuel's brother-in-law (brother of Queen Sarah)
Lord Dalo Stazdiran — deputy prime minister
Yishvav the Babylonian — elderly war strategist
Lord Yosef Diaber — regent
Zecharia Latvias — friend of Istrak
Lord Gedalia Latvias — father of Zecharia
Asher Kafchaver — longtime friend of Istrak, son of Lord Menashe Kafchaver
Lord Gad Baliatar — close friend of King Reuel; governor of the northern princes
Lord Ribak Bati — friend and confidant of Lord Bastian Makan
Lord Nazarel — minister of protocol
Rav Natrunai Ben Masnia — rosh yeshivah of the Royal Beis Medrash; foremost among the Khazari scholars
Lord Menashe Kafchaver — minister of the interior and agriculture; father of Asher

Lord Zavdiel Mitran — minister for internal security
Narma Stazdiran Paz — widowed sister of Lord Dalo Stazdiran

PALACE STAFF

Naitan — Istrak's personal servant; son of Ovadia
Izdru — Istrak's elderly language tutor
Matel — Istrak's personal bodyguard (nobleman)
Minra — Tur's nurse and lady-in-waiting
Ovadia — the king's personal attendant
Difrat — Michoel's tutor
Yehudah — Michoel's bodyguard
Estelle — Unmar's nurse
Avrel — chief waiter

COMMON PEOPLE OF KHAZAR

Kalev Ben Batal — peasant boy; ultimately, Istrak's attendant
Tuval Obseld — painter of portraits
Rivka Obseld — Tuval's wife
Dosa Palev — elderly neighbor of the Obselds
Zerach Palev — Dosa's husband
Calidius Bruchu — cohort of one of the ministers
Ifa Jado — doctor renowned for his potions
Tippias — innkeeper; father of Rivka Obseld
Elkanah — brother of Tippias; uncle of Rivka Obseld
Naftali — yeshiva student; son of Elkanah
Yishai — Mundari; living in the northern region of Khazar
Lista Basbani — master forger

KHAZAR SOLDIERS AND GUARDS

Landon Brach — commander of the palace guard (nobleman)
Miflaeus — guard in the palace (nobleman)
Matrias — commander of the *hostress* troops
Knaz — Mundari; soldier in Khazar's army
Phidos Flair — captain of the mounted cavalry
Boaz — follower of Ruben Min-Hagai
Dan — follower of Ruben Min-Hagai

KAWARIS

Wanana — aged leader of the Kawaris
Ka'hei — future leader of the Kawaris
Yidrat — son of Ka'hei
Te'arah — Ka'hei's lieutenant
Moshe — Kawari who converted to Judaism
Hala — daughter of Ka'hei and Rena

PROLOGUE

He knew it was a dream. Even asleep, he knew that the guards posted at his door would never have allowed the two strangers to enter his room. But knowing that it was only a dream could not quell the fear that gripped him at the men's sudden appearance.

"You are Reuel, king of Khazar?"

"I am."

For a long moment, the pair studied him in silence. Then one of them spoke, his voice neither a request nor a command. "Good. For Khazar's sake, come with us."

Behind the palace, a mountain he had never seen before had suddenly materialized. On the top of the mountain stood a round structure made of pure white marble whose upper reaches kissed the sky. Standing at the top of this tower, flanked by his two mysterious companions, he could see all of Khazar spread before him like a beautifully embroidered patchwork quilt. It was a panorama made up of swatches of color: shades of green, brown, and yellow dotted with thatched roofs and crisscrossed by a complex web of white-gravel roads.

Today, 250 years after Reuel's ancestor King Yosef I had converted to Judaism, the Khazar kingdom — extending from the Platt plains in the northeast to the swamplands and Hungarian mountain ridge in the west — was one of the most stable and prosperous in the region. As Reuel gazed at his country, stretching from horizon to horizon, he could feel the burden of responsibility weigh heavily on his shoulders.

"A beautiful land," one of his companions remarked.

The other pointed upward and said, "Look, Reuel!"

Reuel looked toward the sky — now a perfect, cloudless blue. From the heart of the beautiful blue flew a pure-white dove. As though impelled by some signal from within, he turned his head — just in time to see a large black dot rapidly descending. It took the shape of a giant hawk. With claws like swords, the hawk seized the dove and held it fast.

The dove screeched. A drop of blood dripped from its injured body and seeped into the peaceful earth.

Then all was silent. The two men with him turned and walked away. As they departed, one of them called back over his shoulder, "You cannot say you were not warned, Reuel…"

Left alone, Reuel made his way down. For the first time he noticed that the steps of the white tower were made of black marble, and the tower itself had sprung from an empty patch of ground near the grave of Basya, his first wife — the mother of Istrak, his firstborn and heir.

For a moment he stood transfixed, trying in vain to absorb what had happened. Then he awoke.

He found himself at his desk. Sitting quietly near him was Lord Elranan Shefer, his brother-in-law and study partner.

"I fell asleep," Reuel said, trying to collect his thoughts.

"Only for a moment," Shefer replied. "Your Majesty works too hard."

Reuel's eyes strayed to the window. Through the glass he could see blue sky stretching into the distance. The dream remained fixed in his memory, powerful and alive.

In the Palace

1

"KEEP YOUR BALANCE, BOY!"

Hirlus, the sword master, drew circles with his saber around the son and heir of King Reuel. In the last three minutes, Istrak had managed to stop that saber only once.

"Your shield — lift it higher! It's meant to protect your chest!" Hirlus' sunburned face turned even more crimson with fury. "You're not even trying, Istrak!"

"Yes, I am," Istrak retorted, dropping the arm that held his shield. "Focus on the positive, Hirlus. I'm much better than I was two months ago, aren't I?"

"Yes, you're better," the master acknowledged, wiping the perspiration from his brow with his sleeve. "But you're not good enough!"

"I *am* good enough," Istrak declared. "And you know it as well as I do."

Hirlus grimaced in the semblance of a smile. "As long as someone, even if he's the only one in the world, is able to thrust a saber into your chest without you fending him off, you are no good at all." He retreated a step. "Now, I'm going to come at you from the side. Try and stop me!"

When Istrak had been a child, sword lessons had been fun. The steps he learned were more like a dance than a battle, and when he was told to "defend himself" his teacher had made no real effort to point out that his defense was inadequate. And no one had seriously tried to ward off his saber when it was his turn to go on the offensive.

Everything changed when his father brought Hirlus to the palace. The Greek was a demanding and merciless instructor. Time after time, his blunt practice-saber sent Istrak's flying, leaving him defenseless. The scoldings that followed were extremely distasteful to the crown prince …

"Istrak, are you with me?"

Istrak nodded, dragging his mind back to the present. An instant later, the master's saber tip landed very close to his royal pupil's throat.

"How is this possible?" Hirlus said angrily. "How is this possible, when I've been teaching you for a year and a half? You wanted your grandfather's saber? Your brother is a hundred times worthier than you!"

Istrak drew a deep breath in an effort to stem the rage that was threatening to course through him. What did his birthday present have to do with Michoel, however talented his brother might be? And who had given this gentile permission to speak to him — the future heir of all Khazar — in a tone of such contempt?

His anger suffused him with a force he hardly recognized, and his hand went to the haft of his blunt training saber. Nine years of fairly rigorous practice had etched the sequence of moves into his brain so that they automatically came to the fore.

The instructor responded willingly to his student's challenge. He fought back using his superior height and long arms to attack as well as defend himself from Istrak — who, focused and alert, made maximum use of his agility and flexibility. Their weapons clashed. Drops of sweat were evident on the combatants' foreheads.

The servants standing in a corner of the big hall ceased their chatter. The struggle taking place in the center of the arena was clearly more than just a fencing lesson, and they all turned to watch.

The instructor used the point of his sword; Istrak thrust it back with the side of his own blade and then, without withdrawing his sword, raised it to the sword master's chin.

Hirlus froze in place. An instant later his fingers relaxed, and his sword clattered to the wooden floor.

"So you *can* do it!" he whispered. The heavy-lidded gray eyes sparkled as they peered into Istrak's light ones while his hand gently pushed aside the blade that rested against his neck.

The strange power that had suffused Istrak earlier began to recede, leaving a bad taste in his mouth. Turning sharply away, he lowered his blade and replaced his weapon in its sheath.

"I am honored to tell you, Your Highness — this is the first time in fifteen years that anyone has succeeded in putting his blade to my neck." There was a surprised note of admiration in the sword master's voice, but it didn't last.

"Does Your Highness think we ought to start each of our lessons with a series of insults, just to summon up the stunning talent he displayed today?"

Istrak swallowed his bile. "You are right. Perhaps the time has come to reassess our arrangement, Master Hirlus," he answered formally. He could barely get the words out of his mouth. "I will give you my decision after I've spoken to His Majesty, my father. Naitan!"

A slender youth jumped to attention. "Sir?"

"Remove this protective garment!"

One of the three noblemen who sat at the edge of the training hall during Istrak's lessons approached the center of the room with an energetic stride. "Your lesson is not over yet, Your Highness."

"Thank you, Lord Guardian of the Keys," the heir snapped, "but I believe that the crown prince of Khazar may, by the laws of this kingdom, decide when his lesson is over!"

The nobleman retreated. Istrak flexed his muscles, letting Naitan, his personal servant, tend to the fastenings in the thick protective garment. His blood still boiled in his veins. A measure of calm returned only when he had left the hall and begun to make his way toward the royal archery range.

The double bow, more than any other weapon, had won Khazar its far-reaching dominions. Its Byzantine neighbors used long bows, but these were so heavy that they were hardly fit to serve as effective weapons. The double bow the Khazars used — which, as its name implies, was double the height of an ordinary bow — was incredibly light due to the rare *tamil* wood that grew in the kingdom's northern reaches. Each year competitions were held at the capital, Itil, inviting youths from every part of the kingdom to prove their prowess with the traditional weapon. Istrak, by virtue of his royal position, was disqualified from participating in these contests. However, in training sessions he had several times demonstrated his ability to break the record set the previous year by a youth his own age from the Tanrib province. But today, the same fury that had just won him a surprising victory in the swordmanship arena now caused Istrak to miss his mark on the large, distinct target erected a reasonable distance away.

Or perhaps it was not anger that caused him to miss, but the sound of familiar and very definite footsteps…

"Your Highness?"

Pinras, the Khazar prime minister's third son and Istrak's cousin, stood at arm's length from the crown prince, gazing at him with mingled surprise and empathy. Five years earlier Pinras had been appointed as his mentor.

Istrak did not respond.

"Your Highness, set down that bow!"

Reluctantly, Istrak restored the arrow to its quiver and allowed Naitan to prop the bow against the foot of a tall tree.

"You are not permitted to enter the shooting area unless accompanied by six guards. You know that!"

Istrak liked Pinras, with his pale face and direct gaze, the man whom the king often referred to as "the one who keeps the peace in our kingdom." Somehow Istrak thought that despite his cousin's many fine qualities — or perhaps because of them — he would not understand what had caused him to storm out of the arena like a whirlwind.

"I know that, Pinras," he answered grudgingly.

"And you chose to disobey instructions?"

"I did not obey." Istrak studied the fine scratches that time had etched into the brown marble that bordered the palace courtyard.

"Why? What happened?"

Istrak lifted his eyes, glaring into his tutor's gentle brown ones. "I'm sure you've already received a detailed report about what occurred in my swordmanship lesson. Why should I bother to repeat it?"

"We've talked about this a number of times, Istrak." Pinras' voice was tired as he launched into a well-rehearsed lecture. "Hirlus is the best swordsman we have. His Majesty your father wants to provide you with the best possible training, so that you will be able to lead Khazar's armies into battle and return home at their head, crowned with victory. Your brother Michoel understands that. He —"

"Enough!" Israk said, his tone sharp and commanding. "I've heard enough about Michoel for one day."

Pinras' face softened. His long fingers stroked the small silver beads embroidered into his *ilpak* — the decorative belt that held his *tzitzis* in place. With a quiet smile, he replied, "I will do as you command, Your Highness."

Strangely, Pinras' answer did not make Istrak feel better. It was an effort for him to force his lips into an approximation of a smile.

The sentries near the palace entrance stood at attention and blessed them as they passed. "And may the bestower of this blessing be blessed from the treasury of unearned gifts," Istrak responded, as was the custom. As he did every day, he desired to turn the simple moment beneath the arched gateway into something of significance, both for them and for himself.

Today, he felt, he had not been particularly successful.

Although Istrak liked Izdru, his elderly language tutor, he had no love for the time-consuming lessons that found him seated on a hard stool and memorizing an endless list of words that he had to review between one lesson and the next.

"When the princes of the world come to offer you their good wishes on the occasion of your 17th birthday, you must know how to return their greetings in their own language!" As he spoke, the wrinkles on Izdru's face resembled dried water channels. "In the old days, great kings knew many languages. And the Shanhedrin" — the way the aged teacher, a longtime immigrant to Khazar who observed the seven Noahide laws, pronounced this quintessential Jewish concept was most amusing — "were fluent in numerous languages. Seventy, Istrak! All I am asking you to do is learn six languages and five dialects. That's not such a difficult task."

Istrak stifled a yawn. The dimness in the room made it hard not to doze off.

"I have an idea, Your Highness. A marvelous idea!" The elderly teacher's voluminous cloak rustled as he struggled to his feet. "Just a moment while I consult your mentor…"

Pinras gave his consent.

"You will find it much more congenial on the roof," Izdru said eagerly. "In fact, according to tradition, that is where the ceremony will be held…"

The tutor, a full head shorter than the prince, moved alongside Istrak at a near trot.

Istrak said nothing. The tension in him, he knew, had nothing to do with the dimness of the room or the sweet fragrance emanating from the burning candles. Sunlight and fresh air would do nothing to improve his mood.

"Enough already," Izdru scolded as shadows continued to darken the prince's eyes. "Be a man, Your Highness! The day will come when you will rule all of Khazar…"

"…and then," Istrak finished sardonically, "it will be a very sad thing if I submit to my enemies the way I submit to my low spirits."

"Very true," the tutor agreed. He allowed the words to linger in the air…

Istrak mentally reviewed the list of tasks awaiting him this morning. He fumed at the thought that no one had bothered to consider a single one of the things that *he* wanted to do.

"You sound so much like your father," the old man said suddenly, as though to himself. "He, too, liked to come up here."

This was the last thing Istrak had expected his teacher to say. He stared at Izdru in surprise.

"He was also a child once. Today, he is a man." The teacher pronounced the last word as though it were a compliment of inestimable value. "You, too, will be a man one day." He smiled, and the vast network of wrinkles smiled along with him. "And this old man is here to tell you that it is already obvious that you possess all the qualities needed to rule this kingdom."

An hour later, Istrak descended the stairs leading down from the roof, Izdru's words still echoing in his ears.

He knew, of course, that he was destined to rule — a fact his father never failed to remind him of in their daily talks. But hearing the words on another's lips lent them a much more alarming significance.

Would Istrak, nearly 17, really be worthy of sitting on his father's throne one day and using the great, golden seal that determined destinies? Would he be capable of deciding the fate of so many — among them men as venerable and wise as his teacher, and others who had done their military service back in his grandfather's day, spilling blood in the southern wars? Was he ready to hold in his hands the lives of tens of thousands of innocent children, an entire army of young soldiers, and the anxious parents they had left behind?

His reflection, slightly distorted in the dusky lighting, shimmering back at him from the towering copper gate at the western hall: a tall lad with light eyes and long hair tied back on his neck in the royal manner to leave only the thick *peyos* free at the sides of his face.

He *would* be able to do it, with the Al-mighty's help. If for no other reason than because…he would have no choice.

"Your Highness! Your sister, the Princess Tur, is at the door," Matel, the prince's personal bodyguard, announced. "Shall I let her in?"

"Tur? Yes, let her in. There's no need to ask me *that*, Matel!"

Naitan swiftly gathered the small pieces of parchment on which the prince had supposedly been composing an outline of his forthcoming address, but had instead been covering with doodles for the past half-hour, and slipped them under the tablecloth. Istrak went into the anteroom, ignoring the small knowing smile lurking beneath Matel's mustache.

"Tur!"

"I hope I'm not disturbing you, Istrak…" Tur had already seated herself on one of the small sofas, eyes darting around to gauge any changes in the room since she had last been to visit. "I just happened to be passing by, and having some free time…"

Istrak's brows snapped together in suspicion. No one in the

royal family had "free time," and no one "just happened" to be passing anywhere. Their days were extremely well planned. Too well planned, he thought.

"Can I let Minra go, Istrak? She has some urgent things to attend to. She'll be back to fetch me in about 20 minutes..." Tur spoke in a low voice, a clear plea in her eyes.

"Certainly, Tur. I'm always happy to see you. Mother Minra, please return for Tur in 20 minutes."

"Go on, Minra," Tur said, twinkling mischievously at the woman who served as both nurse and lady-in-waiting. "My brother will take very good care of me. I am sure of that."

"So what do you want?" Istrak asked. He had ushered his sister, just three years his junior, into an inner room and closed the door in Matel's face.

"Just to talk to you, Istrak. You've been so busy lately. I never see you!" Her voice trembled a little. "My only *real* brother..."

Istrak lowered his eyes. He didn't like the tremor in Tur's voice. As she had indicated, she was the only one of his father's surviving children born to his first wife. "If you like," he said, striving for a casual note, "I'll ask Pinras to set up a meeting for us every week or two."

"A meeting! And should we prepare a summary of the topics to be discussed as well? Istrak, you can't be serious!"

Istrak shrugged. "That's our life, Tur." He paused. "Do you want something to drink?"

She didn't answer.

"Tur?"

His sister's eyes were fixed on an obscure spot in the rug, and a light crease of anguish was visible at the corners of her mouth. She seemed genuinely hurt. Had he gone too far this time?

"In just five days, you will turn 17," Tur whispered. "In six months, you can be the king."

"Heaven forbid!" he exclaimed.

"Yes, of course. I only meant that, at 17½, you will be legally empowered to become king if, Heaven forbid..."

"What are you saying, Tur?" Istrak's hand tightened anxiously around the stem of the silver goblet he had lifted from the table.

"I'm sure that Father — and Mother up above, too — are happy to see the way you've grown. How you've begun to train yourself for the kingship…" The princess' slender white fingers played with the fringe of her dress as she spoke.

"That's not the reason you came here."

"Has anyone ever told you that you're a little too impatient, Your Highness?"

"Has anyone ever told *you* that you cry too often, Princess Tur?"

She dabbed at her eyes with the back of her hand. "Yes. Minra tells me so at least once a week. So what?"

He sat down facing her and held out the goblet of water. "It's… hard for me to see you cry — especially when you speak of our mother."

"I'm sorry."

"And don't mention Father in the same breath — may he be spared for life!"

"Istrak, enough!"

He breathed deeply. "All right. I won't say any more about it."

Tur's eyes raked the room, searching for another topic of conversation. "When did you have those wall-hangings changed? They're nice."

"Thank you." Until that moment, Istrak had not noticed that anyone had changed them. He wondered when it had happened.

"What were you doing before I came here?" she asked.

With a pang, he remembered the doodles shoved under the tablecloth. "Nothing special. I was just trying to work on the *d'var Torah* I'll be saying at the feast…"

"On the anniversary of Mother's death, you mean?"

"No, on my birthday, Your Highness."

"What are you going to speak about?"

Dropping his eyes, he gazed at his fingertips. Tur obviously had something on her mind, but was afraid to broach it. It was up to him to help her.

"Is something bothering you, Tur?" he asked finally, trying to inject a note of interest into his voice.

"Yes — very much so."

"Do you want to tell me about it? Is it about your…your upcoming marriage?"

He was not supposed to talk to her about that. Apparently she had no idea that their father, His Majesty the *khagan*, had taken Istrak into his confidence about his correspondence with Meshuel Min-Hagai, her intended's father.

"No." Her voice steadied. "Father knows everything he needs to know about Meshuel's son. I'm sure that Ruben is a good person and that we will be happy together. No, that's not what's troubling me."

"Then what is it?"

Her life was so different from his own. She spent her time chatting and going on outings with her friends, performing assorted acts of charity, doing a bit of fine needlework and embroidery, taking a few lessons in the Holy Scriptures… What could there possibly be to trouble her in such a life?

"It's not *what* is bothering me…it's *who* is bothering me," she said, fixing him with her blue-eyed gaze.

"Who?"

She studied him for a long moment, as though assessing his ability to handle what she was about to say. Then, quietly but with an uncharacteristic firmness, she said, "You."

Istrak looked back at her through narrowed eyes. "I'm sorry to hear that, Your Highness," he drawled. "Do you care to explain?"

"It's a long conversation," Tur said. "And not an easy one."

Istrak's lips stretched into a smile. "I've suffered through worse. Go ahead — tell me!"

At the hour when the royal family was seated in the dining hall, the palace corridors were relatively empty. Only a few sentries, resplendent in their leather uniforms and metallic armor, stood guard in the alcoves.

"Hurry, Your Highness," Pinras urged as they traversed the long passages. "Your father will not be pleased with your being late. Why did you do it?" He looked worried.

Istrak swallowed. He didn't know why he had done it, except that riding in the south pasture, with a fresh wind blowing in his face, had been even more pleasant than usual. So pleasant that when Matel came to inform him that it was time to return to the palace, he had refused. In the face of the prince's insistence on taking one more gallop around the pasture — promising to make all haste in preparing for dinner afterward — Matel had been powerless.

"You know that Matel was punished because of you, Istrak."

Istrak stiffened. No, he hadn't known. It had never occurred to him that Matel's job description included seeing that the young heir adhered to his schedule. Istrak's extra gallop had made the man derelict in his duties. Had he known that, he would certainly have kept his promise to hurry. Instead, he had prepared for the meal in a desultory fashion.

He glanced at his mentor, contrite. "I didn't think of that, Pinras."

"You didn't think!" Pinras' tone hovered between surprise and anger. It seemed to Istrak that, if not for his own exalted position, Pinras would have injected a measure of contempt into the words as well.

"Tell Matel that I'm sorry. I'll make it up to him," Istrak mumbled.

"Make it up to him! Really?" Pinras was slightly breathless with the rapid pace of their walk. "How, exactly?"

Istrak sneaked a glance over his shoulder at a pair of armed guards standing in their niche. Why must Pinras rebuke him in public?

"I'll find a way," he promised.

Pinras offered no reply to this. But the sudden infinitesimal softening of the pale features told Istrak that his mentor approved.

It was strange to reach the dining hall after the doors of *havnei* wood — black and hard as marble — had already been closed, and to view them, for the first time in his life, from the other side. He was astonished to find no less than sixteen guards patrolling the halls while the royal family sat at their dinner.

"Don't say too much, Istrak. Just apologize and ask your father to forgive you and permit you to join them at the table." This time,

Pinras was careful to pitch his voice low. "And fix the fringes of your *tzitzis*!"

Someone, one of the guards, swung open the massive, ornate doors. Pinras, face glowing in the torchlight emanating from the room, pushed Istrak in ahead of him.

The hall was not the largest in the palace. It was family-sized, as the king liked to say. Broad windows were set into two of the walls, with delicate draperies of Roman design cascading from them. On the two opposite walls hung colorful tapestries, expertly woven, depicting famous scenes from Khazar's illustrious history.

In the center of the room stood a low dining table made of marble. Ranged around the table were nine armchairs, eight of them seating members of the royal family — all of them shooting a look of reproach at Istrak. He crossed the room hesitantly.

"You are late, my son."

Reuel II, Istrak's father, was a sturdy, light-haired man of medium height who sported a long scar on his left cheek — a momento from one of the great battles he had fought in his youth. Slowly, and with his characteristic royal calm, he lifted his eyes to Istrak's face.

"I *am* late, Father, and I'm sorry…" The words stuck in Istrak's throat. When he finally succeeded in uttering them, they had an odd ring. "I know that I've disobeyed your wish, and I regret that. I…I will accept with love any punishment I'm given."

The silence in the room was heavy. Michoel and Tur stared in fascination at the globules of fat that had floated to the top of their soup bowls. Little Lissia watched her big brother in wide-eyed astonishment, while 6-year-old Binyamin, 8-year-old Unmar, and 9-year-old Yekavel gazed in turn at Istrak's flaming cheeks and the *khagan*'s stern countenance.

"Come here, Istrak."

At this command, Istrak drew closer to his father's chair. The queen murmured something to the king in a quiet voice.

"You know that I love you, Istrak."

"Yes, Father."

"You know that one day you are destined to become king?"

"Yes, Father."

"There was no justification for your being late today."

"That is true, Father."

"Do you know that it is my obligation to care for the well-being of the Khazar kingdom?"

"Yes, Father."

"Do you understand that a prince who is incapable of obeying his father's instructions, who follows instead the whims of his own heart, can never be a genuine king, as our forefathers were before us?"

"I...I understand, Father."

The *khagan* rose from his chair with a sigh and gazed directly into his son's eyes. A moment later, he slapped Istrak's cheek — a stinging, mortifying blow.

"I do this for your sake, and for the sake of Khazar." The *khagan's* voice was dry. "Your meal will be brought to you in your room. I will not study with you today."

"I...understand, Father." Stunned by the slap, Istrak could think of no clever answer.

"Go."

Istrak hesitated. Then he bowed deeply and left the room, walking backward.

The last thing he saw before the *havnei* doors swung shut was Tur's pain-filled gaze.

Naitan set down Istrak's food, which he had carried up from the kitchen, on the table. Istrak did not even glance at the silver tray. "I don't want to eat, Pinras," he told his mentor, who was sitting across from him.

"That doesn't surprise me."

"Don't *you* be angry at me, too!"

"I'm not permitted to be angry at you, dear prince."

"But you *are* angry," Istrak said.

Pinras blinked. "True, Your Highness. I will leave you alone now. A servant will come by later to accompany you to your lesson with the *rav*. The two guards who escorted us here will stand outside your door until then."

"On my father's orders?"

"Yes, Your Highness. May Hashem bless you."

Two hours. Two full hours stretched ahead of him, hours in which he was not obliged to carry out any specific task. Two hours that conformed to every detail of his dearest wish: he was alone, without Pinras or any other noble companion, and no obligation to fulfill… But tonight, not surprisingly, Istrak found nothing joyful or exciting in the situation.

"It's all Tur's fault!" he said through clenched teeth. "Tur — not me!" His cheek still stung. No one had ever slapped him before.

Tur had infuriated him. Her criticism had been so smug and condescending!

"Your voice is indifferent and your expression aloof," she had said to him that afternoon. "You don't look happy. And that bothers me, because you have no reason to be so bitter. You must learn to be happy," she had continued, and it was only the good manners that Pinras had drilled into him that prevented him from offering his candid opinion of her criticism.

He had been happy for 10 minutes — while riding his horse and forgetting the challenges with which he contended daily in his role as crown prince. And what had come of it? Two hours' imprisonment, with guards outside his door.

He dropped his head on his arms, grateful for the darkness that awaited him there, warm and enveloping. His thoughts whirled through his head in confusion, but they all shared a single, common thread: anger.

The knocking woke him. Groggily, he remembered that he had locked the door before sitting down at the table. "Who's there?"

"It is the vice-commander of the royal guard, Your Highness. In the name of the king — open the door!"

"At once," he replied.

The key was not in the lock. Where had he put it? A glimpse in the mirror as he searched for it showed him a face stained with tears and crisscrossed with red lines — telltale remnants of the restless sleep he had had with his cheeks pillowed on his sleeves.

"Your Highness, open up!"

At last — the key. It must have slipped out of his hand while he slept.

Behind the door stood eight soldiers in full battle dress: shield, sword, large bow, and a quiver of arrows. Their faces were stern and tense.

"How can I help you, goodmen?" An eerie feeling made its way down Istrak's spine.

"By order of His Majesty the king, you are to come with us at once."

Istrak's brow wrinkled. There could be no connection between his late appearance at dinner and these unexpected soldiers at his door. His father's reaction had already been harsher than he had expected it to be. But if there was no link between these soldiers and the slap he had received at his father's hand — what *had* brought them here?

"I'll don my cloak and join you at once."

Whirling around, Istrak started for the inner room, acutely aware of his rumpled appearance.

"There's no time for that, Your Highness."

Why not?

What had happened?

Slowly, Istrak turned back to face the soldiers. Feeling stranger than ever, he stepped out into the passage. In unison, the soldiers raised their shields and formed a tight wall around him, shields facing outward.

It was beneath his dignity to ask where they were taking him. But he would gladly give half the inheritance he had been bequeathed by his mother if someone would just tell him what was going on.

николи, in all his 17 years, had Istrak witnessed such confusion within the palace walls.

Borne along as though by a storm wind amid the armed soldiers who had formed a tight square around him, he glimpsed frightened chambermaids closing shutters with a great clatter, squads of elite *hostress* troops racing to and fro, and groups of noblemen and warriors gathered in the reception hall, all of them speaking loudly and at the same time.

"Hurry, Your Highness!"

He *was* hurrying — but wouldn't anyone tell him *why*? What had happened in the past two hours to justify such agitation?

"To the cellar, Your Highness!"

The usually dim corridors in the cellar level now blazed in the light of a dozen torches. Raised voices emanated from one of the rooms, but he was ushered into the room adjacent to it.

As his human shield dispersed, Istrak was able to see the anxious faces of the distinguished men seated around the long, wooden table. The talking halted abruptly. Silence dominated the space between the bare walls; the only sound to be heard was the scrape of the *khagan*'s chair as he rose to his feet.

"Istrak, my son." The *khagan*'s scar looked more pronounced than usual against his white face. He had exchanged his light dinner robe for a suit of gilded armor.

Istrak bit his tongue. A prince must not be curious; nor was he permitted to display impatience.

"A tragedy has occurred. A tragedy for Khazar, and a tragedy for our family…"

The men around the table cast down their eyes.

"My brother-in-law the *bek* — your uncle Eshal — was murdered in the conference hall just moments ago."

The floor seemed to rock beneath Istrak's feet. The room was very quiet as everyone stared fixedly at him, watching for his reaction to the news of the prime minister's murder.

"*Baruch Dayan ha'emes*," Istrak said, licking his dry lips. Poor Pinras! Had he been informed of his father's death?

"The murder took place here, within the palace walls, only a few minutes ago. Pinras has set out to take the bitter news to my sister, his mother." The king paused, then said, "Come here, my son."

How different this command was from the same words spoken earlier that evening! This time, his father's voice was soft, almost loving.

From somewhere a fur-trimmed cloak was handed to him. Istrak slipped it on over his creased shirt. The chair beside his father's was empty, waiting for him. He sat down hesitantly. This was the first time he had ever been invited to participate in an emergency conference of any kind.

The king's eyes were closed, one hand covering them as though he were reciting the *Shema*. "Let us begin at the beginning," he said after a long moment, removing his hand from his eyes. "Lord Elnatan, you were there. Tell us, in as much detail as possible, what happened."

"Very well, sire." Elnatan's chair scraped over the stone floor as he stood. "Just before Minchah, I received an urgent letter from Eshal, *zichrono livrachah*…" He choked on these last words, finding it difficult to continue. After a pause, he went on.

"He asked me to go to the eastern conference hall immediately after the service to finish the conversation we'd begun this morning — a matter connected to the fund for needy Torah scholars. Eshal…" Again Elnatan paused, his breathing becoming labored. "…was very active in that cause. He personally raised most of the funds necessary for its continued success." Elnatan, minister of education, knew just how vital these funds were.

The *khagan* waved a hand: time was short. Eulogies would have to wait.

"When we reached the room, all the windows were shut and the air was hot and sticky. He himself opened the window… The arrow penetrated the room just seconds later. A single arrow, no more. It struck a death blow."

"Which window?" asked Bastian Makan. Bastian was the supreme commander of the Khazar army. He was also the present queen's brother.

"The third window from the left. The one directly opposite the conference table, facing the chair at the table's head…"

"Was Eshal sitting in that chair?" Bastian asked.

"No. He was in a low armchair, where he always sits during informal talks. Someone knew that."

"Thank you, Lord Elnatan," the king said. "Where is the sentry who came running in at the sound of Elnatan's shout?"

"In the passage, sire."

"Bring him in."

The sentry who entered the room was, like most Khazars, tall and light-haired. The sparse beard on his chin evidenced that he was not much older than Istrak.

"Your name, goodman?"

"Leuman, Your Majesty. Leuman ben Katrel."

"You were patrolling the hall when the prime minister was murdered?"

"I was standing at the left-hand guard post, Your Majesty."

"Why did you enter the conference room?" Bastian demanded.

"I heard him shout." The sentry nodded at Elnatan. "I wanted to help."

"And when you entered the room — what did you see?"

"Him." Another bob of the head toward the minister of education. "Bending over the injured man."

"Injured?" The king's brows lifted in surprise.

"Yes, Your Majesty. When I approached the prime minister, he was still alive. He did not seem to be breathing, but there was a heartbeat. I removed the arrow, as we were taught to do. The wound was mortal — just over the heart. There was not much to be done."

"Who summoned the rest of the guard?" Bastian asked when the king said nothing.

"He did, sir."

"He?"

Leuman pointed to Elnatan. "Yes, Lord Elnatan, sir."

"What else can you tell us?"

The young man's face twisted. Istrak felt a wave of compassion for him. This was probably his first encounter with death.

"The room was hot," the guard said finally. "Very hot, as though someone had turned on the big furnace… After I saw that I could do nothing to help the prime minister, I went to the window, but I saw nothing suspicious."

"Thank you, Leuman. Here is a note to the treasurer. He is to pay you three months' salary and you are to return to your home for a rest…"

Istrak's heart was flooded with love for his good father. He could be counted on to understand the guard's pain. The young man had doubtless not been back home since the start of his training, shortly before his 14th birthday. This leave would be a boon for him.

"Thank you, Your Majesty. May Hashem bless you from the treasury of unearned gifts."

Bastian turned to Istrak. "As a superior archer and vice-commander of the royal archery division, can the Prince tell us where an archer would have to be standing in order to penetrate the eastern conference hall? I'm interested in an exact description of all possible trajectories, as well as —" a cough interrupted the flow of his words — "as well as the Prince's opinion of where the arrow came from."

Only now did Istrak notice the bloodstained arrow lying on a piece of cloth in the center of the table, beside his father's scepter.

"That's a royal arrow!" he exclaimed, noting the golden feather at the arrow's end and the telltale copper thread. "Each fletcher [arrow maker] etches his personal insignia onto the inner side of the tail balance. An expert could easily take apart the arrow to verify that."

"Very good." Bastian was pleased. Apparently, no one but Istrak had remembered this practice among the royal craftsmen.

"What is the maximum distance these arrows can fly, my son?"

"That depends on the quality of the bow and the arm of the archer. If we're talking about an ordinary bow, it would be reasonable to say that it could go no farther than 700 feet."

"And if a double bow was used?"

"If it was, then the situation becomes worse." The deputy prime minister, red-haired Dalo Stazdiran, anticipated Istrak's answer. "By law, as of seventeen years ago, common folk are forbidden to use bows made of *tamil* wood!"

"Thank you, Deputy Prime Minister." A longstanding animosity reigned between Bastian and Dalo Stazdiran. "Honored *Uflah*," — Bastian Makan turned back to Istrak, calling him by his official title — "if one were using a double bow, what is the maximum distance that an experienced archer can achieve?"

"Up to 2,000 feet."

The king and his army commander exchanged a quick glance. Istrak thought he knew what it meant. Even if the anonymous attacker had sent his arrow flying at Uncle Eshal from the maximum range — he had done so within the precincts of the palace.

"Do you have anything to add, my son?"

"I think so, Father. To achieve a shooting strength of 700 feet, the archer must weigh at least 275 pounds. Therefore, the archer cannot be a short or thin man. Also, his two fingers would be scarred by the force of pulling the bowstring."

"Thank you, Prince of Khazar." Bastian's chair creaked as he resumed his seat.

"One of the soldiers has been asked to bring maps of the palace into the next room. I would be pleased, Istrak," his father said slowly, "if you would use them to determine where the archer stood."

"Of course, sire."

Istrak's limbs felt heavy as he stood up. The realization struck him with the force of an unexpected blow: he was not really needed here. Each of the men seated around this table was far more experienced than he. These were men who had fought in wars — unlike himself, a green youth, a spoiled prince who had been lucky enough to be born and raised during a peaceful lull, when Khazar's enemies were afraid to lift their heads. These veterans who knew so much — they didn't need *him*! None of them had "forgotten" the distance an arrow could fly from a double bow. Any child in Khazar knew that! Had he really believed that he was needed to remind them?

Had he really thought that he had been summoned to this emergency meeting because they wanted him there?

He shook his head. What was he thinking?

And how dare he feel sad over this, when Pinras, his dear cousin and mentor, had just been told that his father had been murdered in cold blood?

Yishvav the Babylonian was an old and withered man, lame in both legs, taciturn and impatient. Istrak and Yishvav had worked as a team before, in various military games where Istrak was asked to assess war strategies devised by army commanders and to analyze their strengths and weaknesses. Yishvav was an outstanding strategist. "A *bar samchah* — outstanding in his field," Pinras had labeled the Babylonian. This was one of the few words of praise attributed to the man who, despite his many talents, was not liked by many. It was the old man's presence that was causing Istrak's mood to fluctuate wildly between heroism and despair.

"You have come, Your Highness."

In the last room off the passage he had found Yishvav already seated, the tip of his quill flipping through the maps lying before him. A pair of wooden crutches rested on the table.

"I have come, Yishvav. I see they've already brought the maps here."

"Of course they've brought them," the Babylonian snapped. "But these scribbles, I must tell you, are beneath contempt."

"We'll do the best we can, Yishvav. I hope you haven't been waiting long."

"That's all right." The Babylonian's long fingers tugged at one of the maps. "I want to know where he came from, that killer — may his name be blotted out... Bring me a parchment from over there. Meanwhile, take a look at the general layout of the palace to refresh your memory, Prince. I will need a measuring device as well."

The crown prince obligingly complied. Then, because Yishvav's crutches, sprawled across the table, prevented Istrak from adequately spreading the map, he crouched on the floor and ran an eye over the blueprint of the royal palace.

"Something isn't logical here, Yishvav," he said, his gaze suddenly transfixed. "They're talking about the conference hall in the southeastern corner of the palace, right?"

"Yes, Your Highness. What, exactly, do you find illogical? I'd really like to hear..." Yishvav's tone was mocking.

"This!" Istrak leaped to his feet and thrust the map under Yishvav's nose. "Give me your measure for a minute..."

A careful measurement proved that he had guessed correctly. "I was right. It's impossible to shoot from the garden into a second-story window and strike a person seated on a chair that's lower than the window. Isn't that right? And the angle of a shot from the government building would be equally impossible!"

"Do not say 'impossible,'" Yishvav said, dampening Istrak's ardor. "If we say 'impossible' to everything, our enemies will topple us into the ground before we can say '*Shema* ...'"

"Bring this paper to my father, Yishvav. You may tell him that you are interrupting the meeting on my explicit order. Now, I must go."

"Really!"

"Do as I've told you, Yishvav!" Without conscious intent, Istrak's tone grew harsher.

"And where are you going, if I may ask, my Prince?"

"I have not granted you permission to ask."

It wasn't difficult for Istrak to read the strategist's thoughts, but he didn't care. Let Yishvav think he was behaving like a child. Right now he had more important things to concern him.

Soldiers straightened their backs and greeted him as he passed among them. To his surprise, none of them stopped him to inquire where he was headed. He attributed this to the typical soldier's unpreparedness for coping with emergencies of this kind. Although he was able to take advantage of the situation at the moment, he knew there would be an accounting to render later.

"Soldier!"

A slab of meat went flying from the hand of the young private Istrak had addressed. The soldier scrambled to his feet.

"Yes, Your Highness?"

"You are on your break, if I understand correctly."

"Yes, Your Highness."

"Come here…"

Minutes later, armed with the soldier's shield, helmet, and sword, Istrak climbed the stairs.

"Where to, goodman?" Two of the palace guards emerged from their alcoves and stopped him at sword point.

"I am here by the King's orders. Let me pass!"

The two guards exchanged a suspicious glance. "Which division do you belong to?" asked the taller of the two.

Istrak hesitated. He had donned the soldier's garb in order to forestall recognition by enemies who, he surmised, were present on the palace grounds. What he had not taken into account was that, disguised in a private's uniform, his movements would be severely restricted. Making a snap decision, he drew off the helmet and revealed his face.

The soldiers straightened with a jerk. "May H-Hashem bless you from the treasury of unearned gifts, Your Highness," the shorter guard panted. "But — why is Your Highness dressed in that uniform?"

"Summon sixty *hostress* soldiers to the Path of Knowledge." Istrak whipped off the gold pin that adorned his cloak. "Give this to the commander so that he'll believe you. Hurry!"

Without waiting for their answer, or even turning his head to see if they had obeyed, Istrak broke into a sprint. As he ran, he fumbled with the helmet's straps, trying to refasten them under his chin. In moments he reached the top of the stairs on the entrance level.

"Where to, goodman?" This time he nearly collided with a nobleman clad in armor, who was making his way down to the cellar. "And why do you not show honor to men of position, as the law dictates?"

"Really, Matel!" Istrak grinned. "Let go of my arm, if you please. You're hurting me."

"*You*?" The steely grip on Istrak's forearm loosened at once. Matel looked concerned. "What are you doing here, Your Highness?"

"There is no time to explain. I need you to come with me now."

In the company of the sturdy and good-natured Matel, who was known to everyone in the palace, Istrak's progress through the bustling halls was swift. The soldiers lowered their weapons and permitted the unknown private to pass at will.

"Who gave you leave, Private, to burst into my room?" The sight of Istrak's drawn sword, which he had used to persuade the guards to let him in, inflamed the commander.

"Sheath your sword, Landon Brach," Istrak said quietly. "Don't you recognize me? Apparently, my uncle's murderer is still in the treasury house. We must surround the archery range and seal off the exits leading to the city to prevent the killer from escaping."

Brach's eyes, which had bulged in disbelief at first, shone with understanding. He tensed for battle.

"The archery range, Your Highness?"

"Yes. Take your men out through the Scholars' Gate and encircle the area. You must seal it off completely. Don't let anyone go out to the city that way."

The commander nodded and walked to the door. "Your instructions will be carried out at once. Guards! After me!"

In an incredible display of coordinated movement, the men who had been scattered along the passage were transformed into a single stream flowing through the northern exit.

"Are we finished, Your Highness?" Matel had been patiently silent while Istrak issued orders.

"Not yet, Matel." Istrak went to the window. "The *hostress* will be here soon. We will await them here."

Beads of perspiration dripped from Istrak's helmet. The mail shirt that he had borrowed from the soldier was too narrow in the shoulders for him. And yet, those same shoulders felt far too narrow to bear the heavy burden of responsibility that he had assumed in the wake of the tragedy. If he failed, he would become the target of every jokester in the kingdom.

The minutes that passed until the first of the *hostress* soldiers filtered into the small plaza in front of window felt like an eternity. When they arrived, Istrak prepared to leave.

"You're going out…through the window, sir?"

"Yes, you can stay here, Matel. Thank you for your assistance."

Placing both palms facedown on the windowsill, Istrak leaped up and through to the other side. He landed beside the platoon commander's horse.

"Your Highness?" The metal plates on the commander's chest, worn by all *hostress* troops assigned to the royal compound, gleamed in the sunlight.

"Yes. The treasury house must be surrounded and its guards placed under arrest. Then you must enter the building and search for the prime minister's killer."

"I lack the authority to enter the building, Your Highness," the *hostress* commander said in a low voice to keep his men from hearing. "And apart from the question of authority, not all the troops who are with me are loyal enough or honest enough to be trusted in such a guarded place, sir."

Istrak bit his lip.

"In that case —" he raised his voice — "arrest the treasury-house guards and surround the building! Don't let anyone escape. Wait there until I return to you with explicit instructions from His Majesty."

The platoon commander turned to his men. "Do you hear, *hostress* soldiers?"

The men's shouts of affirmation could be heard a long way off.

"You sent men to surround the archery range."

"Yes, Your Majesty."

"And you instructed sixty *hostress* soldiers to arrest the guards at the treasury and encircle the building."

"Yes, Your Majesty. The maps show it beyond all doubt: it would have been impossible to shoot the prime minister from any other angle than the two southwestern windows of the treasury house."

The king compressed his lips. "Lord Yishvav does not agree with you, Istrak."

"I most certainly do *not* agree, Your Majesty!" came Yishvav's gravelly voice. "The boy is very quick to say, 'Impossible' and 'It can't be.'" His imitation of the crown prince brought suppressed smiles to several of the courtier's faces.

A surge of anger flared in Istrak. "It's been many years since Sir Yishvav has grasped a bow," he replied, trying to maintain a courteous tone while darting a furious glance at Dalo Stazdiran, whose smile had been particularly broad. "Perhaps he no longer remembers the basic rules of the craft. I have yet to hear about the archer who has succeeded in altering the angle of his arrow after it's left the bow. Look at these maps, Your Majesty."

Istrak leaned over the table, tugging with unprincely impatience at the rolled-up maps beside Yishvav. "If we assume that the anonymous archer did not rely on a sudden change in wind direction to carry the arrow in an unnatural path, then we see — right here — that the only two possible trajectories that can strike the prime minister's favorite armchair are these. The first exits from the last window on the treasury building's western wall, and the second from the window next to it. No other trajectories exist."

Silence reigned in the room after Istrak finished demonstrating the trajectories on the parchment.

"Yishvav?"

"The lad appears to be correct, sire." It was clearly difficult for

Yishvav to say the words. "But it is impossible to get into the treasury building!"

A fragile smile touched the king's mouth for the first time. "A talented officer has drilled one basic rule into our troops, Lord Yishvav of Babylon: 'Nothing is impossible!'

"This meeting is now adjourned." Some of the sparkle had returned to his father's eye, much to Istrak's satisfaction. "Lord Dalo, as you have outlined, guards will be posted on the streets of Khazaran-Itil until after the funeral. The army commander will select the troops to patrol the streets and will personally supervise the siege around the treasury building until we find the murderer.

"Lord Elnatan, when the funeral is over, you must deliver a speech to allay the fears of the populace. Promise them, in my name, that the Kingdom of Khazar will not rest until those responsible for this crime have been brought to justice.

"Lord Tobias, Guard of the Treasury — you will go now with members of the palace guard. Until events in the treasury house have been thoroughly investigated, you will reside in guest quarters. You will not participate in the *bek's* funeral.

"My son and I will remain here until we have received a report from the commander regarding the siege. You may be summoned to another meeting tonight. Blessings and sweet sleep."

There was a general scraping of chairs as the men rose to their feet. The babble of voices receded as they moved down the passage. Finally, all was silent. Servants began moving vigorously around the room, preparing it for a long vigil.

"Your Majesty?" whispered Istrak, standing close to his father.

The king did not react. A sigh of disappointment escaped the prince. His father was still angry with him, despite everything. His cheek burned suddenly, as though in memory of the ringing slap it had earlier received.

"Miflaeus! Tell the queen and the children that they may return to their rooms — with the usual security precautions, of course. Istrak has identified the location from where the arrow issued. Strict guard is being kept around the palace. And tell Michoel that I would be pleased to learn with him now. There is a long night ahead of us…"

Miflaeus, scion of a noble family from the south, set down the tray of fruit he had just lifted and hastened from the room, light-footed and silent.

"Father?" Istrak tried again, before his brother appeared.

The *khagan*'s gaze remained fixed on some hidden point.

"Father, I did all right tonight, didn't I?"

The king's only reaction was a quivering muscle at the corner of his mouth. Istrak hesitated. Then he went down on one knee, near his father's chair, as he had often done on official occasions and placed a hand on his father's arm. "Won't you forgive me, Father? I made a mistake, and I was punished. Is that not enough?"

"Rise, Prince of Khazar. You need not kneel."

Prince of Khazar, thought Istrak as he rose. Not Istrak, and not "my son"…

"Hashem has blessed you with many gifts. Gifts without number." The king spoke quietly, and it was only by straining that Istrak was able to hear him. "He has given you wisdom — much wisdom. He has showered you with rare abilities of both body and mind. He has placed you in the highest position that a son of Khazar can aspire to — and you reject it all?"

The *khagan* held up a hand to preempt Istrak's protests. "Do not say a word, son. When you stormed out of your swordmanship lesson, was that not an indication of ingratitude to the Creator Who sent us the best teacher there is to teach you how to defend your own life as well your kingdom in time of need?

"And when you come late to a meal with your father, is that not demonstrating scorn toward the fact that he has freed himself of all his official duties — the weight of which you will appreciate when your own time comes — to dine with you and your siblings?

"You have no idea of the gifts that Hashem has showered upon you, Istrak. If you were truly happy with all the bounty that you've been granted from on High, your life would look different."

A shadow crossed the king's face, and he bowed his head. "You've just seen how easy it is to take away a person's life, no matter how exalted his position. No man knows the number of his years. When

I look at you and see that you're still a boy — an ungrateful child — I become afraid for the fate of Khazar…

"Welcome, Michoel. Have you brought the scroll of tractate *Shabbos*? Good, my son. Ovadia, bring a chair for Prince Michoel."

Istrak stood up. His father would say no more about the subject tonight.

The minutes dragged by slowly, like droplets of persimmon oil dripping from a bottle's mouth. The soldiers' calls, which had sounded at close intervals at the onset of the long night, grew more and more infrequent. The circle around the treasury house was complete, Bastian reported to the king.

"Now, all we need is patience."

Patience. Istrak rubbed his eyes. The letters of the holy Gemara, inscribed on the parchment scroll, seemed to blur, and the blurring did not come from torch smoke or any deficiency on the part of the scribe. Istrak stifled a yawn. His father and Michoel, on the other side of the room, did not appear tired at all.

The king asked a question, and Michoel tried to answer it. In a few words, the father picked apart the son's answer. Ovadia, the king's personal assistant, was sent to bring a Torah scroll from the library.

Istrak brought his eyes back to the parchment. Were it not for his stupid mistake, his father would have been learning with him, not Michoel. Michoel was still a child. His answers were without foundation, and his questions deserved a pitying smile. Nevertheless, the smile on the king's face was not one of pity, but of pleasure — a deep, inner *nachas*.

"Miflaeus," Istrak whispered.

The redheaded nobleman, who had returned to keep guard, rose. "At your service, Your Highness."

"Do you have any idea what time it is?"

"No, Prince of Khazar."

His father lifted his eyes from his scroll and sent them a sharp look.

"All right," Istrak murmured. "I just wanted to know."

Michoel said something, and his father lovingly ruffled the boy's hair. Then the king said something, and Michoel laughed out loud. Miflaeus fetched a light blanket from a closet in a corner of the room and spread it over the crown prince's knees. Istrak had dozed off.

Outside, the sky turned gray, and a new day dawned over Khazar.

"Y OU'VE GOT TO CLIMB THIS HILL," KALEV URGED THE GRAY donkey. "We made this trip yesterday and the day before. You can't get tired today, of all days! Just when the doctor said that we must buy a chicken for Father!"

The donkey gave him a tired look.

"I know I cut back your portion of food today. I trimmed mine, too. Come on, already!" the boy pleaded.

The donkey stirred in melancholy resignation and took a step or two.

"Yes, just like that. You walk forward and I'll help from behind, okay? If you're good, maybe we'll find an old carrot in the marketplace for you. And maybe the *bek's* secretary will have an answer for us today…"

The wooden wagon wheels rolled slowly.

"Very nice, donkey. Let's go!" Despite the predawn chill, Kalev's back was soaked with sweat. The encouraging words he poured into the donkey's ears seemed to be actually aimed at himself…

"You there!" The shout came from the bridge.

"Yes, goodmen?"

The soldiers' arrows were drawn on their bowstrings, and their faces did not look at all friendly.

"Leave the wagon and climb up here. Slowly, with your hands raised!"

The donkey, in a sudden spurt of industry, began dragging the wagon up the hill.

"May I stop my donkey first?" Kalev called, raising his hands. This was not the first time he had been stopped by a patrol, but never had the soldiers sounded so harsh.

"No," came the curt reply.

"Can I put my hands down while I climb the hill? It's hard to climb such a steep slant with my hands in the air!"

"You can do exactly as you're told — if you wish to live to see the sunrise!" There was a distinct threat in the words.

Kalev's sense of humor abruptly abandoned him. This was clearly no laughing matter. Here was no tired patrol wanting to know what a young boy was doing out at such an early hour. It was something else — something much more serious. Arduously, he climbed the slippery slope and presented himself for the soldiers' inspection. His hands, extended high in the air, were beginning to ache.

A well-aimed blow threw him to the ground, where strong arms held him down.

"Forgive our lack of manners, but everyone has his job to do." The voice of the soldier who had him pinned down was dry and insincere, and his face, hovering close to Kalev's, was covered with youthful spots. "I'm going to turn you over now and tie your hands. You'll be treated with respect — as long as you don't resist."

"What did I do?" Tears of pain trickled from the corners of Kalev's eyes. "I've done nothing wrong! Haven't you ever seen a boy trying to help his family earn a living?"

The soldier didn't bother answering.

Kalev, his vision still obscured by the young soldier's pimply face, felt someone conduct a thorough search of his clothing. It was a degrading sensation.

"Captain!"

"Yes?"

"He has a Kawari throwing-axe."

The youthful soldier's grip tightened. "Traitor!" The Kawaris were the Khazars' bitter enemies, and the throwing-axe their national weapon of choice.

"It is *not* a throwing-axe!" Kalev protested. "And the picture on the handle was drawn by my little sister. I'm a woodcutter, and this is just a family joke. Anyway, there are no Kawaris anywhere near here! What do you fellows want from me?"

A rope went around his hands and feet. Then strong arms lifted him — trussed like a lamb on its way to the slaughterer — and deposited him roughly on the floor of an army cart.

"You said that if I raised my hands, I'd get to see the sunrise..." he quipped weakly to another soldier, who was busy tying the rope that bound him to a metal ring screwed into the side of the wagon.

The soldier didn't turn his head. "I'm sorry, but we're taking you to the military prison now."

"Me? You're crazy!"

"Maybe." The soldier sitting on the bench appeared, by the look of his sandals and tanned skin, to have come to Khazarin-Itil, the Khazar capital, from the south. Khazaran-Itil was actually two separate cities: Itil, home of the royal family and the nobility, and Khazaran, surrounding it, for the common folk. "However, right now you have no choice but to come with us."

"At least don't let my donkey run away!" Kalev fumed. "When I'm released, I'll bring you to judgment before the *bek*!"

"What touching innocence," said a mocking voice whose source was invisible to Kalev. "Do you really think anyone will believe that you still don't know that Lord Eshal was murdered last night?"

"The *bek*?" The rooster he had hoped to receive from the prime minister's secretary seemed to crow mockingly in Kalev's ears.

"You didn't know?" the same voice drawled. "Surprise, surprise..."

"Don't mock the boy, Chiel! As long as he's not proved guilty, we must treat him as innocent."

"Innocent, innocent," the wagon wheels seemed to chant in unison.

"Why would I want to kill the prime minister?" Kalev burst out. "Why would anyone want to do such a despicable thing?"

"Quiet, please." The pimple-ridden face leaned over him again. "You'll be able to ask all your questions when you meet the investigating officer. There is justice and there is a judge in Khazar. The truth will out — whether that comforts you or not!"

"I'm sure —"

"I told you to be quiet!" The soldier was obviously annoyed. "Don't force me to use less pleasant methods."

Though he did not specify these methods, the fear that coursed through Kalev made him close his eyes in submission and try his best to still his pounding heart.

The jailhouse was a small white building partially covered with a climbing vine of *partaya*, pretty purple flowers with surprisingly sharp thorns. The warden looked like a kindly old grandfather, and the soldiers on duty appeared much more cheerful and relaxed than the stern-faced military patrol that had arrested him.

The room to which Kalev was taken was also quite pleasant, with whitewashed stone walls, a mattress of medium thickness, and a small, barred window revealing a profusion of more *partaya* blossoms.

Patience, Kalev thought, leaning his head back against the wall. All he needed now was a little patience. The interrogation officer was, he had been informed, due shortly. The truth would be made clear, and he would return home with a riveting tale for his little sister.

It was hard to believe that there was someone who wanted Lord Eshal dead. Who would want to see Stazdiran take his place?

No sane person, that much was certain.

Eshal's hand had been open to all, while his deputy was known to be stingy and tightfisted.

A strange story. A Kawari throwing-axe... Questions flew through Kalev's mind like storks in autumn. How was it that he, out of all the boys in Khazar, had suddenly become a prime suspect in this case? And what would happen if he didn't succeed in dispelling the cloud of guilt that seemed to hover over him? What if all his explanations fell on deaf ears?

But such a thing could not happen. Khazar was known for a civil justice system that was far fairer and more ethical than those of its neighbors. Nevertheless, fear froze the boy's muscles and erased from his memory every chapter of *Tehillim* he had ever known by heart.

The funeral procession of Khazar's prime minister, the Lord Eshal Bluadian, left the Royal House of Study, a place that had been lovingly refurbished by the murdered man. Ten or twelve people rose to eulogize the prime minister and speak in his praise.

Few people had the full facts, which rendered Eshal's death even more tragic. Just two hours earlier, the palace guard had penetrated the treasury house. On the top floor, exactly where Istrak had suspected, they found the corpse of a man who had been in Eshal's service — a simple-minded man of 37. He had killed himself, they surmised, after letting loose the fatal arrow that had felled the *bek*. The man, who all knew to be not quite in his right mind, had recently been seen wandering about the royal plaza, offering to anyone who would listen a litany of complaints against his immediate superior, the man in charge of the *bek's* household who, he claimed, had treated him with contempt and reduced his salary without any justification. He also bore a grudge against the *bek* himself for not agreeing to fire the man.

How foolish to die that way… What a waste, to end such a rich and accomplished life in such a manner. How sad and pointless! So said the dignitaries who delivered the eulogies.

Though the murderer was dead, questions remained. How had the simpleton managed to enter the well-guarded treasure house? And how had he had the presence of mind to plan such a well-aimed attack undetected?

Though the security team acknowledged these as valid questions, the means of the murder were, to their minds, all too clear. It was also clear that someone else had instigated the murder

— someone who had access to the treasury house — and all efforts were now focused on finding out who that was. Soldiers all over Khazar were on high alert, and anyone suspected of taking part in the conspiracy was being arrested and interrogated.

After the funeral, Istrak went to take his leave of his mentor. Pinras closed his eyes for a brief moment.

"Thank you for coming, Istrak."

"Did you think I wouldn't come?" From the corner of his eye, Istrak saw his father part from Pinras' mother, who was the king's sister, as she climbed aboard her carriage.

"I knew you would come. And still — thank you." Pinras' eyes were red.

Istrak murmured, "*HaMakom yenachem eschem besoch she'ar aveilei Tzion viYerushalayim v'lo sosifu l'da'avah od* — May the Almighty console you among the mourners of Zion and Jerusalem and may you never have any more worries."

"Amen."

"You have to go, Pinras. Your mother is waiting."

"Yes…" Pinras passed his handkerchief over his eyes again. "And His Majesty awaits you, Istrak."

The crown prince swallowed. There was so much that he wanted to say, but he didn't know the right words. In silence, the two walked toward the waiting carriages. With a quick embrace, they parted.

"You've been crying," the king remarked as their carriage set out.

"Yes," Istrak affirmed in a low voice.

"When my father died, I was two years older than Pinras," the king said. "Just 28…" Istrak darted a quick look at his father. The king's eyes were half-closed.

"My father had been ill a long time, and still his loss was unimaginable. Just the day before, I'd sat near him, reading the court rulings that required his authorization. I'd taken him into the palace gardens, and we'd watched the sunset together… The next day, our time was over. Parents do not live forever. I didn't understand what that sentence really meant, until that afternoon." He opened his eyes and lifted his lips in a sad smile. "Friends do not live forever, either. I didn't grasp the significance of *that* sentence until yesterday. I trusted Eshal more than I trusted anyone else, apart from my own children."

He paused. "Without detracting from the seriousness of what I told you yesterday — I think that you demonstrated leadership, decisiveness, and a surprising ability to carry out a plan, Istrak."

The carriage rolled to a halt. Through the round window, Istrak saw the palace gardens. One of the king's men opened the carriage door and Istrak leaped out. "Shall I help you, Father?"

How many times in his life had he repeated this small ceremony? From the age of 7, he had supported his father's shoulder whenever the two of them left the same carriage. This was the first time, however, that the youth felt his father's weight, heavy against his own shoulder.

Tuval Obseld's small house stood at the fringes of the city, near the place where green pasture became paved street.

There were advantages and disadvantages to living so far from the center of things. Among the distinct advantages were the wonderful silence and the huge plot of land that Tuval would never have been able to afford in an area closer to the heart of town. On the other hand, this was a less than perfect location for his studio. It was far away from the eyes of art merchants and agents of the wealthy. And then there were the fears he experienced when he left his home each night for Ma'ariv. His neighbors claimed that he saw shadows everywhere, and his wife thought him a coward. As the figure in gray advanced toward him that night, Tuval felt a sense of vindication, despite his fear.

"You are Tuval Obseld?"

"I am." The torch shook in Tuval's hand.

"They say that you are a great artist."

"I'm glad to hear it." The torch's dance slowed somewhat.

"I've seen several of your paintings. They are excellent."

"Thank you."

"I'm prepared to pay a high price — but I expect, in return, skilled work of the highest quality." The man in gray peered hard at Tuval.

Tuval Obseld cleared his throat. After the praise he had just heard, it was a bit uncomfortable to have to put the man off. "I'll be happy to supply what you ask — but right now I'm in a hurry to get to Ma'ariv. If you care to accompany me to the synagogue, we can talk afterward, in my home. I'll show you samples of my work and you can choose the style you prefer. I will also be able to check my calendar to see when I can meet the person whose portrait you want me to paint. Portraits take time, as I'm sure you know."

The stranger's answer was a dissatisfied cough. "I —"

"I can also offer you an herbal drink that my wife prepares, as I see you're suffering from a cold…"

"It —"

"They say there are people who suffer from the scent of growing things in the spring —"

"Would you be quiet already!"

The artist gaped in surprise.

"I'm trying to tell you that it's impossible for you to meet the person whose portrait you are to paint. But you simply won't listen!"

"What do you mean?" Tuval's face furrowed in suspicion. "There is no such thing. Don't make a fool of me, sir!" He turned to walk away.

"You are not going anywhere, Tuval, son of Uriah!" The stranger's hand whipped out of the folds of his large cloak and grasped the artist's arm as he tried to pass. A menacing note had crept into his voice.

"What do you want from me?" Tuval asked, trying in vain to free himself from the steely grip.

"I want to explain what I'd like you to do without having to listen to so much babble!"

Tuval finally managed to extricate himself from the stranger's grasp. He drew himself up, trying to regain some dignity. "I'm listening."

"I want you to paint a portrait of the crown prince, Istrak, and his younger brother, Michoel," the stranger whispered.

"Is that all?" Relief spread through the artist. "That's no problem at all, sir! Come home with me, as I've said, and I'll show you amazing likenesses of both the crown prince and his brother in my shop. You can also purchase a portrait of His Majesty the king himself. I am sure you've heard about our beautiful gilded frames, too! They're the —"

"WILL YOU ALLOW ME TO SPEAK?"

"Yes, yes. Of course, sir." The stranger reminded Tuval of his mother whenever she wanted to stem the tide of his chatter.

"I want a portrait of the royal brothers wearing traveling garments," the customer said through clenched teeth. "I would also like to know what this commission will cost me." In a slightly softer tone, he added, "I require this urgently. How much will I have to pay for you to put aside all your other work?"

While the artist was speaking with the stranger in gray, Tuval's wife, Rivka, was undergoing an even less pleasant experience.

It was a cold, damp evening, and Rivka — mindful of her yeast dough rising on the table — decided to light a fire in the oven. She would cook lentil stew at the same time.

The stone oven that Tuval had built in the small lean-to adjoining the house was perhaps the most beautiful oven in all of Khazaran-Itil and a fine testament to Tuval's artistry. But when it came to actually baking and cooking, the oven bore repeated witness to the fact that Rivka had made a mistake entrusting the job to her husband rather than a professional oven installer.

Seven futile attempts to light the fire brought her to the dismal conclusion that, once again, the chimney was blocked. Because her most recent attempt to clear the chimney had brought several stones tumbling down about her head, Rivka decided to pick up her bowl of dough in one arm and the pot of stew in the other and carry them to her neighbor's house.

Mrs. Palev, who was old enough to be Rivka's mother, was one of Rivka's few friends. Since her marriage to Tuval and their move to this city, Rivka had seen her own mother only once. A warm friendship had soon sprung up between herself and her elderly neighbor.

Rivka filled Dosa Palev's life with youthful cheer, while Dosa provided a sense of stability and taught her the virtues of patience.

Rivka had learned something in the eighteen months since she had first met Dosa. She knocked on the door of the Palev house and waited. When there was no answer — although she could see light coming through chinks in the shutter — she knocked a second time. When this also failed to elicit a response, she began to worry.

Although the couple was neither young nor in particularly good health, they were in better financial shape than most of their neighbors. The valuable jewelry that Dosa wore conveyed that fact to anyone who cared to notice. Could word of her jewelry have reached unscrupulous characters, who had decided to break into the old couple's house and steal what they could?

For a moment, she almost laughed at her own fears. She was becoming as bad as Tuval! Then she heard a noise from inside the house. It was a deep groan — the sound of a person in pain.

"*Dosa?*"

Resolutely, she set her bowl and pot on the ground near the door, and twisted the knob.

"Dosa?" she called again. "Can you hear me? It's Rivka!"

Another groan answered her, followed by a whimper. Dosa, cheeks drained of color, sat on the floor near the wall of the big room and wept.

"Mulush," she sobbed, as a distressed Rivka tried to lift her from the floor. "My Mulush!"

Her normally serene face was wrinkled as a cooked cabbage, and tears had soaked the collar of her dress.

"Has something happened to Mulush?" Rivka was all too afraid she knew the answer, but she could offer no help without a clearer understanding.

Dosa's face crumpled even more. "He's dead," she wailed. "De-e-ead!"

Dead?

Just three days ago, Rivka had seen Dosa's son looking cheerful and resplendent in the uniform he had worn since he began working in the *bek's* household. Mulush had seemed perfectly healthy.

"Where is your husband?" she asked.

"Zerach went to bring him back," Dosa said, huddling even more deeply into herself. "And to make the necessary arrangements…"

"When did it happen?" Rivka asked hesitantly.

"Yesterday!" In a burst of feeling that more closely resembled anger than grief, the older woman added, "They say he killed himself! They say — they say he murdered the *bek*! My Mulush would not do that, Rivka. I am sure of it!" Rivka said nothing. Dosa went back to her sobbing, burbling through the tears, "He always wanted to have many children. He said I'd make a fine grandmother…"

Rivka's hand stroked her friend's arm and kerchiefed head. "Dosa," was all she managed to say. "Oh, Dosa."

Dosa's pain was beyond comforting. "They say he committed suicide," she wept. "It can't be. Someone lured him there, that's for sure. Someone killed him so that there would not be a search for the true guilty party. Someone brought him there… He would never have entered on his own, would he?"

"Where?" Rivka asked.

"The royal treasure-house," Dosa said, before crumpling once again into heartrending sobs.

The window of Tuval's studio faced a zucchini field, which suited him just as well as any flower garden.

"How's the work coming along, Tuval?" asked Rivka, coming in with a glass of juice.

"Could be better," Tuval mumbled, using a fine brush to draw another thin blue line.

"The portrait is beautiful!" she cried, moving the glass closer to her husband.

"I'm missing yellow… That is, I have it, but not the exact shade I need for Istrak's hair."

"His Highness, you mean."

"Yes, of course, His Highness. But I don't have the right yellow! I'll have to go into town." He stood up abruptly. "Maybe Maglazi has some."

There was a time when Rivka found it hard to understand her husband's agitation whenever something was less than perfect in a portrait he was working on. By now she was accustomed to it.

"Prince Michoel's curls are very nice," she said in an effort to distract him.

"They're black. What's so wonderful about that? It's the perfect yellow that I'm missing! If I add orange, the hair will be too dark. Someone ought to make a law stating that princes should have ordinary hair. What does he need that shade for? How will it help him in life?" Still grumbling, he left the house and set off through the zucchini field.

From the window, Rivka watched him with a smile. The portrait would be lovely and lifelike in the end. What troubled her more was the fact that this was already Tuesday afternoon, and the princes' traveling clothes were still no more than two blobs of blue-green paint. Tuval had committed himself to complete the work by tomorrow afternoon. It was hard to believe he would be able to do it.

She sighed, gazing at the unfinished portrait. He was a good man, Tuval, but his head was not always in the world of the practical…

"THE LIST IS SHORT THIS TIME, YOUR HIGHNESS."

Pinras' step, as he entered the room in the middle of Istrak's breakfast, was as energetic as ever — just as though seven whole days had not elapsed since he had last been in the palace. The only change was that his voice was hoarse, as though his throat had been rubbed raw with weeping.

"These were prepared by Miflaeus," indicating the nobleman who had assumed Pinras' duties in his absence. "I have not yet had a chance to fully acquaint myself with the events of the past week in your life…"

Istrak nodded, a signal for Pinras to proceed.

"First of all: the test on the halachos of *eiruvin* has been arranged for Thursday. The *rosh yeshivah* will personally accompany you to the test site, where you'll deal with several problematic points that have arisen in the *eiruv* surrounding Khazaran's eastern neighborhoods. Since a visit to that part of town will naturally elicit a great deal of attention, the three hours following the test are reserved for receiving citizens."

Istrak enjoyed meeting Khazari citizens. His ability to help so many people with so little effort was something that always stunned and exhilarated him. Yet the realization that there were some whom, despite his best intentions, he could not help always detracted from the magic.

"His Majesty the *khagan* has given instructions that you are to attend to him on any day that he deals with government affairs requiring action. The first meeting will take place today, one hour prior to the midday meal... Also, the regent, Lord Diaber, has asked to meet with you. He has a number of documents for you to review before the next government session."

Pinras paused. "I'd like to congratulate you on the new appointments, Istrak."

Istrak grew still, waiting for more. But Pinras sounded merely interested. He did not appear to be offended by the fact that a portion of his murdered father's duties had been transferred to a youth just turned 17.

"...three sets of clothing, ordered by the Keeper of the Wardrobe, are ready for a fitting. And the minister of protocol has sent a reminder that we're to go to his chambers to try on the repaired regent's crown. According to him, additional repairs may be needed, and with the Regency Ceremony fast approaching, my prince, the repairs become urgent.

"One last thing that will make you happy: His Majesty has authorized your attendance at your friend Zecharia Latvias' wedding. You may remain there between the hours of 7:30 and 9. The usual entourage, led by Lord Matel, will escort you there."

Lord Gedalia Latvias looked exactly the way his son would look in forty years' time: tall and slightly stooped, quick of gesture and graced with exquisite manners. But today Zecharia looked entirely different from his father. His tall, erect bearing was enhanced by the gold-embroidered garments he wore. His behavior was not in the least restrained or thoughtful, and the powerful hug he gave Istrak held no hint of either nobility or good manners.

"I'm so glad you came!" he exclaimed, releasing the prince. "And not only because of the honor you do me by joining in my *simchah*, Prince of Khazar. I'm happy, if you'll allow me to say so, because you're my friend."

Friend? Istrak permitted himself a twinge of doubt. "Everyone who loves Khazar loves you, too," Tur had once said to him with her characteristic gaiety. "And there is no person in Khazar who dislikes his native land, Istrak!" There was much logic in her words. Still, Istrak sometimes found himself wondering just how much those who cared for his welfare would have liked him were it not their patriotic duty to do so…

But nothing in the prince's warm smile or handsomely worded answer offered the merest hint that he had not accepted Zecharia's statement at face value.

"Won't you taste something, Your Highness?" Asher Kafchaver — never noted for his slender build — chewed steadily as he spoke. Zecharia had already moved on to greet new arrivals. "The food is very good, believe me!"

Istrak laughed, slowly twirling the wine in the delicate glass goblet he held. "You know I never eat in this manner…," he murmured to his old friend. He understood that it was not appropriate for the king's son to partake of the delicacies. Neither could the prince be seen to be indulging in excessive drinking. Reluctantly he set his half-full cup on a tray carried by a dark-skinned servant.

"Nobility and all that?" Asher asked, still chewing. "You know, I respect you for that. Personally, I can't resist… My father always says that the crown and other possessions can be handed down — but not character."

Istrak shrugged, keenly aware of the nobleman standing silently behind his chair. A week ago he had promised to compensate Matel for the difficulty he had caused him. If his father knew that his son had promised something and then forgotten about it… He bit his lip, failing to remember for the moment his etiquette teacher's strictures about displaying signs of inner tension.

"What an honor — to meet the two noblest young men in Khazar at the same time…"

The chanting cadence of the speech, more than the voice, told Istrak who the speaker was, even before he saw him approaching through the torch-lit trees.

Asher straightened in a gesture of respect. "Lord Diaber — Prince Michoel is not here. Surely it is he who deserves that title."

Yosef Diaber smiled. "His Highness, Prince Michoel, is but a boy, still untested, while you have grown up to become a fine young man, Asher Kafchaver." He reached up to smooth his beard, and the signet ring on his finger reflected the light of the torches. Casually he asked, "How are you, Crown Prince? Are you planning to go to Babylon with Michoel?"

The question caught Istrak by surprise. "To Babylon? With Michoel?"

"Have I made a mistake?" The regent tilted his head to one side with a questioning expression. "It seems to me that when I went to comfort the family of Lord Eshal, may he rest in peace, someone spoke of Michoel's impending trip to Babylon... But perhaps I did not understand correctly. You there!" The finger that wore the diamond beckoned. "Lord Matel, if I'm not mistaken. May His Highness accompany us to the dancing square? This shadowy spot among the trees doesn't suit these young men's lively blood!" A warm smile touched his lips. "The prince has many years of responsibility ahead of him. Right now, let him enjoy himself with his friends..."

Lord Matel murmured something. Lord Diaber, interpreting the murmur in its most liberal sense, led the two youths to the center of the large garden where the festivities were being conducted.

"Isn't it wonderful?" Though he had accepted a second and then a third glass of wine from passing waiters, the regent seemed unaffected by the drink. "Latvias has poured a fortune into this evening. Look at the jeweled tapers, and the crests of both families everywhere... The wine is pouring like water, and as for the food...!" He held a small pastry to his lips and took a delicate bite. "And you've surely heard about the special orchestra he hired for the occasion..."

Asher stifled a giggle.

"What is so amusing?" Istrak threw his friend a curious glance.

"Yes, yes, you probably haven't heard," Diaber said, grasping Istrak's elbow and leading him through the softly lit trees, closer to the musicians' platform. "There are much more important things to occupy your mind..." His manner was gentle and understanding; the empathy he exuded enveloped Istrak like an embrace.

"Latvias has managed to persuade a *ger tzedek* to return to his former profession and be a guest musician at Zecharia's wedding. Before his conversion, he was a member of the same tribe as Wanana, leader of the Kawaris. Unfortunately, the timing of the *ger tzedek's* arrival in Khazaran-Itil was not especially fortuitous: he came the morning after the esteemed prime minister, Lord Eshal, was murdered.

"A most unpleasant episode for everyone involved...but all that belongs to the past. Soon the *chasan* will come out of his room, and the musicians will erupt into song. It will undoubtedly be a unique experience. Just think: musicians who were celebrated in Wanana's court are with us now to gladden the *chasan* and *kallah* in our own Itil... Ah, here they come! Excuse me for a moment, dear boys..."

"I've heard of Moshe the *ger tzedek*," Asher remarked, gazing admiringly at Yosef Diaber's retreating back. "They say he's an extraordinary musician. He's the one who introduced the new style of Jewish music — and Lord Diaber's the one who helped him succeed! Diaber was instrumental in persuading Lord Bastian to release Moshe from prison."

Istrak took a deep breath. "Kawari music and the *simchah* of a mitzvah are not exactly well suited, Asher."

"Why not? What's wrong with the song '*Mi Yovileini Ir Mivtzar*'? There's no boy in Khazar who doesn't enjoy it — and the melody, my father says, is a Kawari battle tune with just a few small changes. *He* doesn't care for it, because it reminds him of the time he was captured — but why shouldn't *you* like the new songs? They're great!"

As though to support his claim, the musicians burst into a merry tune. With the first notes, Istrak — who loved music — realized how remarkably talented they were. The melody was calling for its listeners to dance to it — but a prince of Khazar couldn't be seen to indulge...

"I am the Prince of Khazar, Asher."

"You are the future ruler of Khazar," his friend agreed. "Of course. We all know that. But what's the connection between your position and this music? Don't you want to dance? It's a great merit to rejoice with the *chasan* and *kallah*!"

Want? Istrak's clenched fists throbbed with something that was almost pain. He wanted to dance so much it hurt...

"I am the Prince of Khazar," he repeated solemnly. "This is neither the time nor the place to elaborate on the topic. If you want to discuss it further, I can arrange an appointment for you tomorrow afternoon... You haven't seen my new colt yet, have you? Go ahead and dance now. We'll talk later."

A gleam of understanding, and perhaps pity, shone in Asher's eyes as he bowed deeply and walked backward toward the swaying Brai Stazdiran, son of the deputy prime minister, and Ula Makan, nephew and adopted son of Bastian Makan, Khazar's supreme military commander.

"Your Highness?" Lord Matel's voice brought the prince back to himself. "Hercules here would like to offer you his congratulations in honor of your friend's wedding day. He is a gold merchant from Rome, a relative of the Caesar, and an intimate of Lord Latvias."

Istrak smiled warmly and pressed the Roman's hand as he asked, in Latin, about the gold market — a topic that interested him not a whit. At the end of an unremarkable conversation, he went on to inquire about the royal horse-procurer's crippled daughter, then listened solemnly to the leader of a Khazaran citizens' group, who was insulted by the fact that the date of the prince's visit to the city's eastern sector had been so hastily settled. Why didn't they consult with the citizens? They would have been overjoyed to welcome him with proper ceremony — had anyone bothered telling them about the upcoming visit while there was still time to prepare such a welcome! He asked one of the noblemen who lived in the outlying districts about the situation in his vineyards and listened to an eloquent, detailed answer without betraying by so much as a blink of his eye the rising impatience he felt inside. He accepted condolences over Lord Eshal's demise from three Persians with flowing, impressive mustaches and promised to try to discover why a distant relative of the *chasan's* had failed to be accepted into the Royal House of Study.

And all the while, in the outer circle of those surrounding him, stood a man in simple garb, gazing at Istrak in silence.

"Matel." Istrak seized the opportunity afforded by a momentary lull to whisper to his noble companion.

"Yes, sir?"

"See that fellow over there? The pale one, with the stick?"

"I see him, Your Highness."

"He's been following us everywhere."

Matel was silent, uncomprehending.

"He wants to ask me something. Perhaps there's no one to introduce him," Istrak explained in a whisper.

"Everyone at this wedding would be happy to request something of you, Your Highness. If you were to pay attention to every one of them, you'd have no time for anything else. Those who need help may address you, or other men of position, through normal channels."

Istrak averted his eyes, meeting those of his devoted Naitan. Naitan's look was questioning; Istrak replied with an almost imperceptible nod. Naitan smiled slightly, and Istrak relaxed. Naitan would discover what he needed to know and return to him with all possible speed — and the full story.

"Where do you come by this information, my son?" Obviously exhausted, the king removed the heavy crown from his head and handed it to the Keeper of the Wardrobe, who stood nearby.

Istrak hesitated. "His father attended Zecharia Latvias' wedding," he said at last. "There was no one to introduce him. He stood in the outer circle, watching me, and he seemed sad. I asked Matel to find out what he wanted, but Matel saw no reason why he should receive special attention…" Istrak's voice changed suddenly as a slight note of bitterness crept in. "So I sent one of my own people to talk to the man."

"One of my own people..." the king repeated slowly. He finished unbuttoning the ceremonial cloak he wore and allowed a servant to remove it from his shoulders.

A blush rose to Istrak's face. "All residents of Khazar are your servants, Father. I meant to say, I found out what the man wanted indirectly, without the services of Lord Matel."

"I understand."

The king's voice was measured. Belatedly, Istrak realized that an hour from now — or two, at most, when it came time for the palace servants to have their midday meal, and the Keeper of the Wardrobe went off to dine in the servants' hall — everyone would hear how the crown prince had circumvented Lord Matel's authority last night. And not only that, but he had seen fit to report as much to the king!

The last thing Istrak wanted was for information like this to float through the palace corridors — especially not a mere week after he had already caused Matel considerable unpleasantness. Still, he could not undo what had been done; he could only attempt to control the damage.

"But that's not really important," he said. "What about the matter itself, Father? Why did they imprison Kalev Ben Batal? Dozens of boys his age go out to the forests and fields each morning to help earn the family living!"

The king was silent. His silence continued even after the Keeper of the Wardrobe left the room and Ovadia announced the official in charge of internal communications, who came bearing reports from the provincial governors as he did every Thursday. When he had departed, the *khagan* dismissed Ovadia with an almost imperceptible gesture and gave his son a weary glance.

"You did the right thing in coming to me with the information. I believe this is not the right time to have a serious talk about the manner in which you obtained that information..." The corners of his eyes lifted in a smile. "I will just tell you this: when I was your age, I thought myself very clever whenever I managed to do the kind of thing you did last night. Today, I understand that the protocols of our kingdom were established by men who are better and wiser than we, and that their sole aim was to safeguard Khazar. The aims of those who help you circumvent the law may be different from your own."

Istrak shook his head, thinking of Naitan's blind obedience. "My man is 100 percent loyal to us. I'm sure of it!"

The twinkle in his father's eyes deepened. "Do you know, I feel as if it is I who sit there, in your place, trying with all my might to defend Ovadia, while my father tries to gently explain to me that I am not as wise as I think I am…" The king's eyes nearly disappeared as his smile widened. "Naitan is probably no less loyal than his father — but I will not ask you to give your friend away…"

Istrak gave his father a sheepish smile.

"You asked," the king continued, "why the lad was imprisoned. The answer is simpler than you think. I hope our descendants will never need it, Istrak — but when King Yosef II was forced to flee from the palace about 100 years ago, there was a wagon waiting for him, harnessed to a donkey by an old bridge in the southern portion of the Pelasar Forest."

"An escape tunnel?" Istrak asked with widened eyes.

"Exactly. And since we're on the topic, it would be a good idea for you to memorize the following: 'four by five from the south' — the southernmost corner of the cellar level, fourth row, fifth stone. You'll have to use physical force to remove the stone; a sick or injured person would be incapable of doing it."

Reuel's hand lifted slightly to stem the tide of the many questions Istrak burned to ask. "Now — back to the matter at hand. The boy does appear to be sound. Our best investigators say so. Still, the story is too suspicious for me to simply order his release. He and his donkey were standing alarmingly close to the mouth of the escape tunnel, and he was carrying a Kawari throwing-axe. Also, he began working as a woodcutter just seventeen days before the murder… Isn't the string of coincidences interesting, Istrak?"

The prince spread his hands. "It does look suspicious, Father. But the proofs that his father brought me were very convincing. He gave me the name of the man who owns the pawnshop where the boy got the throwing-axe, six more drawings that the boy's little sister drew that are incredibly like the one that's on the axe, the name of the man who had fired him from his job three weeks before, and the address of their landlord, who threatened to evict them if they did not pay the rent — which led his son, he says, to seek an additional source of income."

The king closed his eyes, cupping his chin in his right hand. "You may pass all these things along to Rumtian, who is in charge of the murder investigation.

"Now, please open the report from the northern district. Two weeks ago, Lord Gad Baliatar sent word about problems in the construction of the central bridge..."

As far as the king was concerned, the discussion of the woodcutter boy's arrest was over. Still dissatisfied, Istrak pulled a large brown envelope from the pile of documents in front of him. The flap was stamped with Lord Baliatar's red seal. Istrak reached for the gilded letter opener. But he never opened the envelope. At that moment, the door burst open behind him.

Istrak hardly had time to think before he saw his father's face turn suddenly gray.

The path was unfamiliar to Calidius Bruchu, and the winding ascent demanded his full attention. The beast stepped slowly, while the rider gnawed his lips. "One false step, and we're over the edge — both of us!" he warned her, mopping rivers of sweat from his brow. "Why does that doctor have to live so high up in the hills anyway? What does he have here that he can't find in our beautiful Khazaran-Itil?"

The beast, as was its way, remained silent; nor did the lofty, verdant hills supply the answer. The rider sighed. When he had entered his master's service, he had not expected to have to travel so far. On the other hand, he had never dreamed of earning so much money and honor either. He supposed that, had both these facts been in his possession when his present mission was proposed, he would still have found himself climbing this steep path on muleback, in search of a village doctor with no formal education. His Excellency compensated his loyal servants with a generous hand.

He mopped his brow again. On the crest of the hills facing him, he glimpsed the cluster of small white cottages that made up the village toward which — according to the map, at any rate — he was headed.

"You live in a remote location, Ifa Jado."

"A doctor must live near his patients, not only near healthy people who can afford his rates, Your Excellency."

The two men took one another's measure. When he had smoothed his beard and donned his official uniform, Calidius Bruchu made an impressive figure. The doctor, in contrast, wore simple but clean garments. His face was gentle, and his tranquil manner made others eager to acquire some of the inner peace that radiated from him.

Calidius was first to lower his eyes. "You wrote my master, saying that you refuse to give the compound to anyone but a Khazari nobleman — someone whose loyalty could be trusted."

Wordlessly, the doctor nodded.

"That is why I — Ribak, of the house of Bati, trusted confidant of Lord Bastian Makan, commander of the Khazari army — am here," Calidius Bruchu said in a tone that conveyed his exalted sense of self-worth. His gaze did not falter as he lied, nor did his conscience suffer a single pang of compunction. "Ula Makan, Lord Bastian's nephew and adopted son, lies on his deathbed. Any delay could lead to tragedy."

"I have no intention of delaying you." The official document, signed with the king's seal, confirming the identity of the messenger — Lord Ribak Bati — and requesting that all who met him was to offer any possible aid, had already undergone the doctor's closest scrutiny. As far as his village intellect could tell, it was not a forgery.

"In that case, why do you hesitate?"

The sudden softness in Calidius' voice made the doctor recoil in suspicion. "This medicine is dangerous for the healthy," he said after a moment. "I'm afraid of its falling into the wrong hands."

"My master handles many important government matters. Is your medicine more important than palace secrets? Than the welfare of Khazar's troops? Than the protection of our borders? You will find no more faithful hands into which to entrust your secret."

The doctor nodded. There was logic in what this messenger said.

"Think of the sick boy!" Calidius pleaded. "Will you deny him a cure for his illness simply because it is impossible to bring him here from Itil? They say you have a compassionate heart, Ifa Jado."

The doctor averted his head. "People say all manner of things," he scoffed. "People can even say that the shadows in the corners of your eyes, Lord Bati, reflect a heart filled with pity for the sick lad."

Once again, the two men silently took each other's measure.

"Will you give me the medicine for my master's nephew? Remember your position, Doctor!"

The doctor's breathing became shorter. "I am a free Jew, and a citizen of Khazar. No one may threaten me!"

"No threat was intended," Calidius said, more gently now. "We need the medicine, that's all. Payment will not be a problem."

"I assumed so. I will not ask you to pay more than I ask other patients. If chicken farmers can afford it, I am sure it will prove no hardship for your master."

Under different circumstances, Calidius would not have allowed such insolence toward his master to go unchecked. However, because his document was a forgery and the only actual thing linking him to Bastian Makan — whom Calidius had disliked since his brother had been wounded in his service — he allowed the words to pass.

"Here is the bottle. The liquid is fatal to healthy people. Take good care of it!"

"That's why I was sent here," Calidius replied, inclining his head in feigned humility.

"Keep it away from water. The patient should take two drops in a glass of milk twice a day for a full year. Should the illness return, the dosage may — under a doctor's supervision — be increased to two drops three times a day. Here is my authorization, Lord Bati."

"Thank you." Calidius Bruchu accepted the rolled parchment. "And if you should chance to come to Itil, remember that the household of the Khazari commander is in your debt."

"I will try to remember that." The doctor half-smiled. "May the Creator protect your going and your coming."

Calidius noted that the doctor's tone was polite, but lacking sincerity. A smile glinted in his eyes. "You don't like me very much, do you?" he remarked. "Why?"

The tranquility vanished from the doctor's face. "I am handing you the most lethal poison ever known to Khazar — and you ask me why?"

"You received all the authorizations that you requested. How else can I calm your fears?"

With a shrug, the doctor followed his visitor to the gate. Despite His Majesty the *khagan's* heavy wax seal on the transit paper, and Lord Makan's family crest embroidered in gold thread on the messenger's uniform, he felt uneasy. The medicine was too dangerous. When administered to healthy individuals, it gave rise to symptoms alarmingly similar to a fatal heart attack. Death inevitably followed.

"I thank you once more in my master's name," Calidius said with a small bow, trying to infuse his gaze with trustworthiness and reassurance. "I will send you a letter of confirmation upon my return to Khazaran-Itil." He threw himself onto the mule's back. "Peace be with you, Ifa Jado."

"Peace with you, Lord Ribak Bati. And may Hashem grant the lad a speedy recovery…"

Calidius bowed his head in an elaborately courteous gesture. "I'll pass on your blessing." Under his prodding, the mule stirred and began trotting forward.

"Take heed on the road!" The doctor called after him. "Take good care of that bottle!"

The messenger lifted his hand in acknowledgment. A moment later, he was lost to sight. The doctor turned back to his modest little cottage.

"Has he gone?" Hanav, the doctor's 15-year-old daughter, peeked out of the room into which she had secluded herself the moment the visitor knocked on their door.

"Yes, he's gone," the doctor answered heavily. "And my heart tells me that it would have been better had he never come."

The girl tossed her head in dismissal. "Oh, you always worry so much, Father!" A fraction of a second later, she added, "Anyway, what evil could possibly come from the house of so honored a man as the commander of the Khazari army?"

"A nice animal, sir."

Calidius straightened up in alarm. He had just finished bathing in a stream, and his formerly black hair was now light brown. How had a shepherd materialized in this remote spot?

His courteous manner held no hint of his inner unease. "Thank you, lad. You have a large flock, I see."

The shepherd gazed contentedly over the flock. "Thanks be to Hashem! I try to do my job faithfully, and the sheep owners are satisfied. So, where did you buy her?"

"Far from here," Calidius said shortly.

"Was she expensive?" the shepherd pressed, gnawing on a hard rind of cheese. "You see, I'm looking to buy myself a mule like that."

"Not too expensive. But she makes a better impression than her actual worth. As a riding animal, she's about average. It's her color — white — that attracts attention…"

The shepherd smiled amiably and nodded.

"And now, if you'll excuse me…" Hastily, Calidius gathered his scattered belongings. "I'm in a great hurry to return home. Farewell!"

"You're not from around here, are you?" The shepherd, lonely and in the mood for company, was not about to let this chance encounter end so soon.

"My sister lives near here," Calidius answered uncomfortably. Had this lad come upon him before he had washed away the dye in his hair, he would have had no objection to whiling away an hour telling him all about the estate of his master, Lord Bastian Makan. But now that he no longer looked like Ribak Bati — although the mule he rode was identical to Bati's — this conversation had become fraught with danger.

Would their entire elaborate plan, and the assumed identity he had taken such precautions to protect, fall apart through the curiosity of an ignorant shepherd?

"Who is your sister's husband?" the shepherd asked with a friendly smile. "Maybe some of his sheep are in my flock. Nearly every self-respecting family in these parts sends its sheep to Shlomo. That's me, in case you haven't figured that out!"

"His name is Subar," Calidius said, uttering the first name that popped into his mind. He clambered onto the mule's back, prepared to flee. He would have to wait until later to wash away her white dye.

Were his master to hear about this, he would not be happy. But Calidius Bruchu had no intention of providing such unpleasant details.

"Father?" Istrak asked worriedly. But the king was looking past him, to the door.

"Gad…" The king put a hand to his forehead. "What are you doing here?"

Istrak turned to look at the man who had dared enter the king's chambers without permission. He waited to see what his father would do about the infraction.

The small, gnarled man bowed his head, glancing down at his stained traveling clothes. "We fell into the river near that red tavern. Where we made a *siyum* on *Yevamos*, remember?"

"Six days' travel," the king said slowly. "Great heavens, couldn't you wait another few hours before coming to see me?"

Gad shrugged. "Three hours can be a long time, sire."

Istrak's eyes moved from his father to the governor of the northern district. "But how did they allow you to enter? That's what I don't understand."

"Later." Gad narrowed his eyes. "Listen, Father of the Khazari people, to what I have to say to you. War is poised to break out with Bulgaria. I don't know when, but I know that it will be soon — today, tomorrow, or perhaps next week."

"War," the king repeated. His face suddenly appeared to be carved of stone.

"Perhaps not, if you act quickly. Ah…" He glanced at Istrak with a pointed look. "Is there a bit of goat's milk in the palace kitchens?"

"Goat's milk, Istrak," the king said, addressing his son. His eyes never left Gad's.

"Goat's milk," Istrak repeated, conquering his shock at the insolence of the governor's demand and the way his father had accepted it. "At once, Your Majesty."

"A good boy," Gad said when Istrak had left the room. In a lowered voice, he added, "They sent a delegation in honor of the regency festivities. As far as that went, all was fine. We received the Bulgarian delegation with all due honor and pomp: flags, banners, exchanging swords…all by the book. Everyone was happy. So was I. They apparently came with goodwill and everything passed peacefully."

"Well?" The description did not accord with Gad's dire prediction of impending war.

"We provided them with a military escort," the small man continued. "Fifteen of our best boys, armed and in uniform. Not too large of a contingent so that we would look suspicious, but enough to restore order should the need arise. All according to instructions. But on Sunday afternoon, shortly before Minchah —"

Lord Baliatar glanced uneasily at Istrak, who had just reentered the room. "Pardon me, Your Highness. I need the goat's milk to be lukewarm — neither very hot nor very cold."

"Istrak is my right hand," the king said. "Don't be afraid to speak in front of him, Gad."

Gad took a deep breath. "Very well. Five days later, a second Bulgarian delegation arrived, identical with the first, Your Majesty."

"Identical?"

"The same prince, the same ministers, the same office-holders wearing the same uniforms and with the same manners. But their faces were totally different from the first group that had entered our kingdom earlier!

"Admittedly, the guard standing watch at the border that afternoon was not particularly bright. By the time someone intelligent was brought to the spot, the Bulgarian prince — Ardamo II — had managed to be insulted to the depths of his royal being. In all honesty, I understand his reaction. The reception he and his people received was deplorable. Two Bulgarian noblemen who attempted to resist arrest by our border police were publicly beaten.

"That intelligent officer stripped the border guard of his rank, and assured the prince that the man would be severely punished. But the prince was not appeased and departed in anger. Again, I must say that I understand him perfectly…" He fell silent.

"Continue, Gad."

Gad spread his hands, and Istrak saw that they contained only three fingers apiece. "That was the Bulgarian incident. The next, and perhaps more urgent question, is…what happened to the first, spurious delegation? I sent a division of troops along the road their carriage took, while I myself came here via the Ashbul Pass in order to bring the news with all possible speed.

"Your Majesty, something bad is brewing within our borders. We must find out what it is — and the sooner, the better."

Lord Nazarel, Khazar's minister of protocol, was a tall, impressive man, so sharp-eyed and vigorous that not even his long white beard was enough to convince strangers that he was already well past his 70th year. For the past quarter-hour he had been trying to get Istrak to focus on the preparations for the Regency Ceremony. He was not succeeding.

"Lord Gad Baliatar," Istrak said, finally expressing what was on his mind. "What can you tell me about him?"

"Lord Gad Baliatar. Governor of the northern province, and a close friend of His Majesty's."

"That's the one."

"The Baliatar family have held central positions in Khazar's military leadership since the year 4141 — even before Khazar was conquered by King Atud I."

Istrak waved this away. The distant past did not interest him.

"The Baliatars are proud of the fact that, in all the years since they received the title, they have always placed a full platoon of trained soldiers at the king's disposal, led by one of their sons. Until now," Nazarel continued, encountering Istrak's questioning look. "Lord Gad's physical condition does not permit him to take part in military exercises. His brothers and sisters died in childhood."

Istrak swallowed. The question he was curious about — whether Gad had always been so small and gnarled — was one he could not ask the minister of protocol. It was beneath the minister's dignity to supply nuggets of random information to a curious youth, even if the youth was the heir to the throne.

"Why are the sons of Baliatar permitted to enter the king's presence without advance notice?" he asked finally.

"His Majesty, King Yosef III, bestowed that right on Lord Henoch Baliatar after Lord Henoch burst into the dining hall and saved the king's two sons — may their merit protect us — from being poisoned. The privilege is contingent on the transfer of a fifth of their property to the king's treasury." He paused. "The Baliatar men have never taken advantage of that right."

"Until today."

If the minister of protocol was surprised by this remark, not a sign of it showed on his face as he bowed courteously to the crown prince. "Now, if we could return to the matter at hand, Your Highness..."

The sun's rays woke Knaz, which surprised him. Hadn't he told Ahaliav to wake him for *tikkun chatzos*? He sat up, watching the pale sun rising in the east. From his place at the edge of the slumbering group — part of the division of troops that Lord Baliatar had sent to follow the path of the bogus delegation — he noticed Ahaliav's sleeping pallet. It was empty.

Strange. Ahaliav's stint of guard duty was supposed to have ended shortly before midnight.

Where was that boy?

His friends often laughed at the almost maternal anxiety he lavished on his nephew. Quickly tying his shoes, Knaz went to find the guard on duty. Perhaps he knew where Ahaliav had gone.

He didn't find the guard on duty. He found Ahaliav. The lad was lying on his back, staring up at the sky. One hand was flung out, fingers spread.

"What are you doing here, Ahaliav?"

His nephew did not answer.

"Ahaliav?" Knaz moved closer, a shiver running down his spine. His nephew's face wore a peaceful expression, almost a smile. But the eyes were wide and empty.

"Ahaliav?" he repeated, bent over the still form. A fly flew from between the young man's lips.

Dry-eyed, Knaz turned his nephew over onto his side. The ground beneath Ahaliav was soaked with blood. A sharp knife protruded from between his ribs. Knaz scrambled to his feet and looked around in alarm. All was deathly quiet.

He made his way back to his companions on legs that felt like lead. The commander's pallet, too, was empty. He woke one of the other men — who discovered Ze'ev, the commander, when he went to wash his hands. The commander's blood was still trickling onto the leaves of the bush onto which he had collapsed. His death had been no easier than Ahaliav's.

They had found the camp they had been seeking. The Bulgarians' tents stood some distance away, wreathed in silence. They had been tracking the impostors for days, and they knew they had been drawing close. Ahaliav must have stumbled on it when he went off to do his guard duty. He must have immediately woken the commander, and the two had been ambushed by the Bulgarian impostors.

"It is with great pain," said Kravil, Ze'ev's deputy commander, "that I am assuming command. Men, scout the perimeter of the impostors' camp. Reim, you come with me."

Reim nodded. Side by side, the two walked toward the grouped tents. The morning was shrouded in peace. Not a breath of wind stirred.

"Where are their horses?" Kravil asked, squinting.

"There are none," Reim said quietly.

"And the servants?"

"Not here." Kravil's eyes widened. Reim dropped to the ground and lifted the flap of the nearest tent.

It was empty.

"I'm not going anywhere."

"Knaz."

"I'm sorry... I can't..."

The sun was in Kravil's eyes, making it hard for him to read Knaz's face. "Knaz, my friend, you've just had a very difficult experience. Someone has to bring Ze'ev and Ahaliav to the city for burial and summon help. Seeing that we number only thirteen now, we will not be able to send an additional escort."

"I don't want an escort, Kravil. I want to remain with you. I want to avenge my nephew's blood."

"His blood will be avenged, Knaz. But a soldier cannot fight when his blood is boiling. Are you capable of putting the kingdom's affairs ahead of your own thirst for revenge?"

"I believe I can."

"And I believe that you cannot."

"You're short of manpower, right? I won't eat or sleep much. Let me go with you!"

"Home. That's an order."

"I cannot go home."

"Are you disobeying a direct order?"

Without another word, Knaz turned and walked away. Through narrowed eyes, the captain watched him collect his belongings and turn to the pair of horses that bore the two corpses.

"Sir?"

"Yes, Reim." Kravil's eyes were still on the mourning soldier.

"I think you're making a mistake. Knaz is the best tracker we have."

"Tracker?"

"He is a Mundari."

Kravil's expression changed. The members of the western tribe were known for their special skill at reading the silent language of the earth. "Very well. Have Knaz examine the Bulgarian camp's perimeter. Let us see what he can find out."

Reim was at least five years older than Kravil and possessed a wealth of experience in battle. Knowing this, the small band of soldiers — in spite of Kravil's higher rank — naturally looked to Reim for leadership. Though all of Reim's decisions were brought to Kravil for authorization, Kravil refused to serve merely as an official stamp. He had been next in rank after the commander, and it was *he* who ought to inherit the commander's role!

There was bad blood brewing between Reim and Kravil. Everyone in the group sensed it, but not one of them knew how to ease the tension in the air.

"Knaz? What is it? What have you found?"

The Mundari straightened. "Something strange, Reim." He spoke slowly, heavily. "I sense that the earth is lying to us."

"The earth?" Reim prompted, puzzled.

"These tracks are lying," Knaz insisted. "I feel it in my bones. The earth is lying — but I don't know exactly how." He let a handful of brown soil slide through his fingers. "Ahaliav, may his memory be a blessing, was a better tracker than I."

"Ahaliav is not here." Reim's voice was gentle. "We're all placing our trust in you now."

Knaz's lips contorted in a twisted smile. "The men are following me — and I feel like a blind *maskuchis*," he said, using the Khazari term for the animal that leads the herd.

"We trust you, Knaz."

"I know that, Reim," Knaz said soberly. "That's exactly what I'm worried about."

Three hours later, Knaz's intuition was proved correct.

The official report of the incident was rather tense:

> The foreign delegation that entered through the northern border disappeared as though swallowed up by the earth. The bodies of nine of the security guard who had escorted them were found in a grove of trees. Their mortal wounds were caused, apparently, by the personal weapon of one of the soldiers who has been declared

missing, along with the other five soldiers of the escort who have still not been found.

Had that one soldier betrayed his companions, or had he been captured by the counterfeit delegation?

With the doors along both sides of the corridor closed, the passageway appeared twice its usual length. In the silence, Istrak and his escorts' footsteps sounded overly loud.

They reached the door of the conference room.

"The crown prince — His Highness, Istrak!" a servant announced.

The king's voice emanated from the head of the long table in the dim, empty room. "Come in, Istrak."

The heavy doors closed behind Istrak. "You wanted to see me, Father?"

"You heard Gad's report today."

"Partially, sir," Istrak replied. "The rest of the time, I was off getting some lukewarm goat's milk from the kitchen."

The king smiled briefly, one hand pressed to his forehead in a gesture of weariness and anxiety. "From what he said, did you grasp what is taking place around us?"

"Not exactly, Father."

"Tell me what you do know."

Istrak took a deep breath and exhaled the air from his lungs in an almost inaudible sigh. "An armed group has infiltrated the Khazari border, pretending to be a delegation from Bulgaria. The real Bulgarians were insulted by the reception they received at the border and are now threatening an all-encompassing incident — in other words, war."

"Yes, war. Do you know what that means, Prince of Khazar?"

Istrak's hands tightened their grip on the chair in front of him. "I hope I will never know that personally, Your Majesty."

"War is a cruel thing," the king said. "And just as it would pain my heart if you were to be killed on the battlefield — other parents' hearts will ache when *their* sons die. Khazar will make every effort to avoid this at all costs."

"I understand."

"However, despite our very strong desire, it is not at all certain that we will succeed. This evening, Lord Bastian Makan, our commander-in-chief, will be sending urgent messages to the captains of the regiments to prepare them for any eventuality."

The king paused. "Come a little closer to me, Istrak. It's not easy to conduct a real conversation with you standing at a distance."

Istrak did as he was bidden. He perched on the edge of the chair nearest his father's.

"You resemble your dear mother," the king said suddenly, his features softening. "When you said, 'I hope I will never know that personally,' it was as if I could hear her voice issuing from your throat…"

Istrak swallowed.

"Istrak, I called you here to discuss another matter. Shortly before your 12th birthday, I told you that it was your mother's wish that you travel to Babylon to complete your studies in Torah and halachah."

Istrak nodded. "I remember, Father."

"You said that it would be too hard for you to leave Khazar for such a long period of time."

Istrak stirred uneasily.

"Looking back, I can see that, although you missed a fine opportunity, your decision may be of benefit to Khazar. These last years you've acquired knowledge and skill that will help you, G-d willing, to conduct your affairs and the affairs of state properly."

The king's gaze moved to the crown resting on a pillow at his left, then returned to the sunburned youth beside him. "In any case, Michoel is interested in taking advantage of the opportunity that was once offered to you. He wishes to go to Babylon."

Istrak stiffened.

"Michoel is a good boy, Istrak. In the future, he can be of great help to you. I will be very happy if I merit to have one son who wears the crown of Torah and the other, the crown of kingship…"

"Stand up straight. And smile — with your eyes, Istrak! Whatever dire news your father's just told you, you can't walk around the palace looking like that."

"There is no dire news, Pinras."

His mentor stopped to regard Istrak in silence. Then he resumed his walk, saying, "If *I* became worried when I saw you, others will feel even more so. Innumerable rumors fly through these corridors. Lord Baliatar's surprise visit, and his willingness to pay such a high price to see the king without delay — all this has lit a fire under the gossipmongers."

"Gossipmongers," Istrak repeated mockingly. "A nice word…" He sighed. "Father wants to send Michoel to Babylon, Pinras."

"To Babylon," his mentor echoed as he followed the young prince through the gate that the soldiers threw open for them.

"The Pumbedisa Yeshivah is the spiritual center of our generation. Michoel has been granted very special gifts, and Father believes that, under the right conditions, he can rise to higher and higher heights. For that reason, and considering the present security situation, Father wishes to send Michoel to Babylon as soon as possible — even if it means his missing the Regency Ceremony."

Istrak's words, like his footsteps, were very rapid. "How much time do I have before dinner?"

"Just a few minutes, Your Highness."

"I don't want to be late again…" A slight smile touched the crown prince's lips. "What would you do if you were in my place, cousin?"

"I would thank G-d that I have a father," his mentor said slowly. "That there's still someone to guide me and make important decisions for me."

"And then?"

Pinras' gaze grew soft with sympathy. "It may not seem that way today, Your Highness — but it is entirely possible that when Michoel returns from Babylon, older and wiser, it will be easier for the two of you to develop a better relationship, free of the taint of the past…"

Despite all the painstaking preparations, the Regency Ceremony did not turn out the way the minister of protocol had described it to Istrak some seven months earlier. In Istrak's opinion, it was Michoel who was to blame for this — just as he had been to blame for any number of more trivial things in the past.

"The king," Pinras had said a few hours earlier, eyeing with affection his splendidly outfitted pupil, "wants to ensure the stability of your future rule. That's the only reason the ceremony was moved up! You should be grateful to your father for his concern."

Thoughtfully, the crown prince regarded his reflection in the mirror.

"Istrak?"

The heir to the throne grimaced at his reflection, pretending to study a tiny scab above his left eyebrow. His mentor folded his arms across his chest, fully aware that his frowning face could be seen in the mirror.

"Here is the proof," Istrak said. "My father believes that the day will come when the people of this kingdom prefer Michoel to me. They'll prefer him so strongly that we have to hurry to preempt them, and tie Michoel's hands with a solemn vow."

As he spoke, he watched the changing play of emotions on his teacher's face.

"Sometimes I, too," Pinras said in response, "am sorry that you are the crown prince."

Istrak swiveled away from the mirror. "Thanks for your honesty, cousin."

"If you were not the prince of Khazar," Pinras continued, measuring his words, "I would be able to smack you across the shoulders and shake you until you understand that your father loves you. Loves you, Istrak! If only my own father, may his memory be a blessing, had poured out half the love on me that your father pours on you. You ungrateful child…"

Unaccountably, Istrak felt his inner turmoil ease at Pinras' words. They were like a cold bucket of water poured over the chaos of hot emotions that had been surging in Istrak these last few days. A new, if temporary, serenity took the place of the old turbulence.

There was the sound of footsteps approaching.

"They've come to escort you," Pinras said. "May it be with *mazal* and *berachah*, my prince. Walk out of this room on your right foot."

Istrak gave a pale smile. Toying with the haft of his sword, he went to the door and stood before it in silence for a long moment. Then he lightly pushed the door, allowing the servants — who had been waiting for this sign — to fling them wide.

According to tradition, twenty-five of Khazar's most respected and influential citizens were to stand outside that closed door, each bearing the insignia of the region over which he presided. Today, three prominent men were among those present: Lord Gad Baliatar, governor of the northern province; Lord Bastian Makan, commander-in-chief of the Khazari army; and Lord Dalo Stazdiran, acting prime minister of Khazar.

Their words floated about Istrak's head, scarcely penetrating his consciousness. They asked his permission to bring him to the place where the ceremony was to be held, and he granted it. They led him out to the empty corridor, and from there up a flight of deserted stairs.

The roof was also painfully bare. There was no music, no celebrating throng, no long speeches — only the star-strewn sky, a solemn quorum of ten men, and three short sentences to encapsulate the essence of the ceremony soberly intoned by the king.

"I am ready, Father," he declared, feeling as if his heart was about to explode from his rib cage. "I am ready to accept the responsibility, the obligations, and the hardships."

"You will not become blinded by the honor? By your personal ambitions and desires?"

A profound silence enveloped the rooftop. Istrak smiled, basking in the wave of warmth that emanated from his father's eyes. "I will try to fulfill my role with faithfulness, integrity, and responsibility."

"The regent, Lord Yosef Diaber!"

The regent's impressive figure stirred from his place. "At your service always, *Khagan* of Khazar."

"Sixteen years ago, you were handed the scepter and crown of the Regent of Khazar — as a pledge, until my firstborn son became of age to serve."

Now the regent spoke. "I have come here today, Father of Khazar, to restore the crown and scepter to you. Your son has matured and is worthy of grasping them."

Yosef Diaber advanced. Standing beside Istrak, before the royal throne, he bent on one knee, removed the crown from his head, and placed it, along with the scepter, on a low table at the foot of the throne.

"Khazar is grateful, Lord Diaber, for your loyal service these past sixteen years, and for the time and effort you have expended for the sake of her growth and development. Will you come to the aid of your people when you are summoned to do so?"

"Khazar and her children are one. Like every son of Khazar, I will be proud to dedicate the best of my abilities to the kingdom."

The king extended a hand to the kneeling man and drew him to his feet. "From today, you will no longer be called 'Regent of Khazar,' but 'Friend of Khazar.' By your readiness to yield your position, you have demonstrated to all that you are interested in the welfare of the people, and not in your personal benefit."

Lord Diaber kissed the king's hand and retreated to his place.

A gust of wind, stronger than usual for the time of year, blew across the roof, bringing the pale-blue and gold royal flag to life. For some reason — perhaps it was the absence of the crowds — the ceremony felt even more serious and moving than Istrak had expected.

"Lords of Khazar," the king said slowly, resting his right hand on Istrak's left shoulder, "you know my firstborn son. You know his strengths and his weaknesses, his speech and his nature. In your opinion, is he too young for the difficult mission that I am about to place on his shoulders?"

"You have already solicited my views, Your Majesty," said Rav Natrunai Ben Masnia, foremost among the Khazari scholars. "I believe that your son is suited to the task and the task is suited to your son."

"He demonstrated initiative and leadership in the case of the *bek's* murder, may he rest in peace," Stazdiran announced. "In his wisdom, he discovered what the best of our people did not see."

"His good heart and compassion are well known," Bastian Makan added in his deep, authoritative voice.

"He is graced with integrity and patience," Lord Kafchaver, minister of the interior and agriculture and Asher's father, said in sonorous tones. "A fine role model for our sons."

"As brother of the departed queen, mother of the heir, perhaps I cannot be trusted to offer testimony about the *uflah*'s character," Lord Diaber said weightily. "However, everyone present here tonight can tell of the heir's courage, and of his warmhearted attitude toward his father's subjects."

"In that case," announced the minister of protocol, stepping forward, "Friend of Khazar, Deputy Prime Minister of Khazar, Commander-in-Chief of Khazar, Minister of Interior of Khazar, Lord Baliatar, Governor of the Northern Province — you may approach."

Lord Diaber placed the crown on Istrak's head. Dalo Stazdiran handed him the long, gilded scepter. Bastian Makan drew the light youth-sword from its sheath and replaced it with the ancient sword of King Yosef I. Menashe Kafchaver spread a cloak embroidered with the symbol of Khazar in gold over the crown prince's shoulders. Lord Baliatar handed him a signet ring and seal adorned with emeralds.

Then it was time for the brother's vow.

Michoel's hands were cold to the touch, and the black velvet sleeve highlighted its paleness. Istrak lifted his eyes and met Michoel's. His brother's gaze was soft and gray. The two had not stood this close to one another in a long time.

"On this day," said Michoel, his hoarse voice rousing in Istrak all the old emotions, "our father has designated you the Crown Prince of Khazar. By this, he has accorded you the highest position that a Khazari can attain in his king's lifetime.

"At our father's wish, I have come to make a solemn vow in the Name of Hashem, and to swear to you, my brother, that I will never dispute this wish of my father's, nor lend my hand or consent to anything that might harm your honor or the power of the position of regent that has been granted you on this day.

"I, Michoel ben Sarah, do hereby swear that, when the time comes, after our father the *khagan* has fulfilled his 120 years of life, I will honor your authority as king. I will stand by your side, I will help you to establish your rule, and I will not dispute it, either directly or indirectly."

Istrak blinked. He knew what he was supposed to say now, but for some reason the words stuck in his throat. Deep silence filled the rooftop.

"I thank you, Michoel," he finally managed to say. The words emerged heavy and graceless. "It is my hope that it will be many long years before your loyalty is put to the test."

The sunrises glowed pink and blue over Khazaran-Itil, and the sunsets blazed crimson, but Istrak had no time to enjoy them. From morning to night he filled out forms, sent letters, and conversed with sober-faced dignitaries. Troop divisions had begun moving toward the border Khazar shared with Bulgaria — which had yet to respond to the messages of apology and friendship that the king had dispatched.

Life was not entirely devoid of pleasures. He enjoyed his regular hour of learning with Asher, he was able to set aside time to practice at the archery range, and his new stature enabled him to arrange a post in the stables for the boy who had been imprisoned on suspicion of abetting the prime minister's murder. But at the end of the day's onerous activities, his eyes smarting from the smoking candles and his brain seething with numbers and facts, not even the thought of the happiness that had engulfed the Ben Batal family when his messenger knocked on their door with news of Kalev's new position was enough to bring a smile to his lips.

"He's pale," the queen said softly after one of their family evenings together, which the king refused to give up despite the tension-filled times. "You mustn't place such heavy responsibility on his shoulders, Reuel."

The father tore his eyes from the window and the view of the peaceful city spread out below. "He is Prince of Khazar."

The queen sighed.

"The security situation is not pretty, Sarah," the king said softly. "The boy must be prepared to lead as the Creator intended him to do."

"The boy," the queen repeated in a whisper.

"He's 17 years old!"

"When you were 17 —"

"Things were different then."

She sighed again. "Isn't it possible to at least lighten some of the load? He's learning, and fulfilling an endless list of tasks that have been placed on his shoulders, and participating in military exercises…"

The king's square chin stiffened beneath his beard. "Khazar doesn't need the boy for his talents or abilities. There are enough clever men who would be happy to contribute their best years to the kingdom. Khazar needs the boy for his future role. He is destined to be king, and he must be prepared to fulfill that function — even if that time should come tomorrow morning."

"Heaven forbid!"

The king's face softened. "We all hope for 120 years of happiness," he said, "but the facts tell us that very few actually get their wish."

"Won't you stay a few more days, Gad?"

There was a faint note of pleading in Reuel's voice. His responsibilities were onerous, and since Eshal's murder, Gad was the only person in all of Khazar with whom he could share the bitter and the difficult, the small failures and the inner struggles.

Gad took the king's hand between his own two gnarled ones. "No, my friend. My duties call me away. You don't need me except to clarify your thoughts. Speak to me even if I am far away."

The king laughed. "You always underestimate your own worth, Gad. This time, I'm the one who will lose by it… So, what is it that you have come to say?"

Gad hesitated. "I've come to implore you to reconsider my suggestion, sire. I know it has not found favor with you…"

"True." In a single, swift movement, the king stood up. "Gad, the arrangements for sending Michoel to Babylon have been more complex than you can imagine. Everything is ready. A caravan set out three weeks ago to organize camping sites and to arrange suitable lodgings for the prince and his entourage in Babylon. Scores of letters have passed between my palace and the caliph's court. The son of Mar Rav Yeshayah HaLevi Gaon has promised to keep an eye on Michoel during the years of his stay there… If we were to halt the plans now, it would be exceedingly difficult to start them up again.

"And apart from that, my son wants to learn Torah. Why keep him here, where there is so much to distract him from his studies?"

Gad gnawed at his lower lip.

"Speak, Gad. That was not a rhetorical question."

"I'm worried about the security situation. A band of murderers, whose purpose in penetrating Khazar is still unclear, is moving about freely in our country. What would make them happier than to set their hands on the prince?"

"I have doubled the number of soldiers escorting the caravan to the border of Byzantium." The king's voice was low. "And don't forget, Gad, that the first murder took place right here, within the very well-protected walls of Itil."

"Who will lead the troops?"

"Landon Brach — commander of the palace guard — will be in charge until Kraten. An additional division of *hostress* troops will join them there, led by Matrias. You may remember him from the old days…"

"Matrias? I remember him well, Your Majesty." Gad's tone was sharp. "He would always lie to avoid a punishment."

"That does not become you, Gad," the king said, gazing steadily into the other's eyes. "Many years have passed since then — many days of forgiveness and atonement. Matrias earned many merit points during those years. However, if you are still wary of him…"

"If you wish to grant me a boon, sire, reconsider the date of Michoel's trip to Babylon."

"I believe we have settled this matter already, Gad. My decision stands."

The small man said nothing.

"You are not a military man, Gad. Security and defense are Bastian Makan's domain. He's approved the plan, and I trust his expertise implicitly."

The silence that fell between the two friends was not an easy one. Gad remained quiet out of deference to the king, while Reuel was discomforted by his friend's troubling obstinacy. Their parting, several minutes later, was actually somewhat of a relief.

IT'S NOT EASY BEING A SUCCESSFUL HOUSEWIFE WHEN YOU are married to an absentminded artist whose notions of fame and fortune are so out of keeping with reality.

If only she had a bit of butter!

If only cows had wings, horses had two heads, and hens would lay diamonds instead of eggs, she told herself mockingly. *Do your job, Rivka! With the tools that Hashem has given you...*

In response to this internal scolding, Rivka tore her gaze from the white clouds and returned to her bowl of dough, trying to stifle the sigh that threatened to burst from her lips. It was hard for her, her mother's daughter, to accustom herself to city fare. Her mother had a huge plot behind the inn where she raised a varied crop for their own use and for sale.

At least they had enough turnips and carrots. The garden was large. Though it had burdened them with a debt they would be paying back for decades to come, it had been worth the price.

"Rivka?"

She lifted her eyes from the bowl. "You're early!" she exclaimed.

"I came just on time," Tuval told her in an odd tone. "Do you realize that there's a goat wandering around the back garden among your cucumber plants...?"

"The Palevs' goat? Why didn't you take it away?" With thin strands of dough clinging to her hands, Rivka shot out of the room and into the garden.

"It's not the Palevs' goat," Tuval called, leaning on the door frame. "It's a black goat."

"A black goat?"

"Maybe she's gone into the woodshed," Tuval said. "She was here just a minute ago…"

Rivka wiped her hands tiredly on the front of her apron. "You should have taken her away," she said irritably, looking for signs of the goat's teeth on her cucumber plants. "By the way, she didn't go into the woodshed. I locked the door this afternoon."

A bleating sounded from the woodshed. Rivka's head jerked up. "What…?"

"There *is* a goat in the woodshed," Tuval said, a twinkle in his eye. "A late *Yom Tov* present, Rivka. I was very upset that I couldn't buy you a present in honor of Pesach, as the halachah obligates me to do."

"A goat!"

"Now you'll have milk," he said.

"Where did you find the money, Tuval?"

"I didn't steal it." Tuval seemed amused by her sharp tone.

"You took a loan!"

"Yes," he admitted. "But not for the whole sum."

"You know we already have enough debts…" she began. "How much did she cost?"

"Two large coins more than what I had in my pocket. Don't you want to see her?"

She followed him to the woodshed, gazing in wonder at the robust-looking goat standing inside, still giving voice.

"How did you come to have so much money in your pocket?" she demanded.

"I was paid for the portrait of the *uflah* and his brother — the one where they're wearing traveling clothes."

"Really? I never believed he'd pay you! He didn't look like a pleasant person to do business with."

Tuval smiled. "It looks as if we both need to have a little more faith in our fellow man. He said that the person who ordered the portrait was very satisfied, and he paid me double my usual fee — on the condition that I don't tell anyone about the commission. He hinted that it's going to be a gift for a very important personage. Who knows — perhaps it's for the king himself!"

"Strange," Rivka mused, absently stroking the goat's head. "Why is it such a secret? Telling your friends that you painted the princes wouldn't diminish the portrait's value."

"Maybe he doesn't want anyone to know that he ordered the portrait from me," Tuval said. This new notion brought a fleeting shadow to his face. "Maybe he'd rather have people think he had it done by one of Khazar's well-known artists."

"You'll be famous, too, one day," Rivka promised, mentally kicking herself for damping down his mood. With feigned gaiety, she added, "Thank you for the gift, Tuval! Do you want to help me try and milk her now?"

He nodded lethargically.

"You can't buy a goat with fame," she consoled him.

But although he tried to pretend that nothing was troubling him, Tuval's expression remained veiled for the rest of the afternoon.

Tur's betrothed was a tall young man with flashing eyes and a merry smile. It was strange to think that when Ruben formally entered their family, he — Michoel — would be very far from home.

"Send us a letter of congratulations on our wedding day," Tur half-requested, half-demanded. "You will rejoice with us from afar, won't you?"

"Of course." Michoel shifted his weight from foot to foot. "Of course I'll rejoice."

"You'll be missed," said Ruben. "The princess will miss you, and so will I. It's been a pleasure getting to know you — although, judging by all the stories I've heard, I haven't had a chance to get to know half of your good qualities."

The young prince gazed forlornly at the bustling room. Everyone was going about their business with such a festive air — with so little sadness and with such obvious calm. And why not? *They* were staying here, together! It was only he who was going far away, over the dark mountains...

When his father had offered him the chance to go to Babylon to study, he had jumped at it. But now that the day was here, the thought of not seeing his family for the next seven years...

"I think it would be a good idea for you to take a stroll in the gardens," said Difrat, his tutor. "Breathe the fresh air and think about something pleasant. Don't dwell on how difficult it will be to part from everyone, but rather on how wonderful it will be to actualize your great dream of sitting among the students of Rav Yeshayah HaLevi Gaon."

Michoel's face brightened. "Where did you learn to read minds, Difrat?"

"It's only *your* thoughts that I've learned to read, my young master." Difrat turned to summon Michoel's bodyguard. "Yehudah! Please escort Prince Michoel. He wishes to walk in the gardens."

The walk did not improve Michoel's mood. In fact, it had the opposite effect.

So many pleasant memories were linked to that garden! Right there, at the end of the central stone plaza, was where Unmar had fallen down at the end of a tumultuous game of tag and pretended to be unconscious. That bench in the corner, by the fountain, was where his mother recited *Tehillim* during the summer months. Near those raspberry bushes was where, after much importuning, Tur had finally taught him how to weave, and under the chestnut tree his father had once surprised him by coming to sit at his side, on the ground, for an apparently aimless chat.

Michoel caught his breath, trying to hold back the tears. He was willing to sacrifice many things to become a *talmid chacham* — but he would miss his father so much! The air escaped his lungs with a gasp. Father, who was always willing to listen, to advise, and to guide, who always found time for his little Michoel...

Michoel's throat hurt. Difrat and Yehudah would be with him

in Babylon — but all their advice and affection would not equal a single one of his father's smiles, or a loving glance from his mother's eyes. By the time he returned home, Unmar would be a young lady — perhaps even the wife of some nobleman. Yekavel would be 16, and doubtless overflowing with awe and admiration for Istrak.

Michoel shook his head, trying to free his mind of its confusion of jumbled thoughts. At some point in his childhood, when he was about 6 or 7, Istrak had stopped liking him. But before that — before that, Istrak had been the best big brother a small boy could possibly wish for.

Istrak was the first one to teach him how to shoot with a bow and arrow. Istrak had taught him how to evade the sharp eyes of the palace servants, and how to coax Yoel the blacksmith into demonstrating how he forged a sword. And when he had given his *d'var Torah* on "Ben chameish lamikra," how many times had Istrak listened to him practice? Fifty? Sixty? He had listened with infinite patience — the same big brother who now looked at him with such coldness...

"Prince Michael, I'm afraid the time for our walk is over. You must return to your room to prepare for your afternoon lessons."

Michoel was suddenly overcome. He longed to have someone promise him that after his long stint away from Khazar, things would remain just as they were today. That his place would not be filled by anyone else, that he would be freshly missed by them all every day, that his sword and shield would be polished regularly, and that, on the great and important occasions that would surely come — they would think of him, their Michoel.

Unmar, despite her many talents and excellent memory, was still merely a baby of 8 years. Yekavel was also too young to offer him any such promises, while Tur — Tur was a woman. Such sentiments came easily to her lips, even if she didn't give a thought to whether they might be true...

Someone was sent to bring the prince a clean tunic. Yehudah's hand supported Michoel's elbow as he walked, unseeing, to the nearest bench.

If only he had a big brother to turn to…

"So, you're back?"

"I'm back, Your Excellency. I've brought the liquid with me."

"Where is it?"

"Right here, Your Excellency."

With deliberate slowness, Calidius untied the drawstrings of the velvet bag and extracted a delicate-looking metal bottle.

"Is that it?" the man in the armchair asked eagerly.

"The most dangerous poison Khazar has ever known," Calidius said impressively, with a small bow.

The diamond ring emitted sparks of light as the man in the armchair removed the bottle's cork and brought it to his nose. "It has a pleasant fragrance."

Calidius bowed again.

"You are a man to be depended on, Calidius Bruchu."

Calidius inclined his head modestly, suppressing his joy at the compliment, which generally was accompanied with a hefty monetary reward.

"Tell me how the trip went."

"It went well," Calidius said, heartbeat accelerating. "Nothing unusual occurred along the way. Everyone I met on the road knows that I was sent to bring back some medicine for the nephew of my 'master,' Lord Bastian Makan."

"No unusual incidents?" his lordship asked, watching him closely.

Calidius's pulse quickened further as he recalled a certain shepherd. People said that his master had been blessed with an uncanny ability to read people's thoughts. "Nothing out of the ordinary, my lord."

The nobleman's eyes narrowed as he studied his man. Calidius returned his gaze confidently.

"I'm pleased to hear that," the nobleman said at last. "I have another mission for you. Linram!"

The lord's personal servant stepped out of the shadows behind the armchair. "At your service, as always, Your Excellency."

"Bring this young gentleman the package."

"The package," the servant repeated. "Right away, my lord."

When the servant returned bearing the package, Calidius knew instantly what it contained. It was the work he had commissioned for his master from the artist in Khazaran. He had not had a chance to examine it closely; he had only had time to deliver it before he left to meet with Ifa Jado.

"Amazing," said the lord, leaning over the contents of the package that the servant had brought. "This work is extraordinary."

"It is almost frightening to speak of Reuel and rebellion in front of it," agreed Calidius. "They look alive!"

"Even a blind man would be able to identify them by this portrait, is that not so?" The nobleman chuckled. "When I am king, I will appoint this artist as my royal portrait painter."

He fell silent, gazing abstractedly at the painting. "Are you not moved by the power of intelligence, young man? Apart from yourself, there are only four people who are working for the big change, and yet, through the power of the mind, we are destined to change the lives of millions..." The notion clearly afforded him pleasure. "All those who help me attain my goal will receive their reward. Take this package, Lord Bruchu, and travel to Matrius, captain of the *hostress* troops encamped at Kraten. He'll know what to do with it."

"Kraten? But I've just returned from a three-week journey!"

The nobleman closed his eyes and leaned his head back, his red beard jutting forward. "Lord Bruchu, governor of the eastern province," he mused as though in a dream. "The title will suit you, Calidius Bruchu."

"Kraten?" Calidius said again, in an entirely different tone of voice. "I will go there gladly, my lord."

"Return in peace."

Calidius hesitated, then dropped to one knee, with his head lowered in obeisance. He straightened, stepped backward, and, with a final bow, left the room.

In the dimly lit room, lost in thought amid the clouds of smoke created by the torches, sat the nobleman who, for the first time in his life, had been granted his life's ambition — an ambition for which he was prepared to kill even his own relatives: the honor due to a king.

The room was dark, he noted groggily. And there could be only one reason for this fierce headache. Calidius propped himself up on an elbow and squinted around him, trying to figure out where he was.

The first cup of wine had not been his fault. Who could have guessed that the skinny fellow whom Calidius had asked to give up his place at the corner table would turn out to be such a ruffian? And who would have guessed that the thug would afterward insist on sharing a cup of wine as a token of peace?

He had not been entirely to blame for the second cup either. The first cup had been of inferior quality, and it was a Khazari's right to receive his money's worth.

It was the third cup that weighed on his conscience. But three cups of wine alone could not have exerted such a baneful influence. He must have drunk at least another half-bottle after that...

Slowly, Calidius sat up on the low bed. Never before had he become drunk while carrying out a mission. And his present mission was more important and fateful than anything he had ever done in his life.

His limbs froze suddenly, as though his master had already fixed him with his piercing gaze. Had he, in his intoxication, blurted out the secret?

Hard to believe. On the other hand, until he had awoken this morning with a pounding headache, he hadn't believed that he could allow himself to get drunk on the job either.

What to do now?

Nothing, he decided. He would go out peacefully on his way to the *beis knesses* and smile at everyone. He would read the expressions of his fellow travelers at this inn and assess the amount of damage he had done…

"He came to the *beis knesses*, Father."

Tippias lifted his eyes from the wagon wheels he was oiling. "And what did he do there?"

The boy rubbed his cold hands together. "What Jews always do in the *beis knesses* — he davened Shacharis."

"Keep an eye on him, Saadia. I don't like the looks of that fellow."

"I know, Father. There's no need to worry. Messi will help me. Go in peace, and return in peace."

"Don't let Messi talk to that fellow too much. I don't like the looks of him." Tippias sighed. "But I think I've told you that already."

Saadia laughed. Then, sobering, he said, "It'll be all right, Father. This is not the first time you've gone to visit Rivka and left us on our own. It's also not the first time people like that drunken fellow have passed through our inn."

"But it *is* the first time both of those things have happened at the same time." He pointed a finger at his eldest son. "Now, make sure that Oshai and Oshoo are milked on time."

"That's Miriam's job," Saadia replied with a shrug. "Anything else, Father?"

His father stroked his mustache, his expression troubled.

"Some man comes here and gets drunk, talks about a secret package, and mentions the name Tuval," the boy said scornfully. "Why are you so worried? Tuval is not involved in anything but painting pictures!"

"Bring the sack of cabbages from your mother and ask her if she's finished preparing the bundle of vegetables," Tippias said shortly. "And when you talk to your father, Saadia, remember what our Creator commanded in the fifth of the Ten Commandments!"

Rivka and Tuval were overjoyed to welcome him.

"We've been waiting for you since yesterday, Father!" Tuval told his father-in-law, pumping the other man's hand warmly. "Rivka was beginning to worry, but I told her there was no cause. Business at the inn probably kept you, right? I knew it!"

Tippias smiled. When he had first come to know Tuval, the incessant chatter had bothered him. But the intervening two years had taught him to see it as an expression of excitement and nothing more.

"Will you have something to drink, Father?" Rivka asked, moving purposefully from the kitchen to the parlor.

"You work too hard, Rivka," he scolded, glancing with amusement at the brimming platters his daughter had set on the table. "I haven't come such a great distance...though it's a pity you two don't live closer."

"We've bought a goat!" Rivka announced. "That is, Tuval bought one."

"A late *Yom Tov* present," Tuval explained with flushed cheeks. "I just happened to have a serious commission, and the customer was so pleased that he paid me very handsomely for it."

Tippias' brows came together. "You bought a goat for the price of a portrait?"

"Well, a large portion of the nobility are folks who have more money than they know how to spend. Many of them pay for work on the basis of how much it pleases them and not its actual worth."

"It was a beautiful portrait," Rivka said, once again bustling from the kitchen. "The prince of Khazar and his brother, Prince Michoel. They looked almost alive."

"Tuval," Tippias said hesitantly, "I know that you're a mature and responsible person. But may I ask you a question?"

"Of course."

"Do you deal only in portraits, or do you do other small things on the side?"

"I paint," Tuval said quietly. "It's not always easy to earn a living from portraits, but so far, with Hashem's help, I've had enough work. I hope that this last portrait will open new doors for me, even though —"

"What are you two whispering about so seriously?" Rivka demanded. "It's nearly time to milk the goat. Do you want to see her, Father?" Her lively eyes darted from one man to the other, trying to piece together the puzzle of Tuval's slightly hurt expression and the tension in her father's face. She pulled a chair over and sat down. "Tuval was paid very nicely for the portrait of the two princes," she said. "You should have seen it, Father. Tuval has a great future ahead of him. I'm sure of that!"

Tuval's mouth turned up in a brief smile. Tippias groped for his handkerchief and mopped his brow. "I know you're afraid I'm going to drag you back into the same argument — but this time I was actually hoping to hear a positive answer. This time I wanted to hear that you're *not* involved in anything else."

"I am an artist," Tuval said. "A person has to use his talents, doesn't he?"

"Why won't you answer me directly, Tuval? Please tell me — yes or no: apart from your painting, have you been involved in any other sort of business?"

"No, Father, unless you're referring to the business of buying a goat," Tuval said with a chuckle. "But no, nothing of the kind of business you're alluding to. With a great deal of patience, Rivka's managed to teach me to work within our means and not to aim too high."

"I have to milk the goat," Rivka declared, getting to her feet. "Do you want to come outside with me, Father? It's a very pleasant day." As she lifted an earthenware jug for the milk, she threw her father an imploring look. When he did not answer at once, she left the two men alone.

"Someone came to the inn yesterday and got drunk," Tippias told his son-in-law quietly. "When he lost control and let his real nature show — I didn't like what I saw." He paused. "He was relatively dark, on the short side and slender, with quick movements and two protruding front teeth. Do you recognize the description?"

Tuval bowed his head. The description was a perfect fit for the man in the gray cloak who had commissioned the portrait of the two princes.

"He mentioned your name," Tippias went on. "Tuval Obseld. He said the name clearly and spoke of some sort of secret package."

"A birthday surprise for someone?" Tuval hazarded. "I had a commission like that recently."

"Perhaps." Tippias folded his handkerchief with painstaking precision. "But it didn't sound that way. Think carefully about who you do business with, Tuval. You are an innocent and good-hearted man, so you may not be able to see the evil in some people's hearts."

"Naive, you mean," Tuval shot back with uncharacteristic acerbity. "That's what you really meant to say, isn't it?"

Tippias was silent. After a moment, he said, "Shall we go see the goat? That will make Rivka happy."

"Can you spare me a bit of hot water, Grandmother?"

The old woman lifted her head from the spindle and looked at the youth standing on the other side of the fence, leaning lightly against it.

"Does the water have to be hot?" she asked.

"If possible." His voice was soft, with an obvious Mundari accent. The shirt he wore was old and frayed.

"There is no hot water in the house," she said. "You'll have to wait until it boils. Is that all right?"

"Of course, Grandmother."

Walking had become difficult for her lately, and the water bucket was heavy. "Can you help me with the pail? You may jump over the fence — my grandsons do it all the time."

He did as she had suggested.

"Wait here," she said, going into the lean-to that served as her kitchen. "I'll bring you the water soon."

"Grandmother?" The youth hesitated. "Do you also have a clean rag? I have no money to pay you…"

She turned her head to stare at him in surprise. "Why do you need a rag?"

"I want to clean a cut and bandage it."

She studied him more closely. He was a pleasant-looking lad, and she wanted to help him. "I'll bring you a rag, young fellow."

"Thank you." He was troubled. The color of the skin around the wound did not look good to him. He had found some *ketutit* in a field, but it didn't seem to be doing the job. He needed help.

"My grandmother told me to ask you if you need anything else." A boy of about 9 popped out of the house and peered curiously at the stranger.

"No, thank you." Discreetly, he pulled up his left sleeve. The edges of the cut were purple, and the area was swollen and tender.

"Grandmother?"

She had returned to her place by the spindle.

"Can I ask you for another kindness?"

She glanced up with the beginnings of annoyance. She had judged him to be a good person who was down on his luck. Now he seemed to be intent on making a pest of himself. "What do you need?"

"You must know about herbal remedies, Grandmother. At first, I thought that a bandage with some *kitutit* would be enough. But now, I'm worried."

"*Kitutit* is a fine herb," she said, mustering her patience. She pictured the youth's own grandmother. She decided she would do what she could for the boy.

"The cut is deep," he said, touching his arm gingerly, "and the flesh around it is purple. The whole area is sensitive…"

"Can I see the wound?"

He rolled up his sleeve again. She looked at the injured place, then up at him.

"*Kitutit* won't be enough, Grandmother, will it?"

"Who did this to you?" She was old enough to know a sword slash when she saw one.

He retreated a step. "Whatever happened, happened. I just want to bandage it"

"Is the muscle all right?"

"More or less. I hope it will improve as my arm heals."

She stared down at the ground, considering. *Saidar* was an expensive item at this time of year, and the boys needed it now and then, when they were hurt and the fear of infection became a cause for alarm.

"I will bring you something better than *kitutit*," she said at last.

"And you, in return, must pray that we will have no need of it until next winter."

"And after."

She smiled. The young man was obviously a good person who was just down on his luck.

The *saidar* would sting his exposed skin. Not even the most brave-hearted could remain impassive in the face of such pain. This wound was so deep that she deemed it best for him to sit on the ground while she poured the oily liquid into the open gash.

He leaned his head back against the fence and breathed deeply, eyelids fluttering.

"When you've recovered, tie the bandage tight," she instructed him. "Do you want something to eat?"

"No, thank you. May the Creator repay you for your kindness." His voice was still shaky from the pain.

"I will give you a little more *saidar* for tomorrow. Do you have a small bottle?"

He looked at her without answering. He was focused on wrapping the bandage around the wound.

"I need something to put the *saidar* into," she clarified, although the matter seemed to her easy enough to understand.

"I won't be able to use *kitutit* by tomorrow?"

"Do you think a wound like that heals overnight?"

His hesitation seemed odd. It was only when he took a small jug with a military crest from his pack that she understood the reason.

"You're a deserter!" she said, instantly regretting the help she had provided.

"Do not say that, Grandmother. I'm loyal to the king with all my heart." His hand still grasped the neck of the small bottle. "I am willing to give Khazar more than my life."

"More than your life?" she repeated. "Is there something more precious than life, young man?"

He nodded. "Death is more precious than life, Grandmother... Will you give me a little of the *saidar*?"

She took the bottle from him and filled it with the costly, yellowish liquid, not fully understanding why she was doing so.

Knaz accepted the filled bottle with quiet thanks. Then he leaped back over the fence and continued on his way, eastward. His heart hammered wildly. He, too, did not understand why the old woman had taken pity on him, or why she hadn't tried to summon the village men to arrest him. From now on, he must stay away from villages — at least, as long as he intended to keep tracking the Bulgarians … a track that was growing more faint with each passing day.

8

THE ROYAL FLAG — THE TWO TABLETS OF THE COVENANT against the background of a double bow — fluttered above the flag-bearer's head, a gleaming medley in blue and gold. The sky was a clear, pale blue, and the grass being trampled beneath the horses' hooves was soft and green. Each evening they stopped in a different place, in some city or town brimming with excitement at the honor of hosting the two princes and their huge entourage. Each day they galloped along new paths, glimpsed new panoramas, and met new people.

The lion's share of Istrak's official responsibilities had been left behind in Khazaran-Itil, to be dealt with by other capable men during the crown prince's absence. This would have been a wonderful outing, he reflected, had he not been forced to be at Michoel's side all the time and to participate in the competition thrust on him by the very fact of his brother's presence.

Whom would the soldiers talk to around the campfire — him or his brother? Who would learn for more hours — he or Michoel? Who would behave more graciously toward their entourage — Michoel or he? The years that separated them should have given him, Istrak, the advantage. But it was an advantage that Istrak felt was disappearing with the swift passage of time.

The road was fine, the sky was clear, and the fragrance of plants and flowers refreshing — but the only thing that chased away the crown prince's dour expression was the knowledge that he would be making his way home without Michoel.

"Your Highness!"

The commander of the *hostress* division galloped up to the prince.

"Yes, Captain Matrias? How can I help you?"

"Our scouts have reported that a bridge has collapsed a distance of a half-day's ride from here. We will not be able to ford the river. The next bridge is far away — near Itra."

Itra was indeed a long distance away. A very long distance.

Istrak wound the reins around his forearm. "Well, what can we do?"

"Not much, sir. By order of the supreme commander, Lord Bastian Makan, we are forbidden to deviate from the route he has authorized."

"Was no alternate route prepared?"

"There is one, Your Highness."

The entire convoy had halted behind the crown prince's horse. The other steeds pawed the ground nervously.

"Then what are we waiting for, Captain Matrias?"

"Lord Brach does not wish to detour the convoy along the alternate route."

Istrak sighed. The power struggle between Matrias and the captain of the palace guard was beginning to grate on his nerves. Had he been older, he would have taken command himself. However — for the moment, at least — this was not an option.

"Will you give the order, Your Highness?"

Something in Matrias' tone caused Istrak's head to come up sharply. He was reminded of the golden feather Gad had given him as a parting gift before returning to his home in the north. Or, more accurately, he remembered the tiny note that had been attached to the gift.

Father liked Gad — and Gad disliked Matrias. Gad had begged

him to be careful. *"Take care of our crown prince and his younger brother,"* he had written at the end of his brief missive. *"The two most valuable lives in Khazar will be your responsibility."*

"Miflaeus!"

The freckle-faced lord detached his gaze from a point on the horizon. "At your service always, Your Highness."

"Please ask Captain Brach, with all due courtesy, to come here for an urgent consultation."

Miflaeus was a superb rider; even the simple action of turning his horse made that clear. Brach, on the other hand, rode up a moment later looking like a sack of potatoes in the saddle.

"You wished to see me, Prince?" His cheeks were pink and his eyes flashed. Istrak wondered what had angered him so much.

"I wished to consult with you, Lord Brach, Commander of the Palace Guard."

If Istrak had hoped that mentioning the man's full title would soothe his anger, he was mistaken — in fact, it seemed to have the opposite effect.

"I am at your service, Prince." Brach's chest rose and fell rapidly.

With whom was Brach so furious, and why?

The *hostress* horses had been trained to stand still for long periods of time. Matrias' horse was quiet, its rider resembling a carved statue. As for Miflaeus, his gaze was once again fixed discreetly on the horizon.

Istrak thought quickly. He was the crown prince. He was the leader. The two men standing on either side of him could not act except on his orders. On the other hand, he was obligated to afford them the full honor that their professional stature demanded.

Did other 17-year-olds have to contend with such nerve-wracking decisions?

Looking away, he encountered his brother's soft gray eyes. Michoel's lips were moving. Michoel could offer him no advice. He was just a boy. Nevertheless, those moving lips gave Istrak an idea.

"We will stop here for the midday meal," he told Miflaeus, who repeated the words out loud so that they were heard by the entire convoy. "We can unharness the horses, eat, and prepare for Minchah."

Istrak was not watching Brach's face. Matrias' lips were pressed tightly together. "Can I invite you to dine with me, Captain Matrias?" he asked. It was hard — almost impossible — to please everybody. But Istrak was determined to return from this journey beloved by all. At least as beloved as Michoel...

The ravine might have been created as a death trap. Its tall walls of stone, narrow opening, and winding curves provided any number of strategic spots for men wielding spears and bows.

No one would see them until they were in shooting range.

The location was excellent — excellent for them, that is. Their "friend" had promised that the princes and their entourage would pass this way. All they had to do now was wait.

The leader of the small band smiled, revealing two perfect rows of teeth. They would wait. They had been waiting already for many years; they could easily wait another three days, or even three weeks if need be.

"Is the prince familiar with the song of the Adrahel division? Perhaps he can hear it sung tonight, around the campfire. My men sing it with a great deal of feeling."

"I know the song, Commander of the Guard."

"The fourth stanza, too?"

"Yes, the fourth stanza, too."

"In that case, all I can say is that the Kina Valley is child's play compared to the Batar Ravine. We are talking about a long path, narrow and winding, with a distance of 200 yards between the first man in line and the last, and no possibility of communication between them. Two soldiers standing on the precipice above could easily block the exit."

"How?"

"With the aid of a bow and arrow, Your Highness. Believe me, it would take no great skill. No more than three horses abreast can pass through the ravine's entrance at one time, and fighters above can find excellent natural cover behind the boulders."

"That sounds bad," Istrak agreed, his gaze on the blue-and-gold flag waving above their heads.

"I, too, believe that it's bad," agreed the captain of the palace guard. "I don't know why *he* thinks otherwise."

"All Captain Matrias wishes to do is lead the men along the route that he was shown by Lord Bastian Makan."

"I will speak honestly, Prince," Lord Brach said earnestly. "I do not know if Your Highness has ever studied a rabbit's burrow close up, but a burrow always has two ways out. The Batar Ravine does not! Anyone who enters at one end is forced to exit at the other end. If Lord Bastian Makan marked the Batar Ravine as an alternate route, that is clear proof that he is beginning to get old."

"You speak harshly, Lord Brach. Harshly, and a little disrespectfully."

"I speak with love, Prince. We did not succeed in preventing the murder of the *bek*, may he rest in Gan Eden. And although the investigation did not reveal even a hint of irregular behavior among my men — I still hold myself to blame."

"And therefore?" Istrak prompted.

"Therefore, I have dared to speak before His Highness, the crown prince, with such openness."

"It's become cold all of a sudden," Istrak remarked inconsequentially. He turned his gaze on the candid face of the commander of the palace guard. "What does Matrias say?"

"He calls my men the 'freckled gang,' " Brach answered quietly. "He says that we know how to fight only when we have a wall to hide behind and a ceiling to protect us, and claims that anyone who does not know how to ride a horse cannot lead a division of mounted troops on the road."

What, indeed, could Istrak respond to that?

The meal was pleasant. Istrak regretted that he had to ruin the atmosphere with questions regarding the alternate route — the purpose for which he had invited Captain Matrias to dine with him.

"I am sure you've heard the views of Lord Brach regarding the Batar Ravine," he said, setting his knife down beside his plate. "Your own opinion is different."

"Completely different, Your Highness."

"He explained to me, at length, all the reasons that lead him to believe that the Batar Ravine is not a desirable route for our convoy — especially in the current situation, with bands of murderers wandering about the countryside. I will be pleased to hear your views, in as much detail as possible."

Captain Matrias wiped his knife on a fragment of bread. His table manners were dreadful, but Istrak was too well bred to call attention to them.

"There's not much to explain, Your Highness. For the past nine years, the Batar Ravine has been guarded by a permanent encampment of troops from the Fourth Division."

Surprise silenced Istrak.

"I would have told him as much, if he hadn't started shouting at me, telling me to be quiet and reminding me again that, by His Majesty's order, he is the leader of this convoy and not I. A soldier is trained to obey his superior officers, Your Highness. In the presence of the captain of the guard, I was forced to hold my tongue."

"I understand." Istrak's father had spoken about this countless times: how most quarrels had their source in a basic lack of understanding. *"If you can only bring the two sides to speak to one another respectfully, and really listen to each other, the problem will disappear with surprising ease,"* Father would tell him.

"He's a good man," Matrias said, crumbling the bread with his fingers. "He is simply unfamiliar with this part of the country and did not prepare adequately for the journey. But I did my homework."

"It's a good thing you did," Istrak said with a smile. "Tomorrow morning, at dawn, we will set out for the Batar Ravine."

The captain of the *hostress* troops returned the prince's smile, but his eyes remained glomy. It was obvious that the insult he had suffered when leadership of the convoy had been granted to Lord Brach still rankled.

To appease Lord Brach, Istrak proposed sending a delegation ahead to meet with the men of the Fourth Division charged with protecting the ravine. They would hear from them whether it was safe to pass. But even the fuming Brach acknowledged that, given the time it would take for such a delegation to set out and to return, such a move would only add considerably to the many delays they had already experienced.

The morning was chillier than usual for the season, and Istrak's mood was not especially sanguine. Naitan, the only one of the men who customarily surrounded him whom he could call a friend, had remained behind in Itil for personal reasons. There was no one else to whom Istrak could comfortably complain.

He was heartily sick of the bickering between the two men who were supposed to make this trip as easy and secure as possible. Instead of assisting him, the two had only made his burden more onerous.

"Servitude," Michoel remarked. "That's what Father calls it."

Istrak lifted his eyes in surprise. There was no rebuke in Michoel's voice, and no trace of envy — only a quiet empathy that acknowledged the burden others failed to recognize.

"I don't understand why they keep quarreling," Istrak admitted, discouraged. "Everything could have been so simple if only they were prepared to talk directly to one another instead of using me as a go-between!"

"There are people who don't understand why *we* quarrel," Michoel remarked, glancing at his brother.

"We? We don't quarrel."

"All right." The boy, nearly 12, lowered his gaze. "Maybe we don't actually argue, but no one could say that you and I have the same kind of relationship as, say, you and Tur."

"Our relationship is fine," Istrak said shortly. "Do you have a problem with it?"

Michoel licked his dry lips. "If I did have a problem — would you be prepared to do something to improve our relationship?"

Istrak was silent, his breath coming faster than usual.

Difrat and Miflaeus entered the tent. "The convoy is ready to set out, Your Highnesses," Miflaeus announced. "Only this tent remains to be dismantled."

Difrat, darting a glance at each of the brothers in turn, asked, "Have we interrupted something, sirs? Would you prefer that we return later?"

"Yes," said Michoel, at the same moment that Istrak, loudly and clearly, said, "No."

Difrat bowed deeply. "In that case — the convoy is ready to set out. Would the princes care to ride at its head?"

Istrak stroked his horse's mane and examined the knots of his reins. He never rode before checking the harness and saddle himself. A person does not hand his life into a stranger's — or a servant's — keeping.

Michoel, beside him, was doing the same thing, his dark hair falling over his face. *"Would you be prepared to do something to improve our relationship?"* The words echoed in Istrak's mind. How nice of his brother to lay the full responsibility on someone else — after six years in which Michoel had done everything he could to show their Father how much better *he* was than his oldest brother.

"We're for the road!" Istrak cried, leaping lightly into the saddle. "For the road, men of Khazar!"

Michoel had not yet completed preparing his horse for travel, but at that moment, Istrak didn't care.

"Wait for me, Istrak!"

From Istrak's perch on the horse, Michoel looked smaller and frailer than usual. How would he look on his return from Babylon? Would his face always remain so soft, his shoulders so slender and hunched?

All at once, the significance of this parting penetrated Istrak's mind. Seven full years. Seven years for Michoel to be on his own in a strange land. Far from his mother, his father, from Yekavel and Unmar. Far from Itil — and from everything that was familiar to him...

A million things could happen in seven years!

Images clouded Istrak's vision as he gave his imagination free rein to consider what those million things could be. A million things *would* happen in the course of the next seven years — and Michoel would not be there to experience them. All he would remember, during those long years, was the way his older brother had ordered the convoy to move while he was still struggling with the harness of his horse.

Istrak pulled on the reins and drew to a halt.

"I'm waiting, Michoel."

Five times a day the leader of the soldiers lying in wait for the ambush insisted that their men study the portrait of the two princes, to engrave the images on their memories. The usual jokes were still heard from time to time, about the crown prince's long nose and his younger brother's pointy chin, but they had largely lost their flavor by now.

"The crown prince will be riding a coal-black stallion," Matt repeated, closing his eyes in an attitude of profound boredom. "The young prince is riding a white mare with red patches... Bolts of thunder!" he swore in disgust. "Does anyone really think I need to review this information five times a day? Am I not smart enough to remember such simple facts after hearing them once?"

Hanba grinned, scratching the sole of one foot on the calf of the other. "Maybe it's me who's the stupid one, not to remember the color of the gray horse that our dear captain of the *hostress* is riding," he said innocently. "What color is it, Matt?"

Matt chuckled softly, leaning his head on the hard, rocky ground. The long hours of waiting as they lay sprawled on the precipice were wearing away at the men's nerves.

Suddenly, on their right, came a deep lowing sound.

"By all the wild geese in the skies!" His hand went instinctively to his weapon. "Did you hear that, Hanba?"

"All waits must come to an end," Hanba replied. For the first time in two weeks, Hanba looked relaxed. He loved battle and blood and hated quiet moments of waiting. "That's what my father taught me when I was just a boy."

The lowing came a second time. Matt returned a lark's whistle.

From a spot 200 yards away came the cry of the jackal, followed by a wildcat's shriek a moment later. All along the ravine, on both sides, various forms of wildlife gave voice.

After that came silence. The special Kawari commando unit was ready for action.

A strange, oppressive feeling filled Istrak as he entered the narrow gorge and contemplated the tall, red-rock walls on either side of the Batar Ravine. He had never experienced such a sensation before, so he had no name for it. The fourth stanza of the Adrahel division's ballad, which had been sung to him endlessly last night, leaped into his mind. He decided that hearing that old story again was the source of the uneasiness that now seemed to pierce him from inside.

Istrak took a deep breath. Riding at the head of the convoy, between the two walls of stone, with Brach's dire warnings echoing in his head, the words of the song seemed to take on a new power.

Weep for the men of Adrahel — alas!
Valiantly they rode to the Batar Pass
Grim walls of stone on either side
Where, fighting to the last, they died.
And so, Khazar, dry not your tears
Remember them through the rush of years
And know this, every mother's son:
Death lies in wait for everyone…

"Another 500 yards, Crown Prince." David Sanpal, the assistant minister of foreign affairs, flashed an encouraging smile. "Only 500 yards more, and this will be behind us…"

Istrak returned his smile. In the distance, framed by the rock walls, he had a glimpse of green fields spreading away from the ravine.

The gorge grew narrower. David slowed his horse's paces, allowing Istrak and Michoel to move ahead, side by side, to lead the convoy.

Lines from the song continued to haunt Istrak.

The battle was over. Home lay ahead
A song on their lips, no intimation of dread
Then fate overtook them (or so the tales tell):
Death lay in ambush for the brave Adrahel…

Istrak shook his head to clear it of the persistent melody. He was only partially successful.

"Michoel," he said, raising his voice to be heard above the noise of the others.

Michoel tilted his head questioningly and drew his horse a little closer.

"I'm sorry about this morning," Istrak continued with difficulty. "I was…impatient. Nervous. I didn't have enough patience to listen. I'm sorry."

"It's all right," Michoel said, sounding rather less than sincere.

Istrak's fingers tightened on the reins. He tried again. "I —"

Something landed on the ground, just a pace in front of his horse. He stared at it in shock. It looked like…an arrow?

The second arrow struck Miflaeus. The good nobleman let out a brief cry, teetered in the saddle, and crashed to the ground.

"Is something wrong, Prince?" called David, riding behind Michoel. "Why —?"

Another arrow sailed through the air. This time, it was David who was its victim.

It was almost too easy. A child could have struck the group of men moving through the narrow channel, helmets dangling on their necks as they chatted lazily with one another.

Cries of fear and pain replaced the carefree chatter soon after the signal was given. Wounded horses rose on their hind legs, pawing the air and threatening to crash down on the riders who had fallen from their backs. Men scrambled and pushed, trying to flee, their one thought to retrace their steps to the ravine's entrance.

"Dismount your horses, men of Khazar!" Lord Brach's voice rose above the clamor. "Join together in a single formation."

Michoel slipped weakly off his horse while Istrak, speechless, did the same. Brach had already proven himself correct once before. It was a pity they hadn't listened to him.

Cries, shouts, and yells carried on the wind. Knaz leaped up. Was he too late? Had his long, difficult journey been in vain? Hastily he shrugged his pack off his shoulder, took out his bowstring, and set it on his curved bow. One more minute — too long — to unbuckle the belt that held his supply of arrows. Then he began running forward, trying not to make a sound. Knaz's left arm, the injured one, trembled with pain as he drew back his bowstring. *Now!*

One of the men sprawled on the ground lost his life without hearing a thing. His companion turned his head, staring in wild confusion at his bleeding friend. Knaz aimed a second time and was rewarded by a cry of alarm from the man on the ground. His arrow had missed.

A third arrow? His left hand would scarcely obey him any longer. This time, though, his arrow found its mark.

It was time to move on. Knaz closed his eyes, trying to pinpoint the exact source of the flying arrows. On the right? The left?

The right.

Silent as the wind that blew among the tents of his tribe, the Mundari slithered along the hard ground, his narrowed eyes seeking additional archers. A fifth, sixth, and seventh arrow flew harmlessly through the air as he tried to strike two more men. The cry of a lark came from one of them as Knaz strained to tauten his bow. Great drops of blood dripped from the gash that had stubbornly refused to knit together.

Night, dark as death, descended over the narrow ravine. In the distance came the cries of wild animals.

Difrat's lips moved with difficulty. "Change your clothes, Michoel. No one needs to know that you're the prince."

"Later," Michoel said, and his voice shook. "Difrat, do you want me to say the *Viduy* with you?"

"You have a good heart, Michoel." Difrat's eyes clouded. "A good heart, but a hasty temper. Watch out for that trait, my child." His face turned even grayer in his effort to draw breath. "May Hashem bless you and protect Khazar.

"Ask my father and mother to forgive me if I did not honor them properly… And I owe Gedalia Latvias 560 gold coins. Please make sure that the debt is repaid."

"I will, Difrat."

The ghost of a smile flickered across the dying man's face.

"*Shema Yisrael*," whispered Michoel, his voice urging his teacher to repeat the words after him. Difrat's lips moved without making a sound. "*Hashem Elokeinu*." The lips moved more slowly as a shudder passed through his body. "*Hashem echad*."

Difrat didn't respond.

There was no star to light the sky that night.

It was a rare moment of peace for the Khazari lord sitting at his window gazing out at the sunset. Still, despite the crimson-and-purple beauty coloring the sky, he was troubled. By his calculations, the pigeon carrying the news of the princes' demise should have arrived by now! He was eager to set the next stage of his plan in motion.

An opulently uniformed servant entered the room bearing a tray with pastries and a small glass of liquor. Silently he placed the tray on the low table by his lord's armchair.

"Bikra!"

The unexpected sound made the tray tremble in the servant's capable hands. "Yes, my lord?"

"Where is Linram?"

"In his room, my lord. He's not feeling well." The servant's manner exuded fear, in spite of the soft, almost dreamy expression on the face of the man in the armchair.

"Tell him, please, that I wish to see him." The nobleman's finely etched brows almost touched as he added, "Urgently."

With a deep bow, the servant left the room.

Linram, paler than usual except for two scarlet blotches on his cheeks, entered moments later.

"You did not find an appropriate time to become ill!" A shade of warmth touched the lord's voice. "You know I need you. Has the pigeon returned yet?"

"Apparently not, sir. I gave explicit orders to be told at once if anything arrived."

"I hate delays." The long, noble fingers wound themselves around the glass of whiskey. "You hate them, too. Don't you, Linram?"

The servant licked his dry lips, trying to maintain his equilibrium in a world gone suddenly unsteady. "Whatever happens, my lord, we must not put off the day."

The nobleman murmured something in response, eyes fixed on an obscure dot on the horizon. Once again, profound silence filled the room.

"HEAR ME WELL, JEWS OF KHAZAR," CAME A VOICE THROUGH the darkness. Though it spoke Khazari, its accent was strange, foreign. "We have pity on your lives. Give us the two princes, and we will not harm you. Our bows line the hills on both sides of the ravine, with arrows in their notches…"

The voice stopped for a moment. The pause was weighty with significance. "We will give you a quarter of an hour's time to decide. You have been warned!"

"It is with a heavy heart that I say this, sir — but it would be a crime to endanger the lives of many in order to protect your life. If those men wished to kill you, they could have done it any time these past few hours…"

Istrak was silent.

"I beg of you, in the name of all the men here, and their parents and children" — Matrius' voice had become lower, and yet somehow more shrill — "go out to those men!"

Michoel leaned tiredly against a boulder. Difrat's death had been a horrific blow.

"I'm sure you'll be returned home within a short time," Matrius said persuasively. "Perhaps His Majesty will have to pay a ransom in gold or land to free you. But think, my prince, how many people stand to lose their lives in the morning if you do not do as they say!"

Istrak closed his eyes in exhaustion. Gad had been right — every word he had written in his little note was true. Matrius, whose speech just now demonstrated how feeble was his loyalty to Khazar and the king, had deliberately led them into this trap. He should have relied implicitly on Brach, may he rest in peace, and not listened to a word this man had said. Pain suffused him, mingling with fear and anger. Had he not been apprehensive that it was only fear and anger that was causing him to think this way, he would already have torn Matrius in two.

"Return a little later, Captain of the Hostress." To Istrak's relief, his voice was dry and laconic. "I must discuss the situation with my brother."

Matrius bowed deeply — perhaps a shade too deeply — and retreated.

"You go, too, Shimon and Gardian. We will call you in a while."

The two moved slowly away, leaving the princes alone among the slain and the wounded.

"I think we have to do it, Michoel." Istrak's hand groped in the dark to find his younger brother's. "I hope we won't suffer too much. I hope Matrius is correct in his theory."

Michoel's hand was cold, as it had been that night on the palace roof. Istrak could not see his eyes.

"We may end up being glad in the end," Michoel said in a broken voice. "It's a big merit to save so many lives. Do you remember the story of the two butchers from Lod?" He was referring to the tale of the two butchers whose self-sacrifice saved the Jews of Lod. The Midrash relates that there is no one who can share their portion in Gan Eden.

"I remember it."

"We have to do it, Istrak."

"That's what I just said, Michoel."

Michoel's fingers tightened around Istrak's. "I'm sorry about all the times I've quarreled with you, my brother."

"It's all right." Istrak's throat felt dry as he spoke. "I'm sorry, too, Michoel. I'm sorry."

"Have you come to a decision, sons of Khazar?" The awful voice shouted down from the heights once more. "Will you send the two princes out to us?"

Istrak's breath caught in his throat. He lifted his head proudly and declared, "No one will be sending the princes out! The princes of Khazar know their obligation to G-d and to their people. They will walk out to you on their own feet, without fear."

"Excellent," the voice said indifferently. "You may be accompanied by two servants — no more. We will await the four at the ravine's exit in five minutes' time."

"We do not need an escort," Istrak shot back.

"Right now, I am the one who decides what is needed, young prince. We will be waiting for you in four and a half minutes at the ravine's exit. Have two men with you, or the arrangement is null."

Hammers seemed to be pounding in Istrak's veins. Everyone began talking at once, each one trying to explain why he need not join the princes.

"I'll go!" a young voice called. "Please! Let me pass!"

A boy walked among the bodies littering the earth until he stood before the prince. He bowed deeply.

"I know you," Istrak murmured.

"My name is Kalev Ben Batal. I work in the royal stables, Your Highness. In your generosity, you gave me the job. I did not know how I could ever repay you — until now. Let me go with you."

Istrak nodded. "I accept, Kalev Ben Batal."

"With your permission, Highness, I, too, will come." A tall figure moved forward to join the princes. In a soft, pain-filled voice, the figure added, "Second Lieutenant Matan, at your service, sir. My wounds are mortal. I have no more than an hour to live. I will be happy to devote it to your service, and to spare the lives of these good men."

Someone lit a fire. A second man took down the princes' saddlebags and removed bits of food, a siddur, tefillin, and several holy books. A third brought Matan a clean, roomy shirt that would conceal his wounds.

"I was supposed to be married a month ago," the soldier told Kalev as the boy loaded a half-empty knapsack onto his back. "Don't you think it a miracle that our parents decided to put off the wedding until the summer? What would have happened if she had been left an *agunah*?"

"Gardian," Michoel stammered to the guard who was preparing his bags, "Difrat owes 560 gold coins to Lord Gedalia Latvias. Please make sure the debt is paid when you return to Itil. He also wanted to ask his parents' forgiveness if he did not honor them properly. I...I'd like to make the same request. Will you do that for me, Gardian?"

"Of course, sire."

Istrak said nothing. King Yosef's sword hung heavy on his hip, and his thoughts weighed even more.

"Do you, too, wish to leave any message, Crown Prince?" Gardian turned to Istrak with an inquiring nod.

"No," Istrak said. "Or...perhaps I do. That is..." He shook his head helplessly. "Tell my father that we did what we had to do. I think that he will find comfort in that. And let someone — perhaps you, Gardian, my friend — apologize to Matel in my name. Ask my father to compensate him for the trouble I caused him. As to Tur's wedding..." His voice suddenly broke. "Tell her not to postpone the wedding for even a day. Tell her to be happy." He filled his lungs with air. "Come, Michoel, my brother, and Kalev, and..."

"Matan," said the tall man quietly. "Lieutenant Matan." Something in his voice made Istrak finish his sentence in a near whisper.

"We have to go. It is time."

"Light the torches!" Gardian called loudly. "Light the torches, my brothers! Light the way before the Crown Prince, the Prince Michoel, and their companions!"

Torch after torch was ignited, and their golden light cast shadows over the men's faces, highlighting the fear, pain, and despair there for all to see.

"After you, Prince of Khazar."

The vast quantity of blood that had been spilled in the ravine in recent hours made the going slippery. Their attempt to avoid touching the wounded and the dead made their walking even harder.

"The rest of you are to stay here," Istrak ordered. How would an escort in the next few minutes avail them in any way?

"As my prince commands." Gardian raised his voice again. "You are to remain here, my brothers. The prince and his companions will make their way alone."

"Say something to them, Prince," Matrius urged, smooth as oil.

Istrak averted his head in disgust. The idea had merit, but everything in him recoiled at the *hostress* captain's manner. Was he right to suspect such a respected man of crass betrayal? Of aiding and abetting the murder of his own people?

"My brothers." The voice that emerged from Istrak's lips was not his voice. It was his father's, speaking through his throat. "My brothers, sons of Khazar. You may think, perhaps, that it was error or betrayal that has brought you to this place. This is a mistake. The King of the world, our Father, is the One Who has brought us here. He is the One Who strengthened the arms of the men holding the bows on the hills, the One Who has taken the lives of the best among us. Parting is painful, but a father does not punish his child unless he is standing near. The pain of the blow is also the pain of love — and our G-d in Heaven loves us. He loves us very much. Be blessed, my brothers, and stand by the king in the difficult days to come."

A stir, quiet but powerful as waves in the sea, swept the group. By the light of the torches Istrak saw them straighten their spines and stand taller. The knowledge that his words had lent them fresh strength was sweet. Istrak's own back grew more erect with a sense of a previously unrecognized inner strength.

"*Hashem Hu ha'Elokim!*" someone called out of the crowd. "Long live the kingdom of Khazar!"

For a quivering instant, a deep silence filled the ravine. Then the call was taken up by the rest, loud, strong, and vibrant.

Someone thrust a torch into Kalev's hand. He grasped it tightly.

Istrak turned his horse until he was facing forward once again. The moment had come.

"Do you hear me, Unmar?"

The young princess nodded, her mind clearly on other things.

"If you heard me," said Estelle, Unmar's nurse, "then perhaps you will explain to me how we are going to join both sides of the pillow?"

Unmar's eyes came to rest on the two pieces of shiny fabric.

"Unmar?"

"I think…this way," the princess answered hesitantly, putting one piece over the other.

"Exactly the opposite," Estelle declared with a dry smile. "Pay attention now, Unmar."

Unmar tried to concentrate, but a moment later her eyes were at the window again.

"I'm worried about Michoel and Istrak," the 8-year-old said unhappily. "I —"

"You must miss them very much," Estelle said gently. "That's not surprising. Everyone in the palace misses our dear princes."

Unmar hung her head. Was it possible that the dread she had been feeling since yesterday afternoon was nothing but a reaction to her brothers' absence? She could feel tears threatening to fall.

She would not cry! She was no less brave than Istrak and no less smart than Michoel. She was no crybaby, like Tur. Not at all!

She stared out at a strip of blue sky where a lone dove swooped into view and then away again.

"Mail has come, Mother Estelle!"

The nurse looked up at the window, but her nearsighted eyes did not discern the small, low-flying bird.

"I want to go to the dovecote!" Unmar cried, all traces of sadness vanished from her face. "Let's go to the dovecote, Estelle, please!"

The nurse stood up with a sigh. This active 8-year-old did not resemble any of the other princesses or noble daughters she had previously had in her care. Unmar could scarcely thread a needle — but she quoted unerringly from the *mishnayos* that her brothers studied. No other princess would dream of going out to the dovecote, or any other place where her clothes could become irreparably soiled. But for Unmar, such adventures were the breath of life! Her father, the king, who preferred to focus on the girl's good qualities, seemed to enjoy her adventurous spirit. He often said that she reminded him of Rena, his deceased sister. His explicit orders in these cases were to let Unmar do as she pleased — much to the dismay of her long-suffering nurse.

"A pigeon came, Lord Kaht. I saw it!" Lord Kaht was in charge of the carrier pigeons.

"Pigeons can come from anywhere, Your Highness." Lord Kaht's beard had turned white in the days of the king's youth, and he walked toward the dovecote with a pronounced limp. "However, I will ask one of the boys to check out the newcomer…"

Estelle walked a step behind. Unmar tried to peek inside the dovecote to see what the boy was doing among the many fluttering birds.

Lord Kaht emerged a moment later. "Our precious Number 301 has returned home." A brown pigeon with a white head rested on Lord Kaht's open palms. "Let's see what she's brought us…"

Estelle and Unmar returned to the small, cluttered office, where they watched him separate a tiny pouch from the pigeon's leg.

"A letter from my brothers?" Unmar asked excitedly.

"Apparently, Your Highness. Number 301 was one of the carrier pigeons that set out with the convoy." He placed the dove in a nearby cage and set to work opening the pouch. "Let us see to whom the letter is addressed. It is entirely possible that it is a purely administrative matter, Your Highness — a message about passing through some town or other…"

Unmar bit her lip with rising impatience while Estelle stifled a sigh. At length, Lord Kaht succeeded in opening the pouch and removing the thin scroll.

"Who is it from?" Unmar asked eagerly.

"It doesn't say," Lord Kaht answered, clearly surprised.

"Well, who is it for?"

"It doesn't say that either." Astonishment intensified on the nobleman's lined face. It was all Unmar could do to restrain a string of further questions and remember how a princess was supposed to behave.

"With your permission, I will open the letter. Those are my orders in such an eventuality."

He unrolled the short parchment scroll, and then shrugged. "It must be a mistake, Princess. There is nothing here except the seal of Lord Brach, commander of the palace guard."

Estelle stood up. "Thank you, Lord Kaht. We will return to the palace now, Princess Unmar."

"May I see the letter?" the princess begged.

There was no reason to refuse the simple request. Lord Kaht handed it to her.

Unmar's eyes scanned the brownish-red seal. They paused at a corner of the missive.

"Lord Kaht?"

"Yes, Your Highness?"

Unmar raised her head. "What is this drop, in the corner?"

He was silent, but she did not wait for his answer. With a flash of intuition well beyond her years, Unmar said, "It looks like blood, does it not?"

Estelle glanced from the princess to the nobleman and decided that it was high time they returned to the princess' room — the sooner, the better.

The scribe's hand moved with lightning swiftness as the minister for internal security dictated to him.

To: the Representatives of His Majesty the Khagan's government
From: the Minister for Internal Security
May Hashem bless you from Zion!

In light of recent developments in your jurisdiction, it is imperative that we increase supervision over the movements of foreigners in the region and report any unusual activity to the governor's office via carrier pigeon.

We will take this opportunity to remind you that when the princes' convoy reaches your jurisdiction, you are to immediately place a pigeon at their disposal to report as much to the government offices.

In the name of the King,
[Signed] Lord Zavdiel Mitran
Minister for Internal Security
Khazaran-Itil

The sixth letter was written and, like the five preceding it, sealed with the official Ministry seal.

"In the next letter," the minister said, halting the scribe's hand in its lightning journey, "instead of 'We will take this opportunity,' please write, 'You are requested to send a division of troops, accompanied by a doctor, to meet the princes' convoy, which should now be making its way from Grat toward your city via the Naat Bridge (preferably) or the Itra Bridge (the alternative choice).' That will be all for today."

" '...the Itra Bridge (the alternative choice),' " the scribe repeated, writing as he spoke. A moment later, he sat back. He had completed his work for the day.

The scribe's chair creaked as he left it, and his step was heavy as he departed the room. He had left his youth behind long ago, but the minister's talk about his childhood region gave him a twinge of nostalgia.

The twin bridges — the Itra and the Naat — stood east and west of his native town. He and his friends used to enjoy hiking across them. Personally, the scribe had always preferred the Batar Ravine to either bridge. It was so quiet there. When you were walking within the stone walls of the deep gorge, you would never guess that a bustling town lay just a short distance away.

A long time had passed since the servants had doused the light and left the room. The voices in the palace courtyard gradually quieted, and the moonlight that had been shining through the window frame was now gone.

"I'll just check," came a whisper from the other side of the door. "If she's sleeping, I won't wake her."

The curtain at the window stirred in the light breeze. The door squeaked slightly, and a stripe of light shone on the floor.

"Unmar?"

Unmar said nothing.

"She's sleeping," the nurse whispered. "I told you that she would be, Your Highness."

Unmar squeezed her eyes tightly shut.

Tur moved aside the hangings around the younger princess' bed. "You're not sleeping. Right, Unmar?"

Without a word, Unmar nodded her head vigorously.

"Are you worried?" Tur's fingers touched her little sister's cheek and met dampness. "Do you want to talk about it, Unmar?"

"I want to sleep." Unmar pulled the bedclothes up over her head.

"But you can't sleep," Tur pointed out — unnecessarily. "You're too worried to sleep. It's no fun lying alone in the dark, worrying…"

"I'm not afraid of the dark!"

"What *are* you afraid of?"

Unmar pulled the bedclothes off her head. Her eyes gleamed in the dark. "If something has happened to Michoel and Istrak, do you think they'll postpone your wedding?"

"It's just a letter, Unmar. An unclear letter. Perhaps the scribe cut his finger, and a drop of blood fell onto the parchment…"

"You don't really believe that, Tur." Unmar sounded far older than her 8 years.

"Unmar, we need patience. Patience and hope. That's what Father said."

"It was a seal of blood," Unmar said, her voice low but clear. "You need a lot of blood to be able to dip a whole seal in it!"

"There are many prayers and many soldiers accompanying that convoy," Tur said, stroking her sister's head. "Istrak and Michoel are well protected. I'm sure of that."

In the course of the night, several brave men tried to exit the ravine and follow the princes' kidnapers. But the men crouched in the hills on either side had good hearing. Gardian, one of those closest to the crown prince, was moderately wounded in the effort. It was only when the sun was shining at full strength that anyone tried to leave the ravine again. This time — as had been promised — no one tried to stop them.

The morning was crisp and clear, the sky free of the slightest trace of cloud, and the fields richly verdant. Slowly, the men began to emerge from the gorge, seeking the tracks of the kidnapers and counting their dead and their wounded.

"Ahoy! Is anybody there?"

A group of armed men on horseback appeared over the crest of a neighboring hill and descended into the valley at a gallop. Nearly the entire population of Pekat, the town nearest the Batar Ravine, came riding over the crest of that hill, bringing food, water, medicine, and carts for bearing away the injured and the dead.

"How did you know?"

It was only after the simple carts began to advance at the head of the damaged convoy that the question was asked.

"The young man reached us," said the village head, a small, round-faced man. "A brave lad."

"Young man?"

"About so high." The villager's hand lifted. "Short beard, an injured arm, yes?"

"Several man attempted to exit the ravine during the night," Matrius said, a shiver running up his spine. "We had no idea that any of them had succeeded."

"When we get to the village, you will see him," the headman promised. "He stayed in my home to rest a bit, brave lad. He also instructed us to set guards on the road — which we have done, of course. May Hashem protect our two precious princes!"

"Yes." Matrius inclined his head. "I will certainly see him…"

But when the village headman opened the door of the room where the young stranger had been resting, he found it empty.

"Eliyahu HaNavi!" his young son shrieked. "He must have been

Eliyahu come to aid the convoy."

Slowly, his father shook his head. Eliyahu HaNavi had no need for the heel of cheese and jug of water that he had left for his guest. And Eliyahu HaNavi — they noted as the day progressed — did not borrow a mule from the richest man in town, or leave a hasty note saying, "*I will return this, or another mule, as soon as I can.*"

The parchment scroll in front of Gardian was still as blank as it had been an hour ago, when the village headman had given it to him. "Someone will be traveling to the region's largest city tomorrow and will make sure to deliver the message to the local regional command — who will see to it that it reaches its destination by carrier pigeon to the royal palace," the headman had said, anxiously aware that a historic episode had just taken place in his territory.

The convoy had set out from Itil equipped with carrier pigeons of their own — sixteen of them. Four had been routinely sent off before the attack and had made their way back to the royal dovecote. The other twelve had taken flight.

In the commotion, the door of their cage had apparently been opened, allowing the birds to escape into the clear sky, far away from the shouting and groaning men on the ground.

Gardian shook his head wearily. His wound was not as serious as he had believed it to be the night before. Still, it had sapped his strength and made it difficult to think.

Was it possible that he, the young son of a noble family who had never held any position of significance, was the lone survivor who remained to lead the convoy?

He leaned his head on the table's surface, staring with glazed eyes at the dirt floor. What was he to write in this horrific letter to be tied to the pigeon's leg?

There was a knock on the door.

It was probably Matrius, deviating for the umpteenth time from his role as a military commander to consult and assist in the decision-making, despite the clear distinction that existed between his responsibility for the convoy's security and Gardian's role as the convoy's temporary leader.

"Just one moment, please," Gardian called. He dipped his quill in ink, shook off the excess, and wrote hastily.

To: the Minister of Internal Security, Lord Zavdiel Mitran
From: Gardian, son of Lord Miel, current leader of the prince's convoy

A shiver ran up the young man's spine. These words would say it all to anyone with eyes in his head. Where were the princes? Where was Lord Lemaneus? Where was David Sanpal, assistant minister of foreign affairs? Where were Avraham and Gideon, sons of Lord Zlatan? Where had Lord Yosef Rakat disappeared?

With stiff fingers, he folded the page in two and continued on the inner side of the parchment,

A tragedy has occurred. As we passed through the Batar Ravine, we were ambushed by anonymous enemies. Only sixty men remain healthy and whole. The princes...

His hand shook as he wrote these words.

...have been captured. Guardposts have been stationed all along the area's roads, and word has been sent to local military forces and the regional commander. No trace has yet been seen of the two prisoners.

Gardian gazed at the crowded lines and sighed. The message must be small enough to be carried by a dove and still manage to convey all the suspicions he harbored. Once again, he dipped quill into ink and scratched hastily on the parchment.

The advantages were all to the enemy.

Was this enough? Would the proper suspicions be aroused in the proper quarters? He was uncertain, so in adding up the facts that led to his conclusion, he decided it was best to hint at his suspicions as minimally as possible. Lord Bastian Makan, commander-in-chief of the Khazari army, had many loyal friends within the palace walls.

For the third time, he dipped the quill.

Yours in sorrow, the lowly Gardian, son of Lord Miel.

Gardian's letter reached the palace late in the afternoon. The minister for internal security, Lord Mitran, was already on his way home when he was called back urgently by a young aide to read it.

After scanning the lines of the missive, Lord Mitran almost raced up the stairs to Lord Bastian Makan's office. Bastian chewed his lip as he read the letter.

"Gardian, son of Miel," he said when had finished. "Is he the only one who survived? There were any number of men in the convoy with more ability than he."

The minister's fingers drummed on the desk. "I wouldn't want to be the one to have to tell…him…this news."

Silence fell in the room, broken only by the steady dripping of the water clock and the minister's drumming fingers.

Bastian grimaced and said, "We will ask the *rav* to come with us." Raising his voice, he called out to his personal secretary. Lord Mitran lowered his head, gazing with captivating interest at the tips of Bastian's sandals peeking out from under the desk. Something about the other man's cool reception of the news felt strange. One was not permitted to suspect the innocent. Nevertheless, Mitran couldn't stop himself from wondering whether the lord facing him — one of the most powerful men in Khazar — had known about recent events even before he had come to tell him about them…

The *rav*, summoned to the room, gasped as he held the letter close to his eyes and read Gardian's painful words. The two lords lowered their own eyes so as not to see the large, heavy tear dropping onto the thin parchment.

Bastian shivered. He had never seen the *rav's* face without its ever-present smile. "I will fetch the doctor," he said, walking heavily to the door. The spectacle was too much for him.

Many eyes followed the four solemn-faced men who passed rapidly through the halls, but no one dared to venture a question. They found the king standing beside the unlit hearth in the reception hall, gazing into the distance.

"Your Majesty," the *rav* began weakly.

The king turned. He was very pale, and a muscle quivered in his cheek. The *rav* took a step forward, slowly crossing the large hall as the king looked on in silence.

Bastian Makan bowed heavily. "A letter has arrived, Your Majesty."

Still the king remained silent. Now there was only a low wooden table between himself and the elderly *rav*. A moment later, the two stood side by side.

"My son," the *rav* said. "Oh, my son…"

The king's face turned gray and his hand went to his chest.

"The King of the world tests only those who are strong," the *rav* said, his age-spotted hand grasping the king's elbow. "Your sons are alive, ruler of Khazar —" he paused — "something that can no longer be said of many of the men in the convoy."

"What happened?" A crimson flush replaced the previous paleness. "Speak, Bastian."

Bastian stepped forward. "A letter has arrived, signed by the son of Lord Miel — calling himself the 'current leader of the princes' convoy.'"

The king looked from Bastian to the *rav* and back again. "Istrak? Michael?"

"I have the letter here, Your Majesty."

Once again the letter changed hands. Slowly, a royal fury engulfed the king. "How did the men come to be in the Batar Ravine, Lord Makan? What sort of insane idea was that?"

The commander-in-chief was breathing rapidly, but his voice was even. "I know nothing, Your Majesty. I gave explicit orders not to deviate from the route I had authorized —"

"And you did not, I hope, authorize passage through that terrible trap!"

"Of course not, Father of Khazar. No."

As the king's head dropped, the precious gems in his crown caught the light and glittered.

"Gardian, son of Miel!" In the silence, the king's whisper could be heard clearly. "But there were…" — he exhalted forcefully — "so many men! Great heavens, so many men…!"

The *rav's* eyes glistened. A quick look passed between them, and an almost imperceptible nod gave the king the permission he sought. With his left hand, he drew his sword from its scabbard and thrust it into the center of the low table at his feet. The noblemen behind the throne bit their lips, and the palace guards turned pale beneath their deep tans. Only the wind continued to play indifferently with the curtains at the window.

"The sword of Khazar has been drawn from its sheath," the king said weightily. "And it will not return to its place until the blood of the slain has been avenged. The murderers will be punished.

"Tonight the Flame of Altik will be lit. We must call all our soldiers to arms."

As the penetrating gray eyes swept the room, all those present seemed to shrink to half their sizes.

"Tomorrow, Khazar goes out to war."

In Captivity

10

IT WAS DIFFICULT TO SEE THE TALL FLAME DURING DAYLIGHT hours, but everyone knew that it burned, on mountaintops the length and breadth of Khazar, heralding the impending war and summoning men and youths to take their places among the ranks of soldiers. With tear-filled eyes, girls baked biscuits and smoked meat while their mothers laundered army uniforms and linens in tight-lipped silence. The blacksmiths sharpened the young men's swords. And the young men stood straighter in the shadow of war, their eyes glowing as though lit from within.

The reasons for the war had yet to reach the more remote villages and towns, but the people trusted their king implicitly. For the past twenty years, he had ruled them with inordinate wisdom and prudence.

When the enemy arrived, they would find the soldiers of Khazar ready for battle.

"It's a boy," smiled the midwife, capably swaddling the newborn baby. "*Mazal tov*, Rivka!"

The new mother smiled back wearily, too exhausted for words. The infant bellowed lustily as though to announce his presence, and the small house suddenly appeared beautiful to Tuval. A son! A male firstborn child! That meant receiving well-wishers in his home on Shabbos night, in honor of the *yeshua haben* [*shalom zachar*]. It meant a *bris milah* and a *pidyon haben*... In vain, he searched for something to say.

"I —" He faltered, finding no suitable way to finish the sentence. "I —"

As though to rescue him, someone chose that moment to knock on the door.

The sun had set hours ago, and the night was dark and cloudy. Who could be knocking now, two hours after midnight?

Tuval went to the door, pausing at the kitchen table on his way to pick up a sharp knife.

"Who's there?"

"Maglazi," came the reply in a deep voice.

Tuval loosened his grasp on the knife and opened the door to greet his friend. "You've come just in time," he smiled, eager to spread the happy news.

"I hope the hour that has brought me here is, indeed, a good hour."

"It has to be a good hour, because —" Tuval tried again.

"I've come for a reason, Tuval." Only now did Tuval notice the army uniform his friend was wearing and the two shadowy figures waiting near the gate.

"Has something happened?"

"The Flame of Altik was lit at midnight," his friend said. "All reservists are being called up. As the recruiting officer, I have come to let you know."

Tuval took a step back. "A son was born to me just now. The midwife is still here."

"*Mazal tov.*" Maglazi's effort to inject some joy into his words was a sincere one, but the result was melancholy. "*Mazal tov*, Tuval. May it be Hashem's will that you merit raising him to Torah, to the *chuppah*, and to good deeds."

"Thank you."

"Say amen," Maglazi recommended. "Considering the impending war, it's an important blessing."

For a long moment the two stood staring at one another. Then Maglazi scratched gloomily at his ear. "In view of the circumstances, I suppose you may stay home tonight... Tomorrow, go to military headquarters and request a deferment. But don't pin your hopes on it, Tuval. We need you, my friend."

"What happened?"

"The Crown Prince and his brother, Prince Michoel, have been taken prisoner." Maglazi turned to go, insensible to the blow he had just struck his friend.

"Prisoner!" Tuval repeated, shaking his head. No...there was no connection. There could not be a connection. Only a man with delusions of grandeur could link his portrait with the princes' capture!

But for some reason, despite his vigorous efforts at denial, not even his firstborn son could restore the broad smile to the new father's face.

"Our younger sister," said the shorter of the two men in a tone of deep sorrow. "You will never believe, my good lady, what a special girl she was!"

The woman glanced with sincere empathy at the girl with the long yellow braids seated in the upholstered carriage, hands manacled to the armrests and mouth muzzled.

"They say," said the taller of the two with a deep sigh, "that there is a doctor in the north, not far from Alda, who is an expert in mental illnesses. He is our last hope. We sold a vineyard and a cow to be able to afford this journey. But we have no choice. There is nothing worse than seeing a beloved younger sister losing her mind, and she is a danger to herself and others."

"Hashem's salvation comes in the blink of an eye," the innkeeper said, the keys in her hand jingling. "A Jew must never lose hope... You will not object if I put you in a room a bit distant from the other guests, will you?"

A quick, sad look passed between the brothers.

Uncomfortably, the innkeeper explained, "People come here to rest. Surely you can understand that... Our good name is important to us." She hesitated, then added, "Please try to keep her as quiet as possible — no screams in the middle of the night or anything of that sort."

The shorter brother sighed and nodded his head, while the taller one climbed back aboard the carriage. With gentle compassion, the two helped their sister into the house, their concern for her welfare abundantly clear. The woman of the house sighed. How many troubles there were in the world!

Soldiers pounded on the inn door, then pushed it open and walked through. Though they were the same age as the woman's oldest son, there was something about their uniforms and their grim expressions that frightened her. She hastened forward, knowing somehow that these men had not come for a warm drink or a late breakfast.

"What's the matter?" she asked.

"We have orders to search this inn," the officer said.

"Search? My inn? But why —"

"General orders, ma'am," the officer said curtly. Raising his voice, he added, "Please stay in your seats, honored guests. We apologize for any inconvenience. In the king's name, we have orders to search this inn for certain individuals."

"Why here?" she protested. "Do you think a criminal could hide here without my knowing about it?"

Ignoring her protests, the officer gave orders and the soldiers commenced their search. Their cool response angered her. Unwillingly, she followed on their heels, jangling her keys.

Room by room they searched, while the innkeeper — even more curt than the officer — supplied information about the guests inhabiting them.

"Poor things," she said at a certain door. "Their sister is, as they say, a little confused... They are traveling to see a big doctor in Alda. Have you heard of him?"

The officer said nothing. With a sure hand he knocked on the door, waking those inside. One of the brothers hurried out, adjusting his clothes. "Quiet, please!" he begged. "Our sister —" Staring in astonishment at the military group, he blurted, "What's going on? But, please — quiet. My sister had an attack last night."

The woman's heart went out to them. "I heard something," she admitted. "I also heard a man shout."

He sighed. "Yes, our sister... It's heartbreaking. I think we'll set out again today. She hasn't had an attack like this in some time. She banged her head on the wall and broke one of your chairs over my brother's head. We will pay you for it, of course." His gaze returned to the soldiers. "Is there something I can do for you?"

"We are conducting a search," the officer said courteously. "May we come inside?"

The man hesitated. "It is not a good time..." He opened the door, then shrugged. "But orders are orders. I, too, was a soldier once. Just give me a minute to get her ready, all right?"

"Poor thing," the woman sighed. "Such a pity..."

From inside the room came a groan, followed by a shrill cry. A moment later, the door opened. Another man, taller and darker than the first, stood in the doorway. "Please. Come in."

There was an unpleasant odor in the room, a combination of dust and perspiration. The woman of the house wrinkled her nose. These three had come here only last night, and already the room smelled this way?

The soldiers scanned the room hastily. The sick girl sat in a chair with a lolling head and a vacant expression on her scratched face. A handkerchief had been tied around her mouth, rendering her mute. A large travel-bag stood open near one of the beds, and articles of crumpled clothing peeked out. Otherwise, the room was like all the others in the inn, simple and spare. There seemed no reason to continue their search in here. Nevertheless, the officer lingered.

"Is there anything else?" Matt asked.

"No," said the officer, his eyes raking the room one last time and pausing at the sick girl huddled in her chair.

"It's just half a year since the first attack," Matt said quietly. "The Hand of G-d has fallen harshly on us."

"A speedy recovery," the officer said, retreating.

"Amen," Matt replied with feeling as he accompanied the officer from the room. "Good luck to you, too. Who are you searching for anyway?"

"His scream in the night — that was our own personal miracle," Matt said when the soldiers were gone. "That woman innkeeper did all the work for me." He laughed, and his laugh was not a pleasant thing to hear. "I told her that our sister tried to hit you with a chair."

"You see?" Hanba's voice held a note of triumph. "Every blow was justified. We had to clarify things to him right from the start! What would have happened if he'd succeeded in escaping, Matt? He was closer to doing that than you imagine! He ought to be beaten with a stick or dunked in the river like a dumb dog!"

Matt did not bother to hide his smile. Glancing at the prince's scratched face, the bloodstains on the woman's garment he wore, and his resigned expression, one would be hard-pressed to classify him as the wildest person in the room now. After a moment, Hanba smiled, too.

As for Istrak, his injured ribs barely allowed him to breathe.

"People will become suspicious at your refusal, Bastian," said Rakel, her hands gripping one another tightly.

"I know." Bastian's voice resembled a low, throaty roar. "I know that all too well."

"Too well?"

"I have enemies, like anyone who has accomplished much in his life. You know that as well as I do. Only a person who never acts never makes a mistake." Bastian passed a weary hand over his brow. "A kingdom does not wage war against the wind, Rakel. You don't start up with a neighboring country on the basis of weak suspicions! The Bulgarians are not as weak as they were twenty years ago, and they are enraged over the reception we accorded their crown prince at the border crossing. This will be a cruel and unnecessary war. I cannot send so many young men to their deaths simply because of guesses! Erroneous guesses, if I may speak freely within the walls of this room."

"Two crown princes," Rakel said softly. "The Bulgarian crown prince and the crown prince of Khazar… Don't you think that's an amazing coincidence? Why are you so convinced that our king, who has not made many errors in his twenty years of rule, is mistaken this time? How do you know this is more than a case of 'an eye for an eye'?"

Bastian paced the room restlessly. "I have information," he said at last. "Reliable information that the king does not possess."

Rakel picked up her embroidery and made a careful stitch. "And you are afraid to give it to him?"

Bastian sighed. "A nobleman is obligated to report all his activities to his king. But corresponding with an honored individual from a neighboring kingdom — one which has been at peace with our own country — is not a crime."

"You sound defensive," Rakel said quietly, fingers busy adjusting the embroidery frame. "What are you so afraid of?"

"A nobleman is not obligated to report that kind of correspondence to his king, Rakel — but it is certainly desirable for him to do so. Especially when the friend I've made is none other than the man second to the Bulgarian king himself."

The ivory needle pierced the fabric again and again. For the moment, Rakel appeared to have lost her tongue.

"We first met at the peace conference, nineteen years ago. Even then we both knew where things would end. I saw my future in the military sphere, while he was in place to inherit his father's position. He is an extremely refined person, very wise and possessed of clear vision. In my opinion, he is the person responsible for the long period of peace and tranquility that we have enjoyed until now. No one believed that peace between our two countries would endure for nearly twenty years!"

"And when was the second time?" Rakel asked, eyes on her needlework.

Bastian spread his hands. "We met there every day over the course of months, Rakel. We were both young and ambitious. He wanted to learn all about the Jewish faith we practice in Khazar, and we spoke at length about the seven Noahide laws... But we only became friends nine years ago, shortly after we legally adopted your nephew." Again he stopped his restless pacing. "Suffering brings people closer together. Bruno Radan is also a bereaved father."

At long last, Rakel lifted her eyes. "Is there any lack of bereaved parents in Khazar?"

A small, sour grimace crossed her husband's face. "If my own wife does not believe me, why should my enemies?" He adjusted the sword that hung from his hip. "This war is a mistake! Do you think there would be any purpose in speaking with my sister?"

Rakel shook her head. Queen Sarah, Bastian's sister, had collapsed at the news of the princes' capture and had not been seen since. The possibility of holding any conversation with her in the coming days was unlikely.

"What do I do, Rakel?"

She set aside her needle and faced him squarely. "There is only one other person who can influence the king."

"And that is...?"

"Unmar, the younger of the two princesses."

"Unmar! But she's only 8!"

"She is as wise and clever as a 13-year-old boy." Lowering her eyes, she added, "Go now, Bastian. It will soon be the little girl's bedtime."

Yekavel kissed his fingertips and carefully rolled up the *sefer mishnayos*.

"You learned well, Yekavel." The smile barely touched the king's lips. "I am certain that your Torah study will be of great benefit to Istrak and Michoel."

"I'll learn more," Yekavel pledged. "Don't worry, Father."

"You encourage me greatly, Yekavel. Go to your room now. We will meet again, please G-d, at Shacharis."

The 9-year-old prince stood up, bowed lightly, and kissed his father's hand. Two servants opened the door for him as he took leave of the king. Outside the room, he paused, staring in surprise at the small figure of Unmar, who had suddenly materialized at his side.

"May I speak to Father now?" Unmar asked in a high, clear voice. "I have something important to tell him, Yekavel!"

Yekavel gazed at his sister in astonishment. Without waiting for his answer, she walked past him into the inner room.

At the sight of his daughter, who should have been safely tucked in bed at this hour, King Reuel wrinkled his brow. "Let us begin with the punishment, Unmar," he said. He led his daughter to the table, trying not to notice how very much the child resembled his departed sister, Rena. "Which meal would you prefer to skip tomorrow?"

"Lunch," Unmar replied solemnly. "I am hungriest at lunchtime."

The king's breath caught. A powerful feeling of love for his daughter suddenly overwhelmed him. Rena, who had been slaughtered so cruelly, looked out at him through her 8-year-old eyes.

"Lunch," he agreed. His hand gripped his daughter's so tightly that tears sprang to her eyes. "And no sweets after breakfast, understand?"

Unmar nodded rapidly.

"And you must apologize to Mother Estelle and make sure to appease her. She is almost certainly frantic by now, wondering where you have gone. She loves you and cares about you. It is not proper to wound her feelings this way. We must honor those who care for us, and be grateful to them. Do you understand?"

Another bob of the head.

"Very good." The king loosened his grip on her hand. "And now, let me hear what was so important as to warrant this urgent meeting." He sat down on his chair. "I am listening."

Unmar's lips pursed. "It's a secret," she said, trying to overcome the tears that threatened to wreak havoc with her vocal cords. "Father, may we speak alone?"

The three noblemen in the room stifled smiles. Even the king looked surprised. But, to their astonishment, the king instructed them to leave the room.

"What is it, Princess Unmar?" he asked when the door had shut behind their backs.

Winding the sash of her dress round and round her hand, she asked, "Do we really have to declare war on Bulgaria, Father? Are you sure that it will help Istrak and Michoel and not harm them?"

"No one can answer that question, Unmar," the king answered. "But my concern for all of the inhabitants of Khazar must come before my concern for the two of them."

She was silent, absorbing this.

"No one wants to go to war, little one. But sometimes there is no other choice. We cannot allow our neighbors to believe that Khazar's military might has been weakened. Victory usually comes to those who attack, and not to those who are compelled to defend themselves." Stroking her curls, he added, "Perhaps there will be no war, after all. Sometimes it is enough merely to make a display of military strength at the border. But whatever happens, my child — we will do our duty."

"Uncle Bas—" Unmar stopped, then, hastily, she went on, "But Bulgaria has been at peace with us until the incident at the border crossing. There is no reason to think that her people would want such a big war now!"

The king closed his eyes for a moment. "You are too young to dabble in politics, Unmar. Tell that to Lord Makan, in my name. And tell him that the next time he makes friends on the other side of the border, I'd like to know about it…

"Now, off to bed, Unmar. Good night."

"They've been captured!" The nobleman's voice was hoarse. "They've been captured!" His fingernails seemed intent on tearing his own flesh. "Do you know what that means for us, Calidius?"

The young nobleman lifted his head. "I understand all too well, Your Excellency."

"What treachery! They promised me that they would kill them, and instead they took them prisoner! I can't understand it!" He fell silent for a moment, then burst out bitterly, "There is no trusting a mercenary!"

Calidius lowered his gaze and compressed his lips. The situation was amusing, but laughter would definitely have been out of place.

"They will hold the princes prisoner under more or less reasonable conditions," he said, slapping his sword in frustration. "They have insinuated that, unless I meet their demands, they will restore the princes to Khazar — a move that will rob me of my kingdom *and* my head!"

"They won't do it," Calidius said with assurance.

"Do you think so?"

"I'm positive, Your Excellency. The captured princes will evince a powerful hatred in the Kawaris — a hatred that will persuade their leaders that it is better for them to continue placing their trust in a wonderful person like yourself, sire."

Slowly lifting his head, Calidius was pleased to see the fury and fear on his lord's face give way to something else more thoughtful and measured. His expression declared that Calidius would play the role of chief advisor and supporter to the future king of Khazar — a role that would supply all of Calidius' practical needs in the years to come.

L IFE MUST GO ON, EVEN WHEN THERE IS A WAR AND TWO OF your beloved sons are missing. The lords of the government were in session, and as much as King Reuel wanted to mount his horse and go after his sons himself, he knew he must stay and fulfill his duty as king of Khazar. The stability of the kingdom depended on him. Speaking of stability…there was still one matter left to be addressed.

"I thank you in the name of my people, Lord Yosef," the king said. Those who were aware of the complicated relationship that existed between the king and the first citizen of Khazar could not help but hear the slight note of dissonance in his words, though only a few knew the reason for it.

"There is one more point that must be raised at this meeting," the king announced. "And that is to officially instate one of the most loyal of our people as Khazar's prime minister — Dalo Stazdiran."

Silence held the hall. Dalo's beard glinted with red highlights as he stood up to acknowledge his colleagues' well wishes. Until now, he had held the title of acting prime minister. And although he had suspected that the king planned to invest his position with greater authority, he had had no clue that the announcement would come so soon — and in such a complimentary fashion!

Struggling to keep from sounding too excited, Dalo Stazdiran answered in the affirmative to the official question posed to him by the minister of protocol.

"Sarah," whispered the king, the lines of his face illuminated by the flickering tapers. "Sarah, you must live. The children need you. I need you..." His voice broke and he hid his face in his hands. The pain was too great for him to bear a second time. He was a king — true. But he was also a human being.

At length, he moved away from his wife's bedside, signaling the doctor to follow him into the adjoining room.

"Her heart is weak," the elderly physician said, lowering his eyes. "We are doing everything we can, Your Majesty."

Had it only been thirteen years since the doctor had stood in a different room in the palace and spoken in the same tone about Basya, the king's first wife and beloved queen?

"You told me that once before," the king said dryly.

The doctor trembled. "We can only do the best we can, Your Majesty. But the Creator — He can do everything."

Despite the doctor's hopeful words, at the fading of the following day, as the sun set behind the hills that surrounded Khazaran-Itil, the queen's soul silently slipped away. Her burial took place a day later, in the presence of Khazar's dignitaries — except for her brother, Lord Bastian Makan, who was already on his way to the Bulgarian border.

Night began to retreat behind the distant hills. A silken gray replaced the deep black, and a chill, predawn northern wind whistled around the guard towers. It was cold on the open balcony, as fingers of wind penetrated the king's thin embroidered cloak.

"How far will you test me, Hashem?"

King David was tested with many more ordeals than yours, the silence replied. *He fought for his life, fled as a fugitive, lost one* child, and then another, and another... His crown was snatched away, and his own subjects made a mockery of him.

Reuel's back curved in a deep bow.

And he — the man who had known every manner of suffering and every flavor of anguish — he had said, and repeated, and written, that everything, *everything*, is imbued with mercy and lovingkindness...

The king trembled. He grasped the balcony railing convulsively.

Mercy? Lovingkindness? Yes. It is impossible that my heart holds insufficient faith to recognize this basic truth!

Mercy! Lovingkindness! Were he not the king, he would have shouted the words out loud and let them find their way to the distant hills. Lovingkindness. *Chesed*!

The skies were still black, but the darkness was gradually dispersing, giving way to light, and not merely because the sun was preparing to rise.

With an edge of his cloak beneath his face, the king sprawled full length on the ground before the One Who owns everything. His prayer was lengthy. When he lifted his face at last, he was surprised to see Unmar standing before him, her cheeks pale within their frame of light curls.

"Were you afraid?" he asked quietly, rising to his feet.

She nodded.

"I was praying," he explained, gazing into her eyes. "Fathers also need to pray quietly sometimes, with no one watching them."

She looked as if she understood.

"Girls sometimes need to pray quietly, too, with no one watching them," he said gently.

She lifted a hand to wipe her eyes, and her pathetic demeanor broke his heart.

The entire kingdom rested on his shoulders and his heart, but there were many people to care about the kingdom. This little girl who had found her way to the balcony in the middle of the night, though surrounded by so many faithful servants, had no one to care for her but himself. Not even a mother.

"What is happening inside your little heart, Unmar?" he asked.

From the trembling of her lips, he guessed at a mountain of words stored up there over the past days.

The king lit a taper. Holding it aloft in one hand and grasping Unmar's hand in the other, he walked slowly with her to the palace courtyard. Their appearance galvanized the palace guard — who hastened to follow them, doing their best to move quietly.

The hunger and thirst that had threatened to rob Istrak of his senses 24 hours earlier were suddenly forgotten, along with the horrendous dizziness and stomach cramps. It had been over 48 hours since he had had anything to drink, but, to his surprise, his mind was incredibly clear. The whole world seemed particularly bright and vivid.

If he ever returned to Khazar, was appointed king and led his people — no one would be able to claim that the man at the helm of their large, wonderful kingdom was unworthy of the job. He was preparing himself for the challenges of kingship at these very moments — although bloodstains, scratched hands, and woman's garb were not exactly the usual way to accomplish it.

His captors were not Khazars. That much he had discovered over the past two days. From their behavior and their speech, he had come to the conclusion that they were members of Wanana's tribe — the Kawaris — who lived on the other side of the border. Right now the two were talking quietly with a third man who had recently arrived. They were apparently discussing their next move. Despite his shackles, Istrak managed to wriggle into a corner from which he could see the trio. The stranger was unloading bags of food from his pack mule.

Working alone, the Kawaris could never have executed such a smooth kidnaping — this much was as obvious to Istrak as his own plight.

Someone had informed them that the princes' convoy would be passing through the Batar Ravine. Someone who had close connections to the royal palace…

Matt's rugged face turned toward the carriage, affording him a glimpse of Istrak's alert and interested expression. Alarmed, he directed his companions' attention to the prince. It was a tiny triumph for Istrak. The pleasure of that triumph did not dissipate even when Matt grabbed his hair and threw him from the wagon.

The underbrush on the ground softened the impact, and their scent reminded Istrak of the palace gardens. A sweet, warm mist replaced the vivid clarity of the past few hours. Was it possible that he was going to die? Just like that...die?

Someone turned him onto his back and removed the handkerchief that sealed his mouth, slightly easing the pain in his lungs.

"Madmen," the stranger said, gazing at the handsome young man's bruised lips and the gap between two side teeth.

"He shouted," explained Matt. "We had to do it, Captain."

"Your orders weren't clear?" The man's voice no longer penetrated Istrak's fading consciousness. "I believe that I forbade any blow that cannot be healed. Did I not?" Silence. "Why did you break his tooth?"

Matt said nothing. Hanba stirred uneasily.

"Bring some water now, fool."

Both of them moved at once, raising an amused grimace.

"I meant Matt. You, Hanba, can take the next disguise out of the bag. Our journey is far from over."

The water that filled his mouth and moistened his face and hair brought Istrak to his senses. Slowly, he opened his eyes and directed them at a pair of cheerful hazel eyes.

"How do you feel, Prince of Khazar?" the man asked, moving the cup of water from the prince's lips. "Of course, the trip is not up to your usual standards, but surely you understand the constraints under which we are working at present... If you have a specific request, I will be glad to fill it."

There was mockery in the man's words, but his tone was more refined than that of the two who had been Istrak's constant companions these past days. With an effort, he tried to focus his thoughts and consider how he should respond.

"I would like to put on my tefillin," he said.

"Anything else?"

Istrak pressed his lips together. Now that his thirst had been partially quenched, he was consumed with hunger pangs once more. He would also have given a great deal to know where his brother Michael was. But the honor of Khazar was too steep a price to pay for satisfying his curiosity, or shortening the length of time until his next meal.

The great Wanana, the terror of the Slavic tribes and the kingdom of Khazar, was not the man he had once been. He was a broken vessel, spending his days lolling on a bed of rabbit fur and remembering his golden days as a warrior and a leader. His name still struck fear into the hearts of the elders of the Platts, but Ka'hei, who regarded himself as worthy of the title of future leader of the united tribes, had already made sure that several stories indicative of the great warrior's weakness had filtered down to the younger set.

His way was not Wanana's way. Where Wanana adored the eagle, Ka'hei preferred the quiet hiss of the field snake. Soon enough, all would learn to acknowledge the correctness of his way: at the risk of a single elite combat unit, he had succeeded in capturing the heart of one of the most powerful men on the other side of the border, and to acquire an outstanding advantage for his tribes — the return of their territory in the years to come and freedom of movement on Khazari land.

"Payment will come," promised the message on the carrier pigeon's leg. It was an effort not to laugh out loud. By now his noble friend had found out about the trap that the tribal leader of the Kawaris had prepared for him. The deal had been to kill the princes of Khazar, which would have allowed the Khazari lord to take control of the kingdom and rule as its king. But this was not in Ka'hei's — or in the Kawaris' — best interests. Although he had never met the Khazari lord, Ka'hei could imagine his reaction to the change of plans.

As it turned out, the depth of the lord's anger and helplessness was something he could not have foreseen.

The metal links rubbing against Kalev's skin never allowed him to forget their presence. These last three days, since his arrival at tribal headquarters, the number of beatings had been reduced. The chain that bound his legs was a fair exchange. The Kawaris, Kalev had discovered, were very fond of the word "fair."

"If you behave properly, our leader will treat you fairly." Old William of the high cheekbones, in charge of Ka'hei's household, could speak a few halting words of Khazari, but from the moment he realized that the boy understood Greek, he had preferred to use that language. "And in my experience, my boy, I can tell you that a slave's life is not as bad as it might seem. It is a pity on your youth and strength. The Kawaris repay fairness with fairness — and unfairness with death. Besides, the road is long and dangerous, our hunters are everywhere, and anyone who sees you with those chains on your legs will know from where you escaped."

He waited a moment or two to allow his words to sink into Kalev's consciousness.

"Those who behave properly and satisfy their masters are rewarded with money and other things. More than a few I've known have succeeded in redeeming themselves by saving up during the years of their servitude. That is the only way to one day return to your own country as a free man."

The wounds on the back of Kalev's neck hurt every time he lowered his head — but he had to lower it. He refused to let the old man see the tears that had sprung to his eyes.

He had had his fill of regret for volunteering to leave the ravine with the two princes. He had been of no use to them; he and Matan had been separated from the princes immediately after they had handed over their weapons to their captors. Matan had died soon after of his mortal wounds, leaving Kalev on his own. Each time Kalev thought of his father and little sister, who had been left to fend for themselves because of his unnecessary sacrifice, he suffered a fresh attack of conscience.

More than 48 hours had passed since his talk with the head of the household. In the course of those hours, Kalev had cleaned the horses' enclosure, and been beaten because someone thought he had not done a thorough job; he had washed dishes in the stream, and been beaten because someone thought he had been too slow about it; and he had swept the small area in front of his master's tent — and been beaten again...did it matter why?

"That's how it is in the beginning," a young slave with dark skin and eyes told him in broken Greek. "After a while, you get used to them and they get used to you. Then things are different. You don't get hit so much."

Kalev nodded, thankful for the encouraging words, and promised himself that he would not remain in this place long enough to see the young slave's words come true.

That evening, the master of the house wished to see him.

Silently, Kalev stood before Ka'hei. The chains on his legs chafed more than ever.

"Your master, the Prince of Khazar, will be arriving here tomorrow, slave," Ka'hei said slowly, studying the round-shouldered youth. "We Kawaris — in contrast to your people — allow everyone to live by his own conscience and faith. I wish foods to be prepared that are permissible for him to eat according to the tenets of his faith. It will be your task to see to this. You will be assisted by three slaves who have expert knowledge of your laws. Your job will be to supervise them and make sure that the prince will be able to eat his fill. Is that clear?"

Kalev nodded in silence, although clarity was the last thing he felt at that moment. *Slaves with expert knowledge of our laws? Really!* Where, exactly, had Ka'hei found such men? And what, exactly, did they know? That the Khazaris were prohibited from eating the meat of a pig? Perhaps these pluralistic Kawaris believed that kashrus was similar to politics: one could cut corners here and bend rules there, all in the name of adapting to the current reality. But he, who had only recently learned how to cook soup, had no idea how he was to cope with the mission that had so suddenly landed on his shoulders.

To Kalev's vast surprise, the slaves turned out to know their work well. They sifted the flour for insects before commencing to make dough for bread. They summoned him to light the fire in the oven and explained to him that the large, juicy figs were forbidden because of the laws of *orlah*.

Orlah!

Stunned, Kalev asked where they had learned all of this.

The slaves merely shrugged their shoulders.

A little beating, a little hunger, a little dirt — was there nothing left of the glory of royal Khazar?

Istrak loathed himself for the weakness he felt, the helplessness and the despair. But after four days of starvation, if all you have to do to obtain food is ask for it — wouldn't you do it?

Was it possible to halt the stream of tears that flowed when he was in pain — real pain? This was not the soreness that resulted from playing a game, an amusing ache that would soon pass.

Could a person present himself as a crown prince and future king when his clothes were caked with dirt and perspiration and dried mud?

As for his captors, the prince's capacity to endure suffering came as a surprise. The serenity with which he seemed to accept his new situation aroused a grudging admiration — though the sentiment was well concealed by their abusive words and coarse behavior.

By the time the primitive wagon rolled into the Kawari encampment, not far from the meeting point of the three great rivers, Istrak was no longer sure he was worthy of being a king.

Ka'hei, leader of the Kawari tribes, had met King Reuel of Khazar when they signed a cease-fire agreement at Tzartaf. Gazing down at the prince bound on the ground before him, he was struck by the powerful resemblance between the prince and the image of the king that remained etched in his memory.

He stood, staring down at the prince for a long moment, arms folded across his broad chest. Istrak's gaze, which had been steady enough, began to falter.

"It's not easy for you, is it?" Ka'hei crouched down beside the bound youth. "The change was too rapid, too extreme."

Istrak said nothing.

"Captivity is not easy," Ka'hei said sympathetically, his hand playing slowly with the haft of a small knife strapped to his thigh. "But the fine upbringing you've had has no doubt prepared you to cope with any situation in which you may find yourself."

A flash of pain, swift as lightning, came and went in the prince's eyes. He, too, had thought so — until two weeks ago.

Silence filled the tent.

The knife blade gleamed between Ka'hei's fingers. It drew Istrak's eyes like a magnet.

"I am Ka'hei, leader of the united thirteen tribes that live on this land. That boy standing there is my son. His name is Yidrat," Ka'hei said, watching the leaping pulse in the prince's throat. "Like you, he is considered an excellent archer. Come here, Yidrat."

The Kawari chief's son took two steps forward and halted. His features were more fragile and of a paler shade of brown than his father's, and his shoulders were narrow. His fingers, long and delicate, were free of any adornment. He did not look like the kind of son of which a tribal warrior would be proud.

From somewhere inside, Istrak discovered an insolence he had not known he possessed.

"It is a pleasure to meet you and your son," he said — but his voice, cracked from prolonged and painful silence, did not convey the desired sarcasm.

"We, too, are pleased at this opportunity to meet you," Ka'hei acknowledged, moving the knife up to Istrak's chest.

Instinctively, Istrak closed his eyes.

Ka'hei pressed the tip of the blade a little more deeply into his prisoner's skin, hard enough to menace and yet softly enough so as not to tear the fine, begrimed cloth. As Ka'hei brought his face closer to the prince's, the blade pressed still more deeply. "I could kill you at this very instant," he said quietly. "Have you ever seen how quickly a butcher works?"

Istrak did not answer.

"Have you?" the Kawari demanded.

The prince nodded his head.

"And you are afraid. Very afraid."

The youth's eyelids fluttered. With difficulty, Istrak said what he knew he must say: "You cannot do anything without the permission of the Master of Creation — and He does not require your help to take any person's life."

The corners of Ka'hei's mouth lifted in a smile. The knife felt smooth and cold in his hand, but it was not for this purpose that he had brought the boy here…

Foolish pride has always been an outstanding characteristic of the Khazars." Ka'hei ran a finger over the ugly cut that ran from the crown prince's eyebrow to his ear, knowing full well the pain he was causing with this seemingly gentle gesture. "But I have looked upon you benevolently, Reuel's son. The day will come when you will thank your Creator for that."

Ka'hei's knife was sharp and his fingers deft. With quick movements he cut through the ropes that bound Istrak and lifted him to his feet to sever the bonds that held his hands together behind his back.

"That's better," he said, gazing at the crown prince, who was struggling to remain upright. "Soon clean clothes will be brought for you and water for washing." He paused, and when he continued, there was an odd note in his voice. "After that, we will be dine together. A special meal has been prepared for you — one that is suitable for your dietary requirements."

After the Kawari chief and his son had left, Istrak stared in silence at the curtain that covered the tent's entrance, still moving slightly in their wake. Numerous guards surrounded the tent, he surmised, since he was left unbound. Still, there was something strange about the way he had been left here, standing alone in the middle of the spacious tent, free of all restraint. What was he supposed to do now?

A polite cough sounded from the other side of the curtain.

Surprised, Istrak called out with equal courtesy — and Kalev entered with laden arms.

Kalev's round, good-natured face beamed with joy. It seemed that the *uflah* had fared better than he had. He thanked Hashem that the prince appeared well and whole.

Kalev bowed deeply. "A clean set of clothes for His Highness, along with a few other necessary items. You will find a washing bowl and a large water pitcher on the other side of the tent."

A wave of cold fury swept Istrak at the sight of the boy. Why, he was nothing but a traitor! A lowly traitor! And he, naive and foolish, had intervened to have the lad released from prison and took pains to find him a job in the palace stables. He must have orchestrated it all from the beginning!

The wave passed as quickly as it had come. A small, pleasant smile rose to Istrak's lips. The moment of triumph would come when he would take his revenge. Revenge for his uncle and the men killed in the convoy. Revenge against this boy, whose soft, open features had fooled the most experienced police interrogators in Khazar.

It was the mare that first noticed something unusual. Ruba's ability as a rider helped him to quickly unravel the riddle of the horse's swerving neck. Someone was lying, curled up, among the bushes and wild grass in the field to their right.

"A person?" Taor asked. The brothers' hunting and selling expedition had not been very successful, and the thought of the mockery that would greet them when they returned to the encampment with nothing more than three sets of new clothing and a single gold necklace made them both cringe.

Ruba's left eyebrow lifted, and Taor nodded his head in agreement. It would be wonderful if they could bring back a new slave. They could always claim that they had acquired him at full price in one of the distant slave markets along the coast.

Grasping their weapons, they dismounted and moved off the main road, both intent on keeping the person at rest among the bushes from hearing their approach. Strangers never understood how the brothers managed to read one another's thoughts, but the matter was really quite simple: their thought processes were so similar that they hardly ever had to pause to explain themselves.

This time, their caution was misplaced. The stranger, weakened by hunger, lay on the ground unconscious. His arm was swollen and flies swarmed around the pus that oozed from it.

"Ugh..." Ruba grimaced.

"Do we continue on our way?" Taor asked, half to his brother and half to himself.

The two stood gazing at the young man, whose long face was flushed with fever that burned him from within.

"A Mundari thief." Ruba shook his big head. "There are plenty of them, on both sides of the border."

"Too bad. They make excellent shepherds and stable hands," Taor commented glumly.

Even with one arm? Ruba's eyes asked.

Even with one arm, Taor's eyes answered. Aloud, he said, "It's worth our while to give it a try, at least."

The Khazar prince who greeted them now looked completely different from the ashen figure who had earlier been covered in dirt and stained with blood. His hair, light and shining, was tied back on his neck in a clumsy plait fashioned by inexpert fingers. The sidelocks to the sides of his face, nearly concealing the ugly gash there. The short-sleeved Kawari shirt revealed his well-developed muscles.

Ka'hei hid a satisfied smile. He had been misled at first by the fire in the prince's eyes, but he knew now that his estimate of the young man's character had been correct. The prince could be manipulated. His entire plan hinged on it. An unpleasant situation would have arisen had the prince stubbornly insisted on remaining in the garb of his own countrymen despite its miserable condition.

"Dinner will be served in just a few minutes in the head tent," Ka'hei said with a smile. "According to what I've heard, you did not get much to eat in these past sixteen days. Tonight, you will have a chance to make up for what you missed." The smile broadened. "The young companion you chose supervised the preparation of the food. It created a great deal of work for our maidservants."

He paused, waiting for some expression of gratitude, but Istrak pressed his lips together. After a moment's awkward silence, Ka'hei shrugged and said, "You are invited to come and dine, Istrak. However, before you do, I'd like to caution you about Yidrat." The Kawari leader's bold eyes peered out of his hard, tanned face. "My son's outward appearance can be a little…misleading. He looks more like a poet than a warrior, but in all of Platt there is no one faster than he at throwing a hammer. And once he has drawn it, not even I, his father, can persuade him to miss his target."

Istrak was silent, though a muscle quivered in his cheek.

"Generally he's a friendly and patient lad," Ka'hei ended cheerfully. "Come, young man. Our escort awaits us outside, and the food is no doubt waiting on the plates… After you, Prince Istrak."

The Khazars tended to laugh at the nomadic culture of the inhabitants of the Platt plain. In light of this, Istrak's astonishment, as he entered the enormous and lavishly furnished head tent, was very understandable. It was also very obvious — so obvious that it was only with difficulty that Yidrat refrained from smiling.

The floor was covered in costly and boldly colored Persian rugs. The low tables were made of valuable wood polished to a high gloss and laden with vast quantities of gold and silver vessels. The amount of food on those tables was double, perhaps triple, the amount that appeared on the Khazar king's table. It was hard for Istrak to believe that ten or fifteen people — the number of men in the tent — would make a dent in that huge meal.

And then there was the music!

Six musicians stood at one side of the tent, playing in perfect harmony, filling the tent with a soft, sweet melody.

"We'll sit here," Ka'hei said, touching Istrak's elbow. "In a moment I will introduce you to the dignitaries present."

From that point, the meal resembled any number of official dinners in which Istrak had participated over the course of his life.

There were mutual bows, courteous comments, and signs of polite interest. It was apparent that the Kawaris had decided to disregard the way the crown prince had been brought to their encampment — and that they expected him, with similar ease, to forget everything that had happened to him in recent weeks.

Kalev served Istrak's meal. "I personally checked the vegetables and sifted the wheat," he whispered to the prince, "and the fish is absolutely fine." He spoke rapidly and in an undertone. The smile he had evidenced earlier had vanished, and a long, fresh burn mark — which had clearly not arrived there by accident — was visible on his arm. But Istrak, reminding himself of the cruel deaths the boy's treachery had caused, could not feel any pity toward him.

Istrak could not fall asleep that night. His thoughts were too weighty, too troubled, too numerous. The behavior of the leader of the united Platt tribes was odd and unexpected, completely different from what he had steeled himself to face since his capture. It was worse in a way — Ka'hei's friendliness was worrisome, almost sinister.

In a tense move that had become almost habitual, Istrak thrust his tongue into the gap left when they broke his tooth. What did Ka'hei really want from him? Why had he been taken prisoner? And what was happening in Khazar right now?

Then there was the matter of the boy. Kalev, who had collapsed at the foot of Istrak's bed after a long day's work, was fast asleep and snoring softly. The monotonous sound enraged the prince.

He suspected that the boy was working for someone — that somehow the Kawaris had managed to find themselves an ally inside Itil itself. Otherwise, how had they known the convoy's planned route?

A suspicion that he had no desire to dwell on now surfaced. He could no longer ignore it: was it possible that Michoel's uncle — minister of war, commander-in-chief of the Khazar army, Lord Bastian Makan — was working hand in glove with the enemy? Where else could that traitor Matrius have been given orders to lead the convoy into the hazardous Batar Ravine?

His father liked Lord Makan. Ever since he could remember,

Istrak had placed his full trust in his father's judgment. Could his father be mistaken this time? Had he fallen into a trap, despite countless warnings by Lord Diaber (the former regent) against the domineering minister of war?

Istrak's fists clenched. It was torture, being in the tent of Khazar's greatest enemy, covered with blue, brown, and purple bruises, and forced to think that everything might have been different if only your father, your king, the person you've followed blindly all your life…

On the ground, Kalev stirred.

Slowly, Istrak opened his clenched hands. His father, after all, was only a human being, and a human being is easy to trust and easy to fool. Istrak, too, was human. He had allowed himself to trust this boy — so wicked inside, but so harmless-looking on the outside.

He flung an arm over his eyes, trying to escape his bitter thoughts and the memory of that gruesome night in the Batar Ravine. There was no point dwelling on the past. He could do that after he returned home. Right now, it was the future that mattered.

The future!

His thoughts ground to a sudden halt. What did the future hold? How should he prepare for it? For the first time in his life, there was no one near to explain, instruct, persuade, and guide him. Alone, he must prepare for the greatest and most difficult test of his life.

If he returned triumphant — the triumph would be his alone.

If he were to be vanquished — the failure would be completely his own.

The sun's rays woke Kalev from a deep sleep filled with uneasy dreams. They lingered on the pale face of the Khazar crown prince, highlighting the dark smudges beneath his eyes and the hard line of his mouth. In the course of one night the crown prince of Khazar had been transformed from a boy into a man.

In the third hour after sunrise, the tent's opening was pushed aside. The leader of the Platt tribes himself stood in the entrance, his face cheerful and his hair swept back to emphasize the high forehead and quiet green eyes. He looked with interest at Kalev, wrapped in Istrak's *tefillin*. Only by a faint crease between his eyes did he betray the surprise he felt at this open cooperation between prince and servant.

"You have woken, Prince of Khazar?"

Istrak's brows lifted slightly. "A prince of Khazar is neither lazy nor idle," he answered curtly. "Shameful will be the day when a prince of Khazar rises after his people."

This appeared to amuse Ka'hei. "In our country, a person of your stature can allow himself to rise a bit after the blacksmiths and shepherds... As long as you are our guest, you may certainly avail yourself of this small pleasure."

He paused a moment for the prince's reaction. When none was forthcoming, he smiled and said, "A breakfast of fresh fruits and vegetables will be served immediately. On future mornings, if you send your boy to the kitchen, we will be happy to provide more respectable fare, prepared according to the laws of your people."

The headman fell silent, waiting — as he had the day before — for some expression of thanks. None was forthcoming. Finally, he added, "We respect the faith and views of every person, whoever he might be. I have instructed my people to fulfill any religious request or need that you may have. I appointed the boy to make sure that your wishes are carried out to the letter, and my servants have been ordered to obey him."

Istrak's eyes narrowed. Ka'hei was at a loss to understand the sudden hostility in the prince's expression.

"After breakfast, you're invited to go out to our training field with me. Some of our Platt youth will be competing with one another. It would be an honor for them if the crown prince of the neighboring kingdom agrees to bestow a silver cup on the winner."

Istrak put his hands behind his back, ignoring the pain the simple move cost him. "I believe," he said, "that I'd prefer to remain here, Ka'hei, leader of the Platt tribes."

When the Khazar prince stood that way, with his head tilted slightly to the right and opposition in his glance, he looked so much like Willok! The memory of his firstborn son, so fair and handsome, tragically killed nearly two years before in a terrible hunting accident, flitted unexpectedly through Ka'hei's mind and stung like a scorpion's bite.

It was not merely his imagination. The two shared many features. The angle of the lips, the sturdy chin, and the stubborn gaze… For a fraction of an instant, memories clouded Ka'hei's consciousness. Despite his mixed lineage, Willok had been blessed with every fine Kawari quality. A very talented lad. If only he had been spared, he would have been destined for greatness…

Why was the Khazar prince alive while his own son lay dead? And why had Willok died, and not Yidrat? He would have paid a great deal to have Yidrat be more like Willok and the bruised and battered but unbowed prince standing before him right now. Despite everything that Istrak had suffered to this point, he remained a prince in every way.

"I believe, my friend," Ka'hei replied mockingly, "that you have no choice in the matter. You would not wish me to break my promise to our young contenders." His eyes locked with Istrak's. "They are waiting impatiently for the prince's arrival. None of them know anything about the circumstances in which you were brought here."

Did Ka'hei think that he ought to feel ashamed for having been captured? In Istrak's view, it had been a noble gesture of self-sacrifice.

Ka'hei's silence lengthened.

All right, Istrak acknowledged to himself. He shouldn't have marched into the narrow and dangerous Batar Ravine the way he had. But *he* was not to blame if a traitor had been appointed to lead the convoy!

Then who *was* to blame?

His father?

He lowered his eyes. Ka'hei chalked up a second private victory.

Shortly after Ka'hei left the tent, Kalev completed his prayers. Carefully he removed the prince's *tefillin*, rolled up the straps, and placed the *batim* into their decorated leather pouch. Then he raised his eyes to the *uflah*.

Istrak sat on the only bed, his head between his hands.

"What worries you, Your Highness?" Kalev asked quietly.

Surprised, Istrak's head jerked up. He stared at the boy as though seeing him for the first time. Apart from the long scar on Kalev's arm, there was no visible sign of the beatings he had suffered. The small smile that was habitual to him further removed all thought of such a possibility.

For a long moment, Istrak held Kalev's eyes. "It is not your concern," he said, and turned away with a decisiveness he had acquired through seventeen years of dwelling in the palace.

Behind his back he heard Kalev's quiet breathing. Istrak imagined that the boy's eyes were still fixed on him, waiting for more. "Thank you for your interest," he added. Then, as though remembering something, he said, "You'd better go see what they've prepared for our next meal."

Kalev's hands clenched. How could the prince, for whom he had sacrificed his freedom and nearly his life, behave toward him in such an arrogant and condescending manner? After everything he had suffered, did he deserve this kind of treatment? It was worse than the treatment he afforded his mule, which at least received full recompense, in the form of carrots and fodder, for its efforts...

Faith, tranquility, and inner joy: these words were carved onto the ancient tombstone of one of his Ben Batal ancestors. Words to live by — no matter the circumstance. Kalev was not about to let anyone cast a shadow on his resolve to remain steadfast — not even the crown prince of Khazar himself. And certainly not the lazy, self-indulgent, and barbaric Kawaris.

Had the tent been possessed of a door, its walls would have shaken with the force of the slam with which Kalev would have liked to shut it behind him. On second thought, had the tent been possessed of a door, perhaps Kalev would have been a little more circumspect in the way he expressed his feelings. The deep respect and admiration he felt for the royal family resulted in his doing nothing more than leave the curtain in the opening swaying slightly in his wake.

THE CHIEF OFFICER OF THE CITY OF KHAZARAN GAZED wearily at the young man with the downcast face. "We need every soldier," he said apologetically. "I can't allow you any further exemptions. Surely you can understand that…" He glanced at the medical note lying on the desk and added with a sigh, "But I also understand that in the present situation you can't leave your wife and the baby on their own in the house…"

Tuval pressed his lips together and did not say a word. Had the officer known him before the war, he would have found this silence astonishing.

"I will issue you temporary orders to join the First Division," the officer decided after a moment's thought, "with special permission to sleep at home. Report to me again two weeks from today."

"Thank you," Tuval said, accepting the document.

The corners of the officer's eyes lifted in a half-smile. "A speedy recovery." At the moment, he was not only an officer but also a man. "Next in line, please."

The sounds of prayer and Torah study filled the air in all directions. With the names of ten soldiers on the battlefield in his hand,

Tuval entered the tent to which he had been assigned.

The soldiers of the First Division occupied Khazar's largest *beis medrash* and the tent city that had sprouted hastily around it. The overwhelming majority of the First Division were Torah scholars, teachers, and yeshivah students. Individuals such as Tuval, who could not be with their own regiments, joined these Torah figures, learning and praying for the safety and success of the soldiers fighting at the front.

Tuval's shoulders were bowed with the weight of responsibility as he found himself a vacant seat. Ever since the birth of his son — who had not had a *bris* until he was 14 days old — his eyes were always damp. If he was unable to protect his own flesh and blood, how could he protect anyone else? What was he, a simple artist, doing here among these men who had devoted their entire lives to drawing close to Hashem?

Ten soldiers. Each of them had a mission in life that only he could help them fulfill. Each of them had his share in revealing Hashem's glory in the world. Each had a family, friends, dreams, and hopes. Each of them wanted to return home to lead happy, peaceful lives. And he had to pray for them… He! And only he knew his true worth, knew the waywardness of his heart, his tendency to chatter, his ambitions….

Weakly, Tuval picked up one of the *Tehillim* scrolls that rested on the table beside him. The moisture in his eyes envolved into large, heavy drops as he began to slowly recite the holy words. Knees buckling, he stood up, ten hours later, for Minchah. The service resembled the Minchah of *erev Yom Kippur*, and it squeezed from him the last of his strength.

Rivka had recovered nicely from childbirth — but the child's condition showed no improvement. Small, yellow, and wrinkled, he lay quietly in his cradle, crying little and eating even less. Most hours of the day found Rivka seated beside him, stroking his small, pinched face and whispering chapters of *Tehillim* through her tears.

This was their son, their little Yosef. And though many babies did not survive, their Yosef just *had* to grow!

In the evenings, Tuval would take her place beside the cradle, often crying softly. Rivka was beside herself with despair.

This evening, she looked at him as she had not really looked at him since the birth, and cold fear gripped her. Tuval's skin, too, was yellowed, and there were great circles of fatigue beneath his eyes. His beard seemed sparser than usual, and a muscle involuntarily twitched in his throat.

"You look ill," she said fearfully.

"I'm not ill," he whispered, eyes locked on the small, suffering visage of their little infant. "Just sad."

"You look ill," she repeated.

"No. I'm not sick at all. I'm fine. But…" He swallowed. "I'm not fine. I have to do *teshuvah*. But I don't know for what, Rivka. Our Father on High wants something from us, but I don't know what it is… You are a good woman and a good mother. You do your job faithfully. And I? I am trying to be better. But our child is still in danger."

Rivka bit her lip. All of her neighbors had expected the baby to succumb by now. She saw the surprise in their eyes every time they came to visit.

A tiny whimper escaped her son. "I'll try to feed him," she said with difficulty.

"And I will try to think. There has to be a reason, Rivka. We have to correct something we did wrong."

The ends of Rivka's kerchief tickled the baby's head as she wiped away another tear. She was afraid that Tuval, like herself, was torturing himself over the same, unanswerable question. But could they have thought of it beforehand, when the portrait was commissioned? Would anyone in the world have thought to question it? Or ought they to have been a little more suspicious in any case — especially after the *bek's* murder?

She sighed.

The questions had no answers, and no real meaning. The only important question was, what could she do with this scrap of information — without hurting Tuval?

One of Rivka's neighbors offered to watch the baby with a

solicitousness that touched Rivka. "It's important for you to get out a little — breathe the fresh air," she urged, leaning on the picket fence. "You must have errands to take care of in the city. Go — and come back soon, all right?"

"He shouldn't be hungry for the next three hours," Rivka said. "I won't be late. I'm only going to take care of a few little things in town."

"Take heed on the road!" her neighbor sang out. "And may Hashem bless your endeavors!"

Rivka smiled and waved her hand. Only Hashem knew just how much she needed those good wishes.

It was a month since she had last stepped past the fence that surrounded the house, so she hadn't seen how the face of Khazaran had altered in that time. Many shops were locked and bolted, while a pair of soldiers stood at every street corner. A strange silence gripped the city.

Suddenly, the war became real for her. Rivka's anxiety intensified. Was it possible that Tuval — and she herself — were responsible for all of this?

She paused near the center of town. A strip of blue sky peeked down at her from between two tall chimneys atop the city soup kitchen, and a ray of afternoon sunshine made her close her eyes. Turning away from the sun, she whispered, "Please help me, Hashem. It's not every day that I have someone to take care of Yosef, and I believe, Hashem, that You want me to do this." There were many more words inside her, jostling to find their way out, but the sound of an argument behind her prompted Rivka to hasten into the women's entrance.

"The meal will be served half an hour after the stars come out," a young woman informed her graciously. She had red cheeks and wore a voluminous white apron as she bustled about setting tables.

"I want to offer my help," Rivka said, licking her dry lips. "Not a permanent position, but I happen to have a few free hours today…"

The young woman's eyes measured her. "In that case, come into the kitchen," she said with a smile. "Speak to Hulda. She's in charge here."

Near the kitchen door stood a large woman chopping carrots into small pieces.

"Who is Hulda?" Rivka asked timidly.

"I am." The woman lifted her head from the carrots. "How can I help you, young lady?"

Young lady. Rivka appreciated this form of address, especially since a glance into the mirror before she had left home had reflected the face of an aging woman. She smiled. "I'd like to help. I have a few free hours…"

"All help is gratefully accepted," Hulda declared with a laugh. "Here, you can take over for me. You've come just in time."

On her way to the huge sink, Rivka glanced surreptitiously around, but there was no clue to what she sought. Which of these woman was Napid, companion of the Princess Tur?

She washed her hands and quickly returned to Hulda.

"Cut them up fine," Hulda instructed. "As though the former regent, Lord Yosef Diaber, were coming here for dinner tonight."

Rivka nodded.

"Very fine!" Hulda repeated. "You know that he stops by sometimes, don't you?"

Rivka smiled. "Very, very fine…"

"Excellent!" Hulda's five chins wobbled approvingly.

It was quiet in the kitchen as the women worked. The setting sun suffused the room with a golden light, but as the sun sank slowly in the west, a creeping gray replaced the golden glow, and the atmosphere in the kitchen became tense. "Quickly!" Hulda urged. "The people will be here soon. You," she called, addressing Rivka, "I don't know your name — cut up some onions."

By now, Rivka knew the names of three of the four women working alongside her. The fourth was too old to be the one she sought. The onions afforded her the opportunity to shed some tears. Was it for nothing that she had left her Yosef? For nothing that she had made this long journey on foot? All for nothing?

The young woman with the rosy cheeks entered the kitchen, wisps of black hair escaping from under her kerchief. "Onion," she said, wrinkling her nose playfully. "It's a good thing Hulda found someone else to give that job to."

"Stop chattering, Guti!" Hulda ordered. "Fill those jugs with water."

"Your kerchief is slipping," Rivka said quietly.

Guti chuckled. "I'm not married yet. The kerchief is just for precaution. Hulda is afraid that a hair will get into the soup…"

Rivka liked her smile. Perhaps this girl would be suitable for Beri, Tuval's younger brother?

Or perhaps not.

Anyway, Beri had to return from the battlefront first. And right now, she had to chop onions.

At last, all was ready.

"Very nice," Hulda nodded. "We can start bringing out the trays."

When the first stars were twinkling in the sky, Rivka took her shawl from the nail on the wall and draped it over her shoulders.

"Come back often," Hulda urged. "I like volunteers who work quietly. And you cut up that onion in a fine dice indeed!"

Guti wrinkled her nose behind Hulda's back and waved her fingers at Rivka as though to say that she, too, would be happy if Rivka came back to chop more onions.

Weariness enveloped Rivka like a thick blanket. The whole effort had been in vain. Now she must start the long trek home…

Slowly, she walked out of the cookhouse. For a long moment she stood by the fence surrounding it, gazing at a small, purple three-leaved flower. She was reluctant to leave, alone with her failure…

Someone else left the cookhouse behind her. "You look a little pale," the older woman said gently. "Are you sure you feel well?"

"Yes," Rivka said, staring at the small flower with unusual intensity — just to make sure that her eyes remained dry.

"You need to drink something," the woman declared. "Maybe something warm? A woman has to protect her health! Have a drink before you leave. Do you have a long way to go?"

"Yes." Rivka hoped that her eyes were still dry. "We live in Kadar, on the outskirts of Khazaran. But it will be all right. I'm used to walking."

"You don't look good," the woman insisted, shaking her head. "If you wait here another minute or two, I'll be able to shorten your trip home." Something in the tone of her voice made Rivka look at her again.

"It will be no trouble," the woman said, pulling a thick wedding band from her coat pocket, along with a pair of diamond-studded rings, and putting them on her fingers as she spoke. "My carriage will be here in just a minute. We even have time to get you a drink. Guti!"

Guti appeared a moment later. She had removed the kerchief from her head. "Yes, my lady."

"Wait here for the carriage. I want to go inside with this young woman."

My lady? Rivka had been told that the wives of the nobility found pleasure in helping at the soup kitchen from time to time, but she had always pictured them as sharp-eyed supervisors, circulating through the kitchen issuing orders and criticism. Certainly not as someone who sprinkled additional salt into the vast soup pot, tasted it thoughtfully, and then washed her own spoon...

Like a little girl, Rivka trailed the older woman inside and accepted a cup of hot water from her.

"That's better." The woman smiled. Glancing out the window and seeing that the carriage had yet to arrive, she added, "So, why have you come here from Kadar? Are there no volunteer centers closer to where you live, Mrs...?"

"Rivka," Rivka said quickly. "Rivka Obseld."

"I am pleased to make your acquaintance, Rivka Obseld. I am Leah Diaber."

The wife of the regent himself stood before her, waiting for a response to her question. Rivka did not hesitate long. Such an opportunity did not come along every day.

"I gave birth one month ago," Rivka whispered. At the other woman's surprised look, her eyes filled with tears. "My little boy is ill. Very ill."

Leah Diaber's face grew sad. "Oh, you poor thing..." Her gaze sharpened as she saw the carriage draw up in front of the cookhouse.

"Come, let us enter the carriage, and you can tell me all about it on the way."

Rivka felt much better after she had unburdened herself. But although Leah Diaber listened attentively and promised to repeat the story to her husband, Rivka had a sense that nothing would come of it.

Well, you've done what you had to do, she told herself firmly as she accepted the baby from her neighbor's arms. "Now let Hashem do His part."

Ka'hei glanced at Te'arah, his lieutenant, with pride and satisfaction. In the field below, the last two pairs of combatants struggled in a fierce battle with each other. The crowd was excited and tense. The presence of the Khazar crown prince had been the catalyst to turn the warriors more warlike and the contestants even more competitive than usual. It was as though the pairs of fighters were intent on winning, not merely a red-painted rock, but the head of a…

Ka'hei shook his head, his good mood dissipating like smoke. So many difficulties and uncertainties lay in wait before he succeeded in achieving his goal! Perhaps it would have been better, after all, to rely on their friends across the border and hope that they would keep their promise to help him win the throne.

A roar rose from the crowd.

One of the fighters fell to the ground in despair, while the other lifted the rock above his head in both arms and gestured with it toward his fallen rival. Yidrat, seated beside Istrak, could hardly sit still. They had won! The Huld side had triumphed!

"Wasn't this a wonderful game, Istrak?" he cried.

The victorious youth, rivulets of sweat glistening on his brow, climbed wearily up to the dignitaries' dais, where Istrak handed him a long-stemmed, silver-rimmed wine goblet. The crowd ran down to the field, some to celebrate with their friends and others to commiserate with them. With slow dignity, those in the upper row stood up and headed to where their horses were tethered.

"Well?" asked Ka'hei. "Did you enjoy the contests?"

The prince, who a moment earlier had appeared alert and interested, seemed to turn to ice. "Your people are clearly well versed in hand-to-hand combat, leader of the Platt tribes," he answered curtly.

"At the start of next week, there will be target-shooting and hammer-throwing competitions as well," Te'arah remarked.

Ka'hei bit his lip. He had deliberately postponed those contests for the following week, fearful of inciting another heated response from the prince on whom he had pinned so many hopes. And if Istrak requested to participate in them, he would not be able to refuse without destroying the image he had worked so patiently to cultivate.

"But a great deal of water will flow in the river before next week comes," Te'arah ended lightly, as though he had divined Ka'hei's thoughts. "This evening there will be a music festival in the black tent, tomorrow morning a horse race, and a performance in the evening... We are determined to turn this visit into a real experience for you, young prince."

"For me, the decisive experience will always be the one that brought me here." The Khazar prince's voice could have cut through diamonds.

Te'arah fell silent, sending an imploring look at Ka'hei, who shrugged and said, "Your father, the king of Khazar, refused to have any contact with us. We could find no other way to bring you here."

Istrak took a deep breath, digesting these words. "Did that justify killing so many men?" he asked quietly.

"We are treading deep waters now — something I generally prefer to do on a full stomach," Ka'hei replied, signaling for one of the servants to approach and untie their horses. "However, as I do not wish to leave you troubled by that question, I will respond with a question of my own: how many men were killed in the Ten Years' War?"

The servant bowed, forehead to the ground, before he dared venture close to the Platt leader and untether his horse. Ka'hei seemed not to see him. His eyes were fixed on Istrak's. Both of them well knew that the Ten Years' War had been a bloodbath for Khazar, just as it had thinned the ranks of the tribal warriors. And it was Khazar that bore full responsibility for the outbreak of that war.

Two servants fanned Ka'hei, while a third wiped his face with a damp, perfumed towel. A fourth and fifth set the table, and the last servant, hair prematurely white, played a three-stringed lyre. Yidrat sat opposite his father, languishing on a special soft cushion and benefiting as well from the fanners' refreshing exertions.

"What did you think of today's events, Yidrat?" his father inquired, plucking a peeled chestnut from the steaming heap in front of him.

Yidrat sighed with satisfaction, chewing a lump of sugar. "You could say it was a successful day."

"Successful — or very successful?"

"Very successful. First of all, the Huld youths won two-thirds of the competitions..." He flashed a smile at his father, proud of his friends and his team. "And I think the prince was impressed as well. He said that such contests strengthen team motivation and unity. When Pluto grabbed the stone from Mara, who'd fought so hard for it, I could see that he was disappointed."

Ka'hei nodded. "That was truly bad luck." He paused. "How do you think he feels here?"

"Under the present conditions — all right," Yidrat answered slowly. Then he added, speaking more rapidly, "He's an impressive young man, that prince of Khazar. Some of those who laughed at him at the start of the day were talking very differently at the end."

"In short, we could say that all is proceeding according to plan?" Ka'hei's perfect teeth ground the chestnut meat.

"It seems so," Yidrat answered thoughtfully. "But I would be wary of those two officers, Hanba and Matt. Right now they're strolling around the tents like a couple of peacocks, swelled with pride and refusing to divulge any information regarding our plan. Still, I wouldn't trust them... Can't you send them away, Father?"

Ka'hei closed his eyes. "Not at the moment, Yidrat." Peering at his son through his lashes, he added, "Their presence frightens Istrak, and that's good." With a deep sigh of satisfaction, he licked his lips, leaned his head back, and slept.

The Kawari tents had no chairs. Instead, the tents of the wealthy featured low couches covered with expensive cloths and soft pillows, while the tents of the poor had mats of animal skin or woven grass.

Istrak's tent held neither. In the course of the past few hours, someone had emptied out the entire place.

The Khazar prince crossed his arms. The game the Kawaris were playing with him was not clear. On the one hand, they treated him with royal honor. On the other... He looked around the tent. Any object that might have been used as a chair had disappeared while he was out at the playing field. If he wished to sit, he could do so only in the dust — or appeal to Ka'hei who, before they parted, had said with total nonchalance, "If you meet with any sort of problem, Istrak, you can always send someone to call me. I want you to feel completely at home here."

Was there a clash of views within the Kawari leadership? Was there someone near the top who would treat the Khazar prince differently than Ka'hei was treating him?

It was reasonable to suppose, Istrak thought, that the Kawaris were already engaged in serious negotiations with the Khazar palace. As long as the Khazars did not sign any kind of agreement, the way the captive prince was treated would remain unknown to them, and so could not influence their decisions. No less reasonable was the assumption that there were more than a few Kawaris who would rejoice at Khazar's degradation and downfall. If the Khazar prince was already in their hands, why not let them "enjoy" it a little?

Istrak's breath quickened. The "prince" he was thinking about was none other than himself. If Hanba and Matt's behavior was anything to go by, he had a pretty clear notion of how the Kawaris wished to treat him. Istrak clenched his jaw, feeling again the gap that his broken tooth had left behind — a keen reminder of that treatment.

If Ka'hei succeeded in mastering those turbulent emotions, then he was a very powerful leader indeed. More powerful than he allowed others to believe from his negligent pose.

Which begged the question: what exactly did Ka'hei hope to achieve with his friendly overtures?

On the surface, the answer seemed simple enough. No one had any doubts about Khazar's military strength and capability. Once Istrak had been restored to his own country, there would be nothing to prevent Khazar from waging a murderous war of revenge against its nomadic neighbors. Only fair and pleasant treatment toward their prince — to demonstrate that the Kawaris were not interested in war, but only in attracting Khazar's attention to a number of issues they had tried, in vain, to have addressed for at least the past fifteen years — would prevent the outbreak of such a war.

Though the answer appeared so obvious — Istrak was not satisfied. If that was really Ka'hei's motive in being so friendly, how did that explain the slaughter in the Batar Ravine? Did the tribal leader believe that his father, a compassionate ruler, would easily forgive the cruel murder of so many of his people? Especially when it had been possible, simply by shooting a number of arrows from both sides of the gorge, to drive home to the convoy their inferior military position and demand the princes' capture without any casualties at all?

The curtain at the tent's entrance stirred behind him. Muscles clenched for battle, Istrak turned swiftly, his hand going automatically to the place where his sword should have been. It was not there, of course — nor did the newcomer call for such alarm. It was only Kalev bearing a tray of lunch, the ubiquitous broad smile plastered across his face.

Three soldiers from Wanana's official guard entered the tent in cadenced step.

"Welcome," Ka'hei greeted them, admirably concealing his surprise at their arrival. "Please, be seated."

"We cannot sit, Commander," said one of the three, stern-faced.

"Why not?" Ka'hei's hearty friendliness threatened to upset several hidebound customs among his fellow tribesmen. This was not the first time that he had carelessly disregarded all distinctions of status, age, and position.

"We have come to summon the commander to the tent of our great leader," said the stern-faced soldier, looking even more sober than before.

Yidrat bit the inside of his lip, trying, as always, to anticipate his father's next move. As always, he guessed wrong.

"The great Wanana wishes me to come and visit him in his tent?" Ka'hei repeated, faithful to the facts but completely altering the subtext of the soldier's message. "I will come at once. Would you care to accompany me?"

Yidrat struggled to contain a smile. His father was a genius! The serious tone of the message made it easy to guess that the tribal leader had ordered his soldiers to summon Ka'hei to his tent. Now, the degrading summons had been turned into a respectful invitation…

"Yidrat!"

"Yes, Commander?"

"Join me in my visit to our leader. Men, I will be right back." Ka'hei's tall figure momentarily dimmed the light of the oil lamp dangling from the tent's central post. "Wait for me here."

From Ka'hei's external appearance, it was impossible to conceive that the 18-year-old youth walking alongside him was his third son. When he stepped out of his tent dressed in his military commander's uniform, a gleaming copper band across his brow, a purple silk cloak rippling from his shoulders, and his green eyes sparkling with the light of battle, he appeared only a few years older than Yidrat.

Wanana — a lump of fat beneath a rabbit-fur blanket, minus one leg and a front tooth that had broken recently when he had bitten into an apple — was well aware of the disparity between them.

"Welcome, young man."

Ka'hei smiled modestly. He had never liked this mode of address, but if it pleased Wanana to be the "wise old man" and made him more tolerant of Ka'hei's decisions, Ka'hei was prepared to endure it.

"Blessed is the speaker, leader of the Platt tribes," Ka'hei responded courteously.

"I asked you here in order to hear a detailed report about the Khazar prisoner you have brought to our camp." Wanana's jowls shook as he spoke, and his speech was not as clear as it had once been. "I have the impression, Ka'hei, that today, as in the past, you prefer to work alone, and on the sly…"

Wanana had not invited him to sit, and now, at these accusatory words, Ka'hei's eyes flashed with barely suppressed anger. "I have reported every action that required authorization. We did nothing we should not have done. If my strategy produced better results than the plans dreamed up by the heads of the other tribes — well, that only proves my point about the need to include mental exercises among the pastimes of our youth."

Wanana groaned, coughed, and shifted into a more comfortable position on the low hammock. "The prisoner must be killed. Let the young men spill his blood. Perhaps we can have it done at the sun festival?"

Not a muscle in Ka'hei's face quivered. "Your will be done, O great tribal chief. No one would question the wisdom of our mighty leader."

Yidrat's lips tightened in disbelief. Wanana, too, wrinkled his brow at this speedy submission by the ambitious and clever military commander. Silence filled the tent, mingling with the fragrance of the medicinal potions.

The silence did not trouble Ka'hei in the least. He stood in a relaxed pose, both arms folded lightly across his chest as rays of light from the oil lamp were reflected on the gleaming copper band on his forehead.

"Explain yourself," Wanana said heavily. "Why did you bring the prisoner here, Ka'hei, when we had agreed that he would be killed?"

"Well," said Ka'hei. "That's a rather long story…" He spoke softly, patiently, as though the young folk at one of the tribal bonfires had asked him to tell the fable of the three-headed deer.

"Fetch yourself a cushion," Wanana said tiredly.

Ka'hei's eyes narrowed. Once again, silence filled the tent, and the scent of the medicinal potions tickled Yidrat's lungs. Wanana waited, too, eyes fixed on the youthful commander with the polite smile.

A moment passed, and then another, and another. Finally, a young soldier stirred from his place and set a pair of cushions on the floor, not far from Wanana's hammock. Ka'hei acknowledged him with a nod and sat down.

"Well," he said, hands on his knees, "the story begins about a year ago, at our end-of-summer festival…when a faithful messenger handed me a letter from a good soldier of ours who had managed to infiltrate the Khazar ranks and establish himself there as a righteous convert."

"Tiapi?" Wanana asked.

"Moshe," Ka'hei pronounced softly. "That is his new name. His position as a successful musician has given him many opportunities for his spying activities…" He fell quiet for a moment, deliberating over his next words. "In his letter," he said finally, "Moshe told me about the great ambitions of a certain Khazar nobleman. For security reasons, I'll not say his name… This power-hungry nobleman has been searching for a way to overthrow the Khazar monarchy for years. I suggested to Moshe that he wait for the appropriate moment and offer the honored lord our assistance — in exchange for certain minor guarantees, such as the return of the Maatal region, free passage for our people in Khazar cities, and nullification of the old law banning travelers to cross the Khazar borders when carrying idols in their baggage.

"Very soon — much sooner than I'd expected — I received a positive reply from the nobleman. He was prepared to agree to all our demands, and even more, if we led an attack on the two older princes — an attack that would lead to their deaths."

Wanana stirred uncomfortably. "There is nothing new in what

you are telling me, young man."

Yidrat hid a smile. His father did not require Wanana's consent — what he wanted was the sparkle that had leaped into the soldiers' eyes when they heard, for the first time, the story from its inception. Wanana's day was over, without a doubt…

Ka'hei squared his shoulders, and the look in his eye held a hint of challenge. "In contrast to those who believed that one can rely on the word of a Khazar who is ready to have his own crown prince murdered, we decided to introduce a small change in the agenda. Instead of providing proof of the deaths of the two princes whose portrait had been handed over to us, we decided to capture them alive — and thereby ensure that the Khazar lord will fulfill every one of his promises."

When Ka'hei finished speaking, Wanana reflected in silence for a moment.

"And if he does not carry them out?" Wanana asked hoarsely.

Ka'hei smiled. "For the past six months, I have been investigating the character of the crown prince. Prince Istrak is not enamored of his life in Khazar. Competitions, horse races, and evenings of song will quickly turn his heart in our favor.

"And then, after Reuel II is murdered, we will be able to restore the young crown prince to his land, where he will sit upon his father's throne — and be happy, very happy, to do whatever I ask of him."

Ka'hei's voice had dropped low on his final words. They seemed to linger in the air, waiting for a response.

Wanana was clearly at a loss. "Bah!" he said finally, in a dismissive tone. "Pretty words."

"Pretty words," Ka'hei said, "build a pretty reality. Khazar will crumble, its power will be lost — and we, without spilling our own blood or the blood of our youth, will walk through its gates to gather the spoils."

"Lunch," announced Kalev, bearing a heavy tray. He looked around in surprise. "Where's the table?"

"Good question, Ben Batal." Istrak's tone was wry — and no warmer than it had been in their previous exchange.

Kalev's long lashes lifted, and his glance, direct and hurt, met the crown prince's. He bent on one knee and placed the heavy tray on the ground.

The gesture evoked in Istrak a powerful sense of pain and loneliness. He turned away from the boy. Through the tent curtains wafted the strains of a lyre and the distant echo of a Greek slave singing.

"They did it deliberately, Your Highness," Kalev said, standing up. "I know them by now, sir. They want you to ask."

Istrak did not react. Kalev added, "Or for you to sit on the sand. They are experts at degradation, Your Highness."

"Ka'hei treats me very well," Istrak said quietly. "Ka'hei's people are very interested in renewing trade ties with Khazar. The kidnaping was the only way they could achieve their goal without a general war."

Kalev nodded doubtfully, gazing around at the large, empty tent. Istrak noticed his skepticism. "But I'm not so sure that Ka'hei is the sole leader here issuing orders. Internal struggles can lead to things like this."

"Things like this?" Kalev echoed, uncomprehending.

"Dualism," explained Istrak. "Double messages."

"Ah," Kalev said with a small smile. "I understand, Your Highness."

The two stared at each other.

"You're laughing at me," Istrak said.

"No." Kalev placed a hand on his heart. "Heaven forbid."

"What is so funny then?"

Kalev's eyes widened. "It wasn't funny, Your Highness."

An unprincely fury washed over Istrak. "Then why did you laugh?"

"I didn't laugh, sir. I only smiled."

The evasion was ludicrous. "Then why did you smile?" Istrak asked between clenched teeth.

Kalev lowered his head. His hair, Istrak noticed, was crusted with dried blood. "Who injured you?" Istrak asked sharply.

"Which injury are you referring to?" Kalev asked with a bark of wry laughter.

"On your head. And don't laugh when you stand before me. It is not respectful."

"I'm sorry, Your Highness." A small smile still lingered in Kalev's eyes.

"Talk," Istrak ordered.

"It was one of the men in charge of the kitchen."

The memory of Miflaeus rose suddenly in Istrak's mind. His lips compressed, and his softened expression vanished. "You had it coming to you," he said.

Only a fluttering curtain in the upper window testified to the fact that, despite the impression created by the old, broken stones lying around, the weeds that had sprouted in the cracks of the walls, and the flourishing wild grass, somebody *did* live in the abandoned watchtower.

The middle-aged doctor adjusted his grip on his medical bag. The elderly teacher whom he was visiting, known as one of the wisest men in all of Itil, had chosen this unusual abode in order to conduct his nighttime stargazing without the interference of city fires. In the doctor's opinion, stars — however beautiful — did not justify such a sacrifice. He would never live in such a desolate spot, not for all the gold in the world.

The doctor pushed open a wooden door swollen with the years and entered the tower.

It always seemed to him that the hardest part about visiting Izdru were the 230 steps he had to climb to reach the modest room at the top where the man chose to live. On this occasion, however, he would have been happy to let the staircase stretch on and on.

What he had come to tell the old teacher would not be easy to say, or digest. But he had to share with someone the suspicion that had been growing inside him these last few days: the certainty that Queen Sarah's death had not been a natural one. Something else, apart from the bad news about the princes, had hastened her death.

A step, and another step, and another. At long last, the doctor stood facing the door. He lifted a hand to knock — and halted at the sound of voices within.

He had always assumed that the teacher lived alone, apart from the company of the stars. Now, embroiled as he was in dark suspicions, the voices seemed to point an accusing finger at the teacher himself. Here was yet another person who presented himself in a way that was different from the truth!

With a sigh, he knocked. The door opened at once. The figure that had opened it made the doctor narrow his eyes and jut out his chin in surprise. "Lord Mitran! What are you doing here, Your Excellency?"

The minister for internal security smiled. "Working." Turning to the teacher, he added, "I didn't know that you were not feeling well, Izdru. But even had I known, I would have been forced to request your help anyway." Then, in deference to the doctor, he explained almost apologetically, "We have no real clue as to where the princes have disappeared to, may Hashem protect them! We're grasping at any straw... A boy reported two wine merchants exchanging some unfamiliar words."

"Words that do not exist," the teacher, an expert in languages, interrupted. "The words that you quoted do not exist, Zavdiel."

The minister inclined his head. "I knew that," he said. "But I thought that you might be able to divine something from the sound of the words or the syllables. You are certain that we have no way of ascertaining from which language those words are derived?" He shook his head. "Understand, we have no footprints, no clues, no lead at all... None of us wants to dwell on what the princes might be suffering right now. We have to find *something*."

The doctor's shoulders slumped. From moment to moment, the burden of his suspicions was growing heavier. It was difficult for him to believe that someone — or several someones — had managed to transport such a large group of people through Khazar without leaving behind, as Lord Zavdiel claimed, the slightest sign. It seemed reasonable to think that one of the searchers was making sure to point the others in the wrong direction… Was that person the man standing before him now — the man in charge of internal security — Lord Zavdiel Mitran? Or was his earlier suspicion the correct one?

The minister accepted the teacher's words with equanimity. "When there are no oxen, even a calf will do," he said. "It is my duty, *our* duty, to do everything, even if it seems to run counter to logic, to bring the princes home. I came to ask for your help, not your comments."

"And I say," the teacher said testily, "that it is impossible to know anything from this chatter. What did the child actually remember after two days had passed? And why did you not immediately set up guard posts along the road? What good will it be to start the search now — more than two weeks after the fact? You are making a fool of us all, Zavdiel!"

The lord's face hardened. "Guard posts were set," he said curtly. "But they did no good. The wine merchants did not remain in the area."

Reuel II had not been feeling well in recent days, and this worried him. He was not accustomed to prolonged fatigue and a rapid heartbeat, and dizziness was something he had only heard about but never experienced.

What was happening to him?

Was it simply a passing weakness, emanating from pain and distress and the heavy burden he must bear? Or was this something else entirely, something that called for the royal physician? Yesterday, when he had nearly fainted, he had been forced to break the fast he had undertaken. But even a glass of sweet drink and a large portion of meat did not succeed in banishing his sudden weakness. On the contrary, it seemed to have only accelerated since then.

Reuel's heartbeat sped up, as it had been doing often in these last few days. With difficulty, he forced his breathing to remain even. His hands rested on a pile of documents requiring his immediate attention. He hoped that none of the men around him had noticed what was happening to him. If word spread that the king was unable to function normally, unnecessary panic would result, and Khazar was already far from calm. The capture and disappearance of his two sons, and the realization that a band of murderers was roaming the countryside with impunity, had caused a great many people sleepless nights. And the latest reports he had received from Bastian Makan, describing tension on both sides of the border, were serious.

Slowly, too slowly, his heart rate settled down and his breathing became easier. It was time to return to the proclamation that would be carried through all of Khazar, containing the king's words to his people at this difficult hour.

But although the latest attack had passed, Reuel's mind was still troubled.

For a long time, much longer than he had planned, Calidius hid among the shadows. At long last, his patience paid off. A burning torch dispelled the darkness as the gray-haired man he had been waiting for approached the dark lane.

Now!

Wearing an arrogant smile beneath his mask, Calidius took one step forward and threw out an arm, blocking the man's way.

"No," gasped the chief waiter, the torch in his hand shaking so that grotesque shapes formed on the walls of the narrow lane. "Not again!"

"What do you mean 'not again'?" Calidius asked. "You have not done a thing, Avrel!"

Avrel's lips whitened. "I did, sir. Exactly what you told me."

"Really?" Calidius' voice was penetrating. "That's very interesting..." After a moment's silence, he added thoughtfully, "How do you spell Bulgaria — B-U-L-G-A-R-I-A, isn't that right? Yes, I think I'll be able to write that without help..."

It was the chief waiter's turn to fall silent. The narrow lane was hushed and dark.

"There is one thing that I fail to understand," Calidius persisted. "How did your oldest son come upon the secrets found in the command documents of your second son? Is it possible that that excellent young man also possesses dark secrets that I have not yet discovered?"

"Beirash is loyal to Khazar," Avrel choked out.

"Beirash is loyal to Khazar…" Calidius mocked. "Yes…the interrogators may believe that. But why should we cause Beirash such uneasiness? They say that the hanging ropes are so itchy…

"I've brought you another vial, Avrel. This time, I warn you, I will not tolerate any mistakes. If I do not see results by the morning after next, a letter will appear on the security officer's desk — and Beirash will have a lot of explaining to do. Understand?"

The chief waiter lowered his head almost imperceptibly, but it was enough for Calidius. He took the torch and, leaving the gray-haired man alone in the darkness, swiftly left the lane.

N O ONE MAY COMMAND THE KING; NOT INFREQUENTLY, he may even bend the law if times call for it. However, in other circumstances, the law could also be frustratingly rigid. The *khagan* of Khazar sighed. This was one of those times.

"Shefer?"

"Here I am, Your Majesty."

Reuel turned his head. "Come, my friend."

The governor of the central region relaxed slightly. He had undertaken this job unwillingly, but to his relief, it looked as if the king was not going to make it too difficult. Quietly, he walked forward and halted near the cliff's edge, a step behind the king.

"The view here is especially lovely," Reuel said in a low voice, gazing at the fields sparkling in the valley below. "In winter, it is even more beautiful." He smiled. "Twenty-three years ago I stood here looking down at the snow-filled valley and decided to say yes to the match with your sister. We were married in the spring."

Lord Shefer lowered his head, his gaze focused on the hem of the king's cloak.

"Seven years later, at the start of the autumn, I stood in the palace garden and listened to the *bek*, may he rest in Gan Eden, relate something very similar to what you have just been telling me."

The king paused. In his mind's eye, he saw his brother-in-law and good friend's elongated face, the lines at the corners of his eyes and the characteristic slant of his mouth. And he heard the echo of his voice:

"The king of Khazar should be a married man, Your Majesty. The law gives you a grace period of four months, but two of those have already passed..." At the memory of the words, the pain returned. Reuel swung around sharply.

"I had two children then, Shefer. Today, I have seven! At least, I hope I have seven..." His voice cracked. "In such circumstances, how can I place myself in a new marriage? What woman would be smart enough and sensitive enough to walk Tur to the *chuppah*, to comfort Yekavel, to soothe Unmar's spirit, to raise Lissia and Binyamin?"

"I have several suggestions, Your Majesty," Shefer replied quietly, only the smallest tremor in his voice betraying his feelings. "All of the proposals have already been presented, of course, to the other side."

The king did not respond. Behind his back, he could feel the sun's rays that shone on the fields of golden-ripe wheat in the valley. Finally, he lifted his head and said, "Tomorrow, at the conclusion of the government meeting, I will hear your suggestions."

Lord Shefer nodded, relieved. But the king was not as sanguine as he seemed.

"Do not move, Governor of the Central Region, until I reach the end of this path. And for your own good, remain silent now. Do not say a word."

It was only as they neared the gates of Itil that Lord Elranan Shefer's horse succeeded in overtaking that of the king of Khazar, who had ridden like a storm wind through trees bowed by the weight of years. As he galloped, Reuel thought about the time and effort required in bending his own will to what was true and necessary. How much longer would he struggle this way? When would he cease to see things as good or bad, but rather as true or false, with a clarity that would allow him to rise above his personal desires?

And then he thought about Unmar, and the very serious talk that he must have with her.

"Enter." The king lifted his head from the parchment scrolls spread across his desk. "I have been waiting for you."

A fire had been built in the fireplace to counter the raw weather. The flames leaped merrily in contrast to the king's sober mien.

"I have brought a list of six proposals," Elranan Shefer said after an exchange of polite courtesies. "Will the king allow me to read them to him?"

Reuel nodded, granting permission.

Shefer unrolled the scroll. "The first suggestion comes from the household of Lord Kafchaver. A modest girl, pious and good-hearted…" He went on to list the merits of each woman on his list, but it was clear to him that the words he was directing at the king were not really penetrating.

"I thank you and your friends for the trouble you've taken in this matter," Reuel said when Lord Shefer was done. "I sense that a genuine concern for Khazar's welfare lies behind your efforts, and therefore they will be blessed by Heaven. Leave the scroll here, my friend. *B'ezras Hashem*, we will discuss this again at a later time."

The lord bowed, kissed the king's outstretched hand, and then slowly straightened. "May Hashem grant the future queen of Khazar the proper feeling and understanding. We are living in a fateful time, when Khazar will need all of a king's wisdom and foresight if it is to survive — but building a family is no less essential for those involved."

"Thank you," Reuel said. Suddenly, he looked exhausted. "Thank you, Elranan. We will speak again tomorrow. *Bli neder*, I will devote my full attention to this scroll and undertake some investigations of my own."

As Elranan Shefer left the room, Unmar entered, looking small and pale. Too small and pale, the king thought, to carry the burden he was about to place on her shoulders. She was only 8 years old, after all. But she, like he, had been born to a position that dwarfed personal needs and desires.

It was only when Unmar had departed, clutching to her heart the big doll her father had given her, that he turned to the list of suggested matches. Although he had not believed it would happen, one of the names caught his eye: Narma Stazdiran Paz, sister of the new *bek* and longtime widow of one of Khazar's *rabbanim*. Not long ago, Sarah, *zichronah livrachah*, had given Narma high praise for the way she was educating her brother's children.

Reuel compressed his lips. Duty came before sensibility. He would summon Ovadia, his personal assistant, and ask him to meet with acquaintances and servants of the new *bek* to learn more about the woman in question.

Rida, Ovadia's wife, found it hard to believe that of all the women in Khazar, the king wanted to know about Narma Stazdiran. "She's nearly 40!" she said, vigorously stirring a pot of onion soup.

"The king is no longer a boy," Ovadia replied, the words emerging somewhat garbled because of the nails that protruded from his mouth.

"But he is the king!" Rida protested. "If you had a daughter of 12, Ovadia, would you not be glad to marry her to the king?"

"You're talking nonsense," her husband said, pounding a nail with rhythmic strokes of his hammer. "The king would never wish to marry our daughter! If anyone were to hear you speak this way, I would blush with shame."

"Still," Rida persisted, "I am certain that there are many lords and honored noblemen who would be happy to hear such a proposal. He does not need to inquire about someone like…that! He is not some widowed woodcutter!"

"What do you mean, 'like that'?"

Rida closed her eyes in despair. Narma Stazdiran's face hovered before her, causing her to shake her head in rejection. There was nothing wrong with Narma. On the contrary, she had no end of wonderful qualities. But the way she looked… In all of Khazar, and perhaps in all the world, Rida was certain, there was no woman as homely as Narma Stazdiran Paz.

"The king said that had heard that she had done an outstanding job of rearing the new *bek's* children," Ovadia said.

"That's true," Rida acknowledged. "The children were raised very properly. They all turned out remarkably well — very different from their father. And all of them lay the credit at Narma's door. My sister says that in her opinion, if Narma had lived in a different generation, she would have been a *neviah,* or at least the mother of one!"

"Women," Ovadia said in amusement. "Can you get me some more information in the next few days? The king is counting on us in this matter. Surely you understand that this is an exceptional honor…"

She nodded. "An honor and a responsibility." In a much lower voice, she added softly, "Unfortunate man."

In a turmoil, Istrak paced the tent. Then he stopped, whirled around to face Kalev, and asked hoarsely, "Well, what shall we do about the furnishings — or I should say, the lack of them?"

The youth tilted his head questioningly.

"I do not want to ask the Kawari for favors," Istrak explained. "That would not reflect well on Khazar's honor. On the other hand, it is undignified for the crown prince of Khazar to sit on" — he stamped on the ground with his foot — "wet sand."

Kalev hesitated.

"Speak," Istrak ordered. With an effort, he added, "My friend."

Kalev shrugged. "My shirt is no substitute for a pillow, but in my humble opinion, it's better than nothing."

"You're a good lad," Istrak said, looking away as Kalev stripped off his shirt. "A very good lad. I have not treated you properly… Things moved too quickly and I became confused."

It was a clear apology, but Kalev did not respond. In silence he spread his shirt on the sand. When he straightened up, he said dryly, "If Your Highness would deign to be seated, I will serve lunch."

"Bless you," said Istrak, staring at the boy. Then, in a tone Kalev had never heard before, he asked, "Is there any room left on the shields of the Ben Batal nobility?"

Flushing bright crimson, Kalev stammered, "Your Highness is too gracious. I only did what I had to do…"

Istrak's eyes were riveted on Kalev's arms and back, on which not a single patch of healthy skin remained. It was all one big, ugly wound.

Kalev bowed his head. Unwillingly, he felt his eyes fill. "For lunch today, we have a medley of root vegetables, fish in white sauce, and cooked wheat…" At that moment, the curtains at the tent's entrance were pushed aside.

"The son of the leader of the Platt tribes, the warrior Yidrat-hai!" somebody announced in an exaggeratedly official voice. Yidrat, sumptuously dressed and smiling cheerfully, entered the tent.

Istrak's muscles quivered. With difficulty, he forced himself to remain seated. He could not let this Kawari youth think that the crown prince of Khazar would rise for him.

Yidrat's eyes widened as he looked around in astonishment. "Istrak! Why are you sitting on the ground?"

Istrak smiled, but his eyes shot sparks. "I am not sitting on the ground. I am sitting on a shirt. Welcome to my abode, warrior Yidrat. You may be seated."

"Where exactly?" Yidrat asked. "Where are all the things that were here, Istrak? Why did you not summon my father or me?"

"It seems to me," Istrak said in a measured tone, "that it is not my job to supply explanations. This was the situation when I arrived here after the competitions."

"They were good, weren't they? The winning team was mine… But what am I babbling about? Wait here a minute, and I will order them to bring you something more respectable than a shirt to sit on." His voice was slightly amused, perhaps even mocking, but his expression as he offered his hand to help Istrak rise was open and friendly.

Istrak preferred to lean on Kalev's bruised arm. Though he tried his best to keep his weight off the arm, the boy winced.

"He needs ointment," Yidrat remarked, ignoring Istrak's disdainful snub of his help, "and bandages. This will be a marvelous opportunity for you to visit our medical tent, Istrak. It is considered — and justifiably so — the most sophisticated in all of the known world... Shall we go now?"

"Certainly," Istrak said. At once, he regretted it. Kalev would not wish to put on his shirt, soiled from the mud. And if he went as he was, with his injuries visible for all to see, that would be truly degrading.

"Is anything wrong?" Yidrat inquired.

Istrak was silent, only the rapid rise and fall of his chest testifying to his inner turmoil. "The boy," he said finally, "needs a clean shirt. It is honorable neither for him nor for me if he were to leave the tent in this way."

"Absolutely," Yidrat agreed. "I thought of that myself... A shirt will be brought here at once. Is there anything else you want, Prince of Khazar?"

Istrak's chest rose and fell again. At last, he blurted, "My *ilpak*. I want it back."

"Gladly." Yidrat's eyes twinkled. "Anything else?"

"Since I do not believe you will provide me with two horses and a sword, I suppose that is all."

Yidrat smiled. "You have a sense of humor, Prince of Khazar."

Istrak nodded, but didn't comment.

"Actually," Yidrat said, after sending someone to carry out the prince's wishes, "I came here for an entirely different reason. A musical evening is planned for tonight, one of the largest we've ever held — 190 musicians in a single tent! There will be singers, too, and the story of Ka'eina, the bear-killer, will be told. My father asked me to assure you that the program has been carefully monitored and is appropriate to your beliefs. Will you attend?"

Istrak did not even have to think about it. "No, I will not."

"My father will not like this refusal," Yidrat said in dismay. "And you will lose by it as well. You will not have many opportunities to hear such an assemblage of instruments. However, your wish, my dear prince, is as important to us as a command... Here is the shirt you requested. Where is the prince's *ilpak*, Brum?"

"I could not find it," the slave said with a deep bow. "The moment the young warrior is pleased to give me leave, I will search for it further."

Kalev took the shirt from the slave. He slipped it on, and the ugly bruises were completely covered. The smile stretched across that freckled face revealed nothing at all of what lay beneath. But in the medical tent, as the wounds were rubbed with ointment, Kalev cried like a baby, and Istrak flushed with discomfort.

On their return to their living quarters, which had been refurnished by Yidrat's people — even more sumptuously than before — there was once again a wall between them. Or, if not precisely a wall, certainly a fence.

Kalev had been summoned to supervise preparations for dinner, and Istrak remained alone in his tent.

No description of captivity that he had ever read, from early childhood until the moment he had foolishly entered the Batar Ravine, was reminiscent of his present imprisonment. For some reason, this made him uneasy. What would he tell Unmar and Tur when he returned home? That as they recited *Tehillim* for his safe return, their brother sat on a leopard-skin rug, eating blackberries? With a gesture of self-loathing, he turned away from the silver bowl. Still, the sweet, blackberries beckoned to him.

Learning for a long period of time makes a man hungry, and reviewing from memory is no different from studying from a scroll — perhaps even more so, since it requires greater concentration and effort. And his lunch had been interrupted by Yidrat, so he hadn't eaten much.

It was all true, all good reasons, but now that Istrak had quieted the demands of his stomach, he regretted that he had eaten.

He was a prisoner, even if his captivity was a pleasant one. He could not forget that even for a moment. A sudden dizziness swept over him as he recalled the long journey from the Batar gorge to this place. His body still ached from the blows he had received, and his broken tooth would never grow back again.

He shook his head, and his long hair fell over his face. He did not need to annoy his captors. It was enough to refrain from being friendly and cooperative. Yes, that was enough.

Feeling easier with his renewed resolve, he stood to daven Minchah.

He had just reached *"Shema Koleinu"* when he heard a throat clearing politely behind him. Immediately, his prayer became slower and more focused. As he bowed and walked backward, he saw from the corner of his eye that Ka'hei himself had entered the tent. He did not turn his head until after he had uttered the last words of *"Aleinu L'Shabe'ach."* Only then did he turn around and speak.

"Welcome, leader of the Platt tribes."

"Greetings to you, Crown Prince of Khazar," Ka'hei returned with a smile. "Your prayer must have been sweet to your G-d."

"He is G-d of the whole world."

Ka'hei chose to ignore this. "I have come to invite you to a musical festival to be held this evening," he said with another of his lazy smiles. "There will be 190 musicians playing, and the story of the great bear massacre will be told by one of our most talented harpists, along with a choir of sixteen. I deliberately ordered that story so that you may enjoy it along with us."

"I thank you for our attentions and your trouble," Istrak said coolly. "However, I will not participate in this gathering."

"You will participate," Ka'hei replied, still smiling.

"I have said my piece, leader of the Platt tribes."

"What have you said? I did not hear a thing. I invited you to a musical evening. There will be 190 musicians at the gathering, and the story of the great bear massacre will be told by one of our talented harpists, along with a choir of sixteen people. I ordered that story specifically for your pleasure."

"And I," answered Istrak, "thanked you for your good intentions, but said that I will not be able to participate in this evening's entertainment."

"You will be able," Ka'hei said warmly. "Of course you will, my dear Istrak. No one will prevent you from doing so. And were I to suspect that the young boy you brought with you is making it difficult for you to behave as a prince should — I will know how to deal with him. Do you understand?"

The overt threat was carefully aimed and razor sharp.

Shortly before the musical evening was scheduled to begin, Yidrat came to Istrak's tent bearing a suit of deerskin embroidered with beads, and a copper diadem to wear on his forehead. "All the measurements," Yidrat said cheerfully, "were taken by my father's eye. Put on the clothes, Istrak, and let's see if he was right."

Taken aback, Istrak looked at the colorful embroidery. "I —"

"Father said that you have already spoken about this," Yidrat said in surprise.

A lump of lead seemed to settle in Istrak's chest. So this, too, was to be included in his deal with Ka'hei?

"Hurry," Yidrat urged. He was just a youth, Istrak's age or perhaps a year younger. If things were different, Istrak wondered, would he have been able to pressure a foreign prince in this way?

"Khazars never hurry," Istrak said slowly, reaching out to take the clothes. "You will have to wait patiently, young man."

"Very patiently," Yidrat agreed. "But no more than five minutes."

Istrak changed his clothes behind the dividing curtain. When he stepped out, Yidrat's jaw dropped. "Amazing!" he exclaimed. "You look completely different — and I mean completely! You…you look like a prince…"

"That is who I am," Istrak reminded him sternly. He was intensely curious to know what had caused Yidrat to become so excited.

"Yes, and now you look like one. Come, let us go over to my tent so you can see yourself."

"That is unnecessary," Istrak said curtly, troubled as much by his own curiosity as by Yidrat's compliments.

Yidrat shrugged. "Your wish is my command." He smiled. "Shall we go?"

It was cold outside. A million stars twinkled in a black velvet sky as throngs of people, dressed in their best, streamed toward the central tent, which was bathed in bright light. A babble of tongues and dialects swirled around him.

So that was why this gathering was so important to Ka'hei. The copper diadem pinched Istrak's brow. No one had told him that he was about to become a walking advertisement for the Kawari's military prowess...

"Istrak!" Ka'hei appeared out of the shadows. "I am very happy to see you here, my boy. Let me introduce you to Ygadrav, Prince of Albania. Ygadrav — meet the heir of Khazar, Prince Istrak."

"I am both surprised and pleased," Ygadrav said, inclining his head slightly, "to meet the prince of Khazar, especially since the kings of the Khazar dynasty are the only relatives I have never met."

The sole familial connection that linked the Albanian kingdom to that of Khazar had been forged sometime in the distant past, three generations before King Yosef had converted to Judaism. The comment made everyone chuckle, including Istrak.

"I hope," Ka'hei smiled, "that from now on you will have many such opportunities. I am certain, Prince Ygadrav, that you will find Prince Istrak to be as fascinating to talk to as I have — especially since, as crown princes of your kingdoms, you have much in common... You must know, Prince Istrak, that for these past five months Prince Ygradav has borne the title of commander of the Albanian army. We are very happy that he has found time to visit."

"Your mission is demanding," Istrak said. "A commander bears a great responsibility. Every soldier has parents, and their hearts are pained if he is wounded — exactly as your own parents would be pained were anything to happen to you."

Ygradav's narrow face twisted in a grimace of surprise. "A commander's job is to care for the state," he said sharply. "Every parent would be happy to sacrifice his son for the sake of his homeland!"

"Ah, but this is not the time for such deep discussions," Ka'hei interjected. "Tomorrow, you will attend the Sabbath feast that will be held for the Khazar prince, and you will find the appropriate setting to talk of such things... Tonight, we have come here to enjoy ourselves." He glanced at Istrak, whose own smile had vanished. "Prince Istrak, I would like to introduce you to the chairman of the Slavic Confederation, the *krat* Adria, who has just now arrived."

"We will meet again," promised Prince Ygradav, taking his cue to depart. He inclined his head once again and brought both fists to his face in an Albanian gesture of courtesy.

"We will meet," Istrak replied, mirroring the gesture. Inwardly, he was seething. How far would Ka'hei be able to squeeze him with threats against Kalev's life? Where was the limit? Life was a thing of inestimable value, justifying any sacrifice — but to conduct a Shabbos meal for all sorts of gentiles?

"It will be all right," Ka'hei murmured near his ear as the Albanian prince entered the main tent. "You are a young man, clever and wise. I am sure that you will be able to conduct a wonderful Sabbath feast and allow us all to join in a spiritual experience that we have never had before..." Aloud, he added, "Here is the chairman of the Slavic Confederacy, ruler of Oduta, the *krat* Waslova Adria, prince. Chairman, may I present the crown prince of Khazar, Prince Istrak, firstborn son of Reuel II."

"Your father is a special man," Waslova Adria said politely. "I met him face to face at the battle of Zraf." He smiled fatuously, and touched his left hand lightly to his right cheek, exposing a large, ugly scar on his palm. "Since then, I have never forgotten him for a single day."

"Chairman Adria and the king of Khazar also met during the peace talks," Ka'hei told Istrak. "And my own humble self was a member of the delegation conducting those talks — the group that removed paragraphs 57, 12, and 59 from his document, along with other subparagraphs scattered here and there. Those were good days, were they not, Chairman Adria?"

"Unforgettable," the Slav agreed. There was a gleam of open hostility in the glance he shot the tribal leader. The sight of it cheered Istrak somewhat. "However, we are all trying to forget what we cannot change. Is that not true, Crown Prince?"

"Forgetfulness is G-d's gift," Istrak replied, his eyes meeting the Slav's directly, "as are peace and tranquility. May He allow these days of peace to continue forever."

"Amen," said Ka'hei. And the Slavic ruler added dryly, "And may they become better and better, like fine wine."

"Like the wine we will soon be tasting." Ka'hei's voice was merry but artificial as he blatantly changed the subject. "And if we are talking about food, my dear Adria, did you know that light refreshments are being served in the tent?...

"Now, I would like to introduce you, Istrak, to another honored personality. This is Prime Minister Platino."

Istrak looked around at Ka'hei's guests. The prince of Albania, the chairman of the Slavic Confederacy, and Prime Minister Platino, elected leader of the Umra people, along with their entourages and hangers-on — this event, Istrak gathered suddenly, was nearly as important as his own Regency Ceremony was meant to be.

For a fleeting instant, his thoughts flew to the softly lit corridors of the palace in Itil, his father's spacious workroom, their upholstered carriage and lavish gardens... How quickly everything changed!

Ka'hei touched his shoulder and dragged him back to the present. "You have been garnering endless compliments," the Kawari leader whispered in his ear. "Continue in this fashion, and within ten months Khazar will have diplomatic ties with half the countries in the region... Come. It is time to go inside."

Raising his voice to the others standing around them, Ka'hei announced, "The festival will begin very shortly. Will our honored guests allow their escorts to lead them to their places?"

One hundred ninety is not such an outlandish number for an orchestra of musicians, Istrak realized as he sat down in a place of honor, between Yidrat's seat and Ka'hei's empty chair — at least, not when they are arranged in orderly rows in an enormous tent and grasping their instruments in complete silence.

Long minutes passed. Istrak took advantage of Ka'hei's absence to withdraw into himself. He had to make some sort of plan. He could not continue to allow that man to manipulate him however he pleased!

Servants moved among the guests, extinguishing the glowing tapers hanging throughout the tent, and the crowd's chatter began to subside. Ka'hei appeared beside them, apparently very satisfied, and lowered himself with a soft sigh into the cushion next to Istrak's. Istrak compressed his lips and turned his face away.

"I have to go outside," he murmured a moment later. "I won't be more than a minute."

Outside, he stuffed into his ears the small pieces of cloth that Kalev had prepared for him, then motioned to his escorts that he was ready to return to his place. The big tent was completely dark by now. Moments later flutes sounded, imitating the chirping of free-winging birds — a sound that penetrated even the wads of fabric in Istrak's ears and filled his eyes with stinging tears.

"Is everything all right?" Ka'hei whispered as Istrak sat down beside him. Istrak nodded pleasantly. Ka'hei stared fixedly at the musicians on the stage. Istrak did the same.

A few seconds later, Ka'hei's hand settled on Istrak's forearm and began to exert pressure. At first, Istrak ignored the uncomfortable sensation, but soon he was struggling silently with pain. He gritted his teeth and dug his fingernails into his palms to prevent himself from turning his head. At last he succumbed and glanced at the Kawari leader.

"No tricks," Ka'hei's lips mouthed clearly. His finger touched his earlobe, and his lips repeated their message: "No tricks."

Sitting in the dark, after removing the wads of cloth from his ears, Istrak wove furious plots of revenge, all directed at Ka'hei, the victor and director of this whole degrading experience. But gradually the music overwhelmed him, and, for a while, all thoughts of revenge were forgotten. It was impossible to think of anything negative while those sweet, tranquil notes uplifted him, willingly or not, until he seemed to float several inches above the ground...

Compared to this music, Istrak was forced to admit to himself, the music of Khazar was primitive. The world had progressed rapidly in the past century. Why did his father stubbornly refuse to release Khazar, mired so firmly in the past?

Late that night, Istrak returned to his tent. At its entrance, he parted from Ka'hei, Yidrat, and six other persons of note. Kalev, who had been sitting just inside the entrance with his head on folded knees, stood tiredly to greet him.

"How was it?" he asked, helping the prince out of his outer coat.

"Amazing." Istrak removed the copper diadem from his forehead. "Really amazing. Stunning."

"Ah." Kalev's fingers unfastened the leather collar.

Istrak passed a thoughtful finger over his upper lip. "There is indeed wisdom among the gentiles, Kalev," he murmured, paraphrasing a well-known *medrash*. "The Kawaris understand music very well."

"They have a great deal of leisure time to devote to it," Kalev said with a touch of bitterness.

"Maybe." Istrak was too weary to let himself be drawn into a long conversation. "The result, at any rate, is remarkable… I must say *Krias Shema* now. Please light more candles, Kalev."

Kalev obeyed, while Istrak lowered himself onto one of the cushions strewn about the floor. "By the way," he said, looking up at Kalev, "Ka'hei is arranging a Shabbos *seudah* for us tomorrow night. We are to be joined by all sorts of local and foreign dignitaries. There are a few basic points of etiquette that you'll need to learn."

"I am always ready to learn," Kalev replied almost inaudibly.

"You will have a busy day tomorrow. You will surely be expected to take charge of the preparations. So perhaps it would be best to do it right now."

Istrak was tired, very tired. This was the last thing he wanted to do, but once again, he had no choice. The honor of Khazar must be upheld.

"First: When there are other people present, you must always address me as 'Crown Prince' and speak to me in the third person. Second: Food is served at the table only with your right hand. Third: When I tell you to sit down beside me, you have to say three times that it is an honor too great for you. Only after the fourth time will you sit.

"Fourth: When I speak to you, do not make the kind of faces that you're making now, neither when we're in public nor when we are alone. You will adopt a courteous mien at all times. Understand?"

"Yes, Crown Prince." Kalev bowed.

Istrak nodded with satisfaction. "Good. Now repeat my instructions. I want to make sure that you understood everything clearly."

Kalev repeated Istrak's instructions to the letter.

"Exactly," Istrak nodded. Then he remembered: "One more thing. No one forced you to come here with me, Kalev. I appreciate the courage and strength that you showed when you volunteered to escort me, and if Hashem ever restores me to my place and position, I will make sure that all of Khazar knows how much the royal family values your devotion. But — unless you've been beaten — I am not prepared to put up with your moods. All right?"

"Yes, Your Highness," Kalev said, barely moving his lips.

"Very good." Istrak adjusted his position on the cushion and resumed reviewing from memory the pages of *Maseches Kiddushin* that he had been learning when Yidrat had come in with the suit of clothing.

A nice suit, that much was certain. The Kawaris knew not only music; they also knew how to sew.

So what if they did? Did it matter?

The holy words of the Gemara struggled wearily with his thoughts. Khazari music was pleasant, but it had not developed much in the past 300 years. From the time King Yosef had converted, the country's leaders had turned their attention to other, more pertinent pastimes. Their clothing was all right. It performed its function admirably, covering the body and keeping it warm. A man couldn't ask for more than that from the cloth he wrapped around himself…

The Gemara gave up the struggle. Istrak leaned his head against the cushion behind him, watching Kalev move around the tent, tidying it quietly.

A prophet must be good-looking — it says that somewhere explicitly. Yosef HaTzaddik was also a handsome man. Is there anything wrong with not looking like a shepherd who had just come back from fighting a hungry wolf? He could not wear the sole Khazari outfit he had in this place — his torn traveling suit stained with dirt and sweat.

Again, his thoughts went to the Batar Ravine, and the smell of blood and death overwhelmed his senses.

"Are you all right, Your Highness?" Kalev asked, suddenly standing beside him.

"I am fine," Istrak said. A future king must be strong. He could not ask for help, not from someone like Kalev.

"You don't look well," the boy said. "And that's no wonder… May I suggest that Your Highness go to sleep now?"

"I need to learn." In a burst of generosity, he added, "Do you want to learn with me?"

Kalev's cheeks burned.

"It's easier to learn with a partner," Istrak said with a smile. "Come, let's learn together."

Kalev hesitated.

"There's no need to refuse, Kalev," Istrak insisted. "And here, between us, there's no need to stand on formality… Take a cushion and sit beside me. In the eyes of Hashem, we are all equal."

The Shabbos *seudah* was a downright disaster.

Istrak knew it — and he knew that Kalev knew it, too. The meal was the exact opposite of the "spiritual experience" that Ka'hei had described, and which, in essence, it was meant to be.

The two prepared for bed in silence.

"I don't think anyone could have done better than I did," Istrak said at last, sitting on a low hammock. "Twelve men against one boy… The game was a little unfair."

"I suspect," Kalev said, "that this was not the first time Your Highness heard such foolish ideas."

"They said nothing terrible," Istrak said, his voice rising slightly. "Nothing very awful. Had they done so, I wouldn't have remained silent for even a minute."

"They destroyed the *kedushah* of Shabbos," the boy replied staunchly. "They forced me to sit on the holiest day and listen to talk about horses! And not just any horses — but the ones embroidered on cloaks!"

Istrak laughed. "Is that the worst thing that's happened to you since your foolish prince ordered his people to enter the Batar

Ravine? I ask, because this is the first time I've seen you become so angry."

Kalev did not answer. Istrak did not appreciate his silence, and he said in a more serious tone, "You're exaggerating, Kalev. Our situation is relatively very good. True, there were a few gentiles at the table who made some not very successful jokes … but nothing terrible happened. You know as well as I that things could be much, much worse."

Kalev just shook his head.

Istrak stared at his young companion, wondering what he wasn't telling him. He sighed. He *was* a fool — a complete dolt. Why, oh why, hadn't he listened to good faithful Brach?

He sat lost in brooding thought for several minutes until suddenly a new notion struck him. "You're not angry because they ruined *kedushas Shabbos*," he said. "You're angry because you enjoyed it. You did enjoy it, didn't you, Kalev?"

Kalev's face twisted. "Yes," he confessed. "I did."

"Anyone in your place would have enjoyed it," Istrak said gently. "The meal was sumptuous, the talk was pleasant, and we were treated well. It is natural that you would enjoy yourself in such circumstances…"

"Your Highness is right." Kalev turned away. "But it is still demeaning."

Istrak fell quiet, swinging lightly on the hammock. "There was nothing bad," he repeated presently. "If anything had been wrong, I would not have allowed the *seudah* to continue. You can depend on me, Kalev."

The boy turned his head sharply, eyes glinting with an unfathomable expression. Istrak offered a calm smile, conscious of the power his strict upbringing provided. "You can depend on me," he promised softly. "Go to sleep, my brother. Everything is all right."

"Yes, sire," Kalev murmured. "At once, Your Highness."

It suddenly struck Istrak that he felt closer to this boy than he ever had to Michael. Briefly he wondered how Michael was faring. He knew he was still alive and assumed he was also being treated well. He wished now that he hadn't been too proud to ask about his brother from the beginning. Since then, any attempt to pry information from Ka'hei or Yidrat about his brother's well-being was brushed aside. "Everything is all right," Istrak repeated in the same quiet tone. "Sweet dreams, Kalev."

It was only much later, when Istrak was asleep and Kalev nearly so, that the magic of Istrak's assurances dissipated. In its place came an overwhelming sadness.

It was all true. And yet…

The longing that was with him constantly now became overwhelming. Kalev wished he were home, surrounded by his family rather than in this foreign place surrounded by gentiles.

He would not let himself admit to another constant emotion, one that was growing stronger every day: the fear that he would never see his family again.

14

How strange to wake up on a Shabbos morning with the sun on your face and a deep, sweet silence all around. Never, since Istrak was a boy of 8, had he had this experience. *Shabbos Kodesh*, the day of respite from the burden of work, was in his father's opinion a marvelous opportunity to make up for all the hours when they were unable to learn and engage in serving their Creator. His father slept no more than one brief hour on Friday night. He expected Istrak, at the very least, to rise before the roosters and donkeys, and not to rest at all in the afternoon.

His father was a special man, a very special man — everyone knew that, even Adria Waslova. Father was never hungry, never angry, never insulted.

Istrak, on the other hand…

He stretched and reached for the water Kalev had prepared for him to use for washing his hands. The basin and cup sat to one side of the bed, with a thick cloth for drying his hands folded neatly beside them.

He stared at his wet hands, for a moment allowing his despair at the situation, which he had been working so hard to suppress, to surface. But no — he couldn't let himself give in to it.

Disturbed, he wiped his hands. He had to take hold of his feelings and remain strong. If he planned — and he did plan — to escape from here as soon as he could, he must be in the best physical shape possible. And he must prepare Kalev for the journey as well.

He remembered the relief he had felt when Kalev volunteered to leave the ravine with them. Now... Why couldn't the boy have waited another minute or two and let others more able and fitting than he offer their own services?

A commotion sounded outside, and Waslova Adria's sharp voice was heard.

"Wake up," Istrak said, tossing the cloth at Kalev. "It's time to daven Shacharis..."

Kalev sat up slowly, blinking in confusion.

"Good morning," said Istrak, a little embarrassed at his action with the towel. "Waslova is outside. I'm afraid he will be coming in here at any moment..."

Kalev's face cleared. Quickly he washed his hands and stood up. When one of the soldiers on guard duty came in to announce that the chairman of the Slavic Confederacy wished to meet with the Khazar crown prince, no one could have guessed that the two young people had woken up only minutes earlier.

"Tell him," Istrak instructed, "that I have not yet prayed to my G-d this morning. I will be pleased to speak with him when the sun is at its zenith."

The soldier saluted and left the tent. A moment later, he reappeared. "The chairman of the Slavic Confederacy believes that the prince of Khazar will regret not seeing him at once."

"The prince of Khazar," Istrak said, growing weary of the soldier's punctilious speech, "cannot see him now. I'll be pleased to meet with the chairman later today."

It was only that evening, after Havdalah, that Adria Waslova reappeared. Behind him were two youthful attendants in colorful garb, bearing, with an air of festivity, a long red box decorated with multicolored engravings.

"Before I return to my homeland," Waslova announced, "I wish to present you with a small gift. I brought it with me in the hope that I would find the Prince of Khazar a person with whom I could talk.

"Unfortunately," continued Waslova, "I was not able to give it to you this morning, even though it was clear to me that you would find it useful in serving your G-d."

Istrak opened his mouth, but Waslova silenced him with a gesture. "Open the gift, Crown Prince of Khazar," he said gaily, "and understand the message that lies behind it. The Slavic Confederacy is interested in friendly ties with your country, but not the kind that come at sword point."

The two attendants moved forward and set the box at Istrak's feet. The prince bent to unfasten the box's clasps. He stared, then quickly stooped to pick up the *Sefer Torah*, hugging it close.

His reaction surprised the chairman. "Do you recognize this scroll?" he asked. "It fell into our hands during the conquest of Latras…"

Istrak didn't know how to react. From the point of view of the man standing before him, returning this *Sefer Torah* was an unparalleled gesture. Of course, Istrak was overjoyed to be able to restore the lost scroll to its rightful place, in Khazar. But he had not yet recovered from the sight of the scroll lying, uncased, in the open box at his feet.

"It was the scroll of King Aharon," Waslova added. "You don't seem pleased. Is anything wrong, Crown Prince?"

"I very much appreciate your gift, as well as the promise of friendship that it symbolizes," Istrak replied with an effort. "However, because the Torah is deserving of honor greater than that of kings, I was disturbed by the way it was brought to me."

Waslova was affronted. "This is a brand-new box! Made of redwood! Lined with combed, dyed wool! I cannot think of a more honorable way to carry your Torah."

"The Khazars," Ka'hei said, walking into the tent with his usual aplomb, "have the custom of carrying their scrolls in their arms, wrapped in an embroidered covering. The Slavs, on the other hand, carry their holy artifacts in a decorated box, made of redwood and lined with combed, dyed wool. But the intentions of both nations are the same: to show honor."

"Cultural differences," said the Slav, as understanding dawned, "have always existed, my young friend. There is nothing to be done to avoid them, apart from talking to one another in a spirit of friendship and honesty."

He thrust out his hand, and Istrak — after passing the Torah into Kalev's waiting arms — put out his own. For a long moment they stood with clasped hands, each grasping the other's elbow, before parting.

"I hope," Waslova said quietly, "that you will look upon me as a friend. May your G-d bless you with the traits that a true leader requires."

"I thank you for your good wishes and for your gift," Istrak answered, this time expressing his pleasure. "And I very much appreciate the honor with which you treated our scroll. You can be sure that I will tell my father about it."

Satisfied, Waslova turned and, with a measured step, left the tent. His attendants followed behind.

Ka'hei remained in the center of the tent. Without offering any explanation as to why he had entered in the first place, he, too, turned and left in the wake of the Slavic dignitary.

The king was not dead, and that was strange, very strange. The chief waiter, shaking with fear, had fervently sworn that he had dripped the liquid into the king's food. In light of the danger that hovered over the chief waiter's two sons, Calidius was inclined to believe him.

And yet — the king was not dead.

The palace dogs, on the other hand, seemed to be suffering from a strange ailment…

Was there a connection between the two? And if there was, who was responsible? The head chef, who was not willing to turn into a murderer — or the king himself, grown suspicious for some reason?

"Arrest the older son," his lord ordered crisply. "After that, we will most likely see more fruitful cooperation."

Ovadia was quiet and efficient. Within 24 hours he had amassed a quantity of information that would have put a professional detective to shame. He summarized for the king what he had learned in a single, satisfying conclusion: Narma Stazdiran Paz had the character and abilities needed, with Hashem's help, to carry out the spectrum of tasks that would fall on her shoulders as wife of the king of Khazar.

Lord Elranan Shefer was more than a little surprised when, at the conclusion of a meeting of the emergency council, the king motioned for him to come close. In a low voice, the king informed him that, for his part, he was prepared to meet that very evening.

"Which one?" Shefer asked.

"Stazdiran," the king replied.

Shefer grew pale. "Why her?" he blurted.

The king's brows came together. "Why not her?"

Lord Shefer coughed.

The king rested his head against the high back of his chair, and waited.

"She …," Shefer said with an effort, when the king's silence had stretched, "that is…my impression is that she is not sufficiently G-d-fearing. She was seen laughing on the Ninth of Av."

"Really?" The information that Ovadia had gathered was, in the king's opinion, more trustworthy than that of Elranan Shefer, who had never been counted among the new *bek's* friends. Nevertheless, the matter called for further investigation. "I hear you," he said thoughtfully. "However, I received different information. Was it not she who established the round-the-clock *Tehillim* group?"

"No," Shefer said. "That was Dalo's sister, Narma."

"Ah! And who were you talking about?"

Shefer's eyes widened. "I was talking about Dalo Stazdiran's daughter."

"And I," said the king, "would like to meet his sister. Subject to your approval, of course."

Somewhat bemused, Lord Shefer left the conference room. The situation had just become uncomfortable. As far as he knew, ever since the death of her husband some fifteen years earlier, Narma Paz had refused to entertain any suggestions for remarriage. Her brother, the new *bek*, on the other hand, had been working strenuously behind the scenes to have his daughter's name included on the list to be presented to the king.

Shefer sighed. His mother — may her memory be a blessing — had always warned him not to become embroiled in matchmaking...

Now he had to find a way to persuade Narma Paz to accede to the king's request, while at the same time try to explain to Stazdiran that he, Elranan Shefer, was not to blame for this ludicrous mistake.

It is always a good idea to listen to your mother.

After much deliberation, Lord Shefer decided it would be prudent to seek assistance before speaking to Lord Stazdiran.

"We must explain to Dalo Stazdiran," he told Lord Yosef Diaber, "that it was not I who made this suggestion. I proposed his daughter to the king — but the king, for reasons of his own, decided to investigate the sister instead. Dalo ought to be pleased that such an illustrious match is being considered for his sister. We must show him that there is no reason for resentment or anger."

Lord Diaber muttered something into his beard. It sounded as if he disagreed with Shefer's logic.

This infuriated Elranan. "His daughter is only 13!" he snapped. "The king is thirty years older than she! Although there is no question that great honor would come with such a match, a father must think first of his child — and not of his own honor as the king's *mechutan*."

"Slowly, now," Diaber cautioned. "Be very careful, my old friend, not to speak slanderously. It is clear to me that the girl would be extremely happy to become the wife of such a wonderful man. Nevertheless..." He shrugged. "Nevertheless, there is no question that this thing is odd."

"Very odd," Shefer agreed.

"I must say..." Yosef Diaber hesitated, as if he deliberating whether he should continue. Shefer waited.

"I must say," Diaber said finally, "that troubling thoughts on this subject have been racing through my mind for days. Dalo Stazdiran is a fine man. We all know that…" He sighed. "It seems to me that ever since Eshal was murdered and the crown prince captured, I have been afraid of my own shadow. Pay no attention to me, Elranan. I've become a nervous wreck."

"That is perfectly understandable. I, too, tend to the theory that there is someone on the inside who is cooperating with the enemy. But what can the Bulgarians, the Turks, or the Kawaris gain by killing the *bek* and taking the princes — as long as the king, may he live long and healthy, remains on the throne?"

"Nothing," returned Diaber. "Nothing at all. And that is the reason for my troubling thoughts…" He coughed, as though trying to direct Elranan's attention to the fact that they were not alone. With a large, artificial smile, he turned to face the minister for internal security, who had entered the conference room with an armload of documents.

"You must safeguard your dignity, Zavdiel," he scolded gently as he helped the minister unload the scrolls onto the big table. "There are any number of clerks and assistants who would be delighted to help you bring the latest orders here…"

Elranan Shefer peered at Lord Diaber. As his two friends chatted in an undertone, he shook his head and brought a hand to his face to massage his brow, trying to make sense of Diaber's suspicions. Suddenly, the fog that had obscured his vision for so long seemed to lift. The facts that they all knew took on a new and much more sinister significance.

The only man in all of Khazar who had benefited from Eshal's death was Stazdiran, who had inherited the murdered man's position. And were it not for the error that had led the king to seek out Stazdiran's sister for a wife, chances were very good that Stazdiran's daughter would have become the new queen. In the absence of the princes — and in accordance with the law that passed down the rule to the prince who was firstborn to his mother — *her* eldest son would have, in time, inherited the throne!

Shefer shook his head again. Stazdiran was not a Torah scholar, nor was he known as a particularly pious man. Nevertheless, his own suspicions seemed wild and improbable to Shefer.

Wildly improbable!

And yet...when the facts were all lined up, they seemed to point a long and accusing finger directly at the Khazari prime minister.

The weather was fine, the sun shone, and the soldiers on either side of the border were well trained. Strangely enough, however, nothing had happened. On one side of the river, the Bulgarian troops were ranked in an age-old military pattern whose flaws were obvious to anyone watching from Khazar's hills. And on the other stood the Khazar army, superior in quality but small in number. On the Bulgarian side, pressure was being exerted on Prince Zarad to attack, while the Khazar officers lifted their brows at Bastian Makan's indifference toward the Bulgarians' clear provocation. What was everyone waiting for?

Day after day, on either side of the border, an eerie silence reigned.

"My men and I," declared Gedalia Latvias, "could easily deliver those Bulgarians a blow they would not soon forget."

Bastian Makan glanced at him. "And what would you gain by it?"

"The Bulgarians are constantly increasing their strength!" Phidos Flair said to buttress Latvias' position. "At first, we had a numerical advantage over them. Now, we are seriously outnumbered. We must not wait any longer, Lord Makan. We must not!"

Bastian Makan's cheeks had become sunken in recent days, and his nose — never especially small or delicate — seemed to have lengthened and grown sharper. With narrowed eyes, he studied the troops across the border.

"Give me two days," he wanted to say. "Two days which, I believe, will eliminate a great deal of bloodshed." What he said instead was, "I will be glad to listen to your plan in greater detail, Gedalia. Please come to my tent at the end of the morning drill. After we have crystallized a clear strategy, I will be pleased if you, Sharet and Baniel, would offer your views as well..."

The two men whose names he had singled out exchanged a swift glance. "With pleasure, sir," Sharet said.

Bastian smiled, but a nervous twitch quivered in his cheek. "May Hashem bless you and restore you and your troops safely to your homes. I will await you in the command tent, Gedalia." He lifted himself slightly in his saddle, inclining his head courteously. With a signal to his aide, the two cantered off.

A strange silence lingered on the hill as the seven officers watched their commander depart. All seven wore a look of open surprise.

"He's waiting for something," Baniel, oldest of the group, declared after a long moment. "That is obvious. The question is — what? And why does Makan think that he can use us as his rubber stamp?"

Phidos Flair, captain of the mounted cavalry, undertook responsibility for the entire affair. Sharet, lower in rank and subordinate to him in most things, was happy to cooperate. Gedalia Latvius, who vigorously opposed the rash step, was asked to remember his youth and lack of military experience. When he stood firm in his views, his three senior officers called him a coward and resolved to leave him out of their secret plans.

A distant cousin of Sharet's, who served as a lieutenant in the communications unit, took the letter that Phidos wrote. Lying practically prone against his horse's neck, he galloped away at top speed and was gone from view in a cloud of dust.

Solemnly, Sharet went to speak to his men.

A bottle of oil and a small box of "ever-fire" were two unusual items that each of his fifty troops was asked to include in his kit. A short time after the evening shadows had darkened into full night, Sharet and his men crossed the Khazar-Bulgaria border, violating the peculiar truce that reigned — apparently without any prior agreement — between the two warring armies.

Without prior agreement?

No one but Gedalia Latvias believed that.

Bastian Makan's tirade, on learning of the secret campaign carried out by his three subordinate officers, was as powerful as a typhoon. It did not move the officers at all. In the distance, across the border, many of the Bulgarian tents burned merrily. In the light of the bonfires the silhouettes of running men could be seen, scrambling desperately to douse the flames.

"Let us not mince words," Phidos Flair said, drawing his sword from its sheath. "Your conduct, Minister of War, has deviated from the dictates of logic. You may summon us to judgment before the king if you wish. I would advise you, as one who was once counted as your friend, to put aside your sword and willingly join the delegation that will accompany you back to the capital, where you may complain about our behavior."

"Rebellion in the field of battle is punishable by death, Phidos," Bastian said quietly.

"Cooperating with the enemy," Baniel said, stepping forward, "is far worse."

"Do you honestly believe, Baniel, tailor's son, in the nonsense you are speaking?" A long, gleaming sword had materialized in Bastian's hand, and the armor he wore under his cloak glinted in response. "Have you never heard of the prohibition against besmirching another's good name?"

"Had Gedalia ben Achikam listened to the people of Jerusalem, the history of the Jewish people would probably be very different," Phidos retorted. "Lay down your sword, Lord Makan. Your judgment will be brought before the king. This tent is surrounded. The soldiers in this camp, Your Excellency, are also of the opinion that the matter should be brought before the ruler of our country."

Bastian's sword rang as it hit the ground. Many of the soldiers present in the tent lowered their eyes. For many of them, Bastian Makan was both a symbol and a role model.

"Take me, if you can," he said. A ray of sunshine, refracted from the fallen sword, raised sparks of gold in his silvering beard. "And tomorrow, when blood will be spilled here, and the number of dead and wounded are recorded, remember that I did everything in my power to prevent its happening."

With no books from which to study, no obligations or goals, no urgent matter requiring the crown prince's attention, no calls for any action that needed to be done that day, an unfamiliar feeling had stolen into Istrak's heart. It was not precisely sadness, nor fear or even homesickness. Could it simply be boredom?

Kalev, in contrast, was extremely busy, and he greeted Istrak's proposal that he teach him some self-defense and attack maneuvers with a sense of helpless frustration. Though he wished to please the prince, he had no time for such things. He was responsible for supervising the cooks, making sure the laundry was done, choosing fish with fins and scales, sweeping the tent, washing the dishes...

The sun had already set that Sunday, and stars began to dot the sky. Kalev had returned to the tent, his face gray with exhaustion — only to be summoned back to the kitchen a moment later. Once again, Istrak was left alone.

He was frustrated by these long periods of solitude. Should he ask Ka'hei to lighten the boy's burden? Not that he was eager to seek out Ka'hei with requests...

A deep silence filled the tent, a silence that stretched and stretched. It was an effort for Istrak to keep his eyes open, but he was determined to stay awake until the boy's return. But Kalev did not appear all that night; his neatly folded bedclothes were mute witnesses to that.

Distressed, Istrak bit his lip. Ka'hei had vowed that as long as the prince conducted himself properly, the boy would not be harmed. Had that been nothing but an empty promise?

Beyond the tent flaps, dawn was breaking and everyday routines starting up again. Someone quipped with the guards, and the sound of their laughter drifted inside. Children shouted, someone called out to a friend, a horse whinnied.

No one came into the tent.

An hour passed, and then another. Istrak said his prayers and learned and did his morning exercises, acknowledging with gritted teeth that recent events had substantially diminished his physical prowess. Afterward he recited *Tehillim* by heart and tried to recall the *mishnayos* that he had memorized when still a young child.

He began to feel hungry. Wasn't it time for lunch?

Where *was* Kalev? What could have happened to cause such a drastic change in Ka'hei's attitude toward his captives?

The anguish-filled events of the past few weeks had blurred the lines of Tur's face and her eyes appeared to have withdrawn into their sockets.

"Istrak insisted that your wedding not be put off even for a day."

As soon as Tur had received her father's summons, she had surmised what it was he wanted to discuss. Now she nodded, looking as though the simple motion pained her.

"It is important to me to fulfill Istrak's request," the king continued heavily. "You must surely understand that, Tur, although in the present circumstances…"

She lowered her eyes, and he sighed, forcing himself to continue. "Based on the date that was established before all this happened, my four months will end during your week of *sheva berachos*."

His words surprised her. Until now, she had not devoted much thought to the idea of her father's remarriage. She had been too absorbed in her own grief, in tending her younger siblings, filling the role of queen inside the palace and outside it, and preparing for her own nuptials.

"And in that case…" His voice broke. He rose to keep his daughter from witnessing his weakness, and strode over to one of the large windows. His faith was as strong as it had been three months earlier, but the pain still threatened to break his heart.

Presently, he succeeded in forcing his body to obey his mind. "In light of these facts," he said, resuming his original place and smiling apologetically at Tur, "your wedding will be advanced. It will take place between next Thursday and the following Tuesday. A notice to that effect has already been sent to Ruben's family." He smiled. "He is a special man, your *chasan*. May Hashem grant the two of you only beautiful days, filled with joy."

His voice had softened as he said these last words — only to harden again as he added, "As my oldest daughter, I offer you the privilege of being the first to hear of the decision I made two hours ago." He fell silent, clenching his right fist. "A month and a half from now, Narma Paz, sister of Dalo Stazdiran, prime minister of Khazar, will, *b'ezras Hashem*, become queen of Khazar. If you can pass the news on to Unmar and Yekavel" — he faltered — "I will be very grateful."

"How did she react?" whispered Puah, the maidservant on night duty.

"All right," answered Estelle, Unmar's nurse. She shrugged. "She reacted well to her mother's death, too — at first."

"Something should be done."

The nurse coughed meaningfully.

"There are people who can help," the younger woman insisted. "My neighbor had a cousin who, after her father died, began pulling out her own hair. They went to see a woman who lives in Gayet, and she managed to help the child come back to herself."

"No problem," Estelle said. "You know who is directly responsible for the girl's education, don't you? You're welcome to make an appointment to see him, and tell him about that woman — what did you say her name was? — who can restore his daughter's balance. Go ahead, it's a fine idea!"

A group of five guards passed on one of their nightly patrols, their long shadows looming on the wall opposite. The two women fell silent.

"It's insufferable," Estelle burst out when the soldiers' steps had died away. "Really insufferable."

"It's as if she's reverted to being 4 years old," Puah agreed.

"I was talking about the soldiers," Estelle said. "They're everywhere now." She returned to the subject at hand. "Unmar was never such a baby, even when she was 3."

Behind the closed door, in the big, canopied bed, an 8-year-old girl lay with soft curls spread on the white pillow and eyes fixed on an invisible point in the distance. If only she were as old as Tur, who would be getting married and leaving this place. If only she were a boy, and Father would let her help with really important things. If only Michoel were here, and Istrak. If only Mother… She shook her head and sat up in bed.

Tur said that Father had no choice, and Tur knew that she was right. But why had Hashem placed her father in such an impossible position?

Quietly, Unmar climbed out of bed and went to the big window. If she went to Father's balcony, would she find him standing and praying there tonight, too?

The wind came through the open window and ruffled her curls. The stone floor felt cold beneath her feet, which were clad only in stockings. Resolutely, using all the weight of her body, Unmar pressed the fourth stone from the floor inward. The stone sank in its place, but there was no familiar squeal to tell her that the metal plates had emerged from between the bricks. Such mishaps occurred from time to time; the palace's secret passageways had not been built by professional artisans. Nonetheless, Unmar was distressed. If anything bad should happen in the palace tonight, Heaven forbid, she would have no way of escaping with the doll that her father had given her.

The royal chief waiter knew Ovadia, the king's personal attendant, only slightly. But with his own life and the lives of his children depending on it, even the smallest acquaintance was enough. He delicately sounded out the situation.

"Is His Majesty, long may he live, displeased with the food?"

Ovadia was at a loss as to how to answer. While he had no wish to lie, he also wanted to avoid both damaging the trust the king had in him and interfering with the king's spiritual life. How to respond sincerely to such a question without exposing the king's practice of fasting for three out of the six days of the week?

His obvious confusion gave the chief waiter the answer he sought.

The poison he had been given by the man in the long cloak might be toxic and lethal — but as long as the king refused to taste the food sent from the kitchen, the chief waiter could not find a way to remove the terrible threat that hovered over his head and those of his two sons.

His hands shook as he returned to the kitchen. His staff noticed his agitation. Shlomko the cook, an old friend with a long beard and a hefty paunch, came to his aid.

When the workday was done, the chief waiter, standing by the stove among the pots with a generous slice of cream cake left from the previous Shabbos, spun the story of the past weeks in choppy, broken sentences. His voice broke as he described the lengths he had been forced to take just to keep his head attached to his neck.

The cook heard him out, pudgy arms crossed in front of him. He had a simple solution to offer, sharp as the sword of Alexander the Great.

"There is a king in Khazar, Avrel," he said. "Apparently, you were too frightened to think of it yourself — but what could be simpler or wiser than lodging a complaint of threats and intimidation?"

As he stared at his friend, the mist before the chief waiter's eyes began to clear.

"Threats?"

"Certainly. Come with me, my friend. There are others who enjoy cream cake and will be happy to listen to what we have to tell them…"

It was more than the cake that turned people into friends of Shlomko the cook. Was it the knowledge that, when the time came that you were in need of help, Shlomko was ever ready to stand up and run from one authority figure to another, pleading and arguing on your behalf without a thought for the lateness of the hour or his own comfort?

As Avrel followed his friend through the palace corridors, mentally arranging his story and deciding which details to include and which to omit, a vast gratitude burgeoned in his heart. What a terrific fellow! Shlomko would help him get out of this sticky situation without destroying his small family… As soon as all this was over, he would buy Shlomko a milk cow and a huge copper pot to show his appreciation, he decided.

After long hours of work in which Shlomko made use of all his social skills — and aided by connections supplied by half his friends — Shlomko and the chief waiter found themselves sitting on a pair of leather-covered chairs, facing the former regent of Khazar himself: Lord Diaber.

Avrel was at ease. From the days of his youth he had come and gone in sumptuous rooms such as this one, though never as a seated visitor. The cook was less comfortable. Though a fervent believer that a person is measured by what he does rather than how expensively upholstered his chairs might be, nevertheless Shlomko tucked his legs under his own chair rather nervously. Diaber's younger brother, who had made use of Shlomko's friendly services in the past and had brought them here tonight, had long since disappeared through one of the heavy wooden doors.

Servants stood in the corners of the room, still as statues. The cook glanced at them in wonder as the minutes stretched into nearly half an hour.

At length, another door swung open, and the two Diaber brothers entered the room.

"His Excellency, Lord Diaber," the younger brother announced, ignoring the two visitors' deep bows, "has agreed to listen to you. Remember that his time is valuable."

The cook cleared his throat significantly, but the chief waiter was struck dumb. Diaber was quiet, and his silence caused Avrel some misgivings. In his experience, quiet servants usually came with a talkative master, issuing orders in loud, commanding tones. Also, this reception seemed out of place to him. Surely Lord Diaber's younger brother did not owe Shlomko *such* a big favor!

Shlomko broke the silence. "Someone," he said, "is trying to poison the king."

"What?" Diaber asked incredulously.

"Someone," the cook repeated, "wants to poison the king."

Yosef Diaber's large, handsome eyes narrowed in disbelief, and his mouth twisted as though he had tasted something foul. "How do you know this?"

"Avrel here is in charge of the kitchen," Shlomko explained. "And I am the head chef."

Diaber nodded as though he understood.

"Someone came to him and threatened to harm him and his family unless he agreed to put poison in the king's food. My friend" — once again, he gestured at the tongue-tied chief waiter — "naturally refused. But he is very frightened. He requires protection."

"The police deal with such matters," said Diaber. "You lodged a complaint with them, I hope?"

Something seemed to burst in the chief waiter's chest. He began to tremble helplessly.

"We lodged no official complaint," Shlomko replied. "But we spoke with the assistant to Zavdiel Mitran, the minister for internal security, and also with the interior minister's secretary." He did not mention Ovadia, the king's personal attendant. Dimly, through his fog, the chief waiter wondered why not.

Silence filled the sumptuous room. Lord Diaber lowered his head to his chest, so that it seemed as though he had fallen asleep. The servants were unmoving as pillars of salt.

Finally, Diaber raised his eyes, and the gleam that emanated from them said that Shlomko had done well to come to this room.

Lord Diaber knew what must be done.

Only thirty guests were present at the *seudah* in honor of the *shidduch*, and the *chasan*'s obvious impatience brought the ceremony to a close more quickly than expected.

"Something is troubling the king," the *kallah* said as she and Reuel stepped onto the open balcony at the end of the dining hall.

The king lowered his head. "I feel as if I am standing alone on the peak of a tall mountain, where I must make decisions whose consequences I have no way of foretelling."

" 'The hearts of kings and ministers are in the hand of Hashem,' " Narma quoted softly. "The king…you…do not make your decisions alone."

He lifted his eyes and, to her surprise, smiled. "You are correct," he said. "I have let myself forget that fact for too long now." After a moment, he added, "Thank you."

After that, they stood in silence for a long time, the cool wind lashing at their faces. Sarah, the king's recently departed wife, had not been capable of standing in such a wind for so long. Reuel happened to enjoy the rushing cold that came off the mountains. But perhaps Narma preferred to go indoors?

At a loss, he asked her.

"In the mornings," she answered obliquely, "you can most likely see the sea from here." She paused. "The children —"

"Tur spoke to them earlier. They understand the situation," he told her, trying in vain to hide his pain and helplessness. "It would be fitting for you to meet them a few more times before the wedding."

"Certainly."

The king sighed. She was not to blame for the fact that the law forced him to marry again so soon — and she surely should not suffer because of the letter…

Nevertheless, it was hard for him to concentrate on anything else. The letter that he had received from the officers at the border shortly before the guests had begun to arrive stung him like fire.

Was it possible that Bastian Makan was a traitor?

The missive from the three officers, which he had read just five minutes before the *shidduch seudah*, had been brief and to the point. In their view, there was no logical or strategic reason for Bastian's long silence. On the contrary, with each passing day the Bulgarians had been strengthening their position, and several openings of which the Khazars might have taken advantage had since been sealed. The Bulgarians' silence — so thought the officers — was equally puzzling. It might point at some sort of collusion.

For all these reasons, they requested that the king remove Bastian Makan from his post and appoint another in his place. Even if Lord Makan was guiltless, their faith in him had been undermined, and they were no longer prepared to serve under him.

The letter was curt and sharp. Those men on the border knew nothing about Bastian Makan's secret correspondence with the Bulgarian vice prime minister.

And yet…

Bastian was his brother-in-law and one of the few people in the world whom he trusted implicitly. The Makan family was among the oldest and most venerable in Khazar. Bastian himself had, in the Ten Years' War, demonstrated a loyalty to the crown that had no equal in Khazar. He was a G-d-fearing man and scrupulous in his mitzvah observance. And even if Reuel was mistaken, and Bastian was not the superior individual he thought him — it was obvious that Bastian would never stoop to the degrading level of kidnaping his own nephews, an act that had led to his only sister's death. The idea was ludicrous.

On the other hand…

The king's head ached.

On the other hand…

The pain between his eyes intensified.

On the other hand…

What was wrong with him? Was *he* the one who had been meant to die, and not Sarah?

That last night lived in his thoughts. He had begged her to be strong for the sake of their other children. He had pleaded with her to eat something. When she had agreed, he had quickly ordered Ovadia to bring her the plate that had been brought to his room just minutes before.

Was it possible that his brother-in-law was responsible for turning his children into orphans?

A great weakness gripped him, along with a terrible pain. He mustn't make decisions now, when he was not fully in control of his faculties. He must not!

"What is the matter?" Narma asked. It was the third time she had asked, but he couldn't answer. He had learned over the years to master his fear and his anger. To subdue his pride and banish sadness. But he had never been afflicted with the kind of pain he had been suffering these last days and weeks. Often — too often — it had succeeded in robbing him of his self-mastery.

In despair, he closed his eyes. He could not go on like this!

Finally, slowly, the wave of pain began to recede, and he was able to speak.

"A few minutes before the *seudah* began," said Reuel, looking steadily at his bride, "I received a letter…"

When the guests had departed and the bride's family had left the palace, the elderly doctor came to the king's room, flustered at the urgent summons and taken aback at the sight of the ruler of Khazar pacing his room like a caged lion — apparently hale and healthy.

"Is it possible," the king asked, still pacing restlessly, "that my wife, Queen Sarah, was poisoned?"

The doctor remained silent, and his silence — even more than the grave expression that suddenly filled his eyes — said that the thought was not new to him.

"Why did you not report this to me?" Reuel asked in a voice like ice.

The doctor groaned in reply.

"Were you waiting for someone else to meet his death in the same manner?"

"The queen was young," the doctor said, shoulders bowed. "There was no prior history, and the attack was acute. It was strange."

"But?" the king prompted.

"There is a certain doctor in the mountains," the aged medical man continued in a quavering voice, "who has developed a potion that is beneficial to the sick and fatal to the healthy…" The words trailed away.

"Talk," the king ordered. "I am listening."

"The symptoms…might be the same."

The king's fingers smoothed his beard over and over again.

"I sent someone to see him," the doctor said, "at the suggestion of Izdru, the language instructor. Two and a half weeks have passed since then. The messenger should return to Khazaran-Itil tomorrow or the next day."

"And what of those who remain here?" the king asked quietly. "What of them, dear doctor?"

The physician breathed hard, blinking his eyes in distress. "I have sinned," he said. "May the King of the world forgive me for going so far in my fear… In the strengthening tonic that I concocted for the king each morning, I placed a tiny bit of that poison."

These last words prompted a sharp movement on the part of the soldiers. "The king understands," the doctor said hoarsely. "Does he not?"

The soldiers, whose constant presence in the room made them as good as invisible — like paper on the wall or a rug underfoot — were all too visible now. They acted quickly. One of them seized the doctor's arms and held them behind his back, while a second drew his sword, awaiting the king's order.

"The body learns," the old doctor continued desperately. "It learns from experience how to defend itself, Your Majesty. You are immune, that poison cannot harm you now."

The king nodded and sat down with a weary sigh. "Let him go," he told the soldiers. He turned to the doctor. "Tell me everything you know about this poison."

"The situation is not good," the nobleman said gloomily.

"It's also not that bad," Calidius said in an encouraging tone. "It would behoove Your Excellency to study the new facts in a cold light.

"First, the chief waiter has shown fresh courage and has sought help.

"Second, the king is protected from the poison, but since we now know that the chief waiter is unprepared to cooperate, that is not as disturbing as it might have been.

"Most important of all" — Calidius's eyes gleamed in anticipation of the gold he would surely be rewarded with once his master heard the good news — "Reuel has decided to arrest Bastian Mak—"

"No!" the nobleman exclaimed, lips curving upward in a broad, incredulous smile.

"Yes," said Calidius. "My information is trustworthy, sir. The king's own scribe told one of our friends in the palace."

"Perfect," said the nobleman, leaning back on his chair, at ease once again. "Just perfect." With a smile, he added, "Let us hammer a final nail into Makan's coffin. Listen well, young Calidius Bruchu!"

15

THE MIDDAY MEAL BROUGHT TO ISTRAK'S TENT BY A SILENT young slave consisted of fresh vegetables, unpeeled and uncooked. Istrak pushed it away in disgust. He was not interested in eating, not now — not as long as a curtain of fog hid Kalev's smiling face from him. Where had the boy disappeared to? Or, more accurately — who had made him disappear?

His decision was not preceded by much thought. It was emotion, more than calculation, that impelled him to stand in one swift motion and go to the tent entrance. The guards on duty on either side of the opening did not seem unduly upset at his appearance, nor did they draw their weapons.

"How may we help you, Prince of Khazar?" one of them asked politely.

"Call Ka'hei," Istrak ordered. "Tell him that as long as I do not know where the boy is, I will not cooperate with him."

"At once," said the second guard, while the first lifted the tent flap for Istrak to return inside.

For a long time, nothing happened. The silence grated on Istrak's nerves and ended by turning a short afternoon nap into a very long one. When he awoke, all was dark.

His head pounded.

Alongside the vegetables sat a second plate of vegetables — his evening repast.

"Where is Kalev?" The question troubled him, and not only because the boy was a subject of his father's.

When morning arrived at last, after endless, sleepless hours, it did not bring an answer — only a headache and profound exhaustion. With an effort, Istrak put on his *tefillin* and said his prayers. Then he sank back onto the cushions, waiting for sleep to overtake him. And it did overtake him, thick, warm, and offering blessed forgetfulness.

Yidrat entered into the tent a short time later and brought him back to the hot, dusty present. "Peace unto you," he greeted Istrak.

"And to you," Istrak replied. He was reminded of another time when he had been interrupted in his sleep and presented himself in less than his best — in crumpled clothing and with creases on his cheeks left by his pillow.

"You must be wondering what happened," Yidrat said.

Istrak's brows lifted, but a frantic search for a clever riposte elicited nothing but a lame, "That would be a reasonable assumption."

"We had no evil intentions," Yidrat apologized. "My father was simply in a hurry to leave headquarters and did not appoint anyone to keep you informed."

"Ah," Istrak said dryly.

Yidrat sighed, looked around, and said, "Would you like to go for a stroll? In the meantime, this tent can be put in order…"

Istrak's face lit up. "A stroll sounds…appealing."

"Good!" Yidrat clapped his hands. "We will go to the lookout point — there is a wonderful view up there. Khazar does not have the beautiful views that we have…"

Istrak smiled at Yidrat's enthusiasm. If the other youth had ever seen the flowering hills, dense forests, and great lakes of Khazar, he would not be so excited over the flat plains of his homeland!

"We will take food with us," said the son of the Kawari leader. "And we will remain there till evening. All right?"

Istrak shook his head vigorously. "One moment. I will not leave until I know what you have done with Kalev. Where is he?" he demanded.

"He is with my father," Yidrat replied. "And we must hurry. It is nearly an hour's ride to the lookout point. If we do not leave now, it will be too late… He is all right, do not worry. Get ready, yes?" With each word he spoke, Yidrat edged closer to the tent flap.

"Is he really all right?" Istrak pressed. The outing, with its offer of fresh air and living greenery, enticed him — but he had to make sure that the boy was well.

"He is perfectly fine," Yidrat assured him. "Did my father not promise you?"

"He did," Istrak acknowledged, content that Ka'hei had remembered his implied vow.

"Then why are you worrying?" Yidrat stepped out of the tent, calling back over his shoulder, "I will be back for you soon. Hurry!"

The ride out to the lookout point was long and pleasant. Istrak's eyes devoured the panorama. Khazar's natural landscape was more beautiful, and the people one met in the fields were warmer and more cheerful. But these vast plains had been tended with a care and precision that were unequaled in Khazar. Istrak recalled the aging fruit trees of his own country, and how the prohibition against cutting them down had caused several main roads to curve like serpents. Here the routes ran parallel in straight lines until they met at the horizon. The grass on either side of the road was scrupulously manicured, and even the wood fences that surrounded the grazing fields had all been painted uniformly.

The Kawaris could definitely give the Khazars a lesson or two on proper land management…

"To the east," Yidrat said, "you can see the tent city of Parashmel, one of our largest and most ancient cities. Perhaps one day I can take you there to show you the ancient ruins, dating from the era of your own Temple in Jerusalem."

"That would be an interesting experience," Istrak said, wrapping the reins around his fingers. "Will you never consider moving into permanent housing, Yidrat?"

The young Kawari made a clucking sound. "Houses rob a warrior of his courage and trap the poet's spirit."

"Ah," Istrak said, and smiled.

"What is so funny?"

"I was thinking of my father, and what he would probably say if he were here with us now."

The horses had cantered along for several minutes before Yidrat spoke again. Trying to mask his curiosity, he asked with feigned nonchalance, "What do you think his reaction would have been?"

Istrak smiled again. "'A nation is not composed solely of poets and warriors. A nation is also comprised of its elderly and its sick, its nursing mothers and barefoot children.'"

"And you?" asked Yidrat, lifting his eyes from the road. "Do you agree with him?"

Istrak did not respond.

On a smooth blanket of grass, with a metal bowl laden with cherries between them, Istrak turned to Yidrat and asked, "What happened to Kalev?"

"Nothing. Your bother, Michoel, was making trouble. He would not eat or sleep. My father said that you would certainly agree to send the boy to him. Your brother is alone there, you know."

"As I am alone here," Istrak said bitterly.

"You are not alone." There was a note in Yidrat's voice that promised friendship. "My father admires you very much. Apart from that, we are seeking someone to take the boy's place as quickly as possible. We will surely find someone soon."

Istrak hugged his knees. "What's wrong with Michoel?"

"Nothing." Yidrat waved a dismissive hand. "He is spoiled, your little brother."

"He's delicate," Istrak corrected. "Not spoiled."

"Semantics," Yidrat said with another wave of the hand. "My father says that the G-d of the Khazars did them a favor by making you the firstborn of your father."

"Thank you. A compliment from someone as discerning as your father is worth far more than another person's praise."

The sun slanted its rays on Yidrat's hair, burnishing it an unnaturally red hue. "Are you bored here?" he asked. "They say that your people work from morning to night, and the list of obligations that everyone must fulfill is never-ending."

A never-ending list of obligations: a simple description that put a smile on Istrak's lips.

"So you *are* bored?" Yidrat had misinterpreted the smile.

"A Khazar is never bored," Istrak wanted to say. Instead, he tightened his arms around his knees and said, "A little."

"What would you wish to do?" Yidrat was in an expansive mood. "Do you draw?"

"No."

"A musical instrument — that would suit you."

"No," repeated Istrak, though a wave of longing suddenly swept over him.

"You never learned how to play?" Yidrat found this hard to believe. "At our music festival, you seemed to drink in the sounds! I was certain that you were an expert musician."

"I love music," Istrak admitted, for the first time in his life. "I think there's something magical about it, something that flows from the composer's heart to the musician's fingers and straight to the heart of the listener..." The description was his father's, who had used it to explain to his firstborn why music that came from across the border could affect him. Istrak believed that, but with a slightly different emphasis.

"Which instrument would you wish to learn to play? The lyre? The lute? Or perhaps the horn?"

"The lyre," said Istrak. "But let it go. I'm too old."

"No, you are not," Yidrat contradicted. "You are only 17."

Istrak lowered his head, gazing at a large, spotted ladybug making its way among the blades of grass. Only? He had never been "only" an age; he had always been "already" that age. Already 5 — time to learn *Chumash*; already 10 — time for *mishnayos*; 13 — ready to assume the burden; 17 — almost an adult...

When he lifted his head, he caught a look of pity on Yidrat's face.

"Seventeen is, by all accounts, too old for children's games," Istrak said. Unwittingly, his voice was a little sad.

"Music is not child's play!" Yidrat scolded.

"True," Istrak said quickly. "Even in our Holy Temple the Levites would accompany the priestly service with music and song. But I am not a Levite, Yidrat. I am a king's son, and my people need me not as a lyre player, but as..." He hesitated, because the term his father habitually used was not suited to foreign ears. How would Yidrat react if he heard that the Khazar crown prince looked upon both his father and himself as a pair of burden-bearing donkeys?

"That may be true," Yidrat said, not noticing Istrak's hesitation. "But now you have the chance. Do you want to?"

"Want to — what?"

"Learn," Yidrat said simply.

Istrak narrowed his eyes in suspicion. Was it possible that, right here, as a captive of a foreign nation, he was being handed his dearest dream on a silver platter?

The youngest of the four Ampi brothers was a strange-looking man. His face was flat and round; his hair, coarse and dark, hung limply on either side. He was short and his accent was odd. But the moment he placed his lyre on his knee and began to play, Istrak forgot all the rest.

"It is not difficult," the musician said when he was done. "The lyre has only four strings, and they make lovely sounds when you pass your hand over them..." He held out the instrument to Istrak, who took it as if mesmerized — paying no heed at all to the fact that he had just crossed an invisible line.

The blacksmith was not careful in his work, and as he welded together the ends of the metal ring around Knaz's leg, he left a great, ugly scar on the flesh.

"It will be your fault if he limps," Taor scolded Ruba. "As though it wasn't bad enough that he's missing the use of one arm. You shouldn't have bickered so much over the price."

Knaz stood by, head down and an apathetic expression on his face. His left arm dangled motionless at his side.

"Let him go out to the field first," Ruba said. "Afterward you can get annoyed."

This reminder irritated Taor even more, as the ungentle hand with which he thumped the slave between the shoulder blades testified.

"Go," he ordered. "Actually — run. The sheep are waiting, fool."

The Mundari lifted his head and then let it hang again. His foot ached, and his arm continued sending intermittent stabs of pain to his brain. But he could do this. He could.

The blacksmith emerged from the house, a large, heavy-looking anvil on his shoulder.

"Which region is he from?" he asked, watching the young man limp away.

"I haven't the slightest idea," Taor told him.

"If he is from the Khazar side," said the blacksmith, "you might want to know that someone came here this morning searching for someone from Khazar to hire."

"Why didn't you say so earlier?" Taor demanded.

Despite the fact that the blacksmith wielded a heavy tool, and his own hands were empty, the former retreated a pace.

"You didn't say he was a Mundari," the blacksmith muttered.

"And how did you suddenly find that out?" Rabu quizzed him.

The blacksmith smiled grimly. "Only a Mundari can remain quiet when his skin is scorched. Go find out, Taor. Drink some water first, and don't hit him if he disappoints you. On such a hot day, it's a pity to waste energy on getting angry."

"It's only hot near your furnace," Rabu said in a friendly way. "A good day to you, my friend."

The dark-haired Kawari studied the slave with disfavor. He didn't like the look of him at all.

"Where are you from?" he asked sternly.

The Mundari lifted his eyes for a moment, then hastily lowered his lids again. The eyes, too, were displeasing to the dark-haired fellow: they held too much strength.

"Where are you from?" he demanded again.

"From here and there," replied the slave. "I am a Mundari, sir."

The Kawari snorted with disdain. As though any fool couldn't tell that much.

"Do you worship Buleh?" Dryly, he pronounced the forbidden name of the ancient Mundari idol.

"The old fat one?" the slave asked rhetorically. "No."

"The G-d of the Jews?"

"The G-d of heaven and earth," the slave answered quietly.

"Do you know Jewish law?"

It was a strange question. Knaz's muscles tensed beneath the stained rags he wore. "A little. Whatever they taught me."

"And what did you do before you were captured?"

The tremor that passed through the Mundari's body did not escape the Kawari's shrewd eyes.

"I went here and there," Knaz said softly. "I am a Mundari, sir."

"Well, apart from going here and there, what else do you know how to do?" Contempt dripped from the Kawari's voice in large droplets.

What *did* he know how to do? He was a good tracker — even a very good one. He had come this far... He was trained in face-to-face combat, at least when his right arm was functioning properly, and his skill with a bow and arrow was excellent. What else?

"I can cook a bit," he said, eyes riveted to the grains of sand near the Kawari's feet. "I can take care of animals and clean."

"With one hand?"

"The arm will heal," Taor said.

"Soon," Rabu added.

"Perhaps," said the Kawari. Moving closer to Knaz, he seized his chin and stared into his eyes. Then he ordered him to open his mouth and take off his shirt. In silence he inspected Knaz's teeth and muscles, as though the Mundari were an ox he was considering for purchase. Finally, he turned away from the slave and said, "If I find nothing better, perhaps I will come back later. But don't count on it. He's no great bargain, this slave of yours."

Immediately after Shacharis, Lord Shefer requested an audience with the king. Granted his request, however, he stood mute before the gilded throne.

"Have you come to ask for your matchmaking fee, Elranan?" It was a weak joke, but in light of the king's despondent state of mind, it testified to the friendship that Khazar's ruler felt toward the governor of the central region.

"No, Your Majesty." Elranan inclined his head.

"Speak," Reuel ordered. "You do not need to be apprehensive with me, old friend."

Shefer stood erect and said, "Perhaps I *am* too nervous, sire. On the other hand, there may be some truth in what I am about to say to the king. It is...a delicate matter."

"The king is listening." Reuel tried to ignore the ominous note of warning in Lord Shefer's voice.

Still Shefer hesitated. "The whole thing may be a mistake. In any case, Your Majesty..."

"Please get to the point," the king requested, staring at his fingertips as they rested on the arm of his throne.

"Well..." Shefer gathered his strength and the words began to erupt, one after the other: "The events that have taken place in the palace over the past few months cannot be placed into the category of coincidence. I speak of Eshal's murder, may he rest in peace, the capture of the princes, the queen's death..."

The king nodded. "Go on."

"I tried," Shefer continued, "to investigate the question of who might profit by all these events. So far, only one person has profited."

"And he is — ?" the king prompted.

Shefer's expression reflected his distress. Every word that he said here would, within hours, reach Stazdiran's ears. Should the king dismiss his accusations out of hand, he, Shefer, would have acquired a formidable enemy. But he should have thought about that earlier. It was too late to retreat now.

"The only one," said Lord Elranan Shefer, "who benefited from the *bek's* death was his successor. And the same man benefited from the death of the queen before her time."

"With your active help," the king said. There was no smile in his voice.

Lord Shefer was silent a moment as two deep creases became

evident on either side of his mouth. "Yes," he admitted. "With my help."

Tuesday was the busiest day of the week for Lord Yosef Diaber, who had assumed the responsibilities of the regent, due to the crown prince's absence. On Tuesday mornings he would make a tour of the network of soup kitchens that had been established throughout the city. He liked to visit their operation for himself and would note any necessary repairs and improvements. In the afternoons he met with the city's charity association, of which he was chairman, devising methods of helping needy families. From there he made his way to the palace for the weekly government meeting. And in the evening, weary from the day's labors, he dealt — as he did every evening — with various requests sent to him from every corner of the city.

Today, as on every Tuesday, Lord Diaber's began his long day shortly after dawn. The king's messenger caught up with him in the fourth hour. He handed him a letter.

The king's scribe, aware of Diaber's busy and important schedule, had written the letter in clear, concise terms: In accordance with the regent's position, and by the third law pertaining to times of crisis, which precluded the king from making certain decisions without the regent's support, the regent was requested to return to the palace without delay. His Majesty thanked the regent in advance for his cooperation.

Now?

Yosef Diaber's eyes darted to and fro, gauging the many small details requiring immediate attention. This soup kitchen, which he had not visited for some three months, had not been managed properly. The cloth on one of the tables was stained, and above the kitchen door was the gray web of an industrious spider. Was this summons really that urgent? His day was filled, and if he did not deal with these things today, he would not be able to devote time to them until next week. Must the poor eat with spiders' webs over their heads simply because their luck had turned?

The king, he reflected — not for the first time — did not really see or understand the needs of his subjects. His throne was too high and too remote; and his understanding, it seemed, too narrow.

Angrily, Diaber broke off his tour of inspection, promising the kitchen's manager that he would return in a week's time and expressing his hope that the various minor problems would be addressed. "Otherwise..." He did not bother to finish the sentence. There were many who would be glad to manage one of Diaber kitchens. The mitzvah — apart from the not inconsiderable salary — was precious. If this fellow did not know how to appreciate the privilege, he could just go home!

Reuel II, with burning eye and sunken cheek, greeted him with a small smile.

"Welcome," he said, gesturing at the seat to his left. "Bless Hashem in my home."

Suspiciously, Lord Diaber took the chair that the king had indicated. It had been years since the king had treated him in such a friendly fashion, and he wondered at the reason for it. He selected a golden exotic fruit from the bowl proffered by one of the servants.

"...*borei pri ha'eitz*," he said, and bit into the sweet, juicy fruit.

"*Ha'adamah*," Reuel corrected him sternly, a shadow passing across his gray eyes.

Lord Diaber made an almost imperceptible gesture with his hand and murmured, "*Rachmana liba bai* [The Merciful One desires sincerity of heart]." Noting the disapproving expression on the king's face, he recited the correct *berachah*, took another bite and then asked, "Why did you summon me, *Khagan* of Khazar?"

Reuel moistened his lips, clearly in need of emotional courage to answer the question. Finally, in a tone that said the topic was not to his liking, he said, "Our officers at the border are not happy with the way Bastian Makan is directing matters." He sighed. "To be more precise — they accuse him of cooperating with the enemy."

"Bastian?" Diaber smiled playfully. "The notion is hardly logical, sire."

"Unfortunately, the matter is not simple. For the past ten years,

Makan has been corresponding with the deputy prime minister of Bulgaria — without letting me know about it even once."

"Ah…" It was hard to tell whether it was surprise that colored Diaber's voice or distress.

"I have decided," the king went on, "to remove Makan from his position. Another man must be appointed in his stead. That is the reason you were summoned here."

"The natural candidate is Phidos Flair," Diaber said. He shook his head. "It's hard to believe. Bastian Makan would not turn traitor, Your Majesty!"

A sad smile played on the king's lips. "That is what I thought, too. For that reason, I did not put a stop to his correspondence with the enemy. Yet I cannot ignore the recent events at the border. I shall appoint Nachum, Bastian's lieutenant, to take his place as minister of war. However, because of the injury he sustained last year, he is unfit to fill Bastian's place in the field. And because I don't wish to encourage intrigue and slander, I am not inclined to appoint Phidos — who was instrumental in having Bastian removed — in his place. On the other hand, if someone else is given the job, Phidos is likely to feel resentful."

"Baniel, commander of the second division, is a few years older than Phidos," Diaber said. "Perhaps Phidos would accept Baniel's appointment with better grace."

"A wise insight." The king's tone was dry. His earlier aspect of friendliness had evaporated without a trace. "When I have crystallized my decision, I'll send a messenger to you with the appointment document so that you may add your signature to mine."

"Certainly." Lord Diaber stood up.

"Not yet," said the king. "There is something else."

Diaber sat down again, but the king did not speak right away. The silence stretched.

Diaber, his patience almost at the breaking point, found his thoughts wandering back to the soup kitchen and its negligent manager.

"Yosef —" the king began.

Diaber stirred. "Yes? I'm listening."

"Another matter is troubling me. It's about Dalo Stazdiran," the king said. "In view of the new relationship that was forged between us the other day upon my betrothal to his sister, the matter has become even more complicated. Someone — an important minister — has turned my attention to the fact that the only person to derive benefit from recent events has been Dalo. He became *bek* in Eshal's place. And his sister…" He stopped, then started speaking again, with difficulty. "The doctor told me yesterday that it is definitely possible the queen was poisoned."

"No!"

The king peered intently at Diaber, noting every twitch.

"These suspicions are altogether too far-fetched," Diaber insisted. "And although I can understand their source, I believe that the minister in question suffers from an excess of nerves and nothing else. Stazdiran could never have dreamed that His Majesty would choose to marry Narma Paz out of all the women of Khazar!"

"Stazdiran," said the king, "might have assumed that, having a daughter of marriageable age of excellent character and possessing influence with those close to me, he might succeed in having her name included in the list of candidates. If you had a chance of one in six to see your daughter become queen, Yosef, would you not be prepared to take the risk?"

"Not at such a price," Diaber said forcefully. "We're speaking of murder, Your Majesty!"

"True," replied the king, a hint of weakness in his voice. "Sadly, I'm all too aware of that fact."

Lately, the chief waiter had begun to hate the long, isolated walk from his home to the gates of Itil, the upper city. But this morning, accompanied by three soft-footed policemen dressed in civilian clothes, he was more to ease.

Apparently, his story had been accepted. The police were sorry for him and the nasty morass into which he had fallen and were ready to make every effort to extricate him from it.

The sky, which for a long time had appeared gray as metal to him, was suddenly bright blue again, and the odor of rotting vegetables that met his nose as he passed through the central market was sweetened by the fragrance of fresh, hot rolls emanating from the baking house. Perhaps he would buy himself one. They looked as enticing as they smelled. Flaky on the outside and soft inside, with a tasty sprinkling of spices on top. The line outside the baking house was not too long. This morning, he could afford the indulgence.

A grimy boy attached himself to the chief waiter as he went to stand at the end of the line.

"Keep your distance," the chief waiter scolded.

"All right."

A moment later, the boy bumped into him again.

"I thought we agreed on something," the chief waiter said, dusting off his right sleeve, which had rubbed against the boy.

"Someone asked me to give this to you." With a grin that was a flash of white in his dirty face, the boy thrust a rolled piece of parchment into the man's hand.

The waiter's chest tightened. Where were those undercover policemen when you needed them?

"Wait a second," he said, digging into his pocket for his purse. "I want to give you something for your trouble…"

The endearing smile widened. The waiter, catching a glimpse of one of the policemen moving decisively forward, allowed himself a smile in return. Why not? It was such a beautiful day!

The boy accepted the coin with thanks and bent over to stick it in his shoe. Even before he had straightened, he felt a touch on his shoulder.

"Boy? Are you looking for some work?"

The 14-year-old stood fully upright with a jerk. "Sure."

"How much would you charge for nine hours?" asked the plainclothed policeman.

"Eight half-coins."

The man eyed him as though measuring his worth. "All right," he said. "Come on."

"Where to?"

"Over there." The man gestured with his chin at a house at the far end of the bustling marketplace, where the police had rented a room on an upper story. The boy followed him, happy at the feel of the coin in his shoe.

With a smile, the chief waiter continued on his way to the palace. In his bag was a large, well-spiced, and fragrant roll.

The apartment to which the policeman led the boy was furnished with nothing but three huge bags filled with tiny glass beads.

"These beads have to be sorted by weight and color," he explained. "Here are some bowls. The work must be exact."

"It will be," the boy promised, crouching beside one of the bags.

The policeman crouched on the other side. For a few moments, the two worked in silence.

"Who is the man you spoke to, over by the baking house?" the policeman asked suddenly.

"Don't know," the boy said with a shrug, as his fingers sorted through the beads with lightning swiftness. "Someone asked me to give him a letter, so I did."

The policeman murmured something about the small green beads, which the boy transferred to an empty bowl.

"Once," said the policeman, "before my father began to deal in these beads, I worked in the palace. That man — the one you spoke to — very much resembles His Majesty, the king. Do you think it possible that the king decided to disguise himself and go out to see the situation in the streets?"

"Maybe." The boy's eyes opened wide. "Do you think I actually talked to the king?"

Though the policeman knew very well that the man who had received the parchment was the royal chief waiter, it suited him to have the boy believe otherwise. Still, he did not want to make that too obvious. "How do I know?" he dissembled. "I didn't see him close up. Who asked you to give him the letter?"

"A man about your height with brown eyes. A little heavier than you."

The policeman chuckled. "Do you have any idea how many

people like that there are in the palace? Dozens! Tell me something more specific."

The boy rubbed his forehead. "He looked completely ordinary," he said. "There was no special sign...except for his collar..."

"Yes? His collar?" the policeman prompted.

"His collar had a symbol on it, sort of round and square, like...like..."

"Like what?"

"Like the symbol on the minister of war's carriage!" the boy said triumphantly. "You could be right! He must have been someone on the minister's staff. So the man I talked to really *might* have been the king! Do you realize what this means? My friends will never believe me!"

"Do I realize what this means?" The shock on the policeman's face was evident. "I think I do..."

16

THE NEWS REACHED THE KING IN THE MIDDLE OF A government meeting. It was scribbled on a small note that had been hastily composed in the anteroom.

The chief investigator, who was not present at the government meeting, wished to inform the *khagan* of Khazar that the evidence against Bastian Makan was gaining credibility. Apparently, the man who had tried to persuade the chief waiter to poison the king was a member of Bastian Makan's staff. The chief investigator wanted to know what were the king's orders in the light of this new evidence.

It was a difficult question. A difficult and painful question.

How could a man whose brother-in-law and very good friend had murdered his wife and kidnaped his sons, proceed to conduct a government meeting as though nothing untoward had occurred?

Did he have any other choice?

A draft blew on the king's neck from the window facing him. Through the glass he could see a strip of pale-blue sky. A single dove had begun building its nest on the sill.

The One Who gave her the knowledge she needs, the king thought as he folded the parchment into four neat squares, *will grant me wisdom as well.*

Closing his hand around the note, he turned to the minister of finance, who continued to rant, with great feeling, about the enormous expense the present state of emergency had cost the kingdom's treasury.

When the meeting finally drew to a close, the king returned to his rooms in a state of inner turmoil. His midday meal, which had long since grown cold, still waited on the table, covered with a silver dome to keep the food fresh.

"This can be returned to the kitchen," he told Ovadia. "It is almost time for the evening meal in any case." He removed his crown and set it on its special cushion.

"A pity," Ovadia said in a fatherly tone.

The king looked up, surprised. There were no more than two years separating them, and the advantage was actually the king's.

"The food is good," Ovadia said. "I personally asked the waiter to taste it."

"I'm not hungry," the king said in quiet apology.

"You are torturing yourself for nothing," Ovadia said with painful sincerity. "You are not to blame for anything, my king."

"I trusted Bastian." The king leaned on the table. "I trusted him, Ovadia. I did not permit the army to deviate from his orders even the smallest bit. Matrias, the commander of the *hostress* troops, has testified under questioning that he opposed Brach, may he rest in peace, who wished to turn the convoy off its designated route. Matrias claimed that there was no logic in taking the convoy through the Batar Ravine."

"Lord Gad Baliatar," Ovadia remarked, "trusted Brach, the commander of the royal guard — but not the *hostress* commander."

The king straightened. "We grew up together, Ovadia. Allow yourself to speak plainly."

"Khazar needs a strong king. A person cannot be strong when he's consumed with guilt. The king must forget the past and look to the future. That's what I heard your father, may his memory be a blessing, say to you when I was 9 years old."

The words propelled an unpleasant memory to the forefront of Reuel's mind. The incident in question had involved a certain potbellied etiquette instructor and three youthful servants who, affronted by the teacher's attitude toward the 11-year-old crown prince, had hidden a piece of hard cheese in the teacher's box of stockings. Three mice, drawn by the smell of cheese, had invaded the box. When they revealed themselves suddenly to the instructor, he ran away, frightened, onto the ice-covered pond — which gave way beneath his weight.

The ensuing apologies, and the beating that the crown prince suffered, eventually appeased the teacher, but the crown prince's pangs of conscience were not forgotten — not even when his back was bloody from the caning he received after the king, his father, realized that the prince had been aware of the nefarious plot but had done nothing to prevent it.

"As it was then, so it is today," Ovadia said. "None of us can anticipate the consequences of our actions."

"I resembled Istrak more than Michoel in my youth," the king said as a wave of memories washed over him. "But I was fortunate to have a father who was wiser than the one he has."

"Istrak is fortunate to have a father who is head and shoulders above the rest," Ovadia answered firmly. "Just as Khazar has been fortunate in its wise and powerful ruler. You must look forward, my king. You must not turn your head to look back over your shoulder for even an instant."

Wordlessly, the king shook his head. He lifted his eyes to the window. "Could Bastian be a traitor?" he whispered.

"At the moment," his man said, "that appears to be a fact."

"At the moment," the king repeated with hope. Then he hid his eyes behind his hand.

"My king." It was one of the noblemen appointed to guard the entrance to the king's chambers. "The chief investigator wishes to see you — urgently."

"Let him enter," said the king. With a sigh, Ovadia picked up the untouched luncheon and left the room as the chief investigator entered.

"The royal physician's messenger returned this morning," he reported, "bearing confirmation of..." He hesitated. "Makan's guilt. A few months ago, a person by the name of Lord Ribak Bati came to see the doctor in the mountains."

The king's face flushed at the sound of the name, and a vein throbbed in his temple.

"He bore a travel visa signed by His Majesty," the chief investigator continued in the same dry tone. "He rode a white donkey. The nobleman asked for medicine for the nephew of his master — our minister of war."

"Have you arrested Bati?" the king asked.

"We have. He, of course, denies the story completely — but is unwilling to tell us where he was during that same period."

Fury raged through the king. "Bring Bastian Makan here," he said, his voice sharp and emotionless. "I will sign an order appointing Baniel, commander of the second division, to take his place."

The official carriage bounded over pits in the dirt road, causing Bastian Makan to bump repeatedly against its walls. He had promoted Phidos Flair to his present position as head of the cavalry. He had personally guided the bungling Baniel and assisted young Sharet's career from afar. And now?

The pair of young officers seated opposite him averted their eyes whenever he glanced their way. But he could feel their gaze when his eyes were riveted to the carriage floor, no doubt envincing their disbelief and even contempt.

In actuality, the pair were feeling stunned and uncertain. Some fourteen or fifteen years earlier, the man facing them had bristled with energy and life. Now he swayed with the carriage, not even gasping the handle to prevent himself from crashing into its walls.

At first, Bastian had been enraged. Then he had submitted to a crushing pain. At this point, all feeling had drained away, leaving him prey to nothing but a powerful desire to sleep. He had never craved sleep so much. Sleep, and the oblivion that came in its wake.

The thousand horses that had galloped constantly inside him, turning him into Khazar's most active and decisive minister, now threatened to trample him beneath their hooves.

Should he, as his officers claimed, have given the order to attack?

That was not the way of Khazar of old — and there was nobody more familiar with the ancient annals than he. The intelligence he had gathered concerning the overtones in the Bulgarian camp had hinted that they, too, were in no hurry to rush into an armed conflict. Indeed, they had not done so. He had been correct.

Why hadn't Sharet and Baniel understood that he was correct?

Phidos Flair had been blinded by the position he might inherit. But the others? Why had Sharet and Baniel followed Flair's lead?

"Your Excellency —" One of the two officers in the carriage leaned forward, a good-natured expression on his face.

"Commander," said Bastian, lifting his head with an effort. "Until the king orders otherwise."

The young officer shrank back as though slapped. Bastian closed his eyes. His temple, which had struck the carriage wall, began to bleed, staining his silvery *peyos*. He was tired, tired to death.

And would it be so terrible to die? He was not perfect, not by a long shot. But after he had been purged and purified from all the bad that he had done, he would be able to sit with his Avraham in a place of endless sweetness and light, and continue learning where they had left off. He remembered precisely the line where they had stopped; he could not forget. Perhaps afterward Ruth would join them, radiant and fine, and ask about something she had not understand in the prayer text…

For years, he had envied those who enjoyed the privilege of raising their children past their youthful years. Over there, he could at least glean some *nachas*. Would it really be so bad?

The carriage slowed, rattling over cobblestones. Bastian Makan did not open his eyes.

A small inn with a thatched roof appeared through the open window.

"We must change horses," the carriage driver called to his passengers, stretching his aching muscles. "Would you like something to eat, Captain?"

"No, thank you," said the senior of the two officers, and his companion joined in his refusal. The visage of the supreme commander of the Khazar army was enough to suppress the appetite of the hungriest of men.

A servant brought low tables into the room, along with bowls of wild fruit and nuts, while a second carefully carried in a large wooden board. When he had set it down, a third servant began to arrange small ivory figures on the board.

"A mind game of the highest order," said Yidrat, watching the servant arrange the figures. "My father believes that it develops mental acuity and broadens one's grasp of strategy. Personally, I like the game simply because it's enjoyable… It is a game for four, but two can also play, if each player uses two sets of figures. Notice, Istrak, that each set has twelve lambs, six ewe, two rams, one shepherd, and three wolves. The goal is to protect your sheep and devour as many of your rival's sheep as you can. Understand? When a wolf jumps over a sheep, that means he's eaten it. And when the shepherd… Are you listening, Istrak?"

"Of course." Istrak tore his eyes away from the ivory figures. "I'm just a little…hungry. It's hard to feel satisfied on a diet of raw vegetables."

"I am sorry." Uncomfortably, Yidrat added, "We have sent men out to comb the area for a servant of your own faith, but it may be a long time before someone like that is found. Is there no way your Torah can permit you to eat our food?"

"Not really," Istrak said, picking up a tiny ivory wolf with bared teeth. "That is, if a person were in danger, it would be permissible. But right now…"

"Danger?" Yidrat asked with interest.

"When a person's life is at risk, the Torah permits a person to transgress some prohibitions if necessary."

Yidrat's forehead wrinkled in perplexity.

"If I am dying of starvation and my life is in peril," Istrak explained patiently, "I would be permitted to eat something to survive. Or if someone were to threaten me with a weapon unless I ate some nonkosher food, then, too, I would be permitted to do so. But as long as things are not that way, I see no reason or method that would make such a thing permissible."

"Arranging such a thing would be no problem at all," Yidrat said, putting a hand on the hilt of his battle-axe. "Shall I do it?"

Istrak laughed. "You have to mean it. Our G-d cannot be fooled. Pass the nuts, please…"

Yidrat did so, then asked, "And your G-d wants you to be dying of starvation before you can eat, say, a piece of our bread? I don't see the logic in that."

"I can't explain it," Istrak confessed.

"And yet you are prepared to unquestioningly obey laws that you do not understand?"

"Yes," he said. "Absolutely, Yidrat. I would not want any of my own citizens, for example, to obey only the laws that they understand."

Yidrat's fingers plucked up a little ivory sheep, then restored it to its place on the board. "Can I say something honestly?" he asked. When there was no reply, he added, "Prince of Khazar?"

"Yes." Istrak inclined his head. "Speak."

"I am glad," Yidrat said, slowly and deliberately, "that I was not born a Khazari."

"That won't help you," Istrak retorted. "You are obligated to obey the seven commandments that G-d gave to Noach's descendants."

"Perhaps." Yidrat shrugged. "But I do not know — nor do I wish to know — anything about that. Do you not envy me, Prince of Khazar?"

"No," Istrak said flatly.

"If I were you," Yidrat said, "I would definitely envy me."

Yidrat won the first two games easily. The third, after Istrak had mastered the complex rules of the game, was longer and more evenly matched. More than once, the balance of points was in Istrak's favor.

"You have great talent," remarked Ka'hei, who had joined them in the middle of the game and sat on the side, watching its progress with interest. "A great talent that has not been developed."

"Thank you." Istrak smiled, tearing his eyes from the board. "It is kind of you to compliment me, leader of the Platt tribes."

"And why should I not compliment you?" Ka'hei's face assumed a remote expression.

It was a good question, and Istrak found it difficult to answer. "A person does not tend to praise his enemies," he finally said.

"You are not an enemy." Ka'hei's handsome green eyes practically skewered the youth seated opposite him. "Perhaps our people are different in personality and beliefs, and no one will try to claim that bloody battles have not been fought at our borders. But we — Yidrat, myself, and you — are not enemies. With my right hand I swear to you that, were you to desire it, I would give you my own daughter as a wife."

These words did not please Istrak, and not only because of the broad menace they carried. "Would you so quickly forget the suffering that the Khazars inflicted on your people?"

"Hordos," said Yidrat, "one of the great philosophers, said that he preferred a brave enemy's hatred to the friendship of a coward."

Yidrat's answer did not make sense to Istrak. Before he could argue, Ka'hei added, "If we do not forget the old hatred and the mutual pain, if we do not erase the past and turn our faces toward a better future — then the pain will continue to fester on either side of the border."

Istrak lowered his head, considering Ka'hei's words. This was an answer he could understand.

"We are not as cruel as Khazari mothers are fond of telling their children," Ka'hei went on. "You have seen that for yourself, Istrak. Even if our priorities are sometimes different, it is not difficult to understand the logic on which they are based. We would like your friendship, Prince. Will you give it to us?"

"I do not have Khazar's authority in this matter," Istrak said, lips dry.

"I know that." The years suddenly made themselves evident on Ka'hei's smooth face. "I know that, Istrak, and I am not asking for that. After all, you are only the crown prince. What I would like — and Yidrat — is your friendship as a person."

Istrak swallowed, eyes moving from Ka'hei to Yidrat, who held out a hand to him. At a loss, Istrak stared at the extended hand. Someone passed near the tent. In a fleeting glimpse, Istrak thought that the fellow resembled Pinras.

Yidrat waited, hand still outstretched.

"I have learned to appreciate you in recent days..." Istrak said, intending to politely reject the Kawari leader's proposal. But Ka'hei did not let him finish.

"Speeches later," he said, a smile in his voice. "Shake hands, boys."

Yidrat's shake was firm and warm.

"Friends?" asked Yidrat.

"Friends," Istrak conceded.

"This calls for a small celebration," Ka'hei announced. "I will send someone for another bottle of wine from your people's sealed bottles, Istrak. May you both succeed in overcoming all the obstacles that will stand in your way as you work to actualize your friendship."

"We will succeed," Yidrat promised.

"With the Creator's help," Istrak added.

The hand that had grasped Yidrat's burned as though it had been branded.

That evening, Ka'hei appeared at the tent once again. He was beaming. "We found who we were seeking!" he said. "Istrak, I'd like to introduce you to Huda." Clearly, he was very proud of his find.

"*Shalom eilecha*," Istrak said, glad to be able to use language he was familiar with after all this time.

"*Aleichem shalom*," returned the old man. His voice was low and frightened.

"My name is Istrak," the youth said, pity stirring in him. "I am the crown prince of Khazar, grandson of King Brachia, son of —"

"Long may he live," the old man said at the mention of Istrak's grandfather. His muddled eyes lit up.

Ka'hei compressed his lips. When he had spoken with the old man a few moments earlier, he had not seemed so confused.

"May he rest in peace," Istrak said. "King Brachia was gathered to his fathers more than twenty years ago. Where are you from, Huda?"

"From up there," he mumbled. The man pointed northward. His Khazari vocabulary was sparse and halting.

"You were born there?"

The old man chuckled, and the chuckle turned into a cough. "Of course not! I am a Khazari, young man."

"Your Highness," Ka'hei rebuked him, revealing for the first time that he had a firm grasp of the language of his neighbors across the border. "This young man is the Khazar crown prince. You must treat him with respect and serve him faithfully. Make sure he lacks for nothing and that all his needs are honorably fulfilled. Understand?"

"Yes, sir," the man said in the Kawari tongue. His shoulders were hunched as though to protect him from what was certainly coming. "Whatever you say, sir."

Now it was Istrak's turn to tighten his lips. A confused old man who hardly remembered his mother tongue did not appear to be the ideal companion.

"I will leave now," said Ka'hei, attempting to minimize the unpleasantness. "My dear Istrak, if you need anything — call me."

The tent flaps stirred, and they were left alone.

"Please sit down, Grandfather Huda," Istrak said gently. "I would like to speak with you a little."

The servant seemed at a loss.

"Sit." Istrak pointed at one of the cushions scattered around. "I'd like to talk with you. To hear some details about your life."

"I am Huda," the old man said with a grimace. "I am quick and good. I came from Khazar. I know halachos."

"I'm glad to hear that." Istrak smiled. "Which halachos do you know, Huda?"

The old man was silent.

"Grandfather Huda, can you tell me how we tell a kosher fish from a nonkosher one?"

Huda brightened. "That's easy. If the fish has a mustache, it's not kosher. If it has no mustache — it's kosher!"

"Mustache," Istrak repeated blankly.

"It is forbidden to eat a fish with a mustache," the old man explained patiently. "Only one without a mustache is permitted. Understand, young man?"

"More or less," Istrak murmured. He struggled not to clench his fists. Had Ka'hei thought him so easy to deceive?

After a short pause, he asked. "Where did you live before?"

The old man's eyes lit up again. "In Khazar," he said proudly. "In beautiful Khazar."

"Where in Khazar?"

"In a little house where the land rises up. My father had a horse, and also a barn. And we never ate fish with a mustache."

"What happened later?"

"Soldiers came. Many soldiers, with such big hats…"

Istrak's anger abandoned him in a flash. The last invasion from Byzantium had taken place in the days of King Istrak II some fifty-eight years earlier. This poor Khazari could not have been more than 6 or 7 when he was taken from his parents' home. "And they took you with them."

"Yes," the old man said sadly.

Istrak's heart constricted. No wonder he knew so little about his own heritage! Why, he had been a slave in foreign lands practically his whole life! "When I get out of here," he vowed, "I will take you with me and return you to Khazar."

The old man's breathing became suddenly labored. "But —"

"But?" Istrak prompted.

"He said they would let me go back afterward."

"Go back where?"

The slave trembled. "To my house," he whispered, gesturing vaguely northward.

What to do with this old Khazari, whose entire knowledge of Jewish law was that it was forbidden to eat a fish with a mustache?

Istrak pitied the old man. He wanted to help him.

If he told Ka'hei that he must find another Khazari slave, chances were that this fellow would be dispatched — one way or another.

Istrak sat on his cushion for a long time, peering into the darkness. Never, in all his life, had he met such a pathetic figure as this Huda. Compared to him, Kalev, for all his childishness and naivete, appeared as the wisest of men...

What need did Michoel have of Kalev anyway? Why did his brother deserve the privilege of having Kalev serve him? For that matter — a surprising thought — why was Ka'hei insisting on keeping them apart? The perfect solution to the whole situation would be to bring Michoel here — not take Kalev to him!

Was it possible that something had happened to Kalev or to Michoel, and Ka'hei was hiding the truth from him with this subterfuge?

The thought galvanized him. It was not all that late, and Ka'hei did not appear to belong to that group of people who retired early...

A cynical smile touched the prince's lips. Even if he was wrong about that, the leader of the Platt tribes — in the name of friendship — would get out of bed for him.

If Ka'hei was surprised at the Khazar prince's unexpected appearance at the entrance of his tent, he did not show it. A moment or two after one of his servants informed him of the prince's arrival, Istrak was invited to enter.

Ka'hei, dressed casually in a long, embroidered shirt over plush velvet trousers, greeted him with a smile. "To what do I owe this honor?" He gestured at a pair of cushions. "Has something happened, Prince of Khazar?"

"Nothing new has happened," Istrak said, sitting on the larger of the two cushions. "Except for a flash of understanding..."

"I'm listening. What's troubling you, young prince?"

"Several things," Istrak replied, trying to buy time to organize his thoughts. "The first is the question of where are my brother and my boy."

"They are in a tented camp about a day's ride from here. Have we not already discussed this, Istrak?"

"If my brother and the boy were only a day's ride from here, you would not have gone to so much trouble to find another companion for me — and you would never have dreamed of proposing such an unfortunate creature as the one you chose. It would have been far easier, and much simpler, to bring Michoel here."

He waited for Ka'hei to respond. When it became evident that the leader of the Platt tribes was in no hurry to speak, Istrak said, "I'm afraid that, in contrast to what I've been told, my brother, Prince Michoel, and the boy —" it was hard to pronounce the words, but he did it anyway — "are no longer among the living. And in that case, leader of the Platt tribes, I rescind everything that was said today."

"A pity," murmured Ka'hei. "Especially since Prince Michoel and your boy are both alive and well."

"Perhaps," Istrak said heavily. "However, since my logic is impeccable and your actions have not been explained, my faith in your promises is gone."

"A pity," Ka'hei said again.

"On the contrary," Istrak said, hands clenched at his sides. "Convince me that I'm wrong."

Ka'hei's jaw worked in a way that Istrak was beginning to recognize. "Have you never heard of the word 'honor,' my boy?"

"I've heard of it."

"In that case —" Ka'hei leaned back on his cushion — "the leader of the nearby tent camp, a very large and important one, is, like many people, enamored of honor. The kind of honor he is accorded by hosting the prince of a neighboring kingdom.

"Despite the unpleasant situation that arose at the death of your brother's companion, I cannot, for reasons I won't go into now, insult that honorable warrior by insisting upon bringing your brother here.

"Do you believe me?" the Kawari asked quietly.

"What you say is logical," Istrak admitted.

"I'm glad to hear it." Ka'hei's smile was as pleasant as ever, but his eyes were serious.

Istrak said nothing. He did not know what to say. Ka'hei, too, was quiet, apparently not at all disturbed by the silence.

"I still don't believe you," Istrak said at last.

"A pity." Ka'hei sighed.

"Yes," said Istrak. "That's true."

"I might," Ka'hei said tentatively, and Istrak was pleased to see that he had been able to bring the confident leader to a state of hesitation, "be able to bring Kalev back here for one day, so that he can tell you himself that you have no cause for worry."

"I'd like that."

"Good." This time, Ka'hei's smile touched his eyes as well. "I will make every effort to find another companion for you — someone more successful. I will have to return Huda to the friend who lent him to me."

"Excellent." Istrak stood up. "Thank you, leader of the Platt tribes."

"You are welcome." Ka'hei stood, too. "And please, call me Ka'hei . After today, there is no need for such formalities."

"Thank you, Ka'hei."

"The pleasure has been all mine. Have a pleasant sleep, young man. As your people are fond of saying, 'Sleep in goodness and wake in compassion.' "

"And the blesser shall be blessed." Istrak smiled. The stone that had been lodged on his heart had rolled off.

"Istrak?" Ka'hei called. Istrak turned back.

"I am honored that you paid me a visit. It would give me much pleasure if you do so again. Good night."

"Good night," said the Khazar prince. Accompanied by the three sentries who had brought him there, he set out into the night.

The next morning was clear and sunny, and the knowledge that he would soon see Kalev again, and would be able to hear from him that Michoel was well, gladdened Istrak and energized him. The birds' twittering filled his heart with song. His morning prayers were long and fervent, and from time to time he ventured to frame the words in a melody and sing them out loud.

He was nearly done when Yidrat walked into his tent.

"How would you like to trap yourself a horse?" the Kawari asked, his voice hoarse with excitement. "There's a herd of them not far from here. We're leaving right now. Come!"

Trap myself a horse?

Istrak mouthed some more words of prayer, but all of his concentration had dissipated. His mind had wandered away, to the Platt plains and wild horses.

Is Ka'hei really prepared to let me use a weapon? This could be my one and only chance to see Kawari combat methods up close!

His murmured prayers continued.

If I trap a horse and tame it — that will open up all sorts of possibilities. Perhaps even escape!

"Are you coming?" asked Yidrat. When there was no answer, he said in annoyance, "We can't wait even a minute, Istrak. If we don't go out now, we won't be able to stick with the herd."

Istrak tried to signal to him.

"I don't understand," Yidrat complained. "Are you coming, or not?"

"Aaaah."

"You're not coming?"

Istrak made a clucking sound.

"You *are* coming?"

"Aaaah."

"Hurry," Yidrat urged. "I'll bring the horses around."

Istrak resumed his prayers, straining to recall the words from memory. He could complete them while riding after the herd; this could undoubtedly be classified as an opportunity not to be missed.

I only hope they don't give me an old, limping nag. If they do that, and the horse drags behind the rest, it will be an embarrassment for all of Khazar. Perhaps it would be better for me not to go?

He shook his head. *Ka'hei has no reason to humiliate Khazar. There's no reason to do that. He is really interested in friendship.*

Hastily, he mumbled words of prayer until Yidrat's voice sounded from outside, calling his name. He unwound his *tefillin* at lightning speed, placed them on the table without rolling up the straps, and left the tent.

"Good!" Yidrat said, already on horseback. "Come on."

Istrak studied the horse he had been given to ride. Even before he had learned to mount a horse, he had been taught that one must not rely on another to tend it. A tiny stone beneath the saddle, or an improperly inserted bit in the horse's mouth, causing pain, could lead to a rampage or even, Heaven forbid, the rider's death.

Had Ka'hei and Yidrat wished him to die, they could have made that happen in any number of other ways. On the other hand, it was best not to deviate from what was correct and proper.

"Come on," Yidrat repeated.

"In a moment." Istrak removed the bit from the horse's mouth.

"What are you doing?"

"Harnessing him myself," Istrak said firmly. "There are things, Yidrat, that one mustn't give up under any circumstances. If you can't wait for me, then go on without me."

Yidrat shrugged. "As you wish, Istrak. But we'll have to gallop like the wind…"

Istrak didn't bother to answer. For long minutes he busied himself adjusting the reins and saddle. Finally, he mounted his horse.

"After you," he said curtly. "At any speed you like."

"That was wonderful!" Istrak slid off his horse's back. "I haven't had an experience like that in a long time. It was…" There was no word in Khazari to express the way he was feeling. In Bulgarian, however — the language in which he and his friendly captors regularly conversed — he found what he was looking for.

"Fun," he said. "It was fun. I enjoyed it!"

"So did we," said Ka'hei, pulling off his thick leather gloves. "Let's hope that we will also succeed in taming the colts we've caught. In any case, the small black colt is yours, Istrak. You've earned him."

Istrak hoped he wasn't blushing. In all honesty, he had thrown his lariat at a different colt. But his lack of experience and control with this sort of weapon had caused the rope to swing wildly in the opposite direction from the one he had intended, winding itself around the black colt's forelegs and toppling it to the ground. Still, an impressive achievement, especially for one who had held the trapping weapon in his hand for the first time that morning.

"Heaven helped me," he murmured.

Yidrat laughed. "Really, Istrak! Why won't you admit that you have some skill?"

"Skill also comes from Heaven," Istrak wanted to say — but did not.

"Will you join us this evening?" Yidrat asked.

"That is not for him," Ka'hei said peremptorily.

"Are you sure?" Yidrat's eyes raced from his father to the Khazar prince and back again while their horses restlessly pawed the ground.

"I have no idea what you're talking about," Istrak said.

"A Greek choir," Ka'hei explained. "A good murder story… But I don't think it's for you."

"If it's not for me," Istrak said, straightening his back, "then it's not for me."

"Exactly." Ka'hei smiled. Then, concerned, he said, "You're a little pale. That is understandable, given the fast that you've imposed on yourself since this morning… You'd better go to your tent now. Would you like to postpone your music lesson?"

"I'm fine," Istrak said, trying to sound cheerful. "Though it wouldn't hurt if you could find someone to cook some food for me…"

Bored, Yidrat turned away to watch the children who were playing in the central square.

"We're working on it," Ka'hei promised. "Messengers have been sent to all the tent camps in the vicinity. And tomorrow afternoon, I hope, you will see your boy."

"With Hashem's help," Istrak said quietly.

Ka'hei inclined his head. "Of course." Impatiently he added, "I'll come see how you are feeling before the performance. Have a pleasant afternoon, Prince of Khazar."

"A pleasant afternoon," Istrak returned politely, taking one step back in the direction of his tent.

The tent was clean and tidy. The befuddled old slave apparently knew his domestic chores, at least. Istrak's *tefillin* were not where he had left them, but a quick search revealed them inside their embroidered bag. Carefully, he removed the *tefillin* and rolled up the straps. He had no doubts about the old man's identity now: only a Jew could know that the *tefillin's* place was in the decorated cloth bag.

He plucked a red apple from the bowl on the table and sprawled on the cushions. The hunt had exhausted him. Even his thoughts were weary.

What would Father say to him if he were here?

Would he, like Istrak, be capable of viewing the leader of the Platt tribes as a person and not a symbol? Once he had come to know them personally, would his father still refuse to accede to their request and allow them to trade with the Khazars? It was certainly not an outrageous demand, especially after twenty years of peace!

Was it possible that even now, with his firstborn son held captive by the Kawaris, his father was still refusing to acquiesce to such a simple request?

An outstanding person like his father, would, like Avraham Avinu, be prepared to sacrifice his son on the altar…

But he — unlike Yitzchak Avinu — was not willing to be sacrificed. He wanted to live.

To live, with everything that implied. To gallop without a destination, to feel the wind in his face and streaming through his hair. To sleep nearly till noon, to chat with a friend, to enjoy a tasty piece of cake, to make music, to laugh, to indulge himself at times.

It would have been far better for him had he not wanted these things — had music been anathema to him and tending horses a waste of time.

The Khazar prince's eyes slowly closed.

How much better it would have been if the Creator had given him a different soul. But since he possessed the soul he had, was there anything wrong in wanting — within the strict confines of halachah, of course — to live the way Ka'hei did?

Was there something unworthy in that?

"As I reported last week, since the kidnaping there have been countless sightings of suspicious figures. We are taking eighty-three of them seriously," said the chief investigator. "Fifty-seven were rejected after a brief inquiry, twenty after being investigated, and five are still a question mark." He paused. "One of them tells of a girl with golden braids who shouted like a man. That sounded promising. The girl's clothes were found in the woods not far from there, but a broader search of the area turned up no further clues. Two platoons of soldiers combed the area, house by house. They found nothing."

"I see," the king said. "Can anything more be done?"

The chief investigator narrowed his eyes in thought. "We might increase the reward for those who cooperate with us. Perhaps a larger sum would persuade one or two of the kidnapers to betray his friends."

"Double the amount," ordered the king. "And announce that the reward will revert to its original sum in twenty days. Any other ideas?"

The chief investigator drew a deep breath. "Your Majesty, I know that I'm overstepping the bounds of my responsibility, but I must repeat what I said earlier. In my opinion, it would be a good idea to pay attention to what is happening on the Kawari side. The place where the girl's clothes were found is no further from that border than it is from our border with Bulgaria."

"We are trying," the king replied curtly.

"If it were up to *me*," the chief investigator pressed on, "I'd send a division of Mundari soldiers across the border. Though they are not trained spies, so many idol-worshiping Mundari wander great expanses of territory that, in my opinion, our men would arouse no suspicion."

The king considered this. "As you said earlier, you are overstepping your bounds. However, I will present your idea to Lord Baniel. Perhaps it is time to expand our investigation. It is time to find out what the Kawaris have been up to lately."

17

Bastian Makan's behavior was that of a guilty man. That was the consensus of everyone who was present at his interview with the king.

Bowed, broken, speaking in meek sentences interspersed with long silences, he did not succeed in convincing anyone of the truth of his assertion that he had delayed attacking the Bulgarians in the belief that they would retreat at the sight of the massed Khazari troops.

Likewise, no one believed his vow that neither he, nor to his knowledge Ribak Bati, a faithful member of his staff, had taken any part in the deeds that had led to his sister's death.

Bastian's reaction to the king's accusation that he had killed Istrak and hidden Michoel, his sister's son, in order to seat him on the throne at some future date was at once the most suspicious and also the most touching. The man did not even try to defend himself. He only sat in his place, his head shaking mutely from side to side. Even Lord Shefer, who before the interview had been convinced of Bastian's innocence, sat afterward with head bent in submission.

But a seedling of doubt sprouted in the king's heart. Bastian was a superb actor. The king knew this, and had even made use of this talent on several occasions in the past. Also, Bastian — like any good military man — always made sure to leave himself an avenue of retreat. Had Bastian Makan been guilty, he would have blustered angrily, hurt and offended. The weakness and apathy he displayed instead, and the absence of any protective cover, did not fit the strong man Reuel had known for so many years. No, it did not fit him at all.

It was shortly after midnight, after hours of stormy inner debate, when the king asked to be taken to Bastian Makan's cell.

The reserved cell, which had been constructed with prisoners of Makan's stature in mind, was furnished with a bed, table, and chair. Nevertheless, when the key turned in the lock and the heavy door swung open, it showed Bastian struggling slowly to his feet from the floor on which he had been sitting.

"Bastian." The king crossed the threshold, overwhelmed with pity. "Where is your strong spirit? If you are not guilty — defend yourself!"

The former minister of war lifted his eyes for a moment, and their redness caused the king to retreat a step.

"I lost my sister," Bastian said hoarsely. "I lost a beloved nephew. I lost my honor and my friend. From where shall I find the strength to fight, King of Khazar?"

"From within your own heart," returned the king. "From your belief in your innocence. From your desire to live and see better days."

Bastian groaned. He glanced up at the king for a fraction of a second, then lowered his eyes again.

"What are you thinking about, Bastian?"

The minister groaned again, and the king hesitantly touched his shoulder. "Speak," he requested. "If you are not guilty, nobody will be happier than I!"

But the minister of war said nothing.

"Think of your wife," the king urged. "Think of your family, of your ancestors, and the desolation that will spread after your death. Think of the pain of all those who have loved and esteemed the illustrious Makan family, and find the strength to defend yourself! If you have anything to tell me — I shall be glad to hear it."

"Thank you," the nobleman whispered. He lifted his head. "Your Majesty —" His voice had grown slightly stronger, and it was obvious that he was trying to take the king's advice. "Is there not a white donkey in your stables, and is it not possible to find a seamstress who could sew the Makan emblem onto the collar of a shirt?"

The king was silent.

"I have said" — Makan's voice increased in strength — "and I say again, that it was not I who instructed the convoy to enter the Batar Ravine. I do not know who was responsible for that, but if the king is seeking my opinion, it would be wise to search for the type of individual who could and would falsify a map." He paused, then spread his hands. "King of Khazar, I can do nothing from this place."

His words were eminently reasonable.

"Who would you choose to head the investigation?" Reuel asked softly.

The minister spent several minutes considering which of his friends were dependable; there were few whom he could trust implicitly. "If the king would be pleased to bring Gad Baliatar here…"

"Thereby granting you at least two more weeks of life," the king said, and there was no cynicism in his voice.

"It would give me hope," Makan admitted, sounding almost like his old self.

The king nodded. To bring Gad here… To have that loyal friend once again at his side. Someone who would listen with all his heart, and be prepared to state his views without endless, polite circumlocutions. The concept was even better than Makan believed it to be. Still, Reuel said, "I must think about it. Who is your second choice?"

Bastian Makan breathed deeply, trying desperately to decide on a second candidate.

Whom should he choose? The minister of protocol, who had, in his youth, set his sights on the Ministry of War?

Lord Shefer, who barely managed to conceal the jealousy he felt over the king's friendship with his brother-in-law?

Lord Kafchaver, who still maintained vigorously, to this day, that the facts that the Makan family had presented to the court — and which had earned them a sizeable portion of Kafchaver land — had been fabricated?

In ordinary times, when they had all sat around one table, these people had managed to suppress their resentment and treat him in a friendly fashion. But Bastian was not at all sure that now, with his guilt so glaring, they would succeed in overcoming their animosities in an impersonal and objective search for the truth.

Whom, then, could he choose?

The king's patience, Bastian sensed, was nearly at an end. He must quickly designate someone else he could trust. His lips were pursed as he prayed without a sound.

Suddenly, the name rose to his mind.

Yosef Diaber! Why hadn't he thought of that before?

Lord Diaber was known throughout Khazar for his monumental *chesed*. Everyone knew he was willing to give up his days and nights in order to help a total stranger. Also, Yosef was, at least officially, the possessor of a prestigious title of his own, which would obviate all jealous and resentment toward himself.

"Yosef Diaber," the minister of war said quietly, looking down at the cell's stone floor.

The trust and empathy that the king had been feeling toward Bastian evaporated in a flash. Was that not the rule? Tell me who your friends are, and I will tell you who you are…

And Yosef, in Reuel's opinion, was capable of perpetuating injustice.

Perhaps Bastian was guilty, after all. Despair, weakness, and a broken heart could also be feigned…

With a wagonload of his wife's cabbages to be sold in the city, Rivka's father came to visit. "How is my grandson?" he boomed from the doorway.

THE BETRAYAL

"Father!" Rivka was surprised to see him. "How nice that you've come… Is everything all right?"

"I asked you first." Tippias walked inside and set a sack of vegetables on the floor.

"He's well, *baruch Hashem*," his daughter was quick to reassure him. "He's a good boy. Please sit, Father, and I'll bring him to you."

"He's still quite small," her father said, taking the baby into his arms.

"Yes," said Rivka. "But Hashem has been good to us. He's been putting on weight."

Tippias studied the child, estimating his weight with an eye experienced in selling produce. "He really has grown," he agreed.

"*Bli ayin hara.* Would you like something to drink, Father?"

He accepted a cup of water mixed with Rivka's cherry wine and praised her on its fine taste. They chatted about the price of cabbages, about Tuval, who had joined the security forces in Khazaran, and about the squeaking hinge on the back door. But Tippias could see that Rivka's thoughts were miles away.

After more of this desultory conversation, he finally asked Rivka what was bothering her.

Hesitantly, Rivka said, "About a week before the princes' convoy set out on its journey, someone ordered a portrait of them from Tuval. In traveling clothes." She fell silent.

Her father knitted his brow. "And what happened?"

"They were kidnaped," Rivka said, her tone despondent. "Maybe that's why the portrait was needed."

"Really! Is that what you think, Rivka?"

She blushed, as though she were a young girl caught with her hand in the cookie jar. "The…the man who ordered the portrait looked like a criminal," she stammered. "And if so many others were killed, but not the princes, they must have known what they looked like."

"That's the first logical thing you've said." Tippias drummed the table with his fingers. "All the rest sounds like complete nonsense. You have a sickly infant, and this is what you're worrying about?"

Insulted, she gathered her faltering courage. "Yes," she said. "This could be a clue to the identity of the kidnapers. It would be a merit for my baby."

"Hm." Her father considered. "The lost vessels of the Beis HaMikdash are in Rome. Can you rescue them from the gentiles? That would also be a merit for your child. I think you heard too many tales of heroes when you were young, Rivka'le. We pray that Yosef will continue to develop nicely, and that we will see much *nachas* from him. It's proper to give *tzedakah* and do *chesed* in his merit. But pursuing foolhardly adventures..." He shook his head.

"I hear you," Rivka said. "I'll try."

"Good!" He restored the baby to his mother's arms and bent to unfasten the bag. "Come see what your mother's sent you."

When Tippias finished selling his cabbages to the vegetable vendors, he did not make his way to shul. Nor did he go home. Instead, he asked one of the local children, playing in the mud, where the nearest Internal Security headquarters was located.

The security people accorded Tippias' story the same kind of reception he had given his daughter that morning. After politely complimenting him for doing his civic duty, they showed him out. He left, feeling like an utter fool.

Calidius Bruchu considered himself a talented fellow, capable of carrying out any task. But when he left the graveyard, the earthenware vessel on his back, he felt for the first time that there was no substitute for a professional.

"You open the cover," Salem explained, perched on one of the headstones. "Like this, yes? Then you grab the end of the tube — like this, yes? — and pull it slowly outward... Very slowly, because if it falls out of your hand, you'll be the first victim, yes?"

"No." Calidius stepped back. "I will not."

"You will," Salem said dryly. "That snake is extremely agitated."

"I meant, I won't break it." Calidius touched the amulet hanging from his neck. Words had power — didn't that fool of a murderer know that?

Salem beamed. "Excellent. You pull the tube very slowly...holding onto its end and keeping it away from your body. Yes?"

"Yes." Calidius nodded, gazing apprehensively at the triangular head sticking out of the vessel.

"Do not be afraid," Salem said. "You mustn't be afraid. The snake cannot move inside the tube. Only its head" — the killer waggled his own dark head to and fro — "and its tongue." He stuck out his own tongue and quickly drew it back. "That's all."

"How long does it take for the poison to take effect?"

"I don't know," Salem chuckled. "But less time than it takes for the doctor to arrive..."

"I understand." The evening wind raised gooseflesh on Calidius' arms.

"Very good." Salem rubbed his hands together. "Afterward, you take the pipe, insert it in the box, like this — holding it tight on the side — close the box and bring back my snake. Yes?"

"Yes."

"If that is not possible," Salem said, "you come here and bring me the same amount of money that you brought me just now."

"All right."

The swarthy man was satisfied. "You learn fast," he complimented. "Here, try it."

A brief practice session reassured both Calidius and Salem.

"Who is it that you wish to kill?" Salem asked curiously as he resealed the box for the third time.

Calidius lied without blinking an eye. "They haven't told me yet. But it's someone important."

"Good luck. You know what they say: All beginnings are hard. It will get easier later."

"And then you stop being afraid?" Calidius asked.

"Oh, you never stop being afraid," Salem answered soberly. "But not necessarily from the same thing you were frightened of in the beginning."

The graveyard was an eerie place at dusk, and the killer's words sent a chill down Calidius' spine. "Meaning?"

Salem sighed. "You, no doubt, are still afraid to die — but that is the worst thing you fear. After one hundred or two hundred times, you will stop being afraid of that. You will see that death can be clean, quick, and easy." He pursed his thick lips. "And then, what you really begin to fear is what will happen to you afterward. At that stage, there's no more hope. G-d will never forgive you." He straightened, wiped his nose with the back of his hand, and said heartily, "But it's better not to think about that too much. That's what the profession's like."

Not many things could fluster Narma, but an epidemic of sneezing, coughing, and bad colds among her household staff, just two days before her nephew Alexander's bar mitzvah almost brought her to the brink of despair.

The event was to be large and impressive. Her brother Dalo's recent advancement meant that there would be double or triple the number of guests who had been present at the previous bar mitzvah four years ago. And *this* was when her servants chose to catch cold!

"Don't blow things out of proportion!" her housekeeper admonished. "All we have to do is hire a few extra servants and ask the butcher to cut up the side of meat for us. There's no reason for such low spirits, Mistress Narma!"

Doubtfully, Narma nodded. Hire extra servants; ask the butcher for his help; find a different tailor, as proficient as the first, to alter the bar mitzvah boy's suit; and make certain that none of the hurriedly hired servants made off with the silver spoons. Pray that the cooks so hastily borrowed from the kitchens of Leah Diaber and Miriam Kafchaver would agree to obey the instructions of a chief chef shaking with fever and chills — the only one of her servants who had left his bed that morning and taken his place by the stove…

And, in the midst of all this, to comfort her 11-year-old niece Shifra, who was deeply regretting her decision to have her dress made of dark-green cloth, which made her look sallow; to soothe Dalo, who felt for some reason that his honor and stature depended on the magnificence of the bar mitzvah *seudah* — and the envy it would arouse in their guests; to make sure that the elderly woman baker who had been hired to prepare the braided loaves did not forget to separate *challah*; to receive Moshe, the Kawari convert, and discuss the music to be played; to listen to her nephew's speech for the umpteenth time; and to personally ensure that His Majesty her *chasan*'s seat was prepared as befit him.

She brightened. The young nobleman, Calidius Bruchu, whom Dalo had sent her, along with letters of recommendation from another lord, a friend of Dalo's, was bright, efficient, and quick. If only she had ten more like him, she might feel a little calmer.

Calidius did not know why he had succumbed to the financial inducements of the king's betrothed and agreed, apart from preparing the dining hall, to also oversee the staff of waiters who would serve Stazdiran's guests. Had it stemmed from a desire to be present at one of the most important events to take place in the history of Khazar? Or was it something else… The same drive that impels a thief to return to the scene of the crime?

Either way, without troubling to analyze his motives, Calidius moved to and fro across the big hall, making sure that every one of the numerous guests would receive perfect service and striving not to cast even a single glance at the still vacant chair of His Majesty the king.

He needn't worry. There was no reason to worry. No one would notice when he attached the tube onto the bottom of the king's chair. No one would notice it until it was too late. And maybe, if luck was with him, no one would notice it even after the uproar began.

The king arrived shortly after the first course was served. Once the excitement always attendant on his entrance had died down, Calidius began to listen expectantly for a cry of pain. But none was forthcoming..

"More wine," Dalo Stazdiran ordered, appearing suddenly at Calidius' side. "Let them start bringing bottles up from the cellar."

"At once, sir," Calidius replied. For the first time that evening, he ventured a glance at the head table.

With three personal guards and two noblemen standing behind him, the king sat in his special chair, his eyes sad. As Calidius watched, Reuel turned his head to the left, as though about to speak to those standing there.

The wine. He had been ordered to bring up more bottles of wine, and for once Calidius was happy to obey orders. What could be better than to go down into the cellar now, and stay there long enough to avoid showing any kind of reaction that might be noted?

And if he heard the cries he was hoping to hear coming from the floor above, he would pour himself one small glass of fine wine from one of the many bottles stored down below. They would not be used for any other purpose this evening.

That evening, strains of song drifted over to Istrak's tent, along with spoken orations following them. The performance, so Istrak understood, had nothing bad in it except for some prayer that the hero addressed to his father's gods. At its conclusion there was a festive dinner. Voices and laughter filled the air as far as Istrak's lonely quarters.

Inside the tent, his elderly servant was puttering around and making it difficult, if not impossible, for Istrak to learn. He tried to practice the basic notes he had learned that day on the four-stringed lyre, but the melancholy notes were all but swallowed up in the chatter and merriment that reached the tent from outside. He was sick and tired of sitting alone, night after night, listening to people chat with their friends. He missed Asher, missed Pinras, even missed Kalev and Michoel. A lyre could not take the place of a friend.

Kalev should be coming tomorrow, with news of Michoel, but he would quickly be sent on his way again. And then what?

The future stretched ahead of him like a gray cloud.

Kalev appeared early the next morning, energetic and smiling.

"Prince Michoel," he said, kissing Istrak's hand, "asked after you. He is well."

"Excellent." Istrak smiled. "I'm glad to hear that. And how are you?"

"I?" The faintest shadow crossed the boy's round face. "Considering the circumstances, Your Highness, I am very well. Pharaoh tells me that you haven't tasted cooked food in four days... If the prince wishes, I'll hurry and arrange something."

"It's not nice to call him 'Pharaoh.' "

"You're right," Kalev agreed. " 'Haman' suits him better."

"His name is Ka'hei," Istrak said, laughing. "And if you bring me something to eat, I'll bless you to the heavens. I'm famished."

Kalev bowed. "At once." With a furtive glance around him, he whispered, "Has she been in touch with you?"

"Who?" Istrak asked curiously. But Ka'hei chose that moment to stride into the tent, radiating smugness.

"It's Kalev, is it not?" he said. "You suspected me falsely, Prince of Khazar... How will you remedy the insult?"

"With friendship," Istrak replied. "But you must admit, leader of the Platt tribes, that the boy's disappearance was very strange."

"Friendship will indeed be a just compensation," the Kawari leader said. Peering at Kalev, he added, "What did you ask the prince just before I walked in, boy?"

Kalev's lips closed tightly.

"Private matters," Istrak said.

"I didn't mean to pry," Ka'hei apologized warmly, eyes darting suspiciously between the blushing boy and the calm prince. "Kalev, prepare the crown prince a hearty breakfast." To Istrak, he announced, "We found someone. We will arrange a meeting so that you can see if he meets your religious standards." He paused. "Unfortunately, the slave's external appearance is unsuited to the service of one as honorable as you."

"I understand," Istrak said, trying to guess what Ka'hei was implying. "It's no matter."

The Kawari leader inclined his head. "I hope you'll think the same after seeing him... But he's the best we could find. Had your father not forced us years ago to free all the Khazari captives, the situation would be completely different..."

"That, I hope, was spoken in jest."

"Certainly," Ka'hei returned, with blatant insincerity. He reached out to touch the lyre. "Ampi says you're very talented," he said, stroking the strings. "I have no musical ability — though I am able to play a few songs. One of them is a Khazari tune. Would you like to hear it?"

"Of course," said Istrak.

Ka'hei ran his fingers lightly along the strings and softly began to sing: *"Baruch atah Hashem Elokeinu melech ha'olam hazan es ha'olam kulo b'tuvo b'chein b'chesed u'verachamim..."*

He sang well, and his accent was perfect. A shiver ran down Istrak's spine. "Stop! That's not a song, Ka'hei. It's a prayer."

"A prayer," Ka'hei repeated, and there was suddenly a threatening note in his voice.

"Yes," Istrak insisted, wondering at the sudden change in the headman's manner. "A prayer that we recite after eating."

The fingers of Ka'hei's hands curled until they were tightly clenched. "How soon after eating?" he demanded.

At a loss, Istrak shrugged. Ka'hei was furious, that much was evident — but what was the cause of his anger? Istrak hadn't a clue.

"It's not important," Ka'hei said, with an effort resuming his ordinary speaking voice. "Do you wish to come with us tomorrow to see how the colts we captured are faring?"

Some time later, Kalev returned with a tray in his arms and an unreadable expression in his eyes.

"There are cooked vegetables, Your Highness," he said, "and grilled fish — and, for dessert, a sweet, delicious dairy pudding."

"Thank you for your trouble, Kalev," Istrak said. "The food looks wonderful."

"A blessing on your innards." Kalev took his own plate from the tray.

"And may the blesser be doubly blessed!" Istrak replied, taking a large spoonful of the vegetables.

"It's strange," Kalev said a moment later, his mouth full, "that they'll let us use knives. If I were them..."

"What could we do with knives?" Istrak asked. "*Katla d'natri* (kill the guards)?"

It took a minute for Kalev to translate the Aramaic words. He almost choked on his food. "That's not a bad idea, Your Highness!" He laughed.

"They know we'd never do such a thing," Istrak said. "They're counting on the Khazari's love for his fellow man and the good *middos* with which our nation has been blessed." He cut a slice of fish. "Hatred, like acid, corrodes the vessel that contains it. Don't let it take hold of you, Kalev."

Kalev said nothing, and the meal continued in silence. It was only when the boy was collecting the plates that he spoke again. "They want me to leave at sunrise tomorrow, Your Highness."

Istrak's face hardened. "A pity." He thumped a pair of cushions and invited Kalev to sit beside him. "I haven't heard a thing from you yet about the days we were separated. How is Michoel?"

"All right. He's very weak, because he hadn't eaten any cooked food for a long time, and he was also not sleeping properly. But the Kawaris treat him with great respect. Almost too much respect, I'd say."

"I'm glad to hear it. When you see him again, please give him my love." To his surprise, Istrak realized that nothing remained of all the hard feeling he had harbored toward his brother before they entered the Batar Ravine.

"I will," Kalev promised. "It's a terrible pity they won't agree to let us be together in one place."

Istrak passed a hand over his eyes, like one waking from a dream. "Who is the person that Ka'hei found?"

"He's a Mundari," Kalev told him, brightening. "A serious young man. He'll have no trouble with the halachos; he knows them better than I do! But..."

"But?"

"He limps," Kalev said. "And one of his arms barely moves. He looks like a walking skeleton."

"An encouraging description," Istrak said dryly.

Kalev chuckled. "He also looks like a good person. The impression

I got was that he manages very well despite his handicaps."

"I see." If he thought it would do any good, he might have suggested that Ka'hei send his "find" to serve Michoel instead. Perhaps he would try, at any rate, to find some way to assuage the other tent camp leader's craving for honor and allow a reunion between himself and his brother...

The sentries, bearing in mind Ka'hei's open invitation, did not try to prevent the young prince from having his way. Glad of a break in the monotonous routine of guarding the prince's tent, they accompanied him to see Ka'hei.

In the light of day, the tent complex was more impressive than it was by night. Istrak gazed in wonder at the painstaking attention to the smallest detail so characteristic of the Kawaris.

Suddenly, he froze. A woman was seated in the entrance of one of the tents used by Ka'hei's wives. She looked familiar…Tur?

The guards stopped short when Istrak stopped. The prince had turned white as a sheet. In a moment he was falling…

In Danger

A SERIES OF SHORT, RHYTHMIC, AND PAINFUL SLAPS ON HIS cheeks, accompanied by the sound of his name, roused Istrak.

"Enough," he mumbled. "Don't shout."

"Open your eyes." Squinting in the sunlight, Istrak saw the blurred outlines of Ka'hei's face hovering above him. Ka'hei asked anxiously, "Are you hurt?"

"No," Istrak said, slowly sitting up. "What happened?"

"That's a good question," Ka'hei said, supporting him. "What *did* happen to you? Why did you faint?"

"I don't know," Istrak said, despising the weakness that still held him pinned to the ground. "I was standing here, looking at the banners hanging among your tents, and then…" He strained to think. "And then I felt you slapping me, and I opened my eyes."

"You fainted. You woke up for a few seconds and then fainted again. It happened twice."

With a feeling of disgust, Istrak felt his damp clothes. "Apart from the fact that I'm soaked, I feel fine."

"I am happy to hear that," Ka'hei said. "You're still pale. I sent someone for the doctor, but it will be a few minutes. You'd better come into my tent and rest. You frightened us very much."

For some reason, Istrak felt contrary. As he rose to his feet in a wobbly fashion, he asked, "Why were you so frightened?"

"Why?" Ka'hei's green eyes grew large. "We're friends, Istrak! If I were to fall unconscious onto the ground, wouldn't you be alarmed?"

But Istrak couldn't answer. Incomprehensively his knees had buckled again, and he was forced to lean on Ka'hei's arm for support.

The doctor arrived a moment or two after Ka'hei helped the Khazar prince wrap himself in a thick fur blanket. He peered into Istrak's eyes, placed his ear to his chest, thumped his ribs, and checked the color of his tongue. "Did something startle you, Prince?"

"I don't think so."

"There is no other reason for your fainting," the doctor said, rising. "If it happens again, we will do a more thorough examination."

"When I was younger," Ka'hei said, "I once fainted from sheer excitement… It was after I succeeded in hunting down a white bear. Have you heard the tales they tell about the land of the white bears, Istrak? It's far, far from here. I had to travel there to bring my mother the spleen of such a bear, so that she would recover from her illness." A thin, delicate film shadowed his eyes. Istrak lowered his own. When his mother became ill, he had been a young child — not much more than a baby.

The doctor, too, was silent. He had never figured out which foolish medical man had believed that the spleen of a white bear would help the poor woman. Sometimes, when a skeptical spirit seized him, he thought that Ka'hei had made up the story to justify the doubtful adventure on which he had embarked while his mother lay dying.

"The land of the white bears is far away from here," Ka'hei continued, "and the people who live there are very odd…" The words came slowly, as though it took an effort to find their way up from the wells of memory. The tale he told was long and interesting, and Istrak — who had begun listening out of mere politeness — was soon mesmerized.

The rays of the setting sun, slanting into the tent with a reddish hue, roused him. "I must say my afternoon prayers," he said. "I'd better return to my tent and change my clothes first."

Kalev was overjoyed to see him. "Your Highness!" he exclaimed with visible relief. "You were away so long!"

With a pang, Istrak remembered his purpose in leaving his tent.

"I fainted," he said, and quickly recounted what had happened. "Ka'hei sent for the doctor, and then he started telling stories..." He paused, remembering. "He's an excellent storyteller! Did you know, Kalev, that in the north there are people who name their dogs after their parents and look upon it as an honor to a deceased mother or father? The world is so varied and so fascinating... Where is my other set of clothes, Kalev?"

"Knaz," Kalev called. "Bring the prince his other garments."

A tall, dark figure appeared at the far end of the tent.

"This is Knaz," Kalev said at Istrak's questioning look. "He is a Mundari who lives in Khazar. He was taken prisoner a short time ago."

"It pains me to meet you under such circumstances," Istrak said warmly.

The Mundari lifted his clear eyes. "I, too," he said, "am sad to meet the prince of Khazar in this way — were the princes of Khazar always so idle and so enamored of folktales?"

Stunned, Istrak lost his tongue. "Never," he said finally.

"Well, no matter," the Mundari said. "There is always a first time."

Lord Yosef Diaber chose to meet with the king's children in Binyamin and Lissia's room. Seated on a large box used to store playthings, clasping one knee with both hands, Diaber did not look as frightening as Unmar imagined him. On the contrary, she thought he appeared the picture of a good-hearted, friendly uncle.

"Princess Unmar, my dear," Diaber said in a soft that oozed compassion. "Come, sit with us."

The great doors swung on their hinges. "Princess Tur!" a servant announced.

In deference to the king's oldest daughter, Diaber stood up and bowed his head. The room was quiet except for the rustle of dresses as Tur and her attendants were seated.

"As I already explained to Yekavel and Binyamin," Lord Diaber began, "I thought it would be a good idea for us to meet here all together, to make sure we grasp the situation." He paused. "Did you all understand what happened yesterday?"

"Someone wanted to kill Father," Lissia said. She frowned. "I'm going to hit him."

"You mustn't hit," Yekavel scolded, tugging at Lissia's hair.

"Hashem did us a big *chesed* by not letting that wicked man succeed in his plot," Lord Diaber said patiently.

Unmar was watching her sister. Tur's eyebrows lifted and her lips grew tight at Diaber's words.

"Look," said Lord Diaber. "In the merit of Lord Tobias, who acted so quickly, most of the poison was sucked out, and the harm to your father — long may he live — was not fatal."

"What does 'fatal' mean?" Lissia asked.

Diaber sighed. "The snake that placed its fangs into your father's leg," he explained, "was very dangerous. Its poison, which was strong enough to kill, paralyzed all of your father's muscles. It's possible that he can hear, and that he understands what we say, but he can't show us if he does. There are people who recover from such a thing. The royal physician says so."

"Many people?" Yekavel asked.

"Not many," Diaber conceded in a muted voice. "That little snake was very poisonous. But we will pray with all our hearts, and Hashem will send a *refuah sheleimah* to the king of Khazar…" He turned his head as the shadow of a bird flitted past the window. "In the meantime, my dears, if you have any question, problem, or misfortune, you can turn to me. During such a difficult time, part of my responsibilities as the newly reappointed regent is to look out for you."

"Will Father get better?" Unmar asked.

"*HaKadosh Baruch Hu* is great, Unmar." Diaber spread his arms as he spoke, as though to symbolize the Creator's greatness. Unmar rested her chin on her fist, clutching the big doll from which she would not be parted for a moment.

"We will all pray," the nobleman concluded. "Does anyone have any questions?"

"I do," said Tur. Her voice was clear and hard. The others turned to her in surprise.

"Yes, Princess?" Diaber sounded surprised as well. "I'm listening."

"Was it really necessary, as early as yesterday, to move my father's chair to the other side of the government table?"

Lord Diaber wondered how the girl had learned this fact. He felt like a person crossing an open field, conscious of hidden archers crouching in wait to defend it.

"Princess, according to the law, government meetings are conducted by the man sitting at the table's head. In our country's present state of war, the government ministers must meet every day… However, I believe that such matters are best clarified in a different, more mature forum."

Tur said nothing. Apprehensively, Unmar stroked her sister's hand. Tur had been acting very strangely since she had heard about their father's injury. The strangest thing of all was that she had not shed a single tear.

"Are there other questions?"

Silence.

"In that case" — Lord Diaber stood up — "I will leave you now. Let's meet again after Ma'ariv and eat the evening meal together."

"We prefer to eat alone," Tur said stiffly.

Diaber filled his lungs with air. "I can request that your meal be served to you in your room, if that is what you prefer, Princess." Belatedly recognizing that her words might be taken as a declaration of war, he added in a gentler tone, "Though I believe that your father, long may he live, would be happy knowing that his family remained united during his illness."

"I agree, Tur," Yekavel said in a low voice.

"Me, too," added Binyamin, who always tended to think exactly as Yekavel did.

"Unmar?"

For a moment, Unmar looked at Diaber, that pleasant gentleman whom her father did not like at all. She looked at Yekavel, standing close to him, and then at the hem of Tur's dress.

"I am just a little girl," she whispered finally. "I don't know what to think."

"And how is your new slave?" asked Ka'hei, as he, Yidrat, and Istrak stood watching the horse trainers attempt to tame the wild horses they had captured.

"He's all right," Istrak said, gazing at his colt. "Hard as a rock on the outside, but his heart's in the right place."

"I told him," Ka'hei said, "that from this day forward, his life has only one purpose: to care for you."

Istrak did not care for the sound of that. "He's doing that."

"Very good."

They continued to watch the horse trainers. Istrak thought they were making some progress, though he couldn't be certain. He had never seen wild horses being tamed before.

Ka'hei spoke again. "Tonight, if the gods will it, we will be enjoying another musical evening. Thirty instruments, and an excellent choir that comes to us once a year. I'm sure you'll enjoy it."

Yidrat, who was sucking a sliver of sugar, chuckled.

"What's so amusing?" Istrak asked.

"Life," said Yidrat. His teeth, as white and perfect as his father's, ground the sugar into tiny particles. "Is this kosher?" He dug in his pocket, extracted several additional slivers of sugar, and handed one to Istrak. "Want one?"

"No." Istrak looked away. A strange thought troubled him, and it had nothing to do with his longing for something sweet. What did his teeth look like? Never before had he given much thought to the question, and the coppery mirrors lent a red-gold hue to everything anyway.

That evening, shortly before it was time to leave for the concert, he decided to ask the Mundari's opinion.

"What color are my teeth?"

Knaz looked at him in surprise. "They're all right," he said. "The tooth near the hole is black. It must have been hit at the same time."

Istrak's tongue went to the gaping hole. "They broke a chair over my head."

"It's a miracle it didn't really hurt you."

Istrak's brow furrowed. "What do you mean, Knaz?"

"For some people, a blow like that could have been a trauma that lasted all their life. Such cruelty, such unwarranted violence, such a lust for blood… You were there. You know."

Something in his voice roused Istrak's suspicions. "And why do you believe that it *hasn't* harmed me?"

The Mundari shrugged. "I have eyes. If someone were to break a chair over *my* head, I would not attend his music festival — ever. And you, no doubt, experienced even worse."

"The soldiers who took me were given orders not to harm me," Istrak said, shaking his head to dispel the memories that rose up from time to time. "They disobeyed them."

The Mundari sighed, biting off a length of thread and trying to insert it into the eye of the needle he held in his other hand.

"Do you need help?" Istrak asked.

"No. You are the Prince of Khazar, Your Highness."

Istrak fell silent, watching the slave struggle to thread the needle. There was a faint cynicism in his voice as he murmured, "So you do know that."

At long last, the thread was through the needle's eye. Carefully, the Mundari pulled it through. "I am distressed," he said, "if I have behaved in a way that has given any other impression."

"You are not distressed," Istrak said sternly.

Knaz lifted his eyes, and once again they held a strange fire. "True," he said quietly.

The man's conduct infuriated Istrak. "Kalev said that you know halachos better than he does. But a Khazar would never behave as you do."

The Mundari gazed studiously at the sock he was darning.

"Answer me when I speak to you," Istrak ordered.

Knaz licked his dry lips. "I am a Mundari," he said. "My forefathers accepted the yoke of Moshe's Torah, and no more. We accept the dominion of the Khazar kings of our own free will. If, one day, we were to decide that we'd had enough of them and their rule, we would get up and move to the other side of the border."

Understanding flashed through Istrak's mind. "Is that how you came here?"

"In simple fact," the Mundari replied, a hint of an odd smile in his eyes, "that's exactly what I did."

"Do you feel no gratitude at all?"

The Mundari's gaze grew remote. "It all depends on how you define 'gratitude.' Personally, I appreciate the cynical use that some people make of the word."

Strange words. But the Mundari's behavior, in general, was stable enough to preclude any suspicion that he might be insane.

"I'm sure things were just perfect across the border," Istrak said sarcastically.

"To tell the truth — no," Knaz admitted. "They weren't."

Istrak waited for the Mundari to explain, but he would say no more. Frustrated, Istrak clapped the copper diadem onto his forehead and left the tent without a word in farewell.

The concert was spectacular. It was even better than the first musical evening he had enjoyed with the Kawaris. Perhaps it was the music, more rhythmic this time, or the fact that he used his sense of sight as well as the one of sound, to take it in. He watched how the musicians' fingers raced over the strings. He saw how they obeyed the conductor's graceful movements, and watched the light play on the silver and copper that adorned the instruments. It was so beautiful, so harmonious, that Istrak felt light as a feather. His troubles, endless as they were, shrank until they nearly disappeared.

On returning to his tent, he was surprised to see the small oil lamp still burning. The table had been tastefully set, and the Mundari was still awake.

"It was nice of you to wait up for me," Istrak said, filled with contentment. "You didn't have to do that."

The slave's expression was cool. "I would be fooling you, Your Highness," he said, "if I did not tell you that I just woke up a moment ago."

"That's good, too." The music had improved Istrak's mood and erased the memory of the unpleasant conversation he had had with Knaz at the start of the evening. "You did so just in time."

"I woke up for *Tikkun Chatzos*," the Mundari clarified.

"Fine," said Istrak. "I understand." He glanced at the tray of vegetables. "I have not met many people who've tried so hard to make me angry at them, Knaz."

"If you like me," the Mundari said stonily, "Ka'hei will send me to Prince Michoel, too."

The words hit Istrak with the force of a blow. "That's not why he did it!" he protested. "Michoel is young and stubborn, and Ka'hei could not persuade..." As he spoke to the young man standing before him, his own words sounded forced and artificial. There was some truth in what the Mundari had said. When he had been furious with Kalev, when he had hated him, when he had been willing to see the boy degraded and hurt, they had been together many hours in the day. It was only after he had realized his error and begun to feel affection for the quiet, patient lad that their hours together had been shortened. Kalev had been given sundry jobs away from the tent, and when he did return for a brief interval, Ka'hei had usually found some way to keep Istrak busy outside...

Istrak's head began to ache. Maybe it was the lateness of the hour, or the smoke from the burning tapers that had filled the music tent. Or maybe — just maybe — it was because of Knaz's insight. Istrak was angry, too; uncharacteristically, he found himself unable to control his anger. It was as though seventeen years of strict upbringing had vanished in an instant.

"You like him," the Mundari said softly, as though he understood something the prince had not yet plumbed.

"What are you talking about?" Istrak snapped.

Knaz was clearly upset. Istrak pressed on. "I asked you to tell me just what you're talking about?"

"You like the leader with the green eyes. You even admire him. It is not pleasant for you to hear that his true image is different from the one he's taken so much trouble to create."

"I do like Ka'hei," Istrak admitted, measuring his words. "I admire him. And I believe that the Khazaris have a great deal to learn from the Kawaris, both in terms of management and culture."

Knaz spat on the ground. "For *you*?" There was a bottomless sorrow in the Mundari's voice. "For you I lost the use of my left arm?"

In shock, Istrak stared at the wet stain on the ground near his foot. He dragged his eyes to the Mundari, whose face was twisted in scorn and anguish. It took him another moment to find his tongue. But Knaz had already retreated to his cot at the far end of the tent. The Mundari sat down with his head on his knees and sadly recited the first verses of *"Al Naharos Bavel"* as he began *Tikkun Chatzos*.

Lord Yosef Diaber was born to lead. Everyone always said so, even when he was just a youth. Now, as he stepped into the highest position in the land, he had a chance to prove, both to himself and to all those who had said it, just how correct they had been.

No one but he could have convinced the body of government ministers that Khazar must appease Bulgaria, even at the price of submission. But he had succeeded — without even a shadow of an argument around the table.

"Recent events have undermined the nation's spirit," he had told them. "The citizens' trust in their leaders has been damaged. Word of the attempted assassination of the king in the prime minister's home has stolen the people's national pride, and Makan's perfidy has stolen their faith in the strength of the military. We cannot win a war that way."

They said nothing, because they knew he was right.

"Better that we come to terms with them and bring our soldiers home without further casualties. This was also the wish of the king, may Hashem extend his days," Diaber added softly. "Once we have brought our young men home, we will seek ways to restore trust, tranquility, and hope to this country."

Lord Kafchaver spoke up. "You are correct. Khazar has no heart for an unnecessary war. We need no additional territory. We should only — and I will not abandon this topic until the day comes when you all understand how right I am — devote enough resources to develop the land that we do have... We also have no need of honor. Khazar is respected and possesses enough strength to serve as a deterrent for our neighbors."

Diaber gave a series of tiny nods, well satisfied. Last night, after an oppressive meal with the king's children, he had ridden over to Kafchaver's house and spoken to him on this subject, promising to implement a land-development program as soon as Khazar had recovered from the war. As anticipated, this had brought the minister of agriculture around to his way of thinking.

Who was left?

Not many.

There was Bastian Makan's second-in-command, who was now serving as minister of war — an injured officer who had been the recipient of a great deal of support, physical, financial, and moral, from Diaber's *chesed* organization as he recovered from his war wound.

Lord Elranan Shefer, who was so anxious about the king's condition that he could not think logically or offer independent opinions.

The minister of protocol, whose offspring had married into the Diaber family and with whom he had been on excellent terms for years.

So, who else?

No one.

Lord Yosef Diaber was born to lead, and he knew how to do it. He knew how to prepare a cure before the ailment struck, how to win friends, and how to explain — without saying it in so many words or using threats, Heaven forbid — that it would be best for all those seated around the big table to raise their hands in favor of the decision to retreat.

The decision was unanimous — something that, in the king's day had been very rare, indeed.

Responsibility, Unmar's father had told her not long ago, is the heaviest burden that a person can bear. And Father, as always, was right.

When the doctor, moved by the girl's solemn, pleading gaze, had allowed her to approach her father's bed, she wanted to tell him so — but the responsibility he had spoken of obligated her to keep quiet.

Could she really escape? Had the time of which her father had spoken now come?

All through dinner she had thought about it, responding absently to Lord Diaber's friendly questions. By the meal's end, she had worked it all out. Tur, instead of Mother, could say *Shema* with Lissia, Binyamin could play with his nurse's children, and Yekavel — who was already a big boy — was not interested in her anyway. After that, things became simple. She would take her village girl's costume from last Purim, and her doll, and leave the palace through one of the escape tunnels.

When she reached the city, she would go to the home of that girl, Dina Ben Batal. Father had told her that the Ben Batal family were good people, and Dina was a well-brought-up girl. Unmar decided that she would give Dina her necklace if she agreed to hide her in her home.

And if she didn't agree?

If not, she would try to find a way to reach Uncle Gad. Uncle Gad would watch over her and her doll. And that, after all, was what her father wanted.

Escaping from the palace was easy. Navigating the city was much, much harder.

The city was big. Very big. It had so many houses, and streets, and people. So many tall people, all in a hurry, all busy, some carrying sacks of vegetables on their shoulders, or leading sheep, or hauling long planks of lumber. People saw her but noticed nothing out of the ordinary. They didn't even see that she was on the brink of tears, which she was holding back only with the most determined effort. Instead, they told her, "Move out of the way!" or "Go find your mother, child. You're being a nuisance." One person even made a shooing motion, just as if she were a cat!

Only much later, when the morning stopped being sunny and pleasant, and day began to feel hot and sticky and her feet were unbearably sore, did women begin to emerge from their homes.

"Excuse me?" Gathering her courage, Unmar approached a young mother. "Where is Lion's Square?"

"I don't know," the young woman said, and crossed the street.

"Excuse me?" Unmar asked an old woman carrying a basket in either hand. "Where can I find Lion's Square?"

"I'm not from here," the woman said with a smile. "Better ask someone else."

"Excuse me," Unmar tried again, addressing a girl in her teens leading a big brown cow by a rope. "Where is Lion's Square?"

"I can't hear you," the girl said. "Please move out of the way!"

"Where is Lion's Square?" Unmar asked again in a shout, running after the girl and nearly crashing into an oil-filled barrel.

"Turn right, and then go straight to the end of the street," said the oil merchant.

Right?

Unmar stood uncertainly in the midst of the noise and bustle. Was her right hand the one with the freckle, or the other one?

"There," the man pointed, noting her confusion.

"Thank you," she mumbled. At that moment, a big, burly boy passed by, grabbed one of the doll's curls, and yanked.

Unmar held on with all her might. "She's mine!" she cried, pale and shaking.

"Leave her alone," the oil merchant told the boy.

"Aw, she probably stole it. It's okay to steal from a robber!"

"Take your cleverness somewhere else," growled the merchant. With a rude laugh, the boy ran off.

Unmar made her escape, leaping awkwardly over a sewage ditch at the side of the pavement, and dirtying her pretty white shoes with the remnants of old vegetables strewn in a layer on the floor of the marketplace.

On reaching the end of the street, she paused, breathing hard, and looked around her. It was a square — but there was nothing at all to suggest lions.

The doll was heavy in her arms, and her head hurt. She was tired and wanted to sleep. But in order to do that, she must find the house with all the rosebushes in the Lion's Square, and hope that Dina Ben Batal agreed to let her stay.

A huge woman — the largest woman Unmar had ever seen — came out of one of the houses. "Are you looking for something, little girl?" she asked as she vigorously swept away the leaves that had fallen on her doorstep.

"Yes," Unmar said tiredly. "Lion's Square."

"That's right here." The woman used her broom to push the leaves into the public domain.

Unmar looked at her doubtfully. "But there are no lions," she ventured.

The woman smiled. "Once, there were."

Unmar was silent, digesting this information. "If this is Lion's Square," she said at last, "where does Dina Ben Batal live?"

"They moved away from here, dear," the woman said. "After the king — may Hashem send him a speedy recovery! — gave them money, they moved somewhere near Itil."

"How can I get there?"

"I have no idea." The woman seemed amused. She added, "You look thirsty, child. Come in and drink something, and then you can go back home."

Go home…

The woman's house was filled with the good smell of simmering onion soup and fresh-baked cookies. Unmar felt dizzy.

"Are you all right?" the woman asked.

"I th-think so," Unmar whispered, tearing her eyes away from the plate of cookies that were resting on the table.

"You're hungry!" the big woman exclaimed. She studied Unmar's expensive garments with a frankly curious eye. "Sit here, my child, and let this be a merit for my husband at the border."

There was no shame in asking for food if you were hungry. Even Dovid HaMelech did that. And anyway, she hadn't even asked… Hesitantly, she sat on the edge of a chair.

"Just like that," the woman said with approval. She lifted the lid of the soup pot. "Where are you from, dear?"

Around the heavy wooden table that stood in the center of the largest of the rooms allotted to the regent sat five men: Lord Elnatan, the minister of education; Refael, his second-in-command; the minister of protocol's young son and a friend he had recommended — and, of course, Yosef Diaber himself.

"I'm glad that you all managed to find space in your busy calendars to attend this meeting," Lord Diaber said. "Unfortunately, our meeting will not be as long as I had intended, as there are several pressing matters that require my attention this morning. However, I very much hope there will be enough time to formulate some sort of plan." He paused for a moment, allowing them to absorb what he had just said.

The morning, which had dawned over the rooftops of Khazaran-Itil two hours earlier, promised to be an extremely busy one — especially in light of the fact that, on top of his crowded schedule as regent and acting ruler of Khazar, Yosef Diaber had to maintain all the *chesed* operations he ran.

"So!" he continued, smiling around the table at those present. "The reason I summoned you all here today is a matter of national concern. Anyone with any intelligence can fathom how far the nation's spirit will have plunged in the aftermath of recent events. When one goes out into the street, the surmise becomes a sad certainty. A number of friends who live in outlying regions tell me that the situation is even worse there, as the news that reaches those parts is often confused and curtailed. In Nadil, for example, it is believed that Bastian Makan joined forces with the Bulgarians and has marched on Itil with a giant army..." He stopped again, watching the other's reactions: disbelief, disdain, amusement, anger.

He went on. "In light of these reports, and others, there is great alarm in the outlying regions. I've reached the conclusion that we must minimize the damage of such rumors by issuing accurate and up-to-date information."

The two younger men nodded enthusiastically, and the education minister's assistant added his own, more measured agreement. Only Lord Elnatan thought to ask, "How, exactly, are we to do this, Regent?"

"These two young men" — Diaber turning to the pair with one of his charming smiles — "have an idea about that. As we all remember, near the end of the reign of King Brachia, the activity of songsters and jesters was forbidden in Khazar because they were not under proper supervision —"

It was just then, at this critical moment, that the new captain of the palace guard knocked on the door.

"Princess Unmar…" the captain said, and faltered.

"Yes? Princess Unmar?" Diaber prompted impatiently.

"She's…disappeared."

"Disappeared," Diaber repeated, this time to give himself time to think.

"Disappeared," the captain confirmed. "She left a letter."

Lord Diaber's brows rose. "And what does the letter say?"

"That she's gone away for a while," the worried officer said. "And that we are not to look for her."

Yosef Diaber sighed. It seemed easier to manage the entire kingdom than to look after those five spoiled orphans. How was he expected to run things properly if every morning another of the children decided to go out "for a while" in the hope that no one would come looking for her?

"Bring me the letter," he ordered. He turned to the men who had taken time from their busy schedules to meet him today. "We will continue this later. I must attend to this situation."

He stalked out of the room mulling over the punishment he would mete out to the young princess once she was found.

19

THE SOFT RAYS OF SUNLIGHT THAT WOKE ISTRAK FILLED HIM with a righteous desire to rise above himself — to put aside all notions of punishment and revenge and treat the Mundari with mercy.

"Good morning," he said in a friendly tone as he washed his hands.

Knaz did not answer, and Istrak's goodwill evaporated as though it had never been. The Mundari would never have had the temerity to behave this way in Khazar, he thought angrily. Did that…that creature…really think that because he, Istrak, was held captive by Ka'hei, he could demean him like this?

His wet hands curled into fists.

The sad truth was — he could. Istrak had no recourse. He could not ask Ka'hei and his people to fight his battles; he could not be one of those who slanders a Jew to non-Jews. He forced himself to relax his muscles, but his hands remained clenched. Though it was a natural reaction, it would be an error — a childish error — to respond with physical violence to his servant's goading. A great deal of water would flow under the bridge before they returned to

Khazar. He could not strike one who is handicapped, and ignoring him seemed pointless. It would be far more mature and intelligent to demonstrate just how great was the gap between them and how inappropriate was Knaz's behavior.

"Is something bothering you, Knaz?" he asked pleasantly.

The Mundari shrugged. "Would it make any difference?"

"I believe it would."

"This will sound terrible," Knaz said, "but it bothers me to see you happy here."

"I'm *not* happy," Istrak wanted to say. He didn't say it. While he wasn't happy in the full sense of the word, in a more limited, daily sense there were things he enjoyed here. The people in this tent camp treated him with great deference. They admired his mastery of so many languages, his ability to speak to and befriend everyone. They had also been excited over his amazing skill at the hunt, refusing to believe that he had trapped the best of the colts by sheer accident. And although the fact that he was a captive troubled him from time to time, he realized that, in the final analysis, he had been no less a captive in his own palace — a prisoner of the customs, laws, and etiquettes that his father seemed to find pleasure in imposing on him.

"Obviously," he said at length, "I'd be happy to return to Khazar."

"Undoubtedly," the Mundari replied. "Especially if, on your return, you'd be able to institute some new practices."

This elicited an unwilling laugh from Istrak. "Who *are* you?" he asked curiously. The man's behavior did not fit the image he had presented until now.

For a long moment, the Mundari was silent. Then he bowed his head. "I am a soldier of His Majesty, your father," he answered quietly.

Istrak was taken aback. "What did you say?" he stammered, and a hot flush rode up his back. If his father received a detailed report of everything that had occurred since Knaz came here...

The Mundari's cheeks appeared more sunken than ever. "I presume that before your convoy set out, you heard the report of a platoon of soldiers that had been sent to escort the Bulgarian crown prince and were ambushed. Everyone was killed, and one soldier went missing."

"And that's you," Istrak said.

Knaz nodded.

"It's not easy, coming face-to-face with death," Istrak said.

"It's even sadder," the Mundari said with a slight bow, "to come face-to-face with life."

"You could have been an excellent government official. I've never met anyone better at saying so much without really saying anything…"

"I prefer the open pasture," Knaz said, "although I doubt if I'll manage to obtain any sort of position with one hand."

Slowly, Istrak filled his lungs with air. "You may find it easier to earn a living after having demonstrated courage in battle on behalf of Khazar."

The Mundari bowed again. "Perhaps."

Still, the memory of the other man's contempt filled Istrak's mind. "If you had two good arms," he said, "I'd force you to apologize."

A thin smile lit the Mundari's face. "If I had two good arms, Your Highness, it's hard for me to believe you'd manage to do it." He hesitated, then bent on one knee. "In truth, sir, you're welcome to try right now."

At a loss, Istrak looked down at the kneeling man. The challenge was open and deliberate, and yet he could not find it within him to knowingly hurt someone who… Who what? His head began to ache. Lately, he had been having headaches more and more frequently. He had never in his life hit anyone in anger. How much more strange and illogical to hurt a person who had been wounded for Khazar's sake, just to force him to apologize…

Istrak turned away. Ignoring the kneeling man, Istrak began to prepare for Shacharis.

His prayers, despite his best efforts, were distracted that morning.

Huddled in the big armchair in the sitting room, clutching the big, wooden doll to her chest, Unmar looked even smaller than she was.

"I don't understand why you did it," Lord Diaber said for the seventh time, pacing back and forth in front of the girl. "Can you explain it to me, Unmar?"

She didn't answer, just as she hadn't answered any of the previous times he'd asked.

"Give me your doll," he ordered.

When she didn't move, he put out his hand and seized the doll by the head.

Unmar's eyes grew large and frightened. "It's mine," she said, holding tight to the doll's wooden legs. "You can't take her."

"You don't deserve this doll," Diaber said sternly, pleased that he had finally made her talk. "When your father gave her to you, he thought you were a smart and mature girl. This is not the way a princess behaves."

"But —" Unmar tightened her grip. Diaber was stronger than she was, and the doll looked pathetic as it dangled by the hair from his fist.

"When you show me that you can behave like a big girl," he said calmly, "you will get the doll back. Until then — I'll keep her for you."

"She's mine!" Unmar tugged. "You have to give her back to me now!"

Diaber gazed at her gloomily. There was something about these children that he had yet to understand. From where did this 8-year-old princess derive her brazen attitude? Had *she* ever had to fight for a piece of bread?

"I will return her to you when you've shown me that you are a big girl," he said again. "And I will be happy to do it this very evening, at dinner — after you apologize, and explain to me why you ran away, and promise to improve your behavior from now on. You may go to your room, Unmar."

The princess stood slowly. Her small legs, clad in delicate white shoes spattered with the dirt of the marketplace, trembled.

"I won't eat anything until you give me back my doll," she said indignantly. "I won't come to dinner, and I won't speak to anyone."

"That would be a mistake," said Diaber. "If you apologize and promise to behave as you ought, you'll get your doll back very quickly."

She didn't answer.

The seamstress carried in a huge armful of dresses, colorful and rustling, and placed them on the low couch. She looked tired. Tur wondered if the woman had been rushed to finish sewing the princess' wedding clothes before the day came when she, Tur, would be forbidden to wear anything new for a whole year…

"Try it on, Tur," Mother Minra urged. Tur had been just 3 years old when she had been placed in Minra's charge, and now, with startling suddenness, here were her wedding and *sheva berachos* dresses, with matching head coverings.

"It's too wide," Minra said, surveying her critically. "And the sleeve is too puffy."

The seamstress, normally quite talkative, merely nodded.

"Do you think we should add additional beads at the bottom?" Minra asked. "It's for the Shabbos *sheva berachos*. It has to be really nice."

Tur lowered her eyes, studying the clusters of beads. In her opinion, any more would be excessive. As it was, the dress looked far too fancy for someone whose father…

She shook her head, pushing the thought away. There was no point thinking this way.

Someone knocked at the door, and then knocked again. A flustered maidservant poked her head through the doorway. "Mother Estelle, Princess Unmar's nurse, wishes to speak to Tur. It's urgent!"

"Let her enter," Mother Minra said, after exchanging a glance with Tur. Estelle, two splotches of color on her cheeks, hurried into the room.

"Unmar has not eaten a thing since yesterday morning!" she said breathlessly. "She says she won't eat until she gets her doll back…" The nurse's voice was hoarse and her eyes were red, obviously she had been weeping. "Nothing I say will move her. Ever since the queen passed away, she's been doing whatever she wants. She just won't listen!"

Tur stared at her, helpless. Such complaints used to reach the queen from time to time, but not her. Never her.

"I'll come right away, Estelle," she said, recovering her wits. "Let me just finish up here."

Unmar's nurse curtseyed and retreated. Minra picked up another dress, this one made of velvet and brocade. Obediently, Tur took it from her.

This dress was also far too wide — as were the third and fourth ones she tried on. Minra said with a hint of accusation, "You're not eating enough! Unmar is not the only one we have to keep an eye on! How will you have the strength to start a new life when your clothes need to be taken in every two months?"

Tur was quiet. What could she say? That she didn't even have the strength right now to lead her old, routine life?

Silently she stood still, allowing the seamstress to do her job. Her lips trembled. Whether or not she had the necessary strength, she must do what she must do.

A few minutes after the seamstress had finished her work and departed with her three helpers, Tur was ready to leave as well. Estelle, and Unmar, were waiting.

The war was almost over, or so her neighbors kept telling her. Rivka just nodded her head and clutched little Yosef more tightly. She would believe it was over — when it was over.

When Tuval came home, she would know that the war was over for her, too.

She had received one letter from him since he had left the city, and that was a long time ago. Many tragedies — not all of them resulting from enemy fire — could happen when a great number of people make their way to a distant location, eating food cooked by strangers and training with weapons intended for killing. When Tuval stepped into the house and boomed out his greeting, when he went out to Ma'ariv at night in a flutter of alarm over all the bad characters who might be lying in wait to harm him — that's when she would know the war was over and life had started again.

Meanwhile, she was alone, and the money that Tuval had left her was nearly gone.

While those around her spoke of historical doings and grew excited over the unexpected political twists that had caused them, she was busy trying to figure out which of her ornaments to sell in order to buy fish in honor of Shabbos.

Someone knocked on the door. She stood up tiredly and went to answer. She set the baby down and he immediately began to wail. An unfamiliar young woman stood there, a large basket over one arm.

"I am from Notzer Chesed," she said.

"I have nothing to give," Rivka said. She knew the organization; Lord Diaber had established it years ago. Its representatives would occasionally come to the inn, where her father emptied the small cash box and counted out silver and copper coins for them.

"We're bringing meals to the families of soldiers who left no means of livelihood behind," the young woman explained. "Khazar has sent those men to war, and Khazar is honored to look after them."

When the woman had left, a pile of foodstuff covered the table. There was also a sum of money — enough to pay someone to chop some wood for her and to clean the chimney.

Rivka sat down at the table and burst into tears. Receiving all this food had made her realize how distressed she had been at the prospect of selling her meager jewelry. She blessed those who contributed to the organization, and blessed, too, Lord Diaber, who stood behind it. May Hashem repay them for their wonderful deeds!

The most beautiful square in Khazaran was the one between Silversmiths Street and the Bakers Market. The square was large, with a capacity for 10,000 people or more. In lieu of that, smaller gatherings tended to go unnoticed. Perhaps that was why the eight pairs of soldiers patrolling the square that afternoon did not, at first, detect an unscheduled gathering that began to take place right under their noses.

By the time they did, the crowd of unfortunates, sickly, and injured had grown into something that was impossible to ignore. The lame, the blind, and the mentally ill… Beggars and amputees… It was frightening to see how many unlucky people lived in the lovely and flourishing city of Khazaran-Itil.

A pleasant wind was gusting through the square, and the flowers that adorned it bowed in the wind, sending their fragrance into the air. The mood of the people was good, and there was a babble of friendly chatter. The soldiers who approached, in pairs, to learn the reason for the gathering, were surprised at the answer they received.

"The regent will be passing here soon, long may he live," an old woman said, holding the hand of her grown, witless son. "We want to be here when he comes."

"Why, Grandmother?" a soldier asked curiously.

"What do you mean, 'why'? To show our support. To tell him that there are people who are praying for him every day. Without him, I would not be walking around today."

"Let him see my little ones," said a woman with four small children, clinging to her hands and her dress. "Let him see that he has made life good for them, even if they have no father."

"To tell him that we're with him!" cried a young farmer with wild-looking hair.

"To show him that we're not ungrateful," his friend explained shyly. "That's all."

A gathering of this size was unlawful, but the people's intentions were so good, and so touching, that the security detail decided to let it happen. A group of mounted police were sent to the area, where they spread out in a watchful circle. The crowd's excitement began to infect them as well.

As the afternoon wore on, the square filled with an enormous throng. Not only the unfortunate, the sickly, and the former criminals who had changed their ways with the help of the support systems that Diaber had set in motion, but a great many ordinary people came as well — Khazars of the lower and middle classes who had heard at second- or third-hand of the wonderful acts of *chesed* perpetrated by the man who stood today at the head of their kingdom. They were all there, poised and expectant, ready to cheer and shout with all their might.

And that is exactly what they did, when a modest carriage rumbled into the square bearing the Diaber crest. The cries of "Long live the regent!" were so loud that they reached even the room where King Reuel II lay unconscious.

Ovadia, hearing it, averted his face in disgust and quickly shut the window. Like his bedridden master, he, too, was a living, breathing dead man. He did not like Yosef Diaber, nor did he trust him even one iota.

In Ovadia's opinion — which he had expressed to the king any number of times — Diaber was the man responsible, directly or indirectly, for everything evil that had taken place in the kingdom in recent months. But the king, though he kept his own distance from the regent, had laughed at these suspicions and waved a dismissive hand.

When the regent and the minister of protocol had finished planning their mutual grandson's *bris*, they turned their attention to more official business: the national mood, the state of the economy, the security situation. Lord Diaber had numerous ideas for improving all these things and was determined to set them in motion at the earliest possible opportunity.

Lord Nazarel listened in silence, from time to time jotting a notation with a stylus on the wax-covered wooden board before him.

"Plans A, B, and D are feasible," said the minister when Diaber had finished speaking. "Apart from the question of finding the money to implement them, I see no reason not to proceed."

Diaber leaned forward. "What problem is there that you did *not* mention?"

"To tax our Torah scholars, you'd have to call a meeting of the steering committee — the council. That's the law, sir."

The regent grimaced. Clearly, the idea did not appeal to him.

"As for the three last sections," the minister continued, "there is no real problem. It's very simple: to sign an order empowering you to negotiate a peace treaty with the Bulgarians, and to confirm Bastian Makan's sentence, you would have to use the royal seal."

"And to do that…?" Diaber sensed trouble.

"To do that, you, along with ten noblemen, would have to go take the seal and ink from the king's work chamber. And," the minister sounded almost gleeful, "because two of those lords must be provincial governors, the earliest the plan can be carried out would be next week."

"We cannot allow the tension on the border to continue another week," Diaber said, shaken. "Do you know how many additional men are likely to leave their wives widowed in a week?"

Lord Nazarel nodded ponderously. "Despite the best intentions of those who came before us, it was impossible for them to foresee every situation that might arise over the course of the generations. Only the Creator can do that."

Lord Diaber did not seem to be listening. "Tell me," he said urgently, breaking into the flow of his *mechutan's* words, "what I would have to do in order to remove one of the provincial governors from his post and replace him with someone from Itil."

The minister's face lit up at this compromise proposal. "If it's only a temporary appointment, as acting governor," he said thoughtfully, "it would be possible to use the small seal in my office…"

"Could we do it immediately?"

"Certainly," said Nazarel, rising. "If you wish. Why don't you have your people summon the scribe?"

He went to the door — which opened as he approached.

"Princess Tur, and her sister, Princess Unmar, request an appointment to speak with the regent," the sentry at the door announced.

Diaber stifled a sigh. The matter of Unmar's doll had not yet been resolved. "Tell them that if Princess Unmar writes me a letter of apology, I will return her doll." He dropped his head to the parchment scrolls spread on the table, feeling the tension in his neck. Dismissing someone from his post — even temporarily — was likely to arouse the ire of any one of the provincial governors. He must be careful. Careful, and clever.

Ah yes! He had the solution! He would appoint Shimon, a

prominent *talmid chacham* studying in the Royal Beis Medrash, who also happened to be the son of the southern province's governor, to take his father's place.

When Lord Nazarel returned with the small seal, they took care of the business with the governor, and Lord Shefer and eight other noblemen were summoned. The lords walked with bowed heads and a heavy tread into the king's outer chamber. The minister of protocol rapped twice on the open door, enabling the regent, followed by the others, to enter.

The seal was not in the top drawer. Nor was it in the three drawers beneath that one. It was not on the open shelves or in the closed cupboard.

"Perhaps it's in the king's bedchamber," Lord Diaber said.

After a brief hesitation, the entire group entered the inner room. They were met with the sorrowful sight of their king lying unmoving and unconscious on his bed. The sharp scent of medicinal herbs filled the room, and the king's labored breathing sounded sad and grotesque. Long moments passed before the noble group was able to begin the task at hand. Their search proved fruitless.

The seal and the ancient ink pad were nowhere to be found.

Abandoning the rules of protocol, they expanded their search. Additional staff were brought in to turn over every room in the palace. Room after room was combed, cupboards were emptied in quick succession, and furniture moved from its place. But not even these intensive efforts brought the royal seal to light.

The minister of protocol was beside himself. "The seal couldn't have just disappeared!" he insisted repeatedly.

"It could have been stolen," Lord Diaber retorted. "And it could have been hidden. The palace, they say, is full of secret places of concealment." He lowered his voice as he said this, and a frown was evident between his eyes. Reuel had not liked him — and, to be perfectly honest, he had not cherished especially warm feelings toward his monarch either. The king had found ways to leach his position of all true impact, leaving him with nothing more than a meaningless title. For more than twenty years, from the time they were youths, Reuel had blocked Diaber's path to any role of real influence over Khazar's citizens. Even now, lying on his sickbed, unconscious, the king had somehow found a way to keep him from wielding any real power.

Where could Reuel have hidden the seal? And of what practical meaning was his position as regent if he could not so much as seal Bastian Makan's verdict?

His fingers gripped the hilt of his sword. Reuel's intent was as transparent as glass. If the seal was not found in the next few days, he would be compelled to call a meeting of every one of Khazar's lords to request their consent and confirmation for the pouring of a new seal in the image of the first. This would afford the perfect opportunity for those who wished him ill to nominate their own candidate for the position of regent.

The thought rattled him. Then intellect dominated emotion. Appointing someone else in his place would necessitate a quorum — three-quarters of the government. The only candidate who might elicit such a show of friendship and loyalty was Meshuel Min-Hagai, whose son, Ruben, was engaged to marry Princess Tur. But Meshuel, as Yosef Diaber well knew, was the last person to agree to accept any position at the price of harming someone else.

Although it would require a great deal more trouble than he had anticipated, his position, he was certain, was secure.

"You can get everything here," Ka'hei said proudly. "From Aristotle's *Poetica* to magical potions." Seeing the look on Istrak's face, he chuckled. "Really, Prince of Khazar!" He gave Istrak's shoulder a friendly thump. "I wouldn't have believed that you'd be afraid of old wives' tales! Those potions don't really work."

"That's reassuring," Istrak said wryly.

"Absolutely," Ka'hei cheerfully agreed.

Ka'hei was taking Istrak on a tour of the big fair that was held near the tent city once a month. This, too, was a new experience for Istrak — the sights, sounds, and smells utterly different from those of the markets in Khazaran-Itil.

They moved on to another stall. "They sell fine instruments here," Ka'hei remarked. "I would be glad to lend you money to buy your own lyre."

Pleasantly surprised, Istrak smiled. He pictured having his own lyre, wood gleaming and strings taut. He imagined himself playing soft lilting melodies and high merry tunes and deep menacing notes without having to be dependent on others' favors.

He envisioned his father's reaction when he returned from captivity, lyre in hand, and his enthusiasm faded. He didn't even have the strength to face the Mundari. What would Knaz have to say about it?

Istrak pondered. He could be one of the few kings to attend weddings and gladden the *chasan* with song... It would be an unforgettable experience. His father would surely soften when he heard that the long hours of practice — apart from the tranquility they induced — also led to practical and worthwhile results.

And the Mundari?

Why should he care what the Mundari thought? Who was this Mundari anyway? A professional soldier who had spent most of his youth running up and down hills! What did he know of protocols and governing? While he, Istrak, was not only the Prince of Khazar and its regent, with all that the position signified, but he had already passed five of the twelve tests the *rav* offered those who desired certification from him! Who was this simple soldier, whose learning doubtless encompassed nothing more than a modicum of *mishnayos* and a bit of halachah, to presume to educate him? It was sheer chutzpah! Istrak's blood boiled and his breathing grew shallow. Resolutely, he tossed his head and galloped after Ka'hei, who had moved ahead, seemingly oblivious to his young guest's brooding.

As he followed Ka'hei from one stall to another, he could not deny that he found the marketplace colorful and interesting. The Platts' approach to economics differed fundamentally from that of the Khazars. These tribes had never heard of market regulation or the complicated laws that legislate against fraud. Nevertheless — or perhaps because of it — the big fair hummed with life.

"Market forces will always outmaneuver outside supervision,"

Ka'hei shouted, trying to make himself heard above the commotion of traders and animals. "There's no need for a black market to develop here, my boy!"

There was some logic in this, Istrak thought. Shlomo HaMelech had long ago written that "stolen waters are sweet." Perhaps, if Khazar eased its supervision over the import of Greek philosophy works, the demand for them would diminish naturally. What need was there to expend so much energy restricting its trade?

As soon as the thought passed through his mind, Istrak felt a twinge of guilt for even thinking it. Immediately he squelched the feeling. He had been brought up to think one way. Here, people thought differently, and maybe that wasn't such a terrible thing. He would learn his lessons privately, he decided. No one, neither Knaz nor Ka'hei, nor even Kalev, need know how much he had learned and absorbed over these past months.

That night, Istrak's sleep was disturbed by a strange dream. He saw Tur sitting in the entrance of one of the tents reserved for Ka'hei's wives, on her face an expression of suffering. When he tried to call out to her, he woke up, heart pounding wildly.

Istrak had never been overly influenced by dreams, but this was something out of the ordinary. It had seemed very real.

The tent was quiet. A light breeze blew through a rip in one of its sides, and a moonbeam shone on his new lyre. Into this idyllic scene floated Tur's tear-stained face...

Dreams are the remnants of daytime thoughts and reflections that have been buried deep in the unconscious. But he had not thought about Tur in at least three days, and he was as certain as the moon was shining that she was safe and sound in their father's palace in Itil.

Why, then, had this strange dream chosen to destroy his peace just now?

A sudden cry sounded in the distance, and a shiver made its way down Istrak's spine. He felt terribly alone. It was a distinctly unpleasant feeling.

20

RUBEN MIN-HAGAI HAD NEVER SEEN HIS FATHER ANGRY, and the fragments of stories he had heard about his father's youthful hotheadedness seemed as remote as the stars to him. There was no other lord in all of Khazar who had such a peaceful and forgiving attitude regarding late tax payments, incomplete remittance of property debts, and the sundry other minor matters that were strewn across his path daily. But the roar that Meshuel emitted now could be construed as nothing but anger. An uncontrollable rage that caused one of his longtime servants to run down to the *beis medrash* on the ground floor and summon the lord's young son.

"What happened, Father?"

"Nothing yet," Meshuel fumed. "But if we don't do something…" His face, already flushed when Ruben entered the room, darkened even further. "He thinks he can do anything he wants in Khazar and that we'll all keep quiet! Is that what he thinks?"

Incomprehension kept Ruben silent. As his father's eldest son, he had been appointed to oversee the estate some years earlier. Nothing out of the ordinary had, to the best of his knowledge, occurred recently to arouse such rage.

"We will *not* be silent! *I* will not be silent!" Meshuel announced forcefully. "And I don't care what price that…that regent exacts from me afterward!"

All at once, the picture became clearer. "What has the regent done?"

His father sank into one of the chairs that dotted the room. "Nothing yet. But he has numerous schemes"

Just as Meshuel Min-Hagai had taken the trouble to plant his own men among Diaber's staff so that they might keep him informed of the regent's plans, so had Diaber, years before, promised Meshuel's scribe a fee for passing on any morsel of information that might interest him. From time to time, Meshuel's scribe sent him missives, for which he was duly paid.

The scribe hoped to add another nice sum to his salary by again betraying his master's trust. Even before all of Meshuel's friends received a letter inviting them to an emergency meeting in his palace at Bagrel, Lord Diaber was aware of the planned meeting.

And it came as a surprise. When plotting his moves and considering the various enemies of whom he must beware, he had not counted Meshuel among their number. Not because Meshuel was any particular friend of his; he had just never considered that Min-Hagai had it in him to oppose him.

Annoyed, Diaber paced his large chamber in the royal palace. He had anticipated that there would be a number of extremists who would object to any change he might try to implement. But never the stolid, unintellectual Meshuel! On the contrary, from what he knew of Meshuel, Diaber believed that he would rejoice in anything that would uplift the people and add color to their lives. The new music he had introduced was a fine example. What had caused Meshuel to change his mind?

Lord Diaber ran a tired hand through his beard. Perhaps Meshuel was more pious than he had given him credit for. Or maybe he wanted to use any justification for seizing the position of regent for himself, or for his son…

Meshuel had many friends who appreciated his generosity and

patience. The approaching nuptials between his fine son, Ruben, and the king's daughter would open a great many doors to him.

Diaber frowned. Meshuel had no idea how hot the fire that he was playing with was. But if he persisted in his stubborn stance, he would very soon find out...

For long hours, Diaber paced his room, trying to piece together the puzzle from the information he had. The picture that emerged in the end was a very serious one. So serious that, on that same day — though he would shortly be leaving the city to attend a nephew's wedding — the regent summoned the minister of the interior for an urgent talk.

Lord Nachliel Pelet was the first guest to arrive at Meshuel's palace in Bagrel. He was welcomed by his host, who was waiting in the doorway.

"What happened?" Lord Pelet asked abruptly, removing his soldier's helmet. "I left my soldiers under the command of a 24-year-old child. I hope this meeting justifies that, Meshuel!"

"I'm afraid it does," Meshuel replied, taking his guest's helmet and traveling cloak. "What do you want to drink?"

"Nothing," said Pelet, striding inside behind his host. "What's wrong, Meshuel? What happened?"

Meshuel sighed. "Nothing — yet. But Diaber..." He lowered his voice. "He has not changed even one iota since we were all youths together."

"So they say," Pelet chuckled. "Still the same displays of generosity to elicit admiration and a boundless superficiality..."

Meshuel nodded. "He wants to have tailors clothe our yeshivah boys in the newest fashions and to dispatch lute-players and singers to the villages. In short, to uproot everything, from the bottom up."

"There will be some," Pelet said thoughtfully, "who won't see anything wrong in that."

Meshuel sank into an armchair. "If they don't understand, we'll have to explain it to them."

Lord Pelet smiled. "What will you explain?"

"I'll let *you* do the explaining. You're usually good at that."

Nachliel Pelet stopped smiling. "Let's say that *I* don't understand, Meshuel," he said quietly. "Perhaps you'll explain it to me?"

Meshuel hesitated. He had been 14 when his teachers had indicated to his father that there would be no point in keeping him glued to the yeshivah bench. Despite his lofty position, his didactic skills were hardly superior to those of the majority of the citizenry.

"I will," he said heavily. "And then we must make the others understand. And if they don't —" he straightened with sudden pride — "then Ruben will explain it to them!"

It was time to send out the invitations. So said her nurse — and the calendar. The royal scribes were waiting for the guest list so they could word the invitations in the manner befitting each invitee. Tur was supposed to have it ready for them by this evening.

Three times she dipped her quill into the ink pot, then let the ink drip uselessly back again. She had never felt so alone in her life.

Her father had always been there, strong and supportive, and her mother, cheerful and interested. And Istrak, headstrong and amusing…

She had never imagined how much she would miss her big brother. Never imagined that he could simply vanish from her life, as though he had been nothing but a dream.

This past Rosh Hashanah Tur had prayed for marriage to a good man, pious and scholarly. She had asked for healthy children. She had never dreamed of all the other things that could slip through her fingers. Life had seemed so uncomplicated then…

Her throat began to ache.

If Unmar had been in her place, she would have known how to cope with all of this. She would have been bursting with energy to honorably fulfill her new roles. Unmar seemed to have inherited all the courage that flowed in the veins of Khazar's princesses. She, Tur, was nothing but a weakling and a coward.

She was so weary. What would happen if she just slipped off to rest a little? Wasn't a young girl, a *kallah*, allowed to be tired sometimes? Did she have to be preparing *all* the time? Couldn't she just forget about guest lists and dresses and everything else, and just have a little bit of peace?

Her fingernail scraped the parchment. She would complete this list as quickly as she could and then go outdoors with Binyamin and Yekavel. Someone had to pay some attention to them. Someone had to provide them with a much-needed sense of warmth, of family…

With a sigh, Tur bent her head and wrote another name.

Someone knocked on the outer door. "Not now!" she called. She had to finish this list!

The knock came again.

"Not *now*!"

The knock sounded a third time.

Tur sighed. Having sent her maidservants away while she worked, she would have to get up and answer the door herself.

On the other side of the door stood Minra, looking nervous. "How are you, Tur?"

"What happened?" Tur asked sharply.

"Nothing. But the regent — that is, Lord Diaber — wants to speak to you."

"With me?" Tur's distaste was blatant.

"Yes. He asked if you can come at once."

Two creases were evident on either side of Tur's nose. "And what happens if I can't? Does he think I do nothing all day?"

"The minister of the interior was with him," Minra said, with obvious reluctance. "Right after that, he asked me to call you."

Tur paled. If the interior minister was involved, this was more serious than a change in the number of wedding guests. It was about Istrak and Michoel. Or…

They say every young bride thinks the world revolves around her and her upcoming wedding. Tur didn't think she belonged in this category, but…could it be…could it possibly be about…Ruben?

Diaber stood up when Tur entered the room. He looked different somehow. Perhaps it was the somber navy-blue cloak he wore, or a certain edginess in his manner.

"I don't know how to begin," he said, his thin face looking suddenly fragile. "I myself am feeling confused and upset... But I felt that the princess must have this new information before we decide on any step."

Tur sat up straight in her chair, hoping that not by the quiver of a muscle was she betraying her inner tension.

"It's like this," Diaber said. He cleared his throat. "That is..." Unhappily, he began again. "I've asked you here because, unfortunately, I see no other choice than to..." He stopped again.

"Lord Meshuel Min-Hagai," he started afresh, talking faster now, "is under suspicion by our interior minister as being involved, up to his neck, in recent events that have taken place in Khazar."

He lifted his downcast eyes to glance at Tur, and then dropped them again. "Internal security," he said, "believes that Meshuel hopes, after his son marries His Majesty the king's daughter, to be able to persuade the lords of Khazar to pass the throne to the king's eldest daughter — to you, Tur — with his son and himself actually running the kingdom."

"But Father admired Meshuel..." She bit her lip. Had she, too, begun to speak of her father in the past tense?

Diaber spread his hands. "Meshuel has already called a meeting of Khazar's lords to work on ousting me. With the wedding so near, it is reasonable to suppose that he will succeed in getting them to appoint him as temporary regent until the festivities are over... Is the princess following me?"

With an effort, Tur nodded.

"If the two princes were here with us, there would be no justifiable reason to request that the throne be passed on to a daughter. However, in the present situation, and adding the fact that Yekavel is too young..." He lowered his voice. "Unfortunately, all men of reason suspect that there has been someone behind these events, Princess Tur."

"Bastian Makan," she said, mustering all her courage.

"That's what we thought," he admitted. "But the evidence is purely circumstantial. The king himself, in discussions with the internal security people, said that any criminal could have sent a messenger disguised as a member of Bastian's staff. And anyone could have sewn the Makan symbol on any sort of garment, Your Highness. Furthermore, it's hard to believe that Bastian would behave in such a way. Ever since —"

Tur lifted her head sharply.

"Ever since the first suspicions arose about the Min-Hagai family, the security people have uncovered some interesting facts." Diaber paused. "Is Your Highness sure she wants to hear all of this now?"

Black spots suddenly filled her field of vision. She shook her head, uttering a feeble, "No. It is quite all right, Lord Diaber. I've heard enough."

Presently, supported by Minra's arm, she left the chamber.

Her legs would scarcely obey her. The walk to her room seemed endless. There was no need to write invitations, no need to try on dresses, no need to muster her strength for a new life. Everything was over even before it had begun.

Seeing the state she was in, Minra led the girl into the nearest room, seeking a chair. It was one of the queen's chambers, now almost completely empty. The only sign of its previous occupant was a single scarf that had, for some reason, been left on the windowsill.

The incoming breeze brought the scarf's fringe's to life. Tur buried her head in its folds and wept like the heartbroken child she was.

Her afternoon rest stretched on and on. Four times, Minra came into the room to see if she could get the princess up and about her daily routine. But, in Tur's mind, there was no longer any point.

The door opened a fifth time. Tur didn't even bother to turn her head.

"Tur?" someone whispered. It was not Minra. Tur sat up, surprised.

"Tur? Can we come in?"

"What are all of you doing here?" she asked, staring at the four heads that peeked into the room. Her voice was rough from not speaking for so many hours.

"We came to see how you're feeling," Yekavel said. "Are you ill?"

"Not exactly." She passed a sleeve across her eyes, which were dry and red. "I'm just sad."

"I love you," Lissia announced, climbing onto the bed.

"Me, too," Binyamin said.

"What happened?" Unmar wanted to know.

Tur could hardly bear to think about the things the regent had said. To repeat them was impossible.

"When you're feeling sad, it's a good idea to jump on the bed," Binyamin suggested. "Whenever I do, it helps." Tur's smile affronted him. "It really *does* help!" he insisted. "Why are you laughing?"

"Try," Unmar urged. "Show her how, Lissia."

The 3-year-old girl jumped vigorously, shaking the bed.

"What it does is shake up the sadness until it's all mixed up," Yekavel offered seriously. "And then it can't remember where it was before…"

They were determined to help her. Tur found herself jumping on the bed with her brothers and sisters, her hair in a braid and tears in her eyes.

Would it be so bad to go on living this way, with her four younger siblings, whom she could raise with love? It was true that this was not what she had dreamed of. But who had ever said that only the realization of one's dreams could bring happiness?

Her father had certainly never thought so.

Little Lissia leaped into the air, her face red with exertion. Unmar gave up and sat down, but Binyamin and Tur kept jumping, battling the sadness that refused to get mixed up.

Finally, Tur surrendered to her breathlessness. Binyamin sank down beside her, eyes shining. "Will you come to the corral with us tomorrow?" he asked. "I'll show you my pony."

"Your pony?"

Six-year-old Binyamin was too young to own such an animal. Yekavel, Michoel, and Istrak had not received ponies of their own until they were 8.

"The regent gave it to me as a present," the boy explained. "It's the nicest pony in the world!" He hesitated, and then added, "You all hate him, for no reason. But he hasn't done anything —"

"Not for no reason," Unmar snapped. "Father said so."

"Father!" Yekavel exclaimed.

"Father spoke to you about the regent, Unmar?" Tur, too, was incredulous.

Unmar was unfazed by their reaction. "Yes," she said, jutting her chin out. "He said that we shouldn't trust him, because he also didn't trust him."

"You dreamed that up," Binyamin taunted.

"Of course!" Unmar said mockingly. "Of course you're right. And Father gave me that doll in a dream, too. Right?"

"What's the connection?" Binyamin asked. "You're not making any sense!"

"Enough," Tur said. "Please, don't fight. We have to help each other. There's no one else to help us."

"There are lots of people," Unmar said, grasping her big sister's cold hand and stroking it. "Lots of people, Tur."

"Maybe." Tur was still hoarse and her eyes stung. Tears were not far behind.

"Then we *are* allowed to fight?" Lissia asked.

"No!" Binyamin said. "You're just a baby."

"It's nearly time for the evening meal," Tur said. "Who wants to go down to the garden first?"

They responded to this invitation with happy cries, glad that their older sister had recovered. After a few moments' preparation, Tur led them all downstairs.

The large garden was quiet in the soft light of the late afternoon. A lone nightingale sang her heart out in the branches above. Legend claimed that nightingales stopped singing when they were happy and satisfied. Did human beings, too, Tur wondered, bring out the best in themselves when times were difficult, and sorrow and loneliness burdened their hearts?

Unmar was dreaming that she was riding a donkey, which pranced and leaped and shook her up and down. It was this dream that kept her from opening her eyes. She was having too much fun.

"Unmar...Unmar!" Tur was not part of the dream. The contradiction caused Unmar to finally wake up.

Tur had thrust a thin taper into the candlestick by Unmar's bed. It cast an orange glow in the dark room.

"What?" Unmar asked drowsily.

"Nothing," Tur said. "Go wash your hands."

As though still locked in a dream, Unmar obeyed. She shook her head, trying to dispel the cobwebs of sleep.

"Good." With quick, efficient motions, Tur toweled her sister's hands dry. "Now, my dear, write your name here. Then you can go back to sleep."

"Why?" Unmar was still tired, but the thick curtain surrounding her was slowly lifting.

"Because you love me," Tur said. "Right?"

Unmar blinked. Something about the answer didn't seem to fit the question, but her bleary brain couldn't quite figure out what it was.

"Here." Tur pointed, her voice soft and loving. "Hurry, Unmar."

With each letter of her name, Unmar's mind cleared a little more. "I didn't write this!" she cried suddenly. "I didn't write any letter to your *chasan*!"

Tur's lips compressed. "I know, Unmar. But if they thought it came from me, it would arouse too much suspicion… Finish writing your name," Tur urged, "and then you can go back to sleep."

Sleep…

The pillow beckoned Unmar, promising all kinds of exciting adventures. With a sigh, the princess allowed herself to obey the twin demands of the pillow and her big sister.

That evening, Princess Tur lingered by her father's bedside longer than usual.

"Thank you," she told Ovadia as she finally took her leave. "No one could have tended him more devotedly."

Ovadia bowed his head.

"Father always valued your loyalty," Tur added, almost inaudibly. "He once said that, ever since you were both boys, he knew that he could count on you implicitly."

Ovadia smiled. Those were good memories, from another world — a world that was growing more distorted with the passage of each successive year. "I would be much happier showing my devotion in any other way than this," he said, the smile leaving his eyes.

"I am sure of that," Tur said. "And I thank you for it."

Again, Ovadia lowered his head. When he lifted it again, Tur and her small entourage had left. Thoughtfully, he took the vials and bottles of medicines from the drawer in which he kept them whenever one of the king's children came to visit. He remembered the king — may Hashem send him a speedy recovery! — telling him that he could never remember his father except the way he looked at the end: crippled, in pain, requiring help to perform the simplest act. Would a pleasant-smelling chamber, flowers, and a table clear of medicines enable Reuel's children to remember the way he had been before he had sunk into this long sleep?

Below, the palace guard began preparing for the night's first change of the watch. As these maneuvers had been coordinated with the doctor's instructions, Ovadia took it as his signal to change the sleeping man's position. This time, however, the task was delayed. Under the blanket, beside the king's body, lay a letter that had not been there before Tur came in.

Curious, Ovadia picked up the letter and untied the ribbons binding the scroll. He spread the parchment on the sick man's blanket. The letter, which had been signed by Unmar, was addressed to Tur's *chasan*.

Was this what Tur had meant when she had expressly thanked him and made such pointed mention of his loyalty to her father?

His brows came together, forming a straight line across his forehead. The girl was only 14 — the same age as his own son. Was her judgment to be relied upon?

There was a rustle in the corridor. Although he didn't expect anyone to walk into the room apart from the doctor and the king's children, he realized it might be prudent to keep the letter concealed until he could deliver it to the right party. After a moment's hesitation, he pulled up his trouser leg and rolled the parchment around his shin. A little extra caution — so said the lawbreakers — never hurt anyone.

So said the lawbreakers…

The thought was both amusing and sorrowful. How hard his master had worked to prevent Yosef Diaber from using the law to suit his own ends! Tears formed in Ovadia's eyes. Ever since he had known him, Reuel had been both an older brother and teacher to him. Now he was alone.

He swallowed hard and lightly stroked the king's hand. Maybe he was making a mistake for which he would pay dearly later — but this would undoubtedly have been the king's wish had he been able to ask him.

Time moved at a strange tempo in the Kawari tent camp. The days passed slowly, relaxed and peaceful, but the weeks flew by as though no time at all had elapsed in between them. The period of time since his capture was blurred in Istrak's mind. Had it happened nine weeks ago? Eleven? Or just six?

The Mundari was more adept than he at observing the times of the year — perhaps because, as a villager, he had learned to study the moon and its phases rather than rely on calendars and palace personnel. Still, Istrak was embarrassed at his own ignorance.

Ka'hei did not seem overly concerned with the passage of time. Each time Istrak inquired as to how negotiations were proceeding between the Kawaris and his father's people, he encountered a dismissive wave and a suggestion for some interesting activity. Since the day Ka'hei had acceded to Istrak's request to attend — as a guest observer — Kawari administrative meetings, there had been no end to these suggestions. The days were brimful with activities.

Activity followed activity and experience flowed from experience. Still, Istrak did not give up a single one of the learning sessions that he had established at the start of his captivity. This afforded him no small measure of satisfaction.

THE BETRAYAL

For some reason — and Istrak decided it was none of his business — Knaz was less satisfied. But life, as everyone knows, can't be perfect.

"At the end of the week," Yidrat said, shaking two playing cubes in the palms of his hands, "when the moon begins to wane, our hunting season will begin."

"Good hunting," Istrak said, eyes on the cubes. The Kawari, for all his charm and friendliness, had a nasty habit of cheating at the game.

"Thanks." Yidrat tossed down the cubes and grimaced at the results. "Will you come to the feast?"

"We'll see." Istrak reached for the pair of shepherds to the far left of the board.

"Father will wish you to honor us with your presence," Yidrat said, moving his sheep inward.

"If the feast is suitable" — Istrak moved his pair of shepherds to the right — "I don't see any reason why I shouldn't be there."

The official invitation came the next day, borne by two hunters around Yidrat's age. Ka'hei, when he encountered Istrak the day after that, claimed to have no knowledge of the invitation.

"The hunters are the ones in charge of the feast," he explained. "I would not have thought, Istrak, that they might want you there. It is truly beyond belief..."

Istrak smiled bashfully. Although his stay in the encampment had dragged on, he still did not know how to react when Ka'hei referred so casually to the long-standing enmity between their two peoples.

"Personal charm is a gift from heaven," Ka'hei added. "It is clear you have been very blessed. I, too, would be pleased if you attended the feast, Istrak. Perhaps you will honor us by delivering a thought from your Torah?"

A *d'var Torah*?

Strange as the idea sounded, Istrak liked it. He would speak about Hashem giving permission for man to fish and hunt and slaughter wild beasts. He could also speak about the seven Noahide laws, about the prohibition against eating the limb of a living creature and also, perhaps, about appointing judges. In so doing, he could weave in a compliment for Ka'hei as the tribe's wise and patient leader… The speech began to take shape in his mind. Who knew? Perhaps it was for this very reason that he had been sent here!

On the third day, the tribesmen began preparing in earnest. The aroma of roasting meat filled the air, along with the strains of practicing musicians and the hoofbeats of horses as they arrived bearing guests. The consistent muffled clamor disturbed the Mundari.

"It would be a good idea to look at the cup as half-full," Istrak suggested after listening to Knaz's grumbling for a good half-hour. "*HaKadosh Baruch Hu* placed us here for a reason. We can have an influence, and we can also learn from the wisdom of the gentiles. I believe, Knaz, that if you examine the situation, you will see that you, too, have something to give and something to gain from being here."

"Absolutely," the Mundari acquiesced sarcastically. "What, for example?"

"Many things. Their systems of administration and supervision, for example, or even their art of wood-carving. And we have a lot to give, too. I, for instance, am going to deliver a speech at their feast about the seven Noahide laws."

"That will doubtless be a great moment," Knaz said. To Istrak's joy, he said it without a trace of mockery.

"I hope so, too."

"A great moment for Ka'hei…," the Mundari continued, as though to himself. "A great moment for the Platt tribes. A great moment for…"

"Enough!" Istrak shouted. "Enough! What is it that you want from me?"

"I want you to choose," the slave said, holding his head erect. "I want you to choose who you are — a Kawari or a Khazari."

The young prince lifted his head as well. "It seems to me," he said, "that you have forgotten to whom you're speaking. I am Istrak, Prince of Khazar."

"Yes." The Mundari retreated a pace. "True. That is where your body belongs. That is where you were born. But your heart loves this place and its customs — and where a person's heart leads, that is where he belongs."

Two frown lines were etched on either side of Istrak's mouth. "One cannot deny beauty," he said, acknowledging for the first time his true feelings. "And a boy of 17 can occasionally want to do something other than to carry out his duties."

"Perhaps." The Mundari's voice was low. "But that boy does not have the right to wear the crown of Khazar. You cannot play Kawari games, play Kawari tunes, love Kawari festivals — and call yourself a Khazari."

"That's fine talk from a man who says that the day he grows fed up with Khazar and its rulers, he will simply get up and cross the border. I am a thousand times the Khazari you are!"

"No, Prince," Knaz said quietly. "You are wrong. Because my heart belongs to the G-d of Khazar, and your heart does not."

21

Money had never been in short supply in the tents that housed Ka'hei's wives, and this enabled Rena to hire other slave girls for the tasks at which she was not proficient. In Khazar, she had never been asked to skin or soften a hide. As for the skills she did possess — the people had come to appreciate the herbal remedies she had learned to concoct. After she had saved the lives of several of the tribe's women, none of them called her "slave" behind her back any longer.

On the outside, she acted the Khazari princess she was — grateful to be alive in the enemy's camp, appreciative of any favors bestowed on her. Inside, however, a different personality had formed: hurting, clever, and continually cautious. But she hadn't been careful enough. When Ka'hei had suddenly become interested in her childhood history, and her memories of Khazar and her father's house, she had assumed he was only mellowing with age.

He had always been proud of the fact that he had returned from the battlefield with a Khazar princess walking behind his horse. Sometimes, it seemed, he looked on her with special favor because of it, favor that had lulled her into a sense of false security, that had led her into thinking his interest was genuine. It was only when her nephew was brought to the tent camp that she had realized her mistake. At night, she tormented herself with the question of how much she and her stories had contributed to the kidnaping operation's success.

If she could manage, with Hashem's help, to frustrate Ka'hei's dangerous plan to destroy Khazar from within, perhaps that would serve as some sort of atonement. So far, however, she had not been able to establish any real communication with either the prince or his servants. Although she helped them in preparing kosher food, Ka'hei always made sure that a loyal soldier or servant was within earshot.

Somehow, some way, she had to get to Istrak.

In a closed box in a corner of her tent, carefully wrapped in strips of white cloth, were the treasures that had earned Rena her special standing in the tribe. Dried flowers from every season, ground leaves from all over the world, and vials of her homemade remedies, formulated with a special steaming device that a blacksmith had built according to her specifications.

Ka'hei laughed at her vials. He said she was no different from the old witches who claimed to be able to bring about salvation in return for a penny. But behind his mockery was fear.

And justly so.

Had Ka'hei not taken her out of there, she would have met her death along with all the others in the great hall. But death would have been preferable to the years that came instead. And if she did owe him any sort of debt of gratitude, she had repaid that debt many times over…

She took one of the small bottles from the box and unwrapped one of the white cloths to choose a tiny bundle of herbs. He had sent word that he was coming to dine with her this afternoon. Here was the opportunity for which she had been waiting.

Her breath grew shallow as she dripped the green liquid into the bottle of wine. She grasped the neck of the bottle tightly and replaced it in the center of the set table.

Now all she had left to do was pray.

One of the hardest things to learn is the skill of silence — a refined, respectful silence that reveals nothing of one's thoughts and feelings. Istrak, his father used to say with a trace of pride, had been born with that skill in his bones.

There had been hundreds, if not thousands, of times when Istrak smiled while strong words burned at the tip of his tongue, and any number of occasions when he had elegantly changed the subject. He knew how to remain quiet. This time, however, he sensed that his silence was unfair.

Were the Mundari's words any more fair?

Once or twice he glanced at Knaz out of the corner of his eye. The slave's expression was rigid as he went about his tasks. This was not the silence for which Istrak's father had praised him. It was not the silence that was meant to protect another person from hurt or insult, or to allow time for feelings to simmer down and hard words to soften, ending a quarrel before it began. This was a different kind of silence, unjustified and unkind.

It was not right to allow a person to stew in the words he had just spoken, without giving him a chance to explain himself, or to apologize.

Apologize?

Had the silence in the tent not been so oppressive, Istrak would have laughed out loud. He had known the other man long enough to know that he would never apologize.

And why should he apologize — when he was right?

In the deepest recesses of his heart, Istrak was able to admit that. Had he been granted the power to choose, perhaps it was very reasonable to suppose that he would have been satisfied with fulfilling his Creator's will by observing the seven Noahide laws.

You're a hypocrite, Tur would have told him had she been here.

A hypocrite?

Had he looked in a mirror, he would have seen that his face was not nearly as expressionless as he thought and that large red patches had formed on his cheeks.

He was *not* a cheat and a hypocrite. Not that.

He did not belong to one nation in his heart, while standing at the head of another nation that scorned their neighbors across the border!

He touched his temples, which had begun to ache. "They're not so bad," he said suddenly, out loud.

The Mundari lifted his head, and his dark, narrow eyes seemed to read the prince's mind. "Yes, they are," he replied quietly.

"We were the ones who started the Ten Years' War," Istrak said, stating a painful truth.

"True," the Mundari acknowledged. "If you don't call years of murder and robbery 'starting'…"

"They've changed," Istrak defended his new friends. "That's a fact."

The Mundari's lip curled. "Really? Ask your aunt if they've changed."

Something suddenly blocked Istrak's windpipe. He couldn't breathe. It had been one of those stories that children aren't supposed to hear, but that reach their ears anyway. There was not one form of death, the grown-ups had whispered, that had not been perpetrated on the 600 residents of the peaceful border district, the one where his aunt had met her no doubt agonizing demise. Were twenty years enough to make a real change? A change that would justify friendship?

"Their culture is beautiful," Istrak insisted. "They're far more advanced than us in many areas."

Knaz said nothing.

Istrak was silent, too, because a picture had suddenly blossomed in his mind's eye: a group of people crowded around a table greedily filling their plates, gravy smearing their white napkins as they shoveled food into their mouths to the strains of enchanting music. There was no charm in the picture, and neither culture nor beauty — though there was plenty of money there, and variety, and attention to detail.

Istrak's heart plummeted.

Knaz was right. A person's mind cannot be focused on two such different things at the same time. He was going to have to choose.

The soldiers who had surrounded the Min-Hagai family estate the previous week returned to their command posts empty-handed. The family, along with a considerable number of their servants and veteran household staff, had vanished as though swallowed up by the earth — or, perhaps, the great forest on their property.

Tur, who remained within the palace walls with the servants' pity and her personal pain, was somewhat encouraged by this news. Her letter, it appeared, had achieved its purpose. If her suspicions had proved correct, that the Min-Hagai household was in danger, they were safe now, for the present at least.

There had been, she acknowledged, a certain brazenness in what she had done. But her father had trusted Meshuel Min-Hagai — enough to give her in marriage to his son. And he had disliked Lord Diaber. She had never doubted her father her entire life. There was no reason to begin now. She was certain Lord Diaber was mistaken — Lord Meshuel would never do anything to harm her.

On the other hand, her father was human. Even kings make mistakes. And so, in addition to writing a missive to her *chasan* to warn him, she had sent a servant to the minister of protocol with a brief note requesting the minutes of government meetings and royal courthouse sessions in the period leading up to the day Istrak and Michoel had embarked on the journey from which they had yet to return. If it turned out that her father had, indeed, made some error that had led to any harm coming to her family, or anyone else, it was her duty to try to rectify it.

The minister of protocol was at home when he received Tur's note. As he read it, he knew that his instincts had been confirmed. Diaber had been wrong to disregard his advice. He should not have reminded the girl that after her marriage her husband — with the consent of the appropriate voting body — would be in a position to claim the regency. The moment she heard this, she had begun meddling in government matters.

Nazarel sighed. His position, passed down to him through his family, had been one of small influence when he had inherited it. After a monumental effort, he had infused it with new life. The king, for all his decisiveness and sober mien, had been far readier to heed his advice than was Lord Nazarel's *mechutan*, the pleasant-spoken Diaber. While Diaber thanked him for every suggestion, in practical terms he had never once deviated from his original schemes.

Power, thought Nazarel, was one of the most potent elixirs in the world. Perhaps, with time, Diaber would learn to listen to those more experienced than he. But he, Nazarel, was growing old. It was becoming more difficult to be patient...

He summoned his manservant and ordered him to prepare the carriage to take him to the palace. Note in hand, he went to see the regent.

Lord Diaber, confident as ever, heard him out with a smile and a derisive gesture. "First of all," he'd said calmly, "if the girl's *chasan* had earned the council's approbation, it would have been a crime to prevent her from receiving what is rightfully hers by law. And second" — he concluded, a gleam in his eye, "I do not believe that the princess ever entertained the kind of notion you've just raised."

Nazarel said stiffly, with a small, ironical bow, "I will be happy to hear the regent's thoughts. *I* cannot think of another reason that would prompt the girl to take an interest in government and legal affairs."

"Perhaps she simply wishes to discover a reason for our recent troubles."

The regent's large, handsome eyes never left the minister's, even when he stood up to indicate that the meeting was over. Nazarel left the room feeling decidedly uneasy.

The king's work habits had differed greatly from that of the regent, who undertook responsibility for everything in the palace — and, indeed, in the country as a whole — with tremendous zeal.

Lord Diaber was an energetic, practical man. If an idea occurred to him in the morning, he contrived to put it into practice by evening. The many committees that the king had established in order to clarify various subjects were not at all to the regent's liking. Too much time elapsed before such committees came up with any sort of decision. His aides' opinions, on the other hand, were very important to him. These men represented "the people," without whom the role of the strongest ruler lacked significance or impact. Ohed, who had been appointed to his personal staff on the day he arrived at the palace, was one of those whose function was to gauge the common folks' reactions.

Hands behind his back in an attitude of submission, Ohed reported, "The kitchen maids have been crying. They said that the princess did not deserve such a thing to happen to her. They wouldn't be surprised if she lost her mind as a result, after all the tragedies she and the other children have already suffered."

Diaber sighed in agreement.

"Someone raised the idea," Ohed continued cautiously, "to send the children to the summer palace for rest and relaxation..."

Diaber's brows rose.

"The servants were excited by the idea," Ohed said. "And that's surprising, considering the fact that they would have to leave their homes and families to accompany the children there. They believe that those poor children could use a period of recuperation, far away from Itil."

Something in Ohed's last words displeased the regent. "Don't call them 'those poor children'!" he said sharply. "They are princes of Khazar."

Ohed bowed his head. "Of course, Your Excellency."

The regent, under the spell of this unexpected new idea, sat lost in thought.

Mother Minra's news surprised Tur. "This is not the time for trips," she said. "Or for taking vacations and having fun."

"That is what you think," Minra said softly. "But others think differently."

Tur twisted her ring as she considered this. Binyamin and Yekavel would benefit from getting away from the palace. Unmar would protest at first, but a stay in the summer palace would revitalize her. It would be nice to see her tracking the movements of ants on an anthill instead of sitting on a bench, knitting socks for the poor like a good little princess.

There was still no change in their father's condition, and

according to the doctor — in words she was not meant to overhear — none was expected. The king might linger this way for as long as fifteen or twenty years.

And then?

"If everyone agrees that it's best, then I won't..." Tur's words trailed off.

"Excellent." The nurse was nothing if not efficient. "What would you like to bring with you, Tur?"

The feeling that woke Tur that night was strong and disturbing, but it had no name. It was neither anger nor sorrow. It was not even the quiet despair that had engulfed her after hearing the regent's suspicions about her *chasan's* family. Still, it was a powerful sensation, this nameless feeling, and it enveloped her from head to toe and made it difficult to breathe.

Something bad was about to happen. She could feel it. That feeling compelled her to go to her father, to make sure he was all right...

Hastily, she washed her hands. The cold water restored clarity to her mind. It would be foolish to wake her maid and instruct her to summon the guard. No need to cause a furor just to see that the king's long sleep was undisturbed. Better to think, to try and understand...

To understand what?

An image — perhaps a fragment of a dream she had just woken from — rose up in her mind. The image was of a narrow, winding path with deep, yawning chasms on either side. All journeys — so said the *Talmud Bavli*, or was it the *Yerushalmi*? — were dangerous. Was it not better at such a time, when heaven's judgment seemed to be focused on them, to avoid entering a situation that called for heavenly mercy at the best of times? So many things could happen to them along the way: Bridges could collapse, horses could go on the rampage, storm winds might hurl trees onto their carriage, drivers could fall asleep at the reins...

The troubling images chased one another through her brain. Try as she might, she could not banish them. Tomorrow, she thought. Tomorrow morning, right after Shacharis, she would inform the regent that she rejected his plan. Her place, and that of her siblings, was here, by their comatose father's side, and near the fresh grave of their recently departed mother. Not on danger-filled roads.

The fire in the hearth had long ago died, and the room was unpleasantly chilled. It would have been better had she reached this decision a day or two earlier, before preparations for their vacation had begun. But even now, she was allowed to change her mind. It would be difficult; the princess hated putting people to trouble for naught. But it was very clear to her now that staying home would be the right thing to do.

In the morning, in the sunlight, the logic of her nighttime fears lost much of its force. Drivers do not fall asleep in their seats after a good night's rest — especially not in the course of transporting five of Khazar's royal family in their carriage. The condition of the bridges could be ascertained before they traversed them, and storms were not a prevalent phenomenon at this time of year.

On the other hand, Lissia's eyes were tired and sad; not even the cake she was offered for dessert prodded her usual enthusiasm. Unmar sat at the edge of her chair and treated Diaber with outlandish politeness — not like herself at all. Yekavel looked as though he hadn't been sleeping much at night, and Binyamin jumped every time the hinges squeaked as the door swung open to admit a newcomer.

A vacation *would* benefit them, all four of them. Was it right to make them give it up because of some unfounded concerns?

On the other hand, there was her decision to find out what had led to her brothers' disappearance and the attempt on her father's life. How would she be able to conduct any sort of investigation if she was sent away?

Tur felt too young to make the decision on her own. If only there were someone she could ask. But who?

The *rav* was always ready to listen to her dilemmas and to offer his advice and his blessing. But he had left the city just hours after Lord Diaber had stepped back into the role of regent and had traveled to the border to encourage the soldiers on duty there. Who, apart from him, could give her advice — good advice, devoid of any personal interest?

Sadly, Tur could think of no one. It looked as if she would have to shoulder the responsibility herself.

For two long hours she debated. After murmuring several chapters of *Tehillim*, Tur decided that it would be better, for now, if her siblings remained in the palace. The regent, receiving her at her request, politely listened to her arguments for five full minutes. When Tur was done, he was silent for a moment. Then he said, "Nevertheless, Princess, it is better that you go."

It was not a question, nor was it an opinion. It was a decision, clear and absolute.

Tur, realizing now that she could not fight it, accepted it with lowered head. And inwardly, truth to tell, she felt relieved that someone had lifted the burden of responsibility from her own puny shoulders.

"Still, Your Excellency, I believe it would be better that you not come here often," the old man said. "That mantle will not prevent people who have met you before from recognizing you."

Ruben Min-Hagai smiled, though the smile did not reach his gray eyes, which were a perfect match to the color of his mantle. "Not often," he promised. "Just exactly as many times as necessary, no more."

In the silence that followed, the three short knocks on the door sounded like thunder.

" 'Tis better to be careful once than regret it many times over,' " the old man said, shuffling toward the entrance. "My father, may his memory be a blessing, used to say that, and he was a wise man."

With an exhaustion that had little to do with the number of hours he had slept, the young nobleman waited in the inner room. He had never enjoyed storms and would not have believed that he would be standing in the heart of one today. But if *HaKadosh Baruch Hu* had placed him here…

In the ten days since he had become an outlaw, sought by those in power, he had grown instinctively wary of eavesdroppers. He lived amid a welter of question marks. Would the regent insist his *kallah* marry someone else? One of Lord Diaber's own sons, perhaps? Would he, Ruben, be forced to accept reality, find some way to come to terms with the regent and return to grow old in his great house in the valley? And what happened if his marriage to Tur did take place, but the council refused to grant Tur the throne?

Every scenario seemed painted with the same sad brush.

Diaber, with a skill no one could have foreseen, had managed to have every leak sealed even before it was sprung, his opponents stymied at every turn.

The old man entered the inner chamber and whispered to Ruben, "It is a messenger from Itil. Someone you will want to see."

Even in the simple gray mantle, Ruben's appearance was impressive as he strode from the inner room. "Welcome, my friend," he said, extending his hand to Naitan, Ovadia's oldest son. "What news have you from the palace?"

The youth squinted, as though the light from the small oil lamp troubled his eyes. "A message from my father," he said. "It's about the children."

"I will be happy to hear it," Ruben said, gesturing toward the inner room.

Yosef Diaber had always been proud of his ability to do several things at once, and to juggle a number of different issues in his mind at the same time. It was, in his estimation, one of the secrets behind his administrative success and the factor that had made his *chesed* operations so incomparably comprehensive. That ability came to his aid now, in running the kingdom and coping with all the many undercurrents gnawing invisibly at the kingdom's very foundations.

The kingdom's non-Jewish citizens, for example. Reuel had been very proud that their numbers had increased during his own and his father's rule. Diaber, however, knew these people better than any lord ever had and was aware that a sizeable percentage of them were only waiting for someone to raise the banner of rebellion and permit them to return to their idol worship. If these had been the only discontented citizens, he would not have been too worried. However, added to theirs were the voices of a group of embittered noblemen along the northern and southeastern borders, who had seen a dwindling of trade in their regions after idol worshipers were forbidden entry to the country. These wealthy men were also unhappy with the division of the tax burden in Khazar: *they* bore the lion's share of that burden, while Khazar's Torah scholars — who earned an easy living, either from their wives' businesses or from lands inherited from their parents — added not a single penny to the kingdom's coffers.

Restoring Khazar's equilibrium and calming all these undercurrents would take time. However, the process could be hurried along through a few small changes…

Diaber sighed. Had he been able to locate the great seal, things would have been easier. With that seal in hand, no one could have stopped him from circumventing all the various royal committees and their decisions. But with the seal lost…

His fist clenched. The seal was not lost. It had been hidden! And *someone* must know where!

But — who?

It was a riddle that, were it not fraught with such negative consequences, would have amused Diaber. It was always entertaining to put himself into another person's shoes, to try to enter his thoughts and see the world from his perspective and in this way solve the riddle. This time, however, Lord Diaber was not amused. And when he caught the one who had hidden the seal, he intended to make sure that amusement was the last thing on the culprit's mind as well.

THE HERBS TOOK EFFECT MORE SLOWLY WHEN THE PERSON tasting them possessed a strong will. And even when she included all the various personalities she had encountered in her childhood, Ka'hei was the strongest-willed man Rena had ever known in her life.

As she cut into the vegetable pastry on her plate, she wondered if she should not have added six instead of four drops of the green concoction to the wine.

"What is troubling you?" Ka'hei asked. The candlelight flickered and shadowed his face as he waited for Rena's answer.

"Nothing," Rena said, taking a deep breath.

"Are you sure?"

She stiffened in her seat. He sensed something. But she, too, possessed a strong will, though up until now she had used it only to preserve a measure of G-dliness in this tent for herself and her daughter.

"It's the whole story with…with Istrak," Rena admitted, drawing courage from the Khazari name. "What good is it all? You've invested so much money and energy into the whole thing, and if it doesn't work —"

"It *will* work!" He thumped his fist on the table. "It will!"

For an instant their eyes clashed. To her relief, Rena noticed a faint clouding at the corners of his eyes. The potion was beginning to do its job.

"It *will* work."

"Who says it will?" she challenged.

"It is working already," Ka'hei said, baring his teeth in a smile.

She shrugged. "That's what you say."

"You're teasing me!" he decided. The herbs she had mixed into his wine and food had combined with the sense of satisfaction he had been experiencing of late, elevating his mood to the point of euphoria. "He is already mine." The thin film covering the whites of his eyes had thickened. "Completely mine. He'll do anything I want. Even..." He fell silent, shaking his head. For some reason, his thoughts were growing confused. This disturbed him.

"You simply have not yet asked him to do anything he would find hard to do," Rena insisted. "Ask him, for instance..." She paused, then, to her own surprise, concluded, "...to marry Hala."

"Our Hala?" Ka'hei's brow creased. "Why?"

"It is a good idea," Rena said. "Think of it. Your daughter could be the queen of Khazar..."

"I will find her a better husband. Not a Khazari. That would be a pity. She's a good girl."

A sudden feeling of despair, cold and cruel, engulfed Rena. It was all she could do to continue playing the lead role in the drama she had woven with such high hopes. "You say that because you're afraid," she said. "Afraid to discover that he's not really yours, as you believe."

"I have never been afraid." The whispered words were filled with venom. "I was not afraid to take you from there, not afraid to bring you here, not afraid to hide you and keep you here..." Again, the corner of his mouth lifted, exposing a row of strong white teeth. "Is that not so?"

Chastened, she nodded.

Satisfied, Ka'hei said, "You just want your daughter to wed a Khazari, that's all. But my grandchildren will not place black prayer cubes on their heads."

"Just as your sons did not," she said submissively. Their three sons had been as like their father as drops of water. Sometimes Rena wondered what role her prayers had played in the unnatural deaths each of them had suffered.

"Just as my sons did not," he agreed. "Exactly so."

Still, her words pierced his heart. Late that night, long after she thought he had fallen asleep, he sat up suddenly. "Rena?"

Rena rose from her corner, where she had been peeling stalks of athelium. "Yes?"

"Are you serious about this?"

The influence of the intoxicating herbs had long since worn off. Ka'hei was clearheaded now, alert and dangerous.

"Yes," she said.

"And the Khazar people?"

"They will not object. By their law, she is a Jewess."

"People want their queen to come from illustrious stock," he protested.

Rena frowned. "Hala's lineage is quite good."

"True. But I, presumably, do not fall into the same category."

"You are a great leader and warrior." She hoped that he would accept her words at face value and not probe further.

"Yes," he agreed, "by the grace of the gods." He glanced at her. "Teach the girl what she has to know in order to carry on a conversation with him: manners, customs, idioms — everything."

It was an outrageous demand, but since Hala, without her father's knowledge, had been raised to this very thing from birth, Rena was not afraid to nod her head and say, "All right."

Ka'hei did not speak again. As Rena returned to her athelium stalks, she mouthed a silent, "Thank you."

The next day, while she prepared his breakfast, she hesitated — and then dripped several drops of the green potion into Ka'hei's salad. A bit of euphoria, she reflected, would make it easier for her self-controlled husband to present his proposal to the boy.

The time that Knaz spent going to and from the fishing nets was, to his mind, the most pleasant part of the day. He could think in peace and pray undisturbed. The other slaves kept their distance, babbling in their incomprehensible mixture of tongues, leaving Knaz to his own thoughts.

At the nets themselves, the picture changed slightly. Everyone wanted to bring his master the nicest fish, and the competition occasionally led to fisticuffs. Since Knaz required not only a sizeable fish, but also one with fins and scales, his task was the hardest of all. Considering that the range of movement of his arm was still compromised, it took all his strength and agility to obtain the necessary fish — and he did not succeed every morning.

Sometimes the mistress' slave helped him. This morning, however, with the catch smaller than usual and the competition consequently fiercer, both of them were left without any kosher fish.

"It is Heaven's will," the Mundari said to the dead fish in his basket. "True?"

As the fish offered no answer, Knaz searched the crowd for someone who might be willing to trade with him.

Eventually, he found someone. As he walked back to the encampment, Knaz began to feel uneasy. The closer he came, the stronger the feeling grew. Finally, on his approach to their tent, he saw that — as usual — his intuition had not misled him. The guard around the tent, which usually numbered six, had been doubled, the soldiers' customary relaxed poses had been replaced by a much more alert stance, clearly visible in the way they held their weapons.

What had happened?

Bypassing the menacing line of guards, Knaz continued on to the cooking area. After depositing his fish there, he would seek out the mistress to ask her advice. Then he would make his way back to the tent to fetch his cooking utensils.

But the mistress was nowhere to be found. And the sinister smiles he glimpsed on several faces caused his brow to wrinkle and a lump to form in his throat.

What had happened?

And why had it happened now — just when he had finally

managed to touch the prince's heart?

Slowly, he covered the fish with damp grasses to preserve its freshness. Without his cooking utensils there was nothing more he could do here. And it was always better to face difficult times with a friend at your side... He was as easily trapped here in the cooking area as in their own tent. He would not forfeit anything by being with the prince.

The return to the tent on that sun-drenched morning seemed endless. And the moment he stepped between the two stony-faced guards — his own manner betraying no cognizance of the change that had taken place since he had last left the tent — was an eternity.

The interior of the tent was, as always, pleasantly dim. But the sense of peace was shattered by the sight of Istrak, lying on his side with one hand on his face and the other stained with blood.

"Istrak?"

The prince stirred. Seeing the Mundari, he sighed with relief.

"You must be satisfied now, aren't you?" Istrak asked, lifting himself into a sitting position. His fingers held closed a rip in his shirt created by a knife slash. An ugly blue bruise mottled one cheekbone. Frowning, Knaz carefully pried the prince's fingers from the cloth and studied the wound in his chest.

"It is only a cut," he said. "A few stitches, some *kitutit*, and it will heal with hardly any scarring." He stood up to obtain the materials he would need to tend to the prince's wound. Before leaving the tent, he paused and asked, "Satisfied with what, Your Highness?"

Had the boy insulted him in private, Ka'hei would still have needed every ounce of his self-control not to obliterate his original plan. But now...now that three soldiers and one officer had witnessed how the boy, in whom he had invested so much, had reacted to his friendly proposal — with blatant mockery — his blood was boiling. Nothing had succeeded in assuaging his fury.

The first thing he would do was deal with Rena, who had conceived this plan in order to degrade him. A *very* thorough dealing. After that, he would find Hala the kind of husband that would make Rena turn over in her grave. And finally...

When his thoughts turned to Istrak, whom he had left on all fours, trying groggily to rise to his feet, Ka'hei's imagination nearly failed. He could, of course, just kill him, slowly and painfully. But that would be tantamount to an admission of failure. He had invested so much money and effort in this operation…

Even so, there would be some justification for his investment. Since he had captured Istrak, a number of changes had taken place in Khazar that had afforded much satisfaction to the neighboring nations. But simply assassinating the two princes would have required nothing more than a single skilled archer. Instead, he had sent in an entire platoon of soldiers, taught them Khazari manners and customs, sunk a fortune into bribing the *hostress* troops, not to mention the endless thought he had given to the camouflage and disguise needed in transporting the kidnaped princes. He smiled as he recalled his cleverness, disguising Istrak as a female and hiding Michoel in a wine barrel in a carriage driven by two "wine merchants"… No, he couldn't kill Istrak without realizing some profit from all of this. The death had to serve some sort of purpose.

But what?

Rena's creative powers would have been useful to him now, but the mere thought of her made the blood pound furiously in his veins. What else had that woman plotted behind his back? How many of the failures that he had experienced in his lifetime did he owe to her?

He would come up with something without her. Could he, for example, frighten Michoel into submitting to the reeducation he had resisted so far — by showing him his brother's severed head?

In short, spare sentences, Istrak described everything that had happened to him from the moment Ka'hei had walked into his tent. He told Knaz of Ka'hei's proposal. "You will be happy with her," Ka'hei had promised. "She has been well brought up."

"What did you tell him?" the Mundari asked.

There was something in the other man's voice that rubbed Istrak the wrong way. "What do you mean? Surely it's obvious."

The Mundari's eyes darkened, and it seemed to Istrak that a wave of hatred filled them.

"Actually," Knaz said slowly, "it is not. I have never met any Jew who lusts after honor as much as you do."

Istrak's breathing became slow and heavy. His 17 years, and the insults he had suffered since his capture, had suffused him with a roiling rage. And yet — in a way he would never understand — he managed to restrain himself.

"Is that what you think?" he asked. "Interesting."

The Mundari did not answer. His silence was somehow more infuriating than any words could have been. As he made a dismissive gesture, Istrak seized his sleeve. "Yesterday you spoke differently," he said. "Just yesterday, you convinced me…"

The Mundari looked at him. "Look how mixed up you are, boy!" he said scornfully. "Explicit prohibitions seem like minor things to you, while a little bit of injured pride leads you to risk your life!"

Without knowing it, Istrak's hand tightened around Knaz's forearm, gripping it to the point of pain. "What," he asked between his teeth, "are you talking about?"

"You might think of your own lineage," the Mundari said. "Even if you had been a descendant of Avraham Avinu — your grandfather would still be Terach. Though it is not ideal, there is nothing forbidden in having a non-Jew for a father-in-law, at least nothing worth risking your life for."

Istrak's fingers loosened their hold. Knaz might be filled with Jewish ardor, but even the warmest heart could not prevail against ignorance.

"She has not converted," Istrak told him compassionately. "And even if she had, the conversion would have no value."

"But why should she convert at all?" the Mundari spat. "Don't you think you're going a little overboard?"

Overboard?!

Istrak passed a hand over his forehead. This conversation was so bizarre that it felt as if it were happening in a nightmare.

"After all," Knaz continued, "she *is* your cousin…"

The words whirled around Istrak before finally penetrating his brain. "What in Heaven's name are you talking about?"

"I'm talking about Ka'hei's daughter." Knaz paused. "And the daughter of Princess Rena."

"*What?!*" A powerful wave of weakness washed over him. "Rena? My *aunt*? But she was killed. We spoke about her only yesterday."

"She was not killed," said Knaz. "She was captured and brought here."

Istrak's stomach clenched and turned over. "But it's been twenty years! Great heavens! I...I..." He had no words. Then, in a tone of vast relief, he said, "It's a trick, Knaz. They're deceiving us."

"I don't think so." Knaz lowered his head. "Forgive me, sir. I judged too hastily."

Somehow, this detail seemed trivial. "What do you mean, you don't think so?" Istrak wanted to know. "Based on what?"

Suddenly his face twisted. A fragment of memory found its way up from the depths of his unconscious mind. Was it possible that the woman he had seen by one of the tents that housed Ka'hei's wives had been, not Tur, but his aunt — Rena?

"The mistress," Knaz said, "helped Kalev and myself in supervising the kashrus of the cooked foods. I was certain, Your Highness, that you already knew this by the time I arrived here."

"I did not know."

"I'm sorry." With a sad smile, the Mundari added, "I know those words can sound a bit superficial..."

"That should only be our biggest problem," Istrak replied curtly. "You should have seen that Kawari's face when he left this tent."

"I saw the guards he placed all around. It looks bad."

"See? Even when I try my best to do the right thing, nothing good comes of it. Only the opposite."

With a feeling of revulsion, he remembered how he had stood up to Knaz, convinced that this was the moment when he would reveal both to the world and to himself exactly where he belonged.

"You did choose," the Mundari objected. "You decided. You were prepared to sacrifice your life for the ideals with which you were brought up. As for the results, there is only One responsible for that..."

Wearily, Istrak rose to his feet. "Bring me my outer garment — and the copper diadem. One has to dress properly to meet one's father-in-law…"

The Mundari did not laugh, or even smile. Neither did Istrak. His attempt at humor hung in the air between them as the Mundari cleaned and bandaged his wound and then helped him dress in his best garments.

It was strange to put on the cloak and diadem in the knowledge that this was what the Master of the universe wanted him to do right now. It was stranger still to tuck his *peyos* behind his ears, leaving the sides of his face bare of any sign of Jewishness. But he did it, in the painful knowledge that it was not only his own life that hung in the balance.

The square-jawed sentries betrayed no emotion when Istrak asked to meet with Ka'hei. They showed neither surprise nor scorn, neither joy nor curiosity. One of them simply separated himself from the line and went off to find the tribe's leader. This lack of reaction made Istrak's heart sink even lower.

Was he really about to do this?

Was he really about to marry at the age of 17½? Marry someone whose existence he had been unaware of until now? Someone about whom he knew nothing, except that her father had fists of steel and perfect manners?

And when he brought her back to Khazar — for this, apparently, was Ka'hei's plan — what then?

In his mind's eye, he saw himself stepping out of the carriage that had brought him to the palace and waiting for his wife to descend. He saw the throng of dignitaries waiting to greet him, wearing their best. And he could hear their thoughts. *The scoundrel,* he could hear them thinking. *How is he not ashamed?*

He could see the minister of protocol's white beard and hear Pinras' clear voice as he made his bow: "I thought better of you than this." And no one would know that it had been a case of *pikuach nefesh* — of saving a life. And not only his own life. This seemed to be the only way to save the girl and her mother from their long, enforced captivity.

That is, if they were even interested in being saved…

His heart sank still lower.

It had been good for him here until yesterday. Until this morning. Until he had decided to choose. Perhaps it was good for them as well. When confronted with the choice, which would they choose?

Deciding to stay was not such a difficult choice, as he knew better than anyone. Especially if you were permitted to continue performing the mitzvos even as you enjoyed all the pleasures the tent camp offered. And, although not a usual practice, it was possible to take a second wife… Or, upon his return to Khazar, no one would be able to prevent him from divorcing this girl. Still…to marry! And now! And to a match that it was doubtful anyone, even a crippled wanderer, would agree to!

He turned his head to study the Mundari standing beside him. If not Knaz — then maybe Michoel?

He liked the idea the moment it came to him. Michoel had always been the self-sacrificing type. Would it be so terrible if he would assume that honor one more time? No one would suspect Michoel of impure motives, as they were sure to do with Istrak. They would never suspect him of wanting her for her beauty, or the honor of her father's house…

Yes, it was a splendid idea. Michoel would marry the girl, and everything would work out for the best.

It sounded good. Very good.

On the other hand, if Michoel did consent to marry the girl, Ka'hei would make very sure — in his exquisitely polite way — that there would be no one else around to contest the crown. Ka'hei would not be satisfied with Istrak's assurances. No, he realized, if a Khazar prince had to marry the girl, it had to be him.

Pikuach nefesh, as the Mundari had pointed out a few minutes earlier, must take priority over a small or even a large amount of injured pride.

Pikuach nefesh? Was there *really* an issue of *pikuach nefesh*? The weeks that Istrak had spent in this encampment had stretched into months, and in all that time no one, by look or hint, had indicated that there was the slightest justification for the powerful hatred the

Khazars felt toward their Platt neighbors. Even Ka'hei — despite the anger he had shown (justifiably!) at Istrak's scornful rejection of his proposal, did not look or behave like a potential murderer. On the contrary, he had shown Istrak on numerous occasions that, although an idol worshiper, he was a generous, educated, and clever man, with a broad range of knowledge and an excellent sense of humor.

If he was not a wicked person — and he had never shown any sign of being one — then why suspect him of such disgraceful behavior? Simply because he was a gentile?

These thoughts literally caused Istrak pain, as though each drilled a separate red-hot nail into his head.

"It is not a question of race or nationality," the Mundari said suddenly. "It would be laughable for a Mundari, a member of one of the most persecuted of tribes, to behave with superiority or racism… It doesn't matter which nation one belongs to, as long as he is a G-d-fearing individual. Such a person is deserving of respect, trust, and admiration. And even if the person in front of you is the crown prince of Khazar himself, if he lives as he chooses and decides for himself what is good and what is bad, it would be better to stay away from him. A value system based on personal opinion can turn out to be very…flexible."

Istrak lifted his eyes and looked at Knaz, but the man offered no explanation for his unsolicited remarks. It was not the first time, Istrak reflected, that the Mundari seemed to be able to read his thoughts.

Knaz laughed. "I do not read minds, Prince Istrak. I read people."

Istrak retreated a step, again studying the man who had been tending his needs these past weeks. The new examination revealed nothing.

"It is a small talent," the Mundari said with a dismissive gesture. "It says nothing about the person, Your Highness."

Istrak found that hard to believe. The tent flaps moved, letting in a beam of light.

"You wished to see me?" asked the leader of the Platt tribes, stepping inside.

Istrak filled his lungs with air. Ka'hei's ringing tones were far removed from the friendly warmth he had formerly shown.

"Yes, I wanted to speak with you." Istrak spoke pleasantly, his voice sounding strange in his own ears. The tent and all its furnishings seemed suddenly surreal, like a picture painted on a canvas.

He had felt the same way at the Regency Ceremony, as he had given voice to his rehearsed answers to his father's questions. But the situation was far different now. Then, all the answers had been pre-scripted. Now, he himself had no idea what the next sentence would bring...

Ka'hei's answer was slow in coming. Was his silence overlong, or was it only that Istrak's sense of time was also blurring?

"For what purpose?" Ka'hei asked finally.

"To try to derive the source of the misunderstanding that caused you to leave this tent in such a rage this morning."

The black pupils in the center of the Kawari's green eyes grew to pinpoints. "And *I* believed that it was a strong mutual understanding that caused it."

"There was definitely some sort of misunderstanding," Istrak's voice said, as he listened, a little surprised, to the words he was speaking. "After all, just a minute or two before..." He shrugged. "Or is that the custom around here?"

Ka'hei shook his head. "Now it is my turn to plead confusion. What is your meaning, Istrak?"

Istrak's cheeks reddened. "I was apparently mistaken," he blurted.

They stared at one another for a second, then two.

"Mistaken — in what?" Ka'hei asked.

"If you will forgive me," Istrak said, "we can skip over these confusing moments and move on. I was mistaken. I thought that..." He fell silent.

Ka'hei waited.

Behind them, the Mundari's voice rang out clearly. "The boy thought that you had honored him with a proposal to join your family."

"And he rejected the proposal," Ka'hei snapped.

"Because that is the custom of our place," the Mundari explained. "Customs vary from country to country, as you know."

A succession of expressions came and went on Ka'hei's face. Disbelief at first, followed by confusion, and finally a measure of relief. A smile lifted the corners of his mouth. "How many further rejections must I suffer, Istrak?" he asked.

Istrak tried to smile, but the one he came up with was more of a sad grimace than anything else.

"Not a single one, leader of the Platt tribes," he said. "Perhaps you will allow me to begin addressing you as 'Father'…right now."

As Ka'hei entered the tent wearing a triumphant smile, a bad feeling crept into Rena's heart.

"He will be here this evening," he said gaily. "Shortly after the stars come out. Perhaps we will be able to spread the word this very night…"

"Really?" She was surprised and bewildered. For some reason, it had never occurred to her that the matter could resolve itself so easily and quickly.

"Yes," Ka'hei said. "What do your people give as a gift for a new bridegroom?"

Your people…

"Like any young Kawari…" she began — and then fell silent. Despite the extraordinary self-confidence he had displayed regarding the boy, Ka'hei would never give a sword to the Khazar prince. "He will be pleased with any gift," she ended. "Just like any young Kawari."

"There's not much time." Ka'hei's voice lost its festive tone and became very practical. "We must prepare quickly."

"Hala is ready," Rena said. "She finished embroidering her robe a year and a half ago."

"Yes," Ka'hei replied absently. Waving a hand, he added, "Tell her."

As Rena nodded her acquiescence, the bad feeling in her heart grew until it enveloped her completely.

Things had progressed too smoothly. And although the boy was a Khazar prince, and though he was scrupulous about *kashrus* and *tefillah*, and it was clear that her brother had given his sons the finest education — it was possible that Ka'hei, and not she, had been more accurate in assessing his personality.

Had she made a mistake? Was the boy actually a shaky edifice, ready to be toppled by any influencing wind — a spineless, pleasure-loving creature?

Her lips went dry. She had acted too hastily. She had been so glad that a Jewish boy had come to the camp just in time: one month after Hala's 13th birthday. And in the intensity of her joy, she had forgotten that even a person with the finest upbringing who had never been seen doing an actual sin might perform the mitzvos only because he had been taught to do so, and not because he recognizes the privilege of belonging to the nation of Hashem's servants.

"What's the matter?" Ka'hei asked.

Rena took a deep breath. Istrak was Hala's brightest hope right now. It would be best if nothing happened to ruin the smooth running of this affair. She should have studied the boy's character while there was still time. And if she had not done so, she must hope and believe that her prayers, and Hala's, had not gone unanswered. Now she must be practical, much more so than anyone around her. Many of the servants were well aware of the mistress' eccentric habits with regard to her *kashrus*, and Hala herself would help supervise them in preparing the wedding feast. But their escape from this place was something that she would have to prepare for alone. Completely alone.

Typically, Ka'hei found an elegant solution to the question of the gift. The pair of slaves that he gave his first son-in-law were worth more than any sword he might have given him. And the robe that

Hala had embroidered for her bridegroom, in the custom of the tribe's young girls, astonished Istrak. The turquoise color Hala had chosen was pronounced by Ka'hei's sons and his three other wives as the perfect complement to the Khazar prince's blond hair.

For his part, Istrak promised his prospective father-in-law that, on their return to Khazar, his *kallah* would receive, as per custom, a crown with a depiction of Jerusalem on it in gold.

Not a word was said, or even hinted, about the bride and groom's family connection, or the unhappy circumstances that had brought about this curious match. And certainly no one breathed a syllable about the dark-blue bruise on Istrak's cheek.

When the last of the food was gone and all the hearty good wishes were heard, the first of the festive occasions marking the approaching nuptials was over. At a signal from Ka'hei, seated at the table's head, family members began rising from their places and moving away. Finally, the large feast tent was empty except for five people: Ka'hei and Istrak — with Knaz standing devotedly behind his chair — at one end of the table, and Rena and her daughter at the other.

Ka'hei, at a loss as to strictures of Jewish law regarding conduct between an engaged couple, stroked his chin and asked, "May the women come a little closer, Istrak? We must discuss when the wedding will take place."

When Istrak did not answer at once, Ka'hei hurried on. "No matter. Let them stay where they are... But the wedding must take place soon, Istrak. I spoke to our astrologer this morning, and the position of the stars is rather complicated. In fifteen days, the Okla will enter the influence of Ziat. From then until next summer, when Ge'al comes along to weaken Ziat's influence, it will be an unpropitious time for a new marriage. I would not wish to put off the wedding for such a lengthy period."

"Khazars do not need astrology," Istrak said, trying to soften his words with a small smile. "Since the time of Avraham, our nation has risen above the influence of the constellations."

Ka'hei refused to be drawn into a theological argument. As long as Istrak remained as he had been up until now — friendly, civilized, and enamored of Kawari life and its various amusements — let him have his beliefs. They did not disturb Ka'hei in the least.

"Nevertheless," he said, "you will surely honor my request to hold the wedding at the earliest possible date."

"For that to happen," Istrak said, "I need my brother and his attendant."

"Witnesses," Rena clarified from her place at the other end of the table. "The marriage will not be valid without the presence of two —" She fell silent, suddenly realizing that Ka'hei might choose to bring Kalev here, but leave Michoel in the other encampment. Such a decision would prevent her from carrying out her escape attempt.

"Two what?" Ka'hei prompted.

"Two witnesses who are not related to the couple," Rena finished. Finding the solution to her dilemma, she added a hasty lie: "Plus one to supervise the ceremony."

"They will be here," Ka'hei promised, "although I cannot guarantee that they will be able to remain here for the festivities in the days following the wedding. What else?"

What else?

The wheels of Rena's mind spun rapidly. In just four days it would be Rosh Chodesh. If Ka'hei held the wedding in two weeks, the moon would be nearly full, lighting the way for both the escapees and their pursuers…

"By Khazari custom," she said, speaking naturally, "it is better not to marry when the moon is increasing."

"Waning," Istrak corrected.

"Increasing," Rena said firmly.

Istrak was troubled. It was only a small error, true, and not a very important one. But this single error could indicate the level of knowledge that this woman — his *kallah's* mother, and her only educator and guide — possessed.

Feeling discouraged, Istrak averted his head, seeking hope and encouragement in Knaz's face.

"Increasing," Knaz said as their eyes met. His voice was every bit as confident as Rena's had been.

Istrak narrowed his eyes. He had been as certain that he was right as he was of his own name. The pair's decisiveness, however, eroded his self-confidence.

"Two against one," Ka'hei said, clapping his hands together. "They've beaten you this time, Istrak. So, my prince, when would you like the wedding to take place?"

That night, Istrak had one of the most interesting conversations in his life. The three who participated in it were — Istrak, Istrak, and his hammock.

"Whoosh," said the hammock.

"*Mazel tov, chasan,*" Istrak said.

"Not a *chasan,*" Istrak said forcefully.

The hammock chuckled. The laughter was clearly heard in the light squeaking sound it made.

"You can deny reality all you want, boy. But this is real," the first voice insisted.

"It won't last long," Istrak promised soundlessly. "I'll run away from here the minute I can."

"You've said that before," he told himself. "And what came of it?"

"Nothing," he admitted.

The hammock laughed again.

"It's not funny!" Had thoughts been able to ignite a flame, Istrak's would have started a bonfire. "I didn't do anything because I was waiting for someone to help me, and no one did. But now — now, everything is different."

It was hard to believe that, just one day's ride from the palace, the world was so different. The views from the window were different, as were the plants that grew in wild profusion in the spacious garden. The food they were served was different. Even the sky looked different…

When things are so changed and unfamiliar, when there are wonderful surprises to be seen in every direction, it is easy to forget painful things.

Trying to conquer her tears, Tur pushed the swing back again, increasing its movement as Lissia, on her lap, had demanded.

It was good for the children here. If she would only allow herself, she could also find pleasure here. If not from the quiet and the panorama, then at least from the fact that the trip had passed safely and uneventfully.

What had she been so afraid of? Why had she entertained the notion of robbing her siblings of this opportunity to savor their childhood despite everything?

Not far away, on the low marble wall that surrounded the pond, sat Unmar, tossing pieces of stale cake to a family of black-and-yellow ducks, her doll — Lord Diaber had finally relented and let her have it — lying on the ground beside her. Yekavel sat nearby, blowing into the small flute the regent had given him as a gift before they departed. Binyamin, very proud that he had managed his first climb into the branches of the old chestnut tree, was embarrassed to confess that he had no idea how to get down. Instead, he was putting a good face on things, and doing his best to aim chestnuts at the center of the pond.

It was all so pleasant and so peaceful. It was a good thing that she had given in.

Something — someone, to be exact — rustled in the leaves behind her. Tur was too absorbed in her thoughts to hear the faint noise, or to glimpse the gleam of metal that caught the sun's rays. Slowly she rocked the swing, back and forth, stroking Lissia's silken curls and feeling — as she had not allowed herself to feel for so long — how very much she missed the two members of her family who were missing from this picture.

Not in her wildest dreams could Tur have imagined the identities of the pair who hid in the bushes. Just as she could never have imagined that, in just two hours' time, her brother Michoel would be attending his elder brother's marriage ceremony…

24

RIVKA DEPOSITED YOSEF'S CRADLE UNDER THE CHESTNUT tree. The baby beamed with joy whenever a ray of sun managed to penetrate the green foliage to caress his cheeks. Nearby, his mother planted turnip seeds in the rich, dark loam. This was not woman's work, but with her husband so far away, she had no choice but to undertake chores that, in different times, she would never have consented to do.

Her back gave another angry twinge. Rivka sighed.

Ever since the regent — may the Creator lengthen his days! — signed a peace treaty with the Bulgarians, many of the men had already returned home. Tuval had not been one of them.

There was a certain logic to the fact that those who had left the city last should return to it last. Still, every time she heard the distant blare of trumpets announcing the return of another division of troops, she would hastily put the house in order and prepare a slightly better meal than she would have made for herself…

Only to be freshly disappointed each time.

At least her disappointment was not laced with fear. For that, Rivka was grateful. Apart from a single skirmish at the border, the dreaded war had not materialized. This peace was a gift of His Excellency, the regent.

Tuval would return home soon, and everything would be as it once was — or almost. For the two of them, this period would always carry an additional significance…

She straightened and smiled at her son — who returned the smile with a joyous one of his own before closing his eyes in drowsy repletion.

Yes, Tuval would be home soon, and everything would be even better than before.

A sudden noise from the yard caused Rivka to stop what she was doing. Her back stiffened with tension. Had Tuval come home? It would be so like him, she thought, hurrying down to the gate with the baby in her arms, to burst in just as though the weeks they had been apart had not stretched into months and to ask if the midday meal was ready.

But Tuval was not waiting patiently for her to open the gate. It was another man.

"Uncle Elkanah!" she cried in astonishment. "Has something happened?"

"Your father is not here yet, I see."

"No," Rivka said, opening the gate. "Has something happened?"

"No. But we arranged to meet here."

"Ah." Rivka nodded, though far from understanding.

"I will sit there, under the tree," he suggested. "I'd be glad for a cup of water."

She blushed, like a little girl caught in some misdemeanor. "Of course! And I have some cookies…"

"Not necessary," her uncle said, his voice, as always, dry and restrained. "By the way — *mazal tov*."

In the kitchen, as she reached for a clean glass, Rivka tried to guess what might have brought her uncle here. Nothing terrible, it seemed, though with Uncle Elkanah one never knew. She had never seen him excited, ecstatic, or confused. His habitual expression was remote, stoic. It was strange to think that such an apparently emotionless man could be such an assiduous doer of *chesed*.

She poured water into the glass from the large jug in the corner and hurried back outside. Her uncle was still seated beneath the tree. Beside him stood her father.

"Father!"

"Hello, hello." Tippias' ubiquitous smile was absent.

"Has anything happened?" she asked, setting down the glass of water near her uncle.

Her father shook his head. "No, nothing."

"Then, why…" She hesitated. There was something in her father's face, and his almost militant stance, that contradicted what he had said.

"It is nothing," Tippias said again. "It's just the regent…" He stopped.

Rivka's brows shot up. "What happened?" she asked yet again.

"Nothing," Tippias answered coolly, yet again. "Shall we go inside, Rivka?"

The house, after yesterday's trumpeting, was ready for unexpected company, sparing Rivka a measure of embarrassment. She also had some tasty food cooking, which she was quick to offer her father and uncle.

"We've received a summons," Uncle Elkanah explained, after spooning up the last of the fresh, hot turnip soup, "to see the vice-regent."

"The vice-regent," Rivka repeated, straining to follow.

"About the charity fund," he added. With that, he began to hum the sad strains of *"Al Naharos Bavel"* prior to reciting *Birkas HaMazon*. Tippias joined him.

Rivka waited with mounting impatience for him to finish. Why in the world would the vice-regent be interested in a charity fund in an outlying city?

"The government wishes to consolidate all charitable activities in the kingdom," her father explained after he had said *Birkas HaMazon*. "Haven't you heard?"

No, she hadn't heard. She'd been too busy watching Yosef's almost imperceptible growth and planting turnip seeds.

"It sounds like it might not be a bad idea," she said cautiously.

"Not bad!" her father said angrily.

Her uncle, however, looked interested. "Why not bad?" he asked, picking up his plate and going in search of the dishpan. "What happens, Rivka, if some poor person does not meet one charity fund's criteria? He should have the option of going to another charity fund until he finds someone who understands his difficulty. But if all charitable activities are under the auspices of the government, with one set of rules…"

He finally found what he was looking for and deposited his soup bowl and wooden spoon inside. "And that," he added thoughtfully, "is even before we bring up those who've been transmitting this news."

Tippias grunted in agreement. Again, Rivka asked for an explanation.

"The wandering minstrels," her father said. "Haven't you heard about them either, Rivka?"

No, she hadn't heard. Since her neighbor had offered to bring basic food supplies from town for her, she hadn't left her home in weeks.

"Khazar is changing," her father said. "Changing completely."

"Now you're exaggerating, Tippias," Uncle Elkanah said.

Tippias sighed. "Time will tell. Time will show which of us is right. I say that Khazar is changing drastically, but because the changes are subtle and quiet, we're all going to wake up when it's too late."

His words drifted above Rivka's head, incomprehensible.

"What happened?" she asked for the umpteenth time. "What's wrong with the wandering minstrels, Father?"

"There's nothing wrong. People need to earn a living somehow. But when the regent — the regent! — is the one who pays them a salary to cause other people to waste their time…and when he permits them, maybe even encourages them, to sing songs that originate who-knows-where, it gives me a pain in my belly!"

"Tippias!" Elkanah chided. "Your aching belly has nothing to do with this and you know it."

Rivka's father sighed again. "Everyone reacts in his own way.

And please don't tell me to drink some soothing potion either."

"Why not? Soothing potions are good for stomachaches."

"Not this kind of stomachache, Elkanah."

The kitchen was so quiet that they could hear the goat bleating out in the yard.

"Maybe you'll feel better, Tippias, if you remember that the songs, as even you will admit, are sometimes very nice. And it's a good thing to have people to transmit news from place to place."

Privately, Rivka agreed with him. It would be a good thing if there were someone to bring news from her to Tuval. He didn't even know that Yosef had begun to smile!

"It may be convenient," Tippias said heavily, "but it's not good. It's not good because we will all pay a price for it."

"What price?" Rivka wanted to ask, but her father had thrown an apprehensive glance at the window. "Minchah!" he cried. In a flash, both men were on their way to the *beis knesses*.

Thoughtfully, Rivka watched them go. Her father had never sounded so...extreme. Not everyone, for example, would have agreed to take an artist for a son-in-law. If he had nothing against artists, why did these traveling singers anger him so?

Perhaps, if she were to meet one of them herself, she would better understand.

All that evening, Tippias worked hard. He drew water from the well and chopped enough firewood to heat the house for at least two weeks.

"It makes me feel young again," he told Rivka, hefting the big axe. "Do you know how many years it's been since I've done this job?"

"You don't have to do it now..." Rivka protested weakly. "There's a boy who will do it for me, and I don't pay him too much..."

"And you have plenty money to spare, right?" he retorted. "When was the last time you tasted meat, my girl?"

Her face lit up. "The regent's organization sent me a basket."

The moment she said it, she realized her error. Now that she had made her father aware of the disastrous state of their finances, he would begin scolding her for the large debts that she and Tuval had undertaken when they decided to buy such a large lot. "They... they give money to families of soldiers who have not yet returned home," she stammered.

"It's nice to hear that they're also busy doing good things," he said dryly, "and don't spend all their time trying to figure out how to take all the power for themselves."

The axe rose and fell rhythmically. Not even Tuval, some thirty years his junior, worked so quickly and with such energy.

"Power?"

He laid down the axe. "Tell me, Rivka. Why does the regent need to bring all the *chesed* organizations in Khazar under his name? If he wants to give money — let him give. If he wants to enact laws — let him enact them. But why place all the charity funds in a single body, which he heads?"

"Well," Rivka said defensively, "any of us would want to be remembered in history as the one who —"

"History!" Tippias repeated scornfully. "Do you hear yourself, Rivka? Do we do *chesed* for history's sake?"

The axe came down with a thud.

"The regent is a good man," Rivka insisted, straining to be heard above the sound of the axe. "He does so much — so many good deeds!"

The axe fell silent. "That's true." Tippias mopped his brow with a pristine handkerchief. "The question is, *why* does he do them? For honor? For history? Or, possibly — just possibly — to carry out Hashem's will?"

That night, Yosef cried continually. As *gabbaim* of their community charity funds, Tippias and Elkanah had been invited to participate in the regent's conference to discuss the plans to consolidate all of Khazar's *chesed* activities. They had arranged to stay with Rivka until the conclusion of the conference. As she paced the room with the baby in her arms, trying in vain to soothe him back to sleep and keep him from waking her guests, Rivka thought about what her father had said.

"Does it really make a difference?" she asked him the next morning. "Does it really matter why he's doing it? Hashem is the One Who knows what's inside a person's heart. All we can do is be satisfied with what we see."

Uncle Elkanah answered her question. "When you were a little girl and were told not to take sweets from a stranger, you understood then that the important part is not what you can see on the surface, isn't that so, Rivka? It's important sometimes to know why people do the things they do. And if the 'why' comes from an ignoble place — I start worrying."

She opened the gate and watched until they were out of sight. Then she hurried back to her turnip seeds, so hastily abandoned the day before. For the next two weeks, the conversation was forgotten.

That morning was one of the most beautiful and meaningful in Yosef Diaber's life. His brilliant plan to bring all the *chesed* organizations in Khazar under one central umbrella, and to guarantee them royal support, had begun to take shape. The mass meeting of charity-fund managers had commenced that morning, and they had already resolved that a supreme, supervisory *chesed* committee would be formed, consisting of sixteen representatives to be selected at that afternoon's session.

From the summer palace came more good news. The children were calm and content; apparently, leaving Itil had been very good for them. This, in itself, would have made Diaber happy. But the fact that the news was sent by the finance minister, who had objected at the time to removing the children from the palace, made him doubly glad.

Everything was moving along nicely. Could he permit himself an extra helping of satisfaction by observing how the government conference on his Torah-support program was progressing?

There was a moment's hesitation — his desk was piled high with numerous matters requiring his attention — but he could not resist the urge. The meeting was being held nearby, within the palace compound, and he was very curious to see how his plan for clothing the *yeshivah bachurim* had been received.

In short order he was on his way to the meeting, leaving in his wake a trail of instructions for his hardworking staff.

The Royal Beis Medrash was considered one of the most beautiful in all of Khazar, and justifiably so. Tall columns adorned with Greek scrollwork supported a vaulted marble ceiling. Surrounding the magnificent central edifice were a number of smaller structures containing everything a yeshivah student might need, from a barbershop to a doctor's office. A precisely clipped hedge with a large gate at the center encircled the entire campus, separating the mundane world outside its perimeter from that which was holy and pure inside it.

Few men were suited to the rigorous life of the yeshivah, or remained in attendance over the long term. Elkanah's gifted 16-year-old son was one of those who were. He had been learning there from the age of 5, never going home even for a brief visit or stepping out into the city. The packages that his mother sent with his father were his sole link to the world on the other side of the living green fence. Elkanah did not speak much about his son, and when he did, his face maintained its usual impassive expression. Only the gleam in his eye whenever he mentioned his son's name hinted at his true feelings.

There were no regular learning sessions or "*sedarim*" at this yeshivah, and no defined breaks. In the kitchen, which was open 24 hours a day, a student could receive sustenance whenever the *sugya* allowed for it. Elkanah, as always, chose to wait there for his son — unaware that, had the boy's friends not hurried off to tell him that his father and uncle had arrived, he would have waited there for two full days. Naftali did not visit the kitchen often. The bread he picked up there twice a week satisfied him…until it ran out.

"You've lost weight," Tippias commented, after their initial greetings. The bulging package was opened, after which a rather constrained silence reigned. Elkanah and Tippias had been sent out by their widowed mother to help support the family before they were 8 years of age, and although the law of compulsory education ensured that they received a basic Jewish grounding, there were not many topics they could discuss with a youth whose whole world was Torah.

"Really?" Naftali asked absently. Then, shaking his head as though to rouse himself, he added, "My tailor says the same thing."

"Your tailor?" Elkanah repeated in surprise. His financial situation did not permit him to splurge on a new suit for his son that year.

"Yes, the tailor!" Naftali laughed. "You have to see it, Father! It's all the regent's doing, long may he live."

"Long may he live," Elkanah echoed tonelessly.

Tippias, more impatient, asked, "*What* is all the regent's doing?"

Upon leaving the palace, Lord Diaber remembered something and paused. After a moment he called for the minister of protocol. Lord Nazarel was surprised at the regent's request, but hastened to carry out his will. The entourage that presently accompanied the regent to the *beis medrash* was nearly double the size it had been originally. Apart from the regent's usual aides, the group included the protocol minister himself, the guardian of the royal emblems, ten members of the palace guard, and two young noblemen, one carrying a gold-embossed table and the other a large wooden box.

The group halted near the gate. A crowd of curious onlookers and passersby began to gather around them. The nobleman with the table carried it respectfully forward, and the regent's companions stepped aside to make way for him. When he was near the regent, he bowed low and set the ornate table down on the ground.

After him came the nobleman with the box. With the appropriate gestures of respect, he placed the box on the table. The guardian of the royal emblems stepped up with a key and unlocked the box.

The minister of protocol, who never missed an opportunity to glorify his role in public, whispered something in the regent's ear. The regent removed the crown from his head and handed it to the minister. Then, in what appeared to be an impulsive gesture, he removed his sumptuous, silver-embroidered cloak and passed this also to Lord Nazarel. The minister of protocol handed the two precious objects to the guardian of the royal emblems, who placed them reverently in the wooden box. He locked the box with his heavy key.

The ten soldiers who had accompanied them stood in a protective circle around the box. Lord Diaber, addressing the interested crowd of onlookers, announced that, in the eyes of the Torah, all were equal. Then he passed beneath the gate and was lost to sight within the yeshivah's precincts.

His aides and companions followed him inside. The minister of protocol, the guardian of the royal emblems, and the quorum of soldiers remained outside with the box to await his return.

For some reason, as he stood near the *tallis* stretched taut between four poles, Istrak could not help feeling that the whole thing was a game. The kind of game that he used to play when his mother was still alive, racing around the big playroom with the sons of their guests…

This was no time for indulging in reminisces — but he couldn't help feeling that now, like then, he was trying to imitate the grownups, who were observing him with tolerant smiles, ready from time to time to help the game along with a helpful hint or prop. Such as a blunt sword, an old robe…or a ring. A ring and a parchment scroll on which the *kesubah* text was inscribed.

For Rena, this was no game, as her anxious attention to detail testified. She had insisted, for example, that Istrak acquire the ring with his own money and not with the funds Ka'hei had given him for this purpose. She had even offered to let him separate strands of wool for her in order to earn the required sum.

The work, which the women seemed to do so easily, was more difficult than it seemed. But Istrak completed the job with a smile on his lips. Not because of the ring — but because of the letter he found tucked under the pile of wool. His aunt, it appeared, was concerned for more than just her own daughter.

Rena's proposal was simple and clear: At the wedding's conclusion, and after Istrak promised not to marry another woman besides her daughter and guaranteed a hefty *tosefes kesubah* — twice the value of his inheritance from his mother — Rena would help her new son-in-law and his three companions escape from the tent camp and return to Khazar.

The terms of the bargain were simple and unambiguous, and Istrak submitted to her conditions for lack of any other choice. He would marry the girl — and what would be would be.

Would their life be a happy one?

He would try to make sure that hers, at least, was happy. As for himself, he could always pour his energy into Torah, and into Khazar. Besides, when he thought about the fact that he was doing the best thing possible under the circumstances, he had a feeling — more subtle than mere joy, and more refined — that prompted him to want to do more. To be stronger, to try harder, to invest more effort still in triumphing over the challenges he faced.

Was this what Pinras had meant when he had claimed that the happiness that came from adventure and the freedom to do as one pleased was only a hint, a shadow, of the real thing?

Preoccupied with his thoughts, he prepared for the ceremony. And suddenly, it occurred to him that his *kallah* faced a similar if not identical dilemma. For the privilege of establishing a mitzvah-observant home, Hala had been prepared to marry someone who was practically a stranger, regarding whose character she knew nothing. He wondered what was sustaining her spirits right now and hoped that the sweetness of doing the right thing was helping her to blunt the edge of fear. If they both did their Creator's will in making the decision to marry, they would undoubtedly build the best and happiest home that a person could desire.

With Knaz walking on one side of him and Kalev on the other, Istrak walked to the *chuppah*. As he placed the ring on her finger, a great peace descended on him, and filled his heart.

Once — and not so long ago, either — Tur's sleep had been so deep that the noise of ten horses would not have woken her. Lately, however, among the many other changes in her life, her sleep had become light and easily disturbed.

Was it the burden of responsibility that made her reluctant to relinquish control and abandon herself to sleep?

Responsibility? Everything was so pleasant here. So good... The children were enjoying themselves. The bright sunshine, and the warmth they received from the palace staff, had softened and blurred the pain that had until recently enveloped them so snugly.

No one but Tur, it seemed, was suffering the torment of wondering what was happening in the palace. Was her father still among the living, or were runners already on their way with the bitter news...

It was this fear, apparently, that was chasing away her sleep night after night. And it was fear that prompted her, after fruitless attempts to fall back asleep, to get out of bed, light a small taper, and murmur several chapters of *Tehillim*.

Tur hid her face in her hands. She was young, and — though she didn't like to admit it — she found it hard to be steadfast in her trust that all would be well. But there was no point in all these reflections, this self-doubt. It was useless. Far better to employ her time in saying *Tehillim*. Encouraged, she reached for the scroll, which opened up to the exact spot where she had left off the day before.

25

LORD DIABER LIKED TO DO THINGS ON A GRAND SCALE. His scheme to clothe each of the 900 *bachurim* in the yeshivah certainly followed that pattern.

Three expert tailors — the best in all of Khazaran-Itil and its environs, who designed and sewed clothing for the country's noble echelons — were invited, along with their assistants, to a spacious, well-lit hall on the yeshivah grounds. The tailors were instructed to sew two sets of clothing for each student from a selection of five patterns, three colors, and a sizeable choice of fabrics that weighed heavily on the shelves that lined the big room. In addition, they were to treat each *bachur* with the deference they would normally have accorded a nobleman.

"The purpose of the project," the regent's representative had explained solemnly, "is to lift the boys' spirits and enable them to feel that their status as *bnei Torah* is the loftiest in Khazar. Therefore, any complaint of impatience or less than perfect service will be severely dealt with."

The tailors were insulted at what they regarded as an unnecessary injunction. It was their privilege and honor to serve these yeshivah students — the next generation's Torah scholars. Still, these words served to reinforce their commitment to providing the best service to the *bachurim*, advising and explaining, demonstrating patterns and fabrics and colors.

"Here we are." Naftali halted. "This is the sewing hall."

Elkanah studied the impressive building. "It's actually our Shabbos dining hall," his son explained. "Sewing clothes, it seems, requires a great deal of light and a lot of space for the rolls of fabric and half-completed suits…"

With a glance at his father and uncle, he added, "The regent has invested a fortune in this project. He's brought the very best tailors and bought the very best materials. He also hired someone to oversee every aspect and to make sure every *bachur* receives the clothes that suit him best."

"Suit him best," Elkanah murmured like an echo.

"After all," Naftali said, "clothing that suits a tall fellow won't suit a short one, and what looks well on a heavy person won't do as well for a thin man."

"Ah," Tippias said guardedly, throwing a fleeting glance at his brother. Elkanah's face was stoic as ever — except for two thin lines evident on either side of his nose, a hint of inner turmoil.

Naftali was baffled. He had hoped that he had hit on a subject that would interest his father and uncle and was at a loss to understand their reaction.

"Shall we go inside?" he asked, grabbing hold of the doorknob. "Or do you have other plans?"

"No, we came to see you," Elkanah said dryly.

Naftali, slightly perplexed, pushed open the door.

The vast hall was surprisingly quiet, though the place was filled with people. The tailors worked silently at their fabric-laden tables, and the men in charge of taking measurements spoke in muted tones. The *bachurim*, taking their cue from the general atmosphere, consulted one another in hushed voices as well.

The overseer of all this activity noticed the small group standing in the doorway and hurried over to greet them with a broad smile.

"Naftali!" He used his phenomenal memory to retrieve the relevant information about the young man in front of him. Looking at Elkanah and Tippias, he added, "Relatives of our young *ilui*? I can see the family resemblance! How may I help you, gentlemen?"

"We only came to have a look," Naftali said. "Is that all right?"

"Certainly, certainly!" The smile broadened just a bit more. "In a moment, I will check the status of your suit of clothes. Perhaps you can take advantage of this opportunity to try it on again. If I am not mistaken, there were several small alterations needed in your everyday suit. In the meantime, you can look around. Perhaps you will begin your tour at the fabric shelves?"

The regent had spared no expense. His staff had raided the three largest fabric warehouses in Khazar, and the huge selection of materials was laid out on a network of hastily assembled shelving.

In silence, Tippias and Elkanah studied the array of fabrics and the six boys who stood debating before the laden shelves.

"There are good and bad points to each one," one of the *bachurim* explained out loud. "The heavy wool will be more durable, while this one looks nicer but can crease. There's no color in the flaxen fabric that I like."

"Color," Elkanah said, as if to himself.

"Vertical pinstripes makes you look taller," another boy remarked. "On the other hand, it also makes you look thinner, and my mother will worry if she hears that I've lost more weight."

His friends chuckled.

"What's so funny?" the speaker demanded. "Weren't *you* debating just now about whether to choose the blue or the gray?"

"Gray," Elkanah murmured.

"Yes, that's the color he picked in the end," Naftali said. "It's a pity I didn't know that you prefer gray, Father, or I'd have chosen it. I took blue instead."

"With a silk collar," said the pinstripe boy. "You have an accomplished son, sir."

Naftali blushed.

"Anyone who's already been tested on half of *Shas* gets a silk collar," the boy explained. "For *all* of *Shas*, you get an extra Shabbos suit or a coat with a fur collar."

"Fur," said Tippias.

"Fur," Elkanah echoed.

"To increase the honor of the Torah," the boys chorused. "This is the regent's personal contribution. It's made the *bachurim* very happy. There have been whole *chaburos* to discuss the question of which is preferable: the coat, or the extra suit."

This time, the two brothers said nothing.

While Naftali was in one of the cubicles having his new suit of clothes tailored, Tippias and Elkanah looked around.

Six tailors labored at alterations for four students.

"Wouldn't it be better to shorten it a bit?" one of the boys asked.

The tailor said that a shorter coat would provide less warmth.

"But it looks better," the boy objected. "Isn't that so?" He seemed to be appealing to Tippias and Elkanah. They did not offer their opinions.

"Is everyone given these suits?" Elkanah asked instead. "All the *bachurim*? They've all been here to choose fabric, and debate colors and styles, and take measurements and have themselves fitted — and then came back to try it on again?"

"The project's only begun," the overseer said apologetically. "But so far, 120 *bachurim* — the cream of the crop — have chosen their fabrics and patterns."

"The cream of the crop," Tippias repeated, looking critically at his nephew, newly emerged from the measuring cubicle. The navy-blue garment brought color to the boy's pale skin and large eyes. The smooth cut, minus the traditional pleats, emphasized his build. Other than the lack of a sword dangling from his hip, he could easily have been mistaken for one of the king's honored dignitaries.

"Is something wrong, Father?" Naftali asked. "Don't you like the color?"

Elkanah spoke in his usual tone, unwittingly shattering the hush in the big room. "What does the color matter?"

Every eye turned to him. Naftali, flushing furiously, mumbled some sort of apology.

"The color doesn't matter to me at all," Elkanah continued. "But there is something that does bother me." He grasped his son's navy-blue sleeve, speaking in his characteristic, unemphatic fashion.

"How is it possible that so many supposed Torah scholars are primping themselves like girls do?"

After a moment, he added into the stunned silence, "I need some extra hands to work the fields. You have five minutes to pack your things."

Naftali stared at him.

"Did you hear me?" Elkanah asked.

"Yes, Father…"

"I did not send you here to try on clothes," Elkanah said, finally showing a flash of real anger. "And *such* clothes!"

Suddenly, he became aware of a new quality in the surrounding silence. He turned around.

Yosef Diaber, regent of Khazar and the force behind this entire project, stood a few steps away. He was wearing a garment cut in exactly the same pattern as Naftali's.

Slack-jawed, Elkanah gaped at the regent, who returned his look with a steady gaze.

"In my opinion," the regent said with a smile, after a momentary pause that felt like an eternity, "the new clothing suits your son very well. And if he has merited to be among the first 120 *bachurim* to be invited here, it would be criminal to turn him from a man of the spirit into a man of the earth."

Though the remark was offered in the guise of personal opinion, anyone with a brain in his head understood the command that lay behind it. It also offered Elkanah a chance to retreat from his harsh remarks.

But Elkanah, his face a mask of surprise and confusion, continued to stare wordlessly at the regent.

This seemed to please Diaber. Recognizing in the man before him one of the representatives who had gathered at the morning's charity-fund conference, he said benevolently, "You will no doubt be happy if your son becomes a *talmid chacham*. Won't you?"

With an effort, Elkanah blinked. Slowly, he replied, "Certainly."

The regent smiled again — a kindly smile.

"That's why," Elkanah continued, "I want him to come home. Because this place" — he waved a hand to encompass the entire hall — "will no longer produce Torah scholars."

The regent's eyes narrowed. "Prophecy," he said, still speaking in a friendly tone, but with an edge now, "has reverted, since the destruction of the Beis HaMikdash, to fools and children."

Elkanah paled. "I am no fool, Your Majesty. Nor am I a prophet. I am —"

"Yes?" the regent prompted. "You are...?"

"A villager," Elkanah said with an effort, "who knows that a seed can produce either a carrot or a turnip, but not both."

The regent lifted his brows, and both Tippias and Naftali exhaled in cautious relief. If Elkanah acted the fool, perhaps they would emerge from this without damage.

Elkanah tried to explain himself. "I meant... That is..."

Lord Diaber waited.

"Your Majesty means well," Elkanah said desperately. "But these boys — if Your Majesty would only *look* at them!"

The regent's eyes slowly left Elkanah's face and scanned the rest of the crowd. The yeshivah students looked exactly the way he had always dreamed of seeing them: erect, poised, and filled with a recognition of their self-worth. The shoulders that had previously been bowed were now straight, and the look in their eyes was alive and alert.

His own eyes returned to the villager. "Do not be afraid of change, my son," he said. "If you gird yourself with a bit of patience, you will see how the *ben Torah*'s new, respected image will positively influence the masses. Your son will be one of the leaders of the revolution, with Hashem's help."

Elkanah was quiet, as was Tippias. Naftali's chest rose and fell rapidly.

"Leave him here," the regent instructed, "and I, personally, will supervise his spiritual ascent."

Elkanah was a man of few words. Tippias, striding along on the boy's other side, felt that the things that needed to be said ought to come from the father. Naftali, walking between the two adults with head slightly bowed, could not find the words with which to express the thoughts that churned through his mind like a fast-boiling cauldron of soup.

For these three reasons, from the moment the regent left them alone to the moment the two brothers parted from Naftali, nothing of any significance was said. It was only after they had parted at the gate, and Naftali had already turned his back to return to the *beis medrash*, that Tippias felt compelled to say something of what was in his heart.

"Naftali?"

The boy turned back to face his uncle.

Tippias passed back beneath the gate and approached Naftali with a rapid step.

"Despite everything," he said, a hand on his nephew's shoulder, "your father still thinks that you are capable of being a fine person. All you have to do is guard yourself against foreign influences."

He paused, and then added, "Your father's example of the carrot and the turnip was actually a very good one. Think about it, Naftali, when you have a free minute." He rejoined Elkanah, and left.

Two *bachurim*, Shevach and Kaniel, came up to Naftali with cries of *"mazal tov!"*

"Our warmest congratulations," added Kaniel, nodding ponderously like a dignitary at a formal occasion.

Each year, each of Khazar's ten districts was permitted to send only nine boys to the Royal House of Study. Occasionally, as is the way of the world, the choice involved considerations of money or status. It might also happen that ability, or an especially sharp mind, might cover up a less than suitable personality. Shevach belonged to the first group. His father, one of the wealthiest men in Khazar, dreamed of seeing his son become one of the next generation's leading Torah figures — an ambition, it must be said, that his son did not share. Kaniel belonged to the second group.

"We have to celebrate!" Shevach announced, linking his arm through Naftali's. "The heavens have opened up before you, friend."

Naftali was in no mood for celebrations. Besides, he wasn't sure what there was to celebrate.

"If the regent said that he'll keep an eye on you, we can start looking forward to interesting news," Kaniel said by way of explanation.

The two boys led Naftali in the direction of the kitchen. Naftali, in the meanwhile, was trying to come up with an excuse to escape. *Bachurim* were crossing the courtyard, hurrying to the Minchah Ketanah service. After his father's outburst in the sewing hall, which had subjected him to the attention of the whole world, Naftali had no desire to be seen talking to these two.

"The regent will propel you higher and higher up the yeshivah ladder," Shevach said with satisfaction, "until the *rosh yeshivah* will have no choice…"

The words hurt Naftali's ears.

"I have to go learn now," he said, spreading his hands. "I wasted enough time today."

"You're pale," Kaniel said pityingly. "You need a hot drink or you won't be able to concentrate. Sometimes you have to waste time in order to use it — you know that."

Most of the ten kitchen workers liked Shevach and were happy to provide a cup of hot tea for Naftali at his request — along with some cream that they had been saving for the evening meal. Shevach added three teaspoons of sugar and piled five baked apples on a plate.

"Eat," Kaniel ordered.

"Don't you know that a person will have to render an accounting for everything his eyes saw that he did not take pleasure from?" Shevach asked.

Other boys, Shevach and Kaniel's friends, had joined their group. "Do you know how many merits we'll all get by answering amen to your *berachos*?" they added, justifying this little...break.

Two kitchen workers — men who were less enamored of Shevach and his cronies — watched the noisy group. The kitchen, warm and cozy in winter and well-ventilated in summer, was open to the students all day long, with no one to supervise the number of cakes each one heaped onto his plate. Most boys in the yeshivah took what they needed to stay alert for their studies and no more. Most boys...

They knew this group, and most of the time they were up to no good. The boy in the center of the group was unfamiliar to them, but from the tone of his companions' remarks it was obvious that he was no newcomer to the yeshivah. This made it even more urgent than usual to put a quick end to the party.

"Run and call Palo and Refael," the first worker requested of the second. "They'll want to be apprised of this." As the other worker ran off, he went into an inner room and fetched a bucket and mop.

The dirty water, as always, began trickling around the boys' legs just when they were really starting to enjoy themselves. It prompted the group to finish eating quickly and go out into the courtyard.

A moment later, two senior students appeared: Palo and Refael, the yeshivah's brightest stars.

Naftali flushed when he saw them, the color creeping from the collar of his shirt all the way to his hairline. The color turned to flaming crimson when the illustrious pair asked him to come with them for a minute.

"You can come back here afterward if you wish," Refael said pleasantly. "We just have to ask you something."

"Don't go with them," Kaniel warned irreverently. "They only want to start a quarrel. They've forgotten that the whole Torah, on one foot, is 'V'ahavta l'rei'acha kamocha.'"

"Storks," Palo said crisply, "stand on one foot. Come, Naftali."

With a friendliness that belied the command in his tone, he placed one hand on Naftali's shoulder. Refael put his hand on the other. When they started walking, Naftali had no choice but to resist or walk quietly between them.

"What's going on?" Refael asked when they had put some distance between themselves and the group of boys still gazing after them.

"Nothing," Naftali said, struggling to free himself from the pair.

"Really?" Palo sounded skeptical.

Naftali stopped struggling. "My father wants to take me home."

"So you decided to start wasting time already?" Refael asked. "If you have only limited time, you have to use every minute."

Naftali's head was beginning to ache. "He said I was a dandy. He said I stand no chance — that with a new suit of clothes, I won't become a *talmid chacham*."

"You've always dressed well," Palo said quietly. "It couldn't have been easy for your parents to pay for your clothes."

This was true, and it confused Naftali even further, intensifying his headache.

"And then the regent got involved," Naftali continued, glad of the opportunity to share the incident with these much older students. "He told my father to leave me alone, and that he would take care of my…my spiritual ascendancy. And my father —" Naftali drew a deep breath — "argued with him."

"A brave man," Refael remarked.

Naftali's eyes darted back and forth between Palo and Refael. "What did you want to ask me?"

The two older students were silent.

"Or did you just want to hear the latest news?" Naftali ventured.

"Every person has his mission to fulfill," Palo said, sticking his hand into a pocket. "Here is our authority, Naftali." He withdrew a parchment scroll and handed it to the boy.

After a bewildered look at Palo and then at Refael, Naftali unrolled the scroll.

> *To Whom It May Concern:*
>
> *Whereas my heart tells me that the decision of Yosef Diaber, who bears the title of regent of Khazar, to send me and six of the best men on the royal yeshivah staff on a journey to strengthen Khazar's soldiers, is one that attempts an illegitimate interference in the yeshivah's management, I have appointed HaRav HeChashuv Palo Machfez as Rosh Yeshivah, and Rav Refael Ben-Achia to oversee the students' spiritual life.*
>
> *These two appointments will be in force for a period of forty-eight months. I ask everyone who cares for the fate of Khazar and the future of the royal yeshivah to obey any instructions that these two might issue and to give them every possible assistance, in terms of money, time, and effort.*
>
> *Signed with an aching heart,*
> *Natrunai Ben Masnia*
> *Former Rosh Yeshivah of the Royal House of Study*

The words hit Naftali like stones dropped into a pond. "What does this mean?" he asked in confusion.

The faces of the two young men standing before him were serious. "It means that you are leaving the yeshivah tonight," Refael said. "You and a few others will be traveling east to join Ruben Min-Hagai and his men."

"Ruben Min-Hagai?" Naftali pronounced the name slowly. "Why?"

Refael smiled. "Let's allow Palo to return to his learning," he said gently, "while you and I pack your things."

It was all so strange and illogical!

First, his father and Uncle Tippias' visit, so embarrassing. Then the regent's intervention, and Kaniel and his group with their friendliness and comforting talk. And finally, these two, with their strange letter of appointment, talking about joining Ruben Min-Hagai, who had been outlawed by...

He passed a hand over his eyes. From earliest childhood, he had been raised to view royal edicts as the essence of goodness. Everyone knew that the king cared deeply and generously about each and every one of his subjects, and that his instructions were intended for his subjects' benefit.

Now he was being told by those he trusted the most to challenge this belief — to rebel against it...

Palo and Rafael were watching him, their faces warm and gentle.

"I don't understand." Naftali shook his head from side to side. "It's like the most convoluted *sugya* in the Gemara!"

Refael smiled at this, but Palo remained sober. "It's a lot simpler than that. Lord Diaber is not King Reuel, may Hashem send him a *refuah sheleimah*."

Naftali closed his eyes, trying to shake off the pounding headache. "The regent is a good man." Opening his eyes, he gazed at the pair facing him. "He does good deeds. He supports us. If the *bachurim* get a little overexcited when they're offered two good suits, that's not our problem."

"A 'good man,' you say. You have no idea how correct you are," said Refael. "Let's send Palo back to his learning now, and go pack your things, all right?"

"How 'correct' I am?" Naftali repeated when they were in his room, standing beside the box that contained all his belongings. He received no answer. He asked again on their way back to the *beis medrash*.

"Refael, what did you mean when you said I was correct about Lord Diaber being a 'good man'?"

Again, no answer.

Later, he approached the pair and requested permission to have his *chavrusa*, his learning partner, join him. After a brief period of reflection, they agreed. Still the question he had asked about the regent troubled him the rest of the day.

It was only as they stood near the wagon that he finally received his answer — this time without asking.

"You said," Refael whispered in his ear, "that Diaber is a good man."

Naftali glanced at him expectantly.

"You did not say," Refael murmured, "that he is a good Jew."

The words surprised Naftali, and angered him. "Isn't that the same thing?"

Refael sighed. "I knew you'd get angry. That's why I didn't want to answer you. When you meet Ruben Min-Hagai, you will be able to discern the differences for yourself."

"Everyone's entitled to make a mistake once in a while," Naftali flared. "He did not outlaw the Min-Hagais from any bad motivation! He thinks they're responsible for all the catastrophes that have occurred these past few months."

"That's what you say," Refael said quietly. "I say otherwise."

"What does the *rosh yeshivah* say?"

"The *rosh yeshivah*," Refael said in a dry voice, "anticipated each and every one of the developments that have taken place in Khazaran-Itil in the last few months, from the time the king was attacked to this very moment."

"Everything?" Naftali asked skeptically.

"Everything...including the fact that his students will have to find great courage to free themselves from the honey that the regent will pour on them and join forces with the one who bears the banner."

"Ruben Min-Hagai, you mean?"

Refael hesitated.

"Is he the man?" Naftali pressed.

"Not necessarily," Rephael answered at last. "But the *rav*'s instructions were clear: the one who most disturbs the regent's peace is the man we must join."

Naftali lowered his head. Ruben Min-Hagai was certainly that man. But he, Naftali, preferred the study hall, to forests and fields

— even if he was given all the time in the world to pursue his learning.

He didn't want to go! The sudden realization struck him like a hammer blow.

"I don't mean to be disrespectful," he said, "but isn't it going a little too far, taking me out of yeshivah just because Diaber promised to keep an eye on me — and because I spent a little time debating the merits of a woolen suit or a flaxen one?"

"No one's trying to get rid of you," Refael said. "Only to bring you closer" — he pointed upward — "to Him."

"But I don't want to go!" Naftali lifted his eyes. "Do I have to?"

"No, Naftali, you don't have to."

"In that case, I'm staying." Naftali reached for his box. "All right?"

"Absolutely. But it would be a good idea if you heard what you can expect if you stay."

Naftali straightened. "I'm listening."

"You'll be learning," Refael said slowly, "and it will be wonderful. The learning will be sweet, and the regent will envelop you with everything good — literally, Torah and greatness in the same place."

That didn't sound so bad.

"And then," Refael continued, "in about five or six years, let us say, the regent will want to make a small change in the halachah. This small change will be in opposition, in the view of several great Torah scholars, to a single line in some remote tractate. They will protest.

"As regent, he will turn to you, and ask you to check out the matter in depth and to write — along with several other *talmidei chachamim* — your opinion on the *sugya*."

Refael drew a breath. "And you, who have been benefiting from the regent's generosity for the past five or six years, buying suits of clothing at his expense and eating at his table on the holidays, will not even sense the twisted nature of your reasoning, or how your view has strayed from the straight path to embrace the regent's..."

After a moment's silence, he added, "And that's the best-case scenario."

The fighting mood that had driven Naftali earlier was nearly dissipated by now, but he could not resist asking, "And in the worst-case scenario?"

"The worst case?" Refael smiled sadly. "In the worst case, you will be the personal fulfillment of the words '*Vayishman Yeshurun vayivat* — Israel will grow fat and reject…' You will become accustomed to wearing the best and most costly clothes. You will know exactly who is for the regent and who is against him, and you will talk about it in the dining hall. The regent will enjoy consulting with you on various topics and will praise your straight thinking. He will invite you to dine with him every evening and will transform you into a circus mouse, who knows nothing but where his cheese is located and what he must do to get it."

He peered at Naftali. "Do you understand?"

Slowly, Naftali shook his head. "No. I really don't. I think I have a strong enough spine to stand up straight and fight back."

"What, exactly, will you fight? Will you struggle against the luxuries you'll receive? Will you give your suits of clothing away to the poor? And what will you do when you are invited to dine at the palace?"

Anger again flared. "The *rosh yeshivah* himself is supported by the king!"

Refael, in contrast, did not raise his voice. "Remember that the king, though extremely generous, never made much noise about the money he gave to the yeshivah. Do you not understand? The regent doesn't just want the *bachurim* to have new suits of clothing in their closets. He wants them to have them on their minds. That may be a minor difference, but it is a very significant one."

Refael was right. And still, Naftali stood with his chin jutting out, angry.

"I'm going to learn now," Refael said. "That is what I am meant to do if I want to make something of myself. You, too, must do what you are meant to do."

Naftali didn't answer. Instead, he removed his hand from his box and turned away.

When he turned back, Refael was gone. In his place stood his *chavrusa*, gazing at him disapprovingly.

26

A MESSENGER WEARING THE UNIFORM OF THE PALACE guard raced up the path leading to the summer palace. Just minutes later, he stood facing the head guard in the palace's spacious entry hall.

His message was concise and clear: In the wake of the dispersal of recently drafted reservists, an urgent need had arisen in Khazaran-Itil for regular troops. Therefore, the summer-palace guard — thirty elite soldiers — were called upon to set out for the capital on receipt of this message.

The officer's eyes darkened. "But there are only forty of us here!" he protested.

The messenger wiped his face with his sleeve. Both of them knew that there was nothing he could do to change the directive he had been ordered to pass on. "I'm only the courier," he said.

"Of course," the head guard agreed, shaking his head. "Go to the kitchen, my good man, and get the meal you deserve. You have done well."

The courier grinned, then hurried away to the kitchen quarters, leaving the frowning officer alone in the hall.

Orders to bring thirty soldiers from the provinces to the capital city! Thirty! Had the situation not been so exasperating, it would have been amusing.

Was there not, in all of Khazaran-Itil, or a more accessible population center, any possibility of drafting a mere thirty additional soldiers? Were there not enough young men who had been drafted into military service to carry out patrol and guard duty in order to free up thirty more experienced soldiers for more complicated duties?

Absurd!

Insane!

To leave the princes of Khazar under no more than a symbolic guard, in order that…

The officer's jaw hardened and his fists clenched.

Such an order would never have been issued, even by General Makan! Unless…

His helpless fury was replaced suddenly by a sense of cold dread. Unless someone, with his own axe to grind, wished to undermine the protective perimeter around the royal children.

The young soldier had been surprised when he, and not some older and more experienced officer, had been appointed to this post. Who, he wondered, could be interested in such a thing?

Ruben Min-Hagai?

Although it was not something that the palace guard spoke about, he personally believed that only a real fool would not have waited until after his marriage to the king's daughter before maneuvering to have the throne transferred to himself.

Dalo Stazdiran?

Since the king had been attacked at Stazdiran's son's bar mitzvah, the prime minister had not shown his face much in public. The officer found it difficult to believe that such a well-connected public figure would choose to harm the king at his own son's bar mitzvah celebration. Surely he could have had someone, in the guise of one of the cleaning crew, infiltrate the government conference hall to hide the snake among the cushions on the king's special chair.

Bastian Makan?

Now that all the fingers of accusation were pointing at Meshuel and Ruben Min-Hagai, suspicion against the veteran military man had gradually diminished. The doctor who had supplied the poison claimed forcefully that Ribak Bati was not the same man who had appeared in his house presenting Bati's papers in order to fraudulently obtain the toxin. And a certain witless, gentile resident had begun circulating in the villages wearing a fancy garment embroidered with the Makan crest. Proudly, he said that the handsome coat had been given to him in exchange for doing a small errand: handing a note to a certain young boy who had been playing with his friends in Khazaran's central marketplace, not far from the big bakery.

The officer shook his head. Though he still stood accused of cooperating with the enemy in wartime, to think that Makan was manipulating all these events from his jail cell — hoping to someday rule the kingdom through his nephew — bordered on the ridiculous.

Who was left?

All of Khazar's many enemies were left: Bulgarians, Kawaris, Barbars, Byzantines, and others. And there was still one more…

Tur was startled when the officer in charge of palace security asked to speak to her in the presence of only little Lissia. But when he had finished speaking, his eyes fixed on the tops of his boots, she realized that her earlier uneasiness was nothing compared to what she felt now.

"What do you recommend that we do?" she asked, her voice small. "How can five children deal with all of the…the forces you've mentioned?"

"I don't think Your Highness quite understands," the officer said patiently. "The problem is not the long-standing enemies across the borders. Khazar can handle the Bulgarians and the Kawaris. The real problem is the person who is cooperating with them."

"Bastian Makan is in jail," Tur pointed out.

The soldier nodded. "And if Ruben Min-Hagai was the one

behind all this, he would have waited until after the wedding to carry out any plans to take over the reins of the kingdom."

"Then who is left?"

When he did not immediately answer, she asked more urgently, "Whom do you suspect, goodman?"

"It is not," the officer said slowly, "for me to say, Your Highness."

"To say what?" Lissia asked, having just toppled her tower of blocks and climbed into Tur's lap.

A smile glimmered in the officer's eye, but his lips remained tightly sealed.

Tur played with her sister's fair curls. It seemed to her that Yosef Diaber ought to be the next suspect on the list. But it was impossible to suspect a man so kindhearted, such a doer of good deeds for the needy. "Actually, at the moment the man's identity is not that important," she said quietly.

The soldier nodded. "I agree, Your Highness. The order that was sent to me, to leave the palace this very night along with the best of my men — leaving only ten soldiers behind — makes me think that someone will try to finish you all off tonight."

"Finish us off?" Lissia asked. "What does that mean?"

Hurriedly, Tur said, "If I request it, can you postpone carrying out the order?"

The officer bit his lip. "I am prepared to do more than that," he said, "but I fear it will be nothing more than flaying a dead horse." At her questioning look, he explained, "If we assume that there are powerful hands stirring this cauldron, then my actions will quickly be labeled an uprising. Within days, this palace will be surrounded. After a few days' siege, the rebellion will be squashed. I will find myself surveying Khazar's scenery from the height of the gallows — and Your Highnesses will find yourselves in the exact same position as you are in now."

"And if we were to leave the palace?"

Shaking his head, he said, "I have no idea, Your Highness, which of my men will cooperate with me, and which will rush away to report any unusual activity."

"Couldn't you claim that the courier gave you a message that was slightly different from the one you actually received?"

"Not as long as he is walking the palace corridors with us."

"I will summon him here and ask him to deviate from the truth."

"Useless, Your Highness. They obey only the orders of their superiors."

Tur sank back in her chair. Silence held the room like a pall.

"You must have come here with some sort of plan," she said finally.

"No," the officer said gently. "Unfortunately, I have not yet managed to come up with one."

Despite the fact that, until Unmar's birth, Tur was the most important girl in all of Khazar, her friends had not agreed to let her have a role in their Chanukah play — so inadequate was her dramatic ability. Now, despite her best effort to appear tranquil and to banish the sense of being a bird trapped in a cage, it was easy to see how worried she was.

Which of her people was loyal?

Who — if anyone — could she turn to for advice?

The officer had insisted that it was best to keep this whole matter a deep secret. With mounting tension, she had asked him how she could be sure *he* was not one of those who wished to harm her and her siblings. Perhaps no messenger had come to the palace at all!

"A good question," he had concurred. After a moment's thought, he added, "And suspicion, in this case, is justified." But he was able to offer no answer to her question.

"Perhaps it would be better to ask someone else for help," he had added with a shrug. "I will obey anything you suggest."

Someone else…Who, exactly?

A small voice interrupted her train of thought. "What's the matter, Tur?"

"Nothing," Tur said, turning away.

"Really." Unmar sounded skeptical. "Why are you lying to me?"

"Because there are some things that grownups have to deal with on their own," Tur explained with an uneasy glance at her maidservants across the room.

"Completely, completely on your own?" Unmar asked. "If you were already married to Ruben, your *chasan*, wouldn't you tell even him?"

With a flash of anger, Tur snapped, "I have no *chasan*. You know that very well."

"I didn't mean to hurt your feelings," Unmar said, unruffled. "I just wanted to say that sometimes you need to confide in someone."

"In whom?" Tur asked, her eyes filling. "Who, exactly, little girl?"

"In me," Unmar said calmly. "I can help you."

"You're a dear girl. I love you."

"Do you need help?" Unmar pressed. "Do you want me to send word to some nice people who can help us?"

Tur studied her with interest. Unmar was not prone to flights of imagination. "Who, for instance?"

Unmar hesitated. Then, glancing right and left, she put her lips to Tur's ear and whispered, "The one you say is not your *chasan* anymore. And his friends."

"That might not be such a bad idea, Unmar," Tur said in a trembling voice. "But it's not very practical, is it?"

"Why not?" Unmar didn't understand. "I just need you to help me write without making mistakes."

Now it was Tur's turn to glance over her shoulder. Grasping Unmar's elbow, she dragged her into a corner of the room.

"What do you mean?" she hissed. "Tell me the whole story, Unmar. Now!"

"They sent me a note," she said. "It said that if we need help, we're to leave a message in the hole."

"Which hole?"

"The squirrel hole. Near the pond where we swim."

"Near the pond," Tur repeated, frowning. "And why have you decided that the note was from my *chasan* and his friends?"

"Because of the question," Unmar replied with satisfaction. "Do you remember that I once asked Ruben a question about the *parshas hashavua*, and he said that he would think about it? Well, in the note, he wrote the answer!"

"Why haven't you told me about this until now?"

Unmar looked at her in surprise. "Was I supposed to tell?"

Near midday, Unmar placed a note in the squirrel hole in the old chestnut tree near the pond. Not long afterward, as he did every day, the elderly water-carrier thrust his hand into the hole. His astonishment upon finding a letter there was considerable. To the guards at the gate, who noticed the change in his expression and asked him about it in a friendly way, he said only that he had been suffering lately from sudden twinges of back pain. He hoped he would make it home...

His backache mysteriously disappeared as soon as he was out of the guards' sight. Had anyone followed that water-carrier, he would have found the man straying from the road that led to the village and entering the forest instead.

Five minutes of shrill whistling finally brought a young man with a sparse beard to the clearing among the trees.

"What happened?"

"A letter," the water-carrier gasped. "From...there." He did not report the contents of the letter. He was unable to read or write.

It was nearly dusk when the water-carrier returned to the palace. The guards at the gate were surprised to see him.

"What's the matter, uncle?" they asked courteously.

"I didn't finish my work this morning. My back sometimes pains me so... May the Kawaris know such backaches!"

"Is the pain gone now?"

"Yes, *baruch Hashem*," he said, and passed inside.

The setting sun cast strange shadows over the garden, making visibility poor. He placed an answering letter into the squirrel hole and was on his way to the kitchen when a heavy hand fell on his shoulder.

"What's wrong, uncle? What have you lost by the pool?"

"N...nothing," the water carrier stammered lamely. His denial was useless. A moment later, the letter was in the soldier's hand.

The older man tensed. While he had no idea of the letter's contents, he could guess that it was no shopping list.

"Listen," he said, seizing the soldier's hand to prevent him from opening the letter. "You do not have permission to read that. It's private!"

"What do you mean?" the soldier demanded.

"I mean that you have no permission to read it. "I... I..." In a rush, a torrent of words tumbled out. He spoke of the year before, when the winter had been hard and he had had no money to heat his home, and his daughter was ill, and they owed money to the doctor from the year before that, and his back constantly plagued him...

"What does all that have to do with this letter?" the soldier asked impatiently.

The water-carrier sighed. Up to this point, he had avoided an outright lie. Did he have any other choice now?

"What does a person do when times are hard?" he asked.

"What?"

"We ask Heaven for help," the water carrier answered his own question. "Right?"

"Yes," the soldier answered. "But I've never heard that a person needs to approach *HaKadosh Baruch Hu* in writing! And leave the message in the courtyard of the royal summer palace!"

"Last winter," the water carrier said, "the royal children were not here..."

The soldier stared at him in open astonishment. "You really did that? I was only joking when I said — This doesn't sound right, uncle! If you'd have at least left the letter in the *aron kodesh* in the *beis haknesses*, I'd understand."

The water-carrier bowed his head. "It is a good idea, what you're saying," he admitted. "But the *gabbaim* might find it there, no?"

The soldier handed back the scroll and said seriously, "Here. And go have a talk with your *rav*, all right?"

"*Bli neder*," the water-carrier agreed, tucking the precious scroll inside his clothes. "I will go on to the kitchen now, if you don't mind."

The soldier nodded, watching the older man lumber heavily off in the direction of the royal kitchens. What notions these ignorant people could get into their heads!

The water-carrier lingered in the kitchen only briefly. On his way back to the gate, he once again placed the letter in the squirrel hole, hoping that it would reach the proper hands as speedily as possible.

In the morning, Tur thanked the head guard for his devotion and his readiness to deviate from orders out of concern for their security. In her opinion, she said, the danger had passed. If an enemy had come to the palace last night and seen how heavily it was guarded, he would not return tonight.

The officer thought otherwise, but was unable to change the princess' mind.

Late that afternoon, most of the palace guard took their leave. The ten soldiers who were left behind had been carefully instructed by their leader, but it was clear to all of them that ten soldiers could not fill the role of forty. Especially when it seemed very likely that one or two of them were cooperating with a possible enemy.

An enemy who was already lying in wait nearby.

They called themselves by the names of great Roman emperors, and were very proud of this — and of the fact that those who knew them were as afraid of them as the Romans had been of Caligula, Julius, Nero, Titus, and Vespasian. The summons that reached them elevated their pride yet another notch.

But the mission they were asked to do was suited to the rawest recruit. There was nothing in it to elicit pride. What was there to be proud of when they had received the key to the side gate and the major portion of the summer palace guard had been cleared away?

At nightfall, the five men left the forest, headed for the nearby palace. The royal children, the summons to action had reported, had their living quarters on the third floor.

In another part of the forest, not very far away, a different group of men, supporters of Ruben Min-Hagai, prepared for action. According to the information that this group had received from their friends within the summer palace, a number of guards were likely to be walking the palace corridors. To avoid bloodshed, the attack was coordinated with the soldiers' regular schedule. The inside information included the fact that at least one royal guard would be constantly posted near the garden gate and three more near the front door. However, on their arrival they found no one barring their way in either place.

They exchanged disquieted glances. Had somebody prepared an ambush in an attempt to catch them in the act? They decided to proceed with the plan, nevertheless, taking extra precautions and staying a good distance apart from one another.

On the half-landing just below the royal children's floor, they encountered two guards who were clearly taken by surprise. Was it shock that prevented them from fighting back, or had they been feeble physical specimens to start with?

"We will not harm you, goodmen," Boaz said as he tied ropes around the two guards, back to back. "Nor will we harm the royal children — if the regent heeds our demands."

With handkerchiefs stuffed into their mouths, the guards looked wide-eyed as small children.

"We apologize," Boaz added, though this was not part of the script that Ruben Min-Hagai had given him, "for having to hurt you."

He strained his ears to listen for any suspicious sound from the third floor, but he heard nothing. The silence was too deep. All he heard was the whisper of an opening door and some too quiet voices. This was strange. It had all happened too easily. Someone, he concluded suddenly, had decided to let them carry out their plan. Once they were captured red-handed, the regent would seize the opportunity to prove to Khazar's populace that the libel he had fabricated about Ruben Min-Hagai was true.

A sound came from the second story, telling him that his realization had come too late.

In a panic, Boaz realized that he had neglected to cover the guards' eyes. With hands made awkward by haste, he attempted to do so now.

Again, it was too late. The guards had already seen the royal children, under no threat of violence, walking calmly down the stairs, dressed in their clothes and each carrying a small bundle. Just behind them came the boys' tutor and Tur's elderly nurse carrying additional bundles. Bringing up the rear of the procession were three servants carrying much larger bundles.

Boaz grimaced in frustration. Now they would be forced to add the two captured guards to this already considerable group. That was not going to make their job any easier…

"Go downstairs," he ordered the children and their escort, his voice unnaturally sharp and tense. In silence, they descended the steps. Not a sound was heard but the padding of feet and the rustling of dresses. The guards stared.

"As you can see for yourselves," Boaz said when the group had moved out of sight, "they trust us completely. Will you come along quietly?"

One of the guards, eyes still fixed on the spot where the group had disappeared, shook his head vehemently.

Boaz sighed. "All right then." His voice hardened. "If we can't do it the easy way, we'll do it the hard way. I'm sorry, but you asked for it…"

Downstairs, near the kitchen door, Ruben Min-Hagai waited impatiently. Hearing the door open at last, he let out his breath with relief and the ball of tension inside him evaporated.

Phase One of the operation had, to his knowledge, ended successfully. Exultant, he stepped out of the shadowy niche in which he had been hiding and moved toward the dimly lit hallway.

The first one to catch sight of him was Yekavel.

A great deal had happened since the last time Yekavel had seen Ruben, and his appearance had altered greatly. Nevertheless, despite the difference between the former elegant garb of *chasan* to the king's daughter and his present hunter's outfit, complete with numerous pockets, Yekavel recognized him instantly.

"Tur," he croaked. "Look!"

Tur lifted her eyes in surprise. In the letter she had received, no mention had been made of the fact that her *chasan* himself would be the one to oversee their escape from the palace. Though she was happy to see him, she realized at the same time that she had made a mistake. Yekavel, with all the fervor of a 9-year-old, very much admired Lord Diaber. And Lord Diaber had done everything in his power to fan the flames of hatred against Min-Hagai and his men.

"It's all right," she reassured her brother. "It's all right, Yekavel. Don't you trust me?"

No. He didn't trust her at all.

In his world, which had been so cruelly shattered and turned upside down, only one figure had remained strong and steadfast and protective. And that dominating figure had constantly spoken out against the man who now stood smiling at them — a taunting smile, it seemed to Yekavel.

His hesitation lasted a fraction of a second. Then he opened his mouth and shrieked.

His scream was loud and piercing, and it reached every corner of the palace. But its duration was not long. A moment after he had screamed, Yekavel found himself lifted into the air, a strong hand clamped over his mouth.

He kicked hard. The person holding him groaned, but did not let go.

"Quick," Min-Hagai said quietly. "Run!"

And, to Yekavel's dismay, they ran.

Rena stole through the shadows, holding her breath.

The darkness was not complete enough to hide her as she stood near the gate surrounding the leader's tent. And the silence was so deep that the slight sound she made as she tried to press against the gate and hide in the shadows reached the ears of one of the sentries.

"Something fell," he told his companion. "Over there."

"It's probably nothing."

"We'd better check," the first insisted, his voice hoarse and tired. "Something fell, I tell you."

A sound came from a certain distance away. This time there was no doubt — something *had* fallen. The soldiers hesitated. From where she stood, Rena could see the changing expressions on their faces. At the sight of their retreating forms, she began to breathe again. The coast was clear for her to traverse the open area without fear. If everything else she had planned had gone as smoothly, then the slave would be waiting by the prince's tent with the dead animals... Unless it had been *he* who had made the noise that caused the sentries to veer off into a different direction. Or — worse — Hala, the young prince, and their three companions.

She had tried her best to plan everything down to the finest detail — but success depended on the very things over which she had no control. And there were so many of them. So many dangers she could not prevent. So many things that could go wrong. So little chance that all would proceed as planned. So many risks...

When the Israelites went out to war, they always left behind one division of troops to speed them on their way with prayer. Was there anyone to pray for them and their escape attempt? Or had everybody despaired of the two princes' lives, leaving their tiny group to find its way completely on its own?

A thin moon appeared suddenly, casting a milky light that was dangerous and encouraging at the same time. With bowed head, Rena crossed the broad plaza and approached the prince's tent.

The sentries, she was glad to see, had been sent away. One of the young people was waiting for her, holding back the tent flap. A moment later, even before she had succeeded in distinguishing her daughter among the shadowy figures, the slave appeared, bent beneath the weight of two medium-sized pigs.

It was the screams, more than the smell, that roused Ka'hei from his sleep. But the instant he awoke, the smell struck his nostrils, powerful and pungent, and telling its own story of great danger. The piercing screams and the odor of scorched flesh could only have one significance.

Fire!

A fire in the camp!

Ka'hei's muscles functioned independently of his mind, moving on instinct. But he paused when his arm struck something in the sleeve of his robe. A rolled parchment scroll.

He had removed the robe when he had entered the tent several hours before, at the wedding's conclusion. Someone had apparently introduced the scroll into his sleeve after he had fallen asleep. Making an effort to suppress his urgency, to throw the scroll aside and race over to the flames, he thrust his hand into the sleeve and removed it. At the tent entrance, in the light of the rampaging flames, he read the inscribed words.

> "The choice is yours: to decide whether to pursue us — or to let the fire do its job."

Fire? Pursue?

It was a juxtaposition of words that offered only one meaning, too terrible to contemplate.

Ka'hei thrust the scroll into the nearest hiding place and hurried outside from his tent to the plaza, from the plaza to the small square, and from there, in a rush, to the source of the tumult — the tent to which all the camp's residents had escorted Hala, his daughter.

"*The choice is yours,*" the black letters on parchment were clear, "*to decide whether to pursue us — or to let the fire do its job.*"

Ka'hei felt dizzy. What was it that the fire was supposed to do?

Was Hala in there, injured, trapped in the flames?

Or maybe…

The flames were tall and cruel. Too tall and cruel to be the natural outcome of negligence or forgetfulness.

Was he the only one to notice this?

Men and women were bringing water, trying to prevent, at the very least, the flames' spread. Only he stood motionless. It seemed to him that the people understood the reason for his rigid stance.

Tonight had been his great moment. And now…

The smell of roasting flesh made everyone avert their eyes from Ka'hei's face. The choice was his, the letters had said. Yes, he must choose — between the lust for revenge and the lust for honor.

It was, he discovered, a very difficult choice to make. His wounded pride demanded vengeance. But vengeance would necessarily lead to a fresh injury to his pride.

How had he been so mistaken about the boy? How had he believed his pretense and thought that he had succeeded in winning his heart and his loyalty?

Through the flames, it seemed he could see Wanana's grinning, mocking face. And the laughter would not stop there; it would spread to all the cynics and rhyme-makers, down through every layer of the camp's population. The shame would afford him no choice but to leave the encampment or seek an honorable death — two options that did not appeal to the Kawari leader in the least.

But...to remain silent? To leave things as they were, with the boy crowing over his victory?

A small, satanic smile touched Ka'hei's lips. His situation, after all, was not so bad. This victory was only temporary.

Even if the boy succeeded in reaching Khazar, there were a few surprises awaiting him there that he could not have anticipated even in his darkest dreams.

In Flight

IT WAS A NIGHTMARE — THAT RACE THROUGH THE NIGHT — that would haunt them all for years to come.

The night was very dark, and the ground riddled with puddles. A sliver of moon hid behind a cloud, and a wind whipped branches into the runners' heads as they passed. The two captured guards had to be dragged along by force.

And then, suddenly, Unmar spoke up.

"Ruben," she panted, trying to keep up with his longer strides, "I left my doll in my room."

"We'll make you a new one," he promised.

"But, Ruben," she said in a thin, tight voice, "I promised my father that I would take care of my doll, no matter what happens."

"Your father," Ruben said without looking at her, "did not mean *any* situation."

"I think he did," she said. And then, all at once, she was no longer beside him.

"Unmar? Un-ma-a-ar!"

"I'll catch her," Ruben said. "The rest of you — run!"

"Let me go after her," Dan said.

Min-Hagai shook his head. "To the horses!" he said breathlessly. "Go!"

"They'll recognize you," Dan protested.

"You don't have to die in my place." Min-Hagai's tone was curt and commanding.

After one helpless look, Dan changed direction. The horses knew him, and he them; others would have had a hard time handling them. Besides, his mother was waiting for him at home. He wanted to help Min-Hagai in his righteous struggle — but, even more, he wished to live.

Unmar ran fast, very fast. The young man who had been designated as her future brother-in-law slipped in a puddle in pursuit. He scrambled to his feet limping and covered in mud. He caught her at last at the foot of the first staircase.

"My doll!" she moaned. "My doll…"

He held back the sharp words that rose to his lips. At this point, all that separated them from the doll were two flights of stairs.

"They'll catch us," he whispered. "Everyone's waiting for us."

"My doll…" Her voice was a feeble whimper, in stark contrast to her vigorous struggle to free herself from him. "The doll with the sea—" She broke off, aghast.

His brows lifted. "Hm? Is that so?"

She paled. It was a secret — and she, like a baby, had let it slip.

His hand, which had been gripping her sleeve, slackened suddenly, and there was reverence in his voice as he said, "Come, Princess. We must hurry."

They hurried.

But there was no need. Five of the soldiers were sound asleep, two others stood guard at the summer palace's outer gate, and the last soldier, who had been patrolling the wall when the "Romans" had invaded, would never bother anyone again.

The doll was tucked beneath Unmar's blanket, her round, wooden eyes staring placidly ahead.

"Excellent." Ruben reached out for it, but Unmar was quicker than him.

"It's mine," she said, plucking up the doll. "My father gave it to me."

She was right, of course. Still, it was not easy for Ruben Min-Hagai to let her race through the palace corridors with the great seal of Khazar in her vulnerable arms. He opened his mouth to object — and then, meeting her stubborn gaze, closed it again. "Come, Princess. I think we'd better hurry."

She smiled in relief. Hugging the doll close, she sprinted over to the door. Something sounded odd to Ruben. Looking down at Unmar's feet, he saw that she was wearing only one shoe.

"You'd better put on your other shoe," he said urgently.

"But I thought you said we have to hurry?"

"You'll move faster with two shoes on." He fought down a rising impatience. "Where do you keep your shoes, Princess Unmar?"

At a loss, she looked around at the big room. "Maybe there…" She gestured vaguely toward the door that led to an inner chamber.

As she made her way to the inner room, he moved over to the window, glad of the brief respite to collect his thoughts and calm his agitation. From the inner room came the sounds of a search: Unmar, apparently, was trying hard to find her missing shoe. Deciding that he had better lend a hand, he left the window and turned his head — to find himself staring directly into the eyes of a huge Roman clad in black.

Very good, the man said to himself. *Very good, Titus. Excellent. You know that they always return to the scene of the crime…* The dagger in his hand glinted. He appeared amused. *Very good*, he said again. *Well, what shall we do with him?*

With his back to the wall and the window, there was not much that Ruben could do — except, perhaps, sink weakly down onto the broad window frame.

"You're afraid of us," pronounced the man with the dagger. "Correct?"

"C-correct," Ruben stammered, pulling his knees up onto the sill.

"Afraid of us, right?" the Roman repeated. "Very, very afraid, right?"

The window sill afforded little protection. Before him stood the tall man with the dagger, and behind him was a thorny rose bed, three floors down. Below, he saw through the window, his men had surrounded his *kallah* and the rest of her group.

Ruben Min-Hagai's breath became quick and shallow.

At one time, back when he was doing his military service, he had been in excellent physical shape. Since ending his army training early because of an injury to his knee, the young nobleman had found more important things to occupy his time.

The man in front of him was stronger and bigger than he. But right now, he was short of options. He must seize his last opportunity...

Ruben lunged off the window sill, unfolding his legs like a jackknife and thrusting them into the man's chest. The mercenary grunted and fell back, his dagger scraping ineffectively against the mud on Ruben's leg. Ruben lunged at him, rolled sideways, and managed to wrest the blade away from his opponent. Both men scrambled to their feet. The fight was far from over.

In the recesses of his mind, Ruben wondered what had become of Unmar. Was she hiding, like a frightened rabbit, among the gowns and shoes in the dressing room? Or would she use these minutes while they were fighting to slip outside to the long corridors with their more numerous nooks and crannies?

A sharp blow to his arm brought him back to his own predicament. The Roman knocked the knife out of his hand, and it flew across the room. Ruben bared his teeth and drew a short sword from the sheath at his hip. The mercenary, not to be outdone, produced a second dagger — this one double-edged...

When it was all over, Ruben Min-Hagai wiped his short blade, for lack of any other option, on the draperies. He replaced the sword in its sheath and made short work of the distance separating him from the dressing-room door.

"Come," he called softly, leaning on the door frame, one hand on his nose to stanch the flowing blood.

She appeared out of the shadows, clutching the doll wordlessly to her chest.

"Let's get out of here," he said.

As they moved into the outer room, he remembered — a fraction of a second too late — what would lie in her field of vision. He stepped forward to block her view. "Look to the right, Princess," he whispered. "I'm sorry. There was nothing else I could do." Then, in a tone of command, "Hurry — after me."

Before they left the room, he stopped again. "Give me the doll. I will return it to you afterward."

She shook her head, both arms clasped tightly around the plaything. Ruben bit his lip in frustration. He had no desire to fight with her, and there was no time to press his point.

"As you wish. Let's go."

The palace corridors were dark and empty. Though there was no sign of any menacing threat, Min-Hagai still felt a sense of dire foreboding.

A shadow protruding from Yekavel and Binyamin's room proved his fears justified. Silently Ruben pointed at the staircase leading toward the roof, indicating to the princess that she should head up there. His other hand went to his sword as he sought a better vantage point than the narrow landing.

This time the scuffle was of longer duration than it had been in Unmar's room. An elaborate wall tapestry came to his assistance. However, when Ruben tried to throw it at his opponent, its metal handles were wrenched from their places and hurled with great force by the black-clad figure at the stair railing behind which Ruben crouched.

This fight, too, ended in victory. But Ruben felt neither triumph in the win nor trembling at the knowledge that he had taken two men's lives that night. His mind, dry and practical, had taken control of his limbs without allowing his heart any say in the matter. It was as though he were observing himself from the outside. Like a very bad dream…

Now, where was Unmar?

Not a trace of the girl was to be seen. Not in the main living quarters, nor on the roof nor on the stairs leading down from it.

He ought to be glad she had found herself a good place of

concealment, but the actual emotion that consumed him was something else entirely. How would he find her now? And if he did not find her — what then? Could he leave the palace without her?

The few seconds he spent pondering these questions felt like an eternity. Finally, he decided to go down and instruct those sitting in the carriages to leave the royal premises. Every minute they lingered here, in this place that swarmed with menace, was one minute too many.

As Ruben ran down the stairs, he encountered two alarmed servants on their way up to the royal living quarters. It was hard to say who was more surprised.

"What happened up there?" they asked.

"Attempted kidnaping," he told them. "Find yourself a safe spot."

"Don't you need help?" one of them, braver than his companion, asked.

"No. The army is already here."

"And who are you?" asked the second, more cowardly, servant.

"Internal security," Min-Hagai said firmly. "Let me pass, please."

They obeyed. As he made his way out to the courtyard, he imagined how they would feel when they had recovered from their surprise and realized the identity of the man they had stopped and allowed to pass. Later, if all ended well, he would apologize to them.

If all ended well…

He forced these thoughts aside and went forward, head bowed against the wind, muscles tensed and ears pricked as he listened for the sound of additional enemies in the area.

When he arrived at the spot where he had left the carriages, he was happy to see only the outline of one of them waiting there. It meant the others had managed to escape to safety. Boaz, in the driver's seat, was just as glad to see him.

"Shall we get out of here, sir?" he whispered, a broad smile indicating his relief.

"You go," Ruben said, his voice muffled because of the hand still trying to stem the flow of blood from his nose. "I'll find my own way out…"

Boaz opened his mouth to protest, but Ruben stopped him. "Don't worry... My father will continue to lead the struggle. Hurry!"

Boaz gaped in incomprehension, though one hand was already uplifted to spur the horses. Then a small voice asked from inside the carriage, "But why?"

"Because of Unmar," Min-Hagai said. "I can't find —" Suddenly, he broke off and flung himself into the carriage. "I couldn't find *you*, Your Highness," he finished as Boaz spurred the horses. "Congratulations, Princess."

"Congratulations?" one of his men asked. "What for?"

But Ruben didn't answer. He simply looked at the doll, seated placidly in Unmar's lap, and smiled.

When the five mercenaries had divided up the task between them, Julius and Vespasian's job had seemed the simplest. They were to remain behind near the servants' entrance to ensure that the retreat route remained open, while Caligula, Nero, and Titus went upstairs to execute the mission itself.

But when Nero, lithe and quick, ran downstairs to tell them that their intended victims had disappeared — adding a description of the child's scream they had heard as they passed through the palace gates — a most unpleasant picture emerged: someone else had snatched their prey from their very fingers!

Nero, youngest of the group, went back upstairs to update Caligula on developments, while Vespasian and Julius raced toward the carriage gate, guessing that the escapees had prepared a means of transportation ahead of time. As they had expected, they found the gate unlocked and took up positions on either side.

Just a minute or two of waiting brought the hoped-for result: a carriage, handled by the capable hands of Dan and carrying the princes and princesses of Khazar, rattled up to the gate.

Vespasian aimed his bow. Nero, a shadow slipping through the trees, had returned to them in time to close in on the coach from behind, and Julius, dagger drawn, ran ahead of it. "Halt!" he shouted in broken Khazari.

Looking down from the height of his coachman's seat, Dan saw Vespasian and his menacing weapon. "Never!" he declared, eyeing the gate. When they had arrived here, Boaz had insisted on climbing down and breaking the lock. Ignoring his friends' remonstrations about wasting precious seconds, he had broken both the tongue of the lock and the elongated metal piece that was meant to be plunged into the ground. Dan was glad now that Boaz had "wasted" those seconds.

Dan took a deep breath and whipped the horses with all his might. Julius, thrust aside by the horse on the left, could do nothing but glare after the carriage as it burst through the gate and barreled off into the darkness.

Vespasian was more efficient. The sequence of arrows he shot off pierced the carriage walls, and one of them — so he claimed — had surely wounded one of the horses.

Julius didn't believe him; Vespasian was prone to boasting. It was Nero who convinced him to nevertheless try to complete the mission they had come here to do.

The mercenaries set out after the carriage. The further they ran, the more signs they saw that there might, after all, be some truth to Vespasian's claims. The wheel tracks were uneven, and after several hundreds yards the tracks showed that one of the horses was behaving extremely erratically. Sounds of kicking reached them from the road.

"If they have any brains at all," Vespasian panted, "they'll jump out of the carriage."

But nobody jumped.

Instead, as they moved behind the rampaging horse, Dan shouted for one of his comrades to climb up onto the coachman's seat and cut the injured horse's reins.

Meanwhile Binyamin, who had fallen from his seat onto the carriage floor, grabbed one of the men's legs, his yells reverberating in the night. When the shouting stopped, a frightening silence took their place. Yekavel was held fast in another man's arms, paralyzed with fear. Tur, ashen in the darkness, covered Lissia's mouth with one hand and held onto the carriage wall with the other, trying not to topple to the floor. Each time the carriage swayed, a tiny groan escaped her lips.

The injured horse galloped into the forest, its torn reins trailing after it. In pain-driven madness, it plowed through the trees and was slashed by the short, sharp branches. The coach wobbled behind the remaining horse on three wheels.

"Good horse," Dan crooned in what he hoped was a soothing voice. "Fine horse…"

"Come on, let's get moving!" called the man who was holding Yekavel. But the carriage was meant to be pulled by two horses, and their one remaining animal — even discounting the exertions of its journey to the summer palace — was incapable of carrying them on its own at anything faster than a turtle's crawl.

"All right." Dan turned to face the others. "We've done our part. Now it's His turn."

"Whose turn?" asked Lissia.

Dan smiled. "His," he said. "The Supreme Leader…"

At this, Tur had to smile, too. The Supreme Leader! What an appropriate name for the Master of the universe. It gave her a feeling of peace. "Everything's all right now," she whispered into Lissia's blonde curls. The little girl was whimpering on her lap. "Everything's all right."

This was not strictly true — not at all. The men who had met them by the gate were still pursuing them. But, in a way, it *was* true, because her faith and trust were freshly energized, and both the forest and the black-clad enemy had lost their terror.

With the carriage now more a liability than a safe means of escape, Dan had decided that they must disembark and continue on foot. Someone took Lissia from Tur and motioned for her to climb out of the carriage. The thought of becoming lost in the forest did not seem at all appealing to her, but she obeyed.

In a frightened near-silence, they emptied the coach. Binyamin, rigid with fear, was held by one of the companions, while Yekavel, his struggles having abated finally, submissively followed Dan through the dense trees.

The carriage and horse remained alone among the trees — but

not for long.

The doctor was an elderly man, old and wrinkled, but until this moment Ovadia had not seen his hands shake. They were shaking now as they held the medical instruments, and the aged eyes were brimming with tears. Alarmed, Ovadia returned his gaze to the king. Reuel's chest rose and fell in the same slow, even tempo as before.

"You are still hoping," the doctor said quietly.

"Hoping and praying," Ovadia replied, hands clasped tightly behind his back.

"Prayers," said the physician, "never return empty-handed. But sometimes they are fulfilled in a different way from the one we asked for."

Ovadia dropped his eyes.

"This will not continue much longer," the doctor spoke in the same quiet tone as the tears coursed down his wrinkled cheeks. "And perhaps it is for the best. *You*, better than anyone, know how much he is suffering."

Ovadia stared at the yellowing hand that lay, as though lifeless, on the coverlet. "He is Khazar's hope!" he blurted, wishing he could hide his own tears. "Everything's begun to change! He *must* come back. He must!"

"Perhaps your prayers," the doctor whispered, "are what are holding him here. But if they are unable to restore him to life or to release him from his suffering..." The silence was long and filled with meaning. "Perhaps it would be better if you were to pray for Khazar's future."

"I do pray for that," Ovadia said. "Every day."

"He was the best king Khazar has ever known," the doctor said softly.

"He still is!" Ovadia's tone was sharp. He busied himself at the dresser, as though seeking something amid the jumble of objects there.

"Makan was not to blame," the physician said, abruptly changing the subject. "And neither, to my mind, was Stazdiran."

Ovadia turned back slowly to face him.

"And I have known Min-Hagai since before his son was born. They are the last ones I would have believed to be embroiled in such a plot." The lined face twisted in pain. "The guilty party is walking the palace corridors a free man. When I entered the field of medicine, I promised to do everything in my power to save lives. But I am a doctor, not a detective..."

The words were seductive — but Ovadia sealed his lips. He might have his suspicions, but suspicions were all he had. If he wanted to keep his head, he had better keep his mouth shut tight.

When he saw he would evince no reaction from Ovadia, the doctor sighed, hefted his medical bag onto one shoulder, and headed to the door. On the threshold, he paused. "When all this is over, I am going to take a long vacation. A very long vacation. If you need me, Ovadia, you'll find me in a village, at my sister's." Fresh lines become evident on his face as he spoke, and his lips took on a grayish hue as he added, "Evil days have fallen on Khazar, Ovadia. Very evil days." And then, so quietly that Ovadia could hardly be sure he heard, the doctor finished, "I never thought I'd regret having lived this long..."

"I don't understand," Ovadia said.

The doctor raised his brows. "He will succeed, and that will be bad. But then — if our prayers are answered — someone else will come and summon the people of Khazar to his banner. And that will be good. But there will be those who will prefer a pot of lentil stew to the birthright... Swords will ring out and clash, the fields will be neglected, and blood will pour instead of water."

"And...in the end?" Ovadia asked reverently. Everyone knew that this man was one of Khazar's righteous men. His words of foresight bore weight.

"In the end?" The doctor spread his hands. "I do not know, my son. All I do know," he added, "is that Khazar will not endure forever. The day will come when people will wonder if this mighty Jewish kingdom, stretching from river to river, ever existed." He bowed his head to his chest. For a moment he stood that way, unmoving. Then he roused himself and left the room without another word.

Ovadia gazed at the door that the doctor had closed behind him. With a sigh, he looked at the king. Was he only imagining it, or were those tears glistening in the corners of the tightly closed eyes?

The second charity-fund conference took place in the early hours of the evening. After much lofty talk about the wonderful merit of their work and a communal Ma'ariv, all the participants were invited to a festive meal at which the regent would be present.

White-jacketed servants led the way to the dining hall, where waiters directed each member to his designated table. The tables were beautiful arranged and laden with an assortment of dishes worthy of the royal kitchens. Tippias and Elkanah found themselves seated on either side of a long, lavish table along with six other *gabba'ei tzedakah* with whom they were not acquainted. All of them managed free-loan funds for the needy and served as trustees for orphans' properties.

The conversation around the table was both interesting and purposeful. They were in the midst of exchanging views about the proper way to invest the money in their charge, when the minister in charge of the gathering clapped his hands and invited His Excellency, Lord Diaber, to say a few words.

Elkanah muttered something under his breath. Tippias stepped on his foot under the table. Silence fell, deep and absolute.

"Good evening." The regent's tone was congenial and welcoming. "I hope that you are all well and have been enjoying the meal. To conclude this long and exciting day, I would like to raise a number of questions that require our attention.

"The first question — one that troubles every responsible *gabbai tzedakah* — is how to know whether the public funds he has been appointed to dole out are indeed used for the purpose for which they've been designated. In other words: how do we know when the needy are truly needy?"

He took a sip of water, allowing the echo of his words to die away before continuing.

"The answer," he said, still holding the stem of the crystal water goblet, "is —"

The regent's voice, which had been clear and resounding, became suddenly hoarse. The muscles of his face twisted in pain. To everyone's astonishment, the goblet fell from his fingers and crashed to the floor. Clutching his chest, he sank weakly into his seat.

"A doctor," he managed to croak. "A doctor...quickly."

Long, precious minutes passed before the doctor arrived — minutes during which the assembled crowd completed several chapters of *Tehillim* for the regent's speedy recovery. Yosef Diaber had been helped into a side room, and it was to this room that the doctor hurried.

There was no immediate, reassuring word for the guests. Only after a considerable period of time had elapsed did word filter out: the same anonymous enemy who had done away with the queen and had dealt the king a mortal blow had struck again. The regent had been poisoned.

A tumult erupted in the big hall. Zavdiel Mitran, minister of internal security, tried to restore order. But it was as though an enormous wave had crashed onto the shore. Every man in that big room wanted to know how it was possible, again and again, for Khazar's enemies to penetrate the most secure places in the kingdom.

"Quiet!" Mitran pleaded, tapping a fork against a glass in an effort to call the crowd to attention. "You are the ones who can provide the answer! Yes — *you*! You, who stand at the very center of the country's *chesed* operations, must ask yourselves how it is that acts of charity are not protecting our people!"

His words finally brought some measure of quiet to the crowd.

"Dogs bite the stick that beats them," Zavdiel said. "The Khazars know that there is a Hand holding the stick. Do not ask me 'how' or 'why.' The answers lie with you — with everyone whose good deeds have not prevented our recent tragedies. This is the time to pray, gentlemen, not to shout or make speeches." That said, he descended the small speakers' platform and gestured for an elderly, white-bearded Jew to take his place and lead the recitation of *Tehillim*.

When they had completed two rounds of the chapters designated specifically for healing the sick, a man of noble bearing entered the room. Those in the know whispered that he was Nazarel, minister of protocol.

Nazarel thanked all those who were praying on the regent's behalf and announced that the stricken man's condition was improving. "With Hashem's mercy," he said, "the regent did not drink much from the glass, but merely wet his lips. The doctor hopes that in light of the minute quantity of poison that passed into the regent's system, the damage to his heart will be gone by morning, without lasting consequences." He cleared his throat. "His Excellency, the regent, begs each and every one of those present here to appear at tomorrow's conference at the appointed hour of the morning. If possible, he will be there in person, as planned. If not, his main proposals will be read out loud." The light-blue eyes twinkled above the luxuriant white beard. "Good night to you all," he concluded and slowly descended the platform.

As though they had waited for this signal, the waiters hastened to serve the last course. After *Birkas HaMazon*, the crowd dispersed — still stunned by what they had witnessed that evening — into the spacious palace gardens.

Glowing lanterns lit the path out of the palace grounds, where a convoy of carriages waited to bear each man off to his night's lodging. A slim, dark-bearded, and sharp-eyed man shared the coach that took Tippias and Elkanah to the outlying suburb where Rivka lived. They exchanged personal details and scrutinized one another.

"It was a good evening," the stranger said. "Except for the tragedy. Or perhaps even with it — it will infuse many people with strength. People need strength."

Elkanah studied the speaker in silence.

Tippias said, "There is something in what you say."

"Something," Elkanah murmured dryly.

"A number of difficult things have happened this year," their fellow traveler remarked. "I was going to return the keys of our charity box to the *rav* — he should live and be well — and let someone else be abused instead of me. Let someone else stay up nights, begging and pleading, only to get punched in the nose in the end!" His eyes burned with the guilelessness of a child. "But now that I've received a bit of respect, my wife and children won't let me give up the job." He paused, then asked abruptly, "How do you think the poison was introduced into the regent's cup?"

Elkanah's drooping eyelids lifted. "Drop by drop," he said.

"Ever since the queen was poisoned, the waiters give the dogs a sip from every bottle of wine that reaches the head table," the man said. "And they are kept under careful supervision."

The carriage drew up in front of Rivka's house before they could hear the man's views on the subject. Bidding their fellow passenger good night, they descended into the darkness, which was far more opaque here than it was in the city.

In the dead of night, when the two brothers were sprawled on the beds that Rivka had made up for them, Elkanah's voice called out softly in the dark.

"Tippias?"

Tippias propped himself up on one elbow. There had been an uncharacteristic note of emotion in his brother's voice. "Yes? What is it?"

"I've been thinking," said Elkanah, "of the fruit whip we were served."

"It was very tasty," Tippias replied, wondering. "But your wife's desserts are even better."

"I think so, too. But isn't it strange, the way the waiters served it so calmly — as though nothing had happened?"

Tippias leaned forward. "What are you trying to say?"

"I don't know. I've just been thinking about the topic His Majesty chose to talk about…"

"What, exactly, are you trying to say, Elkanah?"

"Nothing." With a soft thump, Elkanah lay back on his pillow. "Tomorrow is another day."

Tippias thought of his brother's encounter with the regent earlier in the day. "Don't look for trouble, Elkanah. All right?"

Elkanah didn't answer.

Tippias sighed. For some reason, he found it difficult to believe that his brother had fallen asleep at precisely that instant.

During the course of the night, the regent's health markedly improved. So remarkably, in fact, that he decided — even in the face of the doctor's remonstrance — to call a special emergency meeting at midnight. Diaber led this meeting himself, pausing at frequent intervals to draw air into his lungs. The Khazar ministers and noblemen who had been summoned from their warm mansions to the cold conference room could not help but marvel at the man's amazing resiliency. After a few heartfelt words of thanks to all those whose prayers had sustained him in the last hours, the regent put aside his personal distress to focus exclusively on the kingdom's needs.

"There are a number of crucial areas that need to be addressed," he said. "There is the peace treaty, which has not yet been formally signed, and changes to be made in the internal security framework, which has demonstrated its inability to find and punish those who collaborate with the enemy. All of these issues cannot be resolved because of a problem you are all aware of: the disappearance of the Great Seal."

Diaber paused, obviously exhausted by the effort it took to speak. When his heart rate had returned to normal, he went on. "Every thinking citizen can sense this lack of stability. As Lord Mitran can tell you, the crime rate in Itil has risen noticeably. The people are afraid, and there has been much bartering of hard metals in exchange for flour, sugar, and other staples that can keep for long periods of time. I would guess," he said, "that in the course of the next few days, as news of this latest attack filters out, the panic will increase. We must meet that panic with forethought. We must ensure the nation that Khazar is stable and that nothing — not murder, kidnaping, or the disappearance of the Great Seal — can shake us."

The men around the table stirred uneasily. The state of the kingdom bordered on the catastrophic. Without the Great Seal, the regent's hands were tied.

"That is why I summoned you here," Diaber concluded. "Please divide into groups and try to find possible solutions and means of dealing with this far from simple situation."

The night was extremely well advanced, and none of the men in that conference room had spent the day in sweet slumber or gazing up at the clouds. They were hardworking men, and in their fatigue they found it difficult to think clearly.

The discussion ran along two general lines.

One, the Great Seal made it possible for the arm of the law — specifically, the regent — to do its job.

Two, as long as a regent, and not a king, stood at the helm in Khazar, there was no way to circumvent the legal necessity for the missing seal.

At 4 a.m., utterly spent, they lapsed into silence. It was then — seemingly arising from the ennui that gripped them — that the solution suddenly blossomed: If a king was needed in order to pour a new Great Seal, what was to prevent them, the members of Khazar's highest governing board, from appointing Yosef Diaber as king?

The theory was daring, almost insolent, and its sheer force dispelled their fatigue. Those cold gray walls had never known such turmoil. Men got up from their seats, waved their hands, shouted, and tried in every way possible to express either their support of the idea or their complete disgust with it.

The minister of protocol was among the most vocal of the objectors — not because it was a bad idea, but because its execution was going to be impossible. It would be necessary to circumvent a great many traditions, customs, and laws in order to carry it out. It was impossible, simply impossible.

At the height of the debate, the guards' knock at the door was lost, as was the squeak of its hinges as it opened. But when the chief prison warden and a representative of Zavdiel Mitran's internal security office strode rapidly inside, silence fell over the big room.

The two approached Lord Mitran and spoke to him in an undertone. Eighty pairs of eyes watched the changing expressions on the minister's face as he listened. When he cleared his throat to speak, some of those in the big room had an inkling of what he was about to say.

"It distresses me to have to inform you all," he said, leaning on the table before him, "that Lord Bastian Makan has escaped from his cell tonight."

The others waited with bated breath for him to continue. He obliged, with ill-concealed anger. "Anyone who thinks that this kingdom can be allowed to continue being run in this fashion — raise your hand."

Not a single hand was raised.

Within minutes, a process was begun that had no precedent in Khazar: the country's nobility unanimously proclaimed a voluntary revolution.

The term "voluntary revolution" was easy to say. Its actual implementation was going to be much more complicated — and every member of the governing body knew it.

In order to put the concept into practice, it would be necessary to amend a fundamental portion of Khazar's legal system. It would be necessary as well to explain to the populace, by means of official notices, what the process meant and what its consequences were for the future. And a police-military response must be prepared in advance, in case Min-Hagai's men decided to take advantage of the confusion to usurp control of the kingdom.

In the Ministry of War — which, despite all the upheavals, still held Bastian Makan's stamp — discussions were held about the division of military forces and seizing control of important civilian locations, such as the central crossroads. Beneath one of the large windows in the central hall, three ministers toiled away, with the help of six consultants and two scribes, at formulating the text of the special announcement that would be disseminated by courier throughout the length and breadth of the land, explaining the significance of the revolution. And around the conference table itself sat the statesmen who were preparing to set down on parchment the laws of the "New Khazar," as the regent had dubbed it.

"Nothing will really be different," Lord Shefer said firmly. "That will be the essence of this law."

Diaber, from his armchair, nodded in confirmation.

"Nothing?" Lord Kafchaver leaned across the table. "That isn't like you. As His Majesty's brother-in-law, I would have expected you, Lord Shefer, to be a little more concerned for the family's interests."

The remark was not meant to offend, but only to emphasize the gravity of the move they were contemplating. But Shefer paled, then flushed — until the man seated next to him, believing him to be on the brink of fainting, seized his glass of water and poured it over his head.

"Are you all right? What's the matter?" Lord Kafchaver asked Shefer, taken aback.

"Nothing," Lord Shefer said tersely, wiping his face. It was hard for him to put into words how he had felt upon hearing Kafchaver's comment. It had reminded him of his niece Tur's quiet, submissive face, the face of someone who has learned to give up and to bear down after Diaber shattered her world with his news of a man she should have been able to trust with her life: her *chasan* and soon-to-be husband. Yosef Diaber was a good man, a man who engaged in charity and good deeds, but he had behaved cruelly toward Tur. That was not the way to tell her about the suspicions that had been aroused against her *chasan*. That was not the way! And then there was the reaction of the royal children to this turn of events. What would little Lissia say when someone tried to explain to her that her father was no longer the king?

Around the table, the others were watching him. He shook his head, as if to push away the fog that had clouded his mind during the recent discussions. He had allowed himself to be swept up with the others when the big change was being debated, he realized. Lord Kafchaver's comment had jarred him to think more clearly. Is it possible that Diaber had staged his own poisoning in order to manipulate them?

They had been too hasty. For one thing, the question should have been raised with their great Torah scholars. For another, none of them had considered the tears of children who had already gone through such terrible suffering in recent months…

"Shefer?" A hand touched his, and a concerned face looked into his own.

"I'm all right," he said with an attempt at a smile. "I didn't drink any poison."

The joke, even to his own ears, fell decidedly flat.

PEOPLE CAN UNDERSTAND A CHILD'S DESIRE TO RUN AWAY from school, to gambol in the fields and forests in freedom. But would anyone grant the same understanding to a person who had been freed from a prison cell in which he had been held for so many long months?

When the door to his cell had opened, and one of his jailers had smiled at him and whispered, "You have good friends outside, Your Excellency," Bastian Makan had been filled with an indescribable joy. Subsequently, when he had discovered that there had been no belated recognition of the truth by those charged with his investigation, some of his happiness had dissipated. In its place rose a bitter urge to escape from those who had swallowed the tissue of lies that had been woven around him — and who, even after its falsity had been demonstrated, were in no hurry to beg his pardon.

And so, like those schoolchildren, he had done it. He had yielded to his longing. Glad that there existed those who, despite everything, believed in his innocence, he made his way out into the world.

It was only when his wagon had traveled some distance from

everything that reminded him of the pain and degradation of imprisonment and the betrayal of his friends that Bastian Makan began to weigh what he had done.

He did not like the conclusions he reached.

Until now, his situation had been reasonable, if not pleasant. Ever since the village doctor had declared that it had not been Makan's men who acquired the lethal potion from him, the case had begun to gravitate in his favor. His chances of being acquitted in court had increased, and he had been treated in a deferential manner. Now, with this impulsive bolt, everyone would be convinced that he alone was guilty of all the horrific acts that had shaken the kingdom in recent months. The search for him would be intensive, and any investigation into the identity of another possible suspect or suspects abandoned.

He reached the painful conclusion that his long imprisonment had addled his thought processes. Otherwise, why in the world had it occurred to him to flee?

Beneath his sackcloth shirt — an item that, along with his unkempt appearance, enabled him to pass as an elderly farmer — his heart constricted powerfully. A wave of fear, simple and brutal, overwhelmed the veteran military man.

Perhaps he had been given preferential treatment — but he had still been in jail. The deference for which he had been grateful was comprised of a small private cell — only slightly wider than the bed he had been permitted to bring in — a chair, and any litter removed twice a week instead of the usual once.

He had no desire to return there. He especially did not want to return to the view from his prison window: the tall green pole that served as the gallows.

Never, in his exalted position as minister of war, had he given even passing thought to the cruelty of placing the gallows within view of the condemned men within the prison confines. He allowed himself a sigh of regret. What else had he neglected to think about during his nearly thirty-three years of power and influence?

Bastian Makan's broad, sturdy shoulders hunched forward, the coarse woolen scarf around his neck swaying with the carriage's motion. Eyes closed, he tried to focus on the people he loved and honored most in this world. There were four: his father, his wife, his firstborn son — a golden boy who although still young, had been certain that there was no better man in the world than his father — and Reuel. Even Reuel, despite everything.

All four, he knew, would have urged him to go back.

He made a decision. "Young man," he said, tapping lightly on the wagon-driver's shoulder. "We're going back to Itil."

The driver's protruding front teeth jutted even further as he gaped in astonishment. "To Itil?" he repeated. "What are you looking for there, uncle?"

"The Angel of Death," Bastian replied dryly. "We have an appointment."

The driver's jaw hung slack. "I don't understand."

"I have decided," Bastian said patiently, "to return to prison."

"You don't really mean it, do you?" the driver asked. "That wouldn't be fair to all those who risked their lives to help you escape."

"I am not accustomed to explaining myself or arguing. Please turn the wagon around."

"Impossible. I have my orders. I'm carrying them out."

The man's insolence surprised Bastian. He struggled to maintain his equanimity. "And you have carried out your orders admiringly. But now, I wish you to return me to my prison cell. Turn the wagon around, young man."

The young man appeared as indifferent as the horses plodding along in front of them. His actual orders had been slightly different. He had been explicitly told to make sure that Makan ended up conversing with the angels that very night...and there was a man waiting in a hut in the forest to help him do just that.

"Did you hear me?" Makan demanded.

Rabbit-Teeth shrugged again. "We can return to Itil any time you want," he said, turning off the high road into a lane that led into the forest. "But it would be better to wait until after the guards are off the road. Returning to jail on your own is altogether different from being taken there by force."

Bastian contemplated what the man had advised. There was some truth in his words. If he returned of his own free will, everyone would realize that the search for the true culprits must continue. But if he were apprehended, people would believe exactly what they had come to believe following his escape.

And yet…

A basic military principle states that when facing a strong enemy line, one must seek out every weak spot, even if there is a chance that tomorrow may bring an easier method of penetration. The pressure of what he was feeling inside transformed this "enemy" into an almost unconquerable foe.

"No," Bastian said. "Stop. *Now!*"

Not only did Calidius — for it was he who was driving the wagon that carried Bastian Makan — not stop, but he spurred the horses on to greater speed. Makan's hand, which had been resting on the driver's shoulder, tightened sharply. It hurt, and Calidius — always fearful of attack — reacted to the pain by pulling up the horses and whipping out a knife. Bastian instinctively struck at the other man's forearm, sending the knife flying. Because his seat was lower than the driver's, the knife did not fly down to the ground, but upward, toward the sky. The knife hurtled through the air as though held in an invisible hand, spun once on an unseen hinge, and then plummeted, point down, directly into Calidius' neck.

The blow was so quick that there was no time for so much as a gasp to escape Calidius' lips. The cry that filled the air and brought the hired assassin running from his hut in the forest was uttered by Bastian.

"Has something happened?" the man called, approaching the wagon.

Bastian raised his head from the fallen wagon-driver. "Yes," he said. "Someone has died."

The killer came closer. "Was killed, you mean," he said, studying the scenario with a professional eye.

"G-d killed him," Bastian said sharply, shaking off the responsibility and preparing to engage in a lengthy explanation. To his surprise, the other man nodded. "He had it coming. Yes, he had it coming…"

Bastian, sniffing danger, pulled back.

"There's a beauty in this, don't you think?" the assassin remarked.

"Beauty…in what?" Bastian's voice was steady, but his brain was busy trying to decide whether it would be proper for him — for the purposes of self-defense — to pull the knife out of the dead man's neck.

"In the hand of G-d," the man explained. He nodded at the dead man. "We go back a long way, him and me."

It was reasonable to suppose that no innocent citizen had been recruited to help a prisoner escape from jail. Still, the stranger's reaction interested Bastian. "Yes?" he asked encouragingly.

The assassin pressed his lips together. "He would have died tonight in any case. I would have killed him. But it's nicer that G-d did it."

"How interesting." Bastian tried to keep his voice steady and nonchalant.

"You have no idea," the assassin said, grinning broadly.

Bastian had nothing to say to that.

"He has money for me," the man said. "I want it."

There was no pointing in arguing, and Bastian didn't. Drawing back, he allowed the man to search the body. A bundle of coins was found in the dead man's inner pocket, and the stranger appropriated this with open satisfaction.

"Don't you want to know what the money is for?" he asked, after climbing down from the wagon.

"No."

"He was supposed to give it to me after I killed you," the assassin said. "But if G-d decided to kill him instead — I won't interfere. So what, you may ask again, is the money for?"

It took all of Bastian's will to keep his gaze steady on the other, clearly dangerous man, waiting to see what he would do.

"You are a good man," the assassin announced. "That's what some of my friends told me. The king was a good man, too. If he'd told me that the snake was for *him*, I would never have given it to him. Not at that price..."

Bastian's featured tightened. "Are you saying...? He was the one who...?" He stared down at Calidius in horror. "But...why? Who sent him?"

The assassin grinned. "The same person who sent someone else to pay me to kill him. But my clients count on my discretion. It wouldn't do for me to reveal his name."

Bastian nodded, as though he understood.

"You are a good man," the stranger said again. "That's what my friends say. The king was a good man, too." He gazed into Makan's face before adding, "But Yosef Diaber — no."

"Is that what you think?" Bastian asked thoughtfully.

"If that's what I said, then that's what I think!" The hired killer paused meaningfully. "Take care of yourself. You will be all right on your own, won't you?"

"A Jew is never alone," Makan said. He indicated the dead man. "Was he married?"

The assassin lowered his eyes, as though seeing the corpse as a human being for the first time. "I have no idea, Your Excellency."

"He must be buried. And the authorities in the city where he lived must be notified."

The killer mumbled something, still looking down.

"I can't do it," Bastian went on. "For obvious reasons. And I am also unable to promise you anything in payment."

"You overestimate the influence of my conscience, Your Excellency."

Bastian lowered his head. When he lifted it, the other man was gone.

For a long moment, Bastian Makan sat in the wagon staring at the dead man. Finally he rose, grasped the corpse, placed it on the floor of the wagon, and took his place in the driver's seat. Someone had to bury the poor fellow, and right now there was no one to see to it but himself.

They made slow progress. Although no one in particular was to blame, they all shared the responsibility.

Despite his determination to behave normally, Michoel — who was carrying the old *Sefer Torah* and was weak from lack of food — had to stop from time to time to catch his breath. Hala had twisted her ankle even before they left the tent camp, Kalev turned out not to have much physical stamina, and the Mundari spent considerable time covering their tracks, which entailed a great deal of patient walking on roundabout paths. Knaz, bringing up the rear, seemed not at all troubled by the sight of the morning star rising in the sky. All his attention was riveted on the tiny signs on the surface of the ground. Add to all this the fact that the moon had disappeared behind a blanket of clouds and that a light rain had begun to fall, and it was no wonder they were traveling at a snail's pace.

The cave where Rena had planned for them to spend the remainder of the night and recoup their strength was still far off when the sky began to grow light. She looked around apprehensively. The Kawari encampment was no longer visible, but the distance they had traveled that night with so much exertion could be covered in minutes by armed horsemen.

"We'd better think about finding a place to hide during the daylight hours," the Mundari said, as though reading her thoughts. "Does Your Highness have any ideas?"

"The cave is still far away," Rena said quietly. "We've been making slow progress."

Hala stared down at the ground near her swollen foot. How stupid of her to fall! Knaz looked grave. He, too, took responsibility for the delay — but how could he have acted otherwise?

"I'm trying," Michoel said hoarsely. "I've never been this weak…"

Istrak, with a composure that his new mother-in-law very much appreciated, said, "Berating ourselves will do us no good. We must find a place to conceal ourselves. Are there any feasible places in the area?"

"There are gorges and undergrowth along this way," Hala said tentatively when her mother did not answer immediately. "But…"

"We can't just sit and wait!" Kalev burst out. "*I* can't do it anyway."

"Sometimes there's no choice." Istrak surveyed the small group. "We're all tired." He smiled at Michoel, remembering the moment of rare closeness in the darkness of the Batar Ravine. But Michoel was remembering other things. And those things, along with his brother's smile, made him squirm with mortification. He was weak, true. But that was no reason to embarrass him in front of the others!

Kalev, also misinterpreting Istrak's expression, spoke up in defense of the young prince. "He has not had normal food to eat. Even when I came, there were always questions about the utensils."

Istrak paled. What was Kalev implying? With difficulty, he gathered his wits. "I said that we're *all* tired," he repeated, stressing the penultimate word. "And that's exactly what I meant."

He searched out Michoel's eyes — but those eyes were fixed painfully on some point in the distance. Istrak's stomach clenched. "Father would have been proud of you," he said, each word coming with an effort. "Just as he was always so proud of you."

Michoel turned his head sharply, a question in his eyes.

"It's always been that way," the crown prince continued. "That's no secret."

By the rules of politeness, it was Michoel's turn to deny this claim or to declare it nonsense. But he said nothing, only gazing deep into his brother's eyes.

Behind their backs, Hala's eyes widened in surprise. The Mundari wondered if Istrak should have said those things in the presence of his new bride.

He had no way of knowing it, but it wasn't what Istrak had said that troubled his bride, but rather the way in which he had referred to his father as if he were no longer among the living.

It was Hala who found — at the very last minute — the mouth of a cave concealed behind a thick bush. Knaz cut down some of the foliage so they could enter. Kalev, who had been carefully carrying an earthenware pot that Rena had entrusted to him, made a fire with the coals that it contained. Istrak, after asking the others to move away, hurled the burning coals into the cave and waited beside the entrance, a dagger in his fist.

To their relief, the smoke drew out nothing more dangerous than some befuddled bats. Rena grimaced with distaste. "It will be very dirty in there," she warned. With a quick glance at the pink-tinged horizon, she added, "But today, apparently, we cannot allow ourselves to be overly squeamish."

Istrak glanced at Michoel. Once, back when what now felt like a sweet dream, Michoel had been extremely finicky. To Istrak's surprise, his brother's expression was calm. Rena's comment, and the odor that wafted out of the cave, did not appear to cause the younger prince any undue discomfort.

"Since we'll have to stay here for some time," Rena said, her voice echoing off the cave walls, "we'd better try to improve conditions a bit. Hala and I will clear the surfaces, Kalev and Knaz can gather branches and leaves to sit on, and Your Highnesses —"

"Our Highnesses," Istrak said lightly, "will be cleaning in here. Your Highnesses can wait patiently outside."

Rena smiled. A small smile appeared on Hala's face as well, revealing suddenly how very young she was.

"I'll clean," Istrak said to Michoel when the women had left.

"There's enough work for two," Michoel said. "And the work will go faster…"

"No need for both of us to get dirty," Istrak said cheerfully. He waited a beat, then said, "You've changed."

Michoel turned his head and stared at him, insulted.

"For the better," Istrak added quickly. "You've always been good — in many areas better than me…" It hurt to say the words. "But I've also changed.…"

Once again, politeness bade Michoel contradict his brother's assertions. Again, he was silent. Istrak felt an urge to get up and run as far away as he could.

"You always did what was right," Michoel said after a long silence. "To everyone but me."

"It wasn't personal. It's just that, when it came to you, it became clear that I wasn't right at all. That is, I did what I had to do, but it didn't penetrate inside. It didn't come along with a feeling that this was the right thing to do, and therefore a good thing. Even when I did something perfectly, my heart wasn't really in it. Understand? Like a child, I merely wanted to get credit and avoid punishment. A coward — that's what I was. Not much more than that."

Michoel was gazing at him as though he could not quite grasp what he was hearing.

"I served my Creator," Istrak tried to explain, "but deep down I thought I didn't *want* to serve Him. I wanted…to enjoy life." He looked down at his feet and added, in a near-whisper, "Music, horses, food. With the best *hechsher*, of course… After all, it isn't forbidden to enjoy life, is it?"

"Forbidden?"

"It was all within the confines of halachah." Istrak's lips twisted at the irony. "It's awful to be a person like that, Michoel. But I didn't realize that. I have a *neshamah*. I could sense it, strong and fiery. And what did I do to it? I suffocated it under a mountain of food and music and games…"

Michoel was at a loss. Clearly, he did not understand. After all, he was still only a child himself.

"It's not important," Istrak said tiredly. "Go outside, Michoel, and let me do this job. It won't take long."

"No," Michoel insisted. "We'll do it together."

Istrak looked into his brother's eyes, and then as if he had found what he was seeking, he nodded. "Together," Istrak agreed. "And not only here, my brother."

"*B'ezras Hashem,*" Michoel promised. His hand, as soft and cold as it had been that night on the palace roof, grasped Istrak's tightly. No further words were spoken, but the truce was stronger than anything they might have said.

It was crowded in the wagon. There were ten passengers in a space intended for nine, along with a considerable amount of baggage in the form of bundles and wooden crates. Apart from the driver, who was nearly as uncommunicative as Naftali's father, and Naftali himself, who had yet to understand how matters had evolved in such an unexpected direction, the passengers were in good spirits. They chattered away cheerfully, until Naftali was goaded to snap, "You're running away! I would have expected a more serious attitude."

Several heads turned. His *chavrusa* nudged him. "Not exactly running away," he whispered. "Only you are running away. The rest of them are taking a trip. At worst, they'll be asked to leave the yeshivah."

"And that won't bother us so much," someone else whispered into his other ear. "That's why we went away. Understand?"

No, he did not understand — partly because he didn't want to understand. But despite his lack of clarity, Naftali sat back and remained silent as his fellow passengers started a lively debate on the *sugya* the yeshivah was learning.

Afterward, as the wagon traveled further and further away from the city and the darkness grew ever denser, each of the boys sank into his own thoughts. The road was long. In time, words of Torah were replaced by the words of *Shema* and *HaMapil*. Only Naftali remained awake, trying to banish his troubled thoughts and to focus on the thorny questions posed by the Gemara he was presently learning.

Just when he thought he had succeeded and a marvelous resolution of all the questions began to form in his mind, the horses suddenly reared up in terror, causing the wagon to tilt in a most precarious manner.

The driver's yell, along with the sudden, lurching halt, caused several of the passengers to open their eyes in confusion. Cries of "What is it?" and "What happened?" filled the wagon.

But neither Naftali nor the wagon-driver were there to answer them. They had alighted from the carriage to see what had occurred. On the road before them were pieces of wood and torn bundles. From the distance came a commotion of crashing, dragging noises.

"An injured horse," the driver surmised, lifting his lantern higher to better illuminate the scene. "Or a mad one."

A mad horse? Naftali had never heard of such a thing. But, listening to the jarring sounds in the distance, it sounded entirely possible.

"Let's get back to the others," the driver said. Turning to face the wagon, he called, "We need help here!"

The passengers, tired and befuddled, descended slowly from the wagon. The driver, after lighting a second lantern, asked them to return to the nearest crossroads, take the right-hand road, and search for people who might have jumped or fallen from the disintegrating wagon.

"And we," he said, grabbing Naftali's arm, "are heading there." He pointed up the road.

The thought of approaching a mad horse did not appeal to Naftali. Had he known that three men clad in black were approaching with heavy footfalls, he would probably have been even less pleased with the wagon-driver's proposal.

In contrast to Naftali, who plodded unwillingly in the other man's wake, the wagon-driver did not seem to be afraid. In fact, his mood seemed to have improved.

"I have a way with horses," he said gregariously. "I'll calm it down, that's for sure. And you'll help me, right?"

Naftali, who had always made a point of steering clear of flying hooves, did not know what to say. The closer they came to the source of the commotion, the quieter he became.

And then, just when he could discern the light of a lantern through the trees, silence fell.

"Are they all dead?" the driver wondered aloud.

"Maybe they managed to calm the horse," Naftali offered. Then, reconsidering, he said, "We'd better hurry."

"All of a sudden you're brave," the driver said. "But you're right. Perhaps we'd better..."

Protecting their faces with their arms, they pushed their way through the dense branches. Waiting on the other side was the coach.

There was one horse harnessed to it, breathing hard. The lantern light shone on its perspiring flanks. Of the human beings who had shouted and screamed earlier, there was no sign. Naftali and the wagon-driver stood alone in the forest clearing.

"Is anybody he-e-e-e-re?" the driver shouted.

No answer was forthcoming.

"Strange," he said, half to himself and half to Naftali. "You heard them yelling, too, right?"

The boy nodded.

"Could it have been spirits?"

"Spirits don't need transportation. Anyway, I don't think that should be our first conclusion — not when there's a good chance that there are people nearby who need our help."

"Maybe they think we're robbers," the driver suggested.

"Wonderful," Naftali muttered. "How do we convince them that we're not?"

"Does anybody need any he-e-e-e-lp?" the driver shouted.

The silence remained as deep as before.

"Tell them something," he urged Naftali. "Something that only a *talmid chacham* would know."

This suggestion amused the boy. "I'm no *talmid chacham*, only a *talmid*. But just a minute...listen!"

From the surrounding forest came new noises — voices and breaking branches. Someone was approaching.

Not more than a minute later, three unpleasant-looking men stepped into the clearing.

"Is this your coach?" the wagon-driver asked.

The tallest of the three looked at him coldly.

"I asked, is this your coach?" the driver repeated in his friendly way. "And what happened to the horse?"

"A good question," answered the broad-shouldered one. The Khazari words sounded foreign on his tongue. "Where are our friends?"

"Then you did jump from this coach?" the driver asked with interest. "Why didn't they?"

"Good question," the broad-shouldered one said again. "Where are they now?"

"Good question," the wagon-driver retorted. Tugging at Naftali's sleeve, he said, "Come, sir. It looks like they'll get along fine without us."

But Naftali did not budge.

"Sir?"

Naftali didn't move. "Who are you looking for?" the boy asked suddenly.

"Our friends," the shortest of the three said.

Naftali regarded him in silence, thinking of the robbers that the driver had mentioned.

"Our friends who were on the coach," the shortest one clarified.

"They're not here," Naftali said. "Do you want us to help you search for them?"

"There's no need," the tall one said.

"Of course there is!" the driver said indignantly. "I —"

"I suggest," Naftali said, speaking very forcefully, "that you go summon the soldiers who were traveling with us. There's no reason why they should sleep when there may be people who need their help. Right?"

The driver lifted his brows and tightened his lips. He stared at Naftali, at the empty coach, and at the three strangers. Nodding slowly, he said, "The men? Yes, you're right, sir. At once."

"We're fine on our own," the short one said. A hint of menace had crept into his tone.

"Undoubtedly," Naftali agreed. "But with the help of our men, you'll do much better... I wonder where your friends have disappeared to? They say there are robbers around these parts. Maybe they were kidnaped?"

The driver, who had finally grasped Naftali's meaning, threw an apprehensive look at the black-clad strangers and broke into a run. Since the torch was in his hand, his departure plunged the clearing into gloom.

"I hate the dark," Naftali apologized. "If we take the lantern down from there, it will be easier to manage, won't it?"

The Romans watched him, troubled.

"So I'll take it down," the boy continued. "All right?" As he spoke, he clambered up to the driver's seat and quickly detached the lantern. Its light bobbed and danced in his shaking hand. Suddenly, there was a crash and the tinkle of glass.

"Oops! Sorry about that," Naftali said. "Really, really sorry. The soldiers will be here directly, and they'll bring torches..."

The Romans did not answer. Naftali fell silent as well.

When the driver returned accompanied by the yeshivah students, and the clearing was once again lit — there was no sign of the strangers in black.

The *bachurim*, having been apprised of Naftali's suspicions and the danger that hovered, perhaps, over the occupants of the empty coach, were eager to do something. But what?

Dan had watched the whole scene from a vantage point nearby. With the immediate threat gone, he felt weighed down with responsibility. Finally, he came to a decision. He stepped out from among the trees.

"Hello," he said. "Good evening."

They wheeled around sharply to face him.

"Hello," Dan said again.

"The same to you," answered the wagon-driver. He waited a beat, then asked, "Do you belong to this coach?"

Dan nodded, studying the group with interest.

"What happened to the horse?"

Dan took a deep breath. "It was wounded by arrows." He paused. "Thank you. Those men you chased off — they were chasing us, intending to do us harm."

"You're welcome," the driver said heartily. "Can we help?"

"That's a hard question to answer," Dan said frankly. And because the driver's voice tickled a chord in his memory, he asked, "Do I know you from somewhere?"

The wagon-driver looked at him with fresh eyes. "*Elokei shamayim va'aretz!*" he cried, with a deep bow. Turning to the boys, he said, "This man is one of *his* people — and not just anyone…"

Dan's face, which had lit up at hearing the password — "*Elokei shamayim va'aretz*" — clouded over again. "There's no time for courtesies. We need a safe place to hide. Does anyone know of a small, pleasant but isolated house in the area that belongs to loyal folks?"

The din of a weighty silence answered him.

"It would be best if it were not too far from Itil," Dan added, "and that the owners are not very sociable or known for their opposition to the regent."

"Who is it for?" someone asked.

Dan licked his lips nervously. "Four people." He looked around at the group. "Don't you know anyone at all?"

"I have a cousin who lives on the outskirts of Khazaran," Naftali blurted without taking the time to think it over. "Her husband was conscripted into the army and has not been discharged yet…so maybe it's not so suitable after all…" As soon as he had made the suggestion, he was already having second thoughts.

"It sounds very suitable," Dan declared.

"I —" Naftali began, ready to change the man's mind. But Dan was no longer there. "Wait!" He ran after him.

Dan turned.

"I've never had a serious conversation with them about politics," Naftali said rapidly. "I'm not sure…"

Dan smiled, his eyes gleaming in the dark like a cat's. "You grasped the situation very quickly back there, with those men in black," he complimented, "and acted cleverly to get rid of them. I take that as a sign of your intelligence."

Naftali tried to say something, but Dan stopped him. "They wanted to kill them," he explained.

Naftali's brow wrinkled. "Who?"

"Come with me. I'll show you." Dan led the way through the trees. Naftali followed — and then stopped short.

"Your Highnesses," Dan called softly in greeting. "We are forced to change our plans. This boy will take you to a safer place."

"What do you mean by a 'safer place'?" a woman's voice asked. Naftali retreated a step.

"A small, quiet house," Dan said. "I will escort you there, and Hashem will watch over us."

"And Unmar?"

"Do not worry. Ruben is with her. He'll take care of her."

Naftali stood dumbstruck. It defied all logic, but a moment later four of the seven royal children of Khazar slipped out from among the trees. Still speechless, Naftali led them from the clearing to the wagon and from there — at Dan's orders — directly to his cousin Rivka's house.

Since he knew nothing about the dead man in the wagon, Bastian Makan did not think there was any need for him to speak personally with the *rav* of the *beis knesses* near which he left the body. After tethering the horse and tying a feed bag around its neck, he took his leave of both the horse and the corpse and began walking back in the direction from which he had come — toward the Itil Tower.

The road was long and winding, and he took it in long strides, straightening the shoulders that had for so many years been bent over the conference table. Despite his exertions, his thoughts grew clearer as he went. Suddenly, he saw the recent events in a whole new light.

A cold night wind blew into his face, fanning cheeks grown heated with his walk and his thoughts. If only he knew where to find Meshuel Min-Hagai, he would have enjoyed a brief chat with him before returning to prison...

When he reached the outskirts of Khazaran, he found himself thinking of the gallows. His step slowed, and he paused to rest in a zucchini field.

It seemed as if only moments had passed when he woke with a start. He was surprised to find that he had actually slept, and even more surprised at the sun's position in the sky. More than moments had passed — the time for saying *Krias Shema* had come and gone. Upset, Bastian brushed the dust and dead leaves off his clothes and looked around for water so he could wash his hands.

He noticed a cluster of houses, of the simple style adopted in recent years on the outskirts of the city. For a moment he weighed the dangers. He decided to take the risk. Concocting his cover story as he went, he made his way toward the nearest house.

His loud, insistent knocks finally succeeded in bringing someone to the door, a gaunt man with deep, sunken eyes. Bastian asked if he could wash his hands; after a brief hesitation, the man invited him in.

The furnishings were attractive — which was more than could be said for the odor of neglect and onions that permeated the place. Bastian, accepting an ewer of water with thanks, looked at the man's sunken eyes and at the littered floor. "Widower?" he ventured.

The boldness of the question caused his host to attempt an imitation of a smile. "Bereaved father."

Bastian's fingers grew stiff, and his Adam's apple rose and fell convulsively. "No one knows how painful that is," he said. "I have been where you are. I was ready to die in his place a thousand times." He put the cup down and added gently, "You need a great deal of strength."

His host was silent, his beard lowered onto his chest.

"For them," Bastian explained. "Their memory lives on with us."

The man lifted his eyes, and his gaze was weary. "I tell her that all the time," he said in a lifeless voice. "But she doesn't seem to be consoled."

"That happened to us, too. But then my wife's friends came around, and they forced her to get up and function again."

"Friends?" There was muted anger in the man's face now. "Is there such a thing? Everyone ran away as though our Mulush, our son, was a leper. Only our next-door neighbor tries to help now and then, but she is too young to force Dosa to do anything…"

Bastian looked around, racking his brain. These people needed help, and he needed a place to stay until dark, when he could more safely cross Khazaran to Itil. He would also require some food.

And that was how Khazar's minister of war found himself in the most ramshackle chicken coop he had ever seen, carrying pailful after pailful of fine, natural fertilizer to a heap on the other side of the yard.

When that job was done, his host instructed him to offer a bucketful to the people next door. Resisting the urge to refuse, Bastian lifted a brimming pail and, shovel over his shoulder, left the yard.

He had to knock long and hard on this door as well before it was answered. At length, the woman of the house opened the door, holding a baby in her arms.

"Your neighbors," Makan said, "want to know if you need some fertilizer."

"My neighbors?" she repeated in bewilderment.

"Over there." Bastian gestured toward the house next door.

The housewife hesitated before, somewhat feebly, giving her consent. She followed him to the rear of the house and showed him where to deposit the contents of his bucket.

That was when he saw her.

In all the world, there were probably a good many curly-haired little girls sucking their thumbs. But Bastian Makan had no doubt in the world as to who this was.

"Lis…?" he blurted in shock, before biting his tongue.

Years later, every time Rivka recalled this incident, she would turn red with shame. But at that moment, in the most natural way, she grabbed Bastian's shovel and, with a voice like ice, ordered him to put down the pail and walk backward — into the goat shed.

Bastian was destined to be no fonder of the memory than she. How could he have let a woman holding a baby lock him in a shed? But at that moment, he was so stunned and confused that it never occurred to him to wrest the shovel from her and walk into the house to investigate this mysterious matter for himself.

WHEN UNMAR REALIZED THAT HER SISTERS AND BROTHERS had abandoned her and made their way to some unspecified place of concealment without her, her face grew as gray as dust and her shoulders hunched over the wooden doll she hugged so fiercely.

"It will be all right," Ruben Min-Hagai told her with a smile, trying to convince himself as much as the young princess. "Dan will probably come back here to our main camp tomorrow afternoon, and we'll find a way to bring Your Highness to your sisters and brothers…"

She offered no response.

"In the meantime, my mother and sisters will watch over you," he continued hopefully. "They're very nice. You met them when Tur and I were betrothed. Remember?"

She nodded once, a small, noncommittal bob. Gatherings were something that belonged to long ago, to those days when Father was well and Mother would say *Shema Yisrael* with her every night before she went to bed.

Ruben knew what the girl was afraid of, but he didn't know how to calm her fears. The Great Seal was too valuable to be entrusted to a small child — and yet, that was precisely what the king had elected to do. And if this had been Reuel's decision — reached, no doubt, after long, hard contemplation — then what right did he, Ruben, have to act against it? Were his enemies right? Was he power hungry?

The first time he had heard someone label him this way, it had left a bitter taste in his mouth. Now he was surprised to find that the worst of the pain was gone. Had he grown accustomed to insult — or had he begun to believe that the label was closer to the truth than he had thought?

Such an idea, of course, had never occurred to him. And had Diaber himself not raised the specter of power, it was reasonable to assume that the Min-Hagais would never have dreamed of stepping outside the law. But now that there was a group of people who believed with all their hearts that he was more capable of ruling Khazar than the newly reappointed regent — well, why not?

Why not?

Reuel had loved and esteemed his oldest daughter, and of all the young men of Khazar, he had chosen him, Ruben Min-Hagai, to be her husband. The men surrounding him believed that he could save Khazar from the regent's revolutionary ideas and restore their country to the path that earlier sages had laid out for her. The *rav* believed the same thing. That was why they had all clustered around the Min-Hagai banner.

Did he have the right to disappoint them? To disappoint all those who had elected to go into exile in the forests?

The argument nearly convinced him…but… ultimately he came to the realization that this was not to be his role.

No, he would not disappoint them. Yes, he would lead the rebellion and ensure that the appropriate people ruled this beloved land of theirs. But those appropriate people — as long as the matter rested in his hands — would not include a member of the Min-Hagai family.

Would his decision be sufficient?

How strange to think these thoughts on the road, at night, as the net tightened around him. And yet, despite the absurdity, Ruben could imagine moments of triumph.

He saw the glowing torches illuminating houses of worship humming with humanity, and town squares adorned with colorful banners that young boys looked up to with admiring eyes. He could imagine a *chuppah* and an assembly of the governing council, making the announcement that appeared, at present, like a betrayal of the comatose King Reuel.

Would he be able to find within himself the strength to silence the voices crying, "Long live the regent!"? Would he be strong enough to give someone else the position until Yekavel grew up?

And what if his *kallah*, heeding the voices of the crowd, rejected him?

There was only one force that could stand up to all of this.

He was absolutely quiet for a moment, composing the sentence he would say. Then, his limbs trembling with fear over the deed he was about to do. He swore — using, for the first and only time in his life, the Name of the Creator of heaven and earth — that he would never take the throne, or even the regency, for himself.

His men turned their heads in astonishment at this sudden declaration. Unmar, too, looked bewildered. But after Ruben had done this, he was suffused with a sense of serenity. The imaginary visions receded, and a great peace took their place.

With the strength that this inner peace lent him, he asked, "To whom did your father wish to give this doll, Unmar?"

Unmar blinked back a tear. "He told me to take care of her."

"Until when?" Ruben pressed gently.

"Until Istrak comes back," she whispered. Her voice broke. "But he's not coming back! And Father…"

"He *will* come back," Ruben said compassionately. "But in the meantime…"

"In the meantime, we have to bring her to Gad Baliatar." Unmar's self-control abandoned her entirely. "But he's so f-far away! And there are no lions in the square, like the girl said! And my m-mother d-died…!"

His mother or sisters would have known what to do. Ruben did not — and not only because he was not a woman. As Unmar sobbed into the fur collar of her coat, he stood in stunned disbelief over what she had just said.

Gad Baliatar!

Once, twice, three times he shook his head, trying to force his thoughts into coherence. On the fourth try, he succeeded. And still Unmar sobbed on as though her little heart were breaking.

"Enough!" he said. "This is no way for the Keeper of the Seal to behave!"

The words were followed by a deep and speaking silence. How had he come, unwittingly, to betray the child's secret? The men around him had proven their loyalty; still, the Great Seal called for a special reverence and redoubled caution.

"Very good," he praised her as she struggled to compose herself. He was trying to figure out his next step.

Unmar looked up at him trustingly. "Will you take me to Balata in the north — to Lord Gad?"

He weighed his various options and then, slowly, nodded his head. It was decided. Instead of taking the child to his relatives, he would take her north.

It was nearly noon by the time the lead coach was ready for the long journey. Underneath its benches was an impressive quantity of supplies.

Ruben Min-Hagai, with his characteristic energy, oversaw the preparations. In his preoccupation, he did not at first notice the whispers passing among his men. It was only when the preparations were complete that he realized that the atmosphere had changed. The men were hovering by the coach, and the pine-scented air seemed to be filled with the words they wanted to say.

"Has something happened?" Min-Hagai asked, his light-blue eyes narrowed against the sun.

The men clustered around him didn't answer. Ruben scanned the group and studied their faces. From his father he had learned that his first job as a leader was to love his people, and his own nature helped him excel in this. He loved the elderly for their wisdom and the young for their enthusiasm. His heart went out to the sages for the depth of their knowledge and to the ignorant for their innocence. He loved the poor for their humility and the wealthy for their restraint. Now they all stood in a circle, facing their leader as he perched on the step of the coach. They had left their homes, their parents, their children. They had come here ready to place their lives in his service, and for long months had hidden with him in forests like a herd of restless deer.

And now?

"What happened?" Ruben asked again. "What is troubling you, Jews of Khazar?"

A stir passed through the group, like wind through the treetops. But it was not a good wind.

One of the men ventured to speak. "Your Excellency is traveling?"

"Yes."

The same agitated wind passed among them again. A woodcutter, big and burly, was pushed forward by his friends. "To Balata, in the north?" His voice was as thick as the trees he chopped down. A simple man, almost to the point of coarseness. Ruben smiled at the woodcutter and replied, "Exactly so."

The woodcutter looked around at his friends, at a loss. Their eyes pressed him forward.

"And Your Excellency wishes to…meet with Lord Baliatar and give him…" He paused, filled his lungs with air, and blurted, "The Great Seal?"

The words shattered the quivering silence.

Ruben searched his mind for the right answer. Secrecy would undoubtedly have been best, but it was too late for that now.

"Yes," he said in a measured tone, his glance encompassing the entire group. "Because that was the king's wish."

"The king!" The word burst from the mouth of nearly every man present.

The coach step served as an impromptu stage, and Ruben used it to launch a short and unrehearsed speech. "His Majesty, Reuel II — may the Creator grant him long life — anticipated at least a portion of the recent developments, and he hid the seal in a secret place. His Majesty asked his daughter, Princess Unmar, to reveal the hiding place to Lord Gad Baliatar."

He paused for a moment, readjusted his stance on the step, and added, "His Majesty must have believed Lord Baliatar to be the most fitting man to fill his position."

Ruben's voice was clear and authoritative, and the words he spoke aroused a variety of reactions from the men. There was surprise and disbelief alongside anger and rejection. No one likes to admit that he has made a mistake — that he has dedicated seven long months of his life to the wrong cause.

"That was the king's will," Ruben continued. "And we, you and I, under the leadership of my father, will together carry out his desire. We will set a leader on the throne of this kingdom that the king wished to see there."

His eyes raked the crowd, searching — and not finding — a spark of eagerness. Only three or four of the men knew Lord Gad Baliatar directly. The others knew him only through word of mouth, and this had distorted Baliatar's physique to the point where they thought of him as a sort of monster masquerading as a human being.

Their young leader bit his lip. "Find yourselves a seat and listen."

There was a rustle and a stamping of feet as the men obeyed. Ruben climbed to a higher step and sat down as well. In a soft, mesmerizing voice, he began to speak, transporting the men around him from the dense forest to a palace in Rome, where the Caesar was mocking Rabbi Yehoshua for being ugly.

A shudder ran through the group — a wave of shame. And more than one head hung when Min-Hagai concluded with the Gemara's words about the Torah being present only in one whose mind is humble.

"A person's quality is not measured by his height or the beauty of his features. And I know that you all believe this. If not, you would abandon this forest and cluster around Diaber.

"His Majesty did not choose me to lead the kingdom. I hope the reason he did not do so was only because he anticipated that there would be a bad-hearted person who would accuse the Min-Hagai family of perpetrating the evils that have taken place in Khazar — and that that person would have a great deal of power, forcing loyal men to go into exile with me into the forest. No one bears any suspicion against Lord Baliatar, governor of the northern district. All men of decency will follow him. And because the welfare of Khazar is our primary concern, we will be the first to raise his name to our lips. Say it with me now, brothers: Long Live Gad Baliatar, leader of Khazar!"

They did as he beseeched, and although their enthusiasm was less than when they had cheered him, Ruben was satisfied.

"Good. And now, all you have left to do is wish me a safe and speedy journey."

A sliver of moon, slimmer than it had been the night before, accompanied the band of escapees on the second night of their journey and tried its feeble best to light their way. When they reached the river, however, it abandoned them in a huff, hiding behind a cloud bank as though to reprimand them for their foolishness: one did not cross the river at night — and particularly not at this time of the year!

Knaz felt the same way, but Rena declared with complete confidence that she could locate the ford even in the dark. She claimed, with some justice, that the danger that awaited them if they lingered here another day was greater than the risk the river offered. Istrak, who agreed with her thinking, told the others to do as she had said, and the small band walked slower still, following Knaz as he moved forward at a snail's pace.

"At this rate we'll reach Khazar in about seventy-one years," Kalev said with a grin. "My father will be 111 years old by then, but I'm sure he'll still be happy to see me."

The river ran cold, turning their feet to ice. But it was soon traversed, and Hala exclaimed softly, "How pretty it is here!" Her mother suggested that they stop there for a short rest and a bite to eat.

When they resumed their walk, Istrak found himself impelled forward by a new inner urgency. He set such a rapid pace that the others had to call out to him to slow down.

"I'm sorry," he murmured. His thoughts lay ahead, in Khazar. He was impatient to get home, to see his family again.

It was close to sunrise when they reached the second hiding place that Rena had chosen. "The second and last," she said. "The territory beyond this point is unfamiliar to me. Ka'hei never allowed me to go past here."

"That's a good sign," Hala said, as though to herself. Her mother nodded. Good signs made people happy. Indeed, both Michoel and Kalev wore broad smiles.

But Knaz remained somber, and Istrak's heart was solemn.

"What is troubling His Highness?" Kalev asked later.

Istrak sighed. "I am troubled because I am nothing," he said painfully. "I am an empty, foolish person — a prince with a donkey's ears."

Kalev's eyes grew round. "No," he said. "That's not true."

Istrak stared at the boy and then nodded. "You're right," he said slowly. "I'm exaggerating."

Kalev smiled with relief. "Everyone falls into low spirits now and then. It's human. It's the nature of the world."

Istrak smiled, too. Seventeen years in his father's palace had taught him how to hide his inner pain and keep any trace of it from showing in his face, a skill that came to the fore now. "True. Internal storms need not threaten us."

"They are the work of the *yetzer*," Kalev said, glad that he had managed to soothe his prince's spirit. "That's what my father used to say."

"I'd be glad to make your father's acquaintance when we return to Khazar."

Kalev's smile grew even wider, and his eyes sparkled like twin stars. Istrak felt his heart warming toward the boy. He would have given much to be like him: simple, pure of spirit, lacking in guile and arrogance. But the path the Creator had chosen for him was a different one. And although those who tread that path are undoubtedly wiser and possessed of a more subtle understanding — their chances of reaching the end of the path in safety are correspondingly smaller.

Istrak managed to keep the warm smile on his face until everyone went to sleep. When he was alone once more, he allowed his mouth to droop a little. Once again the images returned to haunt him: pictures of what he was meant to be, and of what he had shown himself to be these past months. He sat down on the ground and rested his head on his knees.

All of nature whispered around him. The bushes stirred, crickets chirped, and a light wind pushed a bank of charcoal cloud in front of the sun. A rustle sounded behind him.

"Your Highness would be better off in the shelter of the trees," Knaz said. "It will rain soon."

The scent of the air told Istrak that Knaz was right. He rose to his feet, brushing off his clothes.

"Nice morning," Knaz said cheerfully. "Isn't it?"

"Is this what you came here to discuss with me? The weather?"

Knaz looked at him, his eyes nearly boring holes in the prince.

"Say it already!" Istrak urged. "Scold me, goad me, tell me that I haven't a hope."

"But…you do."

"Very nice." Istrak was bitter. "You've decided to be polite."

Knaz laughed. Istrak had not heard his laughter often, perhaps not at all. "You are a strong person," the Mundari said obliquely. "If there were a competition for the stoutest heart, you would undoubtedly win one of the top prizes."

He spoke from genuine conviction; that much Istrak could recognize. But his inner vision told him that emotional strength was not enough.

"If you have the will —" Knaz began.

"I have the will. But I also know what will become of all my wanting. That's what hurts."

Knaz jutted out his chin. "So you say."

"I'll be all right," Istrak said bitterly. "Just as I was all right until I met you. But I'll never be a *tzaddik*. How sad to have to acknowledge that..."

The rising wind blew through Istrak's *peyos* and rustled the surrounding foliage. He suddenly noticed a spider's web, woven among the leaves in a nearby bush, and a green-winged fly struggling to escape death.

"And you accept this?"

Istrak closed his eyes wearily. "No, of course not."

"Does it feel bad enough to make you fight?"

"I've fought," Istrak shot back. "I've decided, I've chosen, and all the other nice words. I thought that once was enough. But now I see otherwise: the fight has to be constant; you have to choose again and again. And since the *yetzer hara*'s patience is longer than a person's memory, the impression of words that one has heard or read grows weaker each day — until he falls."

"True," Knaz agreed.

The quick capitulation surprised Istrak. "You were supposed to have an answer!"

"I do have one," Knaz said quietly. "Not one, in fact, but two. One is pleasant and painful, and the other is painful and pleasant."

"Word games."

"The pleasant but painful answer is that you will always be able to find fresh opportunities to strengthen yourself. It's painful because there is a certain risk that you will not always succeed in elevating yourself again to the place you aspire to reach."

"And the second?"

A light drizzle had begun to fall, forming tiny damp spots on their shoulders and faces. Neither of them moved.

"The second possibility hurts," Knaz warned.

"I am not afraid of pain."

A gleam of doubt flashed through Knaz's eyes. This intensified Istrak's stubbornness. "What would I have to do?"

"You would have to undertake to do something — even a small thing — that would stay with you until the end of your life. It would remind you each and every day that you were once young, and that Heaven blessed you — and that you chose your path correctly."

"Is that all?" It didn't sound very hard — let alone painful.

"Yes," Knaz said. "I have a small suggestion: Choose something that will remind you of what it was that you wanted to work on."

"And what did I want to work on?"

Knaz weighed this question with his usual gravity. When he answered, the words came slowly: "A single household may not have two mistresses. In your heart, there were two."

Istrak waited.

"One who sits beside the fire," the Mundari went on, "cannot travel to distant places. And one whose pockets are filled with copper coins cannot bring home gold. *This* world, Your Highness, and the world to come — simply do not go together."

The first man to arrive at the *beis knesses* for early Shacharis was surprised to see a stranger sleeping in an open wagon in the adjacent yard, as though waiting for the service to begin. Sleeping out in the open like that, uncovered, could not be good for his health. Concerned, the man leaned over the stranger to wake him and invite him inside. He recoiled when he realized that the body in the wagon was lifeless.

The man — Tanchum was his name — broke into heartrending cries. "How can we say, 'Our hands did not spill this blood,'" he screamed at two newcomers, "when a Jew has frozen to death because of us?"

"Frozen?" one of the men asked with deep astonishment. The weather had been far from frigid. His companion approached the corpse and touched it, noting the wound in his neck.

This discovery relieved Tanchum as much as it shook the other two. Apprehensively they looked over their shoulders, as though the murderer might still be lurking nearby.

The mayor of that small town had never had to deal with any sort of crime, let alone a murder. He sent his young son to the nearby army base to ask them to handle the case. Those in the know among the townspeople whispered that the mayor suspected that the murderer came from the ranks of those very soldiers, who had come here from a great distance. Was it a coincidence that only a short time after their arrival, the town had known its first murder in one hundred years?

Presently, a group of soldiers came into town. Their superior officer, accompanied by three men of lower rank, made directly for the mayor's home to hear, firsthand, any facts, fears, and suspicions he attached to the case. The rest of the troops remained in the *beis knesses* courtyard, awaiting orders and trying to disregard the curious glances of the many onlookers eager for more news.

Tuval Obseld stood among them. He had been urged by his companions to accompany them in order to draw a picture of the dead man's face for dissemination through the country so that he might be identified. For Tuval, who had nothing to look forward to that day but the repetitive rituals of cleaning his equipment and performing military exercises, the notion held much appeal. It would allow him to leave the army base, whose gray sameness was painful to his artist's eyes, ride out in the morning sun, and return just in time for the evening meal.

But the closer he was to actually carrying out the mission, the tenser he became. Fear clutched at his throat like a dead man's cold fingers. He, Tuval Obseld, who found it hard to carry an slaughtered chicken home from the *shochet*, would be forced to sit in an enclosed area for hours with a corpse, staring at its face and trying to reproduce its features faithfully onto the parchment in front of him…

His extreme unease seemed to him a punishment for his initial lack of sensitivity upon hearing of the murder of a fellow Khazari, and for seeing in the tragedy an opportunity to benefit personally.

The more time that elapsed — and a great deal of time elapsed before the mayor finished telling his story to the army officers, along with his views on the case and his opinion of them, their fellow soldiers, and the kingdom as a whole — the greater Tuval's apprehension grew. By the time the exhausted officers finally emerged from the mayor's house and headed for the small room near the *beis knesses* where the corpse had been placed, poor Tuval's nerves were in a sorry state indeed.

The room to which the dead man had been brought was long and narrow. Flickering candles did little to dispel the gloom and added much to the eerie atmosphere. The soldiers stood clustered together at one end of the room; at the other end, a man in a long white beard sat reciting *Tehillim* in a heartrending chant.

Now that the officers had completed their fact-finding mission, it was Tuval's turn to get to work. Hesitantly he approached the body. Upon seeing the dead man's face, his own changed color and he cried out.

"I know him!"

Tuval recalled the portrait of the two princes in traveling clothes that he had produced at this man's behest — the painting that had troubled the artist's rest for months to come. He had been correct in his fears, and Rivka, his wife, had been correct in her gentle hints: it had not been a true nobleman who had purchased the painting, but a criminal. A despicable individual who had met a criminal's fitting end.

Tuval began to shake. He, and he alone, was responsible for all the terrible things that had taken place in Khazar. If not for his painting — his beautiful painting — things would have turned out so differently…

The others in the room misinterpreted Tuval's distress. They took his quivering body, and the wails that erupted after he had been escorted from the room and given a drink of cold water, as signs of grief over the death of someone close to him.

Patiently, they waited for him to recover. Then, carefully, they asked Tuval to tell them the murdered man's identity, certain that he must, at the very least, be a brother-in-law, a cousin, or a good friend.

When Tuval answered that he had known the man only briefly and not in any personal way, their reactions ran the gamut from astonishment to pity — not for the murdered man, but for the white-faced artist whose hands were shaking so violently that he could not perform the job for which he had been brought here in the first place.

On their return to the base, the superior officer's mind was made up: Tuval Obseld was clearly weaker and more delicate than the average soldier. The man was unfit for military life. Although the officer was not authorized to discharge him from his army duties, he could send him home for a long furlough.

"Get some rest and calm yourself," he advised. "In a week's time, go to the draft office in Itil and find out whether there is any need for you to return here."

Tuval did not show the slightest sign of happiness at this unexpected leave with its veiled promise of a permanent discharge. On the contrary, the thought of a prolonged stay at home — with his sickly baby son and Rivka, whose sharp intuition had long ago told her of the tragedy her husband had brought about for his people — only weighed him down further.

Noting this, his superior officer began to seriously question Tuval's sanity. He wondered if sending him home on his own was the right thing to do. The sight of the supply cart, from which crates of dried fruit and cured meat were being unloaded, helped him make up his mind. It wasn't long before Tuval was bundled onto the empty wagon, along with the modest box of his belongings that his friends had packed for him. And too soon for Tuval, he found himself being off-loaded near the low wooden gate in front of his home.

He had dreamed about home so often in recent weeks. But right now, the place felt like the stuff of nightmares.

Half of the goat shed was used to store firewood. As Dan helped Rivka lock the shed door to secure it, Naftali was alarmed at the thought that their anonymous prisoner need only pelt him and Dan with chunks of wood to make his way out without any real difficulty.

But the prisoner showed no signs of incipient violence; he merely sat placidly on a pile of logs. After a long, penetrating look, he cast his eyes down, waiting.

"Who are you?" Dan asked curtly. "Why have you come here?"

"I am a homeless man," the stranger said. "I am ready to earn my living in any way that I can. The neighbor hired me to clean out his chicken coop."

"That's as may be," Dan replied. "But a homeless man does not recognize the people living in this house, or try to talk to them…"

The prisoner compressed his lips.

"He also does not speak in such a refined manner," Dan continued.

"Not every homeless man has always been homeless," the prisoner remarked.

Naftali, a member of the royal yeshivah, strained to identify the familiar voice. Suddenly, light dawned.

"There's no need to spend any more time discussing this, Dan," he said, tugging at his companion's sleeve. "Sitting before you is Bastian Makan, our former minister of war."

"I do resemble him slightly," the prisoner conceded, seemingly unperturbed. "Once, I considered that an honor. Now, I'm not so sure…"

Naftali shook his head. "He's lying. I'm telling you, Dan, that's him."

"No," the prisoner insisted. "I only look like him."

Ever since Naftali had been a small lad with dreams of being a soldier wielding a bayonet, he had admired Bastian Makan. There was little about the general he did not know. The lingering shreds of that admiration made it difficult for him to use that knowledge against him now. With an effort, he told Dan, "Ask him to show you his left hand. He has a scar."

Bastian said nothing. The scar that wound from his elbow to his shoulder could be neither camouflaged nor explained away. The shed door was closed again while the two young men conferred outside, and Bastian cursed his bad luck. Their voices penetrated the thin walls.

"Let's take him to the city," Dan said briskly, "and hand him over to the security people there."

"You can't do that," Naftali objected. "You can't hand over a person who hasn't been proved guilty to those who want to kill him. And besides —"

The boy's voice dropped, so that Bastian could hear no more of what he was saying, but he drew hope from Naftali's last words. These two, at any rate, were not Lord Diaber's men. It had not been Diaber, then, who had ordered the princes and princesses to be hidden away in this tiny house at the edge of nowhere. And if that were true…

With something like the old sparkle in his eye, Bastian stood up to his full height. "Come inside," he called. "I have a few bits of information that I'll be glad to share with you before you come to a decision."

The young men entered and looked at him, waiting.

"Don't you want to know how I arrived in this place?"

Dan nodded. "Please."

Bastian proceeded to relate the entire tale — from the knock on his cell door in the Itil Tower to the moment he had awoken in a nearby field.

"From what I understand," he went on, "you are not Yosef Diaber's men. And from the presence of those in this house, I can guess who you answer to… Out of all the political players in this game, only the son of Lord Meshuel Min-Hagai would be concerned for the safety of those children and see to it that they were taken to a safe place of concealment."

The affection in Bastian Makan's voice as he spoke the name of Ruben's father, and the sentiment with which he mentioned the royal children, dispelled the last of Dan's suspicions. His stance softened.

Naftali, however, shook his head. "Sir," he said, "your story is very interesting. But surely you understand that we cannot trust what you say."

"True. But you can send a messenger to the town where I left the body of the wagon driver."

Again, Naftali shook his head. "What would that prove? Isn't it possible that the man was killed in some other way than the one you've described?"

"Perhaps." Bastian's newfound optimism faded, and his voice was dry. "If you won't believe me, there is nothing else that I can do — except pray."

On legs that felt suddenly weak, Tuval made his way up the narrow path that led from the gate to his front door. When he was near the house, he stopped. Voices emanated from inside. Cheerful, friendly voices. Prattling, laughing voices. Children's voices. Under the circumstances, the sound tore at his heart.

Would his Yosef ever laugh like that if he discovered what a fool his father was? Would Rivka agree to stay married to a man with blood on his paintbrush and palette?

His knees shook, and an involuntary moan escaped his throat. Never a physically robust person, he felt unequal to his own turbulent emotions. Without stopping to think, he dropped his knapsack near the door and made a bolt for the goat shed, where he could enjoy a quiet cry over his bitter lot.

But the refuge he had sought was denied him. In the shed he found Naftali, his wife's cousin, chatting with two other men.

Naftali was startled to come face to face with the owner of the house they were occupying. "Tuval!" he cried. "Welcome home!"

Tuval's response was a groan. Taking in his disheveled and distraught appearance, Naftali's smile vanished. "I'll be back with you in a minute, Dan," he said quickly, taking his cousin's arm. "Let's go outside, Tuval."

Once they were alone, Naftali let go of Tuval and turned to face him. "What is it, cousin? Why are you so distraught? If it is about your unexpected guests, I can explain..."

Tuval shook his head. "No...no, it isn't that..."

Naftali was a genuine *talmid chacham*, Tuval knew — as were all the students of the royal yeshivah. Perhaps Naftali was the right person to help him unravel his responsibility for the horrors that had taken place in the Batar Ravine...

With trembling lips and halting words, Tuval spun out the story for his young cousin — from the first time had seen the man in the gray cloak to the last time, as a lifeless corpse.

"Am I guilty? Have I done something wicked?" he asked.

The way he uttered the last word touched Naftali's heart. "You did something good," he said softly, also stressing the final word. "Not then...now. Do you know who that older man is, Tuval, sitting in the goat shed on a pile of logs?"

Tuval's unexpected testimony tilted the scales in Bastian's favor. After a whispered conference, Dan and Naftali decided, together with Tuval, to permit the minister of war to remain in the shed under minimal conditions of imprisonment.

By the next morning, however, when it became obvious that Binyamin, Yekavel, and Lissia preferred the company of the man in the goat shed to any other game or pastime, it was unanimously decided to welcome him into the warm house, where the fragrance of baking bread filled the air.

Although there were far too many members of their family circle still missing, it was by far the nicest day the royal children had had lately. Bastian Makan's presence among them was both a stabilizing influence and an encouraging one. His voice, as he learned with Naftali and the children, reminded Tur of her father's. It made her feel lighter, as if a great burden had been lifted from her shoulders. She was no longer obligated to be the one in charge. Finally she could set aside the reins that had been so abruptly thrust into her unready hands. As she held a squirming, gurgling Yosef, blinking back tears of relief, an end to this dreadful period seemed suddenly possible.

31

IN THE WAKE OF THE FIRE IN THE TENT ENCAMPMENT, everyone was quietly respectful of Ka'hei's grief. Their leader had lost, in one fell swoop, both his daughter and his wife, who had apparently raced into the flames in an attempt to rescue her child.

For two full days, a film of thin gray ash continued to hover in the air. On the third day, Ka'hei hired dozens of men from his tribe to cover the heaps of black rubble with a thick layer of dirt. Nearly ninety men loaded buckets of earth onto wagons that Ka'hei had allotted to the task and transported them to the camp. There, under Ka'hei's watchful eye, they dumped the contents of the buckets over the remainder of the opulent tent.

"It is a monument," Ka'hei said, speaking to some point in the distance. "A memorial that will last forever."

Wagon after wagon came up from the riverbank. In addition to the salary he was paying them for the job, Ka'hei offered a hefty bonus to the entire team if they completed the job by week's end. Ka'hei watched them work to ensure that no one would venture to search the rubble for the remains of those who had perished within.

Rena's message, thrust into the sleeve of his cloak and read just before he had gone out to see the flames, had accomplished its purpose. As his wife had recommended, Ka'hei chose the sure thing over the doubtful one: he rejected the possibility of revenge for his outraged pride, in the face of the certain humiliation he would suffer when all realized how his wife and the boy had succeeded in tricking him. This "monument" was intended to prevent anyone from discovering that, underneath the rubble, there were no traces of any human remains at all.

Ka'hei did one other small thing before the moon set on the night of the tragedy. It was something that Rena — even if she had been able to foresee it — would have been incapable of preventing. The escape had forged a new link between his colleague, Khazar's regent, and the Kawari leader. Should Istrak return to Khazar, displace Diaber, and claim the royal throne, the news would quickly spread to the plains, and everyone in the encampment would know what had really happened on this night.

Ka'hei summoned a trusted soldier to gallop with all possible speed for the Khazar border. The messenger had with him two sealed letters: one for Lord Yosef Diaber, and the other for Khazar's highest government council.

Two days later, the messenger made contact with the Mundari who served as Ka'hei's courier for carrying messages into Khazar. His orders were to deliver the letters to Moshe the Kawari musician, who would ensure that the missives reached the right hands. Near evening, just as the members of Moshe's band began lifting the spirits of a Khazari nobleman's guests, the Mundari messenger arrived in Khazaran-Itil. Checking that the six gold coins he had received for his work were secure in his pocket, he made for Moshe's opulent quarters.

A trio of children — ten years old at the most — sat on the stone fence surrounding Moshe's house. Curiously, they watched the Mundari's progress to the heavy front door.

"Moshe isn't home," one of them called.

"He's not here," another clarified.

"He said good-bye to me yesterday," the third put in. "And when I grow up, I'm going to be rich like him!"

The Mundari tried knocking again, harder this time. When no one answered, he sighed. The messenger who had given him the packet of letters had explained that the matter was urgent, and that he was to spare no effort to see that it was placed into the singer's hand at the earliest opportunity.

"You'll never do it," the second boy told the third scornfully. "Your voice is too thin, and you don't stay on tune. If you can't even sing Shabbos *zemiros* properly, how will you ever sing like Moshe? He has a performance today," he concluded, tossing the words at the Mundari by the door. "At Lord Latvias' house."

"They're making a *siyum maseches* there," the first boy added knowledgeably. "My father made one once, too. But he didn't have a singer. It's too expensive, he said."

The messenger turned. "Where does Latvias live?"

"You want to wait for Moshe outside, right?" the second boy asked. "Maybe he'll say hello to you. He gave me a cookie once. I'm saving it."

The messenger laughed. He found this young trio diverting. "Maybe he'll give me one," he joked.

They regarded him solemnly. "He doesn't give them out to just anybody," the first boy said pointedly.

After more banter and bickering, the Mundari finally elicited the address he needed. As he headed up the lane leading to the wealthy man's home, the messenger realized that his job would not be as simple as he had assumed. A long line of beggars straggled away from the front door, passing through the spacious garden and ornate gate into the street, anticipating the donations that Lord Latvias would distribute at the conclusion of the *seudah*. They stood wearily in place, tired of the long wait and anxious lest the bag of coins be emptied before their turn came. There was a suppressed fury in the air that caused the horses, pulling the guests' carriages to the party, to nervously paw the ground.

No one would permit him, the Mundari realized, to simply walk up to the back door and ask someone to summon Moshe.

Still, clutching his packet of letters tightly under one arm, he tried to make his way through the line of paupers and move nearer to the house, from which strains of merry music drifted. Since he was dressed no differently from the others, his action was taken, not unnaturally, as an attempt to get to the head of the line ahead of his turn.

He never knew who lifted the first hand. Perhaps it was a young wagon-driver who decided to put the Mundari in his place...or the old man who gasped the messenger's throat in one bony claw to prevent him from advancing any further...or the hotheaded youngster who grabbed the stranger's shirt. Be that as it may, the Mundari's sharp reaction called forth a similar one. Within minutes, the quiet street had erupted into a melee.

Had circumstances been different, the free-for-all would have been ideal for promoting the messenger's means. He could have slipped up to the house, unnoticed, to find Moshe. As the target of the fight, he was necessarily in the thick of things. Furiously, he dealt blows to those who were trying to teach him a lesson as well as to those who were trying to calm things down.

Cries of "The guards are coming!" finally sent the brawlers fleeing in every direction, and the messenger hurried to crouch behind one of the carriages. As he shook his head to dispel the haze of rage that still surrounded him, he realized to his horror that the packet he had come here to deliver was missing.

Frantically he searched his pockets, then looked around as though expecting to see the packet lying in wait for him somewhere. He bit his lip and brought a hand to his throat, groping for the image of an idol that was there always. What to do now?

Time had lost its meaning. He cowered, frozen, behind the carriage, staring down at his empty hands. The street guards had restored order. Moshe's sweet voice, accompanied by a chorus of youngsters, once again floated through the windows. And still the messenger stooped where he was, helpless.

The package had to be here, somewhere. If he waited for the festivities to end and everyone to leave, perhaps he would find it. Or perhaps not. Perhaps it would fall into someone else's hands...

someone who would hand it over to the stern-faced security men still standing guard all around.

The mere thought turned his skin ashen.

The guards would open the packet to ascertain its owner. When they read its contents, there would be all sorts of questions. Moshe would not be harmed. The Kawari leader had doubtless been canny enough not to put his name down in writing. But if a Mundari with an idol around his neck was seen wandering around searching for a packet that he had lost…

Unhappily, the messenger crept silently back to the opening of the lane, where his donkey awaited him patiently. From there, it was not far to the gates of Itil.

If he never passed the information on, no one would know what was really happening on the other side of the border. Moshe would never know that he had been meant to receive an urgent missive, and the Kawaris would have no idea that their man had not received the urgent letters they had sent.

As for what the security guards would do with the packet — that no longer interested him at all.

Was a good resolution supposed to hurt?

Istrak didn't think so. From the age of 4 or so, he had undertaken — with the approval of his father or mentor —- any number of good resolutions. And although some of them had been difficult to carry out, none of them had been painful.

Why, then, had Knaz spoken of pain?

Even as he asked the question, Istrak knew that he was evading it. Because, although he had chosen his path two weeks earlier, he had not yet taken a knife to cut the cords that bound him to the tent encampment that was growing more distant with every step he took.

The Kawaris were friendly. They were exquisitely polite, they had fine taste, and their accomplishments in various fields — notably, in music — were truly admirable.

Music… An unpleasant shiver went up and down Istrak's spine when he remembered the Kawari melodies.

From the moment Lord Diaber had spread his wings over Moshe, the *ger tzedek* singer, those melodies had begun to infiltrate all of Khazar. They were beautiful, uplifting, merry, agitating the soul and soothing it at the same time. Even while in the palace, Istrak had loved those tunes and had been drawn to them like metal to a magnet.

The shiver became more pronounced. Every soul, it is said, has its own special challenge. For Istrak, those Kawari melodies were an attraction that had no equal.

He loved music, and during the months of his captivity he had discovered that music had the power to enter his heart and give him solace even in his most difficult moments. To give it up now was almost like ripping out a portion of his own personality and hurling it into the sea.

Was this what Knaz had been thinking of when he had used the word "pain"?

He could choose something easier. Something less painful. He could, for example, decide to commemorate his captivity by reciting a chapter of *Tehillim* every day after Shacharis. But Istrak knew that he had to do more than that.

Still, the decision he was contemplating seemed exaggerated to him.

Never again to listen, solely for his own pleasure, to Kawari-style music?

Never?

"All right," he told Knaz. "I've done it."

Knaz lifted his eyes. He knew instantly what Istrak was referring to. "And are you happy?"

"Happy?" Istrak lifted his brows with a scowl. He wanted to say that there was a limit to what could be asked of a person, that the pain was still too great to make room for happiness. But before he could speak, he found, to his surprise, that the sense of lack had suddenly departed without a trace. Along with it went the yearning for those melodies — leaving behind a sense of clear water, serene as a mirror.

This astonished him so much that he smiled. The smile had nothing to do with what the world calls "happiness." He had no desire to laugh out loud, as if in response to a rollicking joke. But he could not deny that he was filled from head to toe with a newfound peace and satisfaction.

No, he was not "happy."

He was content.

The journey took two full weeks. Dusk was falling when the Min-Hagai family finally reached the outskirts of Gad Baliatar's estate.

"It's beautiful here," Meshuel commented from his place beside his son at the reins. Turning to speak to his wife, who sat in the carriage, he added, "Want to move out here, Bruria? It's a nice estate."

Bruria smiled. "An interesting idea. But you'd have to ask the owner's permission, and pay him a tax..."

"Or maybe," Meshuel suggested, "we can simply import a few hundred of these raspberry bushes for our own forest?"

"Our gardener knows how to do that!" Unmar exclaimed. "You have to cut the branches on the diagonal, and then you cover them with a damp cloth..."

Meshuel smiled, he found the young princess to be charming. "You know everything, do you?" he said playfully.

Bruria stroked the girl's curly head, murmuring, "You remind me so much of your aunt, little one. It is a shame you did not know her..."

After that, no one said anything for a long time. Unmar's head was filled with raspberry bushes, and Meshuel's good mood had inexplicably dissipated.

"I like our house better," one of Ruben's three younger sisters said, just to break the silence. "Sometimes I miss it so much, I could cry."

On this optimistic note, the carriage pulled up near the closed gate surrounding the Baliatar estate. They waited for the guards to appear.

Suddenly Ruben was suffused with apprehension. "Maybe this is not such a good idea," he said, gazing at the heavy gates and Lord Baliatar's forbidding palace.

Unmar clutched her doll closer to her chest. By now the dainty dress was badly creased from the constant pressure of her fingers.

"Father, maybe we are trusting him too much. There's no reason to hand him, on a silver platter —" Ruben's voice died away as one of the nobleman's hired soldiers approached their carriage with a sturdy stride. "The chance to arrest us," Ruben ended, very quietly. He leaped down to the ground. "Go from here, Father. I'll meet you at sunset, near the raspberry bushes."

The soldier came closer, his right hand tense on his sword. "Where do you wish to go, please?"

"I have a message for Lord Baliatar," Ruben said, "from friends in Itil."

The soldier scrutinized him. His visage, lacking gentleness or grace, told Ruben that his instincts had not been wrong. Had the carriage not already been moving away, he would have been sorely tempted to climb aboard. It occurred to him how odd he must look: a messenger from the other side of the country, standing before the gates empty-handed, without so much as a knapsack over his shoulder. He smiled warmly at the guard. "It's beautiful here," he remarked.

The soldier's face softened slightly. "Enter," he said, stepping behind Ruben in such a way that the latter could not see him at all.

The two headed through the gate into a stone guardhouse. This tiny building was bare except for a single stone bench, a smoking taper, and a plate bearing the remains of a scanty meal.

"Wait here," the guard ordered, locking the door through which they had just entered. He stepped through the door that led to the palace yard, his ring of keys jangling on his hip. Then this door, too, was locked. Ruben took a deep breath and tried to gird himself with patience.

He stood for a while, leaned against the wall for a while, and then — deciding that it would be prudent to conserve his energy — sat down on the stone bench. How far did the guard have to go just to obtain permission for him to enter the estate? And how was it that Lord Gad Baliatar permitted the gates of such a large estate to remain locked without a guard for such a long stretch of time?

Finally, the second door was reopened, and fresh air flowed into the enclosure. The guard, in a bored voice, said, "I neglected to ask who sent you."

"Pinras, son of the late *bek*," Ruben said wearily. He deliberately named a well-known figure with no overt political affiliations. He leaned his head against the wall, anticipating another long wait. To his surprise, the door was flung open just minutes after it had been relocked. A pair of soldiers — by the looks of them, these were slightly more intelligent than the first — stood in the doorway.

As the pair led him along the path leading to the palatial mansion, Ruben noted that the courtyard was crowded with barrels of water, ladders, stockpiles of arrows, and grim-faced men. The residents of the estate were, by the looks of things, earnestly preparing for war.

"Straight ahead," the guards advised, seeing his interest. "Quickly now."

At the entrance to the house, which more closely resembled a fortress than a palace, they repeated the order. Ruben averted his eyes from the sacks of flour and grain, wondering what could have brought Baliatar and his people to a state of such serious military preparedness.

The mansion's second story was, if anything, an even grimmer spectacle than the ground floor. Here, all the rugs had been put away, so that their footsteps rang hollowly against the bare floor.

"In here, please," one of the guards said. A door was opened in front of him, and Ruben was ushered inside.

This, apparently, was Lord Baliatar's office. But the only person in the room, gazing out the window with his back to Ruben, was a man of Ruben's own height. One of the guards cleared his throat, and the figure at the window slowly turned.

Ruben Min-Hagai was dressed completely differently than he had been at his betrothal ceremony, and the dim lighting aided in obscuring his identity. But he had no trouble recognizing the man who faced him, though fresh lines of worry had been added to his face, and the laughter lines had nearly disappeared.

"Did you say," the man asked quietly, "that it was Pinras, son of the late *bek*, who sent you here?"

Ruben's shock was replace by amusement. "Don't you recognize me, Pinras, son of Lord Eshal?"

Pinras looked at him again. A flash of surprise lit his eyes for a moment, but he had himself well in hand: not a muscle flickered.

"I've come on my own behalf," Ruben said. "Is it possible for me to speak to Lord Baliatar?"

"Let's find out." Pinras instructed the guards, who departed. To Ruben, he said, "Sit down."

Ruben sat slowly, leaning back against the upholstered cushions. Luxuries such as this armchair were some of the things his family had put behind them on the night they left their palace. Pinras stood over him, his gentle eyes narrowed in thought.

"If you wish," Pinras said at last, breaking the silence, "I can order something for you to drink."

"I will be glad for a glass of water," Ruben replied. Then he asked, "When did you leave Itil?"

"Thirteen days ago," Pinras said. "Two days after the revolution was proclaimed."

"Revolution," Ruben repeated. "What do you mean?"

"Diaber's messengers do not, apparently, find their way into the forests," Pinras said dryly. "Our friend the regent, with the help of a few clever men on the council, have decided that, in the absence of the Great Seal and the authority it represents, it is necessary to carry out a 'voluntary revolution' — and to appoint the regent temporary king of the New Khazar."

" 'The New Khazar,' " Min-Hagai echoed, his head pounding painfully.

"The next day," Pinras continued, "word came of the disappearance of the royal family. On the day after that, I decided to accept Lord Baliatar's invitation. I left immediately."

He fell silent, leaning against the wall and studying Ruben as though trying to read his thoughts.

"Does anyone except me," Ruben asked, "understand that something must be done to stop that man?"

"Did you come here to ask that question?"

Min-Hagai shook his head. "Not exactly."

"Then why *are* you here?"

The question had come from a new voice in the doorway.

Recognizing it, Ruben rose to his feet. "I came here to urge Your Excellency to lead the struggle." He bowed slightly. "And to thus carry out the wish of our king."

Gad Baliatar's eyes met those of the crown prince's mentor for a fleeting instant. He crossed the room and sat in one of the armchairs. "Tell me more."

Ruben smiled, picturing his men's reaction to the power emanating from the short-statured man facing him. Passing a hand across his eyes, he began his story from the beginning: from the first letter, signed by Unmar, in which the regent's plans were revealed and concluding with the men in black, a large wooden doll, and the 8-year-old princess' hysterical bout of weeping on a dark night.

When he was done, Gad and Pinras exchanged another glance. Sensing that the two were concealing something from him, Ruben leaned forward, tense.

"I, too," Gad said, "received instructions. They are there, in one of the drawers behind you... They were written some time ago, and given to me on the condition that I open them after the precious writer had completed his 120 years on this earth."

His face twisted. In an effort to overcome his anguish, the next words came rapidly. "I permitted myself to assume that recent events justified an preemptive opening of those orders. And so I did. Istrak was still a child when they were written, and the king asked me..." The rush of words abruptly slowed. "If it was demonstrated that Yosef Diaber had earned the distrust that the king felt toward him, he asked me to make every effort to oust him and to appoint in his place a member of His Majesty's extended family who was deemed suitable for the role."

The words were clear and simple — especially since Pinras, the king's nephew, stood beside him in the flesh.

"I understand." The legs of his chair scraped the floor as Ruben stood up and turned to Pinras. "May I be permitted to congratulate His Majesty on his appointment?"

"You are a good man," Pinras said. "However, much as we need your blessings, we need your help even more."

Baliatar inclined his head in agreement.

"I will follow you," Ruben Min-Hagai said quietly. "You have my loyalty and my obedience."

"Thank you," the tutor said. "But what will your men say?"

"They will be your primary soldiers." Ruben turned to Lord Baliatar. "Is that why you've prepared the water barrels and ladders in the courtyard?"

Lord Baliatar made a noncommittal gesture. "You could say that. You could also say that it constitutes a sort of emotional preparation for whatever steps Yosef Diaber will take after he reads the letter I sent him."

The astounded look on Ruben's face seemed to amuse him.

"Few of Khazar's noblemen will agree to send an army against one of their own countrymen," Gad explained. "Diaber has attempted to persuade them that his plan is valid and necessary. I am demonstrating my vigorous opposition to what they have done."

"And the buckets of water in the yard?"

Gad smiled. "A few military exercises never hurt anybody, and apart from that — let us not forget that the illustrious king of the 'New Khazar' does not actually require the nobility's consent to go out to war."

Ruben's confusion showed on his face. Gad enlightened him.

"To march against the north, Diaber will have to recruit at least two additional divisions. The recruitment notice that will be sent to the young men's homes will provide all the publicity the battle requires."

Ruben tried to absorb the impact of what he had heard. He had promised obedience and must stand by his word. But the steps taken by these two men demonstrated that they were out-of-touch regarding the changes that had begun taking place in Khazar during Yosef Diaber's few months of rule.

Pinras noticed his discomfiture. "What are you thinking?"

Ruben's hands slowly clenched. "The battle has no need for publicity," he said. "What it needs is love. Something to ignite the good people's hearts and call to them, 'Come and fight!' "

"If we were forced to recruit Kawaris or Bulgarians, you would be correct," Pinras replied. "But that fire burns in the Khazar people's hearts already. All we have to do is tell them the northern province awaits their arrival."

Ruben grimaced. "Is that the situation in Itil?"

"No," Pinras admitted. "Diaber has made sure to provide the small creature comforts that blind the people and distract them from the truth. We will get little support there."

"Sadly enough," Min-Hagai said quietly, "the same situation holds true in Khazar's towns and villages."

His companions stared at him in open disbelief.

"You may call me a liar and send me away," Ruben said with a shrug. "But that is the situation. Diaber himself does not visit the villages, perhaps, but his people go there, in the guise of news disseminators, wandering minstrels, and storytellers. With their smiles and their compliments, they have won the people's hearts."

"The people of Khazar are wise," Baliatar stated confidently. "They will read between the lines and find the truth. Then they will flock here to us."

Ruben swallowed. "No," he said. "I wish it were so, Lord Baliatar. But the people have allowed the regent's agents to penetrate their inner hearts and to eradicate years of careful education. You two are prepared to sacrifice everything to restore Khazar's glory. But they, without much effort, will turn you, and the whole issue, into a travesty..."

A few rhymes about a disfigured dwarf and a mentor with delusions of grandeur — that was all it would take. True, there were still some righteous men and women in the villages who would turn their backs on Diaber's lure. But how many soldiers were there among those who deluded themselves with sweet dreams of a home in the city and flute lessons for every child?

"And your recommendation is...?" Pinras prompted.

Ruben closed his eyes, the better to concentrate. "We can do exactly the same thing," he said slowly. "I have some men who can do it very well."

But they would never attain the highly trained caliber of Diaber's people — he could not blind himself to that reality.

"Tell them the story of the Great Seal," Pinras suggested. "About the king's pain as he contemplated the destruction of his people and his country, and his attempt to ensure that even if the worst happened, his subjects would recognize the danger that hovered over them."

"You can begin right now," said Baliatar. "We have men here of sound conscience and sweet voice who would be ready to go out on the road with you."

Me? Ruben bit back the word before it was uttered. With a small bow, he said instead, "Your wish is my command." Still, he stayed where he was.

"We, for our part," Baliatar added, "will compose an open letter to the 'revolutionaries' among Khazar's nobility. I am persuaded that Lord Shefer, for example, and the governor of the eastern province, have held onto their principles and kept their thoughts pure."

"And another letter," Pinras added, "will be sent to the rabbis of the large cities and to the *roshei yeshivah*. The *rosh yeshivah* of the Royal Beis Medrash is not far from here, visiting the soldiers of the Fifth Division. I think it would be helpful if he added a few words of his own."

"I'd like to meet him," Ruben said. Deep down — though he would have been ashamed to admit it — he felt the need for a smile, a look, a word of encouragement to tell him that he had done well in giving up the highest position to which a Khazari could aspire... to become a court clerk.

Two weeks of exhausting walking brought them to the bank of the Four-Colored River. Crimson and purple algae, commonplace greenery, and the violet *slovatia* petals that fell from the trees and were sucked into the current, combined to give the river the unique color that gave it its name.

"We need to replenish our supplies," Rena said. "If the maps are accurate, a three-hour walk will take us to Dair, capital of the Checkats."

"Where the Kawaris are liable to ambush us," Istrak said somberly.

"There is truth in what you say," the Mundari agreed. "It is better that I enter alone at first."

"You're the one who stands out among us," Istrak said with a smile in his eyes that was rarely there these days. "I will do it. What do we need to buy?"

"Going to the shops," said Rena, "is women's business. An older woman who speaks the Checkati tongue and can recognize every face in the Kawari tribe will accomplish the task much faster and more efficiently."

Her logic forestalled further arguments. Moments later Rena was making her way down the slope of the riverbank toward the city, firmly rejecting Hala's offer to accompany her. Alone, she walked among the profuse river foliage, a valiant figure who had permitted nothing in her difficult life to bow her shoulders.

Hala watched her disappear among the tall reeds, a host of indefinable emotions constricting her throat. When she looked back at her own group, she found the men immersed in their learning. Their warm, lively voices caused her eyes to fill. From the time she had been a little girl, her mother had whispered to her — in a language that had then been alien to her — about this day. A day when she would at last enter Khazar's border, married to a man of stature with a heritage she could finally claim openly as her own. Now, faced with the reality of it, she found it even better and more beautiful than she had imagined.

The scents of the river and its abundant growth filled the air. Knaz, too, smiled as he looked at the crown prince of Khazar, who seemed imbued with a new serenity and grace. Hala watched her husband a moment longer and then hurried down to the riverbank. Her mother had told her that the violet flowers were very effective in stanching the flow of blood. Her royal husband, a prince in exile, had no idea what awaited him in his father's kingdom. Better, she thought, to be prepared for any eventuality. She set about packing a quantity of the large purple petals in her pack.

32

IN ALL, THE JOURNEY TOOK MORE THAN A MONTH. AND THEN, one afternoon, the endless trek did — at long last — come to an end. Spread out beneath them, as they perched on the crest of a hill, were the green and brown fields of Khazar in their full glory. As still as the boulders on which they stood, the small group gazed at the dozens of shades of green, gold, and brown that made up the most beautiful panorama they had ever seen.

"We've arrived," Istrak beamed. "We're home. Welcome, all."

Hala smiled, devouring the scene as though she wanted to memorize every detail. Rena's chin quivered, and her hand groped for Hala's shoulder as though for support. Hala turned away. It was strange to see her mother, always a strong woman, in tears.

"We've arrived," Istrak said again. "My father will be so happy to see you, Aunt."

Rena did not answer. She just buried her face more deeply in her daughter's shoulder, sobbing soundlessly.

Beneath them, the round white cottages seemed to wink at them. Tall trees, their luscious fruit looking like pretty colored spots in the distance, could be seen among the houses, and the thin blue smoke coiling up from the chimneys told their tale of simple working folk cooking their dinners.

"Onward," Istrak said finally. "The faster we walk, the sooner we'll get there."

The others stirred, finding it hard to trade the dreamlike sweetness of the moment for practical activity. To spur them on, as well as himself, Istrak said, "What do you say to Minchah with a *minyan*?"

Kalev grinned so widely his face seemed about to split in two. "I'm ready to run all the way to the *beis knesses*," he announced. "Let's go!"

They went. Istrak took the lead, hugging to his chest the ancient *Sefer Torah* and moving in a state of strange exhilaration. The hard-baked earth lent them speed, and the fragrant breeze fanned their faces as they ran down the hill. The round white cottages drew closer.

And then they were at the bottom. On a low stone wall sat a young man munching contentedly on a chicken leg. He looked at them curiously, still chewing.

"Good afternoon," he said. "Welcome to Khazar."

As a reception, it was slightly different from what they had envisioned. Still, the simple friendliness of the words warmed them.

"A good afternoon to you," Istrak returned. "Where are you from?"

"Over there," the man said, gesturing at the tranquil village spread below. "And you?"

"From there," Istrak replied, pointing in the direction of Khazaran-Itil.

"Ah. Then how do you get over there?" The hand holding the chicken leg waved at the great plain, hidden from view now, that sprawled beyond the hill.

"A good question," Istrak said evasively. "And what is your trade, good sir?"

"I am a wandering minstrel."

"A wandering — *what*?"

The singer laughed. "How long has it been since you visited

Khazar, friend? Very soon after the king's collapse, the good old traditions started coming back."

Istrak's tongue suddenly felt glued to his palate, and Michoel's face turned white. "The k-king?" repeated the younger prince. "Collapse?"

"Yes," the singer said, picking up his lute. "Listen!"

As they listened to the sad ballad, their faces grew longer and longer. Kalev put an arm around Michoel, and Michoel dropped his head on Kalev's shoulder. Hala and her mother moved closer to Istrak, while Knaz remained alone in the center, head bowed.

"Everyone cries over that song," the minstrel said with patent satisfaction. "But I've never seen anyone become as emotional as you people!"

"What happened to the king?" Knaz asked slowly. "Speak to the point, Khazari."

"He collapsed. After his son was kidnaped, and then what happened to his wife and all... Diaber, bless him, is running things now, and everything looks different. Much more cheerful, if you ask me."

Istrak's lips were pursed in a long, thin line. Michoel, his head still supported on Kalev's shoulder, did not move. Knaz, after a brief hesitation, decided not to ask the foremost question in all their minds: what had the man meant by "collapsed"?

"What do you mean by saying things are more cheerful?" Istrak asked hoarsely.

The singer scratched his head. "You're not from here," he said. "Or maybe you've been away a long time... Have you ever heard of Lord Diaber?" He plucked a string, emitting a pleasant note.

"To the point," Rena said. "What happened after Diaber came to power?"

"Yes, tell us!" Hala begged.

The minstrel ran his fingers over the lute's strings. "I haven't composed a song about that yet. In fact, that's what I came up here for. There's going to be a big competition in two days' time."

Rena's face was rigid with tension. "What became more cheerful, young man?"

The man sighed. "All right. Madam is right — not everything is more cheerful. The business with Ruben Min-Hagai, for instance…"

"And which business might that be?" Istrak asked sharply.

"There is already a song about that. They all paint him as a criminal, but I met him on the road once. A criminal wouldn't stop his wagon and take me to the city, would he?"

A picture began to form in Istrak's mind, its outlines still blurred and shaky as a child's drawing. It was a picture entirely different from the one he had imagined his homecoming to be.

"That's very interesting, what you said," he remarked. Turning to his companions, he added, "We'd better hurry. We wanted to find a *minyan* for Minchah, remember?"

"You won't get one now," the singer broke in, "unless you have some wings in your knapsacks and can fly there."

"All right then," Istrak said, resigned. "We'll daven here."

Michoel made an inarticulate sound. The brothers' eyes met for a long moment.

"We will pray here," Istrak said, "and we will remember not only Jerusalem in our prayers, but Khazar as well."

Kalev lifted his face as a sign of agreement, and Knaz straightened to an almost military bearing.

The minstrel gazed at them curiously. This was the oddest group he had ever encountered. "I'll join you," he said as the men began removing their packs. "Jerusalem is in that direction." He pointed over the hill. It was obvious that he was puzzled by the strange heaviness that had enveloped the small group that, just moments earlier, had been so merry.

Istrak, not wishing to hurt his feelings, forced a smile. "Thank you."

The sun bathed them in orange-red light, and the evening breeze whistled among the trees and shadows. Such an atmosphere should have been conducive to inspired prayer, but Istrak found his mind whirling with a medley of half-formed thoughts.

If his father was ill, he, Istrak, would be forced to pick up the reins of power. This was what he had been preparing for all his life…

He must be near Father, to ensure that he was receiving the best possible treatment…

He must organize prayers…pay Torah scholars to recite the *Sefer Tehillim* after midnight…

And…what had happened to Michoel's mother?

The thoughts chased one another through his head like wild horses. He tried in vain to chase them away, passing a hand over his forehead time and time again. Did his *yetzer hara* have no pity at all? At this moment, when he needed to be the best person he could be, did it have to continue its rampage, trying to show him how insignificant he really was?

Thinking this, he felt anger rise up inside him. A good, hot anger.

He would not be so easily conquered!

He opened his eyes for a moment, and then closed them again, concentrating on the words of the *tefillah*. Word after word, with no extraneous thought, not even tears and pleading. Just total concentration on the letters and words that the holy sages had arranged. On some level, he knew that it was incumbent on him to hurry, to reach the palace — to act. But at the same time, there was a deeper recognition that this connection to Hashem was the truest and most necessary thing he could foster right now. Banishing anxiety, fear, and every passing thought, he focused on the words. It was the longest and most arduous prayer he had ever said in his life.

By the time he was finished, there were tears in the corners of his eyes — but his heart was at peace.

When he turned around, Istrak saw that the traveling singer had left them, and that his wife and his mother-in-law had built a small campfire and were removing provisions from the packs.

"Yes," Knaz was saying, nodding gravely. "We need time to think."

"Think about what?" Kalev asked.

"About the situation. The regent will not blow the trumpets to celebrate Istrak's return."

"He gave up the position to me once before," Istrak pointed out as he approached the rest of the group.

"Yes." The corners of Knaz's mouth turned up in a small smile. "Before he knew how pleasant a crown can feel on one's head."

Though he knew that Knaz had not meant any insolence, the words nevertheless seemed an attack, not only on Diaber, but on the royal family as well. His father did not enjoy ruling for its own sake; he bore the duty with courage, for his people.

A cold shiver ran down Istrak's spine. Was his father even… alive?

Now that he had finally articulated the fear in his own mind, he looked around and saw that his companions shared it. Michoel was seated near the campfire, face pale and set as he stared into the flames. What was it that the singer had alluded to about Michoel's mother?

Pain engulfed Istrak so thoroughly that he felt compelled, with a murmured apology, to move some distance away from the fire. There, crouched at the foot of a thick tree trunk, he threw up the scant dinner he had just consumed.

Afterward, although his stomach felt better, he remained doubled over with anguish. He could not think of his father without tears. Whether Istrak had wanted it or not, his father had always been there, close and strong. Somehow Istrak had convinced himself that he would always remain that way, wise and patient, waiting for him. And now, suddenly…

Someone was standing beside him, holding out a cup of water. Hala.

"My father," he told her, swallowing the bitterness in his throat. "I need to know what happened to him."

She lowered her eyes.

"This wasn't supposed to happen!" he cried. "He was a strong man. A healthy man. A *tzaddik*. The kind of person who's supposed to live to a hundred…"

"Take this," Hala said softly, handing him the water. As he drank, she added, "My mother just told me to tell you that the man with the cat was Diaber. She said it's important that you know this."

"The man with the cat," Istrak repeated slowly. "What are you talking about, Hala?"

Hala was surprised. "You don't know, do you?"

"Know what?"

It was a story Hala had heard from her mother, a story about an engagement and an injured cat — a story she now related to Istrak.

It was time he knew the truth.

33

P RINCESS RENA WAS LIKE A SMALL, COLORFUL BIRD flitting through life with a song on her lips. Heaven had handed her a bottomless bag of gifts and the intelligence to use them well. Her brothers and sister admired her, her mother showered her with a limitless affection, and her father was prepared to give her anything she wished. The matchmakers pronounced her perfect; her father, King Brachia, with a crease of laughter between his brows, would say that her only flaw was that she had never had to struggle for anything in her life, either material or spiritual.

Indeed, her life flowed pleasantly, illuminated as though by bright spring sunshine. Around the bend, a wedding dress could already be glimpsed, long, white, and beautifully embroidered. Life was wonderful.

A year earlier, Yosef Diaber's father had passed away, and Yosef — barely 20 — inherited the title, obligations, and privileges left by his father's demise. No one who knew him could fail to be impressed by the way he ignored the privileges and set himself to shoulder the obligations. And not only the obligations that his father had carried out before him, but also those that other men had neglected through lack of time, patience, or ability.

Did Yosef Diaber have more time than the average person? This was difficult to believe: young Lord Diaber, like the rest of Khazar's nobility, had been granted only 24 hours in a day; the difference lay in the priorities they set. Diaber's heart was wider and more compassionate than those of his peers. He was also of the opinion that strength multiplied as it was used: the more tired he was, the more strongly motivated he became.

He governed the vast Diaber estate wisely and punctiliously carried out his obligations as a member of Khazar's governing council. The number of laws, for example, that he personally proposed to the council was greater than the number brought forward by his three most energetic fellow members combined. On top of this, he found the time to establish a group whose function was to ensure that animals were not mistreated, which supervised the food and care given to animals on the Diaber estates as well as on the estates of others whom he had persuaded to join his initiative. He also visited his mother's father three times a week, a crusty old gentleman who suffered from a variety of ailments that accompany old age.

The king took note of his activities and took a liking to him. He liked Yosef Diaber so much that he came up with the splendid notion of offering him his own wonderful younger daughter as his bride. One afternoon, near the end of winter, a plate was broken in the king's palace. A week later, Yosef Diaber became officially betrothed to Rena, daughter of Brachia, and gave her a ring as a token of kiddushin.*

Rena's happiness was complete. Proudly she would study the sparkling golden ring on her finger. Whenever she had to remove it, as for washing her hands before a meal, she would later put it back on with a dreamy look that her family soon came to recognize and smile over.

Yosef Diaber was happy, too. His happiness translated into a boundless reservoir of energy. There was much he wished to accomplish before he stood beneath the chuppah.

King Brachia, father of Reuel and Rena, already beginning to suffer

---

* In earlier times marriage consisted of two separate stages. The first, known as *erusin* or *kiddushin,* was effected by the giving of a ring or other object of value. At this point a couple was considered fully married although they did not live together. Should the marriage be terminated, the woman had to be given a *get* (divorce).

with the leg ailment that would, a number of years later, cripple him, was satisfied. Once, when the pain was especially acute, he leaned on his son's shoulder and sighed, "I am not what I once was, my son. If anything should happen to you, Yosef would be able to fill your place." He paused, wincing, and then added, "And he'll do a fine job, too."

Afterward, when the pain had passed, the king tried to backtrack. His efforts at whitewashing what he had said amused his son. But the amusement dwindled as Reuel realized how truly anxious his father was to see him on excellent terms with his future brother-in-law.

Never before had Reuel felt that he had been the cause of his father experiencing any difficulty or distress. It was disturbing to know that he was the reason his father was upset at a time when the king was already suffering physically. Reuel was prepared to do anything to erase that troubled look from his father's eyes — even to invite young Lord Diaber to accompany him on a tour of the military bases near the Bulgarian border. The contingent that was to accompany the prince consisted of the most senior security and military men in the kingdom.

Diaber, assessing the invitation at its true worth, accepted with alacrity.

On a clear morning, three days after Pesach, the two set out accompanied by an illustrious escort. Yosef Diaber, with his characteristic energy and humor, turned what might have been a tedious journey into a pleasant and even amusing one. His vigor and attentiveness went a long way toward helping the delegation meet the goals it had set for itself, and his warm, generous manner endeared him to the men.

Three long, busy weeks went by. With each passing day, Yosef Diaber proved how worthy he was of the compliment Reuel's father had paid him. And then, on the twenty-first day of the journey, as they went down to immerse themselves in the river, something happened that changed everything.

A cat — that was what happened. A very young cat, hardly more than a kitten.

Like all cats, its ears were erect and its eyes round and slanted. Unlike most cats, its white fur was spotted with red. It limped as it made its way, crying, along the riverbank. There was no other name for the sound it was producing. That cat was crying — the cry of an innocent creature, suffering through no fault of its own.

Yosef Diaber spotted it first. He put a hand to his mouth. "Good heavens!" he cried. "Who did that to it?"

None of his companions was able to answer. Then again, no answer was necessary. A moment after the cat came into view, so did its persecutor: a boy, about 7, with a rock in his hand and long brown legs peeking out of his short, dusty trousers.

The boy didn't see them at first, so intent was he on his prey. But a shout from the vice minister of internal security made him lift his eyes, startled, and then bolt in a panic.

"Children can be very cruel sometimes," someone said, looking down at the unfortunate cat.

"Is there any way we can help it?" another said, cautiously approaching the small creature crouched helplessly on the ground.

Yosef Diaber, without a word to anyone, went over to the nearest horse, flung himself onto its back, and galloped away.

Initially, Reuel did not grasp his intention. He was moved by Yosef's heightened sensitivity, which had led him to leave the place in order to hide tears of pain at the sight of the creature's suffering. But he didn't need a horse for that!

Others were quicker to understand.

"He's young," someone said. "And excitable. He thinks he can fix the whole world…"

"He'll soon be back," another said, waving a dismissive hand. "You can't chase a boy like that on a horse…"

Reuel, who was also young and who also believed — as he would believe all his life — in the power of the individual to repair the world, decided to follow Lord Diaber. "Do not come after us," he threw over his shoulder to the others as he signaled Ovadia to join him. "Go about your business. We'll be back as quickly as we can."

They followed the signs of disturbance in the bushes. When they reached the road, the tracks vanished. They were at a loss: in the short time it had taken them to saddle their horses, both Diaber and the boy he had been pursuing had vanished.

Their confusion did not last long. The moment they turned left, in the direction of the thatched huts of the nearby village, they found fresh traces that led them directly to the village square. There, as though following a rehearsed script, stood the small boy — red-faced, with his clothes in tatters — and Yosef Diaber, the king's future son-in-law, resplendent in clothes that boldly accentuated his social status.

The village was populated largely by non-Jewish residents and Muslims. The child, they later learned, was the son of the lone Khazari in the village and had been given the rudiments of a Torah education.

Whether it was because of suppressed jealousy on the part of the non-Jewish residents toward Khazar's majority population, or some other reason, no one came to the abashed child's aid. On both sides of the street shopkeepers watched in silence as he suffered a major tongue-lashing in the village square. The boy stood on his spindly legs and said nothing at all; only by the quivering of his lashes could it be seen that every furious word found its mark.

"You wicked boy!" Diaber shouted, each word lashing like a whip. "Despicable creature!"

The boy lowered his head.

"Cruel! Heartless!"

He shouted so loudly that Reuel could hear him from down the road. He couldn't move. It was as if his muscles had become paralyzed.

"I —" the boy finally said, pale and shaking. "But —"

Diaber's lip curled. "You there!" he called to a pair of boys watching from a safe distance. "Do you know what we call someone who hurts animals?"

One of the boys nodded eagerly. "Wicked," he parroted. "Cruel…"

The boy in the center of the square turned even whiter, and splotches of bright red burned on each cheek. They reminded Reuel, standing frozen in the road, of the splotches of blood on the young cat.

"Wi-cked," chanted the second boy. "Cru-el…"

The paralysis went as suddenly as it had come. Digging his heels into his horse's flank, the crown prince of Khazar galloped into the village square.

"Enough!' he said, struggling with all his might not to utter all the things that trembled on his lips. "Enough! The boy understands."

"And how will that help the cat?" Yosef Diaber demanded. "How can a Jew cause such pain to a living creature, Your Highness? That boy —"

Reuel's jaw clamped shut. He had no desire to insult Diaber, but "that boy," standing pale and trembling before them, deserved protection no less than the cat that his brother-in-law had chosen to champion.

"What kind of Jew," he asked in Latin, "can hurt a fellow human like this, Diaber? Look at him!"

Diaber was taken aback; he seemed honestly not to understand Reuel's meaning. Then he shrugged. "He has to learn a lesson," he replied in the same tongue. Reverting to Khazari, he added, "We must not allow people to walk about Khazar capable of hurting Hashem's creatures without pity." There was a touch of menace in his tone. The boy became even more glassy-eyed with fear.

Reuel could stand no more. "Close your mouth," he said, the Latin words sharp as rocks. "Leave the child alone. That's an order, not a request."

Diaber's eyes widened in shock. Nostrils flaring with anger, he snapped, "Are you willing to take responsibility for the blood of all the cats with broken limbs that will be limping through Khazar for the next eighty years?"

Reuel tilted his head, glancing at the boy and then at Diaber. "Go back to the river," he said. "You have fulfilled your obligation and delivered your rebuke."

"I did not come here to carry out an obligation —"

"I know that," Reuel said coldly. "No one with any sense could have transgressed the prohibition against embarrassing someone, which is akin to murder, in order to rebuke him for transgressing the prohibition of causing pain to animals." Then, in Khazari, "He looks like a good boy. I'm sure he did not behave that way without a reason. Right?"

The boy didn't answer, or even lift his eyes. He stood silently, chin trembling.

"Right?" Reuel asked again, sliding off his horse's back and reaching out to tousle the boy's hair. But the boy recoiled, leaving the crown prince to caress the empty air.

"You are a good boy," Reuel said. "I know that."

The boy finally raised his eyes. "Thank you," he whispered. Then he collapsed onto the ground, sobbing uncontrollably.

Around them, the shopkeepers were motionless. No one understood this battle of wills, or dared to interfere.

"One gold coin," Reuel announced, "to the person who brings me to this boy's father."

The villagers came to life. For a gold coin, they would have been willing to hire out their services for a month. Ovadia chose one of them and ordered him to carry the boy.

"I will do that," Reuel said.

"Sir!" The notion outraged Ovadia. The boy was filthy, and his behavior — it was impossible to ignore it — had been reprehensible.

But Reuel only grinned. "We have to compensate him somehow, don't we?"

When Reuel and Ovadia returned to the group they had abandoned so hastily by the riverbank, they were met by a rather chilly reception. The coolness was understandable in light of the fact that a group of dignitaries had been forced to wait while their prince disappeared without warning for a considerable length of time. But there was an additional message in their demeanor that the prince found difficult to decipher.

Ovadia, quicker to grasp nuances than his master, had a few quiet words with some of the other servants that confirmed his suspicions. Yosef Diaber had returned to the river not long before they did, still fuming. From the disjointed phrases he let fall, the following picture had emerged: When the two of them had arrived in the village, Diaber had tried to educate the boy. But Reuel had prevented this by shouting, scolding, and behaving — according to Diaber — in a manner that put all of Khazar to shame. And furthermore, Reuel had sought to appease the boy and his parents with a gift of cash.

There was a kernel of truth in everything Diaber had said. Reuel had shouted — not at the boy, but at his future brother-in-law. Reuel had indeed embarrassed Lord Diaber by rebuking him in front of the simple villagers. In exchange for a small gold coin, Reuel had discovered who the boy's parents were and — though Diaber did not know this at the time — he had left an additional gift of money at the house. But the interpretation that Yosef Diaber placed on the events, and which his fellow dignitaries accepted, suffered from a lack of exactitude that bordered on the scandalous.

The incident was not yet over.

When Reuel wished to set about doing what he had originally come to the river to do — namely, refresh himself and change his travel-stained garments for cleaner ones — Ovadia and one of the other servants discovered that the cat had died in the interim. It had been laid out on the prince's finest Shabbos garment, wrapped in the cloak as though in a shroud.

The servants, much distressed, claimed to have seen no one handling the prince's things. Ovadia muttered a few choice comments aimed at Diaber. Reuel said nothing.

His struggle was intense. The princely face darkened with the effort to suppress the turmoil within, which lent his eyes a sparkle and straightened his shoulders. His chest rose and fell to the rhythm of his breaths, which had become slow and deep. Better than a hundred witnesses, his clenched hands told the story of the battle being waged within. Afterward, when the war was won, the crimson in his cheeks was replaced by extreme paleness, and his shoulders slowly relaxed.

"Not a word," Reuel said finally. "None of you."

The servants stared at him in confusion.

"Not a word," repeated the crown prince, "to a soul. A small test of your loyalty. If you speak of this, it will mean your immediate dismissal from my service. And because I esteem you all greatly, I am asking each of you to exert the utmost self-control."

"But —"

A shadow passed through Reuel's eyes. "I, too, feel it here," he said, touching his chest. "In here, I feel hot, on fire, hungry for revenge." He glanced at the dead cat, which Ovadia hastily thrust back among the trees. "However, though we may speak of a slight to Khazar's honor, it is reasonable to assume that this was a personal affront." His eyes raked the servants. "I am correct, am I not?"

The men returned his gaze. It was clear that Diaber's insolence had wounded them more than it had the prince.

"I believe I am correct," Reuel said. "And because our blessed Creator has arranged things so that I am the one to decide, I will use the privilege that has been granted me." His eyes probed the men in turn, until each bowed his head in submission. Only then did the crown prince of Khazar walk away.

During the following days, it was obvious to all that Yosef Diaber was braced for some sort of retaliation. It never came. As for Reuel, he managed to convince himself that the entire episode had been a one-time incident, emerging from an unusually heightened emotional state, and so was able to treat Diaber almost normally. The young lord did not return his friendliness.

It was on the third day, a brilliantly clear afternoon, that they encountered the deer.

Full grown and regal, antlers glinting in the sun, the buck stood its ground and gazed at them wisely. It seemed to wish to say something to them, and the military contingent — which was supplied with all the meat it required — returned its gaze as though to indicate its willingness to hear it. The venerable creature lowered its head, and as if on cue its family appeared: a delicate doe and two prancing fawns.

Someone thrust a long, pointed arrow into Reuel's hand.

"Take it, Your Highness," Yosef Diaber said. "And take this bow as well. After all, you enjoy the sight of wounded animals, the blood flowing freely as they cry with pain..."

"I!" Reuel exclaimed. He turned to face the group of dignitaries who were his companions. "Now hear the truth of the tale!" he declared. "The father of that boy who was chasing the cat had been injured by an ox during the threshing. With the money he received as compensation for his suffering, he decided to invest in a small henhouse."

Reuel inhaled deeply. Behind him the deer vanished in the undergrowth. "For the first half-year, the family saw no profit at all. On the contrary, feed for the chickens thinned the already slender family budget. More recently, as the chicks grew into young setting hens, the home was filled with hope. When they sold ten young roosters before Shavuos, the dream seemed to grow firmer. They hoped there would be money to fix the hole in the roof and pay a visit to the used-clothing salesman. The father, a talented man, began to fashion a wooden brace that would hold his leg straight and, perhaps, allow him to walk without a crutch.

"And then, one night, a lovely family of wild cats invaded the coop." The prince's voice grew brittle. "White cats with slanted eyes that left behind a pile of dead bodies and heartbreak..."

"So the boy decided to avenge himself on every cat he met from that day to eternity?"

It was not Diaber who asked this, but a young army officer.

Reuel stared at the soldier in astonishment. "You've glimpsed a single fragment out of an entire life, and you've formulated a theory based on that? If this is the way you construct your military theory, I will be forced to oppose any promotion for you."

The moment he said this, Reuel felt a pang. Was he any better than Diaber? He, too, was engaged in battle on behalf of someone who had been injured and was trampling on others in the process... He felt suddenly weak.

"In any case," he continued, his voice no longer strong and dramatic, "after three such invasions, there was nothing left of that henhouse but a single chicken that refused to sit on its eggs."

The horses pawed the ground restlessly. The road was long, and the position of the sun said that it was high time they were on their way. Though sensing that the men were not with him, Reuel nevertheless concluded the tale.

"They set traps and managed to capture several of the wild cats. They sent the boy down to the river to drown them. The sack was worn and tore on the way..."

None of them understood. None of them, Reuel saw, felt the boy's pain and confusion, the fear that engulfed him when he thought of his mother's reaction and of his father's distress the next morning when they would find, in a litter of bones and blood, the carcass of their last remaining hen.

"The larger cats were too quick for him, but he managed to catch the younger ones, to do as his father had instructed. On his return, he saw that injured white cat making its way slowly back toward the village."

"Injured!" someone said.

Reuel felt some of his battle spirit returning. "Yes, Minister. Human beings are not the only enemies of the wild cat."

"And he didn't throw any stones at it," Yosef Diaber said sarcastically. His tone asked whether the crown prince was always so easily taken in.

"He did throw stones," Reuel replied, "because he wished to catch it."

"As if that's what would it would take to save them," Diaber mocked. "The blood of a little cat."

Reuel shook his head. He could not win here. "Come," he said finally. "Let us move on."

Reuel returned to the capital, after an absence of six long weeks, on an achingly beautiful summer's day. The sun shone sweetly, children played in the streets, and even the adults seemed to search for an excuse to be outdoors, to smile at one another and enjoy the pleasant breeze that was blown in from the sea.

In the palace, the atmosphere was even more cheerful. Knocking on his mother's door, Reuel was invited in to admire the Sefer Torah covering that she had just finished embroidering.

"The sofer says that the Torah will be ready for Rena's chuppah." *Her face glowed as she spoke; she was genuinely fond of Yosef Diaber and was overjoyed that her daughter was to marry him.*

"I...I'll take a look at it later," *Reuel said, retreating.*

"Why not now?"

"It's selfish of me... It's just that I'm so tired..."

"It's not selfish at all!" *His mother stood up quickly.* "I am the one who has been thoughtless. Have you changed your clothes yet? Have you eaten?"

"Not yet."

"Then do it right now," *she said energetically.* "Go ahead, son. You can look at the cover later."

"Very well, Mother. Thank you."

Something in his tone alerted the queen. She studied his face. "Were there any problems on the journey, son?"

"No. It went well. The troops are well organized, their morale is high..."

"Wonderful!"

"Yes." *For the first time, the crown prince smiled, and the smile highlighted his youth.* "It is wonderful." *Then his face grew long again, and he averted his head.*

His mother watched him as he retreated with a last mumbled word of apology. If all had gone well on the military front — what, in Heaven's name, was troubling her son?

Near midday, shortly before the hour designated for the delegation to report to the king, Reuel stood before his father. From the stiffness of his carriage and the tightness of his lips, it was clear that he had not come to impart glad tidings.

He had no desire to do it, but the second option — allowing his younger sister to become the wife of a man with such a distorted set of priorities — was many times worse.

To his surprise, his father's reaction was cold. The eyes that could radiate such warmth stared frigidly at him.

"That's what happened," Reuel said desperately.

The king shook his head. "I would not have believed this of you, Reuel."

Of all possible responses, this was the one Reuel had least expected. The king's words washed over him like icy water, bathing him in confusion. Was he going mad? Could he have been in error? Had it actually been Diaber who had behaved properly, while he, driven by his own character flaws, had made a huge fuss over nothing?

The room seemed to have become flat, two-dimensional. His father's face, too, seemed to lack substance. Fatigued from the journey, Reuel's thoughts were heavy and viscous — almost too heavy for him to formulate the question: "What do you mean, Father?"

The king regarded him in silence. He was a wise man, a man of rich experience. While he loved Reuel dearly, he had never refrained from looking squarely at a person's deficiencies — even if that person was his only son.

"You are jealous of Yosef," *he said at last.* "You are disturbed by the ease with which he has won the hearts of those around him."

Reuel said nothing. He never contradicted his father.

"You were insulted when I praised him," *the king concluded.* "And a sense of personal injury can cause a person to view the world through a distorted glass."

To remain silent now called for an even more heroic effort than the one he had exerted upon finding the dead cat wrapped in his Shabbos garment. Reuel clenched his fists tightly, the nails digging into his palms.

"You must study more works of mussar and ethics," *his father advised, leaning forward.* "A person may rule a mighty kingdom like Khazar, yet be the poorest person in the land — as long as he does not transform his jealousy into something positive."

"I will do so," *Reuel promised.*

"Good." *The king stood. Their talk was over.*

Reuel stood, too, his mind awhirl. If he had indeed become muddled and perceived things incorrectly, that was bad for him. But if he was the only one who had actually succeeded in seeing the truth — that boded only bad for Khazar.

The next afternoon, the prince was again standing before his father. This time he was accompanied by two Khazari dignitaries who had not been numbered among the official military delegation. The king was taken aback as the trio appeared before him. By the looks on their faces, Reuel's companions were equally surprised.

Reuel, in contrast, was pale and tense. He knew exactly what was about to ensue. "I asked these two honored men to come here," he said, "because I require witnesses."

Silence filled the room. After this opening remark, the others were as tense as the crown prince.

"Yesterday," Reuel said heavily, "I caused His Majesty to listen to lashon hara. I thought I fell into the category of a single reliable witness — but I discovered that I was wrong."

The kings' brows moved minutely closer.

"Therefore," Reuel plowed on, "I cannot tell His Majesty several additional details that I have discovered over the course of this past day. I can only ask him to discover them for himself, and to promise him, in the presence of these two witnesses —" Reuel paused to catch his breath, which had suddenly grown short "— that if, after a thorough investigation, His Majesty reaches the conclusion that Lord Yosef Diaber is worthy of marrying my sister, Rena..." Another pause to draw air into his lungs. "If that happens, I am prepared...that is, I've decided to yield all my rights as Regent and Prince of Khazar...to Lord Diaber.

"If it turns out," Reuel continued through parched lips, "that my claims are no more than empty allegations deriving from envy, then I will give Yosef the only thing he lacks." He gave a twisted smile. "On the appropriate day, Yosef will undoubtedly rejoice at being crowned king of Khazar."

"And you?" the king asked. His voice, like his son's, was hoarse.

"I will leave." Reuel's gaze was steady and open. "To remain here, serving under him, would be too much."

The darkness had grown thicker by the time Hala's last words trailed off.

"So what happened in the end?" Istrak asked sharply.

His wife shrugged. "Yosef Diaber did not marry my mother, and your father became king."

The others were silent, digesting this. Istrak tried to incorporate this new information into the mosaic of present-day life in Khazar. Hala, with her characteristic patience, waited for his reaction.

"Why?" he asked at last, passing a hand over his eyes as though waking from a bad dream. "I mean, why did it end that way?"

"My mother didn't tell me," Hala admitted. "But Grandfather—"

Grandfather! Despite everything, he had not yet absorbed the fact that he and his wife, daughter of the Kawari leader, shared the same grandfather.

"— summoned Yosef Diaber a week later and had a long, private talk with him. Afterward, one of the servants was asked to call in the members of the *beis din*. Yosef gave my mother a *get* and the episode was ended.

Istrak permitted himself a doubt. Eighteen months after the events Hala had just described, Yosef Diaber married the orphaned daughter of one of Khazar's wealthiest and most powerful noblemen. The lord, who had not fathered any sons, had bequeathed his house, property, and money to his daughter. Diaber became the owner of the largest estate in Khazar, second only to that of the king himself.

When the king left this world a few years later, Reuel faced an untenable situation: by law, if the king had no son capable of taking on the role of regent, he was required to appoint to the position the largest landowner among Khazar's nobility. In other words, Yosef Diaber.

Diaber became regent of Khazar, but the animosity between himself and Reuel did not abate.

The darkness had become even thicker before Istrak spoke again. "Hala," he said, "even if I believe the story you've told me..."

She lifted her head with a jerk, and he hastened to continue.

"Even if I believe it — and I'm not saying I don't — what exactly would you have me do?"

"What do you mean, what would I have you do?" She was honestly bewildered by the question. "You have to understand whom you're dealing with. Diaber can be very dangerous!"

"Dangerous? Why? Because once, when Yosef Diaber was about 25 or so, he lost his wits for minute or two? Haven't you ever made a mistake?"

Suddenly, his spirits fell. If it was hard to find justification for Yosef Diaber's actions, it was equally hard to find it for his own. He had made so many mistakes. If someone, in some future age, were to try to reconstruct his personality based on these last few months of captivity, the results would not be very flattering...

"No," he said decisively. "I don't think is it fair to decide about someone's character on the basis of a single incident. Diaber was regent of Khazar for decades, and he did only good, Hala. Only good!"

"I am glad to hear," she said angrily, "that my new husband is prepared to be a second Gedalia ben Achikam.* It will be so pleasant to be a young widow."

Istrak cleared his throat. "Don't you think you're getting a little carried away?"

Hala's face clouded. "No, I don't."

"I think you are," Istrak returned. "You grew up in Platt, Hala. You learned to think a certain way. But you're in a very different place now. As of this afternoon, we have entered Khazar."

Hala was hardly more than a silhouette in the black night. "Let me tell you something my mother has always told me," she said, her voice quavering. "She would often say, 'Khazar is in your heart. And you — only you — will decide if you wish to live there.'"

Istrak shrugged. "A nice sentiment. But it has nothing to do with the issue at hand."

Hala closed her eyes, the better to keep back the tears welling

---

* Gedalia, the leader of the Jews who remained in Eretz Yisrael after the destruction of the First Temple, was murdered as a result of his trusting individuals who betrayed him. Tzom Gedalia is observed in remembrance of his assassination.

there. "Don't you understand? Can't you see for yourself?"

Istrak shook his head.

"My mother didn't want me to tell you," she blurted after a moment's hesitation. "But if you don't know this, you will not be able to decide how to act... Your father did not 'collapse,' as they are saying. They hurt him, Istrak. They tried to murder him!"

"They...what?"

Istrak's voice bore no resemblance to that of the young man she had come to know. She hated having to repeat what she had said, and she did so on a deeply apologetic note. "They tried to kill your father. He was gravely hurt. It happened more than six months ago."

A cold wave swept over Istrak, turning him icy-cold from head to toe. "And what has happened since?"

"Nothing, I think." Hala spread her hands helplessly. "His condition is the same, without much hope... But Mother doesn't tell me everything."

Istrak's fingers tightened around a branch of the tree on which he was leaning. "If something's happened to my father, I have to be in Itil. Khazar needs me. I have to rule."

"That's right," Hala whispered. "But Yosef Diaber is also in Itil. And he, with totally different motives, wants to rule, too..."

Istrak closed his eyes and tilted his head back, trying to assuage the convulsions of longing and pain that struck with the force of a tidal wave. "I can't let that stop me. Knaz and I go on to Itil. The rest of you will remain here. If anything should happen to me, Michoel will take my place. He will serve his country well."

Once again, Hala's eyes filled with tears. But she merely nodded.

A sudden weakness assailed Istrak. He put a hand to his eyes. "I know I shouldn't think about it right now, but I don't really feel ready for this job. I need my father. I...I can't go on without him."

"He is with you, Istrak," Hala said, "as Khazar is always with you wherever you are. Though you may not be able to speak to him, you know in your heart what he would tell you to do."

Istrak swallowed, wondering how she could know that the wind was carrying fragments of sentences back to him, all spoken in his father's loving voice, all urging him rise to his feet like a man and do what he knew was right. He longed to go home and prove to his father that he had changed, to show him that there had been a purpose to the endless hours of education, conversation, and molding.

He had never thought for a minute that he would have to prove it in such a manner.

In Command

34

BY THE CUSTOM OF THE KHAZAR ROYAL FAMILY, THE prince's long hair was cut on the morning of his coronation. Istrak found it distressful for his hair to be cut during his father's lifetime. But he knew it was what he must do, and his will triumphed over his emotions. When the group — quieter and graver now — descended the hill the next morning, they left behind, beneath a large stone, long, fair locks shorn from the crown prince's head.

The sleepy town received them indifferently. In the *beis knesses* courtyard, to which the men hastened, no one tried to delve more deeply into Kalev's mumbled cover story, to ask where the furs were that they had ostensibly gone out to buy, or why they had seen fit to take along two women, one older and the other a mere girl. Only their desire to purchase a wagon and an animal to draw it aroused any interest in the village. But even this interest rapidly waned. No one was prepared to sell his horse in exchange for a small, glowing gem. Even the gold chain that Rena produced was scornfully rejected. It became obvious that they had no choice but to continue on their way by foot.

Then the villagers noticed the *Sefer Torah* they carried.

"Is it kosher?" the people asked. There was longing in their voices, and their fingers reached for the scroll without touching it, pleading without words. "We have no *Sefer Torah*. Ours was rendered unfit more than a month ago and we do not have a new one yet."

"This is a very old and delicate Torah," Kalev said, taking a step back and holding the scroll out of their reach. "Careful!"

A sigh rose up from the men around them.

"Are you in a great hurry?" one of them asked. "Can't you stay here for Shabbos? Or at least until Thursday?"

"No," Istrak said, in the face of those pleading eyes. "We must go on. But the *Sefer Torah*…"

"The *Sefer Torah*…" they echoed, imploring him to speak.

"The *Sefer Torah* can remain here in the meanwhile."

The men moved toward Kalev, who threw Istrak an imploring look of his own. Istrak spread his hands slightly. The scroll had belonged to King Aharon, and it had accompanied them on their journey, providing a sense of protection and security. But there was no reason to carry it with them any longer — especially not with a score of Jewish men begging to be allowed to use it as it was meant to be used.

"We will come back one day to retrieve it," he said quietly, when Kalev had reluctantly handed the *Sefer Torah* to the village headman. "This is only a loan."

The headman hugged the Torah tightly. "An invaluable loan. There are no words to express our gratitude."

"There are actions," Rena said, taking a step forward. "We need a horse and cart. Is there no one here prepared to express his gratitude by selling them to us? We will pay a reasonable price and more."

The woman's interference in their conversation startled the men. Istrak, too, felt uncomfortable. His aunt's assertive style had been of tremendous use to them up to this point, but here — as he had told Hala last night — the rules of the game were different.

"I'll do it," someone volunteered. "But my horse is old."

"Too old," someone else said. "It would be scandalous to sell them such a horse. I have a pair of donkeys. You bring the cart."

"Donkeys!" a third exclaimed. "Is that how you treat someone who has given us a *Sefer Torah*? I will give them *my* horse." He turned to Istrak. "Do you need two, perhaps?"

"You'll lose a week's work!" someone scolded. They recognized the minstrel they had encountered at the foot of the hill. "Don't be a fool, Dovid."

The speaker fell silent, shoulder slumping. "Well, maybe two really is going overboard," he said apologetically. "It's hard to find good animals these days. A great many horses and oxen died in the epidemic last year."

"Even one horse is too much," the singer persisted. "Isn't that so?"

An assenting, wordless echo seemed to rise from the circle of men. The warm spirit — so essentially Khazar — had nearly dissipated, replaced by a sense of alienation.

Istrak, who had been feeling so proud of his countrymen just a moment before, stared at them in stupefaction. He had not expected such an enthusiastic response to Rena's challenge — but once they had been roused, and shown themselves prepared to do anything to express their happiness and gratitude, the change was strange and surprising.

"One horse is a lot, son of Khazar," he said, placing a hand on the villager's shoulder. "And I'm proud of you. I'm sure that His Majesty — may Hashem lengthen his days — would be proud of you, too, if he knew how warmhearted a fellow you are."

The minstrel opened his mouth to say something, and then, unexpectedly, closed it with a snap, regarding Istrak with narrowed eyes. The owner of the horses, smiling now, invited them to his home to see the animal for himself.

Knaz inspected the horse carefully, and pronounced himself satisfied. "I am deeply grateful," he said. "Not many people would be willing to sell such a fine beast."

"He's called Shosho," the man said, stroking the horse's mane fondly. "I trained him myself."

"Don't worry," Knaz said with unaccustomed softness. "We'll treat him well."

"I won't," the man lied. "You look like good people. But give him some oats now and then, won't you?"

They promised to do so, and the man seemed calmer. With the price agreed upon, the group proceeded to the house, where hot drinks had been prepared for them.

The kitchen in which they sat was spacious and well equipped. Rena exclaimed aloud over it all, adding warm praise regarding the cleanliness, the tasty food, and the pretty flower baskets hanging in the front hall.

Her enthusiasm seemed a bit overdone to Istrak. Casting a puzzled glance at his wife, he was surprised to see her struggling to conceal a smile. When they finally left, with promises from Rena to pay a return visit when they came to pick up the *Sefer Torah*, Hala whispered to Istrak, "My mother is a fine matchmaker. They have a daughter."

"Ah," Istrak said, with an obvious and complete lack of comprehension.

"She will be perfect for Kalev — like fine wine with a festive meal," Hala said. "You'll see…"

Istrak shrugged. If it were up to him, he would find Kalev a wealthier and more honored father-in-law. But this was not the time to go into that. To tell the truth, the matter did not seem to Istrak all that urgent…

The cart was simple, and it was old, but after having traversed such a considerable distance on foot, even this mode of transportation made them feel fortunate. The horse pulled the wagon at a steady pace. The skies were blue, and a fresh, invigorating scent issued from the fields. But neither the beautiful weather nor the easier mode of travel were able to banish anxiety or anguish.

Michoel, who had been unusually subdued since their first meeting with the wandering minstrel, sat hunched uncommunicatively in a corner of the cart. Knaz looked as though he had not had much sleep the night before, and Kalev spoke gloomily to the horse, urging it to move more quickly.

"We will go with you as far as the city," Istrak announced. "There my aunt can purchase horses for Knaz and myself. Then our paths will separate —"

He was about to outline his plan, when a figure stepped out of the bushes at the side of the road and strode straight ahead, forcing them to stop.

"The singer," Kalev said. "He probably wants a lift."

Kalev was wrong.

When the wagon came to a halt, the minstrel hurried to its side and paused beside Istrak. "You had long hair yesterday, right?" he said, his voice hoarse with excitement. "I...I know who you are!"

"I, too, know who I am," Istrak said. "What interests me more is...who are you?"

"What do you mean?" The singer was genuinely bewildered.

"Think about it," Istrak urged. "When we return to the village to fetch the *Sefer Torah*, I'll be interested in hearing whether you've found the answer to that very important question."

The minstrel's jaw dropped. But whether he would have answered they would never know, since the horses — at last justifying the price they had paid for them — sped away with the wagon, leaving the singer behind in the dust.

"This is not good," Knaz said when they had traveled some distance up the road. On Istrak's instructions, he did not address the prince with the customary titles of honor.

Istrak turned to him. "There is no such thing as 'not good' in this world. There is 'not sweet' or 'unpleasant.' But there is no 'not good.'"

"Very true," Knaz acquiesced. "I stand corrected."

"We must consider the possible ramifications of our meeting with that minstrel," Rena said briskly. "We must consider what actions he might take, and their consequences Then we must consider our counterattack."

Her words catapulted Istrak back to his days in the palace, and the lessons in military strategy in which he had engaged with Yishvav the Babylonian. But this was no game or exercise. The success or failure of whichever course they now chose would determine both their own fate — and the future of all of Khazar.

While Ruben Min-Hagai's literary technique was far from professional, there was no gainsaying the sincerity of his verses, their innate strength, or the tremendous love for Khazar, its children, and its G-d, that flowed from every line. In simple, unsophisticated language, Ruben reminded his fellow countrymen of why they had been put into this world. He patiently explored the goals they wished to live by, and invited them to demonstrate the correctness of their aims by joining those who were not prepared to sit by while their children turned into idlers and street singers. He exhorted the true-hearted to throw in their lot with those who were courageously raising the banner of the authentic Khazar.

His people — who, as followers of Pinras, now called themselves "the Mentor's Men" — sang these verses on the street corners, inner conviction obvious in every word. As they sang, they kept one eye open for the approach of government authorities and the other for those who seemed moved by their words but were afraid to take action. Later, they sought out these people in the prayer houses and marketplaces. "If you believe Hashem is our G-d," Ruben's men whispered in their ears, "then follow Him! Take the path you know He wants you to take …

"Our kingdom is being put to the test," they pressed. "The time has come to choose …"

And the people chose.

Some chose comfort and old habits and a pleasant pipe by the fireside. But others, with courage and honesty, opted for the ranks of the Mentor's Men.

Those who chose this course did not come alone. The tent city that sprang up around Lord Baliatar's fortress grew larger each day. The men who joined were G-d-fearing and spent as much time studying Torah as battle maneuvers. In all, it more closely resembled a yeshivah than an army camp preparing for battle.

"This is Yosafar, one of the largest and wealthiest of the northern cities," Istrak said. "Its prosperity is based mostly on trade in furs and spices. If my memory serves — and if nothing has drastically changed in recent months — Pe'er, Yosef Diaber's oldest son, is mayor of the city."

Kalev paused and looked back. "If that's true, maybe we'd better skip a hot midday meal and keep moving."

Rena laughed. "And how will we gather information?"

"Don't worry," Knaz remarked. "The city's mayor does not wander around in the streets. Besides, His Maj — uh, Istrak looks completely different now. I doubt he will be recognized."

"Michoel doesn't," Istrak said. Then, glancing over at his taciturn brother, he changed his mind. When they had set out on this journey, Michoel had been a fragile, dreamy, innocent boy. Captivity had hardened him, leaving its mark on his skin, his cheeks sunken beneath eyes that no longer held any dreams. "Still, I don't think anyone will recognize him either," he concluded.

Michoel looked at him knowingly. "Only," he said, "if no one steps up to inform the authorities that a strange group consisting of three Khazaris, one Mundari, and two women are about to arrive and disrupt Khazar's peace."

"We will separate, of course," Rena said.

"No," Knaz disagreed. "It will be easier to harm the princes if they are on their own."

Istrak spoke up, his voice calm and decisive. "The correct course is obvious. We divide into two groups, maintaining continuous visual contact. Should that contact be broken, we look for the nearest well and wait for the other group to arrive."

Anxiety for his younger brother tempted Istrak to pass through the city with Michoel under his wing, but logic said otherwise. In their present situation, it was more prudent for the two royal sons to keep their distance from each other. He hesitated for a heartbeat, then decided to keep Kalev with him and to leave Knaz — who, despite his injured arm, was the better bodyguard — with Michoel.

The city of Yosafar suited Pe'er Diaber, Istrak reflected, the way a crown suits a king, or a walking stick a wanderer. Like Pe'er — whom Istrak had known since he was a little boy — the city was calm, sophisticated, and well-established. On Istrak's first and only previous visit, the place had impressed him with the refinement of its inhabitants and the tranquility of their lives. He had admired the cleanliness and the quality of its gardens and landscaping. Now, though, as he walked at Kalev's side along the city's main street, he thought the city had changed — or perhaps the change was only inside him.

How could he have admired a city whose residents — so well dressed and proud of posture — smiled only at their acquaintances, and even then with apathetic eyes? Perhaps he had been enchanted by the fragrance of spices that wafted from the shops and the people's gracious bearing. Today, the graciousness seemed feigned. It seemed to whisper of danger — a feeling that grew stronger with each step he took.

"It's nice here," Kalev remarked.

Istrak nodded wordlessly, keeping his thoughts to himself.

"It's almost nicer than Khazaran-Itil," Kalev added, a shadow crossing his face. "And Itil is the capital city..."

Istrak looked around. Kalev was right. The courtyards that surrounded the stone houses were better tended than those of his home city, their hedges more meticulously trimmed. The paving stones were cleaner, and the uniforms of the servants accompanying their masters to the marketplace were more splendid. In the midst of all this opulence, Michoel and Knaz's ragged garments were a glaring dissonance as they walked along at a distance from Istrak and Kalev. It made them conspicuous, which was the last thing they wanted or needed.

"Kalev," Istrak said, reaching cautiously into his largest pocket for the money his mother-in-law had given him, "unless we want to stand out like a nail from a wall, we're going to need new clothes — and quickly."

After a whispered word to Michoel and Knaz, Istrak was soon standing in a dim, secondhand clothing stall, watching Kalev turn before his eyes — with the help of a set of used garments in good condition — into the image of a young, dandified scion of a noble house. Suddenly he was struck by a surprising notion.

"Very good." Istrak turned to the shopkeeper. "Now bring me, please, a simple suit, as befits my position."

The shopkeeper inclined his head in understanding. From the rear of the shop he brought out a faded suit of clothes, devoid of all adornment. Resisting the impulse to ask who the former owner had been, or whether he had washed the clothes before bringing them to the shop, Istrak tried on the outfit. In the shopkeeper's opinion, it fit him perfectly. After cuffing up the trousers, Istrak agreed. He turned to Kalev.

Kalev, horrified at Istrak's plan, had been rendered temporarily tongue-tied. All he could utter were a few startled coughs.

A few minutes later — after Istrak had, for the first time in his life, engaged in a bargaining session — the clothes were theirs. They stepped out of the gloomy stall into dazzling sunshine, screwing up their eyes.

"I —" Kalev began, staring helplessly down at the lavish outfit Istrak had purchased for him.

"You will continue to be you," Istrak said quickly, "despite the disguise. Don't worry."

Kalev shook his head. "But —" he tried again, gesturing at Istrak.

"It's better this way." The prince of Khazar sounded weary. "Much better, Kalev. Besides, this will give me a chance to repay some of your devoted service. May we proceed now, sir?"

Kalev choked, but Istrak was adamant. Carrying the bundle that Kalev had borne until now, he followed the youth down the streets leading to the central marketplace, trying to conform his thoughts to his new clothes. It was no easy feat to change, in an instant, from the prince of the kingdom to the servant of a young nobleman. But Istrak enjoyed the mental challenge, as well as the chance to see, for the first time, how the other half of Khazar lived.

Their next stop was a small food stall. Kalev, with an anguished face, went inside first, with Istrak following behind to help him deferentially with his coat and to pull out his chair. After informing the owner of the place that his noble master awaited a meal and outlining the desired menu, Istrak walked tentatively toward the rear of the restaurant, where the servants sat on hard benches, eating their fill of bread dipped in thin vegetable broth.

Like their fellow residents of the city, these men did not greet the newcomer, but continued the lively discussion in which they had been engaged. The burning issue of the day was the fear of bankruptcy that hovered over the head of one of the city's wealthiest residents. If the worst came to pass, most of his servants would be forced to seek other employment at a much-reduced salary.

"It will never happen," one of the men at the table stated flatly. "The regent won't let it happen."

At this mention of the regent, Istrak tensed and nearly choked over his soup.

"No, he won't," another, older servant agreed, stuffing more bread into his mouth. "Pe'er Diaber knows how to balance market forces. If salaries go down, so will the people's buying power. It's a cycle that can't be prevented. My master always says —"

He continued in this vein, describing his master's economic theory, but Istrak had stopped paying attention. Had he understood what he had heard correctly? It seemed to him that these people had ascribed the title of regent not to Yosef Diaber — but to his son, Pe'er, the mayor of this city!

"And he also says," the pompous servant concluded with an air of immense satisfaction, "that now, in view of his close family connection, Yosafar will receive extra attention from His Majesty. There is every likelihood that our city will enjoy increased prosperity." He sipped his soup, then glanced at Istrak. "Don't you like what I just said?"

The sudden question startled the prince.

"To tell the truth," he admitted, "I wasn't paying attention."

A scornful expression spread over the servant's face. "It's always that way with you provincials. You're all so preoccupied with growing your food that you don't have the head for anything else."

Repressing the retort that rose to his lips, Istrak gazed humbly down into his soup and allowed the others to preen themselves on their good fortune at having been born in such a successful place as Yosafar. Again and again the name of Pe'er Diaber came up with the title "Regent" attached to it.

A fierce pain burned in Istrak's chest. It was all he could do to maintain his equilibrium in the face of this new knowledge. When he felt that he could speak without a tremor in his voice, he turned to the man next to him.

"Excuse me?"

Unwillingly, his neighbor turned his head.

"Can I ask you something?"

"Maybe later," the fellow said. "I want to hear what they're saying…" He pointed his chin at the others sitting at their table.

Istrak nodded in resignation and sat back against the hard wood. His homecoming was far different than he had envisioned when he had been in captivity.

"What about the princes?" He ventured at last to break into the stream of the conversation around him.

"They have not yet been found," someone answered. "But, to tell the truth, no one cares if they wander around the mountains with Ruben Min-Hagai forever."

"Not exactly," a skinny fellow at the other end of the table spoke up. "Think what would happen if someone were to crop up fifty years from now, claiming to be the son of Lissia or Tur…"

"Nonsense." Soup sprayed into the air as the servant with the pompous economic theories thumped the table. "A grandson from the female line would have no standing. The council has authorized the founding of a new Khazar, with Yosef Diaber as king — period!"

One of the restaurant's employees looked in. "Asher Baza, your master is waiting for *mayim acharonim*."

The man next to Istrak stood up. "Mark my words," the servant told his friends before taking his leave. "The kingdom is secure with Yosef Diaber. Though we must not forget the peacock and the dwarf." A wave of laughter greeted his words. "It's not funny," Asher Baza remonstrated. "You may find, one of these days, that the pale mentor and our dear governor are a power that must be reckoned with."

The laughter ended. "No one would be so foolish as to follow their lead," someone declared. "They have nothing to offer."

Once again the door opened. This time, it was Yosef ben Reuel who was summoned to help his master prepare for the Grace after Meals. Startled at Kalev's free use of his father's name, Istrak stood up. Too late, he saw that the skinny fellow at the other end of the table had done the same.

"Is your name also Yosef ben Reuel?" the man asked. The coincidence had turned Istrak into the focus of attention. "Where are you from, by the way?"

It was a difficult question to answer, especially since he had failed to discuss it with Kalev beforehand.

"What difference does it make?" he asked with feigned carelessness. Thankful that he had not washed his hands for bread — and for his seat near the door — Istrak slipped away at once. He felt most perturbed.

Kalev, looking lost among the noble figures surrounding him, was surprised to see Istrak appear beside him holding a silver washing bowl. Without a word, however, he allowed the crown prince of Khazar to pour the water over his hands.

The price of the meal was slightly more than the cost of the two sets of clothing they had just bought. As they stepped out of the restaurant, to find Michoel and Knaz awaiting them, Istrak's purse was considerably lighter than his heart. In silence, he and Kalev continued on down the street.

"Did you learn anything new?" Kalev asked at last.

"Too much." Istrak raised his eyes from the smooth white pavement stones. "Starting with the fact that my mentor has entered the world of politics…moving on to the fact that the High Council has decided to grant Yosef Diaber the title of 'King' and Pe'er Diaber the title of 'Regent'…and ending with the fact that my brothers and sisters, or at least some of them, are wandering around the mountains with Ruben Min-Hagai!"

35

Pe'er Diaber had never troubled to enforce King Reuel's ban on street musicians in Khazar's cities. When Pe'er's father lifted the royal ban, he had a large amphitheater built in the central marketplace for just these sort of performances — a move that outraged the city's rabbinical leaders. This, too, did not trouble Pe'er. The mayor-turned-regent established a supervisory body known as the "Council of Righteous Guidance." The supervisory body — whose members remained anonymous to the public, and whose salaries Pe'er paid from his own generous pocket — authorized the use of public buildings, and out of seventy requests for permission to hold stage performances of one kind or another, a grand total of eight were turned down. Four of these were requests for mass prayer rallies, which the council found reason to reject. "Prayer is a private matter between a man and his Creator," the council under the guidance of Pe'er Diaber ruled. "It is absolutely not a public event, like those staged by clowns or sword swallowers. Such public displays could lead to a lessening of reverence for prayer among the people."

The organizers of this would-be event were astonished by the council's clarity of vision, and wondered why they themselves had not foreseen the possible negative consequences of the prayer rally. One of them, a good and honest man, even undertook to fast every Monday and Thursday for a solid year, in the hope that the Creator would grant atonement for his error and purify his heart so that he might truly understand the sublime quality of prayer — as the council members so obviously did. And while he fasted and repented, the sword swallowers, clowns, jugglers, minstrels, and comedians continued to appear once or twice each week in Yosafar's central market square. As the fame of these performances spread, there came a steady stream of people to the city: those who wished to be entertained alongside performers who wanted to share the limelight.

Among these performers were Akila and his bear, Lazi.

According to the 8-year-old boy who announced the act in the marketplace, Lazi was a wild bear who came out of the woods one day at the sound of the shepherd Akila's lute and began dancing. Knaz and Michoel, who had struck up a conversation about current events with several street artists, were invited to see the performance. In the cause of deepening their friendship with these two, Knaz graciously accepted. Arm in arm, the quartet walked down the street toward the market square.

Rena and Hala, who had been busy bargaining for some dried herbs, abandoned their negotiations and hurried after them. Istrak, seeing his friends walking away, tried, unsuccessfully, to draw Kalev's attention with a series of discreet throat clearings. He was finally forced to give way to a loud bout of racking coughs before his feigned master turned his head. The two followed their friends, halting near the rope fence that surrounded the arena inside the amphitheater. Akila had just begun playing his lute, accompanying the melody in a low, throaty voice.

The sound drew the she-bear's attention. Dressed in human garments — a short red vest and spangled skirt — she let loose a roar. Abandoning the chunk of meat with which she had been occupied, she slowly rose onto her hind legs and began moving her body in time to the rhythmic notes.

The spectacle was bizarre, Istrak thought, and even unpleasant. The audience seemed to think otherwise. When the performance was over, they applauded vigorously and shouted for an encore. Eyes sparkling, Akila acceded to their request. He took up his stance once more, passed a hand over the strings of his instrument, and began a new song. But the bear, who had returned to her former place, did not seem interested in performing again.

"That's no way to behave, Lazi!" Akila scolded. "Do you want a different song? Which one? How about the one about the king with the scar...yes?"

His fingers plucked at the strings, producing strange sounds. The she-bear stirred. Akila began to sing. By the second verse, Istrak found himself gripping Kalev's arm tightly enough to hurt. Michoel, in another section of the gallery, bit his fingers.

Nothing explicit was said, but anyone possessed of the smallest understanding knew that the big bear was dancing to a song that made fun of Reuel II, Khazar's stricken king. The beat was quick, the lyrics well rhymed, and the barbs sharp and accurately aimed. The king's honor was being blatantly impugned, and no one — not even the internal security men standing around — was doing a thing to stop it.

Michoel tensed, ready to leap into the arena and put a halt to the proceedings. But Knaz's healthy arm went around his shoulder and neck, while the injured one covered his mouth. "Breathe deeply," Knaz said quietly into his ear. "It's over. One more minute, and it's over. Breathe deeply."

No one grabbed Istrak, not even Kalev, who kept mumbling, wide-eyed, "Is he crazy, or what?" The ropes surrounding the arena were right in front of Istrak. All he had to do was leap lightly over them. But his upbringing at the hands of the same man now being taunted in Akila's verses helped him to control the almost uncontrollable impulse.

The singer sang six verses and a repeating chorus, but only pale cheeks and gnawed lips testified to what was taking place in Istrak's heart. Then came the seventh verse, mentioning the *rosh yeshivah*. An instant later, Akila found his elbows grasped in two iron-strong hands, and a hard voice muttering in his ear, "That's enough, you *rasha*." Akila kicked out backward, trying to free himself. But the stranger did not loosen his hold. Akila was forced to drop his instrument.

The song stopped in midstream. The she-bear, confused, dropped down on all fours. The audience, which had been unsure as to whether the disturbance was part of the show, voiced its disapproval. Shouts of "Leave him alone!" and "Security! Call Security!" left Istrak unmoved. Nor was he troubled by the youths who were approaching the rope fence. Holding the screaming Akila high in the air, he turned to the tumultuous audience and demanded loudly, "Where is your respect for the Torah? If these are the sons of Khazar — King Yosef would have been better off dying before he had ever been born!"

People in the audience protested the interruption.

"Leave him!"

"He has permission!"

"The rabbis authorized this performance!"

Istrak knees weakened at the people's shouts across the rope fence. Akila, taking advantage of this, kicked hard and freed himself from Istrak's grasp. He fell into the sand that carpeted the floor of the arena just seconds before Michoel and Knaz climbed over the rope.

"Run!" Knaz yelled, drawing his sword. "Hurry, Istrak!"

Istrak did not grasp his meaning — until he heard Lazi roar, very close to his ear. Turning slowly, he found himself staring into the small, foolish eyes of the she-bear, who was standing on her hind legs just steps away from him, roaring at the top of her lungs.

Complete silence suddenly filled the amphitheater. Almost immediately, the silence was replaced by screams of terror. No one wished to see the bear's long claws tear into the young man. Akila screamed, too, but the bear ignored him and took another step forward.

She was so close now that Istrak could see the raddled fur and the black spots on Lazi's yellow teeth. As the bear lifted one enormous shoulder, poised to descend, fathers covered their children's eyes. Then her eyes suddenly clouded, as if she had forgotten what she was about to do. She uttered a delicate cry, landed on all fours, and remained crouched at Istrak's feet, friendly as a small cub.

Had years of domestication finally mastered the bear's wild nature? Istrak did not know the answer. Either way, a miracle had happened — a clear and unambiguous sign of Hashem's loving concern. Raising his eyes, he scanned the crowd. There were words burning on his lips that the people of Yosafar never had a chance to hear — the internal security men, seeing that the bear no longer constituted a threat, were hurrying into the arena to arrest the young man who had had the temerity to initiate a public disturbance.

Michoel grabbed his brother's sleeve with one hand and the hilt of his sword with the other. "Run away — fast!" he whispered hoarsely. "I'll delay them here."

But this generous offer could not be carried out. Already the guards had surrounded them, staying a safe distance from the bear crouched at Istrak's feet and separating the brothers from Knaz and Kalev.

"Drop your weapons," the security chief ordered, "and lift your hands into the air. Now!"

Istrak didn't move. Michoel followed his brother's example. But the bear, disliking the tone of the head guard's voice, responded with an annoyed roar.

"I'm going to count to eight," the guard snapped. "One...two..."

The sound of counting reminded the bear of her previous trainer. He, too, used to stand like that, with one hand on his hip as he counted. The unpleasant memory made her roar again.

"Three...four..."

A tremor ran through the bear. Always, as her previous trainer counted, the tin he had placed beneath Lazi's feet would grow hotter and hotter. By the time he was done, her feet were scorched, and she was forced to jump and writhe in a grotesque and pathetic dance in an effort to cool her seared soles.

Was the earth going to start burning now, too?

She shook her large, shaggy head, searching for Akila, who had treated her very differently. Unable to see him, and noting only strangers around her, she lost her wits and began advancing rapidly toward the haughty guard.

As had happened moments earlier, when Istrak had seemed threatened, the galleries filled with alarm. Cries flew through the air. All eyes were trained on Akila, who was pushing through the guards, instructing them to lower their weapons and move back. He spoke to the bear in a gentle voice, and by the time she was finally soothed, lowering her head to nuzzle Akila's knees, Istrak, Michoel, and Knaz were at the far end of the street.

Istrak led the way at a sprint, with Michoel right on his heels and Knaz, burdened by the many bundles he carried, bringing up the rear. Passersby gaped at them as they passed, and vendors scolded them as they darted in and out among their stalls with murmured apologies. Then the guards came into view, and the surprised looks and mild chiding were replaced by cries of "Catch those thieves!" They had to escape the marketplace, and quickly.

Cutting to the right, Istrak entered a narrow alley that had only one wagon in it.

"I — can't," Michoel gasped behind him. "No — air."

Istrak swung his head around toward his brother — at the precise moment that someone stuck a foot into his path. He stumbled, lost his balance, and crashed painfully onto the smooth paving stones. Groggily, he shook his head to clear it.

Michoel was at his side at once, heedlessly calling out his name. Knaz, too, halted. But his eyes were not on Istrak, nor on Michoel trying to help his brother to his feet — but on the Mundari who had seized Istrak's other arm with fingers of steel.

"Why did you do that?" Knaz asked in the ancient, guttural tongue of the nomadic tribes.

Startled, the Mundari recoiled. When he saw that the speaker was a fellow countryman, his expression changed.

"Did he not steal?"

Knaz shook his head. "He is a Mundari at heart." With a glance over his shoulder to see if the security men were there, he said urgently, "Get him out of here."

The stranger released the prince. Without a word, he went over to his wagon, where he hastily shifted the sacks that filled it, making room for the three of them. By the time the guards entered the quiet alley, the wagon and its contents were covered and the Mundari was removing the donkey's feed bag, talking to it in a low voice as he prepared for departure.

"Have you seen anyone?" the guards demanded.

"Who?"

"Three men."

"Yes," the Mundari said. "I saw them. They were running. That way." He pointed in the direction from which the security contingent had come.

Without wasting any more time, the guards ran back down the street. When they had vanished from sight, the Mundari climbed into the driver's seat and calmly maneuvered his wagon out of the narrow alley and into the main street. From there it was a short distance to the city gates and open fields.

Yosafar was behind them — and so were Hala, Rena, and Kalev.

When the horses' hooves sounded on hard earth instead of smooth stone, Knaz lifted the cloth cover that his countryman had spread over them, climbed out, and seated himself beside the driver.

At first, the talk was practical. The Mundari stranger wanted to know the reason for the pursuit. Knaz, watching him to gauge his reaction, told him about the scene in the amphitheater. When the Mundari passed the test — heaping praise on Istrak and wondering at the behavior of the Yosafarians — Knaz lowered his voice and spoke further in a very quiet undertone.

It was hot beneath the cloth covering and uncomfortably redolent of goats and sheep. Through cracks in the thick wooden walls only a bit of light entered, giving the princes a very limited view of the passing scenery.

"Does it still hurt?" Michoel whispered.

Gingerly, Istrak moved his fingers, ignoring the gash and the blood that had congealed around it. "Not too much."

The wagon continued to lumber forward, passing jutting boulders and low hedges. For a time silence reigned between them... until something strange about Istrak's breathing alerted Michoel. "Are you sure you're all right?"

"Yes," Istrak said. "Certainly." When Michoel said nothing, he added bitterly, "I'm just lying here and wondering how many faults — in addition to heedlessness and irresponsibility — I'm going to discover in myself over the next eighty years or so. I'm disgusted with myself, Michoel. Completely disgusted. I'm filled to the brim with bad traits. I —"

"Enough," Michoel broke in. "There's no need to whip yourself like this. Of course there are things that can be improved...but not everything in you is bad or needs fixing. There's a great deal of good in you, Istrak. Never stop believing that."

His older brother laughed. "When it comes to character, there's no room for faith. You have to investigate, to dig down deep and try to see what's happening underneath..."

Contrary to his usual practice, Michoel refused to accept his brother's views. "If you keep digging up the earth to see the roots of your plants — nothing will grow. Even if you have the best of intentions."

Istrak had no chance to retort. Just then the wagon ground to a halt.

With the wheels silent, they could hear children's laughter and snatches of talk in Mundari. The wagon began moving once more, only to stop again after several long moments. There was more talk, hard for the brothers to decipher under the muffling cloth. Once again, the wagon started forward. It was only after the fourth pause that the covering was finally removed.

"I'm sorry," the Mundari said. "I did not know about your mission."

Istrak looked around, but Knaz was nowhere to be seen.

"Your companion returned to the city," their host said, understanding his look. "He said that he will continue on to Baliatar on his own."

The news surprised Istrak and left him feeling strangely bereft.

Knaz's move was a logical one. Someone had to return to the city to search for Hala, Rena, and Kalev and bring them to Lord Baliatar's palace. Still, the knowledge that he must make the rest of his way with only Michoel's company weakened him.

"Your friend asked me to supply you with an escort. On our way here, I sent word to four faithful lads." He was silent a moment, listening to sounds inaudible to the two princes. "They are coming."

A moment later, four youths about Istrak's age appeared from among the trees. The Mundari greeted them warmly and began talking rapidly in the ancient language.

"These two are bearing news," he said, indicating the royal brothers. "The present government of Khazar has people out looking for them. They want to prevent them from reaching the gates of Itil."

Four pairs of eyes studied Istrak and Michoel — who studied them in turn.

"Until now," the older Mundari continued, "they were accompanied by one of our own. Before we parted, he asked me to find them another escort. I believe you fellows are well suited to the task."

"What about the sheep?" one of the four asked in a soft, musical voice.

"What kind of news can they be carrying?" asked another.

A third, who by the looks of it was the first one's twin, added, "If any news could bring this country back to the way it was…"

"Of course it can," Istrak said. At the stunned look on the faces of the other five, he recognized his error: despite their participation in Khazari life, the Mundaris stubbornly maintained their separateness. Their use of the ancient tongue, and their refusal to teach it to others, were only two characteristics of that separateness. And now, here was a youth with a servant's garb and a typically Khazari face casually using their language as though he were one of them!

Istrak hesitated, then decided that the element of surprise might speed them toward the desired decision.

"Khazar has hope, and Heaven has chosen me to bear it. Will you agree to bring it to Itil?"

His eyes tested their faces and read in them confusion and hope, astonishment and doubt. Then a spark rose to the eyes of the one with the musical voice. "I will come with you," he said.

Istrak smiled. "I thank you."

"All right," said the twin. "I'll come, too."

"Thank you." With another smile, Istrak waited again.

The fourth young man, who had been silent up till now, stepped forward to offer his services. Thanking him, Istrak waited, but this time the desired result was not forthcoming.

"My place is here," said the last of the youths. "My parents need me."

The older Mundari looked disappointed, but he neither argued nor coaxed. "Are three men enough, sir?" he asked Istrak.

Istrak looked down at his hands. Three men were so few — so few! On the other hand, the larger the group, the more attention they would attract. On the third hand... His adventure in the amphitheater had undermined his faith in his countrymen, and his naive belief in the great joy that would grip Itil on his return had collapsed along with it.

"Is there any possibility of recruiting additional men?"

Two of his three future escorts were silent; the one with the spark in his eye answered for them all. "I'll find them. How many men do you need?"

His friends stared at him in astonishment.

"Our tribe is not large," the older Mundari explained on a note of apology. "And the work is always plentiful."

"I'll find them," the youth repeated, and the spark in his eye turned into a flame. "I'll do it right now, and meet you on the high road."

"What about transportation?" Istrak asked, recalling their trouble that morning. "When the country calms down, the king will surely be quick to reward the man who was prepared to offer such a precious gift for the sake of Khazar."

"I will give you my horse," the Mundari said finally, though it was clear that the offer came with an effort.

The young tribesmen gaped at him. "And how will you bring your baskets to the marketplace?" asked the youth who had elected to stay home.

"On my back. Or in the wagons of generous friends. Anyway, a person's livelihood is determined by Heaven…" Equanimity had returned to the Mundari's voice. "What else must we arrange, sir?"

"Food. And drink, and weapons for those who are coming with us." From the expressions on the others' faces, Istrak knew that he was asking a great deal, and his heart constricted. It was painful to stand there like a beggar and ask for help. "It will all serve a good purpose," he added limply.

"We will try," the Mundari said. He sounded slightly at a loss, but the fiery-eyed youth — his name was Yishai — assured Istrak that he would have everything he needed.

And so it was.

A wagon, food supplies, and weapons appeared from somewhere or other, and within hours a number of young men arrived, ablaze with quiet enthusiasm and a willingness to lend these two messengers every possible assistance.

It was a marvel. Istrak fervently pressed Yishai's hand in wordless gratitude.

"I did only what I had to do," the youth replied bashfully. "Anyone in my place would have done the same."

"Anyone?" Istrak chuckled.

The youth lifted his eyes and looked into those of the prince of Khazar. And his expression told Istrak that he was aware of the identity of the two "messengers."

Moments later they set out. The journey took a full week. On the eighth day, just after dawn, Istrak and Michoel glimpsed the towers of Itil in the distance.

They were home.

36

Despite his heroic resolution, it was hard at first for Ruben Min-Hagai to acknowledge that Pinras was a better leader than he. But as the days succeeded one another, and Pinras' leadership became more widely known, Ruben discovered in the quiet mentor more and more of an ideal leader's qualities.

Not even the most fervent of Pinras' supporters could claim that he was an eloquent man; he certainly came nowhere near Ruben's ability in this area. Nevertheless, the young man was a natural leader, and his influence over his growing group of supporters was astonishing. His simple speeches, while lacking brilliance and dash, became the coinage with which he expressed his love. Many of the younger set exerted themselves to win his smile. Each evening, around the campfires, there could be heard at least one person thanking Heaven for placing "such a man" at their head.

As Ruben entered the fortress' ground level, Pinras rose in greeting and hurried to the door to escort him inside. Ruben added another item in the long list growing in his mind: a true ruler of Khazar was concerned with the honor of those around him more than with his own stature…

"Is there anything new to report?" Gad asked as Pinras poured Min-Hagai a glass of water. "You look excited."

Ruben gave a half-smile. "Maybe I am, and there's a reason for it." His fingers tightened on the stem of his glass. "The moment we all knew was coming has finally arrived. Rumor has it, in the military corridors, that three or four days from now two *hostress* divisions will be setting out, headed by Yosef Diaber himself, on a trip that will combine a coronation tour with a battle against Khazar's enemies living in the north."

"Two divisions of *hostress* troops," Pinras repeated thoughtfully.

Pretending to be insulted, Gad exclaimed, "Only two? Diaber mocks us!"

Ruben hid a smile, but Pinras did not appear to be amused. "I would not wish our men to harm a single one of those soldiers," he said quietly.

Ruben straightened his back, watching the man who sat at the other end of the table. "Yosef Diaber will not willingly hand over to us the crown that he's usurped for himself."

"It will be all right," Lord Baliatar said. "We will do our part, and Hashem will do His. When we hear that Yosef Diaber is actually on his way here, we will review the matter again." His eyes scanned the room, coming to rest on Ruben's tight face. "Don't worry, Ruben. I am certain that only good will come from this kind of decision. Remove the anxiety from your heart."

Ruben was not happy, but all efforts to turn the talk into practical channels failed. Pinras and Gad Baliatar seemed to have forgotten about military strategy. They were content to busy themselves with minor and relatively unimportant details — instead of the enormous problems that confronted them all.

A week later, when a messenger from Itil arrived at the fortress bearing the news they had all been expecting, no change was seen in Gad's face. He merely thanked the messenger for his trouble and warmly urged him to seek out the infirmary. The courier chuckled sheepishly, lifting a hand to his hugely swollen and discolored left eye. "It's nothing," he assured them. "Really nothing. It will heal within a week or two."

"Do as you wish," Lord Baliatar said. "But the mentor would be pleased to know that such a loyal courier as yourself has received the proper treatment."

"It...it didn't happen on my mission," the young messenger stammered. "It happened when I stopped at a kiosk to get something to eat. They wanted to force me to drink to the regent's health — and I refused!" He was very young, and very proud of his resistance and his loyalty. Gad sent him off to the infirmary, then offered his apologies to Ruben and the others in the room. He had just remembered several pressing obligations that forced him to leave them for a time. He departed with tremendous speed — without a word having been exchanged about the expected attack on the northern district by two divisions of *hostress* troops under the leadership of Yosef Diaber.

This was not the first time that Lord Gad Baliatar had left the conference room in the middle of an important discussion on some burning topic. But when his two strategists, at discreet intervals, rose and left in his wake, Ruben felt a sense of urgency that made him stand up as well and go out into the broad corridors where his footsteps echoed loudly. It was just as he had guessed. The teenage boys who were supposed to have been listening to a *shiur* from Pinras at that hour sat alone in their classroom, learning in pairs. Ruben could guess where their pale-faced leader was at that moment: closeted with Lord Gad Baliatar and the two military strategists who had left the conference room on Baliatar's heels.

Anger swept over Ruben in a swift wave. It was quickly replaced by a feeling of humiliation unparalleled in his experience. The humiliation robbed him of his senses and carried him along the corridor like a storm wind. One by one, he pulled people away from what they were doing and asked them to come with him. As he paused before each door prior to knocking, an inner voice implored him to stop — not to shatter, with a single action, the fragile coexistence that had them all working together these past days toward a common goal. But the voice was thin and delicate — while his mortification was like a wild bull on a rampage.

At the head of a small but select group of his men, Ruben Min-Hagai climbed the stairs. The guards, who knew him well by this time, never dreamed of stopping him. Before he knew it, he was standing in front of Gad's door.

The sentries guarding that door said apologetically that there was an urgent conference taking place within, one that must not be disturbed. But the apologetic note only served to inflame Ruben further. It seemed to bring proof that even these guards knew that his place was inside. The only ones oblivious to that fact were the two who had dispatched him to wait at the fringes!

"Tell them that Ruben Min-Hagai wishes to speak with them." His voice had turned gravelly, and there was a stern pride in his eyes as he saw the six faithful companions who had come with him from his father's estate step forward to lend weight to his demand.

The guards held a hasty murmured conference, after which one of them entered the closed room, remained a moment or two, and then came out with an answer that seemed to reverberate inside Ruben's skull: "The ruler of all Khazar says that he will be pleased to meet with Master Min-Hagai tomorrow morning."

The ruler of all Khazar! Master Min-Hagai! Tomorrow morning!

The words whirled around Ruben's head like a flock of startled doves. He felt as though the earth was trembling beneath his feet. Until now, Pinras had treated him as an equal — a crucial ally. What had happened to change his attitude toward the very person whose verses had elevated him to power?

"I see," he said, his tone dry despite his inner turmoil. "Thank you."

His men accompanied him out to the courtyard, which was — as always at this hour of the day — crowded with pairs of duelers working to hone their fighting skills. In the nearby forests and fields were many others, all striving to improve their physical prowess. He had brought them all here.

And what did he get in return?

The words echoed painfully in his mind: *Master Min-Hagai… tomorrow morning…ruler of all Khazar…*

As his mortification began to subside, an overwhelming anger took its place. Even as he felt it, he was glad that he was still able to understand its source: a foolish and distasteful pride.

The pride of a man who had promised obedience but, at the first challenge, failed to stand by his word. A shiver ran through him from head to toe. Had these been any other men than the six faithful companions who had come with him from his father's estate, he would have found it easier to admit that he had erred. But if he lost these men's esteem, he would truly feel alone.

His mentor, in more pleasant days long gone by, used to say that a person's ability to apologize could only elevate him in the eyes of others. There was truth in this. But Ruben wanted and needed these men to believe in and obey him. If he showed himself as petty and weak — a small person wracked by frail desires — why should they follow him at all?

He turned and surveyed them. In their eyes he saw the admiration he craved, along with surprise as they wondered at the reason behind all the recent drama. They were good men and he loved them — each of them individually, and all of them together. And his love for them would not allow him to use them as a bandage for his wounded pride.

"I made a mistake," he admitted finally, "and I must do penance for it. The *bek*'s son is our leader, and I am nothing but a man of flawed character." His face twisted. "I've suddenly discovered that I have a great deal of room for improvement. You men are good friends. Go now, while I calm myself a bit."

There was a strange sense of relief in speaking these words. The image of the glorious leader to which he had clung blew away like smoke. He had confessed to being a person of flawed character. From now, he would be nothing more than an ordinary man. The relief was real, but threaded through with pain and sadness.

"If anyone should need me," he said, with an attempt at a smile, "tell them I will be back by evening."

None of the six were men of words. The two who tried to offer some sort of compliment were silenced with a weary, upraised hand. The only way they could express their admiration, on seeing him mourn the shattering of his self-image, was the same as it ever had been: through total obedience. They went, leaving him alone.

All the rest of that day, Ruben Min-Hagai wandered about Gad Baliatar's estate. As day waned toward evening, his mood began to improve. Near Minchah time, his legs carried him to one of the nearby villages where, in a stark, tiny *beis knesses*, he poured out his heart in one of the best davening sessions he had ever experienced. Afterward he sensed almost tangibly that Heaven had forgiven him his prideful impulse and given a promise to help him cope with it in the future. It was with an uplifted heart that he made his way back to Gad's palace, happy with the inner victory he had won that day.

But the sight of the fortress, of the young sentries at the gate, and the buckets of water in the courtyard, sent his newfound serenity flying away. He was filled with anxious foreboding at the prospect of war. The *hostress* troops were hardy and expertly trained — and Yosef Diaber was capable, beyond a doubt, of inspiring them with his well-chosen words to attack their own blood brothers.

Each morning, after Shacharis and a brief halachah *shiur*, Pinras' men divided up into groups of ten. Each of these groups was granted a certain measure of autonomy regarding how it could schedule its day, but all were bound by the learning and training program that had been established for them on their arrival.

Pinras' own group — which comprised, apart from Gad Baliatar and Ruben Min-Hagai, two of each leader's faithful aides as well as the *talmid chacham* in charge of ruling on halachic issues for the entire camp — tried, despite the many burdens placed on its members, to adhere to the schedule as well. Thus, even before Ruben had an opportunity to discuss yesterday's events with either Pinras or Gad, he found himself seated with them for a joint study session in *Sefer Mishlei*. To his relief, the verses they were studying that morning did not deal with the particular character flaws that had led to his downfall the day before. Though, on second thought, had that been their topic, he might have had the opening he needed to apologize to Pinras, who had been treating Ruben with a chilly and formal politeness all day — in glaring contrast to the genuine, heartfelt respect he had accorded him until now.

The study session finally came to an end. All but two members of the group went outside. Pinras remained seated in his big chair at the head of the table. Ruben stood by the door, waiting for Pinras to rise and leave the room.

For perhaps three minutes they remained that way. Then Ruben moved closer to the man at the head of the table. "I will obey any order you give me," he vowed. When Pinras did not reply, he bowed his head slightly and added, "My men know that I behaved in an unworthy manner yesterday, and I will repeat it to them again today."

Pinras looked at him out of the corner of his eye. The look was penetrating. "Were it not for my sense of pity for your own and your family's honor, I would have called your behavior by its proper name. It was rebellion, Ruben."

Had he heard these words yesterday, at the height of his inner turmoil, Ruben would have battled for his honor. He would have reminded the mentor that, were it not for his abilities, his actions, and his men, Pinras would not have even a quarter of the following he enjoyed at this time. Now, however, he merely cast down his eyes and was silent.

The corridors and the courtyard bustled with life, but the room's thick walls separated the two from the noise and movement that lay beyond. Time passed: an eternity. With difficulty, Ruben forced himself to maintain his submissive posture, like one of the underlings who served his father. The longer Pinras did not speak, the more Ruben's blood began to boil.

"Other challenges will arise," Pinras said finally. "Will you stand up to them?"

It was a good question — and a painful one.

"The sacrifice you have made is greatly appreciated," Pinras went on. "But despite my admiration for all that you've done — and you have surely noticed how moved I have been — there will still be some decisions that I will have to make alone, and contrary to your views."

When Pinras said it, it sounded so logical — something that any thinking person must acknowledge. But the memory of yesterday's hurt was still fresh in Ruben's mind. "I hope that Hashem will give me the strength to meet the challenge," he said honestly. "But it is clear to me that this is the way it must be. You are the ruler of this land, and I, a small man who does his duty. That's all."

His eyes sought Pinras', but the other still seemed remote. Evidently, he had expected a more enthusiastic pledge of loyalty than this. When Pinras next spoke, his voice was brisk and practical. "For some time now, Ruben, I have wanted to ask you to send a letter to your father's friends in Itil, stating that you have given up your claims to the crown and asking them to extend to our people every possible assistance. Will you be able to do that this morning?"

Of all possible requests, this was the one Ruben had least expected. The pinch of degradation inherent in it tickled Min-Hagai's nostrils like pepper powder. "I will do it. Is there anything else?" Despite his efforts, there was an edge to his voice as he spoke. The sound rang in his ears.

Here was the second challenge — and though he had spent a full day preparing for it, he had failed again.

In the room where he had written his verses, from a fervent belief in Pinras' ability to lead the battle on behalf of the Khazari people, Ruben Min-Hagai tried to compose the simple letter that had been requested of him. But the words would not come.

When he had acted from a feeling of greatness and generosity, everything had seemed so simple. Now, having suddenly grasped the true nature of the reality he had helped create, he found himself floundering. His pen had become mute.

"Is Your Majesty listening?"

For the fifth time, the younger and more energetic of the two strategists vied for Pinras' full attention. But although the pale-faced leader was able to repeat and summarize what the three men around the table had said, it was clear that his mind was elsewhere.

"Perhaps it would be better if we stopped now," Gad said. "Let us meet again this afternoon. In the meantime…" Carefully, the governor of the northern district removed his signet ring from his twisted finger. "Ask the quartermaster to collect arms and food and bring them into the fortress. We will deal with the problem of communications later. Most important of all" — he held out the ring to the older of the strategists, who placed it on his own finger, seal facing inward — "summon the seal-maker you were speaking of earlier."

The strategists left. The servants standing outside the door hastened inside to tidy up the room, but were forced to retreat at a gesture from Gad. As they closed the door behind them, Pinras covered his eyes with his hand.

"I was too harsh with him," he burst out. "I could have explained to him… I was unnecessarily cruel. Who needs this job anyway?"

"Khazar does," Gad said firmly. When Pinras did not answer, he added, "Welcome, young man, to the pleasures of rulership."

"Reuel II is Khazar's ruler," Pinras said, lifting his head. He sighed. "I thought I was doing the right thing. But I am a man, with a man's craving for power." After a moment's silence, he added in a near whisper, "And honor."

It was nearly noon when, after tearing up two scrolls into which traces of anger and bitterness had crept, Ruben gave up trying to write directly onto parchment and began writing and erasing an endless number of versions with chalk on the black rock called *tzipchah*, used for drafts and other disposable writings.

At last, the task was done. Exhausted by the inner exertion that had been demanded of him, Ruben summoned a scribe and asked him to copy the letter onto a parchment scroll without any changes. As he left the room, he nearly collided with Lord Gad Baliatar.

"Good afternoon, good afternoon," Gad said. "Was it very difficult?"

"See for yourself," Ruben said. He held up the torn parchment and shook grains of chalk from his clothes. "But I'm glad I did it. His Majesty is a very wise man." It was hard to miss the new note of admiration in his voice.

"I feel the same way," Gad agreed soberly. Moving on, he said, "I won't block your way, young man."

A moment after Ruben had left, Lord Baliatar was at the scribe's side, wordlessly reading over the man's shoulder. After he read what Ruben had written, he picked up the torn parchments and read those, too. Then he gathered them all up and, with an odd smile, left the room with the letters tucked under his arm.

Lista Basbani lived in a modest cottage at the edges of the Baliatar region. He disliked the uniforms worn by Lord Baliatar's guards — and with good reason. Over the past 30-odd years of his life, he had run into those guards too many times to count, and none of the encounters had been pleasant.

Basbani had been lying low in recent months, but the master forger found two men wearing the hated uniforms waiting for him when he came home that evening. The guards deftly caught his arms for him as he tried to clamber out the rear window.

He was not unfamiliar with security headquarters, to which he was promptly escorted. But the other man who greeted him there — a fellow of short build, dark hair, and alert eyes — was a stranger to him.

"So you're Lista, eh?" the stranger asked after the chief guard had left them alone.

Basbani didn't like the other man's probing eyes. "Exactly," he muttered.

The stranger seemed amused by his discomfiture. "Care to sit down, Lista?"

"Why am I here? That's the question."

"You're here to listen to a proposal," the man said pleasantly. "Tell me, how much would you want for a small job, involving ten letters and a seal, which would require you to leave home for two weeks?"

"That's no small job — not if it takes me away from home for two whole weeks," Basbani retorted.

"True," the other man agreed. "But you could be sitting in prison for those two weeks without a penny's profit in exchange."

Now that the terms of the proposal had been clarified, Lista Basbani took a seat and thought it over. He named a price slightly higher than he expected to receive. But the stranger merely nodded and, without negotiating at all, said, "Agreed." With that, he called in the chief guard. "We've cleared up the matter," he explained. "There was no real justification for this man's arrest. Release him."

While this afforded Lista a measure of relief, he could not really call himself happy at the turn of events. In less time than he had thought possible, he had his things packed and was climbing into a closed carriage at the dark-haired stranger's behest. Clutched in his hand were the tools of his trade, which he had rescued from their hiding place behind the stove.

Having been told that he would be away for two weeks, he expected the journey to last several days. But only an hour or two after they set out, the carriage jerked to a halt.

"Come," said the stranger. His tone was not friendly.

Lista was resentful. They would use him, these people, and then toss him away like an old bone. And to whom would he then apply for his payment?

"I want to get paid now," he demanded.

"You shall have it," said his companion, who had introduced himself as Avraham. "Right now, please go inside."

He found himself walking into a small house with a triangular roof and neglected appearance, furnished in the tasteless style of houses that are let for a fee. Not a single personal object was to be seen, apart from a black pouch resting on a table.

"This letter has a copy of the seal we need," Avraham said, pulling a page from the briefcase and tossing it onto the table in front of the forger. "Have you ever seen it up close?"

Lista looked at the page and then up at the confident Avraham. "This…this is the seal of His Majesty…the new king!"

"As far as I'm concerned," Avraham said carelessly, "it could belong to the king of China. Can you copy it?"

Lista studied the wax seal. "I can. But it will cost you double."

"Don't squeeze me. As it is, you're getting more than I make in a whole winter's work."

Lista shrugged. "Then ask for more," he advised. "There's no reason to work if you don't get what you deserve."

"You will have what you deserve," Avraham said decisively. "When can you be finished?"

"This evening. Or this afternoon. It all depends on the payment."

The forged seal was ready that afternoon, handsome and precise down to the last detail. Lista had also prepared the type of wax that the regent habitually used, and careful examination by Avraham discovered no discrepancy between the original seal's imprint and that of the forgery. The final product justified the exorbitant cost.

"Beautiful," Avraham said with immense satisfaction. "Now, for the letters themselves..."

"Time to eat," Lista said, pouring cold water on the other's enthusiasm. "And after that, a short nap..."

His tired face and reddened eyes told Avraham that this was not an attempt at evasiveness. With a sigh, he went to the kitchen.

The midday meal did much to revive Lista. "Let's finish this business," he said briskly. "What has to be written and in what type of script?"

A letter of introduction, its top cut off to conceal the identity of its recipient, answered his second question. Lista nodded. "What do I write?"

Avraham rummaged around in his briefcase. He pulled out one of the versions of Ruben's letter. "This. But wherever it says 'Ruben Min-Hagai,' I want you to write 'Lord Yosef Diaber, Regent of Khazar.'"

It was midnight by the time Lista completed the final forged document. On the table before him lay piles of sealed letters written in Yosef Diaber's hand, all of them affirming that, in view of the fact that King Reuel II had seen fit to pass the Great Seal of Khazar to Lord Baliatar and appointed him to seek an heir to his throne, Diaber had decided to yield that throne to Pinras, son of Eshal, who had been deemed the one most fit to carry out the task.

"I finished quickly, no?" Lista asked. He had wasted no time wondering about the consequences of his forgeries. "You thought it would take two weeks..." There was pride in his tone. "Let's get some sleep now. At first light tomorrow, you can take me home."

"Not so fast," Avraham replied with a half-smile. "You will remain here for the time being, my friend. You will wait patiently while these letters make their way to their destinations — and a few days longer. All this will take, by our estimation, approximately two weeks, give or take a day or two."

The journey, which was meant to be a tour of conquest and triumph in which all of Khazar would witness the greatness of their new king, Yosef Diaber, started off on the wrong foot.

On the very first morning after they left Itil, the filled pastries turned out to be not fully baked. Then, near midday, the edge of the king's most opulent cloak caught on a thornbush and a long thread was pulled out of the fabric. This was no way to enter the small city, about an hour's march away, whose entire population had turned out to greet him. But the king's other traveling garments had not been pressed, and the suggestion that the entire convoy come to a halt while coals were heated for the iron seemed impractical.

As if all this were not enough, it turned out that the crates containing copies of *maseches Pesachim*, which Diaber had intended to learn and to teach during the trip, had disappeared. And then, as the sun was touching the treetops, a messenger galloped into the camp with a letter for Abaye Ben-Elyakim, a young nobleman who was a particular favorite of the new king's.

Abaye accepted the letter with lifted brows and looked at the seal. "It's from my uncle," he said, alarmed. "Something bad must have happened if he was forced to contact me so urgently."

"Maybe he's finally seen the light," someone joked.

"My uncle is a stubborn man," Abaye said grimly.

Another of his friends placed a supportive hand on his shoulder. Abaye opened the letter — and turned pale. "It's my sister," he said, voice quaking. "Or, rather, her twins… I have to be there!"

Someone took the letter from him and quickly scanned its contents. Abaye's uncle reported that his sister's boys had been critically injured in a fire in their home. "Despite our differences of political opinion, I felt obligated to inform you of this," he had written. "Your sister has no one but you in the world. If you can bear to tear yourself away from your false messiah and come home to support her during this difficult time, that would undoubtedly be the right thing to do."

Despite the severity of the news, this reference to their leader made the young men's blood seethe.

"It's supposed to be a private letter," Abaye said hotly, snatching the scroll from his friend's hand. "Who gave you permission to read it at all?"

The two stood facing each other like a pair of roosters squaring off in the dirt. Then the other man shrugged. "I only wanted to help," he apologized. "Pack some food for him," he instructed the others. "He'll need a horse, too. I'll go with him to His Majesty to request permission to leave the convoy."

Permission was granted, though the absence of the energetic and likable Abaye represented yet another stone beneath Diaber's wheels. The friend who had accompanied Abaye to request that permission was much moved by the king's attitude toward his anxious young companion. "He empathized so deeply," he later told the others, "that he looked as though he might burst into tears. Then he gave Abaye a few gold coins and promised him that his place in the convoy would be reserved for him. I was moved to the depths of my soul."

None of his friends had the least idea how far down his soul actually went — nor were they interested. They were all busy expressing their sympathy and encouragement for the unfortunate Abaye, who had already suffered much in his young life and was now faced with yet another tragic incident. After he took his leave, they discussed his history in solemn tones: his father's untimely demise before Abaye's birth, his mother's death on the night before the *bris*. His very name — like that of the *Tanna* Abaye — hinted at his difficult life: according to the *medrash*, the *Tanna*'s real name was Nachmani, but because he had been orphaned of both his father and his mother, he was nicknamed Abaye, an acronym for *"Asher bechah yerucham yasom* — For it is with You that an orphan finds mercy."

As they resumed the meal that the messenger had interrupted, they discussed Abaye's uncle. Had he not been renowned for his heroism on the battlefield during the Ten Years' War, he should have been punished for his insolent opposition to the lawful revolution. And they praised the courageous Abaye, who had been prepared to sever relations with his uncle and his only sister's family to follow the man he loved and admired — Khazar's new king, Yosef Diaber.

And yet, underlying all the fulsome compliments was a strain of envy. Abaye, whose family was neither prosperous nor politically savvy, had found favor in Lord Diaber's eyes and been raised to the level of companion and confidant.

Abaye was aware of the ripple of jealousy that his closeness to the king inspired. But just as he had learned to steel himself against the other difficulties in his life, he succeeded in maintaining his equilibrium over this as well.

Several years earlier, after his uncle overcame his disappointment at the boy's decision to flaunt family tradition by refusing to join the army, he had found Abaye a position as a tutor in the home of a wealthy man in the city. Rumor had it that the man had come by his wealth through less than respectable methods, but Abaye's uncle chose to disregard the rumors in exchange for a stable position for his nephew.

After four years of physical and spiritual suffering, Abaye left the rich man's house a very different person from the one who had come. His regard for both halachah and its teachers had been sadly diminished. Four years of heartache and the need to bow his head to those who were more foolish than he had also given him a fine acting ability. His release after those long years left him feeling disproportionately happy with the mere fact that he was free, and he took a deep pleasure in friendship — something that won the heart of everyone who came into contact with him during his first months in Itil.

Two of his closest friends were Shalvan, Lord Diaber's younger son, and Daniel, Lord Stazdiran's firstborn. Long years of arbitrating between various family members in his role as tutor had taught him the art of discretion. He never spoke about one friend to the other, and so managed to develop a deep bond with each of these two young men, who were polar opposites of each other.

In his few encounters with Shalvan's father, a mutual affection had sprung up between them. Diaber acquired a part-time position for his son's friend as a tutor in the home of a minor nobleman. The salary was reasonable, but, more important, it earned Abaye's gratitude. He was ready to do anything for Lord Diaber.

At the same time, Dalo Stazdiran — at his son Daniel's urging — found Abaye a job as a companion to an honored elderly man who had become blind and needed someone to learn with and read to him. This old man was a sweet and gentle soul, and Abaye — who had spent his entire childhood searching for a father figure to love — became devoted to him. His dedication to all the old man's needs extended far beyond the call of duty.

Before long, Abaye began to feel that he was leading a double life. In the company of the old man and Daniel, he was the golden boy who aspired to spiritual greatness — a person of integrity and the courage to do what was good and proper, even if it displeased those around him. With Diaber's people, he was a man who drank his fill from the cup of life down to the dregs, the one with the witty tongue that could turn any rebuke into a joke — a man who courted danger.

There were a few traits that both "Abayes" shared, such as his consistent evasion of the matchmakers' wiles and an open hand when giving charity. But when he woke in the morning and hurried off to the early Shacharis service at Daniel's side with his head still aching from last night's merriment — or when he ran out to participate in a horse race arranged by Shalvan Diaber while his head resonated with the ethical verses he had just finished reciting with the old man — he felt a powerful sense of alienation. At times, he knew a powerful longing to abandon Shalvan and his cronies and devote himself to his spiritual development, as he knew he ought to do. At other times, he felt that after all the suffering he had known in his life, he was entitled to enjoy life a little. And then, one fateful evening, as Daniel Stzadiran's younger brother celebrated his bar mitzvah, the king was struck down.

The following days were difficult ones for Khazar. Lord Diaber, now the country's acting ruler, invited Abaye to join his growing entourage. The offer stunned Abaye and made his head spin. His bond with Shalvan became stronger than ever. Abaye the merry, the perfect companion, gained the upper hand; Daniel and the sweet old man became images from the past.

It was two months before he next met Daniel. The meeting proved uncomfortable for both of them.

"You've changed," Daniel remarked, scrutinizing his friend from head to toe, from the stylish head covering to the velvet hose folded over his deerskin shoes.

"I was appointed a member of the regent's entourage," Abaye answered with feigned casualness. "Hadn't you heard?"

"No." Daniel's eyes probed Abaye's. "Are you happy there?"

Abaye licked his suddenly dry lips. He liked his new position and enjoyed giving expression to his quick wit and social abilities. But his dream of true friends, devoted to one another to the end, did not seem likely to materialize in the company of men vying for money, influence, and status.

"Yes. Of course," he replied without conviction.

Daniel tilted his head to one side, as though he might, from the corner of his eye, see more than he had glimpsed before. But in the figure before him he saw no sign of the boy he had known so well. "Well, good luck then," he said at last.

"Thank you."

"If you ever feel like visiting, we'd be glad to see you. Our *minyan* misses your *tefillos*."

"The *tefillos* of a suffering man." Abaye laughed. "But the good life is starting now, Daniel. The past is over — dead and buried."

Though he had laughed off Daniel's words, one fine morning Abaye found himself walking toward the *beis knesses* in which he used to pray with his former friends. Those friends looked at him now with astonishment mingled with contempt. They spoke to him very politely, as though to a stranger. And Abaye realized that the past was indeed dead. The realization saddened him. Daniel, following him out, recognized this.

"Abaye —" Daniel placed a hand on his friend's shoulder. "I know better than to try to persuade you to leave your present situation. It's a heady position to be in, so close to Lord Diaber's inner circle. But you, more than I, know the truth."

Abaye stiffened...

"The waters are muddied," Daniel went on. "Don't you agree? Why, for instance, is Diaber persecuting Ruben Min-Hagai? Has he proof that Min-Hagai has actually done anything wrong?"

Abaye lifted his chin and said, more forcefully than necessary, "His Majesty believes that Min-Hagai is behind all the acts of terror that have taken place in Khazar lately."

Daniel bit his lip. "Once we were close," he said in a near whisper, "and I still care about you. If you ever decide that you want to leave — call me. I will come at once."

Abaye bowed mockingly. "I still care about you," he mimicked, "and if *you* ever need help — call me. I will come at once."

"I'll remember that." Daniel put out his hand. "Thanks, Abaye."

Looking at his friend's hand, Abaye hesitated, as though reluctant to stamp their words with undue significance. In the end, the bonds of their former affection bade him place his hand in Daniel's. They shook wordlessly, their eyes doing the talking.

They parted ways. Daniel was certain that Abaye was not truly happy with his choice, while in Abaye's heart was awakened the golden boy who aspired for what was good and right. The memories, once awakened, began to disturb his serenity.

Over the course of the next three months, the two old friends occasionally met. When they did, each studied the other and saw the fear that was permitted to peek out only at such moments. And then, one cold night, as Abaye bounded down the stairs — taking them two at a time, as was his habit — he was stopped by a gray-cloaked figure wearing the large hat favored by the common people. It was Daniel.

Abaye stared. Daniel was unusually pale and his cheeks were sunken. He seemed ill.

"I'm tired of it," Daniel said, grabbing his arm. "Tired of the duplicity and the lying. You must get away from him, Abaye."

"And you mustn't suspect the innocent," Abaye said sharply, though he did not pull away his arm.

"Each of us must choose his own way. I am going to the forest. To join Min-Hagai."

Now Abaye did draw back. "You can do that," he said bitterly. "You have plenty of money, and the connections to save you from the gallows…"

Daniel swayed, as though about to fall over. "Money? Connections? And I thought that you —" His face twisted. Suddenly sapped of energy, he sat on the lowest stair.

"You're ill," Abaye said, leaning over him. He felt the heat radiating from Daniel's fevered brow. "Get up, my friend. Let me take you home."

"Take me to the forest," Daniel pleaded. "Let's go there together."

"When you're better," Abaye promised, just to get his friend moving.

But Daniel did not get better.

Lord Yosef Diaber attended the funeral, a circumstance that prevented Abaye from taking the place he really desired, among the circle of Daniel's shocked and grieving friends — his friends once.

Thirty days later, as the monument was erected at the cemetery, Abaye entered the gates alone. He stood apart from Daniel's family and closest companions, musing over his memories of his departed friend. Suddenly sensing another presence nearby, he turned sharply. Behind him were Pinras and Shaul, two of Daniel's inner circle of friends.

"Khazar has known many tragedies of late," said the missing prince's mentor.

"Yes." There was a giant lump in Abaye's throat. Shaking his head, he strove for a practical tone. "Daniel wanted to go out to the forest. I believe that is the commonplace occurrence among the members of your group."

"Many of us question the interpretation that the regent has placed on recent events in Khazar," Shaul said noncommittally.

Abaye swallowed. "I once promised Daniel that I would help

him. I'd like to keep that promise. If you need help, call me. I will come as soon as I can."

Such words fell strangely from the lips of an orphaned and unconnected young man, especially when spoken to these sons of Khazar's upper echelon. But in truth — and as these men knew well — Abaye was not so unconnected as he thought. His standing within Lord Diaber's entourage grew stronger with each passing week.

"Let us hope there will be no need for that," Pinras said. They stood quietly, contemplating Daniel's headstone.

Abaye was the first to stoop down, pick up a small rock from the ground, and place it on the headstone. He moved away, head down. Shaul hurried after him, and they met near the well. "Your place is with us, Abaye. Daniel thought so until his dying day." His fingers played with the hem of his cloak. "Do you have the courage to cross the line again?"

The question had been posed in a sharp tone, and Abaye found it difficult to answer. "Apparently not," he said finally.

"Even though you know that you're moving in the wrong direction? That Diaber does not represent truth, integrity, or goodness?"

"You are being very presumptuous, Shaul."

"This is no time to mince words. I, too, made a promise to Daniel — that I would look after you. I feel an obligation to help you, the way I would help myself…"

"You care about me only out of obligation," Abaye said harshly. "In Diaber's circle, I'm loved for myself."

"You're avoiding the question."

Abaye's lips curled into a bitter smile. He said nothing.

"In that case" — Pinras had joined them — "if you lack the courage, why did you offer your help? Merely to soothe your conscience?"

The bitter smile vanished. "When the time is right, I'll face any danger," Abaye said. "Right now, let us each go back to our own affairs."

It was with a feeling of intense loneliness that Abaye rejoined his new friends, all Diaber's people. He was secretly proud of the fact that they had no idea just how close he was to crossing the line and returning to his former self — to the boy Daniel had once known. But although each passing day saw Abaye grow more disillusioned with the superficiality of his companions, with the duplicity and the lies, the line remained just as distant as it had been on the day he had been urged to cross it a second time.

Even now, as he spurred his horse down the lane leading from Diaber's camp to the high road, there was that familiar feeling of loneliness in his heart. If only Daniel were here, he thought, or Shaul — or even Pinras, who was so scathingly abused by Khazar's new king these days — he would not have to be making his way alone, exposed to the dangers of the road.

He had no sooner entertained this thought when several figures detached themselves from the shadows and shouted for him to halt. He obeyed, glad that the only money he carried with him were a few gold coins given to him by the king.

But the figures were not after money.

"Take off your hat," they ordered. When he had done so, one of the men took hold of his head and began searching for the streak of red hair that stood out among the brown.

"It's him," he announced. "Do not be concerned, Abaye. We will not harm you. Take him with you, boys."

Not far away, in a clearing in the forest illuminated by a single torch, a familiar figure waited. Abaye snapped his mouth shut to hold back his cry of surprise.

"You pledged your help," Shaul reminded him. "The time has come to keep your promise." He paused. "We're sorry that we couldn't find another way to get you here."

The fire…his sister…the twins… None of it was true! Relief and fury mingled in Abaye's heart. Both rendered him speechless.

"Are you all right?" Shaul asked, his brow wrinkled in concern.

"More or less," Abaye muttered. He felt the king's coins, heavy in his pocket. King Yosef had, after all, been very generous with him. Was it right to betray him? "What do you want?"

"Do I really have to spell it out?"

Abaye chewed his lip. "Yes," he said finally. "But I do not promise to cooperate."

"I understand," said Shaul. "In that case, forgive us for bringing you here. The boys will take you back to the road. Do us a favor and travel from here for at least two weeks. And don't tell anyone what happened."

Abaye lowered his head. "If you called me, it must be important. What is it that you need from me?"

Shaul shook his head. "Forget it. If you are unwilling to keep your promise, that means you are a man of weak character. I cannot place my men's lives at risk merely to satisfy your curiosity."

"Are you still speaking to me because you feel obligated to care about me?" Abaye could not help the bitterness that had crept into his voice as he asked this question.

Shaul smiled. "No. This time I feel obligated to care about the welfare of the nation."

The smile tore at Abaye's heart. "Are you still in touch with the *rosh yeshivah*?" he asked tensely. "Would he say that it is right for me to betray the trust of a man who has done so much for me?"

"Yes." Shaul's brows constricted in puzzlement.

Abaye considered Shaul's words. Finally, with an effort, he said, "Let me hear what the situation is, Shaul. But, as I said, no promises. I can only try…" He spread his hands mutely.

"That is better than nothing. Come." Shaul placed a hand on Abaye's shoulder. "We'll talk privately."

Sitting on a boulder just outside the circle of light, Shaul apoke about the improbable plan, whose absolute success or failure depended on Abaye alone.

"You people are young, naive, and completely without wit," Abaye whispered, disbelieving. "What if I were to say no?"

"I've come here by the order of Khazar's true ruler," Shaul replied, "who insisted that you can be trusted."

A smile rose to Abaye's lips. "And even if I were to say yes," he continued, "what happens then? What will you gain? A day — two days of respite? Is that worth burning all my bridges? Putting everything at risk? What sort of future can I expect if you fail?"

"The same future as the rest of us," Shaul said calmly. "And the understanding that a person's existence is far longer than the eighty years his flesh lasts on this earth. I believe that the investment is worth the cost."

Abaye's fingers played with some twigs. "You did a good job with my uncle's letter," he said presently, wandering from the point. "It was cool, sharp, and unnerving."

Shaul looked at him. "He's an old man. Do you know that he will be turning 70 next week?"

Abaye's mouth turned down. "And what about twenty years ago? Was he a 'poor old man' then? I longed for his love, and he turned his back."

Shaul placed a gentle hand on Abaye's arm. "We have drifted from our topic. The fate of Khazar hangs in the balance."

Abaye gazed up at the dark canopy of foliage above their heads, waiting.

"Besides," Shaul continued, "your sister is still alive, and she loves you, that I know for certain."

"And she is with your people?"

Shaul nodded in confirmation. Abaye bent his head and buried his face in his hands.

Lord Diaber had been good to him from the very first, and Abaye's gratitude had grown with the passage of time. But the more he saw of the new king, the more cracks Abaye glimpsed in the man's carefully constructed image. Yosef Diaber — though generous, clever, and a first-rate tactician — had subtly revealed that he was also vengeful, honor-seeking, and ruthless.

Although Abaye had until now experienced nothing but sweetness at his hand, he could not ignore what he had observed.

"What will you gain?" he asked again. "A day or two's respite? He will come back to Itil and deny everything…"

Shaul sighed. "It is reasonable to suppose that he will do that. But those two days will give us a chance to gather the council and tell its members the truth."

"I owe him so much," Abaye said, his pinched face the picture of misery. "He has given me the most pleasant eight months of my life."

Shaul stopped himself from uttering the sharp retort that rose to his lips. Instead, he said, "Think of how many lives will be saved because of this. Think of it, Abaye."

"And Diaber? What will happen to him?"

Shaul studied him, deliberating as to whether to use the final weapon in his arsenal of persuasion. "Pinras, the true ruler of Khazar, asked me to give you a promise in his name. If you help us, Yosef Diaber will be offered the following choice: his life, in exchange for a public admission of the steps he took to bring about this revolution — and to acquire, illegally, the throne of Khazar."

Lord Kafchaver, Khazar's recently appointed prime minister, was the first of Khazar's governing nobility to receive a visit from the pair of couriers, in strict adherence to the rules of protocol. In disbelief, he read the letter he was handed. Afterward, he questioned one of the couriers, Abaye — whom he knew to be a member of the new king's inner circle — as to the events leading up to Yosef Diaber's hasty surrender of the throne.

Abaye had just spent three full days preparing himself for this question. He answered Lord Kafchaver unhesitatingly, describing the dramatic meeting between the two personalities, the penetrating discussion they had held, and the sight of the Great Seal that had been sought throughout Itil for months. He described the way Diaber, after being persuaded of the truth of Lord Baliatar's story, had embraced Pinras, then removed the crown from his own head and placed it on the former mentor's, saying, "Continue in the tradition of your fathers, and the sons of Khazar will praise you for many generations."

Abaye's story was vivid and convincing. Had Lord Kafchaver not known Yosef Diaber as well as he did, he might have believed it.

"And after that," Abaye went on, "Lord Diaber summoned his personal scribe and dictated — slowly and emotionally, as you can imagine — the letter you are holding."

Lord Kafchaver looked down at the parchment scroll and read its contents a second time. Between the lines, which proclaimed an unshakable loyalty, seeped a faint bitterness tinged with more than a little heartache. This seemed to Kafchaver more genuine than all of Abaye's effusive descriptions.

Yosef Diaber was not the kind of man who easily yielded even a small measure of honor and power...

"I see," the nobleman said. "And I am moved. This comes as a great surprise."

"All of Khazar is moved by the towering spirit of Khazar's former king," Abaye agreed. "This has been a display of awesome and splendid strength that will go down in the annals of Khazari history!"

"Indeed." For the third time, Lord Kafchaver read the scroll. Then he lifted his short, thick neck and asked, "Do you know what the *bek*'s son is planning to do?"

Abaye shrugged. "We set out for Itil the moment the letters were signed. But I tend to believe that the new ruler took Lord Diaber's advice and started for Itil the day after we did."

Lord Kafchaver nodded, three slow, ponderous bobs of the head. "The city must be readied," he reflected aloud. "Flags must be hung, and the streets decorated..." He glanced questioningly at the servant standing to the right of his chair. "What are the colors of the *bek*'s household?"

From Lord Kafchaver's house, the two couriers made their way toward Lord Shefer's home. The closer they came, the more apprehensive Abaye grew. The prime minister had believed them — but then, Kafchaver, though universally admired for his soundness and patience, was not known for his sharp wits. Elranan Shefer was another story entirely. With his quick grasp and patient contemplation, he would be a much more difficult man to fool.

Abaye paused, perspiring despite the coolness in the air and trying in vain to still his pounding heart. While Lord Shefer was not a great supporter of Yosef Diaber's, he had never voiced, or even hinted at, a desire to side with Ruben Min-Hagai or, at a later stage, Pinras' men. His loyalty to the rule of law was total.

Abaye tapped the other messenger — one of Min-Hagai's men — on the shoulder. "Perhaps we should visit Lord Shefer later," he said.

His companion lifted his brows in a silent question. The rules of protocol established a precise order of precedence when it came to official correspondence, rules that were strictly honored even with something as ordinary as sending a letter or an invitation to a minor government functionary.

Abaye swallowed. "I prefer it this way," he said apologetically, though with more than a touch of obstinacy. "Let's go on to Lord Stazdiran's house now."

A visit to Dalo Stazdiran's residence was akin to visiting a home for the infirm. Abaye, who knew the former prime minister well, was nevertheless shocked and saddened at the sight of the frozen stare and apathetic manner. Dismissed from the honored position of Khazar's prime minister after years of incessant toil in politics, Dalo had deteriorated rapidly and lost his zest for life. His son's death had plunged him even more deeply into his depression.

Later, as Abaye rode away, head bowed against the wind, he saw, in his mind's eye, himself at Stazdiran's age, his life sad, dry, and boring. Then the image of Stazdiran was replaced with that of Abaye's uncle, with his erect, military bearing. Would his uncle, too, pay the price for failing to develop his spiritual self? Would he also, once his life's work was taken away, deteriorate into a shell of his former self?

Thinking of it, Abaye's hands tightened on the reins, making his horse rear in alarm. He quickly calmed the steed, but the images remained ingrained in his mind for a long time.

To Abaye's astonishment, Khazar's seven governing noblemen received the news with surprise — but not suspicion. Had he not been so tense, this would have been a compliment to him: such a young man to bring these nine exalted personages news of such a nature!

There was only one scroll left in his pack: the one designated for Lord Shefer. As before, Abaye's instincts warned him against visiting Shefer's home. But there was no longer any way to delay the completion of his mission.

It was just as Abaye had anticipated. Elranan Shefer read the letter with a furrowed brow, and his mouth twisted as though he had tasted something sour.

"What nonsense is this?" He glared at Abaye. "Eh?"

"It is not fitting for a nobleman of Khazar to call His Majesty's letter 'nonsense,'" Abaye said, trying to conceal his panic.

"Of course," Shefer was quick to agree. "I meant to indicate my disbelief at the fact that it was the king of Khazar who actually wrote this letter."

Abaye bowed slightly. "I was at my master's side when he dictated this letter to his scribe. My life is guarantor for its authenticity."

Lord Shefer snorted, as if to show what he thought of the young courier's guarantees. He read the letter again, then studied the seal intently, breaking off a sliver of wax and examining its color. There was no obvious sign of forgery. Lord Shefer seemed satisfied.

After that, the interview progressed more or less along the same lines as it had in the homes of the other noblemen. By the time Abaye stepped outside into the street, his head was spinning.

The first stage of the mentor's crazy plan had been successfully carried out — though nothing but a hefty dose of Heavenly assistance could account for it.

Now all depended on how well they could keep the secret. Only if Pinras' men succeeded, as the plan dictated, in detaining all the messengers that would be sent from the city to the new king — thus preventing word of the false scrolls to reach Diaber's ears — was there a reasonable chance that Pinras would be afforded unimpeded entrance to Itil as its king.

The second possibility was something Abaye preferred not to contemplate.

Baliatar's fortress would provide Pinras and his men with a measure of protection against the *hostress* troops' sharpened arrows. But a clash on the high road could bring nothing but tragedy.

Abaye narrowed his eyes, trying to banish the nightmarish visions that danced about in front of them: Pinras lying sprawled on the road in a pool of his own blood…Shaul's body hanging grotesquely from the gallows…and himself? Where would he find himself in all of this?

A good question. And because it was so good, he was better off leaving it unanswered for now. He lifted his head and deeply inhaled the city air.

If the mentor men managed to safeguard the secret — all would be well.

37

ON THE THIRD NIGHT OF THEIR JOURNEY, AS OVER 500 men sat on the ground in a huge circle around the campfire listening to Ruben Min-Hagai expounded on *midrash* and *aggadah*, leading them to new vistas of wisdom and understanding, something very different was taking place at the other end of the camp.

Three tall, broad-shouldered men slipped out of the shadows and attacked a smaller figure with fists and sticks. After tying the figure up so that it lay bound hand and foot, like a sheep prepared for slaughter, they carried it off into the trees.

Some little time passed. The campfire that served as the focal point of the circle began to die down. Ruben's voice weakened and was spent, and the companions in the circle slowly returned to the world around them — determined to be better men than they had been before.

Unfortunately, a similar determination seemed to animate the shadowy figures, who were now struggling with someone else. They were three, while he was only one. But they wielded sticks — and he drew a sword that gleamed in the moonlight. An instant later, the tall men threw aside their sticks and drew their own swords.

The fight was short and violent, and its outcome predictable from the start: even without their absolute mastery over their weapons, the three had a definite numerical edge.

The men who had been listening to the talk dispersed quietly, still trying to hold onto the words floating in the air. An energetic teenager, rocketing into the crowd in search of Ruben Min-Hagai, attracted considerable attention.

"The ruler," he panted, when he stood face to face with their young leader, "wishes to see Your Excellency at once!"

A shiver went through the group. The tranquility that had been in the air a moment before dissipated at the note of excitement in the breathless youth's voice. Clearly, something was afoot.

Ruben nodded. "At once," he acknowledged. With an apologetic smile at the man with whom he had been conversing, he hurried toward Pinras' tent.

Pinras was waiting for him outside, arms folded across his chest. He wore a stern expression. As Ruben approached, he nodded in greeting and jerked a thumb to the side. They walked away until they stood apart from the others. The mentor went straight to the point. Pinras asked — or, rather, stated — "You are upset with me for not telling you the destination and purpose of this journey."

Responding to the quiet confidence in Pinras' voice, Ruben's answer was a small, dry smile of assent.

"I had a good reason for what I did," Pinras said, on a faint note of apology. "You are invited into my tent to see for yourself."

An unpleasant shiver ran up Ruben's spine. "What is it, sir?"

"Don't be afraid," Pinras said with a weary smile. "I know that you're a good man. You have nothing to fear."

"What happened?" Ruben pressed.

Instead of replying, Pinras went to his tent and moved aside the entrance flap. He gestured for Ruben to precede him inside. Reluctantly, Ruben bent his head and stepped through the low opening. When he straightened, his eyes widened in disbelief.

On the ground lay one of the six men who had accompanied him from his father's house. He was covered with gashes and dripping blood, and wore an expression that was woebegone and angry at the same time.

"I'd like to introduce you," Pinras said behind his back, "to Levi — Diaber's spy."

Ruben whirled around to stare at his leader. "What are you saying?" he asked, with difficulty holding onto his self-control. "What kind of farce is this? Levi has been with me from the start. If he were a spy, I would not be standing here today."

Pinras looked with contempt at the figure on the ground. "It happened recently," he said. "About two months ago. Lately, it's been nearly a daily occurrence."

"No…" Levi blubbered. "It's not true!"

"Do not add falsehood to your crimes." Pinras' eyes flashed fire. To Ruben he added, "His contact was also caught. He provided all the facts."

"That could also be a lie," Ruben said. "An attempt to conceal the real spy's identity."

"We have been shadowing this unpleasant pair for the past ten days." A tremendous exhaustion colored Pinras' voice. "Unfortunately, this is no mere suspicion. This is a sad reality — one that has caused heavy damage."

Ruben dropped his eyes to stare at his bound companion. The look in the fellow's eyes convinced him — more than anything Pinras could say — that the man had betrayed him.

"Why?" he asked. "Why did you do it?"

Levi was quiet for a long time. Then he jutted out his chin. "What do you care? Does it make any difference? Anyway, I needed the money."

Ruben was speechless. Some delicate instrument inside him had broken. A slender string that had continued vibrating throughout this whole difficult period — had snapped.

Only military men between the ages of 17 and 30 had been permitted to join this mysterious trek. Ruben's father, like many others, had remained behind. Ruben felt his absence keenly tonight.

"Ruben?" Pinras placed a hand on his shoulder.

"Yes," he said dully. "How can I help you?"

"I've come to see how you are."

"I am fine, *baruch Hashem*. Thank you."

"Levi was one man, and a foolish one," Pinras said gently. "You've always known that. Do not draw conclusions from what he did."

Ruben twisted his mouth into a semblance of agreement, then hid his eyes to conceal the tears there. Pinras stayed where he was, a stable and supportive presence.

"I did know," Ruben said at last. "You're right."

"We tried to use him, to pass false information on to Diaber," Pinras said. "It was important that he not know we suspected him... And you were with him so often..." He gave Ruben a sideways glance. "I'm sorry."

"You did what you had to do," Ruben said, meeting Pinras' eyes. He lowered his own. "But it hurts."

"Welcome, young man, to the exalted sphere of leaders." Pinras paused, then added, "Our destination is Itil."

Being locked up in the little cottage with the triangular roof was as annoying to Lista Basbani as being incarcerated in an actual prison would have been. The fact that he had been well paid for his work did not make him any happier. The guards posted outside his door would not even help pass the time by wagering their money in a friendly game of chance.

"How are you people any better than the other side?" he fumed at Avraham after five days of this. "You claim to be more ethical, to have a better value system. You don't lie or gamble. You do nothing but pray all day long ... But when the pressure is on, you call Lista and ask him to forge some letters, eh? Aren't you ashamed? You people want to run the government? Then fight like men! Don't sneak in through the back door like a pack of thieves — or lock up a person who's helped you. For shame!"

"Aren't you comfortable here, Lista?" Avraham asked tiredly. The dark rings under his eyes declared that — in contrast to the forger — he had not had much sleep recently. "Isn't the food good enough?"

The gnawed bones on the plate were proof that this was not the problem. Lista frowned.

"The bed?" Avraham inquired politely.

"The logic!" Lista finally shouted. "That is the problem. It just doesn't make sense!"

"It makes perfect sense actually," Avraham said curtly. "It's better to lie than to kill. Because Yosef Diaber has risen against us in war, we are trying to act against him with trickery — to limit the bloodshed." He paused. Then, in an attempt to improve the forger's mood, he added, "It's reasonable to suppose that in the merit of those letters you wrote, the fate of all of Khazar will be altered. Doesn't that make you happy?"

It had always been Lista's policy to honor the views of those who paid him for his work. He mumbled something affirmative. Had his close friends asked the same question, though, his answer would have been decidedly different. The guards outside his door, who did not laugh at his jokes or gamble with him, only reinforced his distaste for the pious. The future, as painted by Yosef Diaber — a future of song, wine, and laughter — was far more appealing to him than the measured, thoughtful reality imposed by King Reuel. And the mentor, by the look of things, intended to follow Reuel's example.

That night, taking advantage of a momentarily distraction in the guards' attention, Lista took his bag of gold, shattered the window in his room, and escaped. He breathed deeply of the free night air as he sprinted away into the darkness.

His first stop was a friend's home — an expert whiskey brewer. His last stop would be Itil. Or, more particularly, the palace of the new king.

Lista was not by nature a traveling man, and the days that passed until he met up with Diaber's convoy were one long nightmare. But he achieved his objective in the end. He, a forger from Baliatar, stood facing the king of Khazar, who smiled at him, thanked him for the vital information he had brought, and promised to meet again to reward him properly for it — when investigation had proved that the information was correct.

"In the meantime," King Yosef said with a smile, "you will stay here with my men. I am sure you will enjoy their company."

While Lista had to admit that the king's caution was justified, the prospect of yet another imprisonment was irritating in the extreme. From his small cell he could hear the *hostress* troops preparing hastily for battle. He heard the snorting of their horses and the clatter of their weapons. Yosef Diaber's voice mingled with the rest.

Diaber spoke words that ignited a flame in the soldiers' eyes and a blaze of anger in their hearts. He was deliberately seeding and nurturing in his men a cruel and powerful thirst for revenge.

"For the sake of a brighter future, for the sake of a happier Khazar, for the fulfillment of all our dreams and hopes —" Slowly, the new king opened his clenched fist. "For the sake of all these things, this will be a war in which no prisoners will be taken. Shoot to kill. Do you hear me, *hostress* soldiers?"

A roar of affirmation rose into the air. But Diaber was not satisfied.

"For the sake of a more compassionate future, for the sake of a freer Khazar, for every Khazari, individually and collectively — what will you do?" he cried. After a split second of silence, the answer came like a thunderclap.

"Very good," said the king. "If your arms are as mighty as your voices, Khazar will be ours. Mount your horses, *hostress* soldiers."

As though synchronized by a master choreographer, the troops swung into their saddles. Khazar's elite fighting unit was ready for battle. They had their orders: *Take no prisoners. Shoot to kill.*

Hearing all this, Lista Basbani was seized with terror. He might be a master forger, but he was no killer. The slaughter that would take place among the Mentor's Men would be his fault. Perhaps, he realized with regret, it would have been better to have simply gone about his own business and left the war games to others.

The guards outside this door were happy for a game of chance with him for copper and silver coins, but Lista's mood was not suited to such games. He lay silently on his bed, staring at the web that a spider was busily weaving in a corner. *The trouble with you, Lista*, his father had always scolded him when he had been a child, *is that you always regret things when it's far too late...*

His father had been right. Strain as he might, Lista could see no way out of this impasse. Unlike the flimsy shutter he had had to break to escape his earlier confinement, the bars of this place were strong and sturdy, the walls made of thick stone, and the guards a suspicious lot. There was no way he could escape and warn the Mentor's Men of what was about to befall them. The unsuspecting lot would continue on their way to Itil — oblivious, confident — and would stumble upon the *hostress* troops, on the march with murder on their minds.

And it would be his fault.

He lay despondent for hours, brooding — until a thought came along that brightened his outlook. The mentor's people might be naive and inexperienced in military tactics, but even the most innocent of them would understand that when a stranger in the possession of military secrets escapes, a change in plans is essential. Exactly so!

If they didn't — the fault would be entirely theirs.

The discussion was stormy. Gad Baliatar and one of his military strategists insisted forcefully that the convoy must hasten to Itil before Diaber's men — if the forger had managed to reach them — could warn the city's residents.

Pinras sided with the second strategist, who was all for returning to Baliatar to avoid the threat altogether.

Ruben was silent. The other four men fixed their eyes on him.

"Walls are not such a wonderful thing — at least, not when you're on the wrong side of them," he said quietly. "We number more than 5,000 men. The Baliatar fortress cannot sustain that many people under humane conditions. It would be impossible to bring in enough food and water for so many. Yosef Diaber will understand this and will besiege us. A siege can only end in surrender — or death."

"And going on to Itil?" Pinras asked tensely.

"If we leave Baliatar province, we will be in the same situation as we are in now — exposed on all sides and open to attack. But now, at least, we can send out scouts to comb the road leading to the city and anticipate an attack before it happens."

"So you recommend that we stay with our original plan?" one of the strategists clarified. "You are for Itil?"

Ruben's fingers tapped the tabletop. "It's been five days since the forger escaped," he said slowly. "I believe that even with a fast horse, he could not have met up with Yosef Diaber's men before today, or perhaps tomorrow. In my opinion, if we make haste, we have a good chance of reaching the capital before them. I recommend that we forge ahead." He nodded twice, as though to underline the statement.

The balance of opinion was now clear: three men for going on with the journey, and two against. But one of those two was the man who had the power to decide.

Pinras was silent, brow furrowed as he considered deeply. "We made a mistake in asking the *rav* to start for Itil before us," he said with a sigh. "This is a question for the *gedolei hador*. But because they are not here, I accept Ruben Min-Hagai's opinion. We will continue on to Itil, at the fastest possible pace. Please ask the trumpeters to sound the call."

Something inside Istrak seemed to burst open at the sight of Itil's soaring walls shining in the morning light. "Look," he said, gesturing. That was all he could say. For a long moment he sat motionless as a pain-filled sweetness spread throughout his body. He was home. But his father was not waiting for him at the palace gates. A banner with an unfamiliar crest flew over the walls beside the Khazari flag. And, as if these things were not enough, he was forced to return to his city like a thief in the night, afraid that revealing his identity could bring tragedy in its wake. Turning to Michoel, he read the same mixture of paralyzing emotions on his brother's face.

"Those houses," he told the Mundaris, pointing at the slumbering streets, "are the first dwellings of Khazaran, the city that circles Itil like a ring. Behind those walls, inside Itil, live the nobility. And in the center of Itil is the royal enclave — our final destination." He paused, struggling to gain control of his voice. "But before we get there, we will have to seek out some friends from among Itil's noble families. Our first stop is the home of Lord Elranan Shefer."

The youths nodded as though they understood, but it was clear to him that they did not grasp the true significance of what he had just said.

"Because Itil's walls are guarded, we must find a way to get inside," Istrak explained. "We'll claim that you were invited here by Lord Kafchaver's farm manager to join his working crew. If that doesn't work, Yishai will start a fight, during which Aharon and I will escape and slip into the city." Istrak fell silent, throwing a glance at Michoel, whose new name for the duration was "Aharon."

He had pounded their cover story into the Mundaris' ears from the moment they had set out. Until now, the patrols they had met on the way accepted Istrak's explanations when they questioned them about the reason for their journey. But now, in the city where every child knew the faces of the royal family, the story would not ring true. Both of them had changed dramatically since their departure from the city — inwardly as well as out. The light-haired Istrak had smeared walnut juice into his hair to darken it to nearly brown. But the difference might not prove adequate. Old acquaintances who might encounter them in the streets were certain to sense something familiar about the pair. And being recognized — at the wrong time and in the wrong place — would be courting disaster.

Istrak scanned his companions' faces. They had been ready to join him on the eight-day journey, to suffer discomfort on a mysterious mission. But which of them would be prepared to risk his own life for the sake of that undefined quest? Only Yishai — who had grasped the whole truth right from the start. The rest still remained in the dark as to his and Michoel's true identity.

Istrak was in a quandary. If he told his young companions the truth, they would instantly recognize the vital nature of their venture, that without their help, Khazar was liable to fall like a ripe fruit into the hands of their enemies both within and without. This would give them the courage they needed to fight with no thought of escape or surrender.

On the other hand, it was dangerous — very dangerous. Should word of the princes' identity spread beyond the bounds of this small group, catastrophe would follow.

But catastrophe could also come about if his companions didn't know the fateful nature of their mission...

There wasn't much time to decide. Just minutes before their wagon reached Khazaran, Istrak asked the driver to detour into the woods.

It was cool and dim among the trees. A breeze shook the branches, making the shadows on the ground shiver. Not far from here, Istrak knew, was concealed the mouth of the secret tunnel leading to the treasury house — the same tunnel his Uncle Eshal's murderer had used to penetrate the treasury house. If only he could locate the exact spot, he and his brother could go home without exposing their whereabouts to Diaber's men, who must surely be guarding all the conventional entrances into the city.

Right now, this was no more than wishful thinking. All he knew was the tunnel's general location — near the Nivgar Bridge. At the moment, the tunnel was of no use to them.

With an effort, Istrak put an end to his galloping thoughts. He inhaled deeply, plastered a smile on his lips, and turned to face his companions. It was time to let them in on his secret.

It was just as he had expected. The knowledge that the two youths in whose company they had been traveling for the past eight days were none other than the lost princes of Khazar struck nine of the Mundaris like a thunderbolt. The tenth bowed his head and murmured, "I knew it all along, Your Highness."

His friends turned to him in wonder.

"That's why I was so stubborn," whispered Yishai. "Stubborn, and ready to make any effort."

Michoel filled the sudden silence. "If only all of us were aware of our duty on this earth," he said, "we would all, every one of us, be stubborn and ready to make every effort in order to carry out that obligation. But we don't value ourselves enough. It is from this that all the problems spring."

Surprised, Istrak stared at his younger brother. A wave of fierce pride suffused him. Where had this young boy found the serenity, in these turbulent days, to evoke a moral lesson from their present reality?

"An enduring concept," he said with a nod of approval. "Positive and inspiring." He looked again at the young Mundaris. "We will continue on to Itil. As I told you earlier, our final destination is the royal enclave." They gaped at him, and he smiled reassuringly. "Nothing has changed. I am Zevulun and this is my brother, Aharon. Try to ignore — to the best of your ability — what I just told you."

Diaber's flag waved beside that of Khazar atop every tall building in Khazaran, testifying to its inhabitants' loyalty to Yosef Diaber. Many of the people wore the flag's colors on their sleeves or around their necks. Even the soldier who stopped them in the market square to ask where they were going wore a cockade of red and yellow ribbons pinned to his collar.

"To my master's palace — Lord Kafchaver," Istrak said pleasantly. "We have come to join his crew of shepherds."

The soldier regarded him doubtfully.

"Don't pay any attention to our clothes," Istrak said, looking directly into the soldier's eyes. "We were robbed on our way here…" The faint scar on his neck served as an unwitting confirmation of his story.

The soldier nodded. "The important thing is, you're alive," he said, and sent them on their way.

But Istrak had one more question. "Where can we buy ribbons like that?" He pointed at the soldier's cockade.

To their surprise, the soldier grimaced. "Everywhere," he said shortly. "At the greengrocer's, at the doctor's, the tailor's and the shoemaker's… In our king's time — may the Creator grant him long life — things were otherwise. No one dreamed of pinning ribbons onto a soldier's collar."

Istrak's brows snapped together in disbelief. "They insist on your wearing them?"

Another grimace. "Not exactly insist…" Belatedly, the soldier remembered his position. "You men may go on your way. Good day to you."

"To you, too," Istrak said, smiling into the man's eyes. "May the Creator bless you from His storehouse of unearned gifts."

The soldier's face softened into a responding smile that made him look suddenly years younger. "And may the bestower of this blessing be blessed," he said quietly. As the wagon started forward, he raised his voice slightly and called, "Thank you."

"Sir, will you become angry if I mention that this is no way to behave if you wish to remain anonymous?" Yiftach, Yishai's twin, asked in mild rebuke. "He will certainly think of you again today, and I would not be at all surprised if he were still watching us…" Instinctively, Istrak glanced over his shoulder. Yiftach was right.

"Perhaps I made a mistake," Istrak admitted. "It was just that he needed it so badly…"

The young men did not grasp his meaning. They had not been raised, as Istrak had been, to be sensitive to the feelings of every one of his subjects and to try and ease their pain. But Michoel understood. Smiling at his brother from the other end of the wagon, he said, "It's all for the best." The smile vanished as he added, "Shall we buy ourselves some of those ribbons?"

Istrak nodded. "Buy pins, too." He reached into his pocket for some coins. "And please ask the seller how to reach Globos Street. Try to avoid having to ask twice."

Two of the Mundaris set about this task. The price of the cockades and pins was steeper than they had expected; eager to avoid notice, they did not bargain. Then they asked for, and received, detailed directions to their destination. They were surprised to discover that the place was very close by — only a few minutes' walk from the shop in which they stood.

Istrak was very pleased. "Excellent!" he said. Then, in a low voice, he instructed them to set in motion the plan he had outlined for them the previous evening.

The bored soldier on duty at the entrance of the military-uniform factory did not realize that an unusual number of Mundaris had just walked down Globos Street. In truth, it would never have occurred to him that anyone might try to break into the building he was so nonchalantly guarding. But someone — more than one person — had that exact intention.

Late that night, one of the building's windows was shattered, and two figures slipped inside. Soundlessly they walked through the large rooms, seeking the storage area, where they filled their arms with clothing from the various shelves. Outside, by moonlight, they matched trousers to shirts and checked the sizes of the uniforms they had taken. While their companions donned the uniforms of the palace guard and pinned on the ribbon cockades, the pair returned to the building they had just left to restore the unneeded uniforms to their places and search for a shelf containing the smallest sizes. But even the most thorough search did not bring to light a single shirt that would fit Michoel.

"We turned the place upside down, sir," one of the pair reported. "No luck."

"I could hide under one of the wagon seats," Michoel offered.

His brother shook his head. Michoel's plan might work for their passage through the gates in the wall separating Itil from Khazaran, but disguise was essential if they were to move freely about after they had left the wagon and entered the inner city.

Yishai broke the tense silence. "Maybe we should all go inside and have a look?"

Again Istrak shook his head. The place had been searched thoroughly. The soldiers-in-disguise were watching him expectantly, awaiting his decision. He gazed off into the distance, praying for inspiration.

"You'll have to wear one of the larger sizes and fold up the sleeves," he told Michoel at last. "And hurry. Staying here is certainly not a good idea."

"No," said Michoel. "I have a better idea. With your permission, stop the wagon in front of a *beis knesses*. At this stage, there's no reason for me to enter Itil with you… Afterward, when everything has been arranged, you can come to the *beis knesses* to get me. I'll be saying *Tehillim* for your swift success."

Michoel's solution was logical. Still, it was hard for Istrak to accept any decision that would once again separate him from his brother. He was loath to leave Michoel behind, with only one or two of the Mundaris for companionship and protection. But he had no other options.

As the others began moving toward the fence, Istrak stopped them. He had an idea. "There's an escape tunnel leading from the treasury house to the Pelasar Forest, near the Nivgar Bridge," he whispered. "I don't know if you will be able to find the opening, but ten Mundari trackers are a force that cannot be ignored."

Yiftach hung his head. "We will do the best we can, sir." He sounded doubtful.

"You must believe in yourself," Istrak urged. "If you do not act from a conviction that you are the person who will determine the fate of the nation, how will you find the strength to do what you must do? And how can I entrust to you the most precious treasure in all of Khazar — my brother?"

"I will believe," Yiftach promised, his lips suddenly dry.

"Good." Istrak smiled. Turning to Michoel, he said quietly, "I don't want to risk leaving you alone in a *beis knesses* where you could be recognized. Go into the forest with the Mundaris. Find the tunnel and follow it to the treasury house. There is always a key hanging on the inner side of the entrance to the treasury-house roof. If you take ropes with you, you'll be able to slide down and enter the palace through Unmar's secret passageway."

Michoel nodded in comprehension. "What if we don't find the opening of the tunnel?"

"Then wait for me in Khazaran's main *beis knesses* until Minchah," Istrak said. "Take two of the Mundaris with you for protection. If I'm not there by then — and you do not receive word from the palace — then do as you think best."

"I know you will succeed, Istrak. You can depend on Lord Shefer," Michoel said with a mixture of confidence and hope.

"If I don't make it to the *beis knesses*, that statement will be in doubt... If that does happen, I would not advise you to turn to him a second time. Nor to Lord Kafchaver." He gazed into Michoel's eyes to make sure he understood. Then he faced the others. "Take good care of him," he said.

The young men nodded. As always, it was Yishai who appeared the most responsible and dedicated of the lot. Istrak stifled a sigh. It was Yishai whom he had intended to take with him.

Conflicting voices argued inside his head. It was he, Istrak, who would be embarking on the more dangerous mission. But Michoel's mission, though less dangerous, was well-nigh impossible… His eyes raked his companions' faces. Yiftach was also clever, brave, and quick. He hesitated.

Michoel, with a twinkle, touched Yishai's shoulder lightly. "Go on, my friend," he said. "Go with my brother. Something tells me he'll need you more than I."

Generally Lord Kafchaver was a very sound sleeper, but he was finding it hard to fall asleep that night. The fantastic story that the young man had told about Yosef Diaber did not sit well with him. And not only him; when he discussed the situation with close friends on the governing council, they had agreed with him that Diaber was not a man to willingly give up the power he had in his grasp. As one sharp-tongued young nobleman put it, it was doubtful if Diaber would be willing to return the crown to King Reuel himself.

Still, none of them could find a trace of forgery in the letters they had received.

The prime minister sat up in bed. Placing his feet one after the other onto the cold floor, he rose heavily. He must think. And he had to do it quickly — before it was too late.

Stepping out onto the balcony in the hope that fresh air would clear his thoughts, he found his son, Asher, along with a couple of friends. Mumbling something, he retreated back inside. He walked the halls of his home with a bowed head, studying the pattern of the floor tiles. By the time he had circled the entire house twice, he was convinced that it had not been Diaber who had written that letter.

Even those close to a person may betray him, he told himself.

Kafchaver was a fairly trusting man. Was it reasonable to suppose that he, of all the Khazari lords, had been the only one to suspect a fraud? Unable to arrive at a clear conclusion, he decided that it was imperative that he share his thoughts with someone.

Upon reflection, he chose Elranan Shefer. Despite his exhaustion, he resolved not to put off the consultation until the morning. The fate of Khazar was at stake. If the letter *was* proven to be a fraud, the day Yosef Diaber was seated on the throne would be the last day they held their high positions — and possibly their last days on earth.

A shiver ran down his spine at the thought of the hundreds of purple cloths he had ordered hung at first light. His fatigue vanished as if it had never been.

Pacing Shefer's study restlessly, Kafchaver poured out the troubled thoughts that had led him to wake Shefer from his sleep. Forgers did exist in the world, and traitors did rear their heads now and then. There was no seal and no wax that could not be counterfeited.

"What are the chances," Lord Shefer asked, "that the tutor's people managed to come up with such an imaginative plot?"

"We view Ruben Min-Hagai and Pinras, Eshal's son, as the two figures behind the attempted uprising," Kafchaver exclaimed. "But we forget that Baliatar stands behind them — and he is no novice. What are you doing, Elranan?"

"Just making sure that we are truly alone," Shefer replied. He opened the door to make sure no one was eavesdropping behind it, then closed it again. Satisfied, he asked, "Do you know who else has not figured prominently enough in our calculations?"

Kafchaver folded his arms across his chest and waited. Shefer checked behind the door a second time, closed it again, and said, "Yosef. He is the person I suspect more than anyone."

"Yosef?" Kafchaver said, tugging at his beard. "Which Yosef?"

"Diaber, of course. I do not believe that Ruben Min-Hagai, Pinras, or even Gad Baliatar concocted such a creative plot. But there is a very reasonable chance that Yosef Diaber himself wishes to…replenish the ranks of Khazar's nobility." He eyed Kafchaver narrowly to see if he had grasped his meaning. "Replenish," he repeated slowly, and made a slashing motion across his neck with the forefinger of his right hand.

Kafchaver seemed thunderstruck. "Are you aware that you are talking about Khazar's new king?"

"I'm speaking of our old childhood friend," Shefer returned, opening the door yet again. "I have become chronically suspicious. Look, Menashe. Diaber can never be 100 percent certain of our loyalty. After all the political games are over, you and I and a few others still believe that the crown is meant to belong to the sons of those who established the throne and sat on it so wisely until now."

"True," Kafchaver agreed. "But there is no one from that family capable of leading the nation at the moment."

"Yes. They've all disappeared in one mysterious fashion or other…"

"Ruben Min-Hagai has kidnaped the children," Menashe Kafchaver reminded him uncomfortably. "And the older boys were ambushed by —"

"Bulgarians, Kawaris, or someone else. But we digress. Let's review the salient points. What would be simpler or easier than accusing all of Khazar's ruling nobility of attempting to rebel and dispatching them to a pleasanter world? Afterward, their property is confiscated by the government and then redistributed among noblemen who will not demonstrate such fealty to Reuel's sons when they return and demand their father's crown." Shefer paused. "But all this is mere guesswork. Fantasy…"

"From which you are extrapolating a full legal tome," Kafchaver said. "How did *you* manage to sleep with all this on your mind?"

Shefer sighed. "No one believes the boy who cries 'Wolf!' over and over. After hundreds of false alarms, even the shepherd teaches himself not to grow afraid of every rustle behind every bush…"

Kafchaver mulled this over in silence for several moments. At last, he said, "All this sounds very logical, Elranan."

"That's always the problem," Shefer answered candidly. "If I were to obey the voice of logic, I'd have no friends left in the world."

Kafchaver brought his fist down on the table. "This time, I'm the one who is saying it. Summon a scribe, Elranan. Together, let us compose a polite letter explaining to the new king that, sensing a trap and a forgery, we cannot respond to his order and hand the mentor's people the throne of Itil on a silver platter. And please hurry!"

Composing the letter took far longer than they had expected. The night was far advanced toward dawn by the time Lord Kafchaver returned to his own home, a copy of the drafted letter in his hand. His head pounded with exhaustion. He went into his study and sat down in his large chair, craving rest and quiet. Through the window wafted a cool, pleasant breeze. Surprisingly, the serenity he craved did not come. He heard laughing voices outside, floating in with the breeze.

He lifted his head in puzzlement. His extensive property was set well back from the street. From where then were the voices coming? If he could hear them, they could be reaching him only from his own, personal courtyard.

He called for a servant. "Please summon my scribe. I know it's late, but this is important."

The servant was back within minutes. "I'm sorry, Your Excellency. The scribe is not in his room."

"Do you have any idea where he is?"

The servant was unable to help him. Again, Kafchaver heard the sounds emanating from his garden. "Tell me, whose voices are those?"

The servant tilted his head, listening. "I believe, Your Excellency, that they are guests at the young master's party."

"Asher? A party? At this hour?"

The servant spread his hands. "If Your Excellency wishes, I can go outside and make sure."

"Wait." Kafchaver stopped him halfway to the door. "I'm coming with you."

At the farthest end of the summer garden, Menashe Kafchaver stopped walking, breathing hard in an effort to regain his self-control. When his anger had begun to subside, he fixed a pleasant expression on his face and entered the enclosed pavilion. As it turned out, he needn't have bothered adjusting his expression — not a single one of the young people present so much as glanced at him. Eight or nine young men — apart from his son, Asher — sat on garden benches with goblets of wine in their hands, listening attentively to one pink-cheeked youth who stood on a table reciting humorous lyrics. Kafchaver noted that his scribe was one of them. Though he found nothing overtly wrong with the lyrics themselves, the entire scene — the late hour, the brimming goblets, the remains of food scattered about, the loud laughter and the idleness — all combined to create an atmosphere contradictory to the lifestyle he wished to see his young son follow.

The young man continued spouting poetry to his appreciative audience. Drawing a long breath, Kafchaver stepped heavily into the center of the circle.

"Good evening, boys," he said. "Or rather, good night. Welcome to my humble abode... Asher, can you step outside for a few minutes?"

"They came for a wedding and got stuck in the city," Asher said quickly, a flush rising to his cheeks. There was a film across his eyes that spoke of much alcohol consumed over the past hours. "So I invited them to sleep over at our house."

"To sleep over," his father repeated with wry humor. "I'm afraid you boys aren't sleeping deeply enough."

Asher chuckled.

"Actually, this is no laughing matter." Every trace of humor had disappeared. "Who are these wild boys? And do you have any idea of the time?"

Asher was insulted. "They're not wild. They're a great bunch... And anyway, Shalvan Diaber throws parties like this at least twice a week, and *his* father doesn't say a word!"

Lord Kafchaver's lips were pinched almost to the vanishing point. "The king apparently is unaware of this. Had he known, he would box his son's ears."

Asher tilted his head and gazed at his father through a cloud of intoxication. "Of course he knows, Father. Do you know how many nights he's sat with us?"

"You're drunk, Asher."

"No, I'm not." To add emphasis to this claim, Asher clapped his chest. "Really I'm not. You don't get drunk on a little pomegranate wine! Shalvan's father is not Istrak's father. He likes to sit with us. He enjoys our company. He says it makes him feel young."

Kafchaver decided to save the rest of his rebuke for the morning. The nonsense Asher was spouting only confirmed his suspicion that his son was in no shape to conduct a reasonable conversation.

"You don't believe me, Father?" Asher, though normally a good boy, was deeply offended. "Have I ever lied to you? Come, let's ask the others."

Lord Kafchaver had no intention of embarrassing his son in public. But Asher was already striding outside. His father hurried after him. To his shock, the guests — drunk as they were — confirmed every word that Asher had spoken.

"I met Yekutiel there, too," Asher said, thumping the poet's back, who had apparently completed his recitation and now sat at the table sipping wine. "He's destined for greatness, this boy!" To his father, he added, "At only 24, he is the king's scribe. But he's also a great poet — with a great future, in my opinion!"

Kafchaver's brow creased. In his years at King Reuel's side, he had met all the scribes who worked in the palace. None had been this young.

"You are King Yosef's scribe?" he asked.

The young man stood up. "His personal scribe," he answered gaily. "And the only one, these past five years!"

Kafchaver paled, but he managed to retain control over his voice. "And why have you not joined him on his coronation tour?"

"My sister's getting married day after tomorrow," the young poet confided. "The king generously agreed to free me so that I could join the family celebrations."

"Very nice," Kafchaver murmured. "It might be a good idea for you to get some sleep now. You must gather your strength for the forthcoming celebration."

The others laughed at this, but the party began to disband. Kafchaver motioned for his scribe to wait for him. He stood in the center of the garden, chin sunk onto his chest as a million thoughts rampaged through his brain like a herd of wild horses.

Though the presence of the king's scribe in the city loomed largest among these thoughts, he could not help reflecting on Shalvan Diaber and his father, King Yosef, spending their nights roistering at youthful, purposeless parties. And he thought of the comatose Reuel, the man who, first and foremost, deserved his loyalty.

A polite cough sounded behind him. "Your Excellency wished to speak with me?"

"Yes." Kafchaver turned to his scribe. "That young poet. You must know him. Is he really King Yosef's personal scribe?"

The other man nodded. "He writes with a very fine hand. Many scribes have tried to imitate his style, but have been unsuccessful."

Kafchaver could think of one person, at least, who had been completely successful.

There was no question about it. The letter had definitely been forged.

Lord Shefer's suspicions were boundless. Even after Menashe Kafchaver told him of the explicit proof that the letter was a forgery — having purportedly been written on the road by a scribe who was actually still in the city — Shefer refused to acknowledge that the forged document had been penned at the mentor's instigation.

"Perhaps this is the trap!" he exclaimed. "Perhaps Yosef had the letter written before he set out from Itil. He left the scribe behind so that he can later accuse us not fulfilling our duty to check whether his scribe might have written the letter."

"Would it be logical for him to demand something like that of us?"

"Or," Shefer plowed on, ignoring the interruption, "he may have been the one to order those young men to stay behind in the city after the wedding, and to come to Asher's house, so that you cannot claim, afterward, not to have known."

Kafchaver sighed. "Enough," he pleaded. "Enough. Just tonight, I discovered that I haven't a clue as to who Asher's friends are. I have a feeling that Yosef Diaber knows more about that than I." He avoided Shefer's eyes. "Anyway, either case would seem to demand the same response: we must send King Yosef a message, telling him about the letter we've received and our suspicion of forgery."

"That's correct," Lord Shefer agreed, brightening slightly. "But what do you mean by 'seem'?"

Kafchaver turned. "May I?" Striding to the door, he imitated his host by opening it a crack and peering out to make sure no one was listening.

"Elranan," he whispered, after closing the door again, "we're friends, aren't we?"

Startled, Elranan nodded. "Certainly."

"I have something to tell you — a secret I have harbored now for a while. To a certain degree, I am placing my life in your hands."

Again, Lord Shefer nodded. "Go on."

Lord Kafchaver cleared his throat. "I am disillusioned with Diaber."

"Disillusioned?"

"With Diaber," Kafchaver repeated. "King Reuel had the man's measure a long time ago. I've just understood it today."

"What have you understood?" Shefer was on his feet now, facing him.

"That we've placed a crown on an animal's head."

Absolute silence reigned for a moment. Shefer broke it. "Animal... an interesting way of putting it."

Bravely, Kafchaver continued. "We all knew that Yosef Diaber is not a Torah scholar and not particularly pious," he said heavily. "But we thought we could disregard those aspects. 'The man does a tremendous amount of *chesed*,' we said. 'His charitable institutions are the biggest in Khazar. His heart is as wide as a house...'"

"True," Shefer said. "All true."

"Yes." Kafchaver lifted his head, and a fighting light sprang into his eyes. "All true. But those facts tell us nothing! His institutions may be large, and he may be ready to battle against anything that strikes him as wrong. But what I learned tonight is that Diaber sees nothing wrong with young men of 20 wasting their nights with rhymes and chatter. He is even prepared to sit with them and laugh at their jokes. I can only repeat what I said before: an animal. The man has no ties to G-d. He is…he is like a donkey, walking on two legs." He swallowed. "Humans and animals have the same flesh. If the soul does not succeed in elevating a person at least a little bit — I see no difference between the two."

"You speak harshly," Shefer said, still watching his friend.

Kafchaver nodded. "As I said, I knew before I began that I was entrusting you with my life."

"That's not what I meant. Forgive me, Menashe, if I sound sharp — but according to your definition you, too, have fallen into the category of 'animal' for most of your life."

Kafchaver's face seemed to crumple. "But there is a difference, isn't there. I, at least, strive to be a human being. I understand that the mitzvos that bind us to Hashem touch on every aspect of our lives. That a person must be a human being at all times — in the *beis medrash*, in the marketplace, and around the governing council's table."

Shefer said nothing, leaving Kafchaver's words dangling in the air.

"Anyway," Kafchaver said, trying to bring the talk back to its original topic, "I am not the king of Khazar, nor the subject of this conversation."

Still Shefer did not speak.

"Elranan, don't you agree with me?"

Lord Shefer's lips formed a thin line. His eyes evaded Kafchaver's.

"You don't need to do a thing," Kafchaver said. "Just sit quietly, suppress your suspicions, and let the Ruben's group enter Itil. I'll worry about the rest."

Lord Shefer swallowed. No response was forthcoming.

"Will you do it?" Kafchaver pressed.

Lord Shefer closed his eyes for a long moment. At last, he opened them. "If you are right," he whispered, "if acts of *chesed* are not sufficient proof of a person's character..." He fell silent once more, passing a hand across his eyes. "Once," he said, "a short time after the troubles began, Yosef came to see me. He drew my attention to the fact that one of Khazar's noblemen — and it was clearly *not* Bastian Makan — must have cooperated with the enemy. He also said, and justifiably so, that the person who received the most benefit from the tragedies is the one who cooperated." His voice faltered slightly. He took a sip of water from the goblet on the table in an effort to ease the sudden dryness in his throat. "At that time, I thought it was Dalo Stazdiran, who inherited the position of prime minister and hoped to marry his daughter to the king. I even spoke of my suspicions to the king himself. However, in the long run, Dalo did not gain at all And...Yosef has become king."

A faint rustle. It was coming from the door. The two lords raised their brows at each other in consternation. But before Shefer could reach the door, a knock sounded on it.

One of the gatekeepers stood there. "Forgive me, Your Excellency, for disturbing you. A young *hostress* officer is outside, requesting an urgent audience with you. Had I known that Your Excellency is in a meeting, I would not have interrupted at such an unusual hour..."

He was still talking, but neither Elranan Shefer nor Menashe Kafchaver were listening. The same thought had just flitted through both of their minds: that Shefer's earlier surmise was correct, and one of Diaber's men had come to warn them against falling into the king's trap.

"Show him in," Shefer ordered, breaking into the man's longwinded apologies. To Kafchaver, he murmured, "I haven't had a night like this since I can remember."

Neither of them had an inkling of the additional tempests this night was yet to bring.

Istrak's fears proved groundless. Entering Itil was easy as child's play. No one stopped the two *hostress* soldiers in the pursuit of their duty, or asked them where they were going. When they were within sight of Lord Shefer's home, Istrak placed a warning hand on Yishai's arm. Without another glance at their destination, he strode on, past Shefer's estate.

Yishai did the same, wondering at the sudden change in plans.

"The guard," Istrak said in an undertone, still walking. "He will recognize me at once..." Despite the situation, the prince smiled. "Just as I recognized him. He worked in the palace for a number of years."

"Where to then?" Yishai asked.

Istrak stopped walking and threw a glance over his shoulder at Shefer's palatial estate. "A good question," he admitted. "There's no one else whom I can trust."

As footsteps sounded behind them, they resumed their walk. "We'll have to wait for a change of the guard," Istrak said, thinking out loud. "We can't wait in any public place — too risky."

Yishai coughed, requesting permission to speak. "If Itil is large enough so that we do not have to go up any street more than twice, we could just keep on walking. As long as we look as though our hurrying is intentional, no one will suspect us."

Three hours of brisk walking — after an already action-filled day — left them drained. When they noted, on their third passage past Lord Shefer's home, that the guard had been changed, their anxiety eased. But when one of the guards they approached went inside to announce them, and the other motioned for them to have a seat on the wooden bench in the gatehouse, Istrak felt all his former tenseness flood back, filling him from the soles of his feet to the top of his head.

He had realized some time ago that one of Khazar's nobility must have cooperated with the enemy. On his return to Khazar, after listening to an account of all that had transpired in the kingdom after Bastian Makan's imprisonment, the circle of his suspicions had expanded. First and foremost among the suspects in his mind was Yosef Diaber, followed by a number of other figures prominent in Khazari government circles, including Dalo Stazdiran, Lord Nazarel, and Menashe Kafchaver. There was not a single one of them whom Istrak was prepared to trust.

Elranan Shefer, his mother's brother, was the only man of influence whose love and trust were, to Istrak, above suspicion. But Shefer might refuse to see him — an anonymous and unannounced visitor in the dead of night. Or, if he did agree, he might not recognize him. Or, if he recognized him, he might refuse to help him. And even if he agreed to help —

His thoughts broke off abruptly at the guard's entrance.

"Lord Shefer has agreed to see you," he announced graciously. "Please follow me."

The corridors where Istrak used to play with his cousins as a young boy had not changed at all. The guard paused before the door of his uncle's study and knocked confidently. At Shefer's call, he opened the door, motioning for the two soldiers to enter.

Istrak crossed the threshold first. The words of greeting he had intended died on his lips. Despite the late hour, his uncle was not alone. Lord Kafchaver was with him, studying the newcomers with interest.

Yishai walked in behind him, prepared to perform one of his final missions on behalf of the prince of Khazar. Once Istrak's uncle had embraced his long-lost nephew, Yishai's job would be over. Men better and certainly more professional than he would take his place, and he would be free to return to the goats he had so hastily abandoned.

"Welcome to my home," Lord Shefer said, calmly and clearly. There was no trace in his voice of either surprise or curiosity at this visit by two *hostress* officers. "How can I help you?"

Yishai glanced at Istrak, waiting for the joyous announcement of his identity. But Istrak said nothing. Ever quick to grasp a situation, Yishai realized that Istrak did not want to speak in the presence of the second man. He took a small step forward and said, "Can we speak to Your Excellency alone?"

Both men stared at him.

"What about?" Lord Shefer demanded.

Yishai's eyes darted to and fro. He repeated, "We must speak with Your Excellency alone."

Shefer cleared his throat, clearly annoyed. "Is this a private matter, or does it deal with issues affecting all of Khazar?" Then, as though struck by lightning, he returned his gaze to the second officer. "Who are you?" he asked urgently. "Where do I know you from?"

"Your Excellency," Yishai broke in, "we have come a long way to speak with you. Can you give us a few moments of your time — in private?"

The determination in his voice surprised Lord Kafchaver and his brow creased in puzzlement. But Lord Shefer was not even listening. He stood up and strode across the room to face the second soldier.

Istrak lowered his head, avoiding his uncle's probing gaze. But one look was enough for Elranan Shefer. With gentle fingers, he lifted Istrak's chin and looked directly into his eyes.

"It's you," he whispered. "How did you get here, child? Where have you been all this time? And how did you know to come here now — at this particular moment?" He retreated a step. "Where were you these last nine months?"

Nine months?

The words ignited a flash of understanding in Kafchaver's brain. "Prince Istrak?" His eyes opened wide in astonishment, making them appear bluer than ever above his reddening cheeks. "Great heavens! You've come just in time, Prince of Khazar!"

Yishai hid a smile, but Lord Shefer did not seem amused by his friend's outburst. Soberly, he said, "Or, perhaps, just a little too late."

"I have seen that for myself," Istrak replied. His voice held a new note that Yishai had never heard before. Both men were silent.

"With your permission..." Istrak gestured at the chairs beside Shefer's desk. At his uncle's nod, he moved toward them and sat down. "You may be seated," he said. The two lords pulled up chairs and sat.

Yishai watched the scene with a sense of shock. For the first time, he understood the significance of the prince with whom, just hours earlier, he had shared a slab of bread. A wave of fresh admiration swept him. All through their journey, both brothers had conducted themselves in a spirit of friendship. There had been no trace of haughtiness in their demeanor. Only now did Yishai recognize their behavior as the quintessence of true nobility.

Istrak placed his hands on the desk and closed his eyes for a moment in silent prayer. Then he looked at Kafchaver and said dryly, "I heard that you were appointed prime minister by Yosef Diaber. Congratulations."

"I believed I was doing the best thing for Khazar," Kafchaver replied slowly. "And I am still prepared to do anything that might be needed — pleasant or not."

"The *bek*, Menashe Kafchaver, arrived here at this unusual hour of the night in order to share with me his suspicions about our new 'king,'" Lord Shefer said. "We both fear, Your Highness, that it was Yosef Diaber who was behind everything, from beginning to end."

Istrak's teeth flashed. "Including the attempt on my father's life?"

It was Kafchaver who answered, almost soundlessly, "It would seem that way."

"I see." Istrak took a deep breath, trying to sort out his feelings and to banish the least favorable of them. For one moment, he surrendered. "My father," he croaked. "Is his condition as grave as everyone is saying it is?"

Shefer put out his hand and laid it on Istrak's. "The doctor believes that these are his final days."

Istrak's muscles tensed and his breath became shrill. "I was afraid of that," he said brokenly, rising with difficulty from his chair. "Please excuse me for a moment..."

Turning his back on the others, he walked to the window looking onto the darkened garden. The two lords bowed their heads in acknowledgment of his anguish; only Yishai disobeyed Istrak's order. For the noblemen, Istrak was first and foremost a prince. For Yishai, he was first and foremost a friend — and friends, he believed, support one another through difficult moments.

Near the window, he hesitated. Then he took another step forward and placed a hand on his friend's arm, lending support by his presence. The two stood this way, in silence, for several minutes.

Istrak turned, and gently removed his arm from Yishai's grasp.

"Thank you," he said, striving for a matter-of-fact note. Holding his back erect, he returned to the table.

"Gentlemen," he said, "I was far away from Khazar for a long period of time —"

"Far from Khazar?" Lord Shefer interrupted anxiously.

"On the Platt plains," Istrak explained shortly. "And therefore, I am not up-to-date on recent events. Tell me, please — which of Khazar's lords is completely loyal to my father?"

Silence was his answer, a silence that stretched beyond the acceptable limits. And still, no one broke it.

"So that's the way it is," Istrak said softly.

"Lords Sanpal and Latvias are not in the city. They were sent to investigate the possibility of a new division of government property," the prime minister said apologetically. "And Lord Lamens, son of the late Lord Lamens, has gone away on a brief vacation in the south."

"And Nachliel was sent to study the problems of agriculture in Khazar," Lord Shefer added. "And all this took place just before Diaber decided to go out to war against Min-Hagai…" His hands curled into tight fists. "How blind we've been, Menashe! Or have we simply been witless fools?"

"Witless fools," Lord Kafchaver echoed. He turned to Istrak. "But there's Min-Hagai, and there are the Mentor's Men. They may be in the city tomorrow or the next day."

In short, concise sentences, unembellished by unnecessary detail, Kafchaver explained about the letter that had reached Itil — a positive forgery with a still unknown perpetrator. "It is reasonable to suppose that Diaber himself is behind the forgery," he concluded. "But there is still hope."

Lord Shefer straightened. "Even if the Mentor's Men should fail, there are still many, many men who will battle for the regime of a direct descendant of our kings. But that will require time, my prince. Meanwhile, it would be best if you left the city. I am honored to offer you my summer estate as a hiding place."

A small, sad smile touched Istrak's lips. His uncle's summer place held happy memories for him. "I will not leave the city until

I have seen my father," he said quietly. "Besides, Michoel is trying to reach the palace as we speak, through one of the secret tunnels leading from the Pelasar Forest."'

"Michoel!"

"Gentlemen." Istrak rose. "Will you accompany me to my father's palace? On the way, I can fill you in on our adventures these past months."

"Now?" Kafchaver asked in surprise. An enormous yawn threatened to escape as he asked the question.

"They will not let us inside, dear prince," Lord Shefer put in. "Come, will you not eat something before dawn?"

Istrak lowered his eyes, gazing at his hands. In the silence that filled the room, Shefer's feet were audible as he moved across the carpet, as was the squeak of the hinges when he opened the door to speak to a servant waiting a short distance away. He was back in a moment. "A light meal will be served to you shortly, my prince," he said warmly.

"Thank you," Istrak said, though food was the last thing on his mind. "Actually, there's no need, Uncle Elranan. Please give the food to the boy."

Lord Shefer inclined his head, then asked, "May I ask Your Highness for more details about your life in these past months?"

Istrak removed his hands from over his eyes. "I married," he said.

The lords shot him looks of astonishment and disbelief. Istrak was not sure why he had proffered that tidbit of information first.

"*Mazal tov*," Lord Shefer said finally. "Who is the lucky girl?"

"My cousin… The daughter of Rena, my father's sister."

The astonishment was replaced by shock. "Your aunt, Princess Rena, who was killed some twenty years ago?" Kafchaver asked gently, as though speaking to someone who had lost his wits.

"My aunt, who was captured by the Kawaris twenty years ago." Istrak's voice was sharp and not at all confused.

"Captured by the Kawaris…" Shefer, of a quicker grasp than his friend the prime minister, understood what Istrak had not said. He tilted his head questioningly at the prince.

"Yes," Istrak affirmed.

"Are you certain it's really her?" Kafchaver asked. "How do you know the Kawaris weren't tricking you?"

It was a serious question, and a difficult one to answer to someone who had not been there, in the Kawari encampment.

"When my aunt arrives in Khazaran-Itil, her former acquaintances will be able to confirm her identity," he replied briefly. "When I last saw them, in Yosafar, I asked my companions to bring her and her daughter to Baliatar's estate." A quiver ran through his voice as he said this. "I hope I was not mistaken in my assessment of his loyalty."

There was a brief silence. "It has been some time," said Lord Shefer, "since I've stopped believing in the purity of men's hearts… Still, if there remain men whose hearts are pure — Gad Baliatar is one of them."

"Thank you." A tired smile touched Istrak's eyes. "Thank you, Uncle."

Silence reigned until the servants entered, bearing a tray with the meal Elranan had ordered. Slowly, they stirred to life.

"Eat, Yishai," Istrak said. "Find yourself a seat — and say the blessing out loud."

Somewhat at a loss, Yishai looked at the ornate tray laden with delicacies.

"I will eat later, sir," he said with a bow. Belatedly, he realized that he had just dismissed a prince's order and had added insult to injury by failing to call him by his proper title. But no one seemed to notice. Istrak rose to his feet with a resolute air, and the two older noblemen followed suit.

"I want to see my father. I do not wish to wait until after Shacharis." The prince's eyes were pinched with sorrow. "From what you say, that may be too late." His fingernails dug into the flesh of his palms in his effort to prevail over his anguish. "Also, it is very possible that Michoel is making his way through the tunnel to the palace this very minute. It never occurred to either of us that we might return to Khazar only to find it necessary to turn around and flee the city like thieves in the night."

Kafchaver buckled first. "The prince is right, Elranan. If you marshal all your creativity, I'm sure you will arrive at a pretext that will afford us entry into the palace at this late hour."

Istrak completed the last leg of the journey to his father's place with his mind and heart a blank. He answered all the lords' questions about his captivity and escape, questions intended to distract him from his worry and pain. His brain did not assimilate what his lips were saying. The air seemed to have been sucked from his heart and lungs, leaving him an empty shell.

He was unaware of when the carriage rolled to a stop, and the familiar corridors did as to penetrate his consciousness. Only the sight of Ovadia, his father's personal servant — awakened in alarm at the lords' knock — succeeded in penetrating the emptiness inside him and brought tears to his eyes.

"Ovadia," he said, throwing caution to the winds, "can I see my father?"

His footsteps sounded overly loud on the marble floor. Hesitantly, step after step, Istrak entered his father's room. The heat that had been pounding through his veins was replaced by a numbing cold. The young man who was afraid of nothing was suddenly filled with fear.

His right hand touched the *mezuzah*, as though beseeching strength. He moved forward to kiss his father's strong, warm hand and to see the beloved face again.

But the hand was soft and cool, and the beloved face was pale and shuttered, as though withdrawn into itself.

"Father," Istrak whispered, stroking the thin hand. "Father, it is I. I've come back. I'm here. I —" He lowered his head, touching his lips to the back of his father's hand. "I have missed you." He did not cry, but his eyes stung. "So much time has passed, my father. My king." Bowing his head again, he buried his face in the sheet. "And so many things have happened."

He stayed in that position for a long time, allowing the ache in his heart to gather in the corners of his eyes, to moisten the sheet and his father's hand. His king's hand. The man who had given him his heart, day after day, who had waited for him to grow up, and to understand. But he had not merited to witness the realization of his dream.

Istrak felt a hand on his head, sliding down toward his shoulder — exactly the way his father used to do when he was satisfied.

Had a miracle occurred?

Slowly, disbelievingly, Istrak raised his head. He looked first at his father's closed eyes, and then at Ovadia, standing beside him.

"You are a good son," Ovadia said, stroking the prince's head again. "A good boy. Please, stand up, Istrak." His voice was quiet and confident. Istrak obeyed.

"We waited for you," Ovadia said. "For months we waited, afraid all along of the disintegration of old rules and the dominance of foolish mediocrity. Of the triumph of evil. And now — you've come. And just as you have come, you must leave."

Istrak squeezed his eyes shut. When he opened them, Ovadia was holding out a shirt of golden mail. "Put this on," he said. "Put it on, my boy."

Istrak's muscles froze. Only his eyes moved.

"Put it on," Ovadia repeated. "And continue your father's battle. There is no one to do it except you." He paused, then added, "It is best that you not tarry, Prince of Khazar."

There was no sound in the room. Outside, the masses were divided on the question of the inheritor to the throne. Here, in this room that bore the scent of approaching death, the throne seemed insubstantial. Very slowly, Istrak shook his head. "I will take an armored shirt from Lord Shefer's house," he whispered.

Ovadia smiled sadly. "No one is perfect," he said. "Everyone was born with his good tendencies and those that are not so pleasant... Even if you were too young to see this, even if it seemed to you that all of his accomplishments happened of their own accord — you must know that your father, too, struggled in his life. There can be nothing that would have afforded him greater pleasure than seeing you wear his uniform and continuing his battle."

Istrak bowed his head. Ovadia, taking this for an assent, placed the armored breastplate over the prince's chest. The coldness of the metal entered his skin through the thin fabric of his garments. But Ovadia was right: there was something about this uniform that imbued Istrak with warmth and strength, and prevented him from repeating his refusal.

As Istrak left his father's chambers, the sun was rising. A new day had dawned, and with it a great hope, and the knowledge that today might be the day he reclaimed his father's throne.

He was not to know that this was the day his father would take his last breath.

Two hours later, the king breathed his last. The *minyan* of men whom Ovadia had hastily summoned stood with tearful eyes, looking down at King Reuel's face. On his lips was a smile, serene and suffused with joy.

When they were just one hour's gallop from Itil's gates, Lord Diaber halted his men for one last rousing talk. Once again, he incited them with a toxic mix of hate, anger, longing, and vengeance. The combination set the blood boiling in their veins. They unsheathed their swords and slashed them in the air as though the enemy were standing before them.

"We are fighting for all that is good and beautiful!" Diaber reminded them. "For a brighter, freer future — the future that the Mentor's Men want to deny you. They will limit you to a life of constraint. They will cut you off from indiscriminately experiencing all the world has to offer. They will turn Khazar back to its years of division and disunity. Will you let them do it?"

The soldiers surged forward with a deafening "NEVER!"

"I ask again — will you let them do it?"

Another shout filled the men's throats, even more powerful than before. "NO!"

Yosef Diaber gazed out at his men — nearly 2,000 soldiers with fire in their eyes.

"May G-d go with you," he told them. "May He strengthen your arms. Commander Matrias — the loyal soldiers of Khazar are ready for your orders."

After Diaber's inflammatory speech, Matrias' orders sounded drier than usual. The men were to surround the section of land near the first bridge on the Minar River. It would be from that direction, they anticipated, that the Mentor's Men would reach Itil. The soldiers were to wait for a triple blast on the trumpet before attacking. When this sounded, they were to use the arrows, with a single goal: to kill everyone who walked on two feet.

The trumpeters' blast spurred the Mentor's Men on to a rapid, reckless gallop. The knowledge that Lord Diaber had learned of their movements only hours before goaded their horses to all possible speed, without pause for explanations, encouragement, or caution.

From time to time the trumpet blasts sounded again, demanding the horsemen to squeeze the last drop of speed from their steeds. But because the majority of the men were using horses more accustomed to pulling a plow than waging war, few were able to maintain the pace set by those at the front of the line.

All along the way, from the camp where they halted for the night to the narrow bridge over the Minar River a short distance from Itil — the Mentor's Men forged on with typical Khazari obstinacy. They spurred their horses ahead to the destination that passed in a whisper from man to man: the capital city's well-guarded gates.

The bridge over the Minar River was too narrow for more than two soldiers to ride abreast. Ruben Min-Hagai and Gad Baliatar crossed it first. Pinras remained on the other side of the Minar, at the rise leading to the bridge, encouraging the men as they rode up. Only after he had offered his calm smile to the last pair of riders did he, too, cross the river. From the heights of the bridge he looked down on the mass of men clustered together into one dense mass. It was not a large group. In truth, they were a meager bunch — painfully so.

"Straighten your back," Baliatar said as Pinras took his place at the head of the line. "Remember that you are coming to the city gates as its king and victor."

Pinras, pale and grave, said quietly, "This is when we have to hope and pray." As he spoke, he gestured to the trumpet bearer, who brought his instrument to his lips. The group straggled forward.

It was no more than a 30-minute gallop to the gates of Itil, but the horses, exhausted by the long trek, had a hard time keeping up with the rapid pace Ruben Min-Hagai set for them. Reluctantly, Ruben slowed down. As he glanced over his shoulder at the men who had survived the night's adventure with him, he wondered how many of them would live to see another sunset. And of what value was his love for them, if he was prepared to lead them toward the equal possibilities of hope or destruction?

There were answers to this question — answers that he had asked himself only yesterday. Right now, however, all the answers seemed feeble and without substance. Thrusting them aside, Ruben lifted his head and narrowed his eyes at the horizon. There was no time for regret. Not far away, behind a clump of trees, was a glint that could be nothing other than the reflection of soldiers' armor.

Diaber's soldiers.

When Istrak expressed a desire to leave the palace grounds via the secret tunnel leading from the treasury house, Menashe Kafchaver rolled his eyes and even Elranan Shefer felt weak. The treasures guarded behind those heavy doors were the most precious in all of Khazar, and the soldiers surrounding it had orders to let no one in except for the king himself.

But Istrak did not stop to listen to the lords' explanations. They were absolutely correct; he knew it even before they had voiced their objections. But Michoel was due to enter the palace that way, and the danger he faced, in his innocence and ignorance of the facts, was very real.

When Kafchaver proved intransigent, Istrak sent him to summon a loyal escort of men to wait for the prince near the bridge in the southern portion of the Pelasar Forest. This suggestion, which absolved the prime minister of all responsibility in this extraordinary situation, appealed to Kafchaver. He quickly took his leave, while Lord Shefer remained behind with the two *"hostress* officers" — one of whom, underneath his military cloak, sported the gold mail shirt of the Khazari king.

When Kafchaver's broad shoulders had passed out of sight inside his carriage, Istrak smiled. "Let's go," he said, including Shefer and Yishai in the command. "You will soon see that this is not so very difficult. All we need is a bit of water."

The pool in the center of the garden provided more than enough of this commodity. Istrak washed his hair, removing the walnut extract that had turned its color dark. With the long, fair *peyos* dangling to his shoulders, there could be no question of his identity.

"This is too dangerous," Shefer insisted.

Istrak shook his head, as much to refute his uncle's claim as to shake the droplets of water from his wet hair. "My brother's life justifies taking much greater risks," he said. "Come, let us make haste"

On their way to the treasury house, Istrak made a brief stop to fetch a large ax from the gardener's shed. He placed the ax in Yishai's hands. Yishai shouldered it without comment and strode on beside the prince.

Four sentries stood guard at various vantage points outside the treasury house, while a pair of higher officers patrolled its perimeter constantly and tested the guards' vigilance. Istrak, firm and resolute, stopped these two on one of their rounds.

"Good morning," he said.

"The same to you," one of the pair answered, studying Istrak with perplexity. "Will Your Excellency identify himself?"

Istrak smiled. "You may do so yourself."

The officers' suspicion grew, but the slight menace in their manner did not seem to trouble the young man facing them. Istrak put a finger to his lips as, with his other hand, he threw open his cloak, revealing his father's armor.

In the split second that followed, the guards' faces betrayed a gamut of emotions. Surprise, shock, disbelief…and, finally, reverence, a feeling that had them bending their knees in a deep bow.

These veteran officers had often been with the prince in various war exercises, and they recognized him now beyond the shadow of a doubt.

"Distract the attention of the guard standing near the door of the building," Istrak ordered, ignoring their gesture of reverence. "Afterward, you may lock the door and position guards in front of it." An uplifted hand silenced their incipient questions. "Lord Shefer will accompany me. We will find our way out of the treasury house on our own — do not trouble yourselves regarding that. You may lock the doors after we have passed inside."

His totally unexpected appearance had shaken the officers' equilibrium. Without a word, they hastened to obey his commands.

When the sentry had moved away from his post by the front door of the treasury, Istrak took the ax and, with four strong, accurate blows, broke the hinges.

The noise was enough to waken the entire palace compound, as Istrak well knew. He urged his trembling uncle to hurry inside the building's thick walls. "They will prevent anyone from coming inside," he breathed into his uncle's neck as he prodded him onward, down the flight of stairs leading to the deepest of the treasury-house cellars. "And not only because I am here. It will be some time before men in a position of authority arrive on the scene. A great deal of time..."

"Yes," Shefer choked out. "But —"

"No 'buts,'" Yishai said, groping carefully but quickly for the next step. "We have arrived, sir. Which way now — right or left?"

"Right," said Istrak, who had managed to retain his sense of direction through the stairs' twists and turns. "That way is south."

The cellar was permeated with a centuries-old chill. Istrak ran his fingers along the cold stones on the wall, counting them in accordance with his father's instructions on that long-ago day when he had attempted to free Kalev from prison.

To his surprise, though he had been told that the fifth stone in the fourth row was very firmly lodged in place, it slipped into his hands without any real effort. Behind it was the handle of the mechanism that allowed a secret, inner door to open.

A moment later, the three men stood in a tunnel whose moist roof dripped lightly onto their heads. The door, with a deep groan, swung shut behind them, leaving them in complete darkness.

"Sometimes I am astounded by our ancestors' technological ability," Shefer said, his voice sounding disembodied in the darkness. "They were brilliant men."

"And organized," Istrak added, removing a small tinderbox from the door handle and lighting a fire in a torch that had been lying there for generations, awaiting this moment. He handed this to the Mundari. "Lead the way, Yishai."

The tunnel was long, and its smoothly paved floor made Istrak mentally endorse Shefer's comment about their ancestors' ingenuity. A surprised cry by Yishai cut short these thoughts.

"Look, sirs," the youth said. "Look at this!"

One of the floor tiles was missing. In the earth below, clearly visible, was a footprint.

"Someone stepped in here and fell down," Yishai said, pointing at another, blurred print.

"How do you know this?" Shefer demanded. But Istrak, having spent long weeks on the road with Knaz, knew enough about the Mundaris' special skill to accept Yishai at his word.

"He came from the palace," Yishai continued. "There is no doubt about that, sir."

Istrak was surprised. It was hard to believe that this footprint was a remnant of King Yosef's historic escape. Shefer's thoughts were more practical. "If the former *bek's* killer entered the palace grounds through this opening, we must assume that those who know about it use this tunnel from time to time for other purposes…"

"The man was holding a sack, which ripped when he fell," Yishai said, holding up a tiny thread he had found on the rock's surface. After a moment's silence as he scanned the area closely, he added, "And things fell out of it."

"Someone found a very efficient way to pad his household income," Shefer remarked. "No one would think of checking whether any golden spoons, for example, had disappeared from the royal treasury."

A sudden impatience seized Istrak. "If the thief had left his name in the dirt, there might be some purpose in our tarrying here," he said. "Right now, we had better keep moving."

The rest of the journey was accomplished in silence. Yishai came to a solid wall and halted suddenly. Istrak apologized for bumping into his uncle; at this juncture, the tunnel had grown so narrow that they had been moving in single file.

Long minutes of searching produced no opening in the wall. Then, struck by inspiration, Istrak raised his head and found what he had been seeking. A rope ladder was hidden in a small niche high on the wall. When he had climbed it and pulled open a small metal tongue in the trap door, he was able to climb out through the tunnel's roof.

It was no easy feat, making an exit while holding the heavy door open with his head and shoulders. However, he did accomplish it in the end and stood up to move the door aside. He filled his lungs with the clean, fresh air of the Pelasar Forest.

A moment later, Yishai was standing beside him, looking around with narrowed eyes. Lord Shefer found it more difficult to wriggle his way out. When he was finally through, he sat down heavily on the tunnel door, breathing hard.

At last, his breathing restored to something approaching normal, he stood up. "I'll close the opening," he said. But he remained standing in place, seemingly transfixed.

"Uncle?" Istrak turned to him.

Elranan's hand moved. "Look," he blurted. "Your wish has come true. The thief did leave his name."

On the underside of the door was a metal plate. Carved into the metal, in ancient Hebrew lettering, were the words: "Completed on the 29th day of the month of Adar, in the thirty-ninth year of the reign of King Aharon II." And then, underneath, "Designed and executed by Adonia Diaber."

Adonia Diaber.

More than 200 years had elapsed since those words were etched into the tunnel door. Was it possible that during all that time, in unsurpassed treachery, the fathers of the Diaber dynasty had passed the secret on to their sons, in anticipation of the day when they could finally put their knowledge to nefarious use?

The answer screamed out at them from the events of recent months.

Despite his impassioned speech to his soldiers, there remained a trace of doubt in Yosef Diaber's heart. Today the people were with him, but it was clear that the nation's collective memory would not take kindly to this sort of mass slaughter. He was uneasily aware that, should the day of reckoning ever come, he would be held accountable. Could he have been certain that killing Pinras, Gad Baliatar, and Ruben Min-Hagai would end the rebellion, he would have been satisfied with the death of only those three. But a tiny, obstinate bird kept whispering in his ear that if those three died, six others would rise up to fight him. And it would not be easy to gather them in one place again and destroy them all.

There was little time for him to decide. The scouts that the *hostress* commander had sent ahead reported that a group of mounted men had been seen advancing from the direction of the Minar River.

With the political considerations being more or less evenly balanced, Yosef Diaber could permit himself to go with his natural inclinations. And those were completely clear.

While Matrias' men started to form their perimeter, on their commander's orders, a plan began to take shape in Diaber's mind. If the Mentor's Men agreed to kill, with their own hands, those who headed their rebellion, he would forgive their insolence and absolve them with fines and forced labor alone. Should they refuse his offer, they would receive a punishment fit for any rebel against the throne. A punishment which, despite the pain, the people of Khazar would understand.

Not far away, Prime Minister Menashe Kafchaver was busy expressing his anguish over Prince Michoel's frail appearance and his joy at the rescue of both royal brothers. The nine Mundari youths, unaccustomed to such vocal expressions of emotion, were hard put not to laugh out loud. Istrak and his companions could not refrain from smiling themselves, but for a different reason: Kafchaver's resonant voice helped them find their way through the trees to the spot where the group was gathered.

"A mighty voice," Istrak remarked to his uncle.

Lord Shefer agreed. "During his year of mourning for his father, the candelabras in the *beis knesses* used to tremble."

Moments later everyone was shaking everyone else's hands or thumping them on the back. Yishai's friends were happy to see him again.

"We will daven Shacharis here," Istrak said. "Afterward, we will start for Lord Shefer's summer estate…"

The Mundaris exchanged quick glances. They had spent the afternoon and the first part of the night crawling on the ground among the undergrowth, as the scratches on their faces and their stained clothing testified. Istrak understood their unspoken comment. "Would you prefer to go down to the river first?" he asked. He glanced at his uncle. "Will we be able to find clean clothes for them at your summer place?"

Shefer nodded. "Certainly. And there is a *Sefer Torah* there, too, Your Highness."

"Excellent." Turning to the others, Istrak said, "Everyone take a horse. All we have to do is cross the Minar. If we hurry, we'll get there before *zeman Krias Shema*."

It was soon clear that Kafchaver, unaware of the large number of the princes' escort, had not brought enough horses. The loyal Mundaris climbed into the rickety wagon that had brought them this far, looking more than ever like a group of beggars.

A moment later, the group was on its way.

The glint of metal told Ruben that their plans had been discovered. Ignoring protocol, which obligated him to consult with those in charge before issuing such an order, he shouted at his men to turn around, recross the bridge, and leave the area with all possible speed.

Alarmed, the men obeyed. The crisp morning air was filled with the neighing of horses and the pawing of hooves. They encountered another, larger group of their men that had not been able to cross the bridge with their leaders. Since the bridge was too narrow to permit the newcomers to turn their horses around, chaos reigned. Horses reared up into the air as their riders cried out in confusion.

The bridge itself added its share of alarm — its central beam began to buckle inward, threatening to collapse. The men were too preoccupied with their need to escape to notice the state of the bridge, which continued to creak and groan until, at last, with a high, shrill scream, the northern end crashed into the water along with its complement of horses and riders.

Many good hands were extended to the men floundering in the river. Busy rescuing their comrades, the Mentor's Men never realized that their single escape route had been sealed off. They were soon surrounded by *hostress* troops, who made no effort to maintain any semblance of secrecy or stealth.

Step after step, marching in a uniform tempo, the *hostress* soldiers completed their ring around Min-Hagai's men and waited in suspense for the triple trumpet blast that was their signal to attack.

But the blast did not come. Instead, Yosef Diaber appeared from among the rows of troops. The milder trumpet notes that sounded beside him drew the attention of all those not occupied with rescue work in the river.

"A good morning to the lawbreakers calling themselves the 'Mentor's Men,'" Diaber said calmly. "The men who have, by their actions, earned themselves the death sentence."

Silence answered him, loud as thunder. The only sound to be heard was the creaking of the bridge — which threatened to complete its collapse momentarily — and the shouts of the men working to extricate the last of those who had fallen into the water.

"I can understand your agony," Diaber continued. "You have grown up with distortion, taught by those who did not understand that our Torah is a Torah of life. Your minds were stuffed with the false idea that our Creator dislikes your pleasure and amusement. As though He desires you to be constricted...imprisoned..."

"It is you who preach distortion, Yosef."

Pinras, whose horse had disappeared in the confusion, strode forward to meet his enemy, his figure fully exposed to Diaber's soldiers.

Only a short tract of land lay between the Pelasar Forest and the Minar, the most beautiful of Khazar's rivers. From their elevation, Istrak and his companions could see the soft morning sun reflecting gold and silver highlights on the green pastures. But that was not the only thing they saw. Near the first bridge over the Minar, an unusual amount of activity seemed to be taking place. *Hostress* troops, distinctive in their special uniforms, had just completed their ring around a small group of men.

"The rebels," Shefer said through dry lips. "It must be them. There is no other possibility."

"Do not say 'rebels,'" Michoel begged. "Say, 'Pinras' men,' or 'Ruben Min-Hagai's men.'"

Kafchaver stirred restlessly in his saddle. "They're all going to die," he said hoarsely. "Down to the last man. You know Diaber, Elranan! You know how he feels about them. Is there nothing we can do?"

"Of course there is." Istrak's voice was quick and resolute. "We must go down there and stop it."

"Absolutely not!" The words came in unison from Kafchaver and Shefer. They sounded forceful and frightened at the same time.

"That is my mission," Istrak said. His voice was strangely calm. "A king, or a king's son, must be prepared to give up his life for each and every one of his subjects. And this is not a matter of a single individual. There are scores of people down there!"

"Yes," Lord Shefer agreed. "What you say is true. But this is an extraordinary case. At stake today is not only your life — but Khazar's future. If you die, there is no one else with the capability to serve as a focal point for the nation and to seize the throne from Diaber."

"The *hostress* soldiers are not the men you once knew," Kafchaver spoke quietly. "They are devoted to Diaber, heart and soul. If he orders them to harm you — and I am certain he will do so — the outcome will be different than you believe."

Istrak turned to Michoel, riding beside him.

"No," Michoel said in a near whisper. "You cannot depend on me. I am still a child. I was not raised to lead, and I am not as good as you are in dealing with people."

"Don't look down there," Kafchaver advised. "Let us turn our horses around and leave this place. We can't help them, Prince of Khazar. It's a painful thing, but we must remember our limitations. Khazar is a changed place, Your Highness. I have seen with my own eyes the way good men have been drawn after Lord Diaber and the culture he espouses. You are not only endangering yourself, my prince. The entire spiritual future of this country hangs in the balance."

"Pinras!" A cruel, thin smile touched Diaber's lips. "It is a shame we must meet again under such unfortunate circumstances."

Pinras flung his head back to gaze at Khazar's new king on horseback.

"Yosef," he said, "behind the walls of constriction that you like to mock has grown the most beautiful civilization on earth. Its members are the happiest people in the world, even without all the amusements you've tried to urge them to seek out. What can you offer against the feeling of satisfaction and joy that come from the knowledge that we are doing what is right and proper in the eyes of Hashem and man? What can you give us?"

"What can I give you?" Diaber sneered disdainfully. "I can give you lives of ongoing pleasure, free of overly rigid constraints. I can give you a cultural feast, live theater, poetry, and literature such as our world has never experienced. I can give you a land where each man is a master of his own thoughts and prepared to acknowledge and place his fealty in the 'new' Khazar." His bright eyes gleamed as his glance passed over each rank of men. "You were mistaken," he told the assembled men softly. "You fell into the trap of false notions. But I am prepared to forgive—"

"Hashem, too, is prepared to forgive!" His voice trembling, Ruben Min-Hagai strode forward to stand by Pinras' side. "The gates of *teshuvah* have not yet shut for you. You propose happiness, Lord Diaber — but you are not happy. Perhaps you started out with good intentions. Perhaps you thought that the Torah could be combined with the culture of appetite. You thought that mitzvos performed by a 'happy' Jew would be more beautiful and more whole. And you believed that the joy you were seeking could be found by indulging in the pleasures of this world.

"But you were mistaken. You did not spend your time learning and adhering to the minutiae of halachah, and yet your life has not been easy, comfortable, or particularly happy. Instead of exerting yourself to fulfill your Creator's will, you worked to fill the emptiness in your soul — to provide it with more pleasure, more honor, more power.

"Look around you now, Lord Diaber. See where your ideas have taken you. How long do you think you will feel happy after we are all dead? Don't you know that, just as all other pleasures have vanished, so will your sense of triumph? The material simply cannot make a person happy — only the spiritual can do that. And the spirit belongs to us."

"It's easy to talk about spirit," Diaber said in an amused tone, ignoring the rebellious leaders to address their men. "No one has ever seen it, and no one knows what it really wants. I am proposing something else entirely: life. A life you can live with joy while performing the practical mitzvos.

"If ten brave men from among you will step forward to punish these two and Gad Baliatar as they deserve — to deliver the punishment of death that is meted out to those who rebel against the throne — I am prepared to pardon the rest of you."

Silence answered him. Even the river, swallowing the last of the bridge's timbers, moved soundlessly. And into the silence came a clear, young voice that struck Yosef Diaber like a bolt of lightning.

Straight-backed, with the morning sun creating a halo effect around him in his golden mail shirt, Istrak galloped among the *hostress* troops. The soldiers retreated to either side, dropping their weapons with startled reverence.

"I know Lord Baliatar and Pinras, the *bek's* son, and Ruben Min-Hagai well," the lost prince of Khazar spoke into the morning breeze. "And I am certain that none of them has *ever* rebelled against my father's throne."

Yosef Diaber's lips opened, but no sound issued from them. Where had the boy sprouted from so suddenly? Was he not far, far away on the Platt plains?

His thoughts became confused, but his amazing sense of preservation came to his rescue one more time, and he rallied quickly.

"Prince of Khazar! What a surprise!" he cried in a voice that dripped with honey. "How did *HaKadosh Baruch Hu* know to send you at just the right moment, to witness the punishment of these rebels? Trumpeter —"

"Halt!"

The trumpeter, who had lifted his instrument, froze.

"Blow," Diaber ordered.

The trumpeter brought the trumpet to his lips.

"Lay down your trumpet," Lord Kafchaver snapped, riding up beside Istrak. "Did you not hear the order of the crown prince of Khazar?"

The trumpeter did not remove the instrument from his lips, but neither did he blow.

Diaber licked his dry lips. This struggle, he understood, was not merely for the lives of this tattered band of rebels. It was over his own right to rule.

"Istrak," he said, "you are *not* the crown prince of Khazar, and it is best that you accept that fact right now. The nation has grown weary of your family's rule, and the high council has passed all your authority to me. I now hold the title of Khazar's new king.

"You are nothing but a small, pathetic child, trying to stick his hands into a dish of cooked food without knowing how hot it is. Go on your way, child. Go far from Khazaran-Itil and political intrigues. I will guarantee that no man shall harm you."

Istrak averted his head in disgust. This morning it had become abundantly clear to him that Yosef Diaber — the man whom all Khazar knew as a goodhearted dispenser of charity — was nothing but a lowly murderer. But because all the facts had not yet been explored to their depths, he could not use the painful revelation to demonstrate to those present where this man's road would lead them.

He could, however, appeal to their souls — to the innermost spark that remains ever faithful to the good and the true.

"Did you hear, *hostress* soldiers and sons of Khazar, what this man who was once known as Lord Yosef Diaber has just said?" he asked. "To whom do you give your loyalty man? To the rightful prince of Khazar — or to an aging, follhardy man? There are very few times in a person's life when he is asked to choose so clearly between right and wrong. For you, this is the moment. *Mi l'Hashem eilai*! All of you who seek to go in the ways of Hashem, join me!"

A whisper passed among the *hostress* troops, moving like a sibilant wave. A single soldier moved forward. For an instant, the world stood still. Then, hesitantly, a small group of about seven horsemen broke free of the *hostress'* orderly lines and moved toward Istrak. They formed a small circle around the prince of Khazar and the two lords that rode with him.

"Fools!" Diaber snapped. "What can this boy give you? What can he offer?"

"Truth," Istrak said gravely. "And joy and satisfaction and self-respect. You cannot give them any of these things. And without those things, anything you *can* give is worthless. Khazari soldiers, do you want a mediocre life, a life of self-loathing and racing after the wind? There is no truth in his words. We already have true pleasure and true happiness. And if you haven't seen this until now — that's because you were busy, all along, with distractions."

It was eerie to see the sturdy *hostress* soldiers bowing their heads. But hundreds of them did so, and their hold on their weapons grew slack.

"Do not be afraid." Istrak's heart filled with compassion and love. "Come."

Yosef Diaber was a smart man — smart enough to retreat rapidly from a battle he was doomed to lose. It was clear to him that the *hostress* soldiers, despite their loyalty to him, would be incapable of harming the prince of Khazar without the appropriate indoctrination. Straightening to his full height in the saddle, a look of disdain on his features, he echoed, "Come."

And the men came, each one choosing his king, his path.

Many of them came to Istrak — but many more of the *hostress* troops massed behind Yosef Diaber's back. Diaber smiled with satisfaction.

"We will meet again," Khazar's new king promised its true prince. "We will meet here, in this place. And then — the outcome of the struggle will be very different."

He motioned to the trumpeter, who sounded the retreat. Spurring his horse with his heels, Diaber rode away, tall and proud, at the head of his troops.

Soberly, Istrak watched the huge number of soldiers ride after Diaber. When they were far enough away so that they looked, in their identical uniforms, like a single long snake winding away along the riverbank, he turned back to his own men.

It was not a large group, and it was comprised of men of many different ages, dressed in an assortment of garments. But there was a common thread that bound them all together: they were, each and every one of them, men of faith and resolution.

They were prepared to begin the year of mourning for Reuel II, who had led them wisely and well until his life was cut short by a diabolical Diaber, and to reestablish the righteous reign of the royal house of Khazar.

They had won a victory today — but there was still a great deal of work ahead of them.

Thank You

To my husband, who was more than a partner in the weaving of the plot and its transfer to the written form.

To my worthy mother, who never tired of listening to me, for her continuous input, and her boundless love.

To my dear father, who taught me to delve into the individual personalities, and for the layers of depth that he added to the heroes (protagonists) of the book.

To my mother-in-law, for the initial proofreading.

To my sister-in-law, Tzippy, for providing me with direction at the onset of the project.

To my friends, Yiscah, Shulamit, and Ruti, the three Kolin sisters for always being there for me; for their constructive criticism and their constant encouragement; to Ruti also for the "Kinnah of Adrael"; and to Shulamit for her meticulous and professional proofreading; I lack the words with which to express my thanks.

And to Esther Rappaport, for her ongoing encouragement.

Without their help and their love, this book would not have seen the light of day

FOR THE ENGLISH EDITION:
Thank you to Libby Lazewnik for a masterful job of translating;
to Suri Brand for her superior editing;
to Judi Dick for the final editing;
to Mindy Stern for proofreading;
to Reizy Ganz for pagination and layout;
to Eli Kroen for the striking cover.